Agatha Christie is known throughout the world as the Queen of Crime. Her books have sold over a billion copies in English with another billion in foreign languages. She is the most widely published author of all time and in any language, outsold only by the Bible and Shakespeare. She is the author of 80 crime novels and short story collections, 20 plays, and six novels written under the name of Mary Westmacott.

Agatha Christie's first novel, *The Mysterious Affair at Styles*, was written towards the end of the First World War, in which she served as a VAD. In it she created Hercule Poirot, the little Belgian detective who was destined to become the most popular detective in crime fiction since Sherlock Holmes. It was eventually published by The Bodley Head in 1920.

In 1926, after averaging a book a year, Agatha Christie wrote her masterpiece. *The Murder of Roger Ackroyd* was the first of her books to be published by Collins and marked the beginning of an author–publisher relationship which lasted for 50 years and well over 70 books. *The Murder of Roger Ackroyd* was also the first of Agatha Christie's books to be dramatized – under the name *Alibi* – and to have a successful run in London's West End. *The Mousetrap*, her most famous play of all, opened in 1952 and is the longest-running play in history.

Agatha Christie was made a Dame in 1971. She died in 1976, since when a number of books have been published posthumously: the bestselling novel *Sleeping Murder* appeared later that year, followed by her autobiography and the short story collections *Miss Marple's Final Cases*, *Problem at Pollensa Bay* and *While the Light Lasts*. In 1998 *Black Coffee* was the first of her plays to be novelized by another author, Charles Osborne.

D0921232

THE AGATHA CHRISTIE COLLECTION

The Man in the Brown Suit
The Secret of Chimneys
The Seven Dials Mystery
The Mysterious Mr Quin
The Sittaford Mystery
The Hound of Death
The Listerdale Mystery
Why Didn't They Ask Evans?
Parker Pyne Investigates
Murder is Easy
And Then There Were None
Towards Zero
Death Comes as the End
Sparkling Cyanide
Crooked House
They Came to Baghdad
Destination Unknown
Ordeal by Innocence
The Pale Horse
Endless Night
Passenger to Frankfurt
Problem at Pollensa Bay
While the Light Lasts

Poirot
The Mysterious Affair at Styles
The Murder on the Links
Poirot Investigates
The Murder of Roger Ackroyd
The Big Four
The Mystery of the Blue Train
Peril at End House
Lord Edgware Dies
Murder on the Orient Express
Three-Act Tragedy
Death in the Clouds
The ABC Murders
Murder in Mesopotamia
Cards on the Table
Murder in the Mews
Dumb Witness
Death on the Nile
Appointment With Death
Hercule Poirot's Christmas
Sad Cypress
One, Two, Buckle My Shoe
Evil Under the Sun
Five Little Pigs
The Hollow
The Labours of Hercules
Taken at the Flood
Mrs McGinty's Dead
After the Funeral
Hickory Dickory Dock

Dead Man's Folly
Cat Among the Pigeons
The Adventure of the Christmas Pudding
The Clocks
Third Girl
Hallowe'en Party
Elephants Can Remember
Poirot's Early Cases
Curtain: Poirot's Last Case

Marple
The Murder at the Vicarage
The Thirteen Problems
The Body in the Library
The Moving Finger
A Murder is Announced
They Do It With Mirrors
A Pocket Full of Rye
4.50 from Paddington
The Mirror Crack'd from Side to Side
A Caribbean Mystery
At Bertram's Hotel
Nemesis
Sleeping Murder
Miss Marple's Final Cases

Tommy & Tuppence
The Secret Adversary
Partners in Crime
N or M?
By the Pricking of My Thumbs
Postern of Fate

Published as Mary Westmacott
Giant's Bread
Unfinished Portrait
Absent in the Spring
The Rose and the Yew Tree
A Daughter's a Daughter
The Burden

Memoirs
An Autobiography
Come, Tell Me How You Live

Play Collections
The Mousetrap and Selected Plays
Witness for the Prosecution
and Selected Plays

Play Adaptations by Charles Osborne
Black Coffee (Poirot)
Spider's Web
The Unexpected Guest

Agatha Christie

1940s

OMNIBUS

·

N OR M?

·

TOWARDS ZERO

·

SPARKLING CYANIDE

·

CROOKED HOUSE

·

HarperCollins*Publishers*

HarperCollins*Publishers*
77–85 Fulham Palace Road,
Hammersmith, London W6 8JB
www.harpercollins.co.uk

This edition first published 2006
3

N or M? © Agatha Christie Limited 1941
Towards Zero © Agatha Christie Limited 1944
Sparkling Cyanide © Agatha Christie Limited 1945
Crooked House © Agatha Christie Limited 1949

ISBN-13   978-0-00-720864-7
ISBN-10   0-00-720864-2

Typeset in Plantin Light and Gill Sans by
Palimpsest Book Production Limited,
Polmont, Stirlingshire

Printed and bound in Great Britain by
Clays Ltd, St Ives plc

CONTENTS

N OR M?

I

Tommy Beresford removed his overcoat in the hall of the flat. He hung it up with some care, taking time over it. His hat went carefully on the next peg.

He squared his shoulders, affixed a resolute smile to his face and walked into the sitting-room, where his wife sat knitting a Balaclava helmet in khaki wool.

It was the spring of 1940.

Mrs Beresford gave him a quick glance and then busied herself by knitting at a furious rate. She said after a minute or two:

'Any news in the evening paper?'

Tommy said:

'The Blitzkrieg is coming, hurray, hurray! Things look bad in France.'

Tuppence said:

'It's a depressing world at the moment.'

There was a pause and then Tommy said:

'Well, why don't you ask? No need to be so damned tactful.'

'I know,' admitted Tuppence. 'There is something about conscious tact that is very irritating. But then it irritates you if I do ask. And anyway I don't *need* to ask. It's written all over you.'

'I wasn't conscious of looking a Dismal Desmond.'

'No, darling,' said Tuppence. 'You had a kind of nailed to the mast smile which was one of the most heartrending things I have ever seen.'

Tommy said with a grin:

'No, was it really as bad as all that?'

'And more! Well, come on, out with it. Nothing doing?'

'Nothing doing. They don't want me in any capacity. I tell you, Tuppence, it's pretty thick when a man of forty-six is made to feel like a doddering grandfather. Army, Navy, Air Force,

Foreign Office, one and all say the same thing – I'm too old. I *may* be required later.'

Tuppence said:

'Well, it's the same for me. They don't want people of my age for nursing – no, thank you. Nor for anything else. They'd rather have a fluffy chit who's never seen a wound or sterilised a dressing than they would have me who worked for three years, 1915 to 1918, in various capacities, nurse in the surgical ward and operating theatre, driver of a trade delivery van and later of a General. This, that and the other – all, I assert firmly, with conspicuous success. And now I'm a poor, pushing, tiresome, middle-aged woman who won't sit at home quietly and knit as she ought to do.'

Tommy said gloomily:

'This war is hell.'

'It's bad enough having a war,' said Tuppence, 'but not being allowed to do anything in it just puts the lid on.'

Tommy said consolingly:

'Well, at any rate Deborah has got a job.'

Deborah's mother said:

'Oh, she's all right. I expect she's good at it, too. But I still think, Tommy, that I could hold my own with Deborah.'

Tommy grinned.

'She wouldn't think so.'

Tuppence said:

'Daughters can be very trying. Especially when they *will* be so kind to you.'

Tommy murmured:

'The way young Derek makes allowances for me is sometimes rather hard to bear. That "poor old Dad" look in his eye.'

'In fact,' said Tuppence, 'our children, although quite adorable, are also quite maddening.'

But at the mention of the twins, Derek and Deborah, her eyes were very tender.

'I suppose,' said Tommy thoughtfully, 'that it's always hard for people themselves to realise that they're getting middle-aged and past doing things.'

Tuppence gave a snort of rage, tossed her glossy dark head, and sent her ball of khaki wool spinning from her lap.

'Are we past doing things? *Are* we? Or is it only that everyone keeps insinuating that we are. Sometimes I feel that we never were any use.'

'Quite likely,' said Tommy.

'Perhaps so. But at any rate we did once feel important. And now I'm beginning to feel that all that never really happened. Did it happen, Tommy? Is it true that you were once crashed on the head and kidnapped by German agents? Is it true that we once tracked down a dangerous criminal – and got him! Is it true that we rescued a girl and got hold of important secret papers, and were practically thanked by a grateful country? Us! You and me! Despised, unwanted Mr and Mrs Beresford.'

'Now dry up, darling. All this does no good.'

'All the same,' said Tuppence, blinking back a tear, 'I'm disappointed in our Mr Carter.'

'He wrote us a very nice letter.'

'He didn't *do* anything – he didn't even hold out any hope.'

'Well, he's out of it all nowadays. Like us. He's quite old. Lives in Scotland and fishes.'

Tuppence said wistfully:

'They might have let us do *something* in the Intelligence.'

'Perhaps we couldn't,' said Tommy. 'Perhaps, nowadays, we wouldn't have the nerve.'

'I wonder,' said Tuppence. 'One feels just the same. But perhaps, as you say, when it came to the point –'

She sighed. She said:

'I wish we could find a job of some kind. It's so rotten when one has so much time to think.'

Her eyes rested just for a minute on the photograph of the very young man in the Air Force uniform, with the wide grinning smile so like Tommy's.

Tommy said:

'It's worse for a man. Women can knit, after all – and do up parcels and help at canteens.'

Tuppence said:

'I can do all that twenty years from now. I'm not old enough to be content with that. I'm neither one thing nor the other.'

The front door bell rang. Tuppence got up. The flat was a small service one.

She opened the door to find a broad-shouldered man with a big fair moustache and a cheerful red face, standing on the mat.

His glance, a quick one, took her in as he asked in a pleasant voice:

'Are you Mrs Beresford?'

'Yes.'

'My name's Grant. I'm a friend of Lord Easthampton's. He suggested I should look you and your husband up.'

'Oh, how nice, do come in.'

She preceded him into the sitting-room.

'My husband, er – Captain –'

'Mr.'

'Mr Grant. He's a friend of Mr Car – of Lord Easthampton's.'

The old *nom de guerre* of the former Chief of the Intelligence, 'Mr Carter', always came more easily to her lips than their old friend's proper title.

For a few minutes the three talked happily together. Grant was an attractive person with an easy manner.

Presently Tuppence left the room. She returned a few minutes later with the sherry and some glasses.

After a few minutes, when a pause came, Mr Grant said to Tommy:

'I hear you're looking for a job, Beresford?'

An eager light came into Tommy's eye.

'Yes, indeed. You don't mean –'

Grant laughed, and shook his head.

'Oh, nothing of that kind. No, I'm afraid that has to be left to the young active men – or to those who've been at it for years. The only things I can suggest are rather stodgy, I'm afraid. Office work. Filing papers. Tying them up in red tape and pigeon-holing them. That sort of thing.'

Tommy's face fell.

'Oh, I see!'

Grant said encouragingly:

'Oh well, it's better than nothing. Anyway, come and see me at my office one day. Ministry of Requirements. Room 22. We'll fix you up with something.'

The telephone rang. Tuppence picked up the receiver.

'Hallo – yes – *what?*' A squeaky voice spoke agitatedly from

the other end. Tuppence's face changed. 'When? – Oh, my dear
– of course – I'll come over right away . . .'

She put back the receiver.

She said to Tommy:

'That was Maureen.'

'I thought so – I recognised her voice from here.'

Tuppence explained breathlessly:

'I'm so sorry, Mr Grant. But I must go round to this friend
of mine. She's fallen and twisted her ankle and there's no one
with her but her little girl, so I must go round and fix up things
for her and get hold of someone to come in and look after her.
Do forgive me.'

'Of course, Mrs Beresford. I quite understand.'

Tuppence smiled at him, picked up a coat which had been
lying over the sofa, slipped her arms into it and hurried out. The
flat door banged.

Tommy poured out another glass of sherry for his guest.

'Don't go yet,' he said.

'Thank you.' The other accepted the glass. He sipped it for a
moment in silence. Then he said, 'In a way, you know, your wife's
being called away is a fortunate occurrence. It will save time.'

Tommy stared.

'I don't understand.'

Grant said deliberately:

'You see, Beresford, if you had come to see me at the Ministry,
I was empowered to put a certain proposition before you.'

The colour came slowly up in Tommy's freckled face. He said:

'You don't mean –'

Grant nodded.

'Easthampton suggested you,' he said. 'He told us you were
the man for the job.'

Tommy gave a deep sigh.

'Tell me,' he said.

'This is strictly confidential, of course.'

Tommy nodded.

'Not even your wife must know. You understand?'

'Very well – if you say so. But we worked together before.'

'Yes, I know. But this proposition is solely for you.'

'I see. All right.'

'Ostensibly you will be offered work – as I said just now – office work – in a branch of the Ministry functioning in Scotland – in a prohibited area where your wife cannot accompany you. Actually you will be somewhere very different.'

Tommy merely waited.

Grant said:

'You've read in the newspapers of the Fifth Column? You know, roughly at any rate, just what that term implies.'

Tommy murmured:

'The enemy within.'

'Exactly. This war, Beresford, started in an optimistic spirit. Oh, I don't mean the people who really knew – we've known all along what we were up against – the efficiency of the enemy, his aerial strength, his deadly determination, and the co-ordination of his well-planned war machine. I mean the people as a whole. The good-hearted, muddle-headed democratic fellow who believes what he wants to believe – that Germany will crack up, that she's on the verge of revolution, that her weapons of war are made of tin and that her men are so underfed that they'll fall down if they try to march – all that sort of stuff. Wishful thinking as the saying goes.

'Well, the war didn't go that way. It started badly and it went on worse. The men were all right – the men on the battleships and in the planes and in the dug-outs. But there was mismanagement and unpreparedness – the defects, perhaps, of our qualities. We don't want war, haven't considered it seriously, weren't good at preparing for it.

'The worst of that is over. We've corrected our mistakes, we're slowly getting the right men in the right place. We're beginning to run the war as it should be run – and we can win the war – make no mistake about that – but only if we don't lose it first. And the danger of losing it comes, not from outside – not from the might of Germany's bombers, not from her seizure of neutral countries and fresh vantage points from which to attack – but from within. Our danger is the danger of Troy – the wooden horse within our walls. Call it the Fifth Column if you like. It is here, among us. Men and women, some of them highly placed, some of them obscure, but all believing genuinely in the Nazi aims and the Nazi creed and desiring to substitute that sternly efficient creed for the muddled easy-going liberty of our democratic institutions.'

Grant leant forward. He said, still in that same pleasant unemotional voice:

'*And we don't know who they are* . . .'

Tommy said: 'But surely –'

Grant said with a touch of impatience:

'Oh, we can round up the small fry. That's easy enough. But it's the others. We know about them. We know that there are at least two highly placed in the Admiralty – that one must be a member of General G –'s staff – that there are three or more in the Air Force, and that two, at least, are members of the Intelligence, and have access to Cabinet secrets. We know that because it must be so from the way things have happened. The leakage – a leakage from the top – of information to the enemy, shows us that.'

Tommy said helplessly, his pleasant face perplexed:

'But what good should I be to you? I don't know any of these people.'

Grant nodded.

'Exactly. You don't know any of them – *and they don't know you.*'

He paused to let it sink in and then went on:

'These people, these high-up people, know most of our lot. Information can't be very well refused to them. I am at my wits' end. I went to Easthampton. He's out of it all now – a sick man – but his brain's the best I've ever known. He thought of you. Over twenty years since you worked for the department. Name quite unconnected with it. Your face not known. What do you say – will you take it on?'

Tommy's face was almost split in two by the magnitude of his ecstatic grin.

'Take it on? You bet I'll take it on. Though I can't see how I can be of any use. I'm just a blasted amateur.'

'My dear Beresford, amateur status is just what is needed. The professional is handicapped here. You'll take the place of the best man we had or are likely to have.'

Tommy looked a question. Grant nodded.

'Yes. Died in St Bridget's Hospital last Tuesday. Run down by a lorry – only lived a few hours. Accident case – but it wasn't an accident.'

Tommy said slowly: 'I see.'

Grant said quietly:

'And that's why we have reason to believe that Farquhar was on to something – that he was getting somewhere at last. By his death that wasn't an accident.'

Tommy looked a question.

Grant went on:

'Unfortunately we know next to nothing of what he had discovered. Farquhar had been methodically following up one line after another. Most of them led nowhere.'

Grant paused and then went on:

'Farquhar was unconscious until a few minutes before he died. Then he tried to say something. What he said was this: *N or M. Song Susie.*'

'That,' said Tommy, 'doesn't seem very illuminating.'

Grant smiled.

'A little more so than you might think. N or M, you see, is a term we have heard before. It refers to two of the most important and trusted German agents. We have come across their activities in other countries and we know just a little about them. It is their mission to organise a Fifth Column in foreign countries and to act as liaison officer between the country in question and Germany. N, we know, is a man. M is a woman. All we know about them is that these two are Hitler's most highly trusted agents and that in a code message we managed to decipher towards the beginning of the war there occurred this phrase – *Suggest N or M for England. Full powers –*'

'I see. And Farquhar –'

'As I see it, Farquhar must have got on the track of one or other of them. Unfortunately we don't know *which*. Song Susie sounds very cryptic – but Farquhar hadn't a high-class French accent! There was a return ticket to Leahampton in his pocket which is suggestive. Leahampton is on the south coast – a budding Bournemouth or Torquay. Lots of private hotels and guesthouses. Amongst them is one called *Sans Souci –*'

Tommy said again:

'Song Susie – Sans Souci – I see.'

Grant said: 'Do you?'

'The idea is,' Tommy said, 'that I should go there and – well – ferret round.'

'That *is* the idea.'

Tommy's smile broke out again.

'A bit vague, isn't it?' he asked. 'I don't even know what I'm looking for.'

'And I can't tell you. I don't know. It's up to you.'

Tommy sighed. He squared his shoulders.

'I can have a shot at it. But I'm not a very brainy sort of chap.'

'You did pretty well in the old days, so I've heard.'

'Oh, that was pure luck,' said Tommy hastily.

'Well, luck is rather what we need.'

Tommy considered a moment or two. Then he said:

'About this place, Sans Souci –'

Grant shrugged his shoulders.

'May be all a mare's nest. I can't tell. Farquhar may have been thinking of "Sister Susie sewing shirts for soldiers". It's all guesswork.'

'And Leahampton itself?'

'Just like any other of these places. There are rows of them. Old ladies, old Colonels, unimpeachable spinsters, dubious customers, fishy customers, a foreigner or two. In fact, a mixed bag.'

'And N or M amongst them?'

'Not necessarily. Somebody, perhaps, who's in touch with N or M. But it's quite likely to be N or M themselves. It's an inconspicuous sort of place, a boarding-house at a seaside resort.'

'You've no idea whether it's a man or a woman I've to look for?'

Grant shook his head.

Tommy said: 'Well, I can but try.'

'Good luck to your trying, Beresford. Now – to details –'

II

Half an hour later when Tuppence broke in, panting and eager with curiosity, Tommy was alone, whistling in an armchair with a doubtful expression on his face.

'Well?' demanded Tuppence, throwing an infinity of feeling into the monosyllable.

'Well,' said Tommy with a somewhat doubtful air, 'I've got a job – of kinds.'

'What kind?'

Tommy made a suitable grimace.

'Office work in the wilds of Scotland. Hush-hush and all that, but doesn't sound very thrilling.'

'Both of us, or only you?'

'Only me, I'm afraid.'

'Blast and curse you. How *could* our Mr Carter be so mean?'

'I imagine they segregate the sexes in these jobs. Otherwise too distracting for the mind.'

'Is it coding – or code breaking? Is it like Deborah's job? Do be careful, Tommy, people go queer doing that and can't sleep and walk about all night groaning and repeating 978345286 or something like that and finally have nervous breakdowns and go into homes.'

'Not me.'

Tuppence said gloomily:

'I expect you will sooner or later. Can I come too – not to work but just as a wife. Slippers in front of the fire and a hot meal at the end of the day?'

Tommy looked uncomfortable.

'Sorry, old thing. I *am* sorry. I hate leaving you –'

'But you feel you ought to go,' murmured Tuppence reminiscently.

'After all,' said Tommy feebly, 'you can knit, you know.'

'Knit?' said Tuppence. '*Knit?*'

Seizing her Balaclava helmet she flung it on the ground.

'I hate khaki wool,' said Tuppence, '*and* Navy wool *and* Air Force blue. I should like to knit something *magenta!*'

'It has a fine military sound,' said Tommy. 'Almost a suggestion of Blitzkrieg.'

He felt definitely very unhappy. Tuppence, however, was a Spartan and played up well, admitting freely that of course he had to take the job and that it didn't *really* matter about her. She added that she had heard they wanted someone to scrub down the First-Aid Post floors. She might possibly be found fit to do that.

Tommy departed for Aberdeen three days later. Tuppence saw him off at the station. Her eyes were bright and she blinked once or twice, but she kept resolutely cheerful.

Only as the train drew out of the station and Tommy saw the forlorn little figure walking away down the platform did he feel a lump in his own throat. War or no war he felt he was deserting Tuppence . . .

He pulled himself together with an effort. Orders were orders.

Having duly arrived in Scotland, he took a train the next day to Manchester. On the third day a train deposited him at Leahampton. Here he went to the principal hotel and on the following day made a tour of various private hotels and guesthouses, seeing rooms and inquiring terms for a long stay.

Sans Souci was a dark red Victorian villa, set on the side of a hill with a good view over the sea from its upper windows. There was a slight smell of dust and cooking in the hall and the carpet was worn, but it compared quite favourably with some of the other establishments Tommy had seen. He interviewed the proprietress, Mrs Perenna, in her office, a small untidy room with a large desk covered with loose papers.

Mrs Perenna herself was rather untidy looking, a woman of middle-age with a large mop of fiercely curling black hair, some vaguely applied make-up and a determined smile showing a lot of very white teeth.

Tommy murmured a mention of his elderly cousin, Miss Meadowes, who had stayed at Sans Souci two years ago. Mrs Perenna remembered Miss Meadowes quite well – such a dear old lady – at least perhaps not really old – very active and such a sense of humour.

Tommy agreed cautiously. There was, he knew, a real Miss Meadowes – the department was careful about these points.

And how was dear Miss Meadowes?

Tommy explained sadly that Miss Meadowes was no more and Mrs Perenna clicked her teeth sympathetically and made the proper noises and put on a correct mourning face.

She was soon talking volubly again. She had, she was sure, just the room that would suit Mr Meadowes. A lovely sea view. She thought Mr Meadowes was so right to want to get out of London. Very depressing nowadays, so she understood, and, of course, after such a bad go of influenza –

Still talking, Mrs Perenna led Tommy upstairs and showed him various bedrooms. She mentioned a weekly sum. Tommy displayed dismay. Mrs Perenna explained that prices had risen so appallingly. Tommy explained that his income had unfortunately decreased and what with taxation and one thing and another –

Mrs Perenna groaned and said:

'This terrible war –'

Tommy agreed and said that in his opinion that fellow Hitler ought to be hanged. A madman, that's what he was, a madman.

Mrs Perenna agreed and said that what with rations and the difficulty the butchers had in getting the meat they wanted – and sometimes too much and sweetbreads and liver practically disappeared, it all made housekeeping very difficult, but as Mr Meadowes was a relation of Miss Meadowes, she would make it half a guinea less.

Tommy then beat a retreat with the promise to think it over and Mrs Perenna pursued him to the gate, talking more volubly than ever and displaying an archness that Tommy found most alarming. She was, he admitted, quite a handsome woman in her way. He found himself wondering what her nationality was. Surely not quite English? The name was Spanish or Portuguese, but that would be her husband's nationality, not hers. She might, he thought, be Irish, though she had no brogue. But it would account for the vitality and the exuberance.

It was finally settled that Mr Meadowes should move in the following day.

Tommy timed his arrival for six o'clock. Mrs Perenna came out into the hall to greet him, threw a series of instructions about his luggage to an almost imbecile-looking maid, who goggled at Tommy with her mouth open, and then led him into what she called the lounge.

'I always introduce my guests,' said Mrs Perenna, beaming determinedly at the suspicious glares of five people. 'This is our new arrival, Mr Meadowes – Mrs O'Rourke.' A terrifying mountain of a woman with beady eyes and a moustache gave him a beaming smile.

'Major Bletchley.' Major Bletchley eyed Tommy appraisingly and made a stiff inclination of the head.

'Mr von Deinim.' A young man, very stiff, fair-haired and blue-eyed, got up and bowed.

'Miss Minton.' An elderly woman with a lot of beads, knitting with khaki wool, smiled and tittered.

'And Mrs Blenkensop.' More knitting – an untidy dark head which lifted from an absorbed contemplation of a Balaclava helmet.

Tommy held his breath, the room spun round.

Mrs Blenkensop! Tuppence! By all that was impossible and unbelievable – Tuppence, calmly knitting in the lounge of Sans Souci.

Her eyes met his – polite, uninterested stranger's eyes.

His admiration rose.

Tuppence!

CHAPTER 2

How Tommy got through that evening he never quite knew. He dared not let his eyes stray too often in the direction of Mrs Blenkensop. At dinner three more habitués of Sans Souci appeared – a middle-aged couple, Mr and Mrs Cayley, and a young mother, Mrs Sprot, who had come down with her baby girl from London and was clearly much bored by her enforced stay at Leahampton. She was placed next to Tommy and at intervals fixed him with a pair of pale gooseberry eyes and in a slightly adenoidal voice asked: 'Don't you think it's really quite safe now? Everyone's going back, aren't they?'

Before Tommy could reply to these artless queries, his neighbour on the other side, the beaded lady, struck in:

'What I say is one mustn't risk anything with children. Your sweet little Betty. You'd never forgive yourself and you know that Hitler has said the Blitzkrieg on England is coming quite soon now – and quite a new kind of gas, I believe.'

Major Bletchley cut in sharply:

'Lot of nonsense talked about gas. The fellows won't waste time fiddling round with gas. High explosive and incendiary bombs. That's what was done in Spain.'

The whole table plunged into the argument with gusto. Tuppence's voice, high-pitched and slightly fatuous, piped out: 'My son Douglas says –'

'Douglas, indeed,' thought Tommy. 'Why Douglas, I should like to know.'

After dinner, a pretentious meal of several meagre courses, all of which were equally tasteless, everyone drifted into the lounge. Knitting was resumed and Tommy was compelled to hear a long and extremely boring account of Major Bletchley's experiences on the North-West Frontier.

The fair young man with the bright blue eyes went out, executing a little bow on the threshold of the room.

Major Bletchley broke off his narrative and administered a kind of dig in the ribs to Tommy.

'That fellow who's just gone out. He's a refugee. Got out of Germany about a month before the war.'

'He's a German?'

'Yes. Not a Jew either. His father got into trouble for criticising the Nazi régime. Two of his brothers are in concentration camps over there. This fellow got out just in time.'

At this moment Tommy was taken possession of by Mr Cayley, who told him at interminable length all about his health. So absorbing was the subject to the narrator that it was close upon bedtime before Tommy could escape.

On the following morning Tommy rose early and strolled down to the front. He walked briskly to the pier returning along the esplanade when he spied a familiar figure coming in the other direction. Tommy raised his hat.

'Good morning,' he said pleasantly. 'Er – Mrs Blenkensop, isn't it?'

There was no one within earshot. Tuppence replied:

'Dr Livingstone to you.'

'How on earth did you get here, Tuppence?' murmured Tommy. 'It's a miracle – an absolute miracle.'

'It's not a miracle at all – just brains.'

'Your brains, I suppose?'

'You suppose rightly. You and your uppish Mr Grant. I hope this will teach him a lesson.'

'It certainly ought to,' said Tommy. 'Come on, Tuppence, tell me how you managed it. I'm simply devoured with curiosity.'

'It was quite simple. The moment Grant talked of our Mr Carter I guessed what was up. I knew it wouldn't be just some miserable office job. But his manner showed me that I wasn't going to be allowed in on this. So I resolved to go one better. I went to fetch some sherry and, when I did, I nipped down to the Browns' flat and rang up Maureen. Told her to ring me up and what to say. She played up loyally – nice high squeaky voice – you could hear what she was saying all over the room. I did my stuff, registered annoyance, compulsion, distressed friend, and rushed off with every sign of vexation. Banged the hall door, carefully remaining inside it, and slipped into the bedroom and eased open the communicating door that's hidden by the tallboy.'

'And you heard everything?'

'Everything,' said Tuppence complacently.

Tommy said reproachfully:

'And you never let on?'

'Certainly not. I wished to teach you a lesson. You and your Mr Grant.'

'He's not exactly my Mr Grant and I should say you have taught him a lesson.'

'Mr Carter wouldn't have treated me so shabbily,' said Tuppence. 'I don't think the Intelligence is anything like what it was in our day.'

Tommy said gravely: 'It will attain its former brilliance now we're back in it. But why Blenkensop?'

'Why not?'

'It seems such an odd name to choose.'

'It was the first one I thought of and it's handy for under-clothes.'

'What do you mean, Tuppence?'

'B, you idiot. B for Beresford. B for Blenkensop. Embroidered on my camiknickers. Patricia Blenkensop. Prudence Beresford. Why did you choose Meadowes? It's a silly name.'

'To begin with,' said Tommy, 'I don't have large B's embroi-dered on my pants. And to continue, I didn't choose it. I was told to call myself Meadowes. Mr Meadowes is a gentleman with a respectable past – all of which I've learnt by heart.'

'Very nice,' said Tuppence. 'Are you married or single?'

'I'm a widower,' said Tommy with dignity. 'My wife died ten years ago at Singapore.'

'Why at Singapore?'

'We've all got to die somewhere. What's wrong with Singapore?'

'Oh, nothing. It's probably a most suitable place to die. I'm a widow.'

'Where did your husband die?'

'Does it matter? Probably in a nursing home. I rather fancy he died of cirrhosis of the liver.'

'I see. A painful subject. And what about your son Douglas?'

'Douglas is in the Navy.'

'So I heard last night.'

'And I've got two other sons. Raymond is in the Air Force and Cyril, my baby, is in the Territorials.'

'And suppose someone takes the trouble to check up on these imaginary Blenkensops?'

'They're not Blenkensops. Blenkensop was my second husband. My first husband's name was Hill. There are three pages of Hills in the telephone book. You couldn't check up on all the Hills if you tried.'

Tommy sighed.

'It's the old trouble with you, Tuppence. You will overdo things. Two husbands and three sons. It's too much. You'll contradict yourself over the details.'

'No, I shan't. And I rather fancy the sons may come in useful. I'm not under orders, remember. I'm a freelance. I'm in this to enjoy myself and I'm going to enjoy myself.'

'So it seems,' said Tommy. He added gloomily: 'If you ask me the whole thing's a farce.'

'Why do you say that?'

'Well, you've been at Sans Souci longer than I have. Can you honestly say you think any of these people who were there last night could be a dangerous enemy agent?'

Tuppence said thoughtfully:

'It does seem a little incredible. There's the young man, of course.'

'Carl von Deinim. The police check up on refugees, don't they?'

'I suppose so. Still, it might be managed. He's an attractive young man, you know.'

'Meaning, the girls will tell him things? But what girls? No

Generals' or Admirals' daughters floating around here. Perhaps he walks out with a Company Commander in the ATS.'

'Be quiet, Tommy. We ought to be taking this seriously.'

'I am taking it seriously. It's just that I feel we're on a wild-goose chase.'

Tuppence said seriously:

'It's too early to say that. After all, nothing's going to be obvious about this business. What about Mrs Perenna?'

'Yes,' said Tommy thoughtfully. 'There's Mrs Perenna, I admit – she does want explaining.'

Tuppence said in a business-like tone:

'What about us? I mean, how are we going to co-operate?'

Tommy said thoughtfully:

'We mustn't be seen about too much together.'

'No, it would be fatal to suggest we know each other better than we appear to do. What we want to decide is the attitude. I think – yes, I think – pursuit is the best angle.'

'Pursuit?'

'Exactly. I pursue you. You do your best to escape, but being a mere chivalrous male don't always succeed. I've had two husbands and I'm on the look-out for a third. You act the part of the hunted widower. Every now and then I pin you down somewhere, pen you in a café, catch you walking on the front. Everyone sniggers and thinks it very funny.'

'Sounds feasible,' agreed Tommy.

Tuppence said: 'There's a kind of age-long humour about the chased male. That ought to stand us in good stead. If we are seen together, all anyone will do is to snigger and say, "Look at poor old Meadowes."'

Tommy gripped her arm suddenly.

'Look,' he said. 'Look ahead of you.'

By the corner of one of the shelters a young man stood talking to a girl. They were both very earnest, very wrapped up in what they were saying.

Tuppence said softly:

'Carl von Deinim. Who's the girl, I wonder?'

'She's remarkably good-looking, whoever she is.'

Tuppence nodded. Her eyes dwelt thoughtfully on the dark passionate face, and on the tight-fitting pullover that revealed the lines of the girl's figure. She was talking earnestly, with emphasis. Carl von Deinim was listening to her.

Tuppence murmured:

'I think this is where you leave me.'

'Right,' agreed Tommy.

He turned and strolled in the opposite direction.

At the end of the promenade he encountered Major Bletchley. The latter peered at him suspiciously and then grunted out, 'Good morning.'

'Good morning.'

'See you're like me, an early riser,' remarked Bletchley.

Tommy said:

'One gets in the habit of it out East. Of course, that's many years ago now, but I still wake early.'

'Quite right, too,' said Major Bletchley with approval. 'God, these young fellows nowadays make me sick. Hot baths – coming down to breakfast at ten o'clock or later. No wonder the Germans have been putting it over on us. No stamina. Soft lot of young pups. Army's not what it was, anyway. Coddle 'em, that's what they do nowadays. Tuck 'em up at night with hot-water bottles. Faugh! Makes me sick!'

Tommy shook his head in melancholy fashion and Major Bletchley, thus encouraged, went on:

'Discipline, that's what we need. Discipline. How are we going to win the war without discipline? Do you know, sir, some of these fellows come on parade in slacks – so I've been told. Can't expect to win a war that way. Slacks! My God!'

Mr Meadowes hazarded the opinion that things were very different from what they had been.

'It's all this democracy,' said Major Bletchley gloomily. 'You can overdo anything. In my opinion they're overdoing the democracy business. Mixing up the officers and the men, feeding together in restaurants – Faugh! – the men don't like it, Meadowes. The troops know. The troops always know.'

'Of course,' said Mr Meadowes, 'I have no real knowledge of Army matters myself –'

The Major interrupted him, shooting a quick sideways glance. 'In the show in the last war?'

'Oh yes.'

'Thought so. Saw you'd been drilled. Shoulders. What regiment?'

'Fifth Corfeshires.' Tommy remembered to produce Meadowes' military record.

'Ah yes, Salonica!'

'Yes.'

'I was in Mespot.'

Bletchley plunged into reminiscences. Tommy listened politely. Bletchley ended up wrathfully.

'And will they make use of me now? No, they will not. Too old. Too old be damned. I could teach one or two of these young cubs something about war.'

'Even if it's only what not to do?' suggested Tommy with a smile.

'Eh, what's that?'

A sense of humour was clearly not Major Bletchley's strong suit. He peered suspiciously at his companion. Tommy hastened to change the conversation.

'Know anything about that Mrs – Blenkensop, I think her name is?'

'That's right, Blenkensop. Not a bad-looking woman – bit long in the tooth – talks too much. Nice woman, but foolish. No, I don't know her. She's only been at Sans Souci a couple of days.' He added: 'Why do you ask?'

Tommy explained.

'Happened to meet her just now. Wondered if she was always out as early as this?'

'Don't know, I'm sure. Women aren't usually given to walking before breakfast – thank God,' he added.

'Amen,' said Tommy. He went on: 'I'm not much good at making polite conversation before breakfast. Hope I wasn't rude to the woman, but I wanted my exercise.'

Major Bletchley displayed instant sympathy.

'I'm with you, Meadowes. I'm with you. Women are all very well in their place, but not before breakfast.' He chuckled a little. 'Better be careful, old man. She's a widow, you know.'

'Is she?'

The Major dug him cheerfully in the ribs.

'*We* know what widows are. She's buried two husbands and if you ask me she's on the look-out for number three. Keep a very wary eye open, Meadowes. A wary eye. That's my advice.'

And in high good humour Major Bletchley wheeled about at the end of the parade and set the pace for a smart walk back to breakfast at Sans Souci.

In the meantime, Tuppence had gently continued her walk along the esplanade, passing quite close to the shelter and the young couple talking there. As she passed she caught a few words. It was the girl speaking.

'But you must be careful, Carl. The very least suspicion –'

Tuppence was out of earshot. Suggestive words? Yes, but capable of any number of harmless interpretations. Unobtrusively she turned and again passed the two. Again words floated to her.

'Smug, detestable English . . .'

The eyebrows of Mrs Blenkensop rose ever so slightly. Carl von Deinim was a refugee from Nazi persecution, given asylum and shelter by England. Neither wise nor grateful to listen assentingly to such words.

Again Tuppence turned. But this time, before she reached the shelter, the couple had parted abruptly, the girl to cross the road leaving the sea front, Carl von Deinim to come along to Tuppence's direction.

He would not, perhaps, have recognised her but for her own pause and hesitation. Then quickly he brought his heels together and bowed.

Tuppence twittered at him:

'Good morning, Mr von Deinim, isn't it? Such a lovely morning.'

'Ah, yes. The weather is fine.'

Tuppence ran on:

'It quite tempted me. I don't often come out before breakfast. But this morning, what with not sleeping very well – one often doesn't sleep well in a strange place, I find. It takes a day or two to accustom oneself, I always say.'

'Oh yes, no doubt that is so.'

'And really this little walk has quite given me an appetite for breakfast.'

'You go back to Sans Souci now? If you permit I will walk with you.' He walked gravely by her side.

Tuppence said:

'You also are out to get an appetite?'

Gravely, he shook his head.

'Oh no. My breakfast I have already had it. I am on my way to work.'

'Work?'

'I am a research chemist.'

'So that's what you are,' thought Tuppence, stealing a quick glance at him.

Carl von Deinim went on, his voice stiff:

'I came to this country to escape Nazi persecution. I had very little money – no friends. I do now what useful work I can.'

He stared straight ahead of him. Tuppence was conscious of some undercurrent of strong feeling moving him powerfully.

She murmured vaguely:

'Oh yes, I see. Very creditable, I am sure.'

Carl von Deinim said:

'My two brothers are in concentration camps. My father died in one. My mother died of sorrow and fear.'

Tuppence thought.

'The way he says that – as though he had learned it by heart.'

Again she stole a quick glance at him. He was still staring ahead of him, his face impassive.

They walked in silence for some moments. Two men passed them. One of them shot a quick glance at Carl. She heard him mutter to his companion:

'Bet you that fellow is a German.'

Tuppence saw the colour rise in Carl von Deinim's cheeks.

Suddenly he lost command of himself. That tide of hidden emotion came to the surface. He stammered:

'You heard – you heard – that is what they say – I –'

'My dear boy,' Tuppence reverted suddenly to her real self. Her voice was crisp and compelling. 'Don't be an idiot. You can't have it both ways.'

He turned his head and stared at her.

'What do you mean?'

'You're a refugee. You have to take the rough with the smooth. You're alive, that's the main thing. Alive and free. For the other

– realise that it's inevitable. This country's at war. You're a German.' She smiled suddenly. 'You can't expect the mere man in the street – literally the man in the street – to distinguish between bad Germans and good Germans, if I may put it so crudely.'

He still stared at her. His eyes, so very blue, were poignant with suppressed feeling. Then suddenly he too smiled. He said:

'They said of Red Indians, did they not, that a good Indian was a dead Indian.' He laughed. 'To be a good German I must be on time at my work. Please. Good morning.'

Again that stiff bow. Tuppence stared after his retreating figure. She said to herself:

'Mrs Blenkensop, you had a lapse then. Strict attention to business in future. Now for breakfast at Sans Souci.'

The hall door of Sans Souci was open. Inside, Mrs Perenna was conducting a vigorous conversation with someone.

'And you'll tell him what I think of that last lot of margarine. Get the cooked ham at Quillers – it was twopence cheaper last time there, and be careful about the cabbages –' She broke off as Tuppence entered.

'Oh, good morning, Mrs Blenkensop, you are an early bird. You haven't had breakfast yet. It's all ready in the dining-room.' She added, indicating her companion: 'My daughter Sheila. You haven't met her. She's been away and only came home last night.'

Tuppence looked with interest at the vivid, handsome face. No longer full of tragic energy, bored now and resentful. 'My daughter Sheila.' Sheila Perenna.

Tuppence murmured a few pleasant words and went into the dining-room. There were three people breakfasting – Mrs Sprot and her baby girl, and big Mrs O'Rourke. Tuppence said 'Good morning' and Mrs O'Rourke replied with a hearty 'The top of the morning to you' that quite drowned Mrs Sprot's more anaemic salutation.

The old woman stared at Tuppence with a kind of devouring interest.

'Tis a fine thing to be out walking before breakfast,' she observed. 'A grand appetite it gives you.'

Mrs Sprot said to her offspring:

'*Nice* bread and milk, darling,' and endeavoured to insinuate a spoonful into Miss Betty Sprot's mouth.

The latter cleverly circumvented this endeavour by an adroit movement of her head, and continued to stare at Tuppence with large round eyes.

She pointed a milky finger at the newcomer, gave her a dazzling smile and observed in gurgling tones: 'Ga – ga bouch.'

'She likes you,' cried Mrs Sprot, beaming on Tuppence as on one marked out for favour. 'Sometimes she's so shy with strangers.'

'Bouch,' said Betty Sprot. 'Ah pooth ah bag,' she added with emphasis.

'And what would she be meaning by that?' demanded Mrs O'Rourke, with interest.

'She doesn't speak awfully clearly yet,' confessed Mrs Sprot. 'She's only just over two, you know. I'm afraid most of what she says is just bosh. She can say Mama, though, can't you, darling?'

Betty looked thoughtfully at her mother and remarked with an air of finality:

'Cuggle bick.'

''Tis a language of their own they have, the little angels,' boomed out Mrs O'Rourke. 'Betty, darling, say Mama now.'

Betty looked hard at Mrs O'Rourke, frowned and observed with terrific emphasis: 'Nazer –'

'There now, if she isn't doing her best! And a lovely sweet girl she is.'

Mrs O'Rourke rose, beamed in a ferocious manner at Betty, and waddled heavily out of the room.

'Ga, ga, ga,' said Betty with enormous satisfaction, and beat with a spoon on the table.

Tuppence said with a twinkle:

'What does Na-zer really mean?'

Mrs Sprot said with a flush: 'I'm afraid, you know, it's what Betty says when she doesn't like anyone or anything.'

'I rather thought so,' said Tuppence.

Both women laughed.

'After all,' said Mrs Sprot, 'Mrs O'Rourke means to be kind but she is rather alarming – with that deep voice and the beard and – and everything.'

With her head on one side Betty made a cooing noise at Tuppence.

'She has taken to you, Mrs Blenkensop,' said Mrs Sprot.

There was a slight jealous chill, Tuppence fancied, in her voice. Tuppence hastened to adjust matters.

'They always like a new face, don't they?' she said easily.

The door opened and Major Bletchley and Tommy appeared. Tuppence became arch.

'Ah, Mr Meadowes,' she called out. 'I've beaten you, you see. First past the post. But I've left you just a *little* breakfast!'

She indicated with the faintest of gestures the seat beside her.

Tommy, muttering vaguely: 'Oh – er – rather – thanks,' sat down at the other end of the table.

Betty Sprot said '*Putch!*' with a fine splutter of milk at Major Bletchley, whose face instantly assumed a sheepish but delighted expression.

'And how's little Miss Bo Peep this morning?' he asked fatuously. 'Bo Peep!' He enacted the play with a newspaper.

Betty crowed with delight.

Serious misgivings shook Tuppence. She thought:

'There must be some mistake. There *can't* be anything going on here. There simply can't!'

To believe in Sans Souci as a headquarters of the Fifth Column needed the mental equipment of the White Queen in *Alice*.

CHAPTER 3

I

On the sheltered terrace outside, Miss Minton was knitting.

Miss Minton was thin and angular, her neck was stringy. She wore pale sky-blue jumpers, and chains or bead necklaces. Her skirts were tweedy and had a depressed droop at the back. She greeted Tuppence with alacrity.

'Good morning, Mrs Blenkensop. I do hope you slept well.'

Mrs Blenkensop confessed that she never slept very well the first night or two in a strange bed. Miss Minton said, Now, wasn't that curious? It was exactly the same with *her*.

Mrs Blenkensop said, 'What a coincidence, and what a very

pretty stitch that was.' Miss Minton, flushing with pleasure, displayed it. Yes, it was rather uncommon, and really quite simple. She could easily show it to Mrs Blenkensop if Mrs Blenkensop liked. Oh, that was very kind of Miss Minton, but Mrs Blenkensop was so stupid, she wasn't really very good at knitting, not at following patterns, that was to say. She could only do simple things like Balaclava helmets, and even now she was afraid she had gone wrong somewhere. It didn't look *right*, somehow, did it?

Miss Minton cast an expert eye over the khaki mass. Gently she pointed out just what had gone wrong. Thankfully, Tuppence handed the faulty helmet over. Miss Minton exuded kindness and patronage. Oh, no, it wasn't a trouble at all. She had knitted for so many years.

'I'm afraid I've never done any before this dreadful war,' confessed Tuppence. 'But one feels so terribly, doesn't one, that one must do *something*.'

'Oh yes, indeed. And you actually have a boy in the Navy, I think I heard you say last night?'

'Yes, my eldest boy. Such a splendid boy he is – though I suppose a mother shouldn't say so. Then I have a boy in the Air Force and Cyril, my baby, is out in France.'

'Oh dear, dear, how terribly anxious you must be.'

Tuppence thought:

'Oh Derek, my darling Derek . . . Out in the hell and mess – and here I am playing the fool – acting the thing I'm really feeling . . .'

She said in her most righteous voice:

'We must all be brave, mustn't we? Let's hope it will all be over soon. I was told the other day on very high authority indeed that the Germans can't possibly last out more than another two months.'

Miss Minton nodded with so much vigour that all her bead chains rattled and shook.

'Yes, indeed, and I believe' – (her voice lowered mysteriously) – 'that Hitler is suffering from a *disease* – absolutely fatal – he'll be raving mad by August.'

Tuppence replied briskly:

'All this Blitzkrieg is just the Germans' last effort. I believe the shortage is something frightful in Germany. The men in the factories are very dissatisfied. The whole thing will crack up.'

'What's this? What's all this?'

Mr and Mrs Cayley came out on the terrace, Mr Cayley putting his questions fretfully. He settled himself in a chair and his wife put a rug over his knees. He repeated fretfully:

'What's that you are saying?'

'We're saying,' said Miss Minton, 'that it will all be over by the autumn.'

'Nonsense,' said Mr Cayley. 'This war is going to last at least six years.'

'Oh, Mr Cayley,' protested Tuppence. 'You don't really think so?'

Mr Cayley was peering about him suspiciously.

'Now I wonder,' he murmured. 'Is there a draught? Perhaps it would be better if I moved my chair back into the corner.'

The resettlement of Mr Cayley took place. His wife, an anxious-faced woman who seemed to have no other aim in life than to minister to Mr Cayley's wants, manipulating cushions and rugs, asking from time to time: 'Now how is that, Alfred? Do you think that will be all right? Ought you, perhaps, to have your sun-glasses? There is rather a glare this morning.'

Mr Cayley said irritably:

'No, no. Don't fuss, Elizabeth. Have you got my muffler? No, no, my silk muffler. Oh well, it doesn't matter. I dare say this will do – for once. But I don't want to get my throat overheated, and wool – in this sunlight – well, perhaps you *had* better fetch the other.' He turned his attention back to matters of public interest. 'Yes,' he said. 'I give it six years.'

He listened with pleasure to the protests of the two women.

'You dear ladies are just indulging in what we call wishful thinking. Now I know Germany. I may say I know Germany extremely well. In the course of my business before I retired I used to be constantly to and fro. Berlin, Hamburg, Munich, I know them all. I can assure you that Germany can hold out practically indefinitely. With Russia behind her –'

Mr Cayley plunged triumphantly on, his voice rising and falling in pleasurably melancholy cadences, only interrupted when he paused to receive the silk muffler his wife brought him and wind it round his throat.

Mrs Sprot brought out Betty and plumped her down with a small woollen dog that lacked an ear and a woolly doll's jacket.

'There, Betty,' she said. 'You dress up Bonzo ready for his walk while Mummy gets ready to go out.'

Mr Cayley's voice droned on, reciting statistics and figures, all of a depressing character. The monologue was punctuated by a cheerful twittering from Betty talking busily to Bonzo in her own language.

'Truckle – truckly – pah bat,' said Betty. Then, as a bird alighted near her, she stretched out loving hands to it and gurgled. The bird flew away and Betty glanced round the assembled company and remarked clearly:

'Dicky,' and nodded her head with great satisfaction.

'That child is learning to talk in the most wonderful way,' said Miss Minton. 'Say "Ta ta", Betty. "Ta ta."'

Betty looked at her coldly and remarked:

'Gluck!'

Then she forced Bonzo's one arm into his woolly coat and, toddling over to a chair, picked up the cushion and pushed Bonzo behind it. Chuckling gleefully, she said with terrific pains:

'Hide! Bow wow. Hide!'

Miss Minton, acting as a kind of interpreter, said with vicarious pride:

'She loves hide-and-seek. She's always hiding things.' She cried out with exaggerated surprise:

'*Where* is Bonzo? Where *is* Bonzo? Where *can* Bonzo have gone?'

Betty flung herself down and went into ecstasies of mirth.

Mr Cayley, finding attention diverted from his explanation of Germany's methods of substitution of raw materials, looked put out and coughed aggressively.

Mrs Sprot came out with her hat on and picked up Betty.

Attention returned to Mr Cayley.

'You were saying, Mr Cayley?' said Tuppence.

But Mr Cayley was affronted. He said coldly:

'That woman is always plumping that child down and expecting people to look after it. I think I'll have the woollen muffler after all, dear. The sun is going in.'

'Oh, but, Mr Cayley, do go on with what you were telling us. It was so interesting,' said Miss Minton.

Mollified, Mr Cayley weightily resumed his discourse, drawing the folds of the woolly muffler closer round his stringy neck.

'As I was saying, Germany has so perfected her system of –'

Tuppence turned to Mrs Cayley, and asked:

'What do you think about the war, Mrs Cayley?'

Mrs Cayley jumped.

'Oh, what do I think? What – what do you mean?'

'Do you think it will last as long as six years?'

Mrs Cayley said doubtfully:

'Oh, I hope not. It's a very long time, isn't it?'

'Yes. A long time. What do you really think?'

Mrs Cayley seemed quite alarmed by the question. She said:

'Oh, I – I don't know. I don't know at all. Alfred says it will.'

'But you don't think so?'

'Oh, I don't know. It's difficult to say, isn't it?'

Tuppence felt a wave of exasperation. The chirruping Miss Minton, the dictatorial Mr Cayley, the nit-witted Mrs Cayley – were these people really typical of her fellow-countrymen? Was Mrs Sprot any better with her slightly vacant face and boiled gooseberry eyes? What could she, Tuppence, ever find out here? Not one of these people, surely –

Her thought was checked. She was aware of a shadow. Some-one behind her who stood between her and the sun. She turned her head.

Mrs Perenna, standing on the terrace, her eyes on the group. And something in those eyes – scorn, was it? A kind of withering contempt. Tuppence thought:

'I must find out more about Mrs Perenna.'

II

Tommy was establishing the happiest of relationships with Major Bletchley.

'Brought down some golf clubs with you, didn't you, Meadowes?'

Tommy pleaded guilty.

'Ha! I can tell you, *my* eyes don't miss much. Splendid. We must have a game together. Ever played on the links here?'

Tommy replied in the negative.

'They're not bad – not bad at all. Bit on the short side, perhaps, but lovely view over the sea and all that. And never very crowded. Look here, what about coming along with me this morning? We might have a game.'

'Thanks very much. I'd like it.'

'Must say I'm glad you've arrived,' remarked Bletchley as they were trudging up the hill. 'Too many women in that place. Gets on one's nerves. Glad I've got another fellow to keep me in countenance. You can't count Cayley – the man's a kind of walking chemist's shop. Talks of nothing but his health and the treatment he's tried and the drugs he's taking. If he threw away all his little pill-boxes and went out for a good ten-mile walk every day he'd be a different man. The only other male in the place is von Deinim, and to tell you the truth, Meadowes, I'm not too easy in my mind about him.'

'No?' said Tommy.

'No. You take my word for it, this refugee business is dangerous. If I had my way I'd intern the lot of them. Safety first.'

'A bit drastic, perhaps.'

'Not at all. War's war. And I've got my suspicions of Master Carl. For one thing he's clearly not a Jew. Then he came over here just a month – only a month, mind you – before war broke out. That's a bit suspicious.'

Tommy said invitingly:

'Then you think –?'

'*Spying* – that's his little game!'

'But surely there's nothing of great military or naval importance hereabouts?'

'Ah, old man, that's where the artfulness comes in! If he were anywhere near Plymouth or Portsmouth he'd be under supervision. In a sleepy place like this, nobody bothers. But it's on the coast, isn't it? The truth of it is the Government is a great deal too easy with these enemy aliens. Anyone who cared could come over here and pull a long face and talk about their brothers in concentration camps. Look at that young man – arrogance in every line of him. He's a Nazi – that's what he is – a Nazi.'

'What we really need in this country is a witch doctor or two,' said Tommy pleasantly.

'Eh, what's that?'

'To smell out the spies,' Tommy explained gravely.

'Ha, very good that – very good. Smell 'em out – yes, of course.'

Further conversation was brought to an end, for they had arrived at the clubhouse.

Tommy's name was put down as a temporary member, he was introduced to the secretary, a vacant-looking elderly man, and the subscription duly paid. Tommy and the Major started on their round.

Tommy was a mediocre golfer. He was glad to find that his standard of play was just about right for his new friend. The Major won by two up and one to play, a very happy state of events.

'Good match, Meadowes, very good match – you had bad luck with that mashie shot, just turned off at the last minute. We must have a game fairly often. Come along and I'll introduce you to some of the fellows. Nice lot on the whole, some of them inclined to be rather old women, if you know what I mean? Ah, here's Haydock – you'll like Haydock. Retired naval wallah. Has that house on the cliff next door to us. He's our local ARP warden.'

Commander Haydock was a big hearty man with a weather-beaten face, intensely blue eyes, and a habit of shouting most of his remarks.

He greeted Tommy with friendliness.

'So you're going to keep Bletchley countenance at Sans Souci? He'll be glad of another man. Rather swamped by female society, eh, Bletchley?'

'I'm not much of a ladies' man,' said Major Bletchley.

'Nonsense,' said Haydock. 'Not your type of lady, my boy, that's it. Old boarding-house pussies. Nothing to do but gossip and knit.'

'You're forgetting Miss Perenna,' said Bletchley.

'Ah, Sheila – she's an attractive girl all right. Regular beauty if you ask me.'

'I'm a bit worried about her,' said Bletchley.

'What do you mean? Have a drink, Meadowes? What's yours, Major?'

The drinks ordered and the men settled on the veranda of the clubhouse, Haydock repeated his question.

Major Bletchley said with some violence:

'That German chap. She's seeing too much of him.'

'Getting sweet on him, you mean? H'm, that's bad. Of course he's a good-looking young chap in his way. But it won't do. It won't do, Bletchley. We can't have that sort of thing. Trading with the enemy, that's what it amounts to. These girls – where's their proper spirit? Plenty of decent young English fellows about.'

Bletchley said:

'Sheila's a queer girl – she gets odd sullen fits when she will hardly speak to anyone.'

'Spanish blood,' said the Commander. 'Her father was half Spanish, wasn't he?'

'Don't know. It's a Spanish name, I should think.'

The Commander glanced at his watch.

'About time for the news. We'd better go in and listen to it.'

The news was meagre that day, little more in it than had been already in the morning papers. After commenting with approval on the latest exploits of the Air Force – first-rate chaps, brave as lions – the Commander went on to develop his own pet theory – that sooner or later the Germans would attempt a landing at Leahampton itself – his argument being that it was such an unimportant spot.

'Not even an anti-aircraft gun in the place! Disgraceful!'

The argument was not developed, for Tommy and the Major had to hurry back to lunch at Sans Souci. Haydock extended a cordial invitation to Tommy to come and see his little place, 'Smugglers' Rest'. 'Marvellous view – my own beach – every kind of handy gadget in the house. Bring him along, Bletchley.'

It was settled that Tommy and Major Bletchley should come in for drinks on the evening of the following day.

III

After lunch was a peaceful time at Sans Souci. Mr Cayley went to have his 'rest' with the devoted Mrs Cayley in attendance. Mrs Blenkensop was conducted by Miss Minton to a depot to pack and address parcels for the Front.

Mr Meadowes strolled gently out into Leahampton and along

the front. He bought a few cigarettes, stopped at Smith's to purchase the latest number of *Punch*, then after a few minutes of apparent irresolution, he entered a bus bearing the legend, 'OLD PIER'.

The old pier was at the extreme end of the promenade. That part of Leahampton was known to house agents as the least desirable end. It was West Leahampton and poorly thought of. Tommy paid 2d, and strolled up the pier. It was a flimsy and weather-worn affair, with a few moribund penny-in-the-slot machines placed at far distant intervals. There was no one on it but some children running up and down and screaming in voices that matched quite accurately the screaming of the gulls, and one solitary man sitting on the end fishing.

Mr Meadowes strolled up to the end and gazed down into the water. Then he asked gently:

'Caught anything?'

The fisherman shook his head.

'Don't often get a bite.' Mr Grant reeled in his line a bit. He said without turning his head:

'What about you, Meadowes?'

Tommy said:

'Nothing much to report as yet, sir. I'm digging myself in.'

'Good. Tell me.'

Tommy sat on an adjacent bollard, so placed that he commanded the length of the pier. Then he began:

'I've gone down quite all right, I think. I gather you've already got a list of the people there?' Grant nodded. 'There's nothing to report as yet. I've struck up a friendship with Major Bletchley. We played golf this morning. He seems the ordinary type of retired officer. If anything, a shade too typical. Cayley seems a genuine hypochondriacal invalid. That, again, would be an easy part to act. He has, by his own admission, been a good deal in Germany during the last few years.'

'A point,' said Grant laconically.

'Then there's von Deinim.'

'Yes, I don't need to tell you, Meadowes, that von Deinim's the one I'm most interested in.'

'You think he's N?'

Grant shook his head.

'No, I don't. As I see it, N couldn't afford to be a German.'

'Not a refugee from Nazi persecution, even?'

'Not even that. We watch, and they know we watch all the enemy aliens in this country. Moreover – this is in confidence, Beresford – very nearly all enemy aliens between 16 and 60 will be interned. Whether our adversaries are aware of that fact or not, they can at any rate anticipate that such a thing might happen. They would never risk the head of their organisation being interned. N therefore must be either a neutral – or else he is (apparently) an Englishman. The same, of course, applies to M. No, my meaning about von Deinim is this. He may be a link in the chain. N or M may not be at Sans Souci, it may be Carl von Deinim who is there and through him we may be led to our objective. That does seem to me highly possible. The more so as I cannot very well see that any of the other inmates of Sans Souci are likely to be the person we are seeking.'

'You've had them more or less vetted, I suppose, sir?'

Grant sighed – a sharp, quick sigh of vexation.

'No, that's just what it's impossible for me to do. I could have them looked up by the department easily enough *but I can't risk it, Beresford*. For, you see, the rot is in the department itself. One hint that I've got my eye on Sans Souci for any reason – and the organisation may be put wise. That's where *you* come in, the outsider. That's why you've got to work in the dark, without help from us. It's our only chance – and I daren't risk alarming them. There's only one person I've been able to check up on.'

'Who's that, sir?'

'Carl von Deinim himself. That's easy enough. Routine. I can have him looked up – not from the Sans Souci angle, but from the enemy alien angle.'

Tommy asked curiously:

'And the result?'

A curious smile came over the other's face.

'Master Carl is exactly what he says he is. His father was indiscreet, was arrested and died in a concentration camp. Carl's elder brothers are in camps. His mother died in great distress of mind a year ago. He escaped to England a month before war broke out. Von Deinim has professed himself anxious to help this country. His work in a chemical research laboratory has been excellent and most helpful on the problem of immunising certain gases and in general decontamination experiments.'

Tommy said:

'Then he's all right?'

'Not necessarily. Our German friends are notorious for their thoroughness. If von Deinim was sent as an agent to England, special care would be taken that his record should be consistent with his own account of himself. There are two possibilities. The whole von Deinim family may be parties to the arrangement – not improbable under the painstaking Nazi régime. Or else this is not really Carl von Deinim but *a man playing the part of Carl von Deinim.*'

Tommy said slowly: 'I see.' He added inconsequently:

'He seems an awfully nice young fellow.'

Sighing, Grant said: 'They are – they nearly always are. It's an odd life this service of ours. We respect our adversaries and they respect us. You usually like your opposite number, you know – even when you're doing your best to down him.'

There was silence as Tommy thought over the strange anomaly of war. Grant's voice broke into his musings.

'But there are those for whom we've neither respect nor liking – and those are the traitors within our own ranks – the men who are willing to betray their country and accept office and promotion from the foreigner who has conquered it.'

Tommy said with feeling:

'My God, I'm with you, sir. That's a skunk's trick.'

'And deserves a skunk's end.'

Tommy said incredulously:

'And there really are these – these swine?'

'Everywhere. As I told you. In our service. In the fighting forces. On Parliamentary benches. High up in the Ministries. We've got to comb them out – we've *got* to! And we must do it quickly. It can't be done from the bottom – the small fry, the people who speak in the parks, who sell their wretched little news-sheets, they don't know who the big bugs are. It's the big bugs we want, they're the people who can do untold damage – and will do it unless we're in time.'

Tommy said confidently:

'We shall be in time, sir.'

Grant asked:

'What makes you say that?'

Tommy said:

'You've just said it – we've *got* to be!'

The man with the fishing line turned and looked full at his subordinate for a minute or two, taking in anew the quiet resolute line of the jaw. He had a new liking and appreciation of what he saw. He said quietly:

'Good man.'

He went on:

'What about the women in this place? Anything strike you as suspicious there?'

'I think there's something odd about the woman who runs it.'

'Mrs Perenna?'

'Yes. You don't – know anything about her?'

Grant said slowly:

'I might see what I could do about checking her antecedents, but as I told you, it's risky.'

'Yes, better not take any chances. She's the only one who strikes me as suspicious in any way. There's a young mother, a fussy spinster, the hypochondriac's brainless wife, and a rather fearsome-looking old Irishwoman. All seem harmless enough on the face of it.'

'That's the lot, is it?'

'No. There's a Mrs Blenkensop – arrived three days ago.'

'Well?'

Tommy said: 'Mrs Blenkensop is my wife.'

'*What?*'

In the surprise of the announcement Grant's voice was raised. He spun round, sharp anger in his gaze. 'I thought I told you, Beresford, not to breathe a word to your wife!'

'Quite right, sir, and I didn't. If you'll just listen –'

Succinctly, Tommy narrated what had occurred. He did not dare look at the other. He carefully kept out of his voice the pride that he secretly felt.

There was a silence when he brought the story to an end. Then a queer noise escaped from the other. Grant was laughing. He laughed for some minutes.

He said: 'I take my hat off to the woman! She's one in a thousand!'

'I agree,' said Tommy.

'Easthampton will laugh when I tell him this. He warned me not to leave her out. Said she'd get the better of me if I did. I wouldn't listen to him. It shows you, though, how damned careful you've got to be. I thought I'd taken every precaution against being overheard. I'd satisfied myself beforehand that you and your wife were alone in the flat. I actually heard the voice in the telephone asking your wife to come round at once, and so – and so I was tricked by the old simple device of the banged door. Yes, she's a smart woman, your wife.'

He was silent for a minute, then he said:

'Tell her from me, will you, that I eat dirt?'

'And I suppose, now, she's in on this?'

Mr Grant made an expressive grimace.

'She's in on it whether we like it or not. Tell her the department will esteem it an honour if she will condescend to work with us over the matter.'

'I'll tell her,' said Tommy with a faint grin.

Grant said seriously:

'You couldn't persuade her, I suppose, to go home and stay home?'

Tommy shook his head.

'You don't know Tuppence.'

'I think I am beginning to. I said that because – well, it's a dangerous business. If they get wise to you or to her –'

He left the sentence unfinished.

Tommy said gravely: 'I do understand that, sir.'

'But I suppose even you couldn't persuade your wife to keep out of danger.'

Tommy said slowly:

'I don't know that I really would want to do that . . . Tuppence and I, you see, aren't on those terms. We go into things – together!'

In his mind was that phrase, uttered years ago, at the close of an earlier war. A *joint venture* . . .

That was what his life with Tuppence had been and would always be – a Joint Venture . . .

CHAPTER 4

I

When Tuppence entered the lounge at Sans Souci just before dinner, the only occupant of the room was the monumental Mrs O'Rourke, who was sitting by the window looking like some gigantic Buddha.

She greeted Tuppence with a lot of geniality and verve.

'Ah now, if it isn't Mrs Blenkensop! You're like myself; it pleases you to be down to time and get a quiet minute or two before going into the dining-room, and a pleasant room this is in good weather with the windows open in the way that you'll not be noticing the smell of cooking. Terrible that is, in all of these places, and more especially if it's onion or cabbage that's on the fire. Sit here now, Mrs Blenkensop, and tell me what you've been doing with yourself this fine day and how you like Leahampton.'

There was something about Mrs O'Rourke that had an unholy fascination for Tuppence. She was rather like an ogress dimly remembered from early fairy tales. With her bulk, her deep voice, her unabashed beard and moustache, her deep twinkling eyes and the impression she gave of being more than life-size, she was indeed not unlike some childhood's fantasy.

Tuppence replied that she thought she was going to like Leahampton very much, and be happy there.

'That is,' she added in a melancholy voice, 'as happy as I can be anywhere with this terrible anxiety weighing on me all the time.'

'Ah now, don't you be worrying yourself,' Mrs O'Rourke advised comfortably. 'Those boys of yours will come back to you safe and sound. Not a doubt of it. One of them's in the Air Force, so I think you said?'

'Yes, Raymond.'

'And is he in France now, or in England?'

'He's in Egypt at the moment, but from what he said in his last letter – not exactly *said* – but we have a little private code if you know what I mean? – certain sentences mean certain things. I think that's quite justified, don't you?'

Mrs O'Rourke replied promptly:

'Indeed I do. 'Tis a mother's privilege.'

'Yes, you see I feel I must know just where he is.'

Mrs O'Rourke nodded the Buddha-like head.

'I feel for you entirely, so I do. If I had a boy out there I'd be deceiving the censor in the very same way, so I would. And your other boy, the one in the Navy?'

Tuppence entered obligingly upon a saga of Douglas.

'You see,' she cried, 'I feel so lost without my three boys. They've never been all away together from me before. They're all so sweet to me. I really do think they treat me more as a *friend* than a mother.' She laughed self-consciously. 'I have to scold them sometimes and *make* them go out without me.'

('What a pestilential woman I sound,' thought Tuppence to herself.)

She went on aloud:

'And really I didn't know quite *what* to do or *where* to go. The lease of my house in London was up and it seemed so foolish to renew it, and I thought if I came somewhere quiet, and yet with a good train service –' She broke off.

Again the Buddha nodded.

'I agree with you entirely. London is no place at the present. Ah! the gloom of it! I've lived there myself for many a year now. I'm by way of being an antique dealer, you know. You may know my shop in Cornaby Street, Chelsea? Kate Kelly's the name over the door. Lovely stuff I had there too – oh, lovely stuff – mostly glass – Waterford, Cork – beautiful. Chandeliers and lustres and punchbowls and all the rest of it. Foreign glass, too. And small furniture – nothing large – just small period pieces – mostly walnut and oak. Oh, lovely stuff – and I had some good customers. But there, when there's a war on, all that goes west. I'm lucky to be out of it with as little loss as I've had.'

A faint memory flickered through Tuppence's mind. A shop filled with glass, through which it was difficult to move, a rich persuasive voice, a compelling massive woman. Yes, surely, she had been into that shop.

Mrs O'Rourke went on:

'I'm not one of those that like to be always complaining – not like some that's in this house. Mr Cayley for one, with his muffler and his shawls and his moans about his business going to pieces.

Of course it's to pieces, there's a war on – and his wife with never boo to say to a goose. Then there's that little Mrs Sprot, always fussing about her husband.'

'Is he out at the Front?'

'Not he. He's a tuppenny-halfpenny clerk in an insurance office, that's all, and so terrified of air raids he's had his wife down here since the beginning of the war. Mind you, I think that's right where the child's concerned – and a nice wee mite she is – but Mrs Sprot she frets, for all that her husband comes down when he can . . . Keeps saying Arthur must miss her so. But if you ask me Arthur's not missing her overmuch – maybe he's got other fish to fry.'

Tuppence murmured:

'I'm terribly sorry for all these mothers. If you let your children go away without you, you never stop worrying. And if you go with them it's hard on the husbands being left.'

'Ah! yes, and it comes expensive running two establishments.'

'This place seems quite reasonable,' said Tuppence.

'Yes, I'd say you get your money's worth. Mrs Perenna's a good manager. There's a queer woman for you now.'

'In what way?' asked Tuppence.

Mrs O'Rourke said with a twinkle:

'You'll be thinking I'm a terrible talker. It's true. I'm interested in all my fellow creatures, that's why I sit in this chair as often as I can. You see who goes in and who goes out and who's on the veranda and what goes on in the garden. What were we talking of now – ah yes, Mrs Perenna, and the queerness of her. There's been a grand drama in that woman's life, or I'm much mistaken.'

'Do you really think so?'

'I do now. And the mystery she makes of herself! "And where might you come from in Ireland?" I asked her. And would you believe it, she held out on me, declaring she was not from Ireland at all.'

'You think she is Irish?'

'Of course she's Irish. I know my own countrywomen. I could name you the county she comes from. But there! "I'm English," she says. "And my husband was a Spaniard" –'

Mrs O'Rourke broke off abruptly as Mrs Sprot came in, closely followed by Tommy.

Tuppence immediately assumed a sprightly manner.

'Good evening, Mr Meadowes. You look very brisk this evening.'

Tommy said:

'Plenty of exercise, that's the secret. A round of golf this morning and a walk along the front this afternoon.'

Millicent Sprot said:

'I took baby down to the beach this afternoon. She wanted to paddle but I really thought it was rather cold. I was helping her build a castle and a dog ran off with my knitting and pulled out yards of it. So annoying, and so difficult picking up all the stitches again. I'm such a bad knitter.'

'You're getting along fine with that helmet, Mrs Blenkensop,' said Mrs O'Rourke, suddenly turning her attention to Tuppence. 'You've been just racing along. I thought Miss Minton said that you were an inexperienced knitter.'

Tuppence flushed faintly. Mrs O'Rourke's eyes were sharp. With a slightly vexed air, Tuppence said:

'I have really done quite a lot of knitting. I told Miss Minton so. But I think she likes teaching people.'

Everybody laughed in agreement, and a few minutes later the rest of the party came in and the gong was sounded.

The conversation during the meal turned on the absorbing subject of spies. Well-known hoary chestnuts were retold. The nun with the muscular arm, the clergyman descending from his parachute and using unclergymanlike language as he landed with a bump, the Austrian cook who secreted a wireless in her bedroom chimney, and all the things that had happened or nearly happened to aunts and second cousins of those present. That led easily to Fifth Column activities. To denunciations of the British Fascists, of the Communists, of the Peace Party, of conscientious objectors. It was a very normal conversation of the kind that may be heard almost every day, nevertheless Tuppence watched keenly the faces and demeanour of the people as they talked, striving to catch some tell-tale expression or word. But there was nothing. Sheila Perenna alone took no part in the conversation, but that might be put down to her habitual taciturnity. She sat there, her dark rebellious face sullen and brooding.

Carl von Deinim was out tonight, so tongues could be quite unrestrained.

Sheila only spoke once toward the end of dinner.

Mrs Sprot had just said in her thin fluting voice:

'Where I do think the Germans made such a mistake in the last war was to shoot Nurse Cavell. It turned everybody against them.'

It was then that Sheila, flinging back her head, demanded in her fierce young voice: 'Why shouldn't they shoot her? She was a spy, wasn't she?'

'Oh, no, not a spy.'

'She helped English people to escape – in an enemy country. That's the same thing. Why shouldn't she be shot?'

'Oh, but shooting a woman – and a nurse.'

Sheila got up.

'I think the Germans were quite right,' she said.

She went out of the window into the garden.

Dessert, consisting of some under-ripe bananas, and some tired oranges, had been on the table some time. Everyone rose and adjourned to the lounge for coffee.

Only Tommy unobtrusively betook himself to the garden. He found Sheila Perenna leaning over the terrace wall staring out at the sea. He came and stood beside her.

By her hurried, quick breathing he knew that something had upset her badly. He offered her a cigarette, which she accepted.

He said: 'Lovely night.'

In a low intense voice the girl answered:

'It could be . . .'

Tommy looked at her doubtfully. He felt, suddenly, the attraction and the vitality of this girl. There was a tumultuous life in her, a kind of compelling power. She was the kind of girl, he thought, that a man might easily lose his head over.

'If it weren't for the war, you mean?' he said.

'I don't mean that at all. I hate the war.'

'So do we all.'

'Not in the way I mean. I hate the cant about it, the smugness – the horrible, horrible patriotism.'

'Patriotism?' Tommy was startled.

'Yes, I hate patriotism, do you understand? All this *country*,

country, country! Betraying your country – dying for your country – serving your country. Why should one's country mean anything at all?'

Tommy said simply: 'I don't know. It just does.'

'Not to me! Oh, it would to you – you go abroad and buy and sell in the British Empire and come back bronzed and full of clichés, talking about the natives and calling for Chota Pegs and all that sort of thing.'

Tommy said gently:

'I'm not quite as bad as that, I hope, my dear.'

'I'm exaggerating a little – but you know what I mean. You believe in the British Empire – and – and – the stupidity of dying for one's country.'

'My country,' said Tommy dryly, 'doesn't seem particularly anxious to allow me to die for it.'

'Yes, but you *want* to. And it's so *stupid*! *Nothing's* worth dying for. It's all an *idea* – talk, talk – froth – high-flown idiocy. My country doesn't mean anything to me at all.'

'Some day,' said Tommy, 'you'll be surprised to find that it does.'

'No. Never. I've suffered – I've seen –'

She broke off – then turned suddenly and impetuously upon him.

'Do you know who my father was?'

'No!' Tommy's interest quickened.

'His name was Patrick Maguire. He – he was a follower of Casement in the last war. He was shot as a traitor! All for nothing! For an idea – he worked himself up with those other Irishmen. Why couldn't he just stay at home quietly and mind his own business? He's a martyr to some people and a traitor to others. I think he was just – *stupid*!'

Tommy could hear the note of pent-up rebellion, coming out into the open. He said:

'So that's the shadow you've grown up with?'

'Shadow's right. Mother changed her name. We lived in Spain for some years. She always says that my father was half a Spaniard. We always tell lies wherever we go. We've been all over the Continent. Finally we came here and started this place. I think this is quite the most hateful thing we've done yet.'

Tommy asked:

'How does your mother feel about – things?'

'You mean – about my father's death?' Sheila was silent a moment, frowning, puzzled. She said slowly: 'I've never really known . . . she never talks about it. It's not easy to know what Mother feels or thinks.'

Tommy nodded his head thoughtfully.

Sheila said abruptly:

'I – I don't know why I've been telling you this. I got worked up. Where did it all start?'

'A discussion on Edith Cavell.'

'Oh yes – patriotism. I said I hated it.'

'Aren't you forgetting Nurse Cavell's own words?'

'What words?'

'Before she died. Don't you know what she said?'

He repeated the words:

'*Patriotism is not enough . . . I must have no hatred in my heart.*'

'Oh.' She stood there stricken for a moment.

Then, turning quickly, she wheeled away into the shadow of the garden.

II

'So you see, Tuppence, it would all fit in.'

Tuppence nodded thoughtfully. The beach around them was empty. She herself leaned against a breakwater, Tommy sat above her and the breakwater itself, from which post he could see anyone who approached along the esplanade. Not that he expected to see anyone, having ascertained with a fair amount of accuracy where people would be this morning. In any case his rendezvous with Tuppence had borne all the signs of a casual meeting, pleasurable to the lady and slightly alarming to himself.

Tuppence said:

'Mrs Perenna?'

'Yes. M not N. She satisfies the requirements.'

Tuppence nodded thoughtfully again.

'Yes. She's Irish – as spotted by Mrs O'Rourke – won't admit the fact. Has done a good deal of coming and going on the Continent. Changed her name to Perenna, came here and started this boarding-house. A splendid bit of camouflage, full of innocuous bores. Her husband was shot as a traitor – she's got every incentive for running a Fifth Column show in this country. Yes, it fits. Is the girl in it too, do you think?'

Tommy said finally:

'Definitely not. She'd never have told me all this otherwise. I – I feel a bit of a cad, you know.'

Tuppence nodded with complete understanding.

'Yes, one does. In a way it's a foul job, this.'

'But very necessary.'

'Oh, of course.'

Tommy said, flushing slightly:

'I don't like lying any better than you do –'

Tuppence interrupted him.

'I don't mind lying in the least. To be quite honest I get a lot of artistic pleasure out of my lies. What gets me down is those moments when one forgets to lie – the times when one is just oneself – and gets results that way that you couldn't have got any other.' She paused and went on: 'That's what happened to you last night – with the girl. She responded to the *real* you – that's why you feel badly about it.'

'I believe you're right, Tuppence.'

'I know. Because I did the same thing myself – with the German boy.'

Tommy said:

'What do you think about him?'

Tuppence said quickly:

'If you ask me, I don't think he's got anything to do with it.'

'Grant thinks he has.'

'Your Mr Grant!' Tuppence's mood changed. She chuckled. 'How I'd like to have seen his face when you told him about me.'

'At any rate, he's made the *amende honorable*. You're definitely on the job.'

Tuppence nodded, but she looked a trifle abstracted.

She said:

'Do you remember after the last war – when we were hunting down Mr Brown? Do you remember what fun it was? How excited we were?'

Tommy agreed, his face lighting up.

'Rather!'

'Tommy – why isn't it the same now?'

He considered the question, his quiet ugly face grave. Then he said:

'I suppose it's really – a question of age.'

Tuppence said sharply:

'You don't think – we're too old?'

'No, I'm sure we're not. It's only that – this time – it won't be *fun*. It's the same in other ways. This is the second war we've been in – and we feel quite different about this one.'

'I know – we see the pity of it and the waste – and the horror. All the things we were too young to think about before.'

'That's it. In the last war I was scared every now and then – and had some pretty close shaves, and went through hell once or twice, but there were good times too.'

Tuppence said:

'I suppose Derek feels like that?'

'Better not think about him, old thing,' Tommy advised.

'You're right.' Tuppence set her teeth. 'We've got a job. We're going to *do* that job. Let's get on with it. Have we found what we're looking for in Mrs Perenna?'

'We can at least say that she's strongly indicated. There's no one else, is there, Tuppence, that you've got your eye on?'

Tuppence considered.

'No, there isn't. The first thing I did when I arrived, of course, was to size them all up and assess, as it were, possibilities. Some of them seem quite impossible.'

'Such as?'

'Well, Miss Minton for instance, the "compleat" British spinster, and Mrs Sprot and her Betty, and the vacuous Mrs Cayley.'

'Yes, but nitwittishness can be assumed.'

'Oh, quite, but the fussy spinster and the absorbed young mother are parts that would be fatally easy to overdo – and these people are quite natural. Then, where Mrs Sprot is concerned, there's the child.'

'I suppose,' said Tommy, 'that even a secret agent might have a child.'

'Not with her on the job,' said Tuppence. 'It's not the kind of thing you'd bring a child into. I'm quite sure about that, Tommy. I *know*. You'd keep a child out of it.'

'I withdraw,' said Tommy. 'I'll give you Mrs Sprot and Miss Minton, but I'm not so sure about Mrs Cayley.'

'No, she might be a possibility. Because she really does overdo it. I mean there can't be many women *quite* as idiotic as she seems.'

'I have often noticed that being a devoted wife saps the intellect,' murmured Tommy.

'And where have you noticed that?' demanded Tuppence.

'Not from you, Tuppence. Your devotion has never reached those lengths.'

'For a man,' said Tuppence kindly, 'you don't really make an undue fuss when you are ill.'

Tommy reverted to a survey of possibilities.

'Cayley,' said Tommy thoughtfully. 'There might be something fishy about Cayley.'

'Yes, there might. Then there's Mrs O'Rourke?'

'What do you feel about her?'

'I don't quite know. She's disturbing. Rather *fee fo fum* if you know what I mean.'

'Yes, I think I know. But I rather fancy that's just the predatory note. She's that kind of woman.'

Tuppence said slowly:

'She – notices things.'

She was remembering the remark about knitting.

'Then there's Bletchley,' said Tommy.

'I've hardly spoken to him. He's definitely your chicken.'

'I *think* he's just the ordinary pukka old school tie. I *think* so.'

'That's just it,' said Tuppence, answering a stress rather than actual words. 'The worst of this sort of show is that you look at quite ordinary everyday people and twist them to suit your morbid requirements.'

'I've tried a few experiments on Bletchley,' said Tommy.

'What sort of thing? I've got some experiments in mind myself.'

'Well – just gentle ordinary little traps – about dates and places – all that sort of thing.'

'Could you condescend from the general to the particular?'

'Well, say we're talking of duck-shooting. He mentions the Fayum – good sport there such and such a year, such and such a month. Some other time I mention Egypt in quite a different connection. Mummies, Tutankhamen, something like that – has he seen that stuff? When was he there? Check up on the answers. Or P & O boats – I mention the names of one or two, say so and so was a comfortable boat. He mentions some trip or other, later I check that. Nothing important, or anything that puts him on his guard – just a check up on accuracy.'

'And so far he hasn't slipped up in any way?'

'Not once. And that's a pretty good test, let me tell you, Tuppence.'

'Yes, but I suppose *if* he was N he would have his story quite pat.'

'Oh yes – the main outlines of it. But it's not so easy not to trip up on unimportant details. And then occasionally you remember too much – more, that is, than a bona fide person would do. An ordinary person doesn't usually remember offhand whether they took a certain shooting trip in 1926 or 1927. They have to think a bit and search their memory.'

'But so far you haven't caught Bletchley out?'

'So far he's responded in a perfectly normal manner.'

'Result – negative.'

'Exactly.'

'Now,' said Tuppence. 'I'll tell you some of my ideas.'

And she proceeded to do so.

III

On her way home, Mrs Blenkensop stopped at the post office. She bought stamps and on her way out went into one of the public call boxes. There she rang up a certain number, and asked for 'Mr Faraday'. This was the accepted method of communication with Mr Grant. She came out smiling and walked slowly homewards, stopping on the way to purchase some knitting wool.

It was a pleasant afternoon with a light breeze. Tuppence curbed the natural energy of her own brisk trot to that leisurely pace that accorded with her conception of the part of Mrs Blenkensop. Mrs Blenkensop had nothing on earth to do with herself except knit (not too well) and write letters to her boys.

She was always writing letters to her boys – sometimes she left them about half finished.

Tuppence came slowly up the hill towards Sans Souci. Since it was not a through road (it ended at Smugglers' Rest, Commander Haydock's house) there was never much traffic – a few trades-men's vans in the morning. Tuppence passed house after house, amusing herself by noting their names. Bella Vista (inaccurately named, since the merest glimpse of the sea was to be obtained, and the main view was the vast Victorian bulk of Edenholme on the other side of the road). Karachi was the next house. After that came Shirley Tower. Then Sea View (appropriate this time), Castle Clare (somewhat grandiloquent, since it was a small house), Trelawny, a rival establishment to that of Mrs Perenna, and finally the vast maroon bulk of Sans Souci.

It was just as she came near to it that Tuppence became aware of a woman standing by the gate peering inside. There was something tense and vigilant about the figure.

Almost unconsciously, Tuppence softened the sound of her own footsteps, stepping cautiously upon her toes.

It was not until she was close behind her, that the woman heard her and turned. Turned with a start.

She was a tall woman, poorly, even meanly dressed, but her face was unusual. She was not young – probably just under forty – but there was a contrast between her face and the way she was dressed. She was fair-haired, with wide cheekbones, and had been – indeed still was – beautiful. Just for a minute Tuppence had a feeling that the woman's face was somehow familiar to her, but the feeling faded. It was not, she thought, a face easily forgotten.

The woman was obviously startled, and the flash of alarm that flitted across her face was not lost on Tuppence. (Something odd here?)

Tuppence said:

'Excuse me, are you looking for someone?'

The woman spoke in a slow, foreign voice, pronouncing the words carefully as though she had learnt them by heart.

'This 'ouse is Sans Souci?'

'Yes. I live there. Did you want someone?'

There was an infinitesimal pause, then the woman said:

'You can tell me please. There is a Mr Rosenstein there, no?'

'Mr Rosenstein?' Tuppence shook her head. 'No. I'm afraid not. Perhaps he has been there and left. Shall I ask for you?'

But the strange woman made a quick gesture of refusal. She said:

'No – no. I make mistake. Excuse, please.'

Then, quickly, she turned and walked rapidly down the hill again.

Tuppence stood staring after her. For some reason, her suspicions were aroused. There was a contrast between the woman's manner and her words. Tuppence had an idea that 'Mr Rosenstein' was a fiction, that the woman had seized at the first name that came into her head.

Tuppence hesitated a minute, then she started down the hill after the other. What she could only describe as a 'hunch' made her want to follow the woman.

Presently, however, she stopped. To follow would be to draw attention to herself in a rather marked manner. She had clearly been on the point of entering Sans Souci when she spoke to the woman; to reappear on her trail would be to arouse suspicion that Mrs Blenkensop was something other than appeared on the surface – that is to say if this strange woman was indeed a member of the enemy plot.

No, at all costs Mrs Blenkensop must remain what she seemed.

Tuppence turned and retraced her steps up the hill. She entered Sans Souci and paused in the hall. The house seemed deserted, as was usual early in the afternoon. Betty was having her nap, the elder members were either resting or had gone out.

Then, as Tuppence stood in the dim hall thinking over her recent encounter, a faint sound came to her ears. It was a sound she knew quite well – the faint echo of a ting.

The telephone at Sans Souci was in the hall. The sound that Tuppence had just heard was the sound made when the receiver of an extension is taken off or replaced. There was one extension in the house – in Mrs Perenna's bedroom.

Tommy might have hesitated. Tuppence did not hesitate for a minute. Very gently and carefully she lifted off the receiver and put it to her ear.

Someone was using the extension. It was a man's voice. Tuppence heard:

'– Everything going well. On the fourth, then, as arranged.'

A woman's voice said: 'Yes, carry on.'

There was a click as the receiver was replaced.

Tuppence stood there, frowning. Was that Mrs Perenna's voice? Difficult to say with only those three words to go upon. If there had been only a little more to the conversation. It might, of course, be quite an ordinary conversation – certainly there was nothing in the words she had overheard to indicate otherwise.

A shadow obscured the light from the door. Tuppence jumped and replaced the receiver as Mrs Perenna spoke.

'Such a pleasant afternoon. Are you going out, Mrs Blenkensop, or have you just come in?'

So it was not Mrs Perenna who had been speaking from Mrs Perenna's room. Tuppence murmured something about having had a pleasant walk and moved to the staircase.

Mrs Perenna moved along the hall after her. She seemed bigger than usual. Tuppence was conscious of her as a strong athletic woman.

She said:

'I must get my things off,' and hurried up the stairs. As she turned the corner of the landing she collided with Mrs O'Rourke, whose vast bulk barred the top of the stairs.

'Dear, dear, now, Mrs Blenkensop, it's a great hurry you seem to be in.'

She did not move aside, just stood there smiling down at Tuppence just below her. There was, as always, a frightening quality about Mrs O'Rourke's smile.

And suddenly, for no reason, Tuppence felt afraid.

The big smiling Irishwoman, with her deep voice, barring her way, and below Mrs Perenna closing in at the foot of the stairs.

Tuppence glanced over her shoulder. Was it her fancy that there was something definitely menacing in Mrs Perenna's upturned face? Absurd, she told herself, absurd. In broad daylight – in a commonplace seaside boarding-house. But the house was so very quiet. Not a sound. And she herself here on the stairs between the two of them. Surely there *was* something a little queer in Mrs O'Rourke's smile – some fixed ferocious quality about it, Tuppence thought wildly, 'like a cat with a mouse'.

And then suddenly the tension broke. A little figure darted

along the top-landing uttering shrill squeals of mirth. Little Betty Sprot in vest and knickers. Darting past Mrs O'Rourke, shouting happily, 'Peek bo,' as she flung herself on Tuppence.

The atmosphere had changed. Mrs O'Rourke, a big genial figure, was crying out:

'Ah, the darlin'. It's a great girl she's getting.'

Below, Mrs Perenna had turned away to the door that led into the kitchen. Tuppence, Betty's hand clasped in hers, passed Mrs O'Rourke and ran along the passage to where Mrs Sprot was waiting to scold the truant.

Tuppence went in with the child.

She felt a queer sense of relief at the domestic atmosphere – the child's clothes lying about, the woolly toys, the painted crib, the sheeplike and somewhat unattractive face of Mr Sprot in its frame on the dressing-table, the burble of Mrs Sprot's denunciation of laundry prices and really she thought Mrs Perenna was a little unfair in refusing to sanction guests having their own electric irons –

All so normal, so reassuring, so everyday.

And yet – just now – on the stairs.

'Nerves,' said Tuppence to herself. 'Just nerves!'

But had it been nerves? Someone *had* been telephoning from Mrs Perenna's room. Mrs O'Rourke? Surely a very odd thing to do. It ensured, of course, that you would not be overheard by the household.

It must have been, Tuppence thought, a very short conversation. The merest brief exchange of words.

'Everything going well. On the fourth as arranged.'

It might mean nothing – or a good deal.

The fourth. Was that a date? The fourth, say of a month?

Or it might mean the fourth seat, or the fourth lamp-post, or the fourth breakwater – impossible to know.

It might just conceivably mean the Forth Bridge. There had been an attempt to blow that up in the last war.

Did it mean anything at all?

It might quite easily have been the confirmation of some perfectly ordinary appointment. Mrs Perenna might have told Mrs O'Rourke she could use the telephone in her bedroom any time she wanted to do so.

And the atmosphere on the stairs, that tense moment, might have been just her own overwrought nerves . . .

The quiet house – the feeling that there was something sinister – something evil . . .

'Stick to facts, Mrs Blenkensop,' said Tuppence sternly. 'And get on with your job.'

CHAPTER 5

I

Commander Haydock turned out to be a most genial host. He welcomed Mr Meadowes and Major Bletchley with enthusiasm, and insisted on showing the former 'all over my little place'.

Smugglers' Rest had been originally a couple of coastguards' cottages standing on the cliff overlooking the sea. There was a small cove below, but the access to it was perilous, only to be attempted by adventurous boys.

Then the cottages had been bought by a London business man who had thrown them into one and attempted half-heartedly to make a garden. He had come down occasionally for short periods in summer.

After that, the cottages had remained empty for some years, being let with a modicum of furniture to summer visitors.

'Then, some years ago,' explained Haydock, 'it was sold to a man called Hahn. He was a German, and if you ask me, he was neither more or less than a spy.'

Tommy's ears quickened.

'That's interesting,' he said, putting down the glass from which he had been sipping sherry.

'Damned thorough fellows they are,' said Haydock. 'Getting ready even then for this show – at least that is my opinion. Look at the situation of this place. Perfect for signalling out to sea. Cove below where you could land a motor-boat. Completely isolated owing to the contour of the cliff. Oh yes, don't tell me that fellow Hahn wasn't a German agent.'

Major Bletchley said:

'Of course he was.'

'What happened to him?' asked Tommy.

'Ah!' said Haydock. 'Thereby hangs a tale. Hahn spent a lot of money on this place. He had a way cut down to the beach for one thing – concrete steps – expensive business. Then he had the whole of the house done over – bathrooms, every expensive gadget you can imagine. And who did he set to do all this? Not a local man. No, a firm from London, so it was said – but a lot of the men who came down were foreigners. Some of them *didn't speak a word of English.* Don't you agree with me that that sounds extremely fishy?'

'A little odd, certainly,' agreed Tommy.

'I was in the neighbourhood myself at the time, living in a bungalow, and I got interested in what this fellow was up to. I used to hang about to watch the workmen. Now I'll tell you this – they didn't like it – they didn't like it at all. Once or twice they were quite threatening about it. Why should they be if everything was all square and above board?'

Bletchley nodded agreement.

'You ought to have gone to the authorities,' he said.

'Just what I did do, my dear fellow. Made a positive nuisance of myself pestering the police.'

He poured himself out another drink.

'And what did I get for my pains? Polite inattention. Blind and deaf, that's what we were in this country. Another war with Germany was out of the question – there was peace in Europe – our relations with Germany were excellent. Natural sympathy between us nowadays. I was regarded as an old fossil, a war maniac, a diehard old sailor. What was the good of pointing out to people that the Germans were building the finest Air Force in Europe and not just to fly round and have picnics!'

Major Bletchley said explosively:

'Nobody believed it! Damned fools! "Peace in our time." "Appeasement." All a lot of blah!'

Haydock said, his face redder than usual with suppressed anger: 'A warmonger, that's what they called me. The sort of chap, they said, who was an obstacle to peace. Peace! I knew what our Hun friends were at! And mind this, they prepare things a long time beforehand. I was convinced that Mr Hahn was up to no good. I didn't like his foreign workmen. I didn't like the way he was spending money on this place. I kept on badgering away at people.'

'Stout fellow,' said Bletchley appreciatively.

'And finally,' said the Commander, 'I began to make an impression. We had a new Chief Constable down here – retired soldier. And he had the sense to listen to me. His fellows began to nose around. Sure enough, Hahn decamped. Just slipped out and disappeared one fine night. The police went over this place with a search-warrant. In a safe which had been built-in in the dining-room they found a wireless transmitter and some pretty damaging documents. Also a big store place under the garage for petrol – great tanks. I can tell you I was cock-a-hoop over that. Fellows at the club used to rag me about my German spy complex. They dried up after that. Trouble with us in this country is that we're so absurdly unsuspicious.'

'It's a crime. Fools – that's what we are – fools. Why don't we intern all these refugees?' Major Bletchley was well away.

'End of the story was I bought the place when it came into the market,' continued the Commander, not to be side-tracked from his pet story. 'Come and have a look round, Meadowes?'

'Thanks, I'd like to.'

Commander Haydock was as full of zest as a boy as he did the honours of the establishment. He threw open the big safe in the dining-room to show where the secret wireless had been found. Tommy was taken out to the garage and was shown where the big petrol tanks had lain concealed, and finally, after a superficial glance at the two excellent bathrooms, the special lighting, and the various kitchen 'gadgets', he was taken down the steep concreted path to the little cove beneath, whilst Commander Haydock told him all over again how extremely useful the whole lay-out would be to an enemy in wartime.

He was taken into the cave which gave the place its name, and Haydock pointed out enthusiastically how it could have been used.

Major Bletchley did not accompany the two men on their tour, but remained peacefully sipping his drink on the terrace. Tommy gathered that the Commander's spy hunt with its successful issue was that good gentleman's principal topic of conversation, and that his friends had heard it many times.

In fact, Major Bletchley said as much when they were walking down to Sans Souci a little later.

'Good fellow, Haydock,' he said. 'But he's not content to let a good thing alone. We've heard all about that business again and again until we're sick of it. He's as proud of the whole bag of tricks up there as a cat of its kittens.'

The simile was not too far-fetched, and Tommy assented with a smile.

The conversation then turning to Major Bletchley's own successful unmasking of a dishonest bearer in 1923, Tommy's attention was free to pursue its own inward line of thought punctuated by sympathetic 'Not reallys?' – 'You don't say so?' and 'What an extraordinary business' which was all Major Bletchley needed in the way of encouragement.

More than ever now Tommy felt that when the dying Farquhar had mentioned Sans Souci he had been on the right track. Here, in this out of the world spot, preparations had been made a long time beforehand. The arrival of the German Hahn and his extensive installation showed clearly enough that this particular part of the coast had been selected for a rallying point, a focus of enemy activity.

That particular game had been defeated by the unexpected activity of the suspicious Commander Haydock. Round one had gone to Britain. But supposing that Smugglers' Rest had been only the first outpost of a complicated scheme of attack? Smugglers' Rest, that is to say, had represented sea communications. Its beach, inaccessible save for the path down from above, would lend itself admirably to the plan. But it was only a part of the whole.

Defeated on that part of the plan by Haydock, what had been the enemy's response? Might not he have fallen back upon the next best thing – that is to say, Sans Souci. The exposure of Hahn had come about four years ago. Tommy had an idea, from what Sheila Perenna had said, that it was very soon after that that Mrs Perenna had returned to England and bought Sans Souci. The next move in the game?

It would seem therefore that Leahampton was definitely an enemy centre – that there were already installations and affiliations in the neighbourhood.

His spirits rose. The depression engendered by the harmless and futile atmosphere of Sans Souci disappeared. Innocent as it seemed, that innocence was no more than skin deep. Behind that innocuous mask things were going on.

And the focus of it all, so far as Tommy could judge, was Mrs Perenna. The first thing to do was to know more about Mrs Perenna, to penetrate behind her apparently simple routine of running her boarding establishment. Her correspondence, her acquaintances, her social or war-working activities – somewhere in all these must lie the essence of her real activities. If Mrs Perenna was the renowned woman agent – M – then it was she who controlled the whole of the Fifth Column activities in this country. Her identity would be known to few – only to those at the top. But communications she must have with her chiefs of staff, and it was those communications that he and Tuppence had got to tap.

At the right moment, as Tommy saw well enough, Smugglers' Rest could be seized and held – by a few stalwarts operating from Sans Souci. That moment was not yet, but it might be very near.

Once the German army was established in control of the channel ports in France and Belgium, they could concentrate on the invasion and subjugation of Britain, and things were certainly going very badly in France at the moment.

Britain's Navy was all-powerful on the sea, so the attack must come by air and by internal treachery – and if the threads of internal treachery were in Mrs Perenna's keeping there was no time to lose.

Major Bletchley's words chimed in with his thoughts:

'I saw, you know, that there was no time to lose. I got hold of Abdul, my syce – good fellow, Abdul –'

The story droned on.

Tommy was thinking:

'Why Leahampton? Any reason? It's out of the mainstream – bit of a backwater. Conservative, old-fashioned. All those points make it desirable. Is there anything else?'

There was a stretch of flat agricultural country behind it running inland. A lot of pasture. Suitable, therefore, for the landing of troop-carrying airplanes or of parachute troops. But that was true of many other places. There was also a big chemical works where, it might be noted, Carl von Deinim was employed.

Carl von Deinim. How did he fit in? Only too well. He was not, as Grant had pointed out, the real head. A cog, only, in the machine. Liable to suspicion and internment at any moment. But in the meantime he might have accomplished what had been his task. He had mentioned to Tuppence that he was working on decontamination problems and on the immunising of certain gases. There were probabilities there – probabilities unpleasant to contemplate.

Carl, Tommy decided (a little reluctantly), was in it. A pity, because he rather liked the fellow. Well, he was working for his country – taking his life in his hands. Tommy had respect for such an adversary – down him by all means – a firing-party was the end, but you knew that when you took on your job.

It was the people who betrayed their own land – from within – that really roused a slow vindictive passion in him. By God, he'd get them!

'– And that's how I got them!' The Major wound up his story triumphantly. 'Pretty smart bit of work, eh?'

Unblushingly Tommy said:

'Most ingenious thing I've heard in my life, Major.'

II

Mrs Blenkensop was reading a letter on thin foreign paper stamped outside with the censor's mark.

Incidentally the direct result of her conversation with 'Mr Faraday'.

'Dear Raymond,' she murmured. 'I was so happy about him out in Egypt, and now, it seems, there is a big change round. All *very* secret, of course, and he can't *say* anything – just that there really is a marvellous plan and that I'm to be ready for some *big surprise* soon. I'm glad to know where he's being sent, but I really don't see why –'

Bletchley grunted.

'Surely he's not allowed to tell you that?'

Tuppence gave a deprecating laugh and looked round the breakfast table as she folded up her precious letter.

'Oh! we have our methods,' she said archly. 'Dear Raymond knows that if only I know where he is or where he's going I don't worry quite so much. It's quite a simple way, too. Just a certain word, you know, and after it the initial letters of the next words spell out the place. Of course it makes rather a funny sentence sometimes – but Raymond is really most ingenious. I'm sure *nobody* would notice.'

Little murmurs arose round the table. The moment was well chosen; everybody happened to be at the breakfast table together for once.

Bletchley, his face rather red, said:

'You'll excuse me, Mrs Blenkensop, but that's a damned foolish thing to do. Movements of troops and air squadrons are just what the Germans want to know.'

'Oh, but I never tell anyone,' cried Tuppence. 'I'm very, very careful.'

'All the same it's an unwise thing to do – and your boy will get into trouble over it some day.'

'Oh, I do hope not. I'm his *mother*, you see. A mother *ought* to know.'

'Indeed and I think you're right,' boomed out Mrs O'Rourke. 'Wild horses wouldn't drag the information from you – we know that.'

'Letters can be read,' said Bletchley.

'I'm very careful never to leave letters lying about,' said Tuppence with an air of outraged dignity. 'I always keep them locked up.'

Bletchley shook his head doubtfully.

III

It was a grey morning with the wind blowing coldly from the sea. Tuppence was alone at the far end of the beach.

She took from her bag two letters that she had just called for at a small newsagent's in the town.

They had taken some time in coming since they had been readdressed there, the second time to a Mrs Spender. Tuppence liked crossing her tracks. Her children believed her to be in Cornwall with an old aunt.

She opened the first letter.

'Dearest Mother,
    'Lots of funny things I could tell you only I mustn't. We're putting

*up a good show, I think. Five German planes before breakfast is
today's market quotation. Bit of a mess at the moment and all that,
but we'll get there all right in the end.*

'*It's the way they machine-gun the poor civilian devils on the
roads that gets me. It makes us all see red. Gus and Trundles want
to be remembered to you. They're still going strong.*

'*Don't worry about me. I'm all right. Wouldn't have missed this
show for the world. Love to old Carrot Top – have the W.O. given
him a job yet?*

'*Yours ever,*
'*Derek.*'

Tuppence's eyes were very bright and shining as she read and
re-read this.

Then she opened the other letter.

'*Dearest Mum,*

'*How's old Aunt Gracie? Going strong? I think you're wonderful
to stick it. I couldn't.*

'*No news. My job is very interesting, but so hush-hush I can't tell
you about it. But I really do feel I'm doing something worthwhile.
Don't fret about not getting any war work to do – it's so silly all these
elderly women rushing about wanting to do things. They only really
want people who are young and efficient. I wonder how Carrots is
getting on at his job up in Scotland? Just filling up forms, I suppose.
Still he'll be happy to feel he is doing something.*

'*Lots of love,*
'*Deborah.*'

Tuppence smiled.

She folded the letters, smoothed them lovingly, and then under
the shelter of a breakwater she struck a match and set them on
fire. She waited until they were reduced to ashes.

Taking out her fountain-pen and a small writing-pad, she wrote
rapidly.

'*Langherne,*
Cornwall.

'*Dearest Deb,*

'*It seems so remote from the war here that I can hardly believe there is a war going on. Very glad to get your letter and know that your work is interesting.*

'*Aunt Gracie has grown much more feeble and very hazy in her mind. I think she is glad to have me here. She talks a good deal about the old days and sometimes, I think, confuses me with my own mother. They are growing more vegetables than usual – have turned the rose-garden into potatoes. I help old Sikes a bit. It makes me feel I am doing something in the war. Your father seems a bit disgruntled, but I think, as you say, he too is glad to be doing something.*

'*Love from your*

'*TUPPENNY MOTHER.*'

She took a fresh sheet.

'*Darling Derek,*

'*A great comfort to get your letter. Send field postcards often if you haven't time to write.*

'*I've come down to be with Aunt Gracie a bit. She is very feeble. She will talk of you as though you were seven and gave me ten shillings yesterday to send you as a tip.*

'*I'm still on the shelf and nobody wants my invaluable services! Extraordinary! Your father, as I told you, has got a job in the Ministry of Requirements. He is up north somewhere. Better than nothing, but not what he wanted, poor old Carrot Top. Still I suppose we've got to be humble and take a back seat and leave the war to you young idiots.*

'*I won't say "Take care of yourself", because I gather that the whole point is that you should do just the opposite. But don't go and be stupid.*

'*Lots of love,*

'*TUPPENCE.*'

She put the letters into envelopes, addressed and stamped them, and posted them on her way back to Sans Souci.

As she reached the bottom of the cliff her attention was caught by two figures standing talking a little way up.

Tuppence stopped dead. It was the same woman she had seen yesterday and talking to her was Carl von Deinim.

Regretfully Tuppence noted the fact that there was no cover. She could not get near them unseen and overhear what was being said.

Moreover, at that moment, the young German turned his head and saw her. Rather abruptly, the two figures parted. The woman came rapidly down the hill, crossing the road and passing Tuppence on the other side.

Carl von Deinim waited until Tuppence came up to him.

Then, gravely and politely, he wished her good morning.

Tuppence said immediately:

'What a very odd-looking woman that was to whom you were talking, Mr Deinim.'

'Yes. It is a Central European type. She is a Pole.'

'Really? A – a friend of yours?'

Tuppence's tone was a very good copy of the inquisitive voice of Aunt Gracie in her younger days.

'Not at all,' said Carl stiffly. 'I never saw the woman before.'

'Oh really. I thought –' Tuppence paused artistically.

'She asked me only for a direction. I speak German to her because she does not understand much English.'

'I see. And she was asking the way somewhere?'

'She asked me if I knew a Mrs Gottlieb near here. I do not, and she says she has, perhaps, got the name of the house wrong.'

'I see,' said Tuppence thoughtfully.

Mr Rosenstein. Mrs Gottlieb.

She stole a swift glance at Carl von Deinim. He was walking beside her with a set stiff face.

Tuppence felt a definite suspicion of this strange woman. And she felt almost convinced that when she had first caught sight of them, the woman and Carl had been already talking some time together.

Carl von Deinim?

Carl and Sheila that morning. '*You must be careful.*'

Tuppence thought:

'I hope – I hope these young things *aren't* in it!'

Soft, she told herself, middle-aged and soft! That's what she was! The Nazi creed was a youth creed. Nazi agents would in all probability be young. Carl and Sheila. Tommy said Sheila wasn't in it. Yes, but Tommy was a man, and Sheila was beautiful with a queer breath-taking beauty.

Carl and Sheila, and behind them that enigmatic figure: Mrs Perenna. Mrs Perenna, sometimes the voluble commonplace guesthouse hostess, sometimes, for fleeting minutes, a tragic, violent personality.

Tuppence went slowly upstairs to her bedroom.

That evening, when she went to bed, she pulled out the long drawer of her bureau. At one side of it was a small japanned box with a flimsy cheap lock. Tuppence slipped on gloves, unlocked the box, and opened it. A pile of letters lay inside. On the top was the one received that morning from 'Raymond'. Tuppence unfolded it with due precautions.

Then her lips set grimly. There had been an eyelash in the fold of the paper this morning. The eyelash was not there now.

She went to the washstand. There was a little bottle labelled innocently: 'Grey powder' with a dose.

Adroitly Tuppence dusted a little of the powder on to the letter and on to the surface of the glossy japanned enamel of the box.

There were no fingerprints on either of them.

Again Tuppence nodded her head with a certain grim satisfaction.

For there should have been fingerprints – her own.

A servant might have read the letters out of curiosity, though it seemed unlikely – certainly unlikely that she should have gone to the trouble of finding a key to fit the box.

But a servant would not think of wiping off fingerprints.

Mrs Perenna? Sheila? Somebody else? Somebody, at least, who was interested in the movements of British armed forces.

IV

Tuppence's plan of campaign had been simple in its outlines. First, a general sizing up of probabilities and possibilities. Second, an experiment to determine whether there was or was not an inmate of Sans Souci who was interested in troop movements and anxious to conceal the fact. Third – who that person was?

It was concerning that third operation that Tuppence pondered as she lay in bed the following morning. Her train of thought was slightly hampered by Betty Sprot, who had pranced in at an early hour, preceding indeed the cup of somewhat tepid inky liquid known as Morning Tea.

Betty was both active and voluble. She had taken a great fancy to Tuppence. She climbed up on the bed and thrust an extremely tattered picture-book under Tuppence's nose, commanding with brevity:

'Wead.'

Tuppence read obediently.

'Goosey goosey gander, whither will you wander?

'Upstairs, downstairs, in my lady's chamber.'

Betty rolled with mirth – repeating in an ecstasy:

'Upstares – upstares – upstares –' and then with a sudden climax, '*Down* –' and proceeded to roll off the bed with a thump.

This proceeding was repeated several times until it palled. Then Betty crawled about the floor, playing with Tuppence's shoes and muttering busily to herself in her own particular idiom:

'Ag do – bah pit – soo – soodah – putch –'

Released to fly back to its own perplexities, Tuppence's mind forgot the child. The words of the nursery rhyme seemed to mock at her.

'Goosey – goosey, gander, whither shall ye wander?'

Whither indeed? Goosey, that was her, Gander was Tommy. It was, at any rate, what they appeared to be! Tuppence had the heartiest contempt for Mrs Blenkensop. Mr Meadowes, she thought, was a little better – stolid, British, unimaginative – quite incredibly stupid. Both of them, she hoped, fitting nicely into the background of Sans Souci. Both such possible people to be there.

All the same, one must not relax – a slip was so easy. She had made one the other day – nothing that mattered, but just a sufficient indication to warn her to be careful. Such an easy approach to intimacy and good relations – an indifferent knitter asking for guidance. But she had forgotten that one evening, her fingers had slipped into their own practised efficiency, the needles clicking busily with the even note of the experienced knitter. Mrs

O'Rourke had noticed it. Since then, she had carefully struck a medium course – not so clumsy as she had been at first – but not so rapid as she could be.

'Ag boo bate?' demanded Betty. She reiterated the question: 'Ag boo bate?'

'Lovely, darling,' said Tuppence absently. 'Beautiful.'

Satisfied, Betty relapsed into murmurs again.

Her next step, Tuppence thought, could be managed easily enough. That is to say with the connivance of Tommy. She saw exactly how to do it –

Lying there planning, time slipped by. Mrs Sprot came in, breathless, to seek for Betty.

'Oh, here she is. I couldn't think where she had got to. Oh, Betty, you naughty girl – oh, dear, Mrs Blenkensop, I am so sorry.'

Tuppence sat up in bed. Betty, with an angelic face, was contemplating her handiwork.

She had removed all the laces from Tuppence's shoes and had immersed them in a toothglass of water. She was prodding them now with a gleeful finger.

Tuppence laughed and cut short Mrs Sprot's apologies.

'How frightfully funny. Don't worry, Mrs Sprot, they'll recover all right. It's my fault. I should have noticed what she was doing. She was rather quiet.'

'I know,' Mrs Sprot sighed. 'Whenever they're quiet, it's a bad sign. I'll get you some more laces this morning, Mrs Blenkensop.'

'Don't bother,' said Tuppence. 'They'll dry none the worse.'

Mrs Sprot bore Betty away and Tuppence got up to put her plan into execution.

CHAPTER 6

I

Tommy looked rather gingerly at the packet that Tuppence thrust upon him.

'Is this it?'

'Yes. Be careful. Don't get it over you.'

Tommy took a delicate sniff at the packet and replied with energy.

'No, indeed. What is this frightful stuff?'

'Asafoetida,' replied Tuppence. 'A pinch of that and you will wonder why your boy-friend is no longer attentive, as the advertisements say.'

'Shades of BO,' murmured Tommy.

Shortly after that, various incidents occurred.

The first was the smell in Mr Meadowes' room.

Mr Meadowes, not a complaining man by nature, spoke about it mildly at first, then with increasing firmness.

Mrs Perenna was summoned into conclave. With all the will to resist in the world, she had to admit that there was a smell. A pronounced unpleasant smell. Perhaps, she suggested, the gas tap of the fire was leaking.

Bending down and sniffing dubiously, Tommy remarked that he did not think the smell came from there. Nor from under the floor. He himself thought, definitely – a dead rat.

Mrs Perenna admitted that she had heard of such things – but she was sure there were no rats at Sans Souci. Perhaps a mouse – though she herself had never seen a mouse.

Mr Meadowes said with firmness that he thought the smell indicated at least a rat – and he added, still more firmly, that he was not going to sleep another night in the room until the matter had been seen to. He would ask Mrs Perenna to change his room.

Mrs Perenna said, 'Of course, she had just been about to suggest the same thing. She was afraid that the only room vacant was rather a small one and unfortunately it had no sea view, but if Mr Meadowes did not mind that –'

Mr Meadowes did not. His only wish was to get away from the smell. Mrs Perenna thereupon accompanied him to a small bedroom, the door of which happened to be just opposite the door of Mrs Blenkensop's room, and summoned the adenoidal semi-idiotic Beatrice to 'move Mr Meadowes' things'. She would, she explained, send for 'a man' to take up the floor and search for the origin of the smell.

Matters were settled satisfactorily on this basis.

II

The second incident was Mr Meadowes' hay fever. That was what he called it at first. Later he admitted doubtfully that he might just possibly have caught cold. He sneezed a good deal, and his eyes ran. If there was a faint elusive suggestion of raw onion floating in the breeze in the vicinity of Mr Meadowes' large silk handkerchief nobody noticed the fact, and indeed a pungent amount of eau de cologne masked the more penetrating odour.

Finally, defeated by incessant sneezing and nose-blowing, Mr Meadowes retired to bed for the day.

It was on the morning of that day that Mrs Blenkensop received a letter from her son Douglas. So excited and thrilled was Mrs Blenkensop that everybody at Sans Souci heard about it. The letter had not been censored at all, she explained, because fortunately one of Douglas's friends coming on leave had brought it, so for once Douglas had been able to write quite fully.

'And it just shows,' declared Mrs Blenkensop, wagging her head sagely, 'how little we know really of what is going on.'

After breakfast she went upstairs to her room, opened the japanned box and put the letter away. Between the folded pages were some unnoticeable grains of rice powder. She closed the box again, pressing her fingers firmly on its surface.

As she left her room she coughed, and from opposite came the sound of a highly histrionic sneeze.

Tuppence smiled and proceeded downstairs.

She had already made known her intention of going up to London for the day – to see her lawyer on some business and to do a little shopping.

Now she was given a good send-off by the assembled boarders and entrusted with various commissions – 'only if you have time, of course'.

Major Bletchley held himself aloof from this female chatter. He was reading his paper and uttering appropriate comments aloud. 'Damned swines of Germans. Machine-gunning civilian refugees on the roads. Damned brutes. If I were our people –'

Tuppence left him still outlining what *he* would do if he were in charge of operations.

She made a detour through the garden to ask Betty Sprot what she would like as a present from London.

Betty ecstatically clasping a snail in two hot hands gurgled appreciatively. In response to Tuppence's suggestions – 'A pussy. A picture-book? Some coloured chalks to draw with?' – Betty decided, 'Betty dwar.' So the coloured chalks were noted down on Tuppence's list.

As she passed on meaning to rejoin the drive by the path at the end of the garden she came unexpectedly upon Carl von Deinim. He was standing leaning on the wall. His hands were clenched, and as Tuppence approached he turned on her, his usually impassive face convulsed with emotion.

Tuppence paused involuntarily and asked:

'Is anything the matter?'

'Ach, yes, everything is the matter.' His voice was hoarse and unnatural. 'You have a saying here that a thing is neither fish, flesh, fowl, nor good red herring, have you not?'

Tuppence nodded.

Carl went on bitterly:

'That is what I am. It cannot go on, that is what I say. It cannot go on. It would be best, I think, to end everything.'

'What do you mean?'

The young man said:

'You have spoken kindly to me. You would, I think, understand. I fled from my own country because of injustice and cruelty. I came here to find freedom. I hated Nazi Germany. But, alas, I am still a German. Nothing can alter that.'

Tuppence murmured:

'You may have difficulties, I know –'

'It is not that. I am a German, I tell you. In my heart – in my feeling. Germany is still my country. When I read of German cities bombed, of German soldiers dying, of German aeroplanes brought down – they are my people who die. When that old fire-eating Major reads out from his paper, when he say "those swine" – I am moved to fury – I cannot bear it.'

He added quietly:

'And so I think it would be best, perhaps, to end it all. Yes, to end it.'

Tuppence took hold of him firmly by the arm.

'Nonsense,' she said robustly. 'Of course you feel as you do. Anyone would. But you've got to stick it.'

'I wish they would intern me. It would be easier so.'

'Yes, probably it would. But in the meantime you're doing useful work – or so I've heard. Useful not only to England but to humanity. You're working on decontamination problems, aren't you?'

His face lit up slightly.

'Ah yes, and I begin to have much success. A process very simple, easily made and not complicated to apply.'

'Well,' said Tuppence, 'that's worth doing. Anything that mitigates suffering is worthwhile – and anything that's constructive and not destructive. Naturally we've got to call the other side names. They're doing just the same in Germany. Hundreds of Major Bletchleys – foaming at the mouth. I hate the Germans myself. "The Germans," I say, and feel waves of loathing. But when I think of individual Germans, mothers sitting anxiously waiting for news of their sons, and boys leaving home to fight, and peasants getting in the harvests, and little shopkeepers and some of the nice kindly German people I know, I feel quite different. I know then that they are just human beings and that we're all feeling alike. That's the real thing. The other is just the war mask that you put on. It's a part of war – probably a necessary part – but it's ephemeral.'

As she spoke she thought, as Tommy had done not long before, of Nurse Cavell's words: 'Patriotism is not enough. I must have no hatred in my heart.'

That saying of a most truly patriotic woman had always seemed to them both the high-water mark of sacrifice.

Carl von Deinim took her hand and kissed it. He said:

'I thank you. What you say is good and true. I will have more fortitude.'

'Oh, dear,' thought Tuppence as she walked down the road into the town. 'How very unfortunate that the person I like best in this place should be a German. It makes everything cock-eyed!'

III

Tuppence was nothing if not thorough. Although she had no wish to go to London, she judged it wise to do exactly as she had said she was going to do. If she merely made an excursion somewhere for the day, somebody might see her and the fact would get round to Sans Souci.

No, Mrs Blenkensop had said she was going to London, and to London she must go.

She purchased a third return, and was just leaving the booking-office window when she ran into Sheila Perenna.

'Hallo,' said Sheila. 'Where are you off to? I just came to see about a parcel which seems to have gone astray.'

Tuppence explained her plans.

'Oh, yes, of course,' said Sheila carelessly. 'I do remember you saying something about it, but I hadn't realised it was today you were going. I'll come and see you into the train.'

Sheila was more animated than usual. She looked neither bad-tempered nor sulky. She chatted quite amiably about small details of daily life at Sans Souci. She remained talking to Tuppence until the train left the station.

After waving from the window and watching the girl's figure recede, Tuppence sat down in her corner seat again and gave herself up to serious meditation.

Was it, she wondered, an accident that Sheila had happened to be at the station just at that time? Or was it a proof of enemy thoroughness? Did Mrs Perenna want to make quite sure that the garrulous Mrs Blenkensop really *had* gone to London?

It looked very much like it.

IV

It was not until the next day that Tuppence was able to have a conference with Tommy. They had agreed never to attempt to communicate with each other under the roof of Sans Souci.

Mrs Blenkensop met Mr Meadowes as the latter, his hay fever somewhat abated, was taking a gentle stroll on the front. They sat down on one of the promenade seats.

'Well?' said Tuppence.

Slowly, Tommy nodded his head. He looked rather unhappy.

'Yes,' he said. 'I got something. But Lord, what a day. Perpetually with an eye to the crack of the door. I've got quite a stiff neck.'

'Never mind your neck,' said Tuppence unfeelingly. 'Tell me.'

'Well, the maids went in to do the bed and the room, of course. And Mrs Perenna went in – but that was when the maids were there and she was just blowing them up about something. And the kid ran in once and came out with a woolly dog.'

'Yes, yes. Anyone else?'

'One person,' said Tommy slowly.

'Who?'

'Carl von Deinim.'

'Oh!' Tuppence felt a swift pang. So, after all –

'When?' she asked.

'Lunch time. He came out from the dining-room early, came up to his room, then sneaked across the passage and into yours. He was there about a quarter of an hour.'

He paused.

'That settles it, I think?'

Tuppence nodded.

Yes, it settled it all right. Carl von Deinim could have had no reason for going into Mrs Blenkensop's bedroom and remaining there for a quarter of an hour save one. His complicity was proved. He must be, Tuppence thought, a marvellous actor . . .

His words to her that morning had rung so very true. Well, perhaps they had been true in a way. To know when to use the truth was the essence of successful deception. Carl von Deinim was a patriot all right; he was an enemy agent working for his country. One could respect him for that. Yes – but destroy him too.

'I'm sorry,' she said slowly.

'So am I,' said Tommy. 'He's a good chap.'

Tuppence said:

'You and I might be doing the same thing in Germany.'

Tommy nodded. Tuppence went on.

'Well, we know more or less where we are. Carl von Deinim working in with Sheila and her mother. Probably Mrs Perenna is the big noise. Then there is that foreign woman who was talking to Carl yesterday. She's in it somehow.'

'What do we do now?'

'We must go through Mrs Perenna's room sometime. There might be something there that would give us a hint. And we must tail her – see where she goes and whom she meets. Tommy, let's get Albert down here.'

Tommy considered the point.

Many years ago Albert, a pageboy in a hotel, had joined forces with the young Beresfords and shared their adventures. Afterwards he had entered their service and been the sole domestic prop of the establishment. Some six years ago he had married and was now the proud proprietor of The Duck and Dog pub in South London.

Tuppence continued rapidly:

'Albert will be thrilled. We'll get him down here. He can stay at the pub near the station and he can shadow the Perennas for us – or anyone else.'

'What about Mrs Albert?'

'She was going to her mother in Wales with the children last Monday. Because of air raids. It all fits in perfectly.'

'Yes, that's a good idea, Tuppence. Either of us following the woman about would be rather conspicuous. Albert will be perfect. Now another thing – I think we ought to watch out for that so-called Polish woman who was talking to Carl and hanging about here. It seems to me that she probably represents the other end of the business – and that's what we're anxious to find.'

'Oh yes, I do agree. She comes here for orders, or to take messages. Next time we see her, one of us must follow her and find out more about her.'

'What about looking through Mrs Perenna's room – and Carl's too, I suppose?'

'I don't suppose you'll find anything in his. After all, as a German, the police are liable to search it and so he'd be careful not to have anything suspicious. The Perenna is going to be difficult. When she's out of the house, Sheila is often there, and there's Betty and Mrs Sprot running about all over the landings, and Mrs O'Rourke spends a lot of time in her bedroom.'

She paused. 'Lunch time is the best.'

'Master Carl's time?'

'Exactly. I could have a headache and go to my room – no,

someone might come up and want to minister to me. I know, I'll just come in quietly before lunch and go up to my room without telling anyone. Then, after lunch, I can say I had a headache.'

'Hadn't I better do it? My hay fever could recrudesce tomorrow.'

'I think it had better be me. If I'm caught I could always say I was looking for aspirin or something. One of the gentlemen boarders in Mrs Perenna's room would cause far more speculation.'

Tommy grinned.

'Of a scandalous character.'

Then the smile died. He looked grave and anxious.

'As soon as we can, old thing. The news is bad today. We must get on to something soon.'

V

Tommy continued his walk and presently entered the post office, where he put through a call to Mr Grant, and reported 'the recent operation was successful and our friend C is definitely involved'.

Then he wrote a letter and posted it. It was addressed to Mr Albert Batt, The Duck and Dog, Glamorgan St, Kennington.

Then he bought himself a weekly paper which professed to inform the English world of what was really going to happen and strolled innocently back in the direction of Sans Souci.

Presently he was hailed by the hearty voice of Commander Haydock leaning from his two-seater car and shouting, 'Hallo, Meadowes, want a lift?'

Tommy accepted a lift gratefully and got in.

'So you read that rag, do you?' demanded Haydock, glancing at the scarlet cover of the *Inside Weekly News*.

Mr Meadowes displayed the slight confusion of all readers of the periodical in question when challenged.

'Awful rag,' he agreed. 'But sometimes, you know, they really do seem to know what's going on behind the scenes.'

'And sometimes they're wrong.'

'Oh, quite so.'

'Truth of it is,' said Commander Haydock, steering rather erratically round a one-way island and narrowly missing collision with a large van, 'when the beggars are right, one remembers it, and when they're wrong you forget it.'

'Do you think there's any truth in this rumour about Stalin having approached us?'

'Wishful thinking, my boy, wishful thinking,' said Commander Haydock. 'The Russkys are as crooked as hell and always have been. Don't trust 'em, that's what I say. Hear you've been under the weather?'

'Just a touch of hay fever. I get it about this time of year.'

'Yes, of course. Never suffered from it myself, but I had a pal who did. Used to lay him out regularly every June. Feeling fit enough for a game of golf?'

Tommy said he'd like it very much.

'Right. What about tomorrow? Tell you what, I've got to go to a meeting about this Parashot business, raising a corps of local volunteers – jolly good idea if you ask me. Time we were all made to pull our weight. So shall we have a round about six?'

'Thanks very much. I'd like to.'

'Good. Then that's settled.'

The Commander drew up abruptly at the gate of Sans Souci.

'How's the fair Sheila?' he asked.

'Quite well, I think. I haven't seen much of her.'

Haydock gave his loud barking laugh.

'Not as much as you'd like to, I bet! Good-looking girl that, but damned rude. She sees too much of that German fellow. Damned unpatriotic, I call it. Dare say she's got no use for old fogies like you and me, but there are plenty of nice lads going about in our own Services. Why take up with a bloody German? That sort of thing riles me.'

Mr Meadowes said:

'Be careful, he's just coming up the hill behind us.'

'Don't care if he does hear! Rather hope he does. I'd like to kick Master Carl's behind for him. Any decent German's fighting for his country – not slinking over here to get out of it!'

'Well,' said Tommy, 'it's one less German to invade England at all events.'

'You mean he's here already? Ha ha! Rather good, Meadowes! Not that I believe this tommy rot about invasion. We never have been invaded and never will be. We've got a Navy, thank God!'

With which patriotic announcement the Commander let in his clutch with a jerk and the car leaped forward up the hill to Smugglers' Rest.

VI

Tuppence arrived at the gates of Sans Souci at twenty minutes to two. She turned off from the drive and went through the garden and into the house through the open drawing-room window. A smell of Irish stew and the clatter of plates and murmur of voices came from afar. Sans Souci was hard at work on its midday meal.

Tuppence waited by the drawing-room door until Martha, the maid, had passed across the hall and into the dining-room, then she ran quickly up the stairs, shoeless.

She went into her room, put on her soft felt bedroom slippers, and then went along the landing and into Mrs Perenna's room.

Once inside she looked round her and felt a certain distaste sweep over her. Not a nice job, this. Quite unpardonable if Mrs Perenna was simply Mrs Perenna. Prying into people's private affairs –

Tuppence shook herself, an impatient terrier shake that was a reminiscence of her girlhood. *There was a war on!*

She went over to the dressing-table.

Quick and deft in her movements, she had soon gone through the contents of the drawers there. In the tall bureau, one of the drawers was locked. That seemed more promising.

Tommy had been entrusted with certain tools and had received some brief instruction on the manipulation of them. These indications he had passed on to Tuppence.

A deft twist or two of the wrist and the drawer yielded.

There was a cash box containing twenty pounds in notes and some piles of silver – also a jewel case. And there were a heap of papers. These last were what interested Tuppence most. Rapidly she went through them; necessarily it was a cursory glance. She could not afford time for more.

Papers relating to a mortgage on Sans Souci, a bank account, letters. Time flew past; Tuppence skimmed through the documents, concentrating furiously on anything that might bear a double meaning. Two letters from a friend in Italy, rambling, discursive letters, seemingly quite harmless. But possibly not so harmless as they sounded. A letter from one Simon Mortimer, of London – a dry business-like letter containing so little of moment that Tuppence wondered why it had been kept. Was Mr Mortimer not so harmless as he seemed? At the bottom of the pile a letter in faded ink signed Pat and beginning '*This will be the last letter I'll be writing you, Eileen my darling –*'

No, not that! Tuppence could not bring herself to read that! She refolded it, tidied the letters on top of it and then, suddenly alert, pushed the drawer to – no time to relock it – and when the door opened and Mrs Perenna came in, she was searching vaguely amongst the bottles on the washstand.

Mrs Blenkensop turned a flustered, but foolish face towards her hostess.

'Oh, Mrs Perenna, do forgive me. I came in with such a blinding headache, and I thought I would lie down on my bed with a little aspirin, and I couldn't find mine, so I thought you wouldn't mind – I know you must have some because you offered it to Miss Minton the other day.'

Mrs Perenna swept into the room. There was a sharpness in her voice as she said:

'Why, of course, Mrs Blenkensop, why ever didn't you come and ask me?'

'Well, of course, yes, I should have done really. But I knew you were all at lunch, and I do so hate, you know, making a *fuss* –'

Passing Tuppence, Mrs Perenna caught up the bottle of aspirin from the washstand.

'How many would you like?' she demanded crisply.

Mrs Blenkensop accepted three. Escorted by Mrs Perenna she crossed to her own room and hastily demurred to the suggestion of a hot-water bottle.

Mrs Perenna used her parting shot as she left the room.

'But you have some aspirin of your own, Mrs Blenkensop. I've seen it.'

Tuppence cried quickly:

'Oh, I know. I know I've got some somewhere, but, so stupid of me, I simply couldn't lay my hands on it.'

Mrs Perenna said with a flash of her big white teeth:

'Well, have a good rest until tea time.'

She went out, closing the door behind her. Tuppence drew a deep breath, lying on her bed rigidly lest Mrs Perenna should return.

Had the other suspected anything? Those teeth, so big and so white – the better to eat you with, my dear. Tuppence always thought of that when she noticed those teeth. Mrs Perenna's hands too, big cruel-looking hands.

She had appeared to accept Tuppence's presence in her bedroom quite naturally. But later she would find the bureau drawer unlocked. Would she suspect then? Or would she think she had left it unlocked herself by accident? One did do such things. Had Tuppence been able to replace the papers in such a way that they looked much the same as before?

Surely, even if Mrs Perenna did notice anything amiss she would be more likely to suspect one of the servants than she would 'Mrs Blenkensop'. And if she did suspect the latter, wouldn't it be a mere case of suspecting her of undue curiosity? There were people, Tuppence knew, who did poke and pry.

But then, if Mrs Perenna were the renowned German agent M., she would be suspicious of counter-espionage.

Had anything in her bearing revealed undue alertness?

She had seemed natural enough – only that one sharply pointed remark about the aspirin.

Suddenly, Tuppence sat up on her bed. She remembered that her aspirin, together with some iodine and a bottle of soda mints, were at the back of the writing-table drawer where she had shoved them when unpacking.

It would seem, therefore, that she was not the only person to snoop in other people's rooms. Mrs Perenna had got there first.

CHAPTER 7

I

On the following day Mrs Sprot went up to London.

A few tentative remarks on her part had led immediately to various offers on the part of the inhabitants of Sans Souci to look after Betty.

When Mrs Sprot, with many final adjurations to Betty to be a very good girl, had departed, Betty attached herself to Tuppence, who had elected to take morning duty.

'Play,' said Betty. 'Play hide seek.'

She was talking more easily every day and had adopted a most fetching habit of laying her head on one side, fixing her interlocutor with a bewitching smile and murmuring '*Peese*'.

Tuppence had intended taking her for a walk, but it was raining hard, so the two of them adjourned to the bedroom where Betty led the way to the bottom drawer of the bureau where her playthings were kept.

'Hide Bonzo, shall we?' asked Tuppence.

But Betty had changed her mind and demanded instead:

'Wead me story.'

Tuppence pulled out a rather tattered book from one end of the cupboard – to be interrupted by a squeal from Betty.

'No, no. Nasty . . . Bad . . .'

Tuppence stared at her in surprise and then down at the book, which was a coloured version of *Little Jack Horner*.

'Was Jack a bad boy?' she asked. 'Because he pulled out a plum?'

Betty reiterated with emphasis:

'B-a-ad!' and with a terrific effort, 'Dirrrty!'

She seized the book from Tuppence and replaced it in the line, then tugged out an identical book from the other end of the shelf, announcing with a beaming smile:

'K-k-klean ni'tice Jackorner!'

Tuppence realised that the dirty and worn books had been replaced by new and cleaner editions and was rather amused. Mrs Sprot was very much what Tuppence thought of as 'the hygienic mother'. Always terrified of germs, of impure food, or of the child sucking a soiled toy.

Tuppence, brought up in a free and easy rectory life, was always rather contemptuous of exaggerated hygiene and had brought up her own two children to absorb what she called a 'reasonable amount' of dirt. However, she obediently took out the clean copy of *Jack Horner* and read it to the child with the comments proper to the occasion. Betty murmuring '*That's* Jack! – Plum! – In a *Pie*!' pointing out these interesting objects with a sticky finger that bade fair to soon consign this second copy to the scrap heap. They proceeded to *Goosey Goosey Gander* and *The Old Woman Who Lived in a Shoe,* and then Betty hid the books and Tuppence took an amazingly long time to find each of them, to Betty's great glee, and so the morning passed rapidly away.

After lunch Betty had her rest and it was then that Mrs O'Rourke invited Tuppence into her room.

Mrs O'Rourke's room was very untidy and smelt strongly of peppermint, and stale cake with a faint odour of moth balls added. There were photographs on every table of Mrs O'Rourke's children and grandchildren and nieces and nephews and great-nieces and great-nephews. There were so many of them that Tuppence felt as though she were looking at a realistically produced play of the late Victorian period.

''Tis a grand way you have with children, Mrs Blenkensop,' observed Mrs O'Rourke genially.

'Oh well,' said Tuppence, 'with my own two –'

Mrs O'Rourke cut in quickly:

'Two? It was three boys I understood you had?'

'Oh yes, three. But two of them are very near in age and I was thinking of the days spent with them.'

'Ah! I see. Sit down now, Mrs Blenkensop. Make yourself at home.'

Tuppence sat down obediently and wished that Mrs O'Rourke did not always make her feel so uncomfortable. She felt now exactly like Hansel or Gretel accepting the witch's invitation.

'Tell me now,' said Mrs O'Rourke. 'What do you think of Sans Souci?'

Tuppence began a somewhat gushing speech of eulogy, but Mrs O'Rourke cut her short without ceremony.

'What I'd be asking you is if you don't feel there's something odd about the place?'

'Odd? No, I don't think so.'

'Not about Mrs Perenna? You're interested in her, you must allow. I've seen you watching her and watching her.'

Tuppence flushed.

'She – she's an interesting woman.'

'She is not then,' said Mrs O'Rourke. 'She's a commonplace woman enough – that is if she's what she seems. But perhaps she isn't. Is that your idea?'

'Really, Mrs O'Rourke, I don't know *what* you mean.'

'Have you ever stopped to think that many of us are that way – different to what we seem on the surface. Mr Meadowes, now. He's a puzzling kind of man. Sometimes I'd say he was a typical Englishman, stupid to the core, and there's other times I'll catch a look or a word that's not stupid at all. It's odd that, don't you think so?'

Tuppence said firmly:

'Oh, I really think Mr Meadowes is *very* typical.'

'There are others. Perhaps you'll know who I'll be meaning?'

Tuppence shook her head.

'The name,' said Mrs O'Rourke encouragingly, 'begins with an S.'

She nodded her head several times.

With a sudden spark of anger and an obscure impulse to spring to the defence of something young and vulnerable, Tuppence said sharply:

'Sheila's just a rebel. One usually is, at that age.'

Mrs O'Rourke nodded her head several times, looking just like an obese china mandarin that Tuppence remembered on her Aunt Gracie's mantelpiece. A vast smile tilted up the corners of her mouth. She said softly:

'You mayn't know it, but Miss Minton's Christian name is Sophia.'

'Oh,' Tuppence was taken aback. 'Was it Miss Minton you meant?'

'It was not,' said Mrs O'Rourke.

Tuppence turned away to the window. Queer how this old woman could affect her, spreading about her an atmosphere of unrest and fear. 'Like a mouse between a cat's paws,' thought Tuppence. 'That's what I feel like . . .'

This vast smiling monumental old woman, sitting there, almost purring – and yet there was the pat pat of paws playing with something that wasn't, in spite of the purring, to be allowed to get away . . .

'Nonsense – all nonsense! I imagine these things,' thought Tuppence, staring out of the window into the garden. The rain had stopped. There was a gentle patter of raindrops off the trees.

Tuppence thought: 'It isn't all my fancy. I'm not a fanciful person. There is something, some focus of evil there. If I could see –'

Her thoughts broke off abruptly.

At the bottom of the garden the bushes parted slightly. In the gap a face appeared, staring stealthily up at the house. It was the face of the foreign woman who had stood talking to Carl von Deinim in the road.

It was so still, so unblinking in its regard, that it seemed to Tuppence as though it was not human. Staring, staring up at the windows of Sans Souci. It was devoid of expression, and yet there was – yes, undoubtedly there was – menace about it. Immobile, implacable. It represented some spirit, some force, alien to Sans Souci and the commonplace banality of English guesthouse life. 'So,' Tuppence thought, 'might Jael have looked, awaiting to drive the nail through the forehead of sleeping Sisera.'

These thoughts took only a second or two to flash through Tuppence's mind. Turning abruptly from the window, she murmured something to Mrs O'Rourke, hurried out of the room and ran downstairs and out of the front door.

Turning to the right she ran down the side garden path to where she had seen the face. There was no one there now. Tuppence went through the shrubbery and out on to the road and looked up and down the hill. She could see no one. Where had the woman gone?

Vexed, she turned and went back into the grounds of Sans Souci. Could she have imagined the whole thing? No, the woman had been there.

Obstinately she wandered round the garden, peering behind bushes. She got very wet and found no trace of the strange woman. She retraced her steps to the house with a vague feeling of foreboding – a queer formless dread of something about to happen.

She did not guess, would never have guessed, what that something was going to be.

II

Now that the weather had cleared, Miss Minton was dressing Betty preparatory to taking her out for a walk. They were going down to the town to buy a celluloid duck to sail in Betty's bath.

Betty was very excited and capered so violently that it was extremely difficult to insert her arms into her woolly pullover. The two set off together, Betty chattering violently: 'Byaduck. Byaduck. For Bettibarf. For Bettibarf,' and deriving great pleasure from a ceaseless reiteration of these important facts.

Two matches, left carelessly crossed on the marble table in the hall, informed Tuppence that Mr Meadowes was spending the afternoon on the trail of Mrs Perenna. Tuppence betook herself to the drawing-room and the company of Mr and Mrs Cayley.

Mr Cayley was in a fretful mood. He had come to Leahampton, he explained, for absolute rest and quiet, and what quiet could there be with a child in the house? All day long it went on, screaming and running about, jumping up and down on the floors –

His wife murmured pacifically that Betty was really a dear little mite, but the remark met with no favour.

'No doubt, no doubt,' said Mr Cayley, wriggling his long neck. 'But her mother should keep her quiet. There are other people to consider. Invalids, people whose nerves need repose.'

Tuppence said: 'It's not easy to keep a child of that age quiet. It's not natural – there would be something wrong with the child if she was quiet.'

Mr Cayley gobbled angrily.

'Nonsense – nonsense – this foolish modern spirit. Letting children do exactly as they please. A child should be made to sit down quietly and – and nurse a doll – or read, or something.'

'She's not three yet,' said Tuppence, smiling. 'You can hardly expect her to be able to read.'

'Well, something must be done about it. I shall speak to Mrs Perenna. The child was singing, singing in her bed before seven o'clock this morning. I had had a bad night and just dropped off towards morning – and it woke me right up.'

'It's very important that Mr Cayley should get as much sleep as possible,' said Mrs Cayley anxiously. 'The doctor said so.'

'You should go to a nursing home,' said Tuppence.

'My dear lady, such places are ruinously expensive and besides it's not the right atmosphere. There is a suggestion of illness that reacts unfavourably on my subconscious.'

'Bright society, the doctor said,' Mrs Cayley explained helpfully. 'A normal life. He thought a guesthouse would be better than just taking a furnished house. Mr Cayley would not be so likely to brood, and would be stimulated by exchanging ideas with other people.'

Mr Cayley's method of exchanging ideas was, so far as Tuppence could judge, a mere recital of his own ailments and symptoms and the exchange consisted in the sympathetic or unsympathetic reception of them.

Adroitly, Tuppence changed the subject.

'I wish you would tell me,' she said, 'of your own views on life in Germany. You told me you had travelled there a good deal in recent years. It would be interesting to have the point of view of an experienced man of the world like yourself. I can see you are the kind of man, quite unswayed by prejudice, who could really give a clear account of conditions there.'

Flattery, in Tuppence's opinion, should always be laid on with a trowel where a man was concerned. Mr Cayley rose at once to the bait.

'As you say, dear lady, I am capable of taking a clear unprejudiced view. Now, in my opinion –'

What followed constituted a monologue. Tuppence, throwing in an occasional 'Now that's very interesting' or 'What a shrewd observer you are', listened with an attention that was not assumed for the occasion. For Mr Cayley, carried away by the sympathy of his listener, was displaying himself as a decided admirer of the Nazi system. How much better it would have been, he hinted, if did not say, for England and Germany to have allied themselves against the rest of Europe.

The return of Miss Minton and Betty, the celluloid duck duly obtained, broke in upon the monologue, which had extended unbroken for nearly two hours. Looking up, Tuppence caught rather a curious expression on Mrs Cayley's face. She found it hard to define. It might be merely pardonable wifely jealousy at the monopoly of her husband's attention by another woman. It might be alarm at the fact that Mr Cayley was being too outspoken in his political views. It certainly expressed dissatisfaction.

Tea was the next move and hard on that came the return of Mrs Sprot from London exclaiming:

'I do hope Betty's been good and not troublesome? Have you been a good girl, Betty?' To which Betty replied laconically by the single word:

'Dam!'

This, however, was not to be regarded as an expression of disapproval at her mother's return, but merely as a request for blackberry preserve.

It elicited a deep chuckle from Mrs O'Rourke and a reproachful:

'Please, Betty, dear,' from the young lady's parent.

Mrs Sprot then sat down, drank several cups of tea, and plunged into a spirited narrative of her purchases in London, the crowd on the train, what a soldier recently returned from France had told the occupants of her carriage, and what a girl behind the stocking counter had told her of a stocking shortage to come.

The conversation was, in fact, completely normal. It was prolonged afterwards on the terrace outside, for the sun was now shining and the wet day a thing of the past.

Betty rushed happily about, making mysterious expeditions into the bushes and returning with a laurel leaf, or a heap of pebbles which she placed in the lap of one of the grown-ups with a confused and unintelligible explanation of what it represented. Fortunately she required little co-operation in her game, being satisfied with an occasional 'How nice, darling. Is it really?'

Never had there been an evening more typical of Sans Souci at its most harmless. Chatter, gossip, speculations as to the course of the war – Can France rally? Will Weygand pull things together? What is Russia likely to do? Could Hitler invade England if he tried? Will Paris fall if the 'bulge' is not straightened out? Was it true that . . . ? It had been said that . . . And it was rumoured that . . .

Political and military scandal was happily bandied about.

Tuppence thought to herself: 'Chatterbugs a danger? Nonsense, they're a safety valve. People *enjoy* these rumours. It gives them the stimulation to carry on with their own private worries and anxieties.' She contributed a nice tit-bit prefixed by 'My son told me – of course this is *quite* private, you understand –'

Suddenly, with a start, Mrs Sprot glanced at her watch.

'Goodness, it's nearly seven. I ought to have put that child to bed hours ago. Betty – Betty!'

It was some time since Betty had returned to the terrace, though no one had noticed her defection.

Mrs Sprot called her with rising impatience.

'Bett – eeee! Where can the child be?'

Mrs O'Rourke said with her deep laugh:

'Up to mischief, I've no doubt of it. 'Tis always the way when there's peace.'

'Betty! I want you.'

There was no answer and Mrs Sprot rose impatiently.

'I suppose I must go and look for her. I wonder where she can be?'

Miss Minton suggested that she was hiding somewhere and Tuppence, with memories of her own childhood, suggested the kitchen. But Betty could not be found, either inside or outside the house. They went round the garden calling, looking all over the bedrooms. There was no Betty anywhere.

Mrs Sprot began to get annoyed.

'It's very naughty of her – very naughty indeed! Do you think she can have gone out on the road?'

Together she and Tuppence went out to the gate and looked up and down the hill. There was no one in sight except a tradesman's boy with a bicycle standing talking to a maid at the door of St Lucian's opposite.

On Tuppence's suggestion, she and Mrs Sprot crossed the road and the latter asked if either of them had noticed a little girl. They both shook their heads and then the servant asked, with sudden recollection:

'A little girl in a green checked gingham dress?'

Mrs Sprot said eagerly:

'That's right.'

'I saw her about half an hour ago – going down the road with a woman.'

Mrs Sprot said with astonishment:

'With a woman? What sort of a woman?'

The girl seemed slightly embarrassed.

'Well, what I'd call an odd-looking kind of woman. A foreigner she was. Queer clothes. A kind of shawl thing and no hat, and a strange sort of face – queer like, if you know what I mean. I've seen her about once or twice lately, and to tell the truth I thought she was a bit wanting – if you know what I mean,' she added helpfully.

In a flash Tuppence remembered the face she had seen that afternoon peering through the bushes and the foreboding that had swept over her.

But she had never thought of the woman in connection with the child, could not understand it now.

She had little time for meditation, however, for Mrs Sprot almost collapsed against her.

'Oh Betty, my little girl. She's been kidnapped. She – what did the woman look like – a gipsy?'

Tuppence shook her head energetically.

'No, she was fair, very fair, a broad face with high cheekbones and blue eyes set very far apart.'

She saw Mrs Sprot staring at her and hastened to explain.

'I saw the woman this afternoon – peering through the bushes at the bottom of the garden. And I've noticed her hanging about. Carl von Deinim was speaking to her one day. It must be the same woman.'

The servant girl chimed in to say:

'That's right. Fair-haired she was. And wanting, if you ask me. Didn't understand nothing that was said to her.'

'Oh God,' moaned Mrs Sprot. 'What shall I do?'

Tuppence passed an arm round her.

'Come back to the house, have a little brandy and then we'll ring up the police. It's all right. We'll get her back.'

Mrs Sprot went with her meekly, murmuring in a dazed fashion:

'I can't imagine how Betty would go like that with a stranger.'

'She's very young,' said Tuppence. 'Not old enough to be shy.'

Mrs Sprot cried out weakly:

'Some dreadful German woman, I expect. She'll kill my Betty.'

'Nonsense,' said Tuppence robustly. 'It will be all right. I expect she's just some woman who's not quite right in her head.' But she did not believe her own words – did not believe for one moment that the calm blonde woman was an irresponsible lunatic.

Carl! Would Carl know? Had Carl something to do with this?

A few minutes later she was inclined to doubt this. Carl von Deinim, like the rest, seemed amazed, unbelieving, completely surprised.

As soon as the facts were made plain, Major Bletchley assumed control.

'Now then, dear lady,' he said to Mrs Sprot. 'Sit down here – just drink a little drop of this – brandy – it won't hurt you – and I'll get straight on to the police station.'

Mrs Sprot murmured:

'Wait a minute – there might be something –'

She hurried up the stairs and along the passage to hers and Betty's room.

A minute or two later they heard her footsteps running wildly along the landing. She rushed down the stairs like a demented woman and clutched Major Bletchley's hand from the telephone receiver, which he was just about to lift.

'No, no,' she panted. 'You mustn't – you mustn't . . .'

And sobbing wildly, she collapsed into a chair.

They crowded round her. In a minute or two, she recovered her composure. Sitting up, with Mrs Cayley's arm round her, she held something out for them to see.

'I found this on the floor of my room. It had been wrapped round a stone and thrown through the window. Look – look what it says.'

Tommy took it from her and unfolded it.

It was a note, written in a queer stiff foreign handwriting, big and bold.

*WE HAVE GOT YOUR CHILD IN SAFE KEEPING.
YOU WILL BE TOLD WHAT TO DO IN DUE COURSE.
IF YOU GO TO THE POLICE YOUR CHILD WILL
BE KILLED. SAY NOTHING. WAIT FOR INSTRUC-
TIONS. IF NOT –*

It was signed with a skull and crossbones.

Mrs Sprot was moaning faintly:

'Betty – Betty –'

Everyone was talking at once. 'The dirty murdering scoundrels'
from Mrs O'Rourke. 'Brutes!' from Sheila Perenna. 'Fantastic,
fantastic – I don't believe a word of it. Silly practical joke' from
Mr Cayley. 'Oh, the dear wee mite' from Miss Minton. 'I do not
understand. It is incredible' from Carl von Deinim. And above
everyone else the stentorian voice of Major Bletchley.

'Damned nonsense. Intimidation. We must inform the police
at once. They'll soon get to the bottom of it.'

Once more he moved towards the telephone. This time a
scream of outraged motherhood from Mrs Sprot stopped him.
He shouted:

'But my dear madam, it's *got* to be done. This is only a crude
device to prevent you getting on the track of these scoundrels.'

'They'll kill her.'

'Nonsense. They wouldn't dare.'

'I won't have it, I tell you. I'm her mother. It's for me
to say.'

'I know. I know. That's what they're counting on – your feeling
like that. Very natural. But you must take it from me, a soldier and
an experienced man of the world, the police are what we need.'

'*No!*'

Bletchley's eyes went round seeking allies.

'Meadowes, you agree with me?'

Slowly Tommy nodded.

'Cayley? Look, Mrs Sprot, both Meadowes and Cayley agree.'

Mrs Sprot said with sudden energy:

'Men! All of you! Ask the women!'

Tommy's eyes sought Tuppence. Tuppence said, her voice
low and shaken:

'I – I agree with Mrs Sprot.'

She was thinking: 'Deborah! Derek! If it were them, I'd feel like her. Tommy and the others are right, I've no doubt, but all the same I couldn't do it. I couldn't risk it.'

Mrs O'Rourke was saying:

'No mother alive could risk it and that's a fact.'

Mrs Cayley murmured:

'I do think, you know, that – well –' and tailed off into incoherence.

Miss Minton said tremulously:

'Such awful things happen. We'd never forgive ourselves if anything happened to dear little Betty.'

Tuppence said sharply:

'You haven't said anything, Mr von Deinim?'

Carl's blue eyes were very bright. His face was a mask. He said slowly and stiffly:

'I am a foreigner. I do not know your English police. How competent they are – how quick.'

Someone had come into the hall. It was Mrs Perenna, her cheeks were flushed. Evidently she had been hurrying up the hill. She said:

'What's all this?' And her voice was commanding, imperious, not the complaisant guesthouse hostess, but a woman of force.

They told her – a confused tale told by too many people, but she grasped it quickly.

And with her grasping of it, the whole thing seemed, in a way, to be passed up to her for judgement. She was the Supreme Court.

She held the hastily scrawled note a minute, then she handed it back. Her words came sharp and authoritative.

'The police? They'll be no good. You can't risk their blundering. Take the law into your own hands. Go after the child yourselves.'

Bletchley said, shrugging his shoulders:

'Very well. If you won't call the police, it's the best thing to be done.'

Tommy said:

'They can't have got much of a start.'

'Half an hour, the maid said,' Tuppence put in.

'Haydock,' said Bletchley. 'Haydock's the man to help us.

He's got a car. The woman's unusual looking, you say? And a foreigner? Ought to leave a trail that we can follow. Come on, there's no time to be lost. You'll come along, Meadowes?'

Mrs Sprot got up.

'I'm coming too.'

'Now, my dear lady, leave it to us –'

'I'm coming too.'

'Oh, well –'

He gave in – murmuring something about the female of the species being deadlier than the male.

III

In the end Commander Haydock, taking in the situation with commendable Naval rapidity, drove the car, Tommy sat beside him, and behind were Bletchley, Mrs Sprot and Tuppence. Not only did Mrs Sprot cling to her, but Tuppence was the only one (with the exception of Carl von Deinim) who knew the mysterious kidnapper by sight.

The Commander was a good organiser and a quick worker. In next to no time he had filled up the car with petrol, tossed a map of the district and a larger scale map of Leahampton itself to Bletchley and was ready to start off.

Mrs Sprot had run upstairs again, presumably to her room to get a coat. But when she got into the car and they had started down the hill she disclosed to Tuppence something in her handbag. It was a small pistol.

She said quietly:

'I got it from Major Bletchley's room. I remembered his mentioning one day that he had one.'

Tuppence looked a little dubious.

'You don't think that –?'

Mrs Sprot said, her mouth a thin line:

'It may come in useful.'

Tuppence sat marvelling at the strange forces maternity will set loose in an ordinary commonplace young woman. She could visualise Mrs Sprot, the kind of woman who would normally declare herself frightened to death of fire-arms, coolly shooting down any person who had harmed her child.

They drove first, on the Commander's suggestion, to the

railway station. A train had left Leahampton about twenty minutes earlier and it was possible that the fugitives had gone by it.

At the station they separated, the Commander taking the ticket collector, Tommy the booking office, and Bletchley the porters outside. Tuppence and Mrs Sprot went into the ladies' room on the chance that the woman had gone in there to change her appearance before taking the train.

One and all drew a blank. It was now more difficult to shape a course. In all probability, as Haydock pointed out, the kidnappers had had a car waiting, and once Betty had been persuaded to come away with the woman, they had made their get-away in that. It was here, as Bletchley pointed out once more, that the co-operation of the police was so vital. It needed an organisation of that kind who could send out messages all over the country, covering the different roads.

Mrs Sprot merely shook her head, her lips pressed tightly together.

Tuppence said:

'We must put ourselves in their places. Where would they have waited in the car? Somewhere as near Sans Souci as possible, but where a car wouldn't be noticed. Now let's *think*. The woman and Betty walk down the hill together. At the bottom is the esplanade. The car might have been drawn up there. So long as you don't leave it unattended you can stop there for quite a while. The only other places are the car park in James's Square, also quite near, or else one of the small streets that lead off from the esplanade.'

It was at that moment that a small man, with a diffident manner and pince nez, stepped up to them and said, stammering a little:

'Excuse me . . . No offence, I hope . . . but I c-c-couldn't help overhearing what you were asking the porter just now' (he now directed his remarks to Major Bletchley). 'I was not listening, of course, just come down to see about a parcel – extraordinary how long things are delayed just now – movements of troops, they say – but really most difficult when it's perishable – the parcel, I mean – and so, you see, I happened to overhear – and really it did seem the most wonderful coincidence . . .'

Mrs Sprot sprang forward. She seized him by the arm.

'You've seen her? You've seen my little girl?'

'Oh really, your little girl, you say? Now fancy that –'

Mrs Sprot cried: 'Tell me.' And her fingers bit into the little man's arm so that he winced.

Tuppence said quickly:

'Please tell us anything you have seen as quickly as you can. We shall be most grateful if you would.'

'Oh, well, really, of course, it may be nothing at all. But the description fitted so well –'

Tuppence felt the woman beside her trembling, but she herself strove to keep her manner calm and unhurried. She knew the type with which they were dealing – fussy, muddle-headed, diffident, incapable of going straight to the point and worse if hurried. She said:

'Please tell us.'

'It was only – my name is Robbins, by the way, Edward Robbins –'

'Yes, Mr Robbins?'

'I live at Whiteways in Ernes Cliff Road, one of those new houses on the new road – most labour-saving, and really every convenience, and a beautiful view and the downs only a stone's throw away.'

Tuppence quelled Major Bletchley, who she saw was about to break out, with a glance, and said:

'And you saw the little girl we are looking for?'

'Yes, I really think it *must* be. A little girl with a foreign-looking woman, you said? It was really the woman I noticed. Because, of course, we are all on the look-out nowadays for Fifth Columnists, aren't we? A sharp look-out, that is what they say, and I always try to do so, and so, as I say, I noticed this woman. A nurse, I thought, or a maid – a lot of spies came over here in that capacity, and this woman was most unusual looking and walking up the road and on to the downs – with a little girl – and the little girl seemed tired and rather lagging, and half-past seven, well, most children go to bed then, so I looked at the woman pretty sharply. I think it flustered her. She hurried up the road, pulling the child after her, and finally picked her up and went on up the path out on to the cliff, which I thought *strange*, you know, because there are no houses there at all – nothing – not until you get to Whitehaven – about five miles over the downs – a favourite walk for hikers. But in this case I thought it odd. I wondered if the woman was going to signal, perhaps. One hears of so much enemy activity, and she certainly looked uneasy when she saw me staring at her.'

Commander Haydock was back in the car and had started the engine. He said:

'Ernes Cliff Road, you say. That's right the other side of the town, isn't it?'

'Yes, you go along the esplanade and past the old town and then up –'

The others had jumped in, not listening further to Mr Robbins.

Tuppence called out:

'Thank you, Mr Robbins,' and they drove off, leaving him staring after them with his mouth open.

They drove rapidly through the town, avoiding accidents more by good luck than by skill. But the luck held. They came out at last at a mass of straggling building development, somewhat marred by proximity to the gas works. A series of little roads led up towards the downs, stopping abruptly a short way up the hill. Ernes Cliff Road was the third of these.

Commander Haydock turned smartly into it and drove up. At the end the road petered out on to bare hillside, up which a footpath meandered upwards.

'Better get out and walk here,' said Bletchley.

Haydock said dubiously:

'Could almost take the car up. Ground's firm enough. Bit bumpy but I think she could do it.'

Mrs Sprot cried:

'Oh yes, please, please . . . We must be quick.'

The Commander murmured to himself:

'Hope to goodness we're after the right lot. That little pipsqueak may have seen any woman with a kid.'

The car groaned uneasily as it ploughed its way up over the rough ground. The gradient was severe, but the turf was short and springy. They came out without mishap on the top of the rise. Here the view was uninterrupted till it rested in the distance on the curve of Whitehaven Bay.

Bletchley said:

'Not a bad idea. The woman could spend the night up here

if need be, drop down into Whitehaven tomorrow morning and take a train there.'

Haydock said:

'No sign of them as far as I can see.'

He was standing up holding some field glasses that he had thoughtfully brought with him to his eyes. Suddenly his figure became tense as he focused the glasses on two small moving dots.

'Got 'em, by Jove . . .'

He dropped into the driver's seat again and the car bucketed forward. The chase was a short one now. Shot up in the air, tossed from side to side, the occupants of the car gained rapidly on those two small dots. They could be distinguished now – a tall figure and a short one – nearer still, a woman holding a child by the hand – still nearer, yes, a child in a green gingham frock. Betty.

Mrs Sprot gave a strangled cry.

'All right now, my dear,' said Major Bletchley, patting her kindly. 'We've got 'em.'

They went on. Suddenly the woman turned and saw the car advancing towards her.

With a cry she caught up the child in her arms and began running.

She ran, not forwards, but sideways towards the edge of the cliff.

The car, after a few yards, could not follow; the ground was too uneven and blocked with big boulders. It stopped and the occupants tumbled out.

Mrs Sprot was out first and running wildly after the two fugitives.

The others followed her.

When they were within twenty yards, the other woman turned at bay. She was standing now at the very edge of the cliff. With a hoarse cry she clutched the child closer.

Haydock cried out:

'My God, she's going to throw the kid over the cliff . . .'

The woman stood there, clutching Betty tightly. Her face was disfigured with a frenzy of hate. She uttered a long hoarse sentence that none of them understood. And still she held the child and looked from time to time at the drop below – not a yard from where she stood.

It seemed clear that she was threatening to throw the child over the cliff.

All of them stood there, dazed, terrified, unable to move for fear of precipitating a catastrophe.

Haydock was tugging at his pocket. He pulled out a service revolver.

He shouted: 'Put that child down – or I fire.'

The foreign woman laughed. She held the child closer to her breast. The two figures were moulded into one.

Haydock muttered:

'I daren't shoot. I'd hit the child.'

Tommy said:

'The woman's crazy. She'll jump over with the child in another moment.'

Haydock said again, helplessly:

'I daren't shoot –'

But at that moment a shot rang out. The woman swayed and fell, the child still clasped in her arms.

The men ran forward, Mrs Sprot stood swaying, the smoking pistol in her hands, her eyes dilated.

She took a few stiff steps forward.

Tommy was kneeling by the bodies. He turned them gently. He saw the woman's face – noted appreciatively its strange wild beauty. The eyes opened, looked at him, then went blank. With a sigh, the woman died, shot through the head.

Unhurt, little Betty Sprot wriggled out and ran towards the woman standing like a statue.

Then, at last, Mrs Sprot crumpled. She flung away the pistol and dropped down, clutching the child to her.

She cried:

'She's safe – she's safe – oh, Betty – *Betty*.' And then, in a low, awed whisper:

'Did I – did I – kill her?'

Tuppence said firmly:

'Don't think about it – don't think about it. Think about Betty. Just think about Betty.'

Mrs Sprot held the child close against her, sobbing.

Tuppence went forward to join the men.

Haydock murmured:

'Bloody miracle. I couldn't have brought off a shot like that. Don't believe the woman's ever handled a pistol before either – sheer instinct. A miracle, that's what it is.'

Tuppence said:

'Thank God! It was a near thing!' And she looked down at the sheer drop to the sea below and shuddered.

CHAPTER 8

I

The inquest on the dead woman was held some days later. There had been an adjournment whilst the police identified her as a certain Vanda Polonska, a Polish refugee.

After the dramatic scene on the cliffs, Mrs Sprot and Betty, the former in a state of collapse, had been driven back to Sans Souci, where hot bottles, nice cups of tea, ample curiosity, and finally a stiff dollop of brandy had been administered to the half-fainting heroine of the night.

Commander Haydock had immediately got in touch with the police, and under his guidance they had gone out to the scene of the tragedy on the cliff.

But for the disturbing war news, the tragedy would probably have been given much greater space in the papers than it was. Actually it occupied only one small paragraph.

Both Tuppence and Tommy had to give evidence at the inquest, and in case any reporters should think fit to take pictures of the more unimportant witnesses, Mr Meadowes was unfortunate enough to get something in his eye which necessitated a highly disfiguring eyeshade. Mrs Blenkensop was practically obliterated by her hat.

However, such interest as there was focused itself entirely on Mrs Sprot and Commander Haydock. Mr Sprot, hysterically summoned by telegraph, rushed down to see his wife, but had to go back again the same day. He seemed an amiable but not very interesting young man.

The inquest opened with the formal identification of the body by a certain Mrs Calfont, a thin-lipped, gimlet-eyed woman who had been dealing for some months with refugee relief.

Polonska, she said, had come to England in company with a cousin and his wife who were her only relatives, so far as she knew. The woman, in her opinion, was slightly mental. She understood from her that she had been through scenes of great horror in Poland and that her family, including several children, had all been killed. The woman seemed not at all grateful for anything done for her, and was suspicious and taciturn. She muttered to herself a lot, and did not seem normal. A domestic post was found for her, but she had left it without notice some weeks ago and without reporting to the police.

The coroner asked why the woman's relatives had not come forward, and at this point Inspector Brassey made an explanation.

The couple in question were being detained under the Defence of the Realm Act for an offence in connection with a Naval dockyard. He stated that these two aliens had posed as refugees to enter the country, but had immediately tried to obtain employment near a Naval base. The whole family was looked upon with suspicion. They had had a larger sum of money in their possession than could be accounted for. Nothing was actually known against the deceased woman Polonska – except that her sentiments were believed to have been anti-British. It was possible that she also had been an enemy agent, and that her pretended stupidity was assumed.

Mrs Sprot, when called, dissolved at once into tears. The coroner was gentle with her, leading her tactfully along the path of what had occurred.

'It's so awful,' gasped Mrs Sprot. 'So awful to have killed someone. I didn't mean to do that – I mean I never thought – but it was Betty – and I thought that woman was going to throw her over the cliff and I had to stop her – and oh, dear – I don't know how I did it.'

'You are accustomed to the use of firearms?'

'Oh, no! Only those rifles at regattas – at fairs – when you shoot at booths, and even then I never used to hit anything. Oh, dear – I feel as though I'd *murdered* someone.'

The coroner soothed her and asked if she had ever come in contact with the dead woman.

'Oh, *no*. I'd never seen her in my life. I think she must have been quite mad – because she didn't even *know* me or Betty.'

In reply to further questions, Mrs Sprot said that she had attended a sewing party for comforts for Polish refugees, but that that was the extent of her connection with Poles in this country.

Haydock was the next witness, and he described the steps he had taken to track down the kidnapper and what had eventually happened.

'You are clear in your mind that the woman was definitely preparing to jump over the cliff?'

'Either that or to throw the child over. She seemed to be quite demented with hate. It would have been impossible to reason with her. It was a moment for immediate action. I myself conceived the idea of firing and crippling her, but she was holding up the child as a shield. I was afraid of killing the child if I fired. Mrs Sprot took the risk and was successful in saving her little girl's life.'

Mrs Sprot began to cry again.

Mrs Blenkensop's evidence was short – a mere confirming of the Commander's evidence.

Mr Meadowes followed.

'You agree with Commander Haydock and Mrs Blenkensop as to what occurred?'

'I do. The woman was definitely so distraught that it was impossible to get near her. She was about to throw herself and the child over the cliff.'

There was little more evidence. The coroner directed the jury that Vanda Polonska came to her death by the hand of Mrs Sprot and formally exonerated the latter from blame. There was no evidence to show what was the state of the dead woman's mind. She might have been actuated by hate of England. Some of the Polish 'comforts' distributed to refugees bore the names of the ladies sending them, and it was possible that the woman got Mrs Sprot's name and address this way, but it was not easy to get at her reason for kidnapping the child – possibly some crazy motive quite incomprehensible to the normal mind. Polonska, according to her own story, had suffered great bereavement in her own country, and that might have turned her brain. On the other hand, she might be an enemy agent.

The verdict was in accordance with the coroner's summing up.

II

On the day following the inquest Mrs Blenkensop and Mr Meadowes met to compare notes.

'Exit Vanda Polonska and a blank wall as usual,' said Tommy gloomily.

Tuppence nodded.

'Yes, they seal up both ends, don't they? No papers, no hints of any kind as to where the money came from that she and her cousins had, no record of whom they had dealings with.'

'Too damned efficient,' said Tommy.

He added: 'You know, Tuppence, I don't like the look of things.'

Tuppence assented. The news was indeed far from reassuring.

The French Army was in retreat and it seemed doubtful if the tide could be turned. Evacuation from Dunkirk was in progress. It was clearly a matter of a few days only before Paris fell. There was a general dismay at the revelation of lack of equipment and of material for resisting the Germans' great mechanised units.

Tommy said:

'Is it only our usual muddling and slowness? Or has there been deliberate engineering behind this?'

'The latter, I think, but they'll never be able to prove it.'

'No. Our adversaries are too damned clever for that.'

'We are combing out a lot of the rot now.'

'Oh, yes, we're rounding up the obvious people, but I don't believe we've got at the brains that are behind it all. Brains, organisation, a whole carefully thought-out plan – a plan which uses our habits of dilatoriness, and our petty feuds, and our slowness for its own ends.'

Tuppence said:

'That's what we're here for – and we haven't got results.'

'We've done something,' Tommy reminded her.

'Carl von Deinim and Vanda Polonska, yes. The small fry.'

'You think they were working together?'

'I think they must have been,' said Tuppence thoughtfully. 'Remember I saw them talking.'

'Then Carl von Deinim must have engineered the kidnapping?'

'I suppose so.'

'But why?'

'I know,' said Tuppence. 'That's what I keep thinking and thinking about. It doesn't make *sense*.'

'Why kidnap that particular child? Who are the Sprots? They've no money – so it isn't ransom. They're neither of them employed by Government in any capacity.'

'I know, Tommy. It just doesn't make any sense at all.'

'Hasn't Mrs Sprot any idea herself?'

'That woman,' said Tuppence scornfully, 'hasn't got the brains of a hen. She doesn't think at all. Just says it's the sort of thing the wicked Germans would do.'

'Silly ass,' said Tommy. 'The Germans are efficient. If they send one of their agents to kidnap a brat, it's for some reason.'

'I've a feeling, you know,' said Tuppence, 'that Mrs Sprot *could* get at the reason if only she'd *think* about it. There must be *something* – some piece of information that she herself has inadvertently got hold of, perhaps without knowing what it is exactly.'

'*Say nothing. Wait for instructions,*' Tommy quoted from the note found on Mrs Sprot's bedroom floor. 'Damn it all, that means *something*.'

'Of course it does – it must. The only thing I can think of is that Mrs Sprot, or her husband, has been given something to keep by someone else – given it, perhaps, just because they are such humdrum ordinary people that no one would ever suspect they had it – whatever "it" may be.'

'It's an idea, that.'

'I know – but it's awfully like a spy story. It doesn't seem real somehow.'

'Have you asked Mrs Sprot to rack her brains a bit?'

'Yes, but the trouble is that she isn't really interested. All she cares about is getting Betty back – that, and having hysterics because she's shot someone.'

'Funny creatures, women,' mused Tommy. 'There was that

woman, went out that day like an avenging fury, she'd have shot down a regiment in cold blood without turning a hair just to get her child back, and then, having shot the kidnapper by a perfectly incredible fluke, she breaks down and comes all over squeamish about it.'

'The coroner exonerated her all right,' said Tuppence.

'Naturally. By Jove, I wouldn't have risked firing when she did.'

Tuppence said:

'No more would she, probably, if she'd known more about it. It was sheer ignorance of the difficulty of the shot that made her bring it off.'

Tommy nodded.

'Quite Biblical,' he said. 'David and Goliath.'

'Oh!' said Tuppence.

'What is it, old thing?'

'I don't quite know. When you said that something twanged somewhere in my brain, and now it's gone again!'

'Very useful,' said Tommy.

'Don't be scathing. That sort of thing does happen sometimes.'

'Gentlemen who draw a bow at a venture, was that it?'

'No, it was – wait a minute – I think it was something to do with Solomon.'

'Cedars, temples, a lot of wives and concubines?'

'Stop,' said Tuppence, putting her hands to her ears. 'You're making it worse.'

'Jews?' said Tommy hopefully. 'Tribes of Israel?'

But Tuppence shook her head. After a minute or two she said:

'I wish I could remember who it was that woman reminded me of.'

'The late Vanda Polonska?'

'Yes. The first time I saw her, her face seemed vaguely familiar.'

'Do you think you had come across her somewhere else?'

'No, I'm sure I hadn't.'

'Mrs Perenna and Sheila are a totally different type.'

'Oh, yes, it wasn't them. You know, Tommy, about those two. I've been thinking.'

'To any good purpose?'

'I'm not sure. It's about that note – the one Mrs Sprot found on the floor in her room when Betty was kidnapped.'

'Well?'

'All that about its being wrapped round a stone and thrown through the window is rubbish. It was put there by someone – ready for Mrs Sprot to find – and I think it was Mrs Perenna who put it there.'

'Mrs Perenna, Carl, Vanda Polonska – all working together.'

'Yes. Did you notice how Mrs Perenna came in just at the critical moment and clinched things – not to ring up the police? She took command of the whole situation.'

'So she's still your selection for M.'

'Yes, isn't she yours?'

'I suppose so,' said Tommy slowly.

'Why, Tommy, have you got another idea?'

'It's probably an awfully dud one.'

'Tell me.'

'No, I'd rather not. I've nothing to go on. Nothing whatever. But if I'm right, it's not M we're up against, but N.'

He thought to himself.

'Bletchley. I suppose he's all right. Why shouldn't he be? He's a true enough type – almost too true, and after all, it was he who wanted to ring up the police. Yes, but he could have been pretty sure that the child's mother couldn't stand for the idea. The threatening note made sure of that. He could afford to urge the opposite point of view –'

And that brought him back again to the vexing, teasing problem to which as yet he could find no answer.

Why kidnap Betty Sprot?

III

There was a car standing outside Sans Souci bearing the word Police on it.

Absorbed in her own thoughts Tuppence took little notice of that. She turned in at the drive, and entering the front door went straight upstairs to her own room.

She stopped, taken aback, on the threshold, as a tall figure turned away from the window.

'Dear me,' said Tuppence. 'Sheila?'

The girl came straight towards her. Now Tuppence saw her more clearly, saw the blazing eyes deep set in the white tragic face.

Sheila said:

'I'm glad you've come. I've been waiting for you.'

'What's the matter?'

The girl's voice was quiet and devoid of emotion. She said:

'They have arrested Carl!'

'The police?'

'Yes.'

'Oh, dear,' said Tuppence. She felt inadequate to the situation. Quiet as Sheila's voice had been, Tuppence was under no apprehension as to what lay behind it.

Whether they were fellow-conspirators or not, this girl loved Carl von Deinim, and Tuppence felt her heart aching in sympathy with this tragic young creature.

Sheila asked:

'What shall I do?'

The simple forlorn question made Tuppence wince. She said helplessly:

'Oh, my dear.'

Sheila said, and her voice was like a mourning harp:

'They've taken him away. I shall never see him again.'

She cried out:

'What shall I do? What shall I do?' And flinging herself down on her knees by the bed she wept her heart out.

Tuppence stroked the dark head. She said presently, in a weak voice:

'It – it may not be true. Perhaps they are only going to intern him. After all, he is an enemy alien, you know.'

'That's not what they said. They're searching his room now.'

Tuppence said slowly, 'Well, if they find nothing –'

'They will find nothing, of course! What should they find?'

'I don't know. I thought perhaps you might?'

'I?'

Her scorn, her amazement were too real to be feigned. Any suspicions Tuppence had had that Sheila Perenna was involved died at this moment. The girl knew nothing, had never known anything.

Tuppence said:

'If he is innocent –'

Sheila interrupted her.

'What does it matter? The police will make a case against him.'

Tuppence said sharply:

'Nonsense, my dear child, that really isn't true.'

'The English police will do anything. My mother says so.'

'Your mother may say so, but she's wrong. I assure you that it isn't so.'

Sheila looked at her doubtfully for a minute or two. Then she said:

'Very well. If you say so. I trust you.'

Tuppence felt very uncomfortable. She said sharply:

'You trust too much, Sheila. You may have been unwise to trust Carl.'

'Are you against him too? I thought you liked him. He thinks so too.'

Touching young things – with their faith in one's liking for them. And it was true – she had liked Carl – she did like him.

Rather wearily she said:

'Listen, Sheila, liking or not liking has nothing to do with facts. This country and Germany are at war. There are many ways of serving one's country. One of them is to get information – and to work behind the lines. It is a brave thing to do, for when you are caught, it is' – her voice broke a little – 'the end.'

Sheila said:

'You think Carl –'

'Might be working for his country that way? It is a possibility, isn't it?'

'No,' said Sheila.

'It would be his job, you see, to come over here as a refugee, to appear to be violently anti-Nazi and then to gather information.'

Sheila said quietly:

'It's not true. I know Carl. I know his heart and his mind. He cares most for science – for his work – for the truth and the knowledge in it. He is grateful to England for letting him work here. Sometimes, when people say cruel things, he feels German and bitter. But he hates the Nazis always, and what they stand for – their denial of freedom.'

Tuppence said: 'He would say so, of course.'

Sheila turned reproachful eyes upon her.

'So you believe he is a spy?'

'I think it is' – Tuppence hesitated – 'a possibility.'

Sheila walked to the door.

'I see. I'm sorry I came to ask you to help us.'

'But what did you think I could do, dear child?'

'You know people. Your sons are in the Army and Navy, and I've heard you say more than once that they knew influential people. I thought perhaps you could get them to – to do – something?'

Tuppence thought of those mythical creatures, Douglas and Raymond and Cyril.

'I'm afraid,' she said, 'that they couldn't do anything.'

Sheila flung her head up. She said passionately:

'Then there's no hope for us. They'll take him away and shut him up, and one day, early in the morning, they'll stand him against a wall and shoot him – and that will be the end.'

She went out, shutting the door behind her.

'Oh, damn, damn, damn the Irish!' thought Tuppence in a fury of mixed feelings. 'Why have they got that terrible power of twisting things until you don't know where you are? If Carl von Deinim's a spy, he deserves to be shot. I must hang on to that, not let this girl with her Irish voice bewitch me into thinking it's the tragedy of a hero and a martyr!'

She recalled the voice of a famous actress speaking a line from *Riders to the Sea*:

'It's the fine quiet time they'll be having . . .'

Poignant . . . carrying you away on a tide of feeling . . .

She thought: 'If it weren't true. Oh, if only it weren't true . . .'

Yet, knowing what she did, how could she doubt?

IV

The fisherman on the end of the Old Pier cast in his line and reeled it cautiously in.

'No doubt whatever, I'm afraid,' he said.

'You know,' said Tommy, 'I'm sorry about it. He's – well, he's a nice chap.'

'They are, my dear fellow, they usually are. It isn't the skunks and the rats of a land who volunteer to go to the enemy's country. It's the brave men. We know that well enough. But there it is, the case is proved.'

'No doubt whatever, you say?'

'No doubt at all. Among his chemical formulae was a list of people in the factory to be approached, as possible Fascist sympathisers. There was also a very clever scheme of sabotage and a chemical process that, applied to fertilisers, would have devastated large areas of food stocks. All well up Master Carl's street.'

Rather unwillingly, Tommy said, secretly anathematising Tuppence, who had made him promise to say it:

'I suppose it's not possible that these things could have been planted on him?'

Mr Grant smiled, rather a diabolical smile.

'Oh,' he said. 'Your wife's idea, no doubt.'

'Well – er – yes, as a matter of fact it is.'

'He's an attractive lad,' said Mr Grant tolerantly.

Then he went on:

'No, seriously, I don't think we can take that suggestion into account. He'd got a supply of secret ink, you know. That's a pretty good clinching test. And it wasn't obvious as it would have been if planted. It wasn't "The mixture to be taken when required" on the wash hand-stand, or anything like that. In fact, it was damned ingenious. Only came across the method once before, and then it was waistcoat buttons. Steeped in the stuff, you know. When the fellow wants to use it, he soaks a button in water. Carl von Deinim's wasn't buttons. It was a shoelace. Pretty neat.'

'Oh!' Something stirred in Tommy's mind – vague – wholly nebulous . . .

Tuppence was quicker. As soon as he retailed the conversation to her, she seized on the salient point.

'A shoelace? Tommy, that explains it!'

'What?'

'Betty, you idiot! Don't you remember that funny thing she did in my room, taking out my laces and soaking them in water.

I thought at the time it was a funny thing to think of doing. But, of course, she'd seen Carl do it and was imitating him. He couldn't risk her talking about it, and arranged with that woman for her to be kidnapped.'

Tommy said, 'Then that's cleared up.'

'Yes. It's nice when things begin to fall into shape. One can put them behind you and get on a bit.'

'We need to get on.'

Tuppence nodded.

The times were gloomy indeed. France had astonishingly and suddenly capitulated – to the bewilderment and dismay of her own people.

The destination of the French Navy was in doubt.

Now the coasts of France were entirely in the hands of Germany, and the talk of invasion was no longer a remote contingency.

Tommy said:

'Carl von Deinim was only a link in the chain. Mrs Perenna's the fountain head.'

'Yes, we've got to get the goods on her. But it won't be easy.'

'No. After all, if she's the brains of the whole thing one can't expect it to be.'

'So M is Mrs Perenna?'

Tommy supposed she must be. He said slowly:

'You really think the girl isn't in this at all?'

'I'm quite sure of it.'

Tommy sighed.

'Well, you should know. But if so, it's tough luck on her. First the man she loves – and then her mother. She's not going to have much left, is she?'

'We can't help that.'

'Yes, but supposing we're wrong – that M or N is someone else?'

Tuppence said rather coldly:

'So you're still harping on that? Are you sure it isn't a case of wishful thinking?'

'What do you mean?'

'Sheila Perenna – that's what I mean.'

'Aren't you being rather absurd, Tuppence?'

'No, I'm not. She's got round you, Tommy, just like any other man –'

Tommy replied angrily:

'Not at all. It's simply that I've got my own ideas.'

'Which are?'

'I think I'll keep them to myself for a bit. We'll see which of us is right.'

'Well, I think we've got to go all out after Mrs Perenna. Find out where she goes, whom she meets – everything. There must be a link somewhere. You'd better put Albert on to her this afternoon.'

'You can do that. I'm busy.'

'Why, what are you doing?'

Tommy said:

'I'm playing golf.'

CHAPTER 9

I

'Seems quite like old times, doesn't it, madam?' said Albert. He beamed happily. Though now, in his middle years, running somewhat to fat, Albert had still the romantic boy's heart which had first led him into associations with Tommy and Tuppence in their young and adventurous days.

'Remember how you first came across me?' demanded Albert. 'Cleanin' of the brasses, I was, in those top-notch flats. Coo, wasn't that hallporter a nasty bit of goods? Always on to me, he was. And the day you come along and strung me a tale! Pack of lies it was too, all about a crook called Ready Rita. Not but what some of it didn't turn out to be true. And since then, as you might say, I've never looked back. Many's the adventures we had afore we all settled down, so to speak.'

Albert sighed, and, by a natural association of ideas, Tuppence inquired after the health of Mrs Albert.

'Oh, the missus is all right – but she doesn't take to the Welsh much, she says. Thinks they ought to learn proper English, and as for raids – why, they've had two there already, and holes in the field what you could put a motor-car in, so she says. So – how's that for safety? Might as well be in Kennington, she says, where she wouldn't have to see all the melancholy trees and could get good clean milk in a bottle.'

'I don't know,' said Tuppence, suddenly stricken, 'that we ought to get you into this, Albert.'

'Nonsense, madam,' said Albert. 'Didn't I try and join up and they were so haughty they wouldn't look at me. Wait for my age-group to be called up, they said. And me in the pink of health and only too eager to get at them perishing Germans – if you'll excuse the language. You just tell me how I can put a spoke in their wheel and spoil their goings on – and I'm there. Fifth Column, that's what we're up against, so the papers say – though what's happened to the other four they don't mention. But the long and short of it is, I'm ready to assist you and Captain Beresford in any way you like to indicate.'

'Good. Now I'll tell you what we want you to do.'

II

'How long have you known Bletchley?' asked Tommy as he stepped off the tee and watched with approval his ball leaping down the centre of the fairway.

Commander Haydock, who had also done a good drive, had a pleased expression on his face as he shouldered his clubs and replied:

'Bletchley? Let me see. Oh! About nine months or so. He came here last autumn.'

'Friend of friends of yours, I think you said?' Tommy suggested mendaciously.

'Did I?' The Commander looked a little surprised. 'No, I don't think so. Rather fancy I met him here at the club.'

'Bit of a mystery man, I gather?'

The Commander was clearly surprised this time.

'Mystery man? Old Bletchley?' He sounded frankly incredulous.

Tommy sighed inwardly. He supposed he was imagining things.

He played his next shot and topped it. Haydock had a good

iron shot that stopped just short of the green. As he rejoined the other, he said:

'What on earth makes you call Bletchley a mystery man? I should have said he was a painfully prosaic chap – typical Army. Bit set in his ideas and all that – narrow life, an Army life – but mystery!'

Tommy said vaguely:

'Oh well, I just got the idea from something somebody said –'

They got down to the business of putting. The Commander won the hole.

'Three up and two to play,' he remarked with satisfaction.

Then, as Tommy had hoped, his mind, free of the preoccupation of the match, harked back to what Tommy had said.

'What sort of mystery do you mean?' he asked.

Tommy shrugged his shoulders.

'Oh, it was just that nobody seemed to know much about him.'

'He was in the Rugbyshires.'

'Oh, you know that definitely?'

'Well, I – well, no, I don't know myself. I say, Meadowes, what's the idea? Nothing wrong about Bletchley, is there?'

'No, no, of course not.' Tommy's disclaimer came hastily. He had started his hare. He could now sit back and watch the Commander's mind chasing after it.

'Always struck me as an almost absurdly typical sort of chap,' said Haydock.

'Just so, just so.'

'Ah, yes – see what you mean. Bit too much of a type, perhaps?'

'I'm leading the witness,' thought Tommy. 'Still perhaps something may crop up out of the old boy's mind.'

'Yes, I do see what you mean,' the Commander went on thoughtfully. 'And now I come to think of it I've never actually come across anyone who knew Bletchley before he came down here. He doesn't have any old pals to stay – nothing of that kind.'

'Ah!' said Tommy, and added, 'Shall we play the bye? Might as well get a bit more exercise. It's a lovely evening.'

They drove off, then separated to play their next shots. When they met again on the green, Haydock said abruptly:

'Tell me what you heard about him.'

'Nothing – nothing at all.'

'No need to be so cautious with me, Meadowes. I hear all sorts of rumours. You understand? Everyone comes to me. I'm known to be pretty keen on the subject. What's the idea – that Bletchley isn't what he seems to be?'

'It was only the merest suggestion.'

'What do they think he is? A Hun? Nonsense, the man's as English as you and I.'

'Oh, yes, I'm sure he's quite all right.'

'Why, he's always yelling for more foreigners to be interned. Look how violent he was against that young German chap – and quite right, too, it seems. I heard unofficially from the Chief Constable that they found enough to hang von Deinim a dozen times over. He'd got a scheme to poison the water supply of the whole country and he was actually working out a new gas – working on it in one of our factories. My God, the short-sightedness of our people! Fancy letting the fellow inside the place to begin with. Believe anything, our Government would! A young fellow has only to come to this country just before war starts and whine a bit about persecution, and they shut both eyes and let him into all our secrets. They were just as dense about that fellow Hahn –'

Tommy had no intention of letting the Commander run ahead on the well-grooved track. He deliberately missed a putt.

'Hard lines,' cried Haydock. He played a careful shot. The ball rolled into the hole.

'My hole. A bit off your game today. What were we talking about?'

Tommy said firmly:

'About Bletchley being perfectly all right.'

'Of course. Of course. I wonder now – I did hear a rather funny story about him – didn't think anything of it at the time –'

Here, to Tommy's annoyance, they were hailed by two other men. The four returned to the clubhouse together and had drinks. After that, the Commander looked at his watch and remarked that he and Meadowes must be getting along. Tommy had accepted an invitation to supper with the Commander.

Smugglers' Rest was in its usual condition of apple-pie order. A tall middle-aged manservant waited on them with the professional deftness of a waiter. Such perfect service was somewhat unusual to find outside of a London restaurant.

When the man had left the room, Tommy commented on the fact.

'Yes, I was lucky to get Appledore.'

'How did you get hold of him?'

'He answered an advertisement as a matter of fact. He had excellent references, was clearly far superior to any of the others who applied and asked remarkably low wages. I engaged him on the spot.'

Tommy said with a laugh:

'The war has certainly robbed us of most of our good restaurant service. Practically all good waiters were foreigners. It doesn't seem to come naturally to the Englishman.'

'Bit too servile, that's why. Bowing and scraping doesn't come kindly to the English bulldog.'

Sitting outside, sipping coffee, Tommy gently asked:

'What was it you were going to say on the links? Something about a funny story – apropos of Bletchley.'

'What was it now? Hallo, did you see that? Light being shown out at sea. Where's my telescope?'

Tommy sighed. The stars in their courses seemed to be fighting against him. The Commander fussed into the house and out again, swept the horizon with his glass, outlined a whole system of signalling by the enemy to likely spots on shore, most of the evidence for which seemed to be non-existent, and proceeded to give a gloomy picture of a successful invasion in the near future.

'No organisation, no proper co-ordination. You're an LDV yourself, Meadowes – you know what it's like. With a man like old Andrews in charge –'

This was well-worn ground. It was Commander Haydock's pet grievance. He ought to be the man in command and he was quite determined to oust Col Andrews if it could possibly be done.

The manservant brought out whisky and liqueurs while the Commander was still holding forth.

'– and we're still honeycombed with spies – riddled with 'em. It was the same in the last war – hairdressers, waiters –'

Tommy, leaning back, catching the profile of Appledore as the latter hovered deft-footed, thought – 'Waiters? You could call that fellow Fritz easier than Appledore . . .'

Well, why not? The fellow spoke perfect English, true, but then many Germans did. They had perfected their English by years in English restaurants. And the racial type was not unlike. Fair-haired, blue-eyed – often betrayed by the shape of the head – yes, the head – where had he seen a head lately . . .

He spoke on an impulse. The words fitted in appositely enough with what the Commander was just saying.

'All these damned forms to fill in. No good at all, Meadowes. Series of idiotic questions –'

Tommy said:

'I know. Such as "What is your name?" Answer N or M.'

There was a swerve – a crash. Appledore, the perfect servant, had blundered. A stream of crême de menthe soaked over Tommy's cuff and hand.

The man stammered, 'Sorry, sir.'

Haydock blazed out in fury:

'You damned clumsy fool! What the hell do you think you're doing?'

His usually red face was quite purple with anger. Tommy thought, 'Talk of an Army temper – Navy beats it hollow!' Haydock continued with a stream of abuse. Appledore was abject in apologies.

Tommy felt uncomfortable for the man, but suddenly, as though by magic, the Commander's wrath passed and he was his hearty self again.

'Come along and have a wash. Beastly stuff. It would be the crême de menthe.'

Tommy followed him indoors and was soon in the sumptuous bathroom with the innumerable gadgets. He carefully washed off the sticky sweet stuff. The Commander talked from the bedroom next door. He sounded a little shamefaced.

'Afraid I let myself go a bit. Poor old Appledore – he knows I let go a bit more than I mean always.'

Tommy turned from the wash-basin drying his hands. He did not notice that a cake of soap had slipped on to the floor. His foot stepped on it. The linoleum was highly polished.

A moment later Tommy was doing a wild ballet dancer step. He shot across the bathroom, arms outstretched. One came up against the right-hand tap of the bath, the other pushed heavily against the side of a small bathroom cabinet. It was an extravagant gesture never likely to be achieved except by some catastrophe such as had just occurred.

His foot skidded heavily against the end panel of the bath.

The thing happened like a conjuring trick. The bath slid out from the wall, turning on a concealed pivot. Tommy found himself looking into a dim recess. He had no doubt whatever as to what occupied that recess. It contained a transmitting wireless apparatus.

The Commander's voice had ceased. He appeared suddenly in the doorway. And with a click, several things fell into place in Tommy's brain.

Had he been blind up to now? That jovial florid face – the face of a 'hearty Englishman' – was only a mask. Why had he not seen it all along for what it was – the face of a bad-tempered overbearing Prussian officer. Tommy was helped, no doubt, by the incident that had just happened. For it recalled to him another incident, a Prussian bully turning on a subordinate and rating him with the Junker's true insolence. So had Commander Haydock turned on his subordinate that evening when the latter had been taken unawares.

And it all fitted in – it fitted in like magic. The double bluff. The enemy agent Hahn, sent first, preparing the place, employing foreign workmen, drawing attention to himself and proceeding finally to the next stage in the plan, his own unmasking by the gallant British sailor Commander Haydock. And then how natural that the Englishman should buy the place and tell the story to everyone, boring them by constant repetition. And so N, securely settled in his appointed place, with sea communications and his secret wireless and his staff officers at Sans Souci close at hand, is ready to carry out Germany's plan.

Tommy was unable to resist a flash of genuine admiration. The whole thing had been so perfectly planned. He himself had never suspected Haydock – he had accepted Haydock as the genuine article – only a completely unforeseen accident had given the show away.

All this passed through Tommy's mind in a few seconds. He knew, only too well, that he was, that he must necessarily be, in deadly peril. If only he could act the part of the credulous thick-headed Englishman well enough.

He turned to Haydock with what he hoped was a natural-sounding laugh.

'By Jove, one never stops getting surprises at your place. Was this another of Hahn's little gadgets? You didn't show me this the other day.'

Haydock was standing still. There was a tensity about his big body as it stood there blocking the door.

'More than a match for me,' Tommy thought. 'And there's that confounded servant, too.'

For an instant Haydock stood as though moulded in stone, then he relaxed. He said with a laugh:

'Damned funny, Meadowes. You went skating over the floor like a ballet dancer! Don't suppose a thing like that would happen once in a thousand times. Dry your hands and come into the other room.'

Tommy followed him out of the bathroom. He was alert and tense in every muscle. Somehow or other he must get safely away from this house with his knowledge. Could he succeed in fooling Haydock? The latter's tone sounded natural enough.

With an arm round Tommy's shoulders, a casual arm, perhaps (or perhaps not), Haydock shepherded him into the sitting-room. Turning, he shut the door behind them.

'Look here, old boy, I've got something to say to you.'

His voice was friendly, natural – just a shade embarrassed. He motioned to Tommy to sit down.

'It's a bit awkward,' he said. 'Upon my word, it's a bit awkward! Nothing for it, though, but to take you into my confidence. Only you'll have to keep dark about it, Meadowes. You understand that?'

Tommy endeavoured to throw an expression of eager interest upon his face.

Haydock sat down and drew his chair confidentially close.

'You see, Meadowes, it's like this. Nobody's supposed to know it but I'm working on Intelligence MI42 BX – that's my department. Ever heard of it?'

Tommy shook his head and intensified the eager expression.

'Well, it's pretty secret. Kind of inner ring, if you know what I mean. We transmit certain information from here – but it would be absolutely fatal if that fact got out, you understand?'

'Of course, of course,' said Mr Meadowes. 'Most interesting! Naturally you can count on me not to say a word.'

'Yes, that's absolutely vital. The whole thing is extremely confidential.'

'I quite understand. Your work must be most thrilling. Really most thrilling. I should like so much to know more about it – but I suppose I mustn't ask that?'

'No, I'm afraid not. It's very secret, you see.'

'Oh yes, I see. I really do apologise – a most extraordinary accident –'

He thought to himself, 'Surely he can't be taken in? He can't imagine I'd fall for this stuff?'

It seemed incredible to him. Then he reflected that vanity had been the undoing of many men. Commander Haydock was a clever man, a big fellow – this miserable chap Meadowes was a stupid Britisher the sort of man who would believe anything! If only Haydock continued to think that.

Tommy went on talking. He displayed keen interest and curiosity. He knew he mustn't ask questions but – He supposed Commander Haydock's work must be very dangerous? Had he ever been in Germany, working there?

Haydock replied genially enough. He was intensely the British sailor now – the Prussian officer had disappeared. But Tommy, watching him with a new vision, wondered how he could ever have been deceived. The shape of the head – the line of the jaw – nothing British about them.

Presently Mr Meadowes rose. It was the supreme test. Would it go off all right?

'I really must be going now – getting quite late – feel terribly apologetic, but can assure you will not say a word to anybody.'

('It's now or never. Will he let me go or not? I must be ready – a straight to his jaw would be best –')

Talking amiably and with pleasurable excitement, Mr Meadowes edged towards the door.

He was in the hall . . . he had opened the front door . . .

Through the door on the right he caught a glimpse of Appledore setting the breakfast things ready on a tray for the morning. (The damned fools were going to let him get away with it!)

The two men stood in the porch, chatting – fixing up another match for next Saturday.

Tommy thought grimly: 'There'll be no next Saturday for you, my boy.'

Voices came from the road outside. Two men returning from a tramp on the headland. They were men that both Tommy and the Commander knew slightly. Tommy hailed them. They stopped. Haydock and he exchanged a few words with them, all standing at the gate, then Tommy waved a genial farewell to his host and stepped off with the two men.

He had got away with it.

Haydock, damned fool, had been taken in!

He heard Haydock go back to his house, go in and shut the door. Tommy tramped carefully down the hill with his two new-found friends.

Weather looked likely to change.

Old Monroe was off his game again.

That fellow Ashby refused to join the LDV. Said it was no damned good. Pretty thick, that. Young Marsh, the assistant caddy master, was a conscientious objector. Didn't Meadowes think that matter ought to be put up to the committee. There had been a pretty bad raid on Southampton the night before last – quite a lot of damage done. What did Meadowes think about Spain? Were they turning nasty? Of course, ever since the French collapse –

Tommy could have shouted aloud. Such good casual normal talk. A stroke of providence that these two men had turned up just at that moment.

He said goodbye to them at the gate of Sans Souci and turned in.

He walked up the drive whistling softly to himself.

He had just turned the dark corner by the rhododendrons when something heavy descended on his head. He crashed forward, pitching into blackness and oblivion.

CHAPTER 10

·····················

I

'Did you say Three Spades, Mrs Blenkensop?'

Yes, Mrs Blenkensop had said Three Spades. Mrs Sprot, returning breathless from the telephone: 'And they've changed the time of the ARP exam, again, it's *too* bad,' demanded to have the bidding again.

Miss Minton, as usual, delayed things by ceaseless reiterations.

'Was it Two Clubs I said? Are you sure? I rather thought, you know, that it might have been one No Trump – Oh yes, of course, I remember now. Mrs Cayley said One Heart, didn't she? I was going to say one No Trump although I hadn't quite got the count, but I do think one should play a plucky game – and then Mrs Cayley said One Heart and so I had to go Two Clubs. I always think it's so difficult when one has two short suits –'

'Sometimes,' Tuppence thought to herself, 'it would save time if Miss Minton just put her hand down on the table to show them all. She was quite incapable of not telling exactly what was in it.'

'So now we've got it right,' said Miss Minton triumphantly. 'One Heart, Two Clubs.'

'Two Spades,' said Tuppence.

'I passed, didn't I?' said Mrs Sprot.

They looked at Mrs Cayley, who was leaning forward listening. Miss Minton took up the tale.

'Then Mrs Cayley said Two Hearts and I said Three Diamonds.'

'And I said Three Spades,' said Tuppence.

'Pass,' said Mrs Sprot.

Mrs Cayley sat in silence. At last she seemed to become aware that everyone was looking at her.

'Oh dear,' she flushed. 'I'm so sorry. I thought perhaps Mr Cayley needed me. I hope he's all right out there on the terrace.'

She looked from one to the other of them.

'Perhaps, if you don't mind, I'd better just go and *see*. I heard rather an odd noise. Perhaps he's dropped his book.'

She fluttered out of the window. Tuppence gave an exasperated sigh.

'She ought to have a string tied to her wrist,' she said. 'Then he could pull it when he wanted her.'

'Such a devoted wife,' said Miss Minton. 'It's very nice to see, isn't it?'

'Is it?' said Tuppence, who was feeling far from good-tempered.

The three women sat in silence for a minute or two.

'Where's Sheila tonight?' asked Miss Minton.

'She went to the pictures,' said Mrs Sprot.

'Where's Mrs Perenna?' asked Tuppence.

'She said she was going to do accounts in her room,' said Miss Minton. 'Poor dear. So tiring, doing accounts.'

'She's not been doing accounts all evening,' said Mrs Sprot, 'because she came in just now when I was telephoning in the hall.'

'I wonder where she'd been,' said Miss Minton, whose life was taken up with such small wonderments. 'Not to the pictures, they wouldn't be out yet.'

'She hadn't got a hat on,' said Mrs Sprot. 'Nor a coat. Her hair was all anyhow and I think she'd been running or something. Quite out of breath. She ran upstairs without a word and she glared – positively glared at me – and I'm sure *I* hadn't done anything.'

Mrs Cayley reappeared at the window.

'Fancy,' she said. 'Mr Cayley has walked all round the garden by himself. He quite enjoyed it, he said. Such a mild night.'

She sat down again.

'Let me see – oh, do you think we could have the bidding over again?'

Tuppence suppressed a rebellious sigh. They had the bidding all over again and she was left to play Three Spades.

Mrs Perenna came in just as they were cutting for the next deal.

'Did you enjoy your walk?' asked Miss Minton.

Mrs Perenna stared at her. It was a fierce and unpleasant stare. She said:

'I've not been out.'

'Oh – oh – I thought Mrs Sprot said you'd come in just now.'

Mrs Perenna said:

'I just went outside to look at the weather.'

Her tone was disagreeable. She threw a hostile glance at the meek Mrs Sprot, who flushed and looked frightened.

'Just fancy,' said Mrs Cayley, contributing her item of news. 'Mr Cayley walked all round the garden.'

Mrs Perenna said sharply:

'Why did he do that?'

Mrs Cayley said:

'It is such a mild night. He hasn't even put on his second muffler and he *still* doesn't want to come in. I do *hope* he won't get a chill.'

Mrs Perenna said:

'There are worse things than chills. A bomb might come any minute and blow us all to bits!'

'Oh, dear, I hope it won't.'

'Do you? *I* rather wish it would.'

Mrs Perenna went out of the window. The four bridge players stared after her.

'She seems very *odd* tonight,' said Mrs Sprot.

Miss Minton leaned forward.

'You don't think, do you –' She looked from side to side. They all leaned nearer together. Miss Minton said in a sibilant whisper:

'You don't suspect, do you, that she drinks?'

'Oh, dear,' said Mrs Cayley. 'I wonder now? That would explain it. She really is so – so unaccountable sometimes. What do you think, Mrs Blenkensop?'

'Oh, I don't *really* think so. I think she's worried about something. Er – it's your call, Mrs Sprot.'

'Dear me, what shall I say?' asked Mrs Sprot, surveying her hand.

Nobody volunteered to tell her, though Miss Minton, who had been gazing with unabashed interest into her hand, might have been in a position to advise.

'That isn't Betty, is it?' demanded Mrs Sprot, her head upraised.

'No, it isn't,' said Tuppence firmly.

'She felt that she might scream unless they could get on with the game.

Mrs Sprot looked at her hand vaguely, her mind still apparently maternal. Then she said:

'Oh, One Diamond, I *think*.'

The call went round. Mrs Cayley led.

'When in doubt lead a Trump, they say,' she twittered, and laid down the Nine of Diamonds.

A deep genial voice said:

''Tis the curse of Scotland that you've played there!'

Mrs O'Rourke stood in the window. She was breathing deeply – her eyes were sparkling. She looked sly and malicious. She advanced into the room.

'Just a nice quiet game of bridge, is it?'

'What's that in your hand?' asked Mrs Sprot, with interest.

''Tis a hammer,' said Mrs O'Rourke amiably. 'I found it lying in the drive. No doubt someone left it there.'

'It's a funny place to leave a hammer,' said Mrs Sprot doubtfully.

'It is that,' agreed Mrs O'Rourke.

She seemed in a particularly good humour. Swinging the hammer by its handle she went out into the hall.

'Let me see,' said Miss Minton. 'What's trumps?'

The game proceeded for five minutes without further interruption, and then Major Bletchley came in. He had been to the pictures and proceeded to tell them in detail the plot of *Wandering Minstrel*, laid in the reign of Richard the First. The Major, as a military man, criticised at some length the crusading battle scenes.

The rubber was not finished, for Mrs Cayley, looking at her watch, discovered the lateness of the hour with shrill little cries of horror and rushed out to Mr Cayley. The latter, as a neglected invalid, enjoyed himself a great deal, coughing in a sepulchral manner, shivering dramatically and saying several times:

'*Quite* all right, my dear. I hope you enjoyed your game. It doesn't matter about *me* at all. Even if I *have* caught a severe chill, what does it really matter? There's a war on!'

II

At breakfast the next morning, Tuppence was aware at once of a certain tension in the atmosphere.

Mrs Perenna, her lips pursed very tightly together, was distinctly acrid in the few remarks she made. She left the room with what could only be described as a flounce.

Major Bletchley, spreading marmalade thickly on his toast, gave vent to a deep chuckle.

'Touch of frost in the air,' he remarked. 'Well, well! Only to be expected, I suppose.'

'Why, what has happened?' demanded Miss Minton, leaning forward eagerly, her thin neck twitching with pleasurable anticipation.

'Don't know that I ought to tell tales out of school,' replied the Major irritatingly.

'Oh! Major Bletchley!'

'*Do* tell us,' said Tuppence.

Major Bletchley looked thoughtfully at his audience: Miss Minton, Mrs Blenkensop, Mrs Cayley and Mrs O'Rourke. Mrs Sprot and Betty had just left. He decided to talk.

'It's Meadowes,' he said. 'Been out on the tiles all night. Hasn't come home yet.'

'*What?*' exclaimed Tuppence.

Major Bletchley threw her a pleased and malicious glance. He enjoyed the discomfiture of the designing widow.

'Bit of a gay dog, Meadowes,' he chortled. 'The Perenna's annoyed. Naturally.'

'Oh dear,' said Miss Minton, flushing painfully. Mrs Cayley looked shocked. Mrs O'Rourke merely chuckled.

'Mrs Perenna told me already,' she said. 'Ah, well, the boys will be the boys.'

Miss Minton said eagerly:

'Oh, but surely – perhaps Mr Meadowes has met with an accident. In the black-out, you know.'

'Good old black-out,' said Major Bletchley. 'Responsible for a lot. I can tell you, it's been an eye-opener being on patrol in the LDV. Stopping cars and all that. The amount of wives "just seeing their husbands home". And different names on their identity cards! And the wife or the husband coming back the other way alone a few hours later. Ha ha!' He chuckled, then quickly composed his face as he received the full blast of Mrs Blenkensop's disapproving stare.

'Human nature – a bit humorous, eh?' he said appeasingly.

'Oh, but Mr Meadowes,' bleated Miss Minton. 'He may really have met with an accident. Been knocked down by a car.'

'That'll be his story, I expect,' said the Major. 'Car hit him and knocked him out and he came to in the morning.'

'He may have been taken to hospital.'

'They'd have let us know. After all, he's carrying his identity card, isn't he?'

'Oh dear,' said Mrs Cayley, 'I wonder what Mr Cayley will say?'

This rhetorical question remained unanswered. Tuppence, rising with an assumption of affronted dignity, got up and left the room.

Major Bletchley chuckled when the door closed behind her.

'Poor old Meadowes,' he said. 'The fair widow's annoyed about it. Thought she'd got her hooks into him.'

'Oh, Major *Bletchley*,' bleated Miss Minton.

Major Bletchley winked.

'Remember your Dickens? *Beware of widders, Sammy.*'

III

Tuppence was a little upset by Tommy's unannounced absence, but she tried to reassure herself. He might possibly have struck some hot trail and gone off upon it. The difficulties of communication with each other under such circumstances had been foreseen by them both, and they had agreed that the other one was not to be unduly perturbed by unexplained absences. They had arranged certain contrivances between them for such emergencies.

Mrs Perenna had, according to Mrs Sprot, been out last night. The vehemence of her own denial of the fact only made that absence of hers more interesting to speculate upon.

It was possible that Tommy had trailed her on her secret errand and had found something worth following up.

Doubtless he would communicate with Tuppence in his special way, or else turn up, very shortly.

Nevertheless, Tuppence was unable to avoid a certain feeling of uneasiness. She decided that in her role of Mrs Blenkensop it would be perfectly natural to display some curiosity and even anxiety. She went without more ado in search of Mrs Perenna.

Mrs Perenna was inclined to be short with her upon the subject. She made it clear that such conduct on the part of one of her lodgers was not to be condoned or glossed over. Tuppence exclaimed breathlessly:

'Oh, but he may have met with an *accident*. I'm sure he *must* have done. He's not at all that sort of man – not at all loose in his ideas, or *anything* of that kind. He must have been run down by a car or something.'

'We shall probably soon hear one way or another,' said Mrs Perenna.

But the day wore on and there was no sign of Mr Meadowes.

In the evening, Mrs Perenna, urged on by the pleas of her boarders, agreed extremely reluctantly to ring up the police.

A sergeant called at the house with a notebook and took particulars. Certain facts were then elicited. Mr Meadowes had left Commander Haydock's house at half-past ten. From there he had walked with a Mr Walters and a Dr Curtis as far as the gate of Sans Souci, where he had said goodbye to them and turned into the drive.

From that moment, Mr Meadowes seemed to have disappeared into space.

In Tuppence's mind, two possibilities emerged from this.

When walking up the drive, Tommy may have seen Mrs Perenna coming towards him, have slipped into the bushes and then have followed her. Having observed her rendezvous with some unknown person, he might then have followed the latter, whilst Mrs Perenna returned to Sans Souci. In that case, he was probably very much alive, and busy on a trail. In which case the well-meant endeavours of the police to find him might prove most embarrassing.

The other possibility was not so pleasant. It resolved itself into two pictures – one that of Mrs Perenna returning 'out of breath and dishevelled' – the other, one that would not be laid aside, a picture of Mrs O'Rourke standing smiling in the window, holding a heavy hammer.

That hammer had horrible possibilities.

For what should a hammer be doing lying outside?

As to who had wielded it, that was more difficult. A good deal depended on the exact time when Mrs Perenna had re-entered the house. It was certainly somewhere in the neighbourhood of half-past ten, but none of the bridge party happened to have noted the time exactly. Mrs Perenna had declared vehemently that she had not been out except just to look at the weather. But one does not get out of breath just looking at the weather. It was clearly extremely vexing to her to have been seen by Mrs Sprot. With ordinary luck the four ladies might have been safely accounted for as busy playing bridge.

What had the time been exactly?

Tuppence found everybody extremely vague on the subject.

If the time agreed, Mrs Perenna was clearly the most likely suspect. But there were other possibilities. Of the inhabitants of Sans Souci, three had been out at the time of Tommy's return. Major Bletchley had been out at the cinema – but he had been to it alone, and the way that he had insisted on retailing the whole picture so meticulously might suggest to a suspicious mind that he was deliberately establishing an alibi.

Then there was the valetudinarian Mr Cayley who had gone for a walk all round the garden. But for the accident of Mrs Cayley's anxiety over her spouse, no one might have ever heard of that walk and might have imagined Mr Cayley to have remained securely encased in rugs like a mummy in his chair on the terrace. (Rather unlike him, really, to risk the contamination of the night air so long.)

And there was Mrs O'Rourke herself, swinging the hammer, and smiling . . .

IV

'What's the matter, Deb? You're looking worried, my sweet.'

Deborah Beresford started, and then laughed, looking frankly into Tony Marsdon's sympathetic brown eyes. She liked Tony. He had brains – was one of the most brilliant beginners in the coding department – and was thought likely to go far.

Deborah enjoyed her job, though she found it made somewhat strenuous demands on her powers of concentration. It was tiring, but it was worthwhile and it gave her a pleasant feeling of importance. This was real work – not just hanging about a hospital waiting for a chance to nurse.

She said:

'Oh, nothing. Just *family*! *You* know.'

'Families *are* a bit trying. What's yours been up to?'

'It's my mother. To tell the truth, I'm just a bit worried about her.'

'Why? What's happened?'

'Well, you see, she went down to Cornwall to a frightfully trying old aunt of mine. Seventy-eight and completely ga ga.'

'Sounds grim,' commented the young man sympathetically.

'Yes, it was really very noble of Mother. But she was rather hipped anyway because nobody seemed to want her in this war. Of course, she nursed and did things in the last one – but it's all quite different now, and they don't want these middle-aged people. They want people who are young and on the spot. Well, as I say, Mother got a bit hipped over it all, and so she went off down to Cornwall to stay with Aunt Gracie, and she's been doing a bit in the garden, extra vegetable growing and all that.'

'Quite sound,' commented Tony.

'Yes, much the best thing she could do. She's quite active still, you know,' said Deborah kindly.

'Well, that sounds all right.'

'Oh yes, it isn't *that*. I was quite happy about her – had a letter only two days ago sounding quite cheerful.'

'What's the trouble, then?'

'The trouble is that I told Charles, who was going down to see his people in that part of the world, to go and look her up. And he did. And she wasn't there.'

'Wasn't *there*?'

'No. And she hadn't been there! Not at all apparently!'

Tony looked a little embarrassed.

'Rather odd,' he murmured. 'Where's – I mean – your father?'

'Carrot Top? Oh, he's in Scotland somewhere. In one of those dreadful Ministries where they file papers in triplicate all day long.'

'Your mother hasn't gone to join him, perhaps?'

'She can't. He's in one of those area things where wives can't go.'

'Oh – er – well, I suppose she's just slopped off somewhere.'

Tony was decidedly embarrassed now – especially with Deborah's large worried eyes fixed plaintively upon him.

'Yes, but why? It's so *queer*. All her letters – talking about Aunt Gracie and the garden and everything.'

'I know, I know,' said Tony hastily. 'Of course, she'd want you to think – I mean – nowadays – well, people *do* slope off now and again if you know what I mean –'

Deborah's gaze, from being plaintive, became suddenly wrathful.

'If you think Mother's just gone off weekending with someone you're absolutely wrong. Absolutely. Mother and Father are devoted to each other – really devoted. It's quite a joke in the family. She'd never –'

Tony said hastily:

'Of course not. Sorry. I really didn't mean –'

Deborah, her wrath appeased, creased her forehead.

'The odd thing is that someone the other day said they'd seen Mother in Leahampton, of all places, and of course I said it couldn't be her because she was in Cornwall, but now I wonder –'

Tony, his match held to a cigarette, paused suddenly and the match went out.

'Leahampton?' he said sharply.

'Yes. Just the last place you could imagine Mother going off to. Nothing to do and all old Colonels and maiden ladies.'

'Doesn't sound a likely spot, certainly,' said Tony.

He lit his cigarette and asked casually:

'What did your mother do in the last war?'

Deborah answered mechanically:

'Oh, nursed a bit and drove a General – Army, I mean, not a bus. All the usual sort of things.'

'Oh, I thought perhaps she'd been like you – in the Intelligence.'

'Oh, Mother would never have had the head for this sort of work. I believe, though, that she and Father did do something in the sleuthing line. Secret papers and master spies – that sort of thing. Of course, the darlings exaggerate it all a good deal and make it all sound as though it had been frightfully important. We don't really encourage them to talk about it much because you know what one's family is – the same old story over and over again.'

'Oh, rather,' said Tony Marsdon heartily. 'I quite agree.'

It was on the following day that Deborah, returning to her digs, was puzzled by something unfamiliar in the appearance of her room.

It took her a few minutes to fathom what it was. Then she rang the bell and demanded angrily of her landlady what had happened to the big photograph that always stood on the top of the chest of drawers.

Mrs Rowley was aggrieved and resentful.

She couldn't say, she was sure. She hadn't touched it herself. Maybe Gladys –

But Gladys also denied having removed it. The man had been about the gas, she said hopefully.

But Deborah declined to believe that an employee of the Gas Co. would have taken a fancy to and removed the portrait of a middle-aged lady.

Far more likely, in Deborah's opinion, that Gladys had smashed the photograph frame and had hastily removed all traces of the crime to the dustbin.

Deborah didn't make a fuss about it. Sometime or other she'd get her mother to send her another photo.

She thought to herself with rising vexation:

'What's the old darling up to? She might tell me. Of course, it's absolute nonsense to suggest, as Tony did, that she's gone off with someone, but all the same it's very queer . . .'

CHAPTER 11

I

It was Tuppence's turn to talk to the fisherman on the end of the pier.

She had hoped against hope that Mr Grant might have had

some comfort for her. But her hopes were soon dashed. He stated definitely that no news of any kind had come from Tommy.

Tuppence said, trying her best to make her voice assured and business-like:

'There's no reason to suppose that anything has – happened to him?'

'None whatever. But let's suppose it has.'

'*What?*'

'I'm saying – supposing it has. What about you?'

'Oh, I see – I – carry on, of course.'

'That's the stuff. *There is time to weep after the battle.* We're in the thick of the battle now. And time is short. One piece of information you brought us has been proved correct. You overheard a reference to the *fourth.* The fourth referred to is the fourth of next month. It's the date fixed for the big attack on this country.'

'You're sure?'

'Fairly sure. They're methodical people, our enemies. All their plans neatly made and worked out. Wish we could say the same of ourselves. Planning isn't our strong point. Yes, the fourth is The Day. All these raids aren't the real thing – they're mostly reconnaissance – testing our defences and our reflexes to air attack. On the fourth comes the real thing.'

'But if you know that –'

'We know The Day is fixed. We know, or think we know, roughly, *where* . . . (But we may be wrong there.) We're as ready as we can be. But it's the old story of the siege of Troy. They knew, as we know, all about the forces without. It's the forces within we want to know about. The men in the Wooden Horse! For they are the men who can deliver up the keys of the fortress. A dozen men in high places, in command, in vital spots, by issuing conflicting orders, can throw the country into just that state of confusion necessary for the German plan to succeed. We've *got* to have inside information in time.'

Tuppence said despairingly:

'I feel so futile – so inexperienced.'

'Oh, you needn't worry about that. We've got experienced people working, all the experience and talent we've got – but when there's treachery within we can't tell who to trust. You and Beresford are the irregular forces. Nobody knows about you. That's why you've got a chance to succeed – that's why you *have* succeeded up to a certain point.'

'Can't you put some of your people on to Mrs Perenna? There *must* be some of them you can trust absolutely?'

'Oh, we've done that. Working from "information received that Mrs Perenna is a member of the IRA with anti-British sympathies". That's true enough, by the way – but we can't get proof of anything further. Not of the vital facts we want. So stick to it, Mrs Beresford. Go on, and do your darndest.'

'The fourth,' said Tuppence. 'That's barely a week ahead?'

'It's a week exactly.'

Tuppence clenched her hands.

'We *must* get *something*! I say *we* because I believe Tommy is on to something, and that that's why he hasn't come back. He's following up a lead. If I could only get something too. I wonder how. If I –'

She frowned, planning a new form of attack.

II

'You see, Albert, it's a possibility.'

'I see what you mean, madam, of course. But I don't like the idea very much, I must say.'

'I think it might work.'

'Yes, madam, but it's exposing yourself to attack – that's what I don't like – and I'm sure the master wouldn't like it.'

'We've tried all the usual ways. That is to say, we've done what we could keeping under cover. It seems to me that now the only chance is to come out into the open.'

'You are aware, madam, that thereby you may be sacrificing an advantage?'

'You're frightfully BBC in your language this afternoon, Albert,' said Tuppence, with some exasperation.

Albert looked slightly taken aback and reverted to a more natural form of speech.

'I was listening to a very interesting talk on pond life last night,' he explained.

'We've no time to think about pond life now,' said Tuppence.

'Where's Captain Beresford, that's what I'd like to know?'

'So should I,' said Tuppence, with a pang.

'Don't seem natural, his disappearing without a word. He ought to have tipped you the wink by now. That's why –'

'Yes, Albert?'

'What I mean is, if *he's* come out in the open, perhaps *you'd* better not.'

He paused to arrange his ideas and then went on.

'I mean, they've blown the gaff on *him*, but *they mayn't know about you* – and so it's up to you to keep under cover still.'

'I wish I could make up my mind,' sighed Tuppence.

'Which way were you thinking of managing it, madam?'

Tuppence murmured thoughtfully:

'I thought I might lose a letter I'd written – make a lot of fuss about it, seem very upset. Then it would be found in the hall and Beatrice would probably put it on the hall table. Then the right person would get a look at it.'

'What would be in the letter?'

'Oh, roughly – that I'd been successful in discovering the *identity of the person in question* and that I was to make a full report personally tomorrow. Then, you see, Albert, N or M would have to come out in the open and have a shot at eliminating me.'

'Yes, and maybe they'd manage it, too.'

'Not if I was on my guard. They'd have, I think, to decoy me away somewhere – some lonely spot. That's where *you'd* come in – because they don't know about you.'

'I'd follow them up and catch them red-handed, so to speak?'

Tuppence nodded.

'That's the idea. I must think it out carefully – I'll meet you tomorrow.'

III

Tuppence was just emerging from the local lending library with what had been recommended to her as a 'nice book' clasped under her arm when she was startled by a voice saying:

'Mrs Beresford.'

She turned abruptly to see a tall dark young man with an agreeable but slightly embarrassed smile.

He said:

'Er – I'm afraid you don't remember me?'

Tuppence was thoroughly used to the formula. She could have predicted with accuracy the words that were coming next.

'I – er – came to the flat with Deborah one day.'

Deborah's friends! So many of them, and all, to Tuppence, looking singularly alike! Some dark like this young man, some fair, an occasional red-haired one – but all cast in the same mould – pleasant, well-mannered, their hair, in Tuppence's view, just slightly too long. (But when this was hinted, Deborah would say, 'Oh, *Mother*, don't be so terribly 1916. I can't *stand* short hair.')

Annoying to have run across and been recognised by one of Deborah's young men just now. However, she could probably soon shake him off.

'I'm Anthony Marsdon,' explained the young man.

Tuppence murmured mendaciously, 'Oh, of course,' and shook hands.

Tony Marsdon went on:

'I'm awfully glad to have found you, Mrs Beresford. You see, I'm working at the same job as Deborah, and as a matter of fact something rather awkward has happened.'

'Yes?' said Tuppence. 'What is it?'

'Well, you see, Deborah's found out that you're not down in Cornwall as she thought, and that makes it a bit awkward, doesn't it, for you?'

'Oh, bother,' said Tuppence, concerned. 'How did she find out?'

Tony Marsdon explained. He went on rather diffidently:

'Deborah, of course, has no idea of what you're really doing.'

He paused discreetly, and then went on:

'It's important, I imagine, that she shouldn't know. My job, actually, is rather the same line. I'm supposed to be just a beginner in the coding department. Really my instructions are to express views that are mildly Fascist – admiration of the German system, insinuations that a working alliance with Hitler wouldn't be a bad thing – all that sort of thing – just to see what response I get. There's a good deal of rot going on, you see, and we want to find out who's at the bottom of it.'

'Rot everywhere,' thought Tuppence.

'But as soon as Deb told me about you,' continued the young man, 'I thought I'd better come straight down and warn you so that you can cook up a likely story. You see, I happen to know what you are doing and that it's of vital importance. It would be fatal if any hint of who you are got about. I thought perhaps you could make it seem as though you'd joined Captain Beresford in Scotland or wherever he is. You might say that you'd been allowed to work with him there.'

'I might do that, certainly,' said Tuppence thoughtfully.

Tony Marsdon said anxiously:

'You don't think I'm butting in?'

'No, no, I'm very grateful to you.'

Tony said rather inconsequentially:

'I'm – well – you see – I'm rather fond of Deborah.'

Tuppence flashed him an amused quick glance.

How far away it seemed, that world of attentive young men and Deb with her rudeness to them that never seemed to put them off. This young man was, she thought, quite an attractive specimen.

She put aside what she called to herself 'peace-time thoughts' and concentrated on the present situation.

After a moment or two she said slowly:

'My husband isn't in Scotland.'

'Isn't he?'

'No, he's down here with me. At least he was! Now – he's disappeared.'

'I say, that's bad – or isn't it? Was he on to something?'

Tuppence nodded.

'I think so. That's why I don't think that his disappearing like this is really a bad sign. I think, sooner or later, he'll communicate with me – in his own way.' She smiled a little.

Tony said, with some slight embarrassment:

'Of course, you know the game well, I expect. But you ought to be careful.'

Tuppence nodded.

'I know what you mean. Beautiful heroines in books are always easily decoyed away. But Tommy and I have our methods. We've got a slogan,' she smiled. *'Penny plain and tuppence coloured.'*

'What?' The young man stared at her as though she had gone mad.

'I ought to explain that my family nickname is Tuppence.'

'Oh, I see.' The young man's brow cleared. 'Ingenious – what?'

'I hope so.'

'I don't want to butt in – but couldn't I help in any way?'

'Yes,' said Tuppence thoughtfully. 'I think perhaps you might.'

CHAPTER 12

I

After long aeons of unconsciousness, Tommy began to be aware of a fiery ball swimming in space. In the centre of the fiery ball was a core of pain, the universe shrank, the fiery ball swung more slowly – he discovered suddenly that the nucleus of it was his own aching head.

Slowly he became aware of other things – of cold cramped limbs, of hunger, of an inability to move his lips.

Slower and slower swung the fiery ball . . . It was now Thomas Beresford's head and it was resting on solid ground. Very solid ground. In fact something suspiciously like stone.

Yes, he was lying on hard stones, and he was in pain, unable to move, extremely hungry, cold and uncomfortable.

Surely, although Mrs Perenna's beds had never been unduly soft, this could not be –

Of course – Haydock! The wireless! The German waiter! Turning in at the gates of Sans Souci . . .

Someone, creeping up behind him, had struck him down. That was the reason of his aching head.

And he'd thought he'd got away with it all right! So Haydock, after all, hadn't been quite such a fool?

Haydock? Haydock had gone back into Smugglers' Rest, and closed the door. How had he managed to get down the hill and be waiting for Tommy in the grounds of Sans Souci?

It couldn't be done. Not without Tommy seeing him.

The manservant, then? Had he been sent ahead to lie in wait? But surely, as Tommy had crossed the hall, he had seen

Appledore in the kitchen of which the door was slightly ajar? Or did he only fancy he had seen him? Perhaps that was the explanation.

Anyway it didn't matter. The thing to do was to find out where he was now.

His eyes, accustomed to the darkness, picked out a small rectangle of dim light. A window or small grating. The air smelt chilly and musty. He was, he fancied, lying in a cellar. His hands and feet were tied and a gag in his mouth was secured by a bandage.

'Seems rather as though I'm for it,' thought Tommy.

He tried gingerly to move his limbs or body, but he could not succeed.

At that moment, there was a faint creaking sound and a door somewhere behind him was pushed open. A man with a candle came in. He set down the candle on the ground. Tommy recognised Appledore. The latter disappeared again and then returned carrying a tray on which was a jug of water, a glass, and some bread and cheese.

Stooping down he first tested the cords binding the other limbs. He then touched the gag.

He said in a quiet level voice:

'I am about to take this off. You will then be able to eat and drink. If, however, you make the slightest sound, I shall replace it immediately.'

Tommy tried to nod his head which proved impossible, so he opened and shut his eyes several times instead.

Appledore, taking this for consent, carefully unknotted the bandage.

His mouth freed, Tommy spent some minutes easing his jaw. Appledore held the glass of water to his lips. He swallowed at first with difficulty, then more easily. The water did him the world of good.

He murmured stiffly:

'That's better. I'm not quite so young as I was. Now for the eats, Fritz – or is it Franz?'

The man said quietly:

'My name here is Appledore.'

He held the slice of bread and cheese up and Tommy bit at it hungrily.

The meal washed down with water, he then asked:

'And what's the next part of the programme?'

For answer, Appledore picked up the gag again.

Tommy said quickly:

'I want to see Commander Haydock.'

Appledore shook his head. Deftly he replaced the gag and went out.

Tommy was left to meditate in darkness. He was awakened from a confused sleep by the sound of the door reopening. This time Haydock and Appledore came in together. The gag was removed and the cords that held his arms were loosened so that he could sit up and stretch his arms.

Haydock had an automatic pistol with him.

Tommy, without much inward confidence, began to play his part.

He said indignantly:

'Look here, Haydock, what's the meaning of all this? I've been set upon – kidnapped –'

The Commander was gently shaking his head.

He said:

'Don't waste your breath. It's not worth it.'

'Just because you're a member of our Secret Service, you think you can –'

Again the other shook his head.

'No, no, Meadowes. You weren't taken in by that story. No need to keep up the pretence.'

But Tommy showed no signs of discomfiture. He argued to himself that the other could not really be sure. If he continued to play his part –

'Who the devil do you think you are?' he demanded. 'However great your powers you've no right to behave like this. I'm perfectly capable of holding my tongue about any of our vital secrets!'

The other said coldly:

'You do your stuff very well, but I may tell you that it's immaterial to me whether you're a member of the British Intelligence, or merely a muddling amateur –'

'Of all the damned cheek –'

'Cut it out, Meadowes.'

'I tell you –'

Haydock thrust a ferocious face forwards.

'Be quiet, damn you. Earlier on it would have mattered to find out who you were and who sent you. Now it doesn't matter. The time's short, you see. And you didn't have the chance to report to anyone what you'd found out.'

'The police will be looking for me as soon as I'm reported missing.'

Haydock showed his teeth in a sudden gleam.

'I've had the police here this evening. Good fellows – both friends of mine. They asked me all about Mr Meadowes. Very concerned about his disappearance. How he seemed that evening – what he said. They never dreamt, how should they, that the man they were talking about was practically underneath their feet where they were sitting. It's quite clear, you see, that you left this house well and alive. They'd never dream of looking for you here.'

'You can't keep me here for ever,' Tommy said vehemently.

Haydock said with a resumption of his most British manner:

'It won't be necessary, my dear fellow. Only until tomorrow night. There's a boat due in at my little cove – and we're thinking of sending you on a voyage for your health – though actually I don't think you'll be alive, or even on board, when they arrive at their destination.'

'I wonder you didn't knock me on the head straight away.'

'It's such hot weather, my dear fellow. Just occasionally our sea communications are interrupted, and if that were to be so – well, a dead body on the premises has a way of announcing its presence.'

'I see,' said Tommy.

He did see. The issue was perfectly clear. He was to be kept alive until the boat arrived. Then he would be killed, or drugged, and his dead body taken out to sea. Nothing would ever connect this body, when found, with Smugglers' Rest.

'I just came along,' continued Haydock, speaking in the most natural manner, 'to ask whether there is anything we could – er – do for you – afterwards?'

Tommy reflected. Then he said:

'Thanks – but I won't ask you to take a lock of my hair to the little woman in St John's Wood, or anything of that kind. She'll miss me when pay day comes along – but I dare say she'll soon find a friend elsewhere.'

At all costs, he felt, he must create the impression that he was playing a lone hand. So long as no suspicion attached itself to Tuppence, then the game might still be won through, though he was not there to play it.

'As you please,' said Haydock. 'If you did care to send a message to – your friend – we would see that it was delivered.'

So he was, after all, anxious to get a little information about this unknown Mr Meadowes? Very well, then, Tommy would keep him guessing.

He shook his head. 'Nothing doing,' he said.

'Very well.' With an appearance of the utmost indifference Haydock nodded to Appledore. The latter replaced the bonds and the gag. The two men went out, locking the door behind them.

Left to his reflections, Tommy felt anything but cheerful. Not only was he faced with the prospect of rapidly approaching death, but he had no means of leaving any clue behind him as to the information he had discovered.

His body was completely helpless. His brain felt singularly inactive. Could he, he wondered, have utilised Haydock's suggestion of a message? Perhaps if his brain had been working better . . . But he could think of nothing helpful.

There was, of course, still Tuppence. But what could Tuppence do? As Haydock had just pointed out, Tommy's disappearance would not be connected with him. Tommy had left Smugglers' Rest alive and well. The evidence of two independent witnesses would confirm that. Whoever Tuppence might suspect, it would not be Haydock. And she might not suspect at all. She might think that he was merely following up a trail.

Damn it all, if only he had been more on his guard –

There was a little light in the cellar. It came through the grating which was high up in one corner. If only he could get his mouth free, he could shout for help. Somebody might hear, though it was very unlikely.

For the next half-hour he busied himself straining at the cords that bound him, and trying to bite through the gag. It was all in vain, however. The people who had adjusted those things knew their business.

It was, he judged, late afternoon. Haydock, he fancied, had gone out; he had heard no sounds from overhead.

Confound it all, he was probably playing golf, speculating at the clubhouse over what could have happened to Meadowes!

'Dined with me night before last – seemed quite normal, then. Just vanished into the blue.'

Tommy writhed with fury. That hearty English manner! Was everyone blind not to see that bullet-headed Prussian skull? He himself hadn't seen it. Wonderful what a first-class actor could get away with.

So here he was – a failure – an ignominious failure – trussed up like a chicken, with no one to guess where he was.

If only Tuppence could have second sight! She might suspect. She had, sometimes, an uncanny insight . . .

What was that?

He strained his ears listening to a far-off sound.

Only some man humming a tune.

And here he was, unable to make a sound to attract anyone's attention.

The humming came nearer. A most untuneful noise.

But the tune, though mangled, was recognisable. It dated from the last war – had been revived for this one.

'If you were the only girl in the world and I was the only boy.'

How often he had hummed that in 1917.

Dash this fellow. Why couldn't he sing in tune?

Suddenly Tommy's body grew taut and rigid. Those particular lapses were strangely familiar. Surely there was only one person who always went wrong in that one particular place and in that one particular way!

'Albert, by gosh!' thought Tommy.

Albert prowling round Smugglers' Rest. Albert quite close at hand, and here he was, trussed up, unable to move hand or foot, unable to make a sound . . .

Wait a minute. Was he?

There was just one sound – not so easy with the mouth shut as with the mouth open, but it could be done.

Desperately Tommy began to snore. He kept his eyes closed, ready to feign a deep sleep if Appledore should come down, and he snored, he snored . . .

Short snore, short snore, short snore – pause – long snore, long snore, long snore – pause – short snore, short snore, short snore . . .

II

Albert, when Tuppence had left him, was deeply perturbed.

With the advance of years he had become a person of slow mental processes, but those processes were tenacious.

The state of affairs in general seemed to him quite wrong.

The war was all wrong to begin with.

'Those Germans,' thought Albert gloomily and almost without rancour. Heiling Hitler, and goose-stepping and over-running the world and bombing and machine-gunning, and generally making pestilential nuisances of themselves. They'd got to be stopped, no two ways about it – and so far it seemed as though nobody had been able to stop them.

And now here was Mrs Beresford, a nice lady if there ever was one, getting herself mixed up in trouble and looking out for more trouble, and how was he going to stop her? Didn't look as though he could. Up against this Fifth Column and a nasty lot they must be. Some of 'em English-born, too! A disgrace, that was!

And the master, who was always the one to hold the missus back from her impetuous ways – the master was missing.

Albert didn't like that at all. It looked to him as though 'those Germans' might be at the bottom of that.

Yes, it looked bad, it did. Looked as though he might have copped one.

Albert was not given to the exercise of deep reasoning. Like most Englishmen, he felt something strongly, and proceeded to muddle around until he had, somehow or other, cleared up the mess. Deciding that the master had got to be found, Albert, rather after the manner of a faithful dog, set out to find him.

He acted upon no settled plan, but proceeded in exactly the same way as he was wont to embark upon the search for his wife's missing handbag or his own spectacles when either of those essential articles were mislaid. That is to say, he went to the place where he had last seen the missing objects and started from there.

In this case, the last thing known about Tommy was that he

had dined with Commander Haydock at Smuglers' Rest, and had then returned to Sans Souci and been last seen turning in at the gate.

Albert accordingly climbed the hill as far as the gate of Sans Souci, and spent some five minutes staring hopefully at the gate. Nothing of a scintillating character having occurred to him, he sighed and wandered slowly up the hill to Smugglers' Rest.

Albert, too, had visited the Ornate Cinema that week, and had been powerfully impressed by the theme of *Wandering Minstrel*. Romantic, it was! He could not but be struck by the similarity of his own predicament. He, like that hero of the screen, Larry Cooper, was a faithful Blondel seeking his imprisoned master. Like Blondel, he had fought at that master's side in bygone days. Now his master was betrayed by treachery, and there was none but his faithful Blondel to seek for him and restore him to the loving arms of Queen Berengaria.

Albert heaved a sigh as he remembered the melting strains of 'Richard, O mon roi', which the faithful troubadour had crooned so feelingly beneath tower after tower.

Pity he himself wasn't better at picking up a tune.

Took him a long time to get hold of a tune, it did.

His lips shaped themselves into a tentative whistle.

Begun playing the old tunes again lately, they had.

'If you were the only girl in the world and I was the only boy –'

Albert paused to survey the neat white-painted gate of Smugglers' Rest. That was it, that was where the master had gone to dinner.

He went up the hill a little farther and came out on the downs.

Nothing here. Nothing but grass and a few sheep.

The gate of Smugglers' Rest swung open and a car passed out. A big man in plus fours with golf clubs drove out and down the hill.

'That would be Commander Haydock, that would,' Albert deduced.

He wandered down again and stared at Smugglers' Rest. A tidy little place. Nice bit of garden. Nice view.

He eyed it benignly. 'I would say such wonderful things to you,' he hummed.

Through a side door of the house a man came out with a hoe and passed out of sight through a little gate.

Albert, who grew nasturtiums and a bit of lettuce in his back garden, was instantly interested.

He edged nearer to Smugglers' Rest and passed through the open gate. Yes, tidy little place.

He circled slowly round it. Some way below him, reached by steps, was a flat plateau planted as a vegetable garden. The man who had come out of the house was busy down there.

Albert watched him with interest for some minutes. Then he turned to contemplate the house.

Tidy little place, he thought for the third time. Just the sort of place a retired Naval gentleman would like to have. This was where the master had dined that night.

Slowly Albert circled round and round the house. He looked at it much as he had looked at the gate of Sans Souci – hopefully, as though asking it to tell him something.

And as he went he hummed softly to himself, a twentieth-century Blondel in search of his master.

'There would be such wonderful things to do,' hummed Albert. 'I would say such wonderful things to you. There would be such wonderful things to do –' Gone wrong somewhere, hadn't he? He'd hummed that bit before.

Hallo, funny, so the Commander kept pigs, did he? A long-drawn grunt came to him. Funny – seemed almost as though it were underground. Funny place to keep pigs.

Couldn't be pigs. No, it was someone having a bit of shut-eye. Bit of shut-eye in the cellar, so it seemed . . .

Right kind of day for a snooze, but funny place to go for it. Humming like a bumble bee Albert approached nearer.

That's where it was coming from – through that little grating. Grunt, grunt, grunt, snoooooore. Snooooooore, snooooooooore – grunt, grunt, grunt. Funny sort of snore – reminded him of something . . .

'Coo!' said Albert. 'That's what it is – SOS. Dot, dot, dot, dash, dash, dash, dot, dot, dot.'

He looked round him with a quick glance.

Then kneeling down, he tapped a soft message on the iron grille of the little window of the cellar.

CHAPTER 13

I

Although Tuppence went to bed in an optimistic frame of mind, she suffered a severe reaction in those waking hours of early dawn when human morale sinks to its lowest.

On descending to breakfast, however, her spirits were raised by the sight of a letter sitting on her plate addressed in a painfully backhanded script.

This was no communication from Douglas, Raymond or Cyril, or any other of the camouflaged correspondence that arrived punctually for her, and which included this morning a brightly coloured Bonzo postcard with a scrawled, 'Sorry I haven't written before. All well, Maudie,' on it.

Tuppence thrust this aside and opened the letter.

> *Dear Patricia* (it ran),
>
> '*Auntie Grace is, I am afraid, much worse today. The doctors do not actually say she is sinking, but I am afraid that there cannot be much hope. If you want to see her before the end I think it would be well to come today. If you will take the 10.20 train to Yarrow, a friend will meet you with his car.*
>
> '*Shall look forward to seeing you again, dear, in spite of the melancholy reason.*
>
> '*Yours ever,*
> '*Penelope Playne.*'

It was all Tuppence could do to restrain her jubilation.

Good old Penny Plain!

With some difficulty she assumed a mourning expression – and sighed heavily as she laid the letter down.

To the two sympathetic listeners present, Mrs O'Rourke and Miss Minton, she imparted the contents of the letter, and enlarged freely on the personality of Aunt Gracie, her indomitable spirit, her indifference to air raids and danger, and her vanquishment by illness. Miss Minton tended to be curious as to the exact nature of Aunt Gracie's sufferings, and compared them interestedly with the diseases of her own cousin Selina. Tuppence, hovering slightly between dropsy and diabetes, found herself slightly confused, but compromised on complications with the kidneys. Mrs O'Rourke displayed an avid interest as to whether Tuppence would benefit pecuniarily by the old lady's death and learned that dear Cyril had always been the old lady's favourite grand-nephew as well as being her godson.

After breakfast, Tuppence rang up the tailor's and cancelled a fitting of a coat and skirt for that afternoon, and then sought out Mrs Perenna and explained that she might be away from home for a night or two.

Mrs Perenna expressed the usual conventional sentiments. She looked tired this morning, and had an anxious harassed expression.

'Still no news of Mr Meadowes,' she said. 'It really is *most* odd, is it not?'

'I'm sure he must have met with an accident,' sighed Mrs Blenkensop. 'I always said so.'

'Oh, but surely, Mrs Blenkensop, the accident would have been reported by this time.'

'Well, what do you think?' asked Tuppence.

Mrs Perenna shook her head.

'I really don't know *what* to say. I quite agree that he can't have gone away of his own free will. He would have sent word by now.'

'It was always a most unjustified suggestion,' said Mrs Blenkensop warmly. 'That horrid Major Bletchley started it. No, if it isn't an accident, it must be loss of memory. I believe that is far more common than is generally known, especially at times of stress like those we are living through now.'

Mrs Perenna nodded her head. She pursed up her lips with rather a doubtful expression. She shot a quick look at Tuppence.

'You know, Mrs Blenkensop,' she said, 'we don't know very much *about* Mr Meadowes, do we?'

Tuppence said sharply: 'What do you mean?'

'Oh, please, don't take me up so sharply. *I* don't believe it – not for a minute.'

'Don't believe what?'

'This story that's going round.'

'What story? I haven't heard anything.'

'No – well – perhaps people wouldn't tell you. I don't really know how it started. I've an idea that Mr Cayley mentioned it first. Of course he's rather a suspicious man, if you know what I mean?'

Tuppence contained herself with as much patience as possible.

'Please tell me,' she said.

'Well, it was just a suggestion, you know, that Mr Meadowes might be an enemy agent – one of these dreadful Fifth Column people.'

Tuppence put all she could of an outraged Mrs Blenkensop into her indignant:

'I never *heard* of such an absurd idea!'

'No. I don't think there's anything in it. But of course Mr Meadowes was seen about a good deal with that German boy – and I believe he asked a lot of questions about the chemical processes at the factory – and so people think that perhaps the two of them might have been working together.'

Tuppence said:

'*You* don't think there's any doubt about Carl, do you, Mrs Perenna?'

She saw a quick spasm distort the other woman's face.

'I wish I *could* think it was not true.'

Tuppence said gently: 'Poor Sheila . . .'

Mrs Perenna's eyes flashed.

'Her heart's broken, the poor child. Why should it be that way? Why couldn't it be someone else she set her heart upon?'

Tuppence shook her head.

'Things don't happen that way.'

'You're right.' The other spoke in a deep, bitter voice. 'It's got to be sorrow and bitterness and dust and ashes. It's got to be the way things tear you to pieces. . . . I'm sick of the cruelty – the unfairness of this world. I'd like to smash it and break it – and let us all start again near to the earth and without these rules and laws and the tyranny of nation over nation. I'd like –'

A cough interrupted her. A deep, throaty cough. Mrs O'Rourke was standing in the doorway, her vast bulk filling the aperture completely.

'Am I interrupting now?' she demanded.

Like a sponge across a slate, all evidence of Mrs Perenna's outburst vanished from her face – leaving in their wake only the mild worried face of the proprietress of a guesthouse whose guests were causing trouble.

'No, indeed, Mrs O'Rourke,' she said. 'We were just talking about what had become of Mr Meadowes. It's amazing the police can find no trace of him.'

'Ah, the police!' said Mrs O'Rourke in tones of easy contempt. 'What good would they be? No good at all, at all! Only fit for fining motor-cars, and dropping on poor wretches who haven't taken out their dog licences.'

'What's your theory, Mrs O'Rourke?' asked Tuppence.

'You'll have been hearing the story that's going about?'

'About his being a Fascist and an enemy agent – yes,' said Tuppence coldly.

'It might be true now,' said Mrs O'Rourke thoughtfully. 'For there's been something about the man that's intrigued me from the beginning. I've watched him, you know,' she smiled directly at Tuppence – and like all Mrs O'Rourke's smiles it had a vaguely terrifying quality – the smile of an ogress. 'He'd not the look of a man who'd retired from business and had nothing to do with himself. If I was backing my judgement, I'd say he came here with a purpose.'

'And when the police got on his track he disappeared, is that it?' demanded Tuppence.

'It might be so,' said Mrs O'Rourke. 'What's your opinion, Mrs Perenna?'

'I don't know,' sighed Mrs Perenna. 'It's a most vexing thing to happen. It makes so much *talk*.'

'Ah! Talk won't hurt you. They're happy now out there on the terrace wondering and surmising. They'll have it in the end that the quiet, inoffensive man was going to blow us all up in our beds with bombs.'

'You haven't told us what you think?' said Tuppence.

Mrs O'Rourke smiled, that same slow ferocious smile.

'I'm thinking that the man is safe somewhere – quite safe . . .'

Tuppence thought:

'She might say that if she knew . . . but he isn't where she thinks he is!'

She went up to her room to get ready. Betty Sprot came running out of the Cayleys' bedroom with a smile of mischievous and impish glee on her face.

'What have you been up to, minx?' demanded Tuppence.

Betty gurgled:

'Goosey, goosey gander . . .'

Tuppence chanted:

'Whither will you wander? *Up*stairs!' She snatched up Betty high over her head. '*Down*stairs!' She rolled her on the floor –

At this minute Mrs Sprot appeared and Betty was led off to be attired for her walk.

'Hide?' said Betty hopefully. 'Hide?'

'You can't play hide-and-seek now,' said Mrs Sprot.

Tuppence went into her room, donned her hat (a nuisance having to wear a hat – Tuppence Beresford never did – but Patricia Blenkensop would certainly wear one, Tuppence felt).

Somebody, she noted, had altered the position of the hats in her hat-cupboard. Had someone been searching her room? Well, let them. They wouldn't find anything to cast doubt on blameless Mrs Blenkensop.

She left Penelope Playne's letter artistically on the dressing-table and went downstairs and out of the house.

It was ten o'clock as she turned out of the gate. Plenty of time. She looked up at the sky, and in doing so stepped into a dark puddle by the gatepost, but without apparently noticing it she went on.

Her heart was dancing wildly. Success – success – they were going to succeed.

II

Yarrow was a small country station where the village was some distance from the railway.

Outside the station a car was waiting. A good-looking young man was driving it. He touched his peaked cap to Tuppence, but the gesture seemed hardly natural.

Tuppence kicked the off-side tyre dubiously.

'Isn't this rather flat?'

'We haven't got far to go, madam.'

She nodded and got in.

They drove, not towards the village, but towards the downs. After winding up over a hill, they took a side-track that dropped sharply into a deep cleft. From the shadow of a small copse of trees a figure stepped out to meet them.

The car stopped and Tuppence, getting out, went to meet Anthony Marsdon.

'Beresford's all right,' he said quickly. 'We located him yesterday. He's a prisoner – the other side got him – and for good reasons he's remaining put for another twelve hours. You see, there's a small boat due in at a certain spot – and we want to catch her badly. That's why Beresford's lying low – we don't want to give the show away until the last minute.'

He looked at her anxiously.

'You do understand, don't you?'

'Oh, yes!' Tuppence was staring at a curious tangled mass of canvas material half-hidden by the trees.

'He'll be absolutely all right,' continued the young man earnestly.

'Of course Tommy will be all right,' said Tuppence impatiently. 'You needn't talk to me as though I were a child of two. We're both ready to run a few risks. What's that thing over there?'

'Well –' The young man hesitated. 'That's just it. I've been ordered to put a certain proposition before you. But – but well, frankly, I don't like doing it. You see –'

Tuppence treated him to a cold stare.

'Why don't you like doing it?'

'Well – dash it – you're Deborah's mother. And I mean – what would Deb say to me if – if –'

'If I got it in the neck?' inquired Tuppence. 'Personally, if I were you, I shouldn't mention it to her. The man who said explanations were a mistake was quite right.'

Then she smiled kindly at him.

'My dear boy, I know exactly how you feel. That it's all very well for you and Deborah and the young generally to run risks, but that the mere middle-aged must be shielded. All complete nonsense, because if anyone is going to be liquidated it is much better it should be the middle-aged, who have had the best part of their lives. Anyway, stop looking upon me as that sacred object, Deborah's mother, and just tell me what dangerous and unpleasant job there is for me to do.'

'You know,' said the young man with enthusiasm, 'I think you're splendid, simply splendid.'

'Cut out the compliments,' said Tuppence. 'I'm admiring myself a good deal, so there's no need for you to chime in. What exactly *is* the big idea?'

Tony indicated the mass of crumpled material with a gesture.

'That,' he said, 'is the remains of a parachute.'

'Aha,' said Tuppence. Her eyes sparkled.

'There was just an isolated parachutist,' went on Marsdon. 'Fortunately the LDVs around here are quite a bright lot. The descent was spotted, and they got her.'

'*Her?*'

'Yes, *her*! Woman dressed as a hospital nurse.'

'I'm sorry she wasn't a nun,' said Tuppence. 'There have been so many good stories going around about nuns paying their fares in buses with hairy muscular arms.'

'Well, she wasn't a nun and she wasn't a man in disguise. She was a woman of medium height, middle-aged, with dark hair and of slight build.'

'In fact,' said Tuppence, 'a woman not unlike me?'

'You've hit it exactly,' said Tony.

'Well?' said Tuppence.

Marsdon said slowly:

'The next part of it is up to you.'

Tuppence smiled. She said:

'I'm *on* all right. Where do I go and what do I do?'

'I say, Mrs Beresford, you really *are* a sport. Magnificent nerve you've got.'

'Where do I go and what do I do?' repeated Tuppence, impatiently.

'The instructions are very meagre, unfortunately. In the woman's pocket there was a piece of paper with these words on it in German. "Walk to Leatherbarrow – due east from the stone cross. 14 St Asalph's Rd. Dr Binion."'

Tuppence looked up. On the hilltop nearby was a stone cross.

'That's it,' said Tony. 'Signposts have been removed, of course.

But Leatherbarrow's a biggish place, and walking due east from the cross you're bound to strike it.'

'How far?'

'Five miles at least.'

Tuppence made a slight grimace.

'Healthy walking exercise before lunch,' she commented. 'I hope Dr Binion offers me lunch when I get there.'

'Do you know German, Mrs Beresford?'

'Hotel variety only. I shall have to be firm about speaking English – say my instructions were to do so.'

'It's an awful risk,' said Marsdon.

'Nonsense. Who's to imagine there's been a substitution? Or does everyone know for miles round that there's been a parachutist brought down?'

'The two LDV men who reported it are being kept by the Chief Constable. Don't want to risk their telling their friends how clever they have been!'

'Somebody else may have seen it – or heard about it?'

Tony smiled.

'My dear Mrs Beresford, every single day word goes round that one, two, three, four, up to a hundred parachutists have been seen!'

'That's probably quite true,' agreed Tuppence. 'Well, lead me to it.'

Tony said:

'We've got the kit here – and a policewoman who's an expert in the art of make-up. Come with me.'

Just inside the copse there was a tumble-down shed. At the door of it was a competent-looking middle-aged woman.

She looked at Tuppence and nodded approvingly.

Inside the shed, seated on an upturned packing case, Tuppence submitted herself to expert ministrations. Finally the operator stood back, nodded approvingly and remarked:

'There, now, I think we've made a very nice job of it. What do you think, sir?'

'Very good indeed,' said Tony.

Tuppence stretched out her hand and took the mirror the other woman held. She surveyed her own face earnestly and could hardly repress a cry of surprise.

The eyebrows had been trimmed to an entirely different shape, altering the whole expression. Small pieces of adhesive plaster hidden by curls pulled forward over the ears that tightened the skin of the face and altered its contours. A small amount of nose putty had altered the shape of the nose, giving Tuppence an unexpectedly beak-like profile. Skilful make-up had added several years to her age, with heavy lines running down each side of the mouth. The whole face had a complacent, rather foolish look.

'It's frightfully clever,' said Tuppence admiringly. She touched her nose gingerly.

'You must be careful,' the other woman warned her. She produced two slices of thin india-rubber. 'Do you think you could bear to wear these in your cheeks?'

'I suppose I shall have to,' said Tuppence gloomily.

She slipped them in and worked her jaws carefully.

'It's not really too uncomfortable,' she had to admit.

Tony then discreetly left the shed and Tuppence shed her own clothing and got into the nurse's kit. It was not too bad a fit, though inclined to strain a little over the shoulders. The dark blue bonnet put the final touch to her new personality. She rejected, however, the stout square-toed shoes.

'If I've got to walk five miles,' she said decidedly, 'I do it in my own shoes.'

They both agreed that this was reasonable – particularly as Tuppence's own shoes were dark blue brogues that went well with the uniform.

She looked with interest into the dark blue handbag – powder; no lipstick; two pounds fourteen and sixpence in English money; a handkerchief and an identity card in the name of Freda Elton, 4 Manchester Road, Sheffield.

Tuppence transferred her own powder and lipstick and stood up, prepared to set out.

Tony Marsdon turned his head away. He said gruffly:

'I feel a swine letting you do this.'

'I know just how you feel.'

'But, you see, it's absolutely vital – that we should get some idea of just where and how the attack will come.'

Tuppence patted him on the arm. 'Don't you worry, my child. Believe it or not, I'm enjoying myself.'

Tony Marsdon said again:

'I think you're simply wonderful!'

III

Somewhat weary, Tuppence stood outside 14 St Asalph's Road and noted that Dr Binion was a dental surgeon and not a doctor.

From the corner of her eye she noted Tony Marsdon. He was sitting in a racy-looking car outside a house farther down the street.

It had been judged necessary for Tuppence to walk to Leather-barrow exactly as instructed, since if she had been driven there in a car the fact might have been noted.

It was certainly true that two enemy aircraft had passed over the downs, circling low before making off, and they could have noted the nurse's lonely figure walking across country.

Tony, with the expert policewoman, had driven off in the opposite direction and had made a big detour before approaching Leatherbarrow and taking up his position in St Asalph's Road. Everything was now set.

'The arena doors open,' murmured Tuppence. 'Enter one Christian *en route* for the lions. Oh, well, nobody can say I'm not seeing life.'

She crossed the road and rang the bell, wondering as she did so exactly how much Deborah liked that young man. The door was opened by an elderly woman with a stolid peasant face – not an English face.

'Dr Binion?' said Tuppence.

The woman looked her slowly up and down.

'You will be Nurse Elton, I suppose.'

'Yes.'

'Then you will come up to the doctor's surgery.'

She stood back, the door closed behind Tuppence, who found herself standing in a narrow linoleum-lined hall.

The maid preceded her upstairs and opened a door on the first floor.

'Please to wait. The doctor will come to you.'

She went out, shutting the door behind her.

A very ordinary dentist's surgery – the appointments somewhat old and shabby.

Tuppence looked at the dentist's chair and smiled to think that for once it held none of the usual terrors. She had the 'dentist feeling' all right – but from quite different causes.

Presently the door would open and 'Dr Binion' would come in. Who would Dr Binion be? A stranger? Or someone she had seen before? If it was the person she was half expecting to see –

The door opened.

The man who entered was not at all the person Tuppence had half fancied she might see! It was someone she had never considered as a likely starter.

It was Commander Haydock.

CHAPTER 14

I

A flood of wild surmises as to the part Commander Haydock had played in Tommy's disappearance surged through Tuppence's brain, but she thrust them resolutely aside. This was a moment for keeping all her wits about her.

Would or would not the Commander recognise her? It was an interesting question.

She had so steeled herself beforehand to display no recognition or surprise herself, no matter whom she might see, that she felt reasonably sure that she herself had displayed no signs untoward to the situation.

She rose now to her feet and stood there, standing in a respectable attitude, as befitted a mere German woman in the presence of a Lord of creation.

'So you have arrived,' said the Commander.

He spoke in English and his manner was precisely the same as usual.

'Yes,' said Tuppence, and added, as though presenting her credentials: 'Nurse Elton.'

Haydock smiled as though at a joke.

'Nurse Elton! Excellent.'

He looked at her approvingly.

'You look absolutely right,' he said kindly.

Tuppence inclined her head, but said nothing. She was leaving the initiative to him.

'You know, I suppose, what you have to do?' went on Haydock. 'Sit down, please.'

Tuppence sat down obediently. She replied:

'I was to take detailed instructions from you.'

'Very proper,' said Haydock. There was a faint suggestion of mockery in his voice.

He said:

'You know the day?'

'The fourth.'

Haydock looked startled. A heavy frown creased his forehead.

'So you know that, do you?' he muttered.

There was a pause, then Tuppence said:

'You will tell me, please, what I have to do?'

Haydock said:

'All in good time, my dear.'

He paused a minute, and then asked:

'You have heard, no doubt, of Sans Souci?'

'No,' said Tuppence.

'You haven't?'

'No,' said Tuppence firmly.

'Let's see how you deal with this one!' she thought.

There was a queer smile on the Commander's face. He said:

'So you haven't heard of Sans Souci? That surprises me very much – since I was under the impression, you know, *that you'd been living there for the last month . . .*'

There was a dead silence. The Commander said:

'What about that, Mrs Blenkensop?'

'I don't know what you mean, Dr Binion. I landed by parachute this morning.'

Again Haydock smiled – definitely an unpleasant smile.

He said:

'A few yards of canvas thrust into a bush create a wonderful illusion. And I am not Dr Binion, dear lady. Dr Binion is, officially, my dentist – he is good enough to lend me his surgery now and again.'

'Indeed?' said Tuppence.

'Indeed, Mrs Blenkensop! Or perhaps you would prefer me to address you by your real name of Beresford?'

Again there was a poignant silence. Tuppence drew a deep breath.

Haydock nodded.

'The game's up, you see. "*You've walked into my parlour,*" said *the spider to the fly.*'

There was a faint click and a gleam of blue steel showed in his hand. His voice took on a grim note as he said:

'And I shouldn't advise you to make any noise or try to arouse the neighbourhood! You'd be dead before you got so much as a yelp out, and even if you did manage to scream it wouldn't arouse attention. Patients under gas, you know, often cry out.'

Tuppence said composedly:

'You seem to have thought of everything. Has it occurred to you that I have friends who know where I am?'

'Ah! Still harping on the blue-eyed boy – actually brown-eyed! Young Anthony Marsdon. I'm sorry, Mrs Beresford, but young Anthony happens to be one of our most stalwart supporters in this country. As I said just now, a few yards of canvas creates a wonderful effect. You swallowed the parachute idea quite easily.'

'I don't see the point of all this rigmarole!'

'Don't you? We don't want your friends to trace you too easily, you see. *If* they pick up your trail it will lead to Yarrow and to a man in a car. The fact that a hospital nurse, of quite different facial appearance, walked into Leatherbarrow between one and two will hardly be connected with your disappearance.'

'Very elaborate,' said Tuppence.

Haydock said:

'I admire your nerve, you know. I admire it very much. I'm sorry to have to coerce you – but it's vital that we should know just exactly how much you *did* discover at Sans Souci.'

Tuppence did not answer.

Haydock said quietly:

'I'd advise you, you know, to come clean. There are certain – possibilities – in a dentist's chair and instruments.'

Tuppence merely threw him a scornful look.

Haydock leant back in his chair. He said slowly:

'Yes – I dare say you've got a lot of fortitude – your type often has. But what about the other half of the picture?'

'What do you mean?'

'I'm talking about Thomas Beresford, your husband, who has lately been living at Sans Souci under the name of Mr Meadowes, and who is now very conveniently trussed up in the cellar of my house.'

Tuppence said sharply:

'I don't believe it.'

'Because of the Penny Plain letter? Don't you realise that that was just a smart bit of work on the part of young Anthony. You played into his hands nicely when you gave him the code.'

Tuppence's voice trembled.

'Then Tommy – then Tommy –'

'Tommy,' said Commander Haydock, 'is where he has been all along – completely in my power! It's up to you now. If you answer my questions satisfactorily, there's a chance for him. If you don't – well, the original plan holds. He'll be knocked on the head, taken out to sea and put overboard.'

Tuppence was silent for a minute or two – then she said:

'What do you want to know?'

'I want to know who employed you, what your means of communication with that person or persons are, what you have reported so far, and exactly what you know?'

Tuppence shrugged her shoulders.

'I could tell you what lies I choose,' she pointed out.

'No, because I shall proceed to test what you say.' He drew his chair a little nearer. His manner was now definitely appealing. 'My dear woman – I know just what you feel about it all, but believe me when I say I really do admire both you and your husband immensely. You've got grit and pluck. It's people like you that will be needed in the new State – the State that will arise in this country when your present imbecile Government is vanquished. We want to turn some of our enemies into friends – those that are worthwhile. If I have to give the order that ends your husband's life, I shall do it – it's my duty – but I shall feel really badly about having to do it! He's a fine fellow – quiet, unassuming and clever. Let me impress upon you what so few people in this country seem to understand. Our Leader does not intend to conquer this country in the sense that you all think. He aims at creating a new Britain – a Britain strong in its own power – ruled over, *not* by Germans, but by Englishmen. And the best *type* of Englishmen – Englishmen with brains and breeding and courage. *A brave new world*, as Shakespeare puts it.'

He leaned forward.

'We want to do away with muddle and inefficiency. With bribery and corruption. With self-seeking and money-grabbing – *and in this new state we want people like you and your husband* – brave and resourceful – enemies that have been, friends to be. You would be surprised if you knew how many there are in this country, as in others, who have sympathy with and belief in our aims. Between us all we will create a new Europe – a Europe of peace and progress. Try and see it that way – because, I assure you – it *is* that way . . .'

His voice was compelling, magnetic. Leaning forward, he looked the embodiment of a straightforward British sailor.

Tuppence looked at him and searched her mind for a telling phrase. She was only able to find one that was both childish and rude.

'*Goosey, goosey gander!*' said Tuppence . . .

II

The effect was so magical that she was quite taken aback.

Haydock jumped to his feet, his face went dark purple with rage, and in a second all likeness to a hearty British sailor had vanished. She saw what Tommy had once seen – an infuriated Prussian.

He swore at her fluently in German. Then, changing to English, he shouted:

'You infernal little fool! Don't you realise you give yourself away completely answering like that? You've done for yourself now – you and your precious husband.'

Raising his voice he called:

'Anna!'

The woman who had admitted Tuppence came into the room. Haydock thrust the pistol into her hand.

'Watch her. Shoot if necessary.'

He stormed out of the room.

Tuppence looked appealingly at Anna, who stood in front of her with an impassive face.

'Would you really shoot me?' said Tuppence.

Anna answered quietly:

'You need not try to get round me. In the last war my son was killed, my Otto. I was thirty-eight, then – I am sixty-two now – but I have not forgotten.'

Tuppence looked at the broad, impassive face. It reminded her of the Polish woman, Vanda Polonska. That same frightening ferocity and singleness of purpose. Motherhood – unrelenting! So, no doubt, felt many quiet Mrs Joneses and Mrs Smiths all over England. There was no arguing with the female of the species – the mother deprived of her young.

Something stirred in the recesses of Tuppence's brain – some nagging recollection – something that she had always known but had never succeeded in getting into the forefront of her mind. Solomon – Solomon came into it somewhere . . .

The door opened. Commander Haydock came back into the room.

He howled out, beside himself with rage.

'Where is it? Where have you hidden it?'

Tuppence stared at him. She was completely taken aback. What he was saying did not make sense to her.

She had taken nothing and hidden nothing.

Haydock said to Anna:

'Get out.'

The woman handed the pistol to him and left the room promptly.

Haydock dropped into a chair and seemed to be striving to pull himself together. He said:

'You can't get away with it, you know. I've got you – and I've got ways of making people speak – not pretty ways. You'll have to tell the truth in the end. Now then, *what have you done with it?*'

Tuppence was quick to see that here, at least, was something that gave her the possibility of bargaining. If only she could find out what it was she was supposed to have in her possession.

She said cautiously:

'How do you know I've got it?'

'From what you said, you damned little fool. You haven't got it on you – that we know, since you changed completely into this kit.'

'Suppose I posted it to someone?' said Tuppence.

'Don't be a fool. Everything you posted since yesterday has been examined. You didn't post it. No, there's only one thing you *could* have done. Hidden it in Sans Souci before you left this morning. I give you just three minutes to tell me where that hiding-place is.'

He put his watch down on the table.

'Three minutes, Mrs Thomas Beresford.'

The clock on the mantelpiece ticked.

Tuppence sat quite still with a blank impassive face.

It revealed nothing of the racing thoughts behind it.

In a flash of bewildering light she saw everything – saw the whole business revealed in terms of blinding clarity and realised at last who was the centre and pivot of the whole organisation.

It came quite as a shock to her when Haydock said:

'Ten seconds more . . .'

Like one in a dream she watched him, saw the pistol arm rise, heard him count:

'One, two, three, four, five –'

He had reached *eight* when the shot rang out and he collapsed forward on his chair, an expression of bewilderment on his broad red face. So intent had he been on watching his victim that he had been unaware of the door behind him slowly opening.

In a flash Tuppence was on her feet. She pushed her way past the uniformed men in the doorway, and seized on a tweed-clad arm.

'Mr Grant.'

'Yes, yes, my dear, it's all right now – you've been wonderful –'

Tuppence brushed aside these reassurances.

'Quick! There's no time to lose. You've got a car here?'

'Yes.' He stared.

'A fast one? We must get to Sans Souci *at once*. If only we're in time. Before they telephone here, and get no answer.'

Two minutes later they were in the car, and it was threading its way through the streets of Leatherbarrow. Then they were out in the open country and the needle of the speedometer was rising.

Mr Grant asked no questions. He was content to sit quietly whilst Tuppence watched the speedometer in an agony of apprehension. The chauffeur had been given his orders and he drove with all the speed of which the car was capable.

Tuppence only spoke once.

'Tommy?'

'Quite all right. Released half an hour ago.'

She nodded.

Now, at last, they were nearing Leahampton. They darted and twisted through the town, up the hill.

Tuppence jumped out and she and Mr Grant ran up the drive. The hall door, as usual, was open. There was no one in sight. Tuppence ran lightly up the stairs.

She just glanced inside her own room in passing, and noted the confusion of open drawers and disordered bed. She nodded and passed on, along the corridor and into the room occupied by Mr and Mrs Cayley.

The room was empty. It looked peaceful and smelt slightly of medicines.

Tuppence ran across to the bed and pulled at the coverings.

They fell to the ground and Tuppence ran her hand under the mattress. She turned triumphantly to Mr Grant with a tattered child's picture-book in her hand.

'Here you are. It's all in here –'

'What on –?'

They turned. Mrs Sprot was standing in the doorway staring.

'And now,' said Tuppence, '*let me introduce you to M*! Yes. *Mrs Sprot!* I ought to have known it all along.'

It was left to Mrs Cayley arriving in the doorway a moment later to introduce the appropriate anticlimax.

'Oh *dear*,' said Mrs Cayley, looking with dismay at her spouse's dismantled bed. 'Whatever *will* Mr Cayley say?'

CHAPTER 15

I

'I ought to have known it all along,' said Tuppence.

She was reviving her shattered nerves by a generous tot of old brandy, and was beaming alternately at Tommy and at Mr Grant – and at Albert, who was sitting in front of a pint of beer and grinning from ear to ear.

'Tell us all about it, Tuppence,' urged Tommy.

'You first,' said Tuppence.

'There's not much for me to tell,' said Tommy. 'Sheer accident let me into the secret of the wireless transmitter. I thought I'd get away with it, but Haydock was too smart for me.'

Tuppence nodded and said:

'He telephoned to Mrs Sprot at once. And she ran out into the drive and laid in wait for you with the hammer. She was only away from the bridge table for about three minutes. I *did* notice she was a little out of breath – but I never suspected her.'

'After that,' said Tommy, 'the credit belongs entirely to Albert. He came sniffing round like a faithful dog. I did some impassioned morse snoring and he cottoned on to it. He went off to Mr Grant with the news and the two of them came back late that night. More snoring! Result was, I agreed to remain put so as to catch the sea forces when they arrived.'

Mr Grant added his quota.

'When Haydock went off this morning, our people took charge at Smugglers' Rest. We nabbed the boat this evening.'

'And now, Tuppence,' said Tommy. 'Your story.'

'Well, to begin with, I've been the most frightful fool all along! I suspected everybody here except Mrs Sprot! I *did* once have a terrible feeling of menace, as though I was in danger – that was after I overheard the telephone message about the fourth of the month. There were three people there at the time – I put down my feeling of apprehension to either Mrs Perenna or Mrs O'Rourke. Quite wrong – it was the colourless Mrs Sprot who was the really dangerous personality.

'I went muddling on, as Tommy knows, until after he disappeared. Then I was just cooking up a plan with Albert when suddenly, out of the blue, Anthony Marsdon turned up. It seemed all right to begin with – the usual sort of young man that Deb often has in tow. But two things made me think a bit. First I became more and more sure as I talked to him that I *hadn't* seen him before and that he never had been to the flat. The second was that, though he seemed to know all about my working at Leahampton, he assumed that *Tommy* was in Scotland. Now, that seemed all wrong. If he knew about anyone, it would be *Tommy* he knew about, since I was more or less unofficial. That struck me as very odd.

'Mr Grant had told me that Fifth Columnists were everywhere – in the most unlikely places. So why shouldn't one of them be working in Deborah's show? I wasn't convinced, but I was suspicious enough to lay a trap for him. I told him that Tommy and I had fixed up a code for communicating with each other. Our real one, of course, was a Bonzo postcard, but I told Anthony a fairy tale about the Penny plain, tuppence coloured saying.

'As I hoped, he rose to it beautifully! I got a letter this morning which gave him away completely.

'The arrangements had been all worked out beforehand. All I had to do was to ring up a tailor and cancel a fitting. That was an intimation that the fish had risen.'

'Coo-er!' said Albert. 'It didn't half give me a turn. I drove up with a baker's van and we dumped a pool of stuff just outside the gate. Aniseed, it was – or smelt like it.'

'And then –' Tuppence took up the tale. 'I came out and walked in it. Of course it was easy for the baker's van to follow me to the station and someone came up behind me and heard me book to Yarrow. It was after that that it might have been difficult.'

'The dogs followed the scent well,' said Mr Grant. 'They picked it up at Yarrow station and again on the track the tyre had made after you rubbed your shoe on it. It led us down to the copse and up again to the stone cross and after you where you had walked over the downs. The enemy had no idea we could follow you easily after they themselves had seen you start and driven off themselves.'

'All the same,' said Albert, 'it gave me a turn. Knowing you were in that house and not knowing what might come to you. Got in a back window, we did, and nabbed the foreign woman as she came down the stairs. Come in just in the nick of time, we did.'

'I knew you'd come,' said Tuppence. 'The thing was for me to spin things out as long as I could. I'd have pretended to tell if I hadn't seen the door opening. What was really exciting was the way I suddenly saw the whole thing and what a fool I'd been.'

'How did you see it?' asked Tommy.

'*Goosey, goosey, gander,*' said Tuppence promptly. 'When I said that to Commander Haydock he went absolutely livid. And not just because it was silly and rude. No, I saw at once that it *meant* something to him. And then there was the expression on that woman's face – Anna – it was like the Polish woman's, and then, of course, I thought of Solomon and I saw the whole thing.'

Tommy gave a sigh of exasperation.

'Tuppence, if you say that once again, I'll shoot you myself. Saw all *what*? And what on earth has Solomon got to do with it?'

'Do you remember that two women came to Solomon with a baby and both said it was hers, but Solomon said, "Very well, cut it in two." And the false mother said, "All right." But the real mother said, "No, let the other woman have it." You see, she couldn't face her child being killed. Well, that night that Mrs Sprot shot the other woman, you all said what a miracle it was and how easily she might have shot the child. Of course, it ought to have been quite plain then! If it had been her child, she *couldn't* have risked that shot for a minute. It meant that Betty *wasn't* her child. And that's why she absolutely had to shoot the other woman.'

'Why?'

'Because, of course, the other woman was *the child's real mother*.' Tuppence's voice shook a little.

'Poor thing – poor hunted thing. She came over a penniless refugee and gratefully agreed to let Mrs Sprot adopt her baby.'

'Why did Mrs Sprot want to adopt the child?'

'*Camouflage*! Supreme psychological camouflage. You just can't conceive of a master spy dragging her kid into the business. That's the main reason why I never considered Mrs Sprot seriously. Simply because of the child. But Betty's real mother had a terrible hankering for her baby and she found out Mrs

Sprot's address and came down here. She hung about waiting for her chance, and at last she got it and went off with the child.

'Mrs Sprot, of course, was frantic. At all costs she didn't want the police. So she wrote that message and pretended she found it in her bedroom, and roped in Commander Haydock to help. Then, when we'd tracked down the wretched woman, she was taking no chances, and shot her . . . Far from not knowing anything about firearms, she was a very fine shot! Yes, she killed that wretched woman – and because of that I've no pity for her. She was bad through and through.'

Tuppence paused, then she went on:

'Another thing that ought to have given me a hint was the likeness between Vanda Polonska and Betty. It was *Betty* the woman reminded me of all along. And then the child's absurd play with my shoelaces. How much more likely that she'd seen her so-called mother do that – not Carl von Deinim! But as soon as Mrs Sprot saw what the child was doing, she planted a lot of evidence in Carl's room for us to find and added the master touch of a shoelace dipped in secret ink.'

'I'm glad that Carl wasn't in it,' said Tommy. 'I liked him.'

'He's not been shot, has he?' asked Tuppence anxiously, noting the past tense.

Mr Grant shook his head.

'He's all right,' he said. 'As a matter of fact I've got a little surprise for you there.'

Tuppence's face lit up as she said:

'I'm terribly glad – for Sheila's sake! Of course we were idiots to go on barking up the wrong tree after Mrs Perenna.'

'She was mixed up in some IRA activities, nothing more,' said Mr Grant.

'I suspected Mrs O'Rourke a little – and sometimes the Cayleys –'

'And I suspected Bletchley,' put in Tommy.

'And all the time,' said Tuppence, 'it was that milk and water creature we just thought of as – Betty's mother.'

'Hardly milk and water,' said Mr Grant. 'A very dangerous woman and a very clever actress. And, I'm sorry to say, English by birth.'

Tuppence said:

'Then I've no pity or admiration for her – it wasn't even her country she was working for.' She looked with fresh curiosity at Mr Grant. 'You found what you wanted?'

Mr Grant nodded.

'It was all in that battered set of duplicate children's books.'

'The ones that Betty said were "nasty",' Tuppence exclaimed.

'They *were* nasty,' said Mr Grant dryly. '*Little Jack Horner* contained very full details of our naval dispositions. *Johnny Head in Air* did the same for the Air Force. Military matters were appropriately embodied in: *There Was a Little Man and He Had a Little Gun.*'

'And *Goosey, Goosey, Gander?*' asked Tuppence.

Mr Grant said:

'Treated with the appropriate reagent, that book contains written in invisible ink a full list of all prominent personages who are pledged to assist an invasion of this country. Amongst them were two Chief Constables, an Air Vice-Marshal, two Generals, the Head of an Armaments Works, a Cabinet Minister, many Police Superintendents, Commanders of Local Volunteer Defence Organisations, and various military and naval lesser fry, as well as members of our own Intelligence Force.'

Tommy and Tuppence stared.

'*Incredible!*' said the former.

Grant shook his head.

'You do not know the force of the German propaganda. It appeals to something in man, some desire or lust for power. These people were ready to betray their country not for money, but in a kind of megalomaniacal pride in what they, *they themselves*, were going to achieve for that country. In every land it has been the same. It is the Cult of Lucifer – Lucifer, Son of the Morning. Pride and a desire for *personal glory*!'

He added:

'You can realise that, with such persons to issue contradictory orders and confuse operations, how the threatened invasion would have had every chance to succeed.'

'And now?' said Tuppence.

Mr Grant smiled.

'And now,' he said, '*let them come! We'll be ready* for them!'

CHAPTER 16

....

I

'Darling,' said Deborah. 'Do you know I almost thought the most terrible things about you?'

'Did you?' said Tuppence. 'When?'

Her eyes rested affectionately on her daughter's dark head.

'That time when you sloped off to Scotland to join Father and I thought you were with Aunt Gracie. I almost thought you were having an affair with someone.'

'Oh, Deb, did you?'

'Not really, of course. Not at your age. And of course I knew you and Carrot Top are devoted to each other. It was really an idiot called Tony Marsdon who put it into my head. Do you know, Mother – I think I might tell you – he was found afterwards to be a Fifth Columnist. He always did talk rather oddly – how things would be just the same, perhaps better if Hitler did win.'

'Did you – er – like him at all?'

'Tony? Oh no he was always rather a bore. I must dance this.'

She floated away in the arms of a fair-haired young man, smiling up at him sweetly. Tuppence followed their revolutions for a few minutes, then her eyes shifted to where a tall young man in Air Force uniform was dancing with a fair-haired slender girl.

'I do think, Tommy,' said Tuppence, 'that our children are rather nice.'

'Here's Sheila,' said Tommy.

He got up as Sheila Perenna came towards their table.

She was dressed in an emerald evening dress which showed up her dark beauty. It was a sullen beauty tonight and she greeted her host and hostess somewhat ungraciously.

'I've come, you see,' she said, 'as I promised. But I can't think why you wanted to ask me.'

'Because we like you,' said Tommy smiling.

'Do you really?' said Sheila. 'I can't think why. I've been perfectly foul to you both.'

She paused and murmured:

'But I am grateful.'

Tuppence said:

'We must find a nice partner to dance with you.'

'I don't want to dance. I loathe dancing. I came just to see you two.'

'You will like the partner we've asked to meet you,' said Tuppence smiling.

'I –' Sheila began. Then stopped – for Carl von Deinim was walking across the floor.

Sheila looked at him like one dazed. She muttered:

'You –'

'I, myself,' said Carl.

There was something a little different about Carl von Deinim this evening. Sheila stared at him, a trifle perplexed. The colour had come up on her cheeks, turning them a deep glowing red.

She said a little breathlessly:

'I knew that you would be all right now – but I thought they would still keep you interned?'

Carl shook his head.

'There is no reason to intern me.'

He went on:

'You have got to forgive me, Sheila, for deceiving you. I am not, you see, Carl von Deinim at all. I took his name for reasons of my own.'

He looked questioningly at Tuppence, who said:

'Go ahead. Tell her.'

'Carl von Deinim was my friend. I knew him in England some years ago. I renewed acquaintanceship with him in Germany just before the war. I was there then on special business for this country.'

'You were in the Intelligence?' asked Sheila.

'Yes. When I was there, queer things began to happen. Once or twice I had some very near escapes. My plans were known when they should not have been known. I realised that there was something wrong and that "the rot", to express it in their terms, had penetrated actually into the service in which I was. I had been let down by my own people. Carl and I had a certain superficial likeness (my grandmother was a German), hence my suitability for work in Germany. Carl was not a Nazi. He was interested solely in his job – a job I myself had also practised – research chemistry. He decided, shortly before war broke out, to escape to England. His brothers had been sent to concentration camps. There would, he thought, be great difficulties in the way of his own escape, but in an almost miraculous fashion all these difficulties smoothed themselves out. The fact, when he mentioned it to me, made me somewhat suspicious. Why were the authorities making it so easy for von Deinim to leave Germany when his brothers and other relations were in concentration camps and he himself was suspected because of his anti-Nazi sympathies? It seemed as though they wanted him in England for some reason. My own position was becoming increasingly precarious. Carl's lodgings were in the same house as mine and one day I found him, to my sorrow, lying dead on his bed. He had succumbed to depression and taken his own life, leaving a letter behind which I read and pocketed.

'I decided then to effect a substitution. I wanted to get out of Germany – and I wanted to know why Carl was being encouraged to do so. I dressed his body in my clothes and laid it on my bed. It was disfigured by the shot he had fired into his head. My landlady, I knew, was semi-blind.

'With Carl von Deinim's papers I travelled to England and went to the address to which he had been recommended to go. The address was Sans Souci.

'Whilst I was there I played the part of Carl von Deinim and never relaxed. I found arrangements had been made for me to work in the chemical factory there. At first I thought that the idea was I should be compelled to do work for the Nazis. I realised later that the part for which my poor friend had been cast was that of scapegoat.

'When I was arrested on faked evidence, I said nothing. I wanted to leave the revelation of my own identity as late as possible. I wanted to see what would happen.

'It was only a few days ago that I was recognised by one of our people and the truth came out.'

Sheila said reproachfully:

'You should have told me.'

He said gently:

'If you feel like that – I am sorry.'

His eyes looked into hers. She looked at him angrily and proudly – then the anger melted. She said:

'I suppose you had to do what you did . . .'

'Darling –'

He caught himself up.

'Come and dance . . .'

They moved off together.

Tuppence sighed.

'What's the matter?' said Tommy.

'I do hope Sheila will go on caring for him now that he isn't a German outcast with everyone against him.'

'She looks as though she cares all right.'

'Yes, but the Irish are terribly perverse. And Sheila is a born rebel.'

'Why did he search your room that day? That's what led us up the garden path so terribly.'

Tommy gave a laugh.

'I gather he thought Mrs Blenkensop wasn't a very convincing person. In fact – while we were suspecting him he was suspecting us.'

'Hallo, you two,' said Derek Beresford as he and his partner danced past his parents' table. 'Why don't you come and dance?'

He smiled encouragingly at them.

'They are so kind to us, bless 'em,' said Tuppence.

Presently the twins and their partners returned and sat down. Derek said to his father:

'Glad you got a job all right. Not very interesting, I suppose?'

'Mainly routine,' said Tommy.

'Never mind, you're doing something. That's the great thing.'

'And I'm glad Mother was allowed to go and work too,' said Deborah. 'She looks ever so much happier. It wasn't too dull, was it, Mother?'

'I didn't find it at all dull,' said Tuppence.

'Good,' said Deborah. She added: 'When the war's over, I'll be able to tell you something about my job. It's really frightfully interesting, but very confidential.'

'How thrilling,' said Tuppence.

'Oh, it is! Of course, it's not so thrilling as flying –'

She looked enviously at Derek.

She said, 'He's going to be recommended for –'

Derek said quickly:

'Shut up, Deb.'

Tommy said:

'Hallo, Derek, what have you been up to?' .

'Oh, nothing much – sort of show all of us are doing. Don't know why they pitched on me,' murmured the young airman, his face scarlet. He looked as embarrassed as though he had been accused of the most deadly of sins.

He got up and the fair-haired girl got up too.

Derek said:

'Mustn't miss any of this – last night of my leave.'

'Come on, Charles,' said Deborah.

The two of them floated away with their partners.

Tuppence prayed inwardly:

'Oh let them be safe – don't let anything happen to them . . .'

She looked up to meet Tommy's eyes. He said, 'About that child – shall we?'

'Betty? Oh, Tommy, I'm glad you've thought of it, too! I thought it was just me being maternal. You really mean it?'

'That we should adopt her? Why not? She's had a raw deal, and it will be fun for us to have something young growing up.'

'Oh Tommy!'

She stretched out her hand and squeezed his. They looked at each other.

'We always do want the same things,' said Tuppence happily.

Deborah, passing Derek on the floor, murmured to him:

'Just look at those two – actually holding hands! They're rather sweet, aren't they? We must do all we can to make up to them for having such a dull time in this war . . .'

TOWARDS ZERO

To Robert Graves

Dear Robert,
Since you are kind enough to say you like my stories, I
venture to dedicate this book to you. All I ask is that you
should sternly restrain your critical faculties (doubtless
sharpened by your recent excesses in that line!) when
reading it.

This is a story for your pleasure and *not* a candidate
for Mr Graves' literary pillory!
Your friend,

Agatha Christie

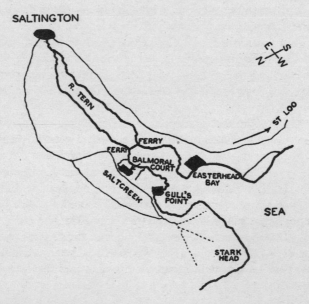

November 19th

The group round the fireplace was nearly all composed of lawyers or those who had an interest in the law. There was Martindale the solicitor, Rufus Lord, KC, young Daniels who had made a name for himself in the Carstairs case, a sprinkling of other barristers, Mr Justice Cleaver, Lewis of Lewis and Trench and old Mr Treves. Mr Treves was close on eighty, a very ripe and experienced eighty. He was a member of a famous firm of solicitors, and the most famous member of that firm, he was said to know more of backstairs history than any man in England and he was a specialist on criminology.

Unthinking people said Mr Treves ought to write his memoirs. Mr Treves knew better. He knew that he knew too much.

Though he had long retired from active practice, there was no man in England whose opinion was so respected by the members of his own fraternity. Whenever his thin precise little voice was raised there was always a respectful silence.

The conversation now was on the subject of a much talked of case which had finished that day at the Old Bailey. It was a murder case and the prisoner had been acquitted. The present company was busy trying the case over again and making technical criticisms.

The prosecution had made a mistake in relying on one of its witnesses – old Depleach ought to have realized what an opening he was giving to the defence. Young Arthur had made the most of that servant girl's evidence. Bentmore, in his summing up, had very rightly put the matter in its correct perspective, but the mischief was done by then – the jury had believed the girl. Juries were funny – you never knew what they'd swallow and what they wouldn't. But let them once get a thing into their heads and no one was ever going to get it out again. They believed that the girl was speaking the truth about the crowbar and that was that.

The medical evidence had been a bit above their heads. All those long terms and scientific jargon – damned bad witnesses, these scientific johnnies – always hemmed and hawed and couldn't say yes or no to a plain question – always 'in certain circumstances that might take place' – and so on!

They talked themselves out, little by little, and as the remarks became more spasmodic and disjointed, a general feeling grew of something lacking. One head after another turned in the direction of Mr Treves. For Mr Treves had as yet contributed nothing to the discussion. Gradually it became apparent that the company was waiting for a final word from its most respected colleague.

Mr Treves, leaning back in his chair, was absent-mindedly polishing his glasses. Something in the silence made him look up sharply.

'Eh?' he said. 'What was that? You asked me something?'

Young Lewis spoke.

'We were talking, sir, about the Lamorne case.'

He paused expectantly.

'Yes, yes,' said Mr Treves. 'I was thinking of that.'

There was a respectful hush.

'But I'm afraid,' said Mr Treves, still polishing, 'that I was being fanciful. Yes, fanciful. Result of getting on in years, I suppose. At my age one can claim the privilege of being fanciful, if one likes.'

'Yes, indeed, sir,' said young Lewis, but he looked puzzled.

'I was thinking,' said Mr Treves, 'not so much of the various points of law raised – though they were interesting – very interesting – if the verdict had gone the other way there would have been good grounds for appeal. I rather think – but I won't go into that now. I was thinking, as I say, not of the points of law but of the – well, of the *people* in the case.'

Everybody looked rather astonished. They had considered the people in the case only as regarding their credibility or otherwise as witnesses. No one had even hazarded a speculation as to whether the prisoner had been guilty or as innocent as the court had pronounced him to be.

'Human beings, you know,' said Mr Treves thoughtfully. 'Human beings. All kinds and sorts and sizes and shapes of 'em. Some with brains and a good many more without. They'd come from all over the place, Lancashire, Scotland – that restaurant proprietor from Italy and that school teacher woman from somewhere out Middle West. All caught up and enmeshed in the thing and finally all brought together in a court of law in London on a grey November day. Each one contributing his little part. The whole thing culminating in a trial for murder.'

He paused and gently beat a delicate tattoo on his knee.

'I like a good detective story,' he said. 'But, you know, they begin in the wrong place! They begin with the murder. But the murder is the *end*. The story begins long before that – years before sometimes – with all the causes and events that bring certain people to a certain place at a certain time on a certain day. Take that little maid servant's evidence – if the kitchenmaid hadn't pinched her young man she wouldn't have thrown up her situation in a huff and gone to the Lamornes and been the principal witness for the defence. That Guiseppe Antonelli – coming over to exchange with his brother for a month. The brother is as blind as a bat. He wouldn't have seen what Guiseppe's sharp eyes saw. If the constable hadn't been sweet on the cook at No. 48, *he* wouldn't have been late on his beat . . .'

He nodded his head gently:

'All converging towards a given spot . . . And then, when the time comes – over the top! *Zero Hour*. Yes, all of them converging towards zero . . .'

He repeated: 'Towards zero . . .'

Then gave a quick little shudder.

'You're cold, sir, come nearer the fire.'

'No, no,' said Mr Treves. 'Just someone walking over my grave, as they say. Well, well, I must be making my way homewards.'

He gave an affable little nod and went slowly and precisely out of the room.

There was a moment of dubious silence and then Rufus Lord, KC, remarked that poor old Treves was getting on.

Sir William Cleaver said:

'An acute brain – a very acute brain – but Anno Domini tells in the end.'

'Got a groggy heart, too,' said Lord. 'May drop down any minute, I believe.'

'He takes pretty good care of himself,' said young Lewis.

At that moment Mr Treves was carefully stepping into his smooth-running Daimler. It deposited him at a house in a quiet square. A solicitous butler valet helped him off with his coat. Mr Treves walked into his library where a coal fire was burning. His bedroom lay beyond, for out of consideration for his heart he never went upstairs.

He sat down in front of the fire and drew his letters towards him.

His mind was still dwelling on the fancy he had outlined at the Club.

'Even now,' thought Mr Treves to himself, 'some drama – some murder to be – is in course of preparation. If I were writing one of these amusing stories of blood and crime, I should begin now with an elderly gentleman sitting in front of the fire opening his letters – going, unbeknownst to himself – towards zero . . .'

He slit open an envelope and gazed down absently at the sheet he abstracted from it.

Suddenly his expression changed. He came back from romance to reality.

'Dear me,' said Mr Treves. 'How extremely annoying! Really, how very vexing. After all these years! This will alter all my plans.'

'OPEN THE DOOR AND HERE ARE THE PEOPLE'

January 11th

The man in the hospital bed shifted his body slightly and stifled a groan.

The nurse in charge of the ward got up from her table and came down to him. She shifted his pillows and moved him into a more comfortable position.

Angus MacWhirter only gave a grunt by way of thanks.

He was in a state of seething rebellion and bitterness.

By this time it ought to have been over. He ought to have been out of it all! Curse that damned ridiculous tree growing out of the cliff! Curse those officious sweethearts who braved the cold of a winter's night to keep a tryst on the cliff edge.

But for them (and the tree!) it would have been over – a plunge into the deep icy water, a brief struggle perhaps, and then oblivion – the end of a misused, useless, unprofitable life.

And now where was he? Lying ridiculously in a hospital bed with a broken shoulder and with the prospect of being hauled up in a police court for the crime of trying to take his own life.

Curse it, it was his *own* life, wasn't it?

And if he had succeeded in the job, they would have buried him piously as of unsound mind!

Unsound mind, indeed! He'd never been saner! And to commit suicide was the most logical and sensible thing that could be done by a man in his position.

Completely down and out, with his health permanently affected, with a wife who had left him for another man. Without a job, without affection, without money, health or hope, surely to end it all was the only possible solution?

And now here he was in this ridiculous plight. He would shortly be admonished by a sanctimonious magistrate for doing the common-sense thing with a commodity which belonged to him and to him only – his life.

He snorted with anger. A wave of fever passed over him.

The nurse was beside him again.

She was young, red-haired, with a kindly, rather vacant face.

'Are you in much pain?'

'No, I'm not.'

'I'll give you something to make you sleep.'

'You'll do nothing of the sort.'

'But –'

'Do you think I can't bear a bit of pain and sleeplessness?'

She smiled in a gentle, slightly superior way.

'Doctor said you could have something.'

'I don't care what doctor said.'

She straightened the covers and set a glass of lemonade a little nearer to him. He said, slightly ashamed of himself:

'Sorry if I was rude.'

'Oh, that's all right.'

It annoyed him that she was so completely undisturbed by his bad temper. Nothing like that could penetrate her nurse's armour of indulgent indifference. He was a patient – not a man.

He said:

'Damned interference – all this damned interference . . .'

She said reprovingly:

'Now, now, that isn't very nice.'

'Nice?' he demanded. '*Nice?* My God.'

She said calmly: 'You'll feel better in the morning.'

He swallowed.

'You nurses. You *nurses*! You're inhuman, that's what you are!'

'We know what's best for you, you see.'

'That's what's so infuriating! About you. About a hospital. About the world. Continual interference! Knowing what's best for other people. I tried to kill myself. You know that, don't you?'

She nodded.

'Nobody's business but mine whether I threw myself off a bloody cliff or not. I'd finished with life. I was down and out!'

She made a little clicking noise with her tongue. It indicated abstract sympathy. He was a patient. She was soothing him by letting him blow off steam.

'Why shouldn't I kill myself if I want to?' he demanded.

She replied to that quite seriously.

'Because it's wrong.'

'Why is it wrong?'

She looked at him doubtfully. She was not disturbed in her own belief, but she was much too inarticulate to explain her reaction.

'Well – I mean – it's wicked to kill yourself. You've got to go on living whether you like it or not.'

'Why have you?'

'Well, there are other people to consider, aren't there?'

'Not in my case. There's not a soul in the world who'd be the worse for my passing on.'

'Haven't you got any relations? No mother or sisters or anything?'

'No. I had a wife once but she left me – quite right too! She saw I was no good.'

'But you've got friends, surely?'

'No, I haven't. I'm not a friendly sort of man. Look here, nurse, I'll tell you something. I was a happy sort of chap once. Had a good job and a good-looking wife. There was a car accident. My boss was driving the car and I was in it. He wanted me to say he was driving under thirty at the time of the accident. He wasn't. He was driving nearer fifty. Nobody was killed, nothing like that, he just wanted to be in the right for the insurance people. Well, I wouldn't say what he wanted. It was a lie. I don't tell lies.'

The nurse said:

'Well, I think you were quite right. Quite right.'

'You do, do you? That pigheadedness of mine cost me my job. My boss was sore. He saw to it that I didn't get another. My wife got fed up seeing me mooch about unable to get anything to do. She went off with a man who had been my friend. He was doing well and going up in the world. I drifted along, going steadily down. I took to drinking a bit. That didn't help me to hold down jobs. Finally I came down to hauling – strained my inside – the doctor told me I'd never be strong again. Well, there wasn't much to live for then. Easiest way, and the cleanest way, was to go right out. My life was no good to myself or anyone else.'

The little nurse murmured:

'You don't know that.'

He laughed. He was better-tempered already. Her naïve obstinacy amused him.

'My dear girl, what use am I to anybody?'

She said confusedly:

'You don't know. You may be – someday –'

'Someday? There won't be any someday. Next time I shall make sure.'

She shook her head decidedly.

'Oh, no,' she said. 'You won't kill yourself now.'

'Why not?'

'They never do.'

He stared at her. '*They never do.*' He was one of a class of would-be suicides. Opening his mouth to protest energetically, his innate honesty suddenly stopped him.

Would he do it again? Did he really mean to do it?

He knew suddenly that he didn't. For no reason. Perhaps the right reason was the one she had given out of her specialized knowledge. Suicides didn't do it again.

All the more he felt determined to force an admission from her on the ethical side.

'At any rate I've got a right to do what I like with my own life.'

'No – no, you haven't.'

'But why not, my dear girl, why?'

She flushed. She said, her fingers playing with the little gold cross that hung round her neck:

'You don't understand. God may need you.'

He stared – taken aback. He did not want to upset her childlike faith. He said mockingly:

'I suppose that one day I may stop a runaway horse and save a golden-haired child from death – eh? Is that it?'

She shook her head. She said with vehemence and trying to express what was so vivid in her mind and so halting on her tongue:

'It may be just by *being* somewhere – not doing anything – just by being at a certain place at a certain time – oh, I can't say what I mean, but you might just – just walk along a street some day and just by doing that accomplish something terribly important – perhaps even without knowing what it was.'

The red-haired little nurse came from the west coast of Scotland and some of her family had 'the sight'.

Perhaps, dimly, she saw a picture of a man walking up a road on a night in September and thereby saving a human being from a terrible death . . .

February 14th

There was only one person in the room and the only sound to be heard was the scratching of that person's pen as it traced line after line across the paper.

There was no one to read the words that were being traced. If there had been, they would hardly have believed their eyes. For what was being written was a clear, carefully detailed project for murder.

There are times when a body is conscious of a mind controlling it – when it bows obedient to that alien something that controls its actions. There are other times when a mind is conscious of owning and controlling a body and accomplishing its purpose by using that body.

The figure sitting writing was in the last-named state. It was a mind, a cool, controlled intelligence. This mind had only one thought and one purpose – the destruction of another human being. To the end that this purpose might be accomplished, the scheme was being worked out meticulously on paper. Every eventuality, every possibility was being taken into account. The thing had got to be absolutely fool-proof. The scheme, like all good schemes, was not absolutely cut and dried. There were certain alternative actions at certain points. Moreover, since the mind was intelligent, it realized that there must be intelligent provision left for the unforeseen. But the main lines were clear and had been closely tested. The time, the place, the method, the victim! . . .

The figure raised its head. With its hand, it picked up the sheets of paper and read them carefully through. Yes, the thing was crystal-clear.

Across the serious face a smile came. It was a smile that was not quite sane. The figure drew a deep breath.

As man was made in the image of his Maker, so there was now a terrible travesty of a creator's joy.

Yes, everything planned – everyone's reaction foretold and allowed for, the good and evil in everybody played upon and brought into harmony with one evil design.

There was one thing lacking still . . .

With a smile the writer traced a date – a date in September.

Then, with a laugh, the paper was torn in pieces and the pieces carried across the room and put into the heart of the glowing fire. There was no carelessness. Every single piece was consumed and destroyed. The plan was now only existent in the brain of its creator.

March 8th

Superintendent Battle was sitting at the breakfast table. His jaw was set in a truculent fashion and he was reading, slowly and carefully, a letter that his wife had just tearfully handed to him. There was no expression visible on his face, for his face never did register any expression. It had the aspect of a face carved out of wood. It was solid and durable and, in some way, impressive. Superintendent Battle had never suggested brilliance; he was, definitely, not a brilliant man, but he had some other quality, difficult to define, that was nevertheless forceful.

'I can't believe it,' said Mrs Battle, sobbing. 'Sylvia!'

Sylvia was the youngest of Superintendent and Mrs Battle's five children. She was sixteen and at school near Maidstone.

The letter was from Miss Amphrey, headmistress of the school in question. It was a clear, kindly and extremely tactful letter. It set out, in black and white, that various small thefts had been puzzling the school authorities for some time, that the matter had at last been cleared up, that Sylvia Battle had confessed, and that Miss Amphrey would like to see Mr and Mrs Battle at the earliest opportunity 'to discuss the position'.

Superintendent Battle folded up the letter, put it in his pocket, and said: 'You leave this to me, Mary.'

He got up, walked round the table, patted her on the cheek and said, 'Don't worry, dear, it will be all right.'

He went from the room, leaving comfort and reassurance behind him.

That afternoon, in Miss Amphrey's modern and individualistic drawing-room, Superintendent Battle sat very squarely on his chair, his large wooden hands on his knees, confronting Miss Amphrey and managing to look, far more than usual, every inch a policeman.

Miss Amphrey was a very successful headmistress. She had personality – a great deal of personality, she was enlightened and up to date, and she combined discipline with modern ideas of self-determination.

Her room was representative of the spirit of Meadway. Everything was of a cool oatmeal colour – there were big jars of daffodils and bowls of tulips and hyacinths. One or two good copies of the antique Greek, two pieces of advanced modern sculpture, two Italian primitives on the walls. In the midst of all this, Miss Amphrey herself, dressed in a deep shade of blue, with an eager face suggestive of a conscientious greyhound, and clear blue eyes looking serious through thick lenses.

'The important thing,' she was saying in her clear well-modulated voice, 'is that this should be taken the right way. It

is the girl herself we have to think of, Mr Battle. Sylvia herself!
It is most important – *most* important, that her life should not be
crippled in any way. She must not be made to assume a burden
of *guilt* – blame must be very very sparingly meted out, if at all.
We must arrive at the reason *behind* these quite trivial pilferings.
A sense of inferiority, perhaps? She is not good at games, you
know – an obscure wish to shine in a different sphere – the desire
to assert her ego? We must be very very careful. That is why I
wanted to see you alone first – to impress upon you to be very
very careful with Sylvia. I repeat again, it's very important to get
at what is *behind* this.'

'That, Miss Amphrey,' said Superintendent Battle, 'is why I
have come down.'

His voice was quiet, his face unemotional, his eyes surveyed
the school mistress appraisingly.

'I have been very gentle with her,' said Miss Amphrey.

Battle said laconically:

'Good of you, Ma'am.'

'You see, I really love and understand these young things.'

Battle did not reply directly. He said:

'I'd like to see my girl now, if you don't mind, Miss Amphrey.'

With renewed emphasis Miss Amphrey admonished him to be
careful – to go slow – not to antagonize a child just budding into
womanhood.

Superintendent Battle showed no signs of impatience. He just
looked blank.

She took him at last to her study. They passed one or two girls
in the passages. They stood politely to attention but their eyes
were full of curiosity. Having ushered Battle into a small room,
not quite so redolent of personality as the one downstairs, Miss
Amphrey withdrew and said she would send Sylvia to him.

Just as she was leaving the room, Battle stopped her.

'One minute, Ma'am, how did you come to pitch upon Sylvia
as the one responsible for these – er – leakages?'

'My methods, Mr Battle, were psychological.'

Miss Amphrey spoke with dignity.

'Psychological? H'm. What about the evidence, Miss Amphrey?'

'Yes, yes, I quite understand, Mr Battle – you would feel that
way. Your – er – profession steps in. But psychology is beginning

to be recognized in criminology. I can assure you that there is no mistake – Sylvia freely admits the whole thing.'

'Yes, yes – I know that. I was just asking how you came to pitch upon her to begin with.'

'Well, Mr Battle, this business of things being taken out of the girls' lockers was on the increase. I called the school together and told them the facts. At the same time, I studied their faces unobtrusively. Sylvia's expression struck me at once. It was guilty – confused. I knew at that moment who was responsible. I wanted, not to *confront* her with her guilt, but to get her to admit it *herself*. I set a little test for her – a word association.'

Battle nodded to show he understood.

'And finally the child admitted it all.'

Her father said:

'I see.'

Miss Amphrey hesitated a minute, then went out.

Battle was standing looking out of the window when the door opened again.

He turned round slowly and looked at his daughter.

Sylvia stood just inside the door, which she had closed behind her. She was tall, dark, angular. Her face was sullen and bore marks of tears. She said timidly rather than defiantly:

'Well, here I am.'

Battle looked at her thoughtfully for a minute or two. He sighed.

'I should never have sent you to this place,' he said. 'That woman's a fool.'

Sylvia lost sight of her own problems in sheer amazement.

'Miss Amphrey? Oh, but she's *wonderful*. We all think so.'

'H'm,' said Battle. 'Can't be quite a fool, then, if she sells the idea of herself as well as that. All the same, Meadway wasn't the place for you – although I don't know – this might have happened anywhere.'

Sylvia twisted her hands together. She looked down. She said:

'I'm – I'm sorry, Father. I really am.'

'So you should be,' said Battle shortly. 'Come here.'

She came slowly and unwillingly across the room to him. He took her chin in his great square hand and looked closely into her face.

'Been through a good deal, haven't you?' he said gently.

Tears started into her eyes.

Battle said slowly:

'You see, Sylvia, I've known all along with you, that there was *something*. Most people have got a weakness of some kind or another. Usually it's plain enough. You can see when a child's greedy, or bad-tempered, or got a streak of the bully in him. You were a good child, very quiet – very sweet-tempered – no trouble in any way – and sometimes I've worried. Because if there's a flaw you don't see, sometimes it wrecks the whole show when the article is tried out.'

'Like me!' said Sylvia.

'Yes, like you. You've cracked under strain – and in a damned queer way too. It's a way, oddly enough, I've never come across before.'

The girl said suddenly and scornfully:

'I should think you'd come across thieves often enough!'

'Oh yes – I know all about them. And that's why, my dear – not because I'm your father (fathers don't know much about their children) but because I'm a *policeman* I know well enough you're not a thief. *You* never took a thing in this place. Thieves are of two kinds, the kind that yields to sudden and overwhelming temptation – (and that happens damned seldom – it's amazing what temptation the ordinary normal honest human being can withstand) and there's the kind that just takes what doesn't belong to them almost as a matter of course. You don't belong to either type. You're not a thief. You're a very unusual type of liar.'

Sylvia began, 'But –'

He swept on.

'You've admitted it all? Oh yes, I know *that*. There was a saint once – went out with bread for the poor. Husband didn't like it. Met her and asked what there was in her basket. She lost her nerve and said it was roses – he tore open her basket and roses it was – a miracle! Now if you'd been Saint Elizabeth and were out with a basket of roses, and your husband had come along and asked what you'd got, you'd have lost your nerve and said "Bread".'

He paused and then said gently:

'That's how it happened, isn't it?'

There was a longer pause and then the girl suddenly bent her head.

Battle said:

'Tell me, child. What happened exactly?'

'She had us all up. Made a speech. And I saw her eyes on me and I knew she thought it was me! I felt myself getting red – and I saw some of the girls looking at me. It was awful. And then the others began looking at me and whispering in corners. I could see they all thought so. And then the Amp had me up here with some of the others one evening and we played a sort of word game – she said words and we gave answers –'

Battle gave a disgusted grunt.

'And I could see what it meant – and – and I sort of got paralysed. I tried not to give the wrong word – I tried to think of things quite outside – like squirrels or flowers – and the Amp was there watching me with eyes like gimlets – you know, sort of boring inside one. And after that – oh, it got worse and worse, and one day the Amp talked to me quite kindly and so – so *understandingly* – and – and I broke down and said I *had* done it – and oh! Daddy, the relief!'

Battle was stroking his chin.

'I see.'

'You do understand?'

'No, Sylvia, I don't understand, because I'm not made that way. If anyone tried to make me say I'd done something I hadn't I'd feel more like giving them a sock on the jaw. But I see how it came about in your case – and that gimlet-eyed Amp of yours has had as pretty an example of unusual psychology shoved under her nose as any half-baked exponent of misunderstood theories could ask for. The thing to do now is clear up this mess. Where's Miss Amphrey?'

Miss Amphrey was hovering tactfully near at hand. Her sympathetic smile froze on her face as Superintendent Battle said bluntly:

'In justice to my daughter, I must ask that you call in your local police over this.'

'But, Mr Battle, Sylvia herself –'

'Sylvia has never touched a thing that didn't belong to her in this place.'

'I quite understand that, as a father –'

'I'm not talking as a father, but as a policeman. Get the police to give you a hand over this. They'll be discreet. You'll find the things hidden away somewhere and the right set of fingerprints on them, I expect. Petty pilferers don't think of wearing gloves. I'm taking my daughter away with me now. If the police find evidence – *real* evidence – to connect her with the thefts, I'm prepared for her to appear in court and take what's coming to her, but I'm not afraid.'

As he drove out of the gate with Sylvia beside him some five minutes later, he asked:

'Who's the girl with fair hair, rather fuzzy, very pink cheeks and a spot on her chin, blue eyes far apart? I passed her in the passage.'

'That sounds like Olive Parsons.'

'Ah, well, I shouldn't be surprised if she were the one.'

'Did she look frightened?'

'No, looked smug! Calm smug look I've seen in the police court hundreds of times! I'd bet good money she's the thief – but you won't find her confessing – not much!'

Sylvia said with a sigh:

'It's like coming out of a bad dream. Oh Daddy, I am sorry! Oh, I *am* sorry! How could I be such a fool, such an utter fool? I do feel awful about it.'

'Ah, well,' said Superintendent Battle, patting her on the arm with a hand he disengaged from the wheel, and uttering one of his pet forms of trite consolation. 'Don't you worry. These things are sent to try us. Yes, these things are sent to try us. At least, I suppose so. I don't see what else they can be sent for . . .'

April 19th

The sun was pouring down on Nevile Strange's house at Hindhead.

It was an April day such as usually occurs at least once in a month, hotter than most of the June days to follow.

Nevile Strange was coming down the stairs. He was dressed in white flannels and held four tennis racquets under his arm.

If a man could have been selected from amongst other Englishmen as an example of a lucky man with nothing to wish for, a Selection Committee might have chosen Nevile Strange. He was a man well known to the British public, a first-class tennis player and all-round sportsman. Though he had never reached the finals at Wimbledon, he had lasted several of the opening rounds and in the mixed doubles had twice reached the semi-finals. He was, perhaps, too much of an all-round athlete to be a Champion tennis player. He was scratch at golf, a fine swimmer and had done some good climbs in the Alps. He was thirty-three, had magnificent health, good looks, plenty of money, an extremely beautiful wife whom he had recently married and, to all appearances, no cares or worries.

Nevertheless as Nevile Strange went downstairs this fine morning a shadow went with him. A shadow perceptible, perhaps, to no eyes but his. But he was aware of it, the thought of it furrowed his brow and made his expression troubled and indecisive.

He crossed the hall, squared his shoulders as though definitely throwing off some burden, passed through the living-room and out on to a glass-enclosed veranda where his wife, Kay, was curled up amongst cushions drinking orange juice.

Kay Strange was twenty-three and unusually beautiful. She had a slender but subtly voluptuous figure, dark red hair, such a perfect skin that she used only the slightest make-up to enhance it, and those dark eyes and brows which so seldom go with red hair and which are so devastating when they do.

Her husband said lightly:

'Hullo, Gorgeous, what's for breakfast?'

Kay replied: 'Horribly bloody-looking kidneys for you – and mushrooms – and rolls of bacon.'

'Sounds all right,' said Nevile.

He helped himself to the aforementioned viands and poured out a cup of coffee. There was a companionable silence for some minutes.

'Oo,' said Kay voluptuously, wriggling bare toes with scarlet manicured nails. 'Isn't the sun lovely? England's not so bad after all.'

They had just come back from the South of France.

Nevile, after a bare glance at the newspaper headlines, had turned to the Sports page and merely said 'Um . . .'

Then, proceeding to toast and marmalade, he put the paper aside and opened his letters.

There were a good many of these, but most of them he tore across and chucked away. Circulars, advertisements, printed matter.

Kay said: 'I don't like my colour scheme in the living-room. Can I have it done over, Nevile?'

'Anything you like, beautiful.'

'Peacock blue,' said Kay dreamily, 'and ivory satin cushions.'

'You'll have to throw in an ape,' said Nevile.

'You can be the ape,' said Kay.

Nevile opened another letter.

'Oh, by the way,' said Kay. 'Shirty has asked us to go to Norway on the yacht at the end of June. Rather sickening we can't.'

She looked cautiously sideways at Nevile and added wistfully: 'I would love it so.'

Something, some cloud, some uncertainty, seemed hovering on Nevile's face.

Kay said rebelliously:

'Have we got to go to dreary old Camilla's?'

Nevile frowned.

'Of course we have. Look here, Kay, we've had this out before. Sir Matthew was my guardian. He and Camilla looked after me. Gull's Point is my home, as far as any place is home to me.'

'Oh all right, all right,' said Kay. 'If we must, we must. After all, we get all that money when she dies, so I suppose we have to suck up a bit.'

Nevile said angrily:

'It's not a question of sucking up! She's no control over the money. Sir Matthew left it in trust for her during her lifetime and to come to me and my wife afterwards. It's a question of *affection*. Why can't you understand that?'

Kay said, after a moment's pause:

'I do understand really. I'm just putting on an act because – well because I know I'm only allowed there on sufferance as it were. They hate me! Yes, they do! Lady Tressilian looks down that long nose of hers at me and Mary Aldin looks over my shoulder when she talks to me. It's all very well for *you*. You don't see what goes on.'

'They always seem to be very polite to you. You know quite well I wouldn't stand for it if they weren't.'

Kay gave him a curious look from under her dark lashes.

'They're polite enough. But they know how to get under my skin all right. I'm the interloper, that's what they feel.'

'Well,' said Nevile, 'after all, I suppose – that's natural enough, isn't it?'

His voice had changed slightly. He got up and stood looking out at the view with his back to Kay.

'Oh yes, I daresay, it's natural. They were devoted to Audrey, weren't they?' Her voice shook a little. 'Dear, well-bred, cool, colourless Audrey! Camilla's not forgiven me for taking her place.'

Nevile did not turn. His voice was lifeless, dull. He said: 'After all, Camilla's old – past seventy. Her generation doesn't really like divorce, you know. On the whole I think she's accepted the position very well considering how fond she was of – of Audrey.'

His voice changed just a little as he spoke the name.

'They think you treated her badly.'

'So I did,' said Nevile under his breath, but his wife heard.

'Oh Nevile – don't be so stupid. Just because she chose to make such a frightful fuss.'

'She didn't make a fuss. Audrey never made fusses.'

'Well, you know what I mean. Because she went away and was ill, and went about everywhere looking broken-hearted. That's what I call a fuss! Audrey's not what I call a good loser. From my point of view if a wife can't hold her husband she ought to give him up gracefully! You two had nothing in common. She never played a game and was as anaemic and washed up as – as a dish rag. No life or go in her! If she really cared about you, she ought to have thought about your happiness first and been glad you were going to be happy with someone more suited to you.'

Nevile turned. A faintly sardonic smile played around his lips.

'What a little sportsman! How to play the game in love and matrimony!'

Kay laughed and reddened.

'Well, perhaps I was going a bit too far. But at any rate once the thing had happened, there it was. You've got to accept these things!'

Nevile said quietly:

'Audrey accepted it. She divorced me so that you and I could marry.'

'Yes, I know –' Kay hesitated.

Nevile said: 'You've never understood Audrey.'

'No, I haven't. In a way, Audrey gives me the creeps. I don't know what it is about her. You never know what she's thinking . . . She's – she's a little frightening.'

'Oh, nonsense, Kay.'

'Well, she frightens *me*. Perhaps it's because she's got brains.'

'My lovely nitwit!'

Kay laughed.

'You always call me that!'

'Because it's what you are!'

They smiled at each other. Nevile came over to her and, bending down, kissed the back of her neck.

'Lovely, lovely Kay,' he murmured.

'Very good Kay,' said Kay. 'Giving up a lovely yachting trip to go and be snubbed by her husband's prim Victorian relations.'

Nevile went back and sat down by the table.

'You know,' he said. 'I don't see why we shouldn't go on that trip with Shirty if you really want to so much.'

Kay sat up in astonishment.

'And what about Saltcreek and Gull's Point?'

Nevile said in a rather unnatural voice:

'I don't see why we shouldn't go there early in September.'

'Oh, but Nevile, surely –' She stopped.

'We can't go in July and August because of the Tournaments,' said Nevile. 'But we'd finish up at St Loo the last week in August, and it would fit in very well if we went on to Saltcreek from there.'

'Oh, it would fit in all right – beautifully. But I thought – well, *she* always goes there for September, doesn't she?'

'Audrey, you mean?'

'Yes. I suppose they could put her off, but –'

'Why should they put her off?'

Kay stared at him dubiously.

'You mean, we'd be there at the same time? What an extraordinary idea.'

Nevile said irritably:

'I don't think it's at all an extraordinary idea. Lots of people do it nowadays. Why shouldn't we all be friends together? It makes things so much *simpler*. Why, you said so yourself only the other day.'

'*I* did?'

'Yes, don't you remember? We were talking about the Howes, and you said it was the sensible civilized way to look at things, and that Leonard's new wife and his Ex were the best of friends.'

'Oh, *I* wouldn't mind. I *do* think it's sensible. But – well, I don't think Audrey would feel like that about it.'

'Nonsense.'

'It isn't nonsense. You know, Nevile, Audrey really was terribly fond of you . . . I don't think she'd stand it for a moment.'

'You're quite wrong, Kay. Audrey thinks it would be quite a good thing.'

'Audrey – what do you mean, Audrey thinks? How do you know what Audrey thinks?'

Nevile looked slightly embarrassed. He cleared his throat a little self-consciously.

'As a matter of fact, I happened to run into her yesterday when I was up in London.'

'You never told me.'

Nevile said irritably:

'I'm telling you now. It was absolute chance. I was walking across the Park and there she was coming towards me. You wouldn't want me to run away from her, would you?'

'No, of course not,' said Kay, staring. 'Go on.'

'I – we – well, we stopped, of course, and then I turned round and walked with her. I – I felt it was the least I could do.'

'Go on,' said Kay.

'And then we sat down on a couple of chairs and talked. She was very nice – very nice indeed.'

'Delightful for you,' said Kay.

'And we got talking, you know, about one thing and another. She was quite natural and normal and – and all that.'

'Remarkable!' said Kay.

'And she asked how you were –'

'Very kind of her!'

'And we talked about you for a bit. Really, Kay, she couldn't have been nicer.'

'Darling Audrey!'

'And then it sort of came to me – you know – how nice it would be if – if you two could be friends – if we could all get together. And it occurred to me that perhaps we might manage it at Gull's Point this summer. Sort of place it could happen quite naturally.'

'*You* thought of that?'

'I – well – yes, of course. It was all my idea.'

'You've never said anything to me about having any such idea.'

'Well, I only happened to think of it just then.'

'I see. Anyway, you suggested it and Audrey thought it was a marvellous brainwave?'

For the first time, something in Kay's manner seemed to penetrate to Nevile's consciousness.

He said:

'Is anything the matter, gorgeous?'

'Oh no, nothing! Nothing at all! It didn't occur to you or Audrey whether *I* should think it a marvellous idea?'

Nevile stared at her.

'But, Kay, why on earth should *you* mind?'

Kay bit her lip.

Nevile went on:

'You said yourself only the other day –'

'Oh, don't go into all that again! I was talking about other people – not *us*.'

'But that's partly what made me think of it.'

'More fool me. Not that I believe that.'

Nevile was looking at her with dismay.

'But, Kay, why should you mind? I mean, there's nothing for you to mind about!'

'Isn't there?'

'Well, I mean – any jealousy or that – would be on the other side.' He paused, his voice changed. 'You see, Kay, you and I treated Audrey damned badly. No, I don't mean that. It was nothing to do with you. *I* treated her very badly. It's no good just saying that I couldn't help myself. I feel that if this could come off I'd feel better about the whole thing. It would make me a lot happier.'

Kay said slowly: 'So you haven't been happy?'

'Darling idiot, what do you mean? Of course I've been happy, radiantly happy. But –'

Kay cut in.

'*But* – that's it! There's always been a "*but*" in this house. Some damned creeping shadow about the place. Audrey's shadow.'

Nevile stared at her.

'You mean to say you're jealous of Audrey?' he asked.

'I'm not jealous of her. I'm afraid of her . . . Nevile, you don't know what Audrey's like.'

'Not know what she's like when I've been married to her for over eight years?'

'You don't know,' Kay repeated, 'what Audrey is like.'

April 30th

'Preposterous!' said Lady Tressilian. She drew herself up on her pillow and glared fiercely round the room. 'Absolutely preposterous! Nevile must be mad.'

'It does seem rather odd,' said Mary Aldin.

Lady Tressilian had a striking-looking profile with a slender bridged nose down which, when so inclined, she could look with telling effect. Though now over seventy and in frail health, her native vigour of mind was in no way impaired. She had, it is true, long periods of retreat from life and its emotions when she would lie with half-closed eyes, but from these semi-comas she would emerge with all her faculties sharpened to the uttermost, and with an incisive tongue. Propped up by pillows in a large bed set across one corner of her room, she held her court like some French Queen. Mary Aldin, a distant cousin, lived with her and looked after her. The two women got on together excellently. Mary was thirty-six, but had one of those smooth ageless faces that change little with passing years. She might have been thirty or forty-five. She had a good figure, an air of breeding, and dark hair to which one lock of white across the front gave a touch of individuality. It was at one time a fashion, but Mary's white lock of hair was natural and she had had it since her girlhood.

She looked down now reflectively at Nevile Strange's letter which Lady Tressilian had handed to her.

'Yes,' she said. 'It does seem rather odd.'

'You can't tell me,' said Lady Tressilian, 'that this is Nevile's own idea! Somebody's put it into his head. Probably that new wife of his.'

'Kay. You think it was Kay's idea?'

'It would be quite like her. New and vulgar! If husbands and wives *have* to advertise their difficulties in public and have recourse to divorce, then they might at least part decently. The new wife and the old wife making friends is quite disgusting in my mind. Nobody has any *standards* nowadays!'

'I suppose it is just the modern way,' said Mary.

'It won't happen in my house,' said Lady Tressilian. 'I consider I've done all that could be asked of me having that scarlet-toed creature here at all.'

'She is Nevile's wife.'

'Exactly. Therefore I felt that Matthew would have wished it. He was devoted to the boy and always wanted him to look on this as his home. Since to refuse to receive his wife would have made an open breach, I gave way and asked her here. I do *not* like her – she's quite the wrong wife for Nevile – no background, no roots!'

'She's quite well born,' said Mary placatingly.

'Bad stock!' said Lady Tressilian. 'Her father, as I've told you, had to resign from all his clubs after that card business. Luckily he died shortly after. And her mother was notorious on the Riviera. What a bringing up for the girl. Nothing but Hotel life – and that mother! Then she meets Nevile on the tennis courts, makes a dead set at him and never rests until she gets him to leave his wife – of whom he was extremely fond – and go off with her! I blame her entirely for the whole thing!'

Mary smiled faintly. Lady Tressilian had the old-fashioned characteristic of always blaming the woman and being indulgent towards the man in the case.

'I suppose, strictly speaking, Nevile was equally to blame,' she suggested.

'Nevile was very much to blame,' agreed Lady Tressilian. 'He had a charming wife who had always been devoted – perhaps too devoted – to him. Nevertheless, if it hadn't been for that girl's persistence, I am convinced he would have come to his senses. But she was determined to marry him! Yes, my sympathies are entirely with Audrey. I am very fond of Audrey.'

Mary sighed. 'It has all been very difficult,' she said.

'Yes, indeed. One is at a loss to know how to act in such difficult circumstances. Matthew was fond of Audrey, and so am I, and one cannot deny that she was a very good wife to Nevile though perhaps it is a pity that she could not have shared his amusements more. She was never an athletic girl. The whole business was very distressing. When I was a girl, these things simply did not happen. Men had their affairs, naturally, but they were not allowed to break up married life.'

'Well, they happen now,' said Mary bluntly.

'Exactly. You have so much common sense, dear. It is of no use recalling bygone days. These things happen, and girls like Kay Mortimer steal other women's husbands and nobody thinks the worse of them!'

'Except people like you, Camilla!'

'I don't count. That Kay creature doesn't worry whether I approve of her or not. She's too busy having a good time. Nevile can bring her here when he comes and I'm even willing to receive her friends – though I do not much care for that very theatrical-looking young man who is always hanging round her – what is his name?'

'Ted Latimer?'

'That is it. A friend of her Riviera days – and I should very much like to know how he manages to live as he does.'

'By his wits,' suggested Mary.

'One might pardon that. I rather fancy he lives by his looks. *Not* a pleasant friend for Nevile's wife! I disliked the way he came down last summer and stayed at the Easterhead Bay Hotel while they were here.'

Mary looked out of the open window. Lady Tressilian's house was situated on a steep cliff overlooking the River Tern. On the other side of the river was the newly created summer resort of Easterhead Bay, consisting of a big sandy bathing beach, a cluster of modern bungalows and a large Hotel on the headland looking out to sea. Saltcreek itself was a straggling picturesque fishing village set on the side of a hill. It was old-fashioned, conservative and deeply contemptuous of Easterhead Bay and its summer visitors.

The Easterhead Bay Hotel was nearly exactly opposite Lady Tressilian's house, and Mary looked across the narrow strip of water at it now where it stood in its blatant newness.

'I am glad,' said Lady Tressilian, closing her eyes, 'that Matthew never saw that vulgar building. The coastline was *quite* unspoilt in his time.'

Sir Matthew and Lady Tressilian had come to Gull's Point thirty years ago. It was nine years since Sir Matthew, an enthusiastic sailing man, had capsized his dinghy and been drowned almost in front of his wife's eyes.

Everybody had expected her to sell Gull's Point and leave Saltcreek, but Lady Tressilian had not done so. She had lived on in the house, and her only visible reaction had been to dispose of all the boats and do away with the boathouse. There were no boats available for guests at Gull's Point. They had to walk along to the ferry and hire a boat from one of the rival boatmen there.

Mary said, hesitating a little:

'Shall I write, then, to Nevile and tell him that what he proposes does not fit in with our plans?'

'I certainly shall not dream of interfering with Audrey's visit. She has always come to us in September and I shall not ask her to change her plans.'

Mary said, looking down at the letter:

'You did see that Nevile says Audrey – er – approves of the idea – that she is quite willing to meet Kay?'

'I simply don't believe it,' said Lady Tressilian. 'Nevile, like all men, believes what he wants to believe!'

Mary persisted:

'He says he has actually spoken to her about it.'

'What a very odd thing to do! No – perhaps, after all, it isn't!'

Mary looked at her inquiringly.

'Like Henry the Eighth,' said Lady Tressilian.

Mary looked puzzled.

Lady Tressilian elaborated her last remark.

'Conscience, you know! Henry was always trying to get Catherine to agree that the divorce was the right thing. Nevile knows that he has behaved badly – he wants to feel *comfortable* about it all. So he has been trying to bully Audrey into saying everything is all right and that she'll come and meet Kay and that she doesn't mind at all.'

'I wonder,' said Mary slowly.

Lady Tressilian looked at her sharply.

'What's in your mind, my dear?'

'I was wondering –' She stopped, then went on: 'It – it seems so *unlike* Nevile – this letter! You don't think that, for some reason, Audrey *wants* this – this meeting?'

'Why should she?' said Lady Tressilian sharply. 'After Nevile left her she went to her aunt, Mrs Royde, at the Rectory, and had a complete breakdown. She was absolutely like a ghost of her former self. Obviously it hit her terribly hard. She's one of those quiet self-contained people who feel things intensely.'

Mary moved uneasily.

'Yes, she is intense. A queer girl in many ways . . .'

'She suffered a lot . . . Then the divorce went through and Nevile married the girl, and little by little Audrey began to get over it. Now she's almost back to her old self. You can't tell me she wants to rake up old memories again?'

Mary said with gentle obstinacy: 'Nevile says she does.'

The old lady looked at her curiously.

'You're extraordinarily obstinate about this, Mary. Why? Do you *want* to have them here together?'

Mary Aldin flushed. 'No, of course not.'

Lady Tressilian said sharply:

'It's not *you* who have been suggesting all this to Nevile?'

'How can you be so absurd?'

'Well, I don't believe for a minute it's really his idea. It's not *like* Nevile.' She paused a minute, then her face cleared. 'It's the 1st of May tomorrow, isn't it? Well, on the 3rd Audrey is coming to stay with the Darlingtons at Esbank. It's only twenty miles away. Write and ask her to come over and lunch here.'

May 5th

'Mrs Strange, m'lady.'

Audrey Strange came into the big bedroom, crossed the room to the big bed, stooped down and kissed the old lady and sat down in the chair placed ready for her.

'Nice to see you, my dear,' said Lady Tressilian.

'And nice to see you,' said Audrey.

There was a quality of intangibility about Audrey Strange. She was of medium height with very small hands and feet. Her hair was ash-blonde and there was very little colour in her face. Her eyes were set wide apart and were a clear pale grey. Her features were small and regular, a straight little nose set in a small oval pale face. With such colouring, with a face that was pretty but not beautiful, she had nevertheless a quality about her that could not be denied nor ignored and that drew your eyes to her again and again. She was a little like a ghost, but you felt at the same time that a ghost might be possessed of more reality than a live human being . . .

She had a singularly lovely voice; soft and clear like a small silver bell.

For some minutes she and the old lady talked of mutual friends and current events. Then Lady Tressilian said:

'Besides the pleasure of seeing you, my dear, I asked you to come because I've had rather a curious letter from Nevile.'

Audrey looked up. Her eyes were wide, tranquil and calm. She said:

'Oh yes?'

'He suggests – a preposterous suggestion, *I* call it! – that he and – and Kay should come here in September. He says he wants you and Kay to be friends and that you yourself think it a good idea?'

She waited. Presently Audrey said in her gentle placid voice:

'Is it – so preposterous?'

'My dear – do you really want this to happen?'

Audrey was silent again for a minute or two, then she said gently:

'I think, you know, it might be rather a good thing.'

'You really want to meet this – you want to meet Kay?'

'I do think, Camilla, that it might – simplify things.'

'Simplify things!' Lady Tressilian repeated the words helplessly.

Audrey spoke very softly.

'Dear Camilla. You have been so good. If Nevile wants this –'

'A fig for what Nevile wants!' said Lady Tressilian robustly. 'Do *you* want it, that's the question?'

A little colour came in Audrey's cheeks. It was the soft delicate glow of a sea shell.

'Yes,' she said. 'I do want it.'

'Well,' said Lady Tressilian. 'Well –'

She stopped.

'But, of course,' said Audrey. 'It is entirely your choice. It is your house and –'

Lady Tressilian shut her eyes.

'I'm an old woman,' she said. 'Nothing makes sense any more.'

'But of course – I'll come some other time. Any time will suit me.'

'You'll come in September as you always do,' snapped Lady Tressilian. 'And Nevile and Kay shall come too. I may be old but I can adapt myself, I suppose, as well as anyone else, to the changing phases of modern life. Not another word, that's settled.'

She closed her eyes again. After a minute or two she said, peering through half-shut lids at the young woman sitting beside her: 'Well, got what you want?'

Audrey started.

'Oh, yes, yes. Thank you.'

'My dear,' said Lady Tressilian, and her voice was deep and concerned, 'are you sure this isn't going to hurt you? You were very fond of Nevile, you know. This may reopen old wounds.'

Audrey was looking down at her small gloved hands. One of them, Lady Tressilian noticed, was clenched on the side of the bed.

Audrey lifted her head. Her eyes were calm and untroubled. She said:

'All that is quite over now. *Quite* over.'

Lady Tressilian leaned more heavily back on her pillows. 'Well, you should know. I'm tired – you must leave me now, dear. Mary is waiting for you downstairs. Tell them to send Barrett to me.'

Barrett was Lady Tressilian's elderly and devoted maid.

She came in to find her mistress lying back with closed eyes.

'The sooner I'm out of this world the better, Barrett,' said Lady Tressilian. 'I don't understand anything or anyone in it.'

'Ah! don't say that, my lady, you're tired.'

'Yes, I'm tired. Take that eiderdown off my feet and give me a dose of my tonic.'

'It's Mrs Strange coming that's upset you. A nice lady, but *she* could do with a tonic, I'd say. Not healthy. Always looks as though she's seeing things other people don't see. But she's got a lot of character. She makes herself *felt*, as you might say.'

'That's very true, Barrett,' said Lady Tressilian. 'Yes, that's very true.'

'And she's not the kind you forget easily, either. I've often wondered if Mr Nevile thinks about her sometimes. The new Mrs Strange is very handsome – very handsome indeed – but Miss Audrey is the kind you remember when she isn't there.'

Lady Tressilian said with a sudden chuckle:

'Nevile's a fool to want to bring those two women together. *He's* the one who'll be sorry for it!'

May 29th

Thomas Royde, pipe in mouth, was surveying the progress of his packing with which the deft-fingered Malayan No. 1 boy was busy. Occasionally his glance shifted to the view over the plantations. For some six months he would not see that view which had been so familiar for the past seven years.

It would be queer to be in England again.

Allen Drake, his partner, looked in.

'Hullo, Thomas, how goes it?'

'All set now.'

'Come and have a drink, you lucky devil. I'm consumed with envy.'

Thomas Royde moved slowly out of the bedroom and joined his friend. He did not speak, for Thomas Royde was a man singularly economical of words. His friends had learned to gauge his reactions correctly from the quality of his silences.

A rather thickset figure, with a straight solemn face and observant thoughtful eyes, he walked a little sideways, crablike. This, the result of being jammed in a door during an earthquake, had contributed towards his nickname of the Hermit Crab. It had left his right arm and shoulder partially helpless which, added to an artificial stiffness of gait, often led people to think he was feeling shy and awkward when in reality he seldom felt anything of the kind.

Allen Drake mixed the drinks.

'Well,' he said. 'Good hunting!'

Royde said something that sounded like 'Ah hum.'

Drake looked at him curiously.

'Phlegmatic as ever,' he remarked. 'Don't know how you manage it. How long is it since you went home?'

'Seven years – nearer eight.'

'It's a long time. Wonder you haven't gone completely native.'

'Perhaps I have.'

'You always did belong to Our Dumb Friends rather than to the human race! Planned out your leave?'

'Well – yes – partly.'

The bronze impassive face took a sudden and a deeper brick-red tinge.

Allen Drake said with lively astonishment:

'I believe there's a girl! Damn it all, you *are* blushing!'

Thomas Royde said rather huskily: 'Don't be a fool!'

And he drew very hard on his ancient pipe.

He broke all previous records by continuing the conversation himself.

'Dare say,' he said, 'I shall find things a bit changed.'

Allen Drake said curiously:

'I've always wondered why you chucked going home last time. Right at the last minute, too.'

Royde shrugged his shoulders.

'Thought that shooting trip might be interesting. Bad news from home about then.'

'Of course. I forgot. Your brother was killed – in that motoring accident.'

Thomas Royde nodded.

Drake reflected that, all the same, it seemed a curious reason for putting off a journey home. There was a mother – he believed a sister also. Surely at such a time – then he remembered something. Thomas had cancelled his passage *before* the news of his brother's death arrived.

Allen looked at his friend curiously. Dark horse, old Thomas! After a lapse of three years he could ask:

'You and your brother great pals?'

'Adrian and I? Not particularly. Each of us always went his own way. He was a barrister.'

'Yes,' thought Drake, 'a very different life. Chambers in London, parties – a living earned by the shrewd use of the tongue.' He reflected that Adrian Royde must have been a very different chap from old Silent Thomas.

'Your mother's alive, isn't she?'

'The mater? Yes.'

'And you've got a sister, too.'

Thomas shook his head.

'Oh, I thought you had. In that snapshot –'

Royde mumbled, 'Not a sister. Sort of distant cousin or something. Brought up with us because she was an orphan.'

Once more a slow tide of colour suffused the bronzed skin.

Drake thought, 'Hullo – o –?'

He said: 'Is she married?'

'She was. Married that fellow Nevile Strange.'

'Fellow who plays tennis and racquets and all that?'

'Yes. She divorced him.'

'And you're going home to try your luck with her,' thought Drake.

Mercifully he changed the subject of the conversation.

'Going to get any fishing or shooting?'

'Shall go home first. Then I thought of doing a bit of sailing down at Saltcreek.'

'I know it. Attractive little place. Rather a decent old-fashioned Hotel there.'

'Yes. The Balmoral Court. May stay there, or may put up with friends who've got a house there.'

'Sounds all right to me.'

'Ah hum. Nice peaceful place, Saltcreek. Nobody to hustle you.'

'I know,' said Drake. 'The kind of place where nothing ever happens.'

May 29th

'It is really *most annoying*,' said old Mr Treves. 'For twenty-five years now I have been to the Marine Hotel at Leahead – and now, would you believe it, the whole place is being pulled down. Widening the front or some nonsense of that kind. Why they can't let these seaside places alone – Leahead always had a peculiar charm of its own – Regency – pure Regency.'

Rufus Lord said consolingly:

'Still, there are other places to stay there, I suppose?'

'I really don't feel I can go to Leahead at all. At the Marine, Mrs Mackay understood my requirements perfectly. I had the same rooms every year – and there was hardly ever a change in the service. And the cooking was excellent – quite excellent.'

'What about trying Saltcreek? There's rather a nice old-fashioned Hotel there. The Balmoral Court. Tell you who keeps it. Couple of the name of Rogers. She used to be cook to old Lord Mounthead – he had the best dinners in London. She married the butler and they run this hotel now. It sounds to me just your kind of place. Quiet – none of these jazz bands – and first-class cooking and service.'

'It's an idea – it's certainly an idea. Is there a sheltered terrace?'

'Yes – a covered-in veranda and a terrace beyond. You can get sun or shade as you prefer. I can give you some introductions in the neighbourhood, too, if you like. There's old Lady Tressilian – she lives almost next door. A charming house and she herself is a delightful woman in spite of being very much of an invalid.'

'The judge's widow, do you mean?'

'That's it.'

'I used to know Matthew Tressilian, and I think I've met her. A charming woman – though, of course, that's a long time ago. Saltcreek is near St Loo, isn't it? I've several friends in that part of the world. Do you know, I really think Saltcreek is a very good idea. I shall write and get particulars. The middle of August is when I wish to go there – the middle of August to the middle of September. There is a garage for the car, I suppose? And my chauffeur?'

'Oh yes. It's thoroughly up-to-date.'

'Because, as you know, I have to be careful about walking uphill. I should prefer rooms on the ground floor, though I suppose there is a lift.'

'Oh yes, all that sort of thing.'

'It sounds,' said Mr Treves, 'as though it would solve my problem perfectly. And I should enjoy renewing my acquaintance with Lady Tressilian.'

July 28th

Kay Strange, dressed in shorts, and a canary-coloured woolly, was leaning forward watching the tennis players. It was the semi-final of the St Loo tournament, men's singles, and Nevile was playing young Merrick, who was regarded as the coming star in the tennis firmament. His brilliance was undeniable – some of his serves quite unreturnable – but he occasionally struck a wild patch when the older man's experience and court crafts won the day.

The score was three all in the final set.

Slipping on to a seat next to Kay, Ted Latimer observed in a lazy ironic voice:

'Devoted wife watches her husband slash his way to victory!'

Kay started.

'How you startled me. I didn't know you were there.'

'I am always there. You should know that by this time.'

Ted Latimer was twenty-five and extremely good-looking – even though unsympathetic old colonels were wont to say of him:

'Touch of the Dago!'

He was dark and beautifully sunburnt and a wonderful dancer.

His dark eyes could be very eloquent, and he managed his voice with the assurance of an actor. Kay had known him since she was fifteen. They had oiled and sunned themselves at Juan les Pins, had danced together and played tennis together. They had been not only friends but allies.

Young Merrick was serving from the left-hand court. Nevile's return was unplayable, a superb shot to the extreme corner.

'Nevile's backhand is good,' said Ted. 'It's better than his forehand. Merrick's weak on the backhand and Nevile knows it. He's going to pound at it all he knows how.'

The game ended. '*Four three – Strange leads.*'

He took the next game on his service. Young Merrick was hitting out wildly.

'*Five three.*'

'Good for Nevile,' said Latimer.

And then the boy pulled himself together. His play became cautious. He varied the pace of his shots.

'He's got a head on him,' said Ted. 'And his footwork is first-class. It's going to be a fight.'

Slowly the boy pulled up to five all. They went to seven all, and Merrick finally won the match at nine seven.

Nevile came up to the net, grinning and shaking his head ruefully, to shake hands.

'Youth tells,' said Ted Latimer. 'Nineteen against thirty-three. But I can tell you the reason, Kay, why Nevile has never been actual championship class. He's too good a loser.'

'Nonsense.'

'It isn't. Nevile, blast him, is always the complete good sportsman. I've never seen him lose his temper over losing a match.'

'Of course not,' said Kay. 'People don't.'

'Oh yes, they do! We've all seen them. Tennis stars who give way to nerves – and who damn' well snatch every advantage. But old Nevile – he's always ready to take the count and grin. Let the best man win and all that. God, how I hate the public school spirit! Thank the lord I never went to one.'

Kay turned her head.

'Being rather spiteful, aren't you?'

'Positively feline!'

'I wish you wouldn't make it so clear you don't like Nevile.'

'Why should I like him? He pinched my girl.'

His eyes lingered on her.

'I wasn't your girl. Circumstances forbade.'

'Quite so. Not even the proverbial tuppence a year between us.'

'Shut up. I fell in love with Nevile and married him –'

'And he's a jolly good fellow – and so say all of us!'

'Are you trying to annoy me?'

She turned her head as she asked the question. He smiled – and presently she returned his smile.

'How's the summer going, Kay?'

'So, so. Lovely yachting trip. I'm rather tired of all this tennis business.'

'How long have you got of it? Another month?'

'Yes. Then in September we go to Gull's Point for a fortnight.'

'I shall be at the Easterhead Bay Hotel,' said Ted. 'I've booked my room.'

'It's going to be a lovely party!' said Kay. 'Nevile and I, and Nevile's Ex, and some Malayan planter who's home on leave.'

'That does sound hilarious!'

'And the dowdy cousin, of course. Slaving away round that unpleasant old woman – and she won't get anything for it, either, since the money comes to me and Nevile.'

'Perhaps,' said Ted, 'she doesn't know that?'

'That would be rather funny,' said Kay.

But she spoke absently. She stared down at the racquet she was twiddling in her hands. She caught her breath suddenly.

'Oh Ted!'

'What's the matter, sugar?'

'I don't know. It's just sometimes I get – I get cold feet! I get scared and feel queer.'

'That doesn't sound like you, Kay.'

'It doesn't, does it? Anyway,' she smiled rather uncertainly, 'you'll be at the Easterhead Bay Hotel.'

'All according to plan.'

When Kay met Nevile outside the changing rooms, he said:

'I see the boy friend's arrived.'

'Ted?'

'Yes, the faithful dog – or faithful lizard might be more apt.'

'You don't like him, do you?'

'Oh, I don't mind him. If it amuses you to pull him around on a string –'

He shrugged his shoulders.

Kay said:

'I believe you're jealous.'

'Of Latimer?' His surprise was genuine.

Kay said:

'Ted's supposed to be very attractive.'

'I'm sure he is. He has that lithe South American charm.'

'You *are* jealous.'

Nevile gave her arm a friendly squeeze.

'No, I'm not, Gorgeous. You can have your tame adorers – a whole court of them if you like. I'm the man in possession, and possession is nine points of the law.'

'You're very sure of yourself,' said Kay with a slight pout.

'Of course. You and I are Fate. Fate let us meet. Fate brought us together. Do you remember when we met at Cannes and I was going on to Estoril and suddenly, when I got there, the first person I met was lovely Kay! I knew then that it was Fate – and that I couldn't escape.'

'It wasn't exactly Fate,' Kay said. 'It was me!'

'What do you mean by "it was me"?'

'Because it was! You see, I heard you say at Cannes you were going to Estoril, so I set to work on Mums and got her all worked up – and that's why the first person you saw when you got there was Kay.'

Nevile looked at her with a rather curious expression. He said slowly: 'You never told me that before.'

'No, because it wouldn't have been good for you. It might have made you conceited! But I always *have* been good at planning. Things don't happen unless you make them! You call me a nitwit sometimes – but in my own way I'm quite clever. I make things happen. Sometimes I have to plan a long way beforehand.'

'The brainwork must be intense.'

'It's all very well to laugh.'

Nevile said with a sudden curious bitterness:

'Am I just beginning to understand the woman I've married? For Fate – read Kay!'

Kay said:

'You're not cross, are you, Nevile?'

He said rather absently:

'No – no, of course not. I was just – thinking . . .'

August 10th

Lord Cornelly, that rich and eccentric peer, was sitting at the monumental desk which was his especial pride and pleasure. It had been designed for him at immense expense and the whole furnishing of the room was subordinated to it. The effect was terrific and only slightly marred by the unavoidable addition of Lord Cornelly himself, an insignificant and rotund little man completely dwarfed by the desk's magnificence.

Into this scene of City splendour there entered a blonde secretary, also in harmony with the luxury furnishings.

Gliding silently across the floor, she laid a slip of paper before the great man.

Lord Cornelly peered down at it.

'MacWhirter? MacWhirter? Who's he? Never heard of him. Has he got an appointment?'

The blonde secretary indicated that such was the case.

'MacWhirter, eh? Oh! *MacWhirter! That* fellow! Of course! Send him in. Send him in at once.'

Lord Cornelly chuckled gleefully. He was in high good-humour.

Throwing himself back in his chair, he stared up into the dour unsmiling face of the man he had summoned to an interview.

'You're MacWhirter, eh? Angus MacWhirter?'

'That's my name.'

MacWhirter spoke stiffly, standing erect and unsmiling.

'You were with Herbert Clay? That's right, isn't it?'

'Yes.'

Lord Cornelly began to chuckle again.

'I know all about you. Clay got his driving-licence endorsed, all because you wouldn't back him up and swear he was going at twenty miles an hour! Livid about it he was!' The chuckle increased. 'Told us all about it in the Savoy Grill. "That damned pig-headed Scot!" That's what he said! Went on and on. D'you know what *I* was thinking?'

'I've not the least idea.'

MacWhirter's tone was repressive. Lord Cornelly took no notice. He was enjoying his remembrance of his own reactions.

'I thought to myself: "That's the kind of chap I could do with!

Man who can't be bribed to tell lies." You won't have to tell lies for *me*. I don't do my business that way. I go about the world looking for honest men – and there are damned few of them!'

The little peer cackled with shrill laughter, his shrewd monkey-like face wrinkled with mirth. MacWhirter stood solidly, not amused.

Lord Cornelly stopped laughing. His face became shrewd, alert.

'If you want a job MacWhirter, I've got one for you.'

'I could do with a job,' said MacWhirter.

'It's an important job. It's a job that can only be given to a man with good qualifications – you've got those all right – I've been into that – and to a man who can be trusted – absolutely.'

Lord Cornelly waited. MacWhirter did not speak.

'Well, man, can I depend upon you absolutely?'

MacWhirter said dryly:

'You'll not know that from hearing me answer that of course you can.'

Lord Cornelly laughed.

'You'll do. You're the man I've been looking for. Do you know South America at all?'

He went into details. Half an hour later MacWhirter stood on the pavement, a man who had landed an interesting and extremely well-paid job – and a job that promised a future.

Fate, after having frowned, had chosen to smile upon him. But he was in no mood to smile back. There was no exultation in him, though his sense of humour was grimly tickled when he thought back over the interview. There was a stern poetic justice in the fact that it was his former employer's diatribes against him that had actually got him his present advancement!

He was a fortunate man, he supposed. Not that he cared! He was willing to address himself to the task of living, not with enthusiasm, not even with pleasure, but in a methodical day after day spirit. Seven months ago, he had attempted to take his own life; chance, and nothing but chance, had intervened, but he was not particularly grateful. True, he felt no present disposition to do away with himself. That phase was over for good. You could not, he admitted, take your life in cold blood. There had to be some extra fillip of despair, of grief, of desperation or of passion. You could not commit suicide merely because you felt that life was a dreary round of uninteresting happenings.

On the whole he was glad that his work would take him out of England. He was to sail for South America the end of September. The next few weeks would be busy getting together certain equipment and being put in touch with the somewhat complicated ramifications of the business.

But there would be a week's leisure before he left the country. He wondered what he should do with that week? Stay in London? Go away?

An idea stirred nebulously in his brain.

Saltcreek?

'I've a damned good mind to go down there,' said MacWhirter to himself.

It would be, he thought, grimly amusing.

August 19th

'And bang goes my holiday,' said Superintendent Battle disgustedly.

Mrs Battle was disappointed, but long years as the wife of a police officer had prepared her to take disappointments philosophically.

'Oh well,' she said, 'it can't be helped. And I suppose it *is* an interesting case?'

'Not so that you'd notice it,' said Superintendent Battle. 'It's got the Foreign Office in a twitter – all those tall thin young men rushing about and saying Hush Hush here, there and everywhere. It'll straighten out easy enough – and we shall save everybody's face. But it's not the kind of case I'd put in my Memoirs, supposing I was ever foolish enough to write any.'

'We could put our holiday off, I suppose –' began Mrs Battle doubtfully, but her husband interrupted her decisively.

'Not a bit of it. You and the girls go off to Britlington – the rooms have been booked since March – pity to waste them. I tell you what I'll do – go down and spend a week with Jim when this blows over.'

Jim was Superintendent Battle's nephew, Inspector James Leach.

'Saltington's quite close to Easterhead Bay and Salt- creek,' he went on. 'I can get a bit of sea air and a dip in the briny.'

Mrs Battle sniffed.

'More likely he'll rope you in to help him over a case!'

'They don't have any cases this time of the year – unless it's a woman who pinches a few sixpennyworths from Woolworth's. And anyway Jim's all right – he doesn't need his wits sharpening for him.'

'Oh well,' said Mrs Battle. 'I suppose it will work out all right, but it is disappointing.'

'These things are sent to try us,' Superintendent Battle assured her.

SNOW WHITE AND RED ROSE

I

Thomas Royde found Mary Aldin waiting for him on the platform at Saltington when he got out of the train.

He had only a dim recollection of her, and now that he saw her again he was rather surprisedly aware of pleasure in her brisk capable way of dealing with things.

She called him by his Christian name.

'How nice to see you, Thomas. After all these years.'

'Nice of you to put me up. Hope it isn't a bother.'

'Not at all. On the contrary. You'll be particularly welcome. Is that your porter? Tell him to bring the things out this way. I've got the car right at the end.'

The bags were stowed in the Ford. Mary took the wheel and Royde got in beside her. They drove off and Thomas noticed that she was a good driver, deft and careful in traffic and with a nice judgement of distance and spaces.

Saltington was seven miles from Saltcreek. Once they were out of the small market town and on the open road, Mary Aldin reopened the subject of his visit.

'Really, Thomas, your visit just now is going to be a godsend. Things are rather difficult – and a stranger – or partial stranger is just what is needed.'

'What's the trouble?'

His manner, as always, was incurious – almost lazy. He asked the question, it seemed, more from politeness than because he had any desire for the information. It was a manner particularly soothing to Mary Aldin. She wanted badly to talk to someone – but she much preferred to talk to someone who was not too much interested.

She said:

'Well – we've got rather a difficult situation. Audrey is here, as you probably know?'

She paused questioningly and Thomas Royde nodded.

'And Nevile and his wife also.'

Thomas Royde's eyebrows went up. He said after a minute or two: 'Bit awkward – what?'

'Yes it is. It was Nevile's idea.'

She paused. Royde did not speak, but as though aware of some current of disbelief issuing from him, she repeated assertively: 'It *was* Nevile's idea.'

'Why?'

She raised her hands for a moment from the steering-wheel.

'Oh, some modern reaction! All sensible and friends together. That idea. But I don't think, you know, it's working very well.'

'Possibly it mightn't.' He added, 'What's the new wife like?'

'Kay? Good-looking, of course. Really very good-looking. And quite young.'

'And Nevile's keen on her?'

'Oh yes. Of course they've only been married a year.'

Thomas Royde turned his head slowly to look at her. His mouth smiled a little. Mary said hastily:

'I didn't mean that exactly.'

'Come now, Mary. I think you did.'

'Well, one can't help seeing that they've really got very little in common. Their friends, for instance –' She came to a stop.

Royde asked:

'He met her, didn't he, on the Riviera? I don't know much about it. Only just the bare facts that the mater wrote.'

'Yes, they met first at Cannes. Nevile was attracted, but I should imagine he'd been attracted before – in a harmless sort of way. I still think myself that if he'd been left to himself nothing would have come of it. He *was* fond of Audrey, you know.'

Thomas nodded.

Mary went on:

'I don't think he wanted to break up his marriage – I'm sure he didn't. But the girl was absolutely determined. She wouldn't rest until she'd got him to leave his wife – and what's a man to do in those circumstances? It flatters him, of course.'

'Head over heels in love with him, was she?'

'I suppose it may have been that.'

Mary's tone sounded doubtful. She met his inquiring glance with a flush.

'What a cat I am! There's a young man always hanging about – good-looking in a gigolo kind of way – an old friend of hers – and I can't help wondering sometimes whether the fact that Nevile is very well off and distinguished and all that didn't have something to do with it. The girl hadn't a penny of her own, I gather.'

She paused, looking rather ashamed. Thomas Royde merely said: 'Uh hum,' in a speculative voice.

'However,' said Mary, 'that's probably plain cat! The girl is what one would call glamorous – and that probably rouses the feline instincts of middle-aged spinsters.'

Royde looked thoughtfully at her, but his poker face showed no recognizable reaction. He said, after a minute or two:

'But what, exactly, is the present trouble about?'

'Really, you know, I haven't the least idea! That's what's so odd. Naturally we consulted Audrey first – and she seemed to have no feeling against meeting Kay – she was charming about it all. She *has* been charming. No one could have been nicer. Audrey, of course, in everything she does is always just right. Her manner to them both is perfect. She's very reserved, as you know, and one never has any idea of what she is really thinking or feeling – but honestly I don't believe she *minds at all.*'

'No reason why she should,' said Thomas Royde. He added, rather belatedly, 'After all, it's three years ago.'

'Do people like Audrey forget? She was very fond of Nevile.'

Thomas Royde shifted in his seat.

'She's only thirty-two. Got her life in front of her.'

'Oh, I know. But she *did* take it hard. She had quite a bad nervous breakdown, you know.'

'I know. The mater wrote me.'

'In a way,' said Mary, 'I think it was good for your mother to have Audrey to look after. It took her mind off her own grief – about your brother's death. We were so sorry about that.'

'Yes. Poor old Adrian. Always did drive too fast.'

There was a pause. Mary stretched out her hand as a sign she was taking the turn that led down the hill to Saltcreek.

Presently, as they were slipping down the narrow twisting road, she said:

'Thomas – you know Audrey very well?'

'So so. Haven't seen much of her for the last ten years.'

'No, but you knew her as a child. She was like a sister to you and Adrian?'

He nodded.

'Was she – was she at all unbalanced in any way? Oh I don't mean that quite the way it sounds. But I've a feeling that there is something very wrong with her now. She's so completely detached, her poise is so unnaturally perfect – but I wonder sometimes what is going on behind the façade. I've a feeling, now and then, of some really powerful emotion. And I don't quite know what it is! But I do feel that she isn't *normal*. There's *something*! It worries me. I do know that there's an atmosphere in the house that affects everybody. We're all nervous and jumpy. But I don't know what it is. And sometimes, Thomas, it frightens me.'

'Frightens you?' His slow wondering tone made her pull herself together with a little nervous laugh.

'It sounds absurd . . . But that's what I meant just now – your arrival will be good for us – create a diversion. Ah, here we are.'

They had slipped round the last corner. Gull's Point was built on a plateau of rock overlooking the river. On two sides it had sheer cliff going down to the water. The gardens and tennis court were on the left of the house. The garage – a modern after-thought – was actually farther along the road, on the other side of it.

Mary said:

'I'll put the car away now and come back. Hurstall will look after you.'

Hurstall, the aged butler, was greeting Thomas with the pleasure of an old friend.

'Very glad to see you, Mr Royde, after all these years. And so will her ladyship be. You're in the east room, sir. I think you'll find everyone in the garden, unless you want to go to your room first.'

Thomas shook his head. He went through the drawing-room to the window which opened on to the terrace. He stood there for a moment, watching, unobserved himself.

Two women were the only occupants of the terrace. One was sitting on the corner of the balustrade looking out over the water. The other woman was watching her.

The first was Audrey – the other, he knew, must be Kay Strange. Kay did not know she was being overlooked and she took no pains to disguise her expression. Thomas Royde was not, perhaps, a very observant man where women were concerned, but he could not fail to notice that Kay Strange disliked Audrey Strange very much.

As for Audrey, she was looking out across the river and seemed unconscious of, or indifferent to, the other's presence.

It was seven years since Thomas had seen Audrey Strange. He studied her now very carefully. Had she changed, and, if so, in what way?

There was a change, he decided. She was thinner, paler, altogether more ethereal-looking – but there was something else, something he could not quite define. It was as though she were holding herself tightly in leash, watchful over every movement – and yet all the time intensely aware of everything going on round her. She was like a person, he thought, who had a secret to hide. But what secret? He knew a little of the events that had befallen her in the last few years. He had been prepared for lines of sorrow and loss – but this was something else. She was like a child who, by a tightly clenched hand over a treasure – calls attention to what it wants to hide.

And then his eyes went to the other woman – the girl who was now Nevile Strange's wife. Beautiful, yes. Mary Aldin had been right. He rather fancied dangerous, too. He thought: I wouldn't like to trust her near Audrey if she had a knife in her hand . . .

And yet, why should she hate Nevile's first wife? All that was over and done with. Audrey had no part or parcel in their lives nowadays. Footsteps rang out on the terrace as Nevile came round the corner of the house. He looked warm and was carrying a picture paper.

'Here's the *Illustrated Review*,' he said. 'Couldn't get the other –'

Then two things happened at precisely the same minute.

Kay said: 'Oh good, give it to me,' and Audrey, without moving her head, held out her hand almost absent-mindedly.

Nevile had stopped half-way between the two women. A dawn of embarrassment showed in his face. Before he could speak, Kay said, her voice rising with a slight note of hysteria, 'I want it. Give it me! Give it me, Nevile!'

Audrey Strange started, turned her head, withdrew her hand and murmured with just the slightest air of confusion:

'Oh sorry. I thought you were speaking to me, Nevile.'

Thomas Royde saw the colour come up brick-red in Nevile Strange's neck. He took three quick steps forward and held out the picture paper to Audrey.

She said, hesitating, her air of embarrassment growing:

'Oh, but –'

Kay pushed back her chair with a rough movement. She stood up, then, turning, she made for the drawing-room window. Royde had no time to move before she had charged into him blindly.

The shock made her recoil; she looked at him as he apologized. He saw then why she had not seen him, her eyes were brimming with tears – tears, he fancied, of anger.

'Hullo,' she said. 'Who are you? Oh, of course, the man from Malay!'

'Yes,' said Thomas. 'I'm the man from Malay.'

'I wish to God I was in Malay,' said Kay. 'Anywhere but here! I loathe this beastly lousy house! I loathe everyone in it!'

Emotional scenes always alarmed Thomas. He regarded Kay warily and murmured nervously:

'Ah – hum.'

'Unless they're very careful,' said Kay, 'I shall kill someone! Either Nevile or that whey-faced cat out there!'

She brushed past him and went out of the room, banging the door.

Thomas Royde stood stock-still. He was not quite sure what to do next, but he was glad that young Mrs Strange had gone. He stood and looked at the door that she had slammed so vigorously. Something of a tiger cat, the new Mrs Strange.

The window was darkened as Nevile Strange paused in the space between the french doors. He was breathing rather fast.

He greeted Thomas vaguely.

'Oh – er – hullo, Royde, didn't know you'd arrived. I say, have you seen my wife?'

'She passed through about a minute ago,' said the other.

Nevile in his turn went out through the drawing-room door. He was looking annoyed.

Thomas Royde went slowly through the open window. He was not a heavy walker. Not until he was a couple of yards away did Audrey turn her head.

Then he saw those wide-apart eyes open wider, saw her lips part. She slipped down from the wall and came towards him, hands outstretched.

'Oh Thomas,' she said. 'Dear Thomas! How glad I am you've come.'

As he took the two small white hands in his and bent down to her, Mary Aldin in her turn arrived at the french windows. Seeing the two on the terrace she checked herself, watched them for a moment or two, then slowly turned away and went back into the house.

II

Upstairs Nevile had found Kay in her bedroom. The only large double-bedroom in the house was Lady Tressilian's. A married couple was always given the two rooms with the communicating door and a small bathroom beyond on the west side of the house. It was a small isolated suite.

Nevile passed through his own room and on into his wife's. Kay had flung herself down on her bed. Raising a tear-stained face, she cried angrily:

'So you've come! About time, too!'

'What *is* all this fuss about? Have you gone quite crazy, Kay?'

Nevile spoke quietly, but there was a dent at the corner of his nostril that registered restrained anger.

'Why did you give that *Illustrated Review* to her and not to me?'

'Really, Kay, you are a child! All this fuss about a wretched little picture paper.'

'You gave it to her and not to me,' repeated Kay obstinately.

'Well, why not? What does it matter?'

'It matters to me.'

'I don't know what's wrong with you. You can't behave in this hysterical fashion when you're staying in other people's houses. Don't you know how to behave in public?'

'Why did you give it to Audrey?'

'Because she wanted it.'

'So did I, and I'm your wife.'

'All the more reason, in that case, for giving it to an older woman and one who, technically, is no relation.'

'She scored off me! She wanted to and she did. You were on her side!'

'You're talking like an idiotic jealous child. For goodness' sake, control yourself, and try to behave properly in public!'

'Like she does, I suppose?'

Nevile said coldly: 'At any rate Audrey can behave like a lady. She doesn't make an exhibition of herself.'

'She's turning you against me! She hates me and she's getting her revenge.'

'Look here, Kay, will you stop being melodramatic and completely foolish? I'm fed up!'

'Then let's go away from here! Let's go tomorrow. I hate this place!'

'We've only been here four days.'

'It's quite enough! Do let's go, Nevile.'

'Now look here, Kay, I've had enough of this. We came here for a fortnight and I'm going to stay for a fortnight.'

'If you do,' said Kay, 'you'll be sorry. You and your Audrey! You think she's wonderful!'

'I don't think Audrey is wonderful. I think she's an extremely nice and kindly person whom I've treated very badly and who has been most generous and forgiving.'

'That's where you're wrong,' said Kay. She got up from the bed. Her fury had died down. She spoke seriously – almost soberly.

'Audrey hasn't forgiven you, Nevile. Once or twice I've seen her looking at you . . . I don't know what is going on in her mind but something is – She's the kind that doesn't let anyone know what they're thinking.'

'It's a pity,' said Nevile, 'that there aren't more people like that.'

Kay's face went very white.

'Do you mean that for me?' There was a dangerous edge to her voice.

'Well – you haven't shown much reticence, have you? Every bit of ill temper and spite that comes into your mind you blurt straight out. You make a fool of yourself and you make a fool of me!'

'Anything more to say?'

Her voice was icy.

He said in an equally cold tone:

'I'm sorry if you think that was unfair. But it's the plain truth. You've no more self-control than a child.'

'You never lose your temper, do you? Always the self-controlled charming-mannered little pukka sahib! I don't believe you've got any feelings. You're just a *fish* – a damned cold-blooded *fish*! Why don't you let yourself go now and then? Why don't you shout at me, swear at me, tell me to go to Hell?'

Nevile sighed. His shoulders sagged.

'Oh lord,' he said.

Turning on his heel he left the room.

III

'You look exactly as you did at seventeen, Thomas Royde,' said Lady Tressilian. 'Just the same owlish look. And no more conversation now than you had then. Why not?'

Thomas said vaguely,

'I dunno. Never had the gift of the gab.'

'Not like Adrian. Adrian was a very clever and witty talker.'

'Perhaps that's why. Always left the talking to him.'

'Poor Adrian. So much promise.'

Thomas nodded.

Lady Tressilian changed the subject. She was granting an audience to Thomas. She usually preferred her visitors one at a time. It did not tire her and she was able to concentrate her attention on them.

'You've been here twenty-four hours,' she said. 'What do you think of our Situation?'

'Situation?'

'Don't look stupid. You do that deliberately. You know quite well what I mean. The eternal triangle which has established itself under my roof.'

Thomas said cautiously: 'Seems a bit of friction.'

Lady Tressilian smiled rather diabolically.

'I will confess to you, Thomas, I am rather enjoying myself. This came about through no wish of mine – indeed I did my utmost to prevent it. Nevile was obstinate. He would insist on bringing these two together – and now he is reaping what he has sown!'

Thomas Royde shifted a little in his chair.

'Seems funny,' he said.

'Elucidate,' snapped Lady Tressilian.

'Shouldn't have thought Strange was that kind of chap.'

'It's interesting your saying that. Because it is what I felt. It was uncharacteristic of Nevile. Nevile, like most men, is usually anxious to avoid any kind of embarrassment or possible unpleasantness. I suspected that it wasn't originally Nevile's idea – but, if not, I don't see whose idea it can have been.' She paused and said with only the slightest upward inflection, 'It wouldn't be Audrey's?'

Thomas said promptly, 'No, not Audrey.'

'And I can hardly believe it was that unfortunate young woman, Kay's, idea. Not unless she is a remarkable actress. You know, I have almost felt sorry for her lately.'

'You don't like her much, do you?'

'No. She seems to me empty-headed and lacking in any kind of poise. But, as I say, I do begin to feel sorry for her. She is blundering about like a daddy-long-legs in lamp-light. She has no idea of what weapons to use. Bad temper, bad manners, childish rudeness – all things which have a most unfortunate effect upon a man like Nevile.'

Thomas said quietly:

'I think Audrey is the one who is in a difficult position.'

Lady Tressilian gave him a sharp glance.

'You've always been in love with Audrey, haven't you, Thomas?'

His reply was quite imperturbable. 'Suppose I have.'

'Practically from the time you were children together?'

He nodded.

'And then Nevile came along and carried her off from under your nose?'

He moved uneasily in his chair.

'Oh well – I always knew I hadn't a chance.'

'Defeatist,' said Lady Tressilian.

'I always have been a dull dog.'

'Dobbin!'

'Good old Thomas! – that's what Audrey feels about me.'

'"True Thomas",' said Lady Tressilian. 'That was your nickname, wasn't it?'

He smiled as the words brought back memories of childish days. 'Funny! I haven't heard that for years.'

'It might stand you in good stead now,' said Lady Tressilian. She met his glance clearly and deliberately.

'Fidelity,' she said, 'is a quality that anyone who has been through Audrey's experience might appreciate. The dog-like devotion of a lifetime, Thomas, does sometimes get its reward.'

Thomas Royde looked down, his fingers fumbling with a pipe.

'That,' he said, 'is what I came home hoping.'

IV

'So here we all are,' said Mary Aldin.

Hurstall, the old butler, wiped his forehead. When he went into the kitchen, Mrs Spicer, the cook, remarked upon his expression.

'I don't think I can be well, and that's the truth,' said Hurstall. 'If I can so express myself, everything that's said and done in this house lately seems to me to mean something that's different from what it sounds like – if you know what I mean?'

Mrs Spicer did not seem to know what he meant, so Hurstall went on:

'Miss Aldin, now, as they all sat down to dinner – she says "*So*

here we all are" – and just that gave me a turn! Made me think
of a trainer who's got a lot of wild animals into a cage, and then
the cage door shuts. I felt, all of a sudden, as though we were
all caught in a trap.'

'Law, Mr Hurstall,' said Mrs Spicer, 'you must have eaten
something that's disagreed.'

'It's not my digestion. It's the way everyone's strung up. The
front door banged just now and Mrs Strange – our Mrs Strange,
Miss Audrey – she jumped as though she had been shot. And
there's the silences, too. Very queer they are. It's as though, all of
a sudden, everybody's afraid to speak. And then they all break out
at once just saying the things that first come into their heads.'

'Enough to make anyone embarrassed,' said Mrs Spicer.

'Two Mrs Stranges in the house. What I feel is, it isn't
decent.'

In the dining-room, one of those silences that Hurstall had
described was proceeding.

It was with quite an effort that Mary Aldin turned to Kay
and said:

'I asked your friend, Mr Latimer, to dine tomorrow night!'

'Oh good,' said Kay.

Nevile said:

'Latimer? Is he down here?'

'He's staying at the Easterhead Bay Hotel,' said Kay.

Nevile said:

'We might go over and dine there one night. How late does
the ferry go?'

'Until half-past one,' said Mary.

'I suppose they dance there in the evenings?'

'Most of the people are about a hundred,' said Kay.

'Not very amusing for your friend,' said Nevile to Kay.

Mary said quickly:

'We might go over and bathe one day at Easterhead Bay. It's
quite warm still and it's a lovely sandy beach.'

Thomas Royde said in a low voice to Audrey:

'I thought of going out sailing tomorrow. Will you come?'

'I'd like to.'

'We might all go sailing,' said Nevile.

'I thought you said you were going to play golf,' said Kay.

'I did think of going over to the links. I was right off my wooden shots the other day.'

'What a tragedy!' said Kay.

Nevile said good-humouredly:

'Golf's a tragic game.'

Mary asked Kay if she played.

'Yes – after a fashion.'

Nevile said:

'Kay would be very good if she took a little trouble. She's got a natural swing.'

Kay said to Audrey:

'You don't play any games, do you?'

'Not really. I play tennis after a fashion – but I'm a complete rabbit.'

'Do you still play the piano, Audrey?' asked Thomas.

She shook her head.

'Not nowadays.'

'You used to play rather well,' said Nevile.

'I thought you didn't like music, Nevile,' said Kay.

'I don't know much about it,' said Nevile vaguely. 'I always wondered how Audrey managed to stretch an octave, her hands are so small.'

He was looking at them as she laid down her dessert knife and fork.

She flushed a little and said quickly:

'I've got a very long little finger. I expect that helps.'

'You must be selfish then,' said Kay. 'If you're unselfish you have a short little finger.'

'Is that true?' asked Mary Aldin. 'Then I must be unselfish. Look, my little fingers are quite short.'

'I think you are very unselfish,' said Thomas Royde, eyeing her thoughtfully.

She went red – and continued, quickly.

'Who's the most unselfish of us? Let's compare little fingers. Mine are shorter than yours, Kay. But Thomas, I think, beats me.'

'I beat you both,' said Nevile. 'Look,' he stretched out a hand.

'Only one hand, though,' said Kay. 'Your left hand little finger is short but your right hand one is much longer. And your left hand is what you are born with and the right hand is what you make of your life. So that means that you were born unselfish but have become more selfish as time goes on.'

'Can you tell fortunes, Kay?' asked Mary Aldin. She stretched out her hand, palm upward. 'A fortune-teller told me I should have two husbands and three children. I shall have to hurry up!'

Kay said:

'Those little crosses aren't children, they're journeys. That means you'll take three journeys across water.'

'That seems unlikely too,' said Mary Aldin.

Thomas Royde asked her: 'Have you travelled much?'

'No, hardly at all.'

He heard an undercurrent of regret in her voice.

'You would like to?'

'Above everything.'

He thought in his slow reflective way of her life. Always in attendance on an old woman. Calm, tactful, an excellent manager. He asked curiously:

'Have you lived with Lady Tressilian long?'

'For nearly fifteen years. I came to be with her after my father died. He had been a helpless invalid for some years before his death.'

And then, answering the question she felt to be in his mind:

'I'm thirty-six. That's what you wanted to know, wasn't it?'

'I did wonder,' he admitted. 'You might be – any age, you see.'

'That's rather a two-edged remark!'

'I suppose it is. I didn't mean it that way.'

That sombre thoughtful gaze of his did not leave her face. She did not find it embarrassing. It was too free from self-consciousness for that – a genuine thoughtful interest. Seeing his eyes on her hair, she put up her hand to the one white lock.

'I've had that,' she said, 'since I was very young.'

'I like it,' said Thomas Royde simply.

He went on looking at her. She said at last, in a slightly amused tone of voice:

'Well, what is the verdict?'

He reddened under his tan.

'Oh, I suppose it is rude of me to stare. I was wondering about you – what you are really like.'

'Please,' she said hurriedly and rose from the table. She said as she went into the drawing-room with her arm through Audrey's:

'Old Mr Treves is coming to dinner tomorrow, too.'

'Who's he?' asked Nevile.

'He brought an introduction from the Rufus Lords. A delightful old gentleman. He's staying at the Balmoral Court. He's got a weak heart and looks very frail, but his faculties are perfect and he has known a lot of interesting people. He was a solicitor or a barrister – I forget which.'

'Everybody down here is terribly old,' said Kay discontentedly.

She was standing just under a tall lamp. Thomas was looking that way, and he gave her that same slow interested attention that he gave to anything that was immediately occupying his line of vision.

He was struck suddenly with her intense and passionate beauty. A beauty of vivid colouring, of abundant and triumphant vitality. He looked across from her to Audrey, pale and mothlike in a silvery grey dress.

He smiled to himself and murmured:

'Red Rose and Snow White.'

'What?' It was Mary Aldin at his elbow.

He repeated the words. 'Like the old fairy story, you know –'

Mary Aldin said: 'It's a very good description . . .'

V

Mr Treves sipped his glass of port appreciatively. A very nice wine. And an excellently cooked and served dinner. Clearly Lady Tressilian had no difficulties with her servants.

The house was well managed, too, in spite of the mistress of it being an invalid.

A pity, perhaps, that the ladies did not leave the dining-room when the port went round. He preferred the old-fashioned routine. But these young people had their own ways.

His eyes rested thoughtfully on that brilliant and beautiful young woman who was the wife of Nevile Strange.

It was Kay's night tonight. Her vivid beauty glowed and shone in the candlelit room. Beside her, Ted Latimer's sleek dark head bent to hers. He was playing up to her. She felt triumphant and sure of herself.

The mere sight of such radiant vitality warmed Mr Treves' old bones.

Youth – there was really nothing like youth!

No wonder the husband had lost his head and left his first wife. Audrey was sitting next to him. A charming creature and a lady – but then that was the kind of woman who invariably did get left, in Mr Treves' experience.

He glanced at her. Her head had been down and she was staring at her plate. Something in the complete immobility of her attitude struck Mr Treves. He looked at her more keenly. He wondered what she was thinking about. Charming the way the hair sprang up from that small shell-like ear . . .

With a little start, Mr Treves came to himself as he realized that a move was being made. He got hurriedly to his feet.

In the drawing-room, Kay Strange went straight to the gramophone and put on a record of dance music.

Mary Aldin said apologetically to Mr Treves:

'I'm sure you hate jazz.'

'Not at all,' said Mr Treves, untruly but politely.

'Later, perhaps, we might have some bridge?' she suggested. 'But it is no good starting a rubber now, as I know Lady Tressilian is looking forward to having a chat with you.'

'That will be delightful. Lady Tressilian never joins you down here?'

'No, she used to come down in an invalid chair. That is why we had a lift put in. But nowadays she prefers her own room. There she can talk to whomsoever she likes, summoning them by a kind of Royal Command.'

'Very aptly put, Miss Aldin. I am always sensible of the Royal touch in Lady Tressilian's manner.'

In the middle of the room Kay was moving in a slow dance step.

She said: 'Just take that table out of the way, Nevile.'

Her voice was autocratic, assured. Her eyes were shining, her lips parted.

Nevile obediently moved the table. Then he took a step towards her, but she turned deliberately towards Ted Latimer.

'Come on, Ted, let's dance.'

Ted's arm went round her immediately. They danced, swaying, bending, their steps perfectly together. It was a lovely performance to watch.

Mr Treves murmured:

'Er – quite professional.'

Mary Aldin winced slightly at the word – yet surely Mr Treves had spoken in simple admiration. She looked at his little wise nut-cracker face. It bore, she thought, an absent-minded look as though he were following some train of thought of his own.

Nevile stood hesitating a moment, then he walked to where Audrey was standing by the window.

'Dance, Audrey?'

His tone was formal, almost cold. Mere politeness, you might have said, inspired his request. Audrey Strange hesitated a minute before nodding her head and taking a step towards him.

Mary Aldin made some commonplace remarks to which Mr Treves did not reply. He had so far shown no signs of deafness and his courtesy was punctilious – she realized that it was absorption that held him aloof. She could not quite make out if he was watching the dancers, or was staring across the room at Thomas Royde, standing alone at the other end.

With a little start Mr Treves said:

'Excuse me, my dear lady, you were saying?'

'Nothing. Only that it was an unusually fine September.'

'Yes, indeed – rain is badly needed locally, so they tell me at my hotel.'

'You are comfortable there, I hope?'

'Oh yes, though I must say I was vexed when I arrived to find –'

Mr Treves broke off.

Audrey had disengaged herself from Nevile. She said with an apologetic little laugh:

'It's really too hot to dance.'

She went towards the open window and out on to the terrace.

'Oh! go after her, you fool,' murmured Mary. She meant the remark to be under her breath, but it was loud enough for Mr Treves to turn and stare at her in astonishment.

She reddened and gave an embarrassed laugh.

'I'm speaking my thoughts aloud,' she said ruefully. 'But really he does irritate me so. He's so *slow*.'

'Mr Strange?'

'Oh no, not Nevile. Thomas Royde.'

Thomas Royde was just preparing to move forward, but by now Nevile, after a moment's pause, had followed Audrey out of the window.

For a moment Mr Treves' eye, interestedly speculative, rested on the window, then his irritation returned to the dancers.

'A beautiful dancer, young Mr – Latimer, did you say the name was?'

'Yes. Edward Latimer.'

'Ah yes, Edward Latimer. An old friend, I gather, of Mrs Strange?'

'Yes.'

'And what does this very – er – decorative young gentleman do for a living?'

'Well, really, I don't quite know.'

'In-deed,' said Mr Treves, managing to put a good deal of comprehension into one harmless word.

Mary went on:

'He is staying at the Easterhead Bay Hotel.'

'A very pleasant situation,' said Mr Treves.

He added dreamily after a moment or two: 'Rather an interesting shaped head – a curious angle from the crown to the neck – rendered less noticeable by the way he has his hair cut, but distinctly unusual.' After another pause, he went on still more dreamily: 'The last man I saw with a head like that got ten years' penal servitude for a brutal assault on an elderly jeweller.'

'Surely,' exclaimed Mary, 'you don't mean –?'

'Not at all, not at all,' said Mr Treves. 'You mistake me entirely. I am suggesting no disparagement of a guest of yours. I was merely pointing out that a hardened and brutal criminal can be in appearance a most charming and personable young man. Odd, but so it is.'

He smiled gently at her. Mary said: 'You know, Mr Treves, I think I am a little frightened of you.'

'Nonsense, dear lady.'

'But I am. You are – such a very shrewd observer.'

'My eyes,' said Mr Treves complacently, 'are as good as ever they were.' He paused and added: 'Whether that is fortunate or unfortunate, I cannot at the moment decide.'

'How could it be unfortunate?'

Mr Treves shook his head doubtfully.

'One is sometimes placed in a position of responsibility. The right course of action is not always easy to determine.'

Hurstall entered bearing the coffee tray.

After taking it to Mary and the old lawyer, he went down the room to Thomas Royde. Then, by Mary's directions, he put the tray down on a low table and left the room.

Kay called over Ted's shoulder. 'We'll finish out this tune.'

Mary said: 'I'll take Audrey's out to her.'

She went to the french windows, cup in hand. Mr Treves accompanied her. As she paused on the threshold he looked out over her shoulder.

Audrey was sitting on the corner of the balustrade. In the bright moonlight her beauty came to life – a beauty born of line rather than colour. The exquisite line from the jaw to the ear, the tender modelling of chin and mouth, and the really lovely bones of the head and the small straight nose. That beauty would be there when Audrey Strange was an old woman – it had nothing to do with the covering flesh – it was the bones themselves that were beautiful. The sequinned dress she wore accentuated the effect of the moonlight. She sat very still and Nevile Strange stood and looked at her.

Nevile took a step towards her.

'Audrey,' he said, 'you –'

She shifted her position, then sprang lightly to her feet and clapped a hand to her ear:

'Oh! my ear-ring – I must have dropped it.'

'Where? Let me look –'

They both bent down, awkward and embarrassed – and collided in doing so. Audrey sprang away. Nevile exclaimed:

'Wait a sec – my cuff button – it's caught in your hair. Stand still.'

She stood quite still as he fumbled with the button.

'Oo – you're pulling it out by the roots – how clumsy you are, Nevile, do be quick.'

'Sorry I – I seem to be all thumbs.'

The moonlight was bright enough for the two onlookers to see what Audrey could not see, the trembling of Nevile's hands as he strove to free the strand of fair silvery hair.

But Audrey herself was trembling too – as though suddenly cold.

Mary Aldin jumped as a quiet voice said behind her:

'Excuse me –'

Thomas Royde passed between them and out.

'Shall I do that, Strange?' he asked.

Nevile straightened up and he and Audrey moved apart.

'It's all right. I've done it.'

Nevile's face was rather white.

'You're cold,' said Thomas to Audrey. 'Come in and have coffee.'

She came back with him and Nevile turned away staring out to sea.

'I was bringing it out to you,' said Mary. 'But perhaps you'd better come in.'

'Yes,' said Audrey, 'I think I'd better come in.'

They all went back into the drawing-room. Ted and Kay had stopped dancing.

The door opened and a tall gaunt woman dressed in black came in. She said respectfully:

'Her ladyship's compliments and she would be glad to see Mr Treves up in her room.'

VI

Lady Tressilian received Mr Treves with evident pleasure.

He and she were soon deep in an agreeable flood of reminiscences and a recalling of mutual acquaintances.

At the end of half an hour Lady Tressilian gave a deep sigh of satisfaction.

'Ah,' she said, 'I've enjoyed myself! There's nothing like exchanging gossip and remembering old scandals.'

'A little malice,' agreed Mr Treves, 'adds a certain savour to life.'

'By the way,' said Lady Tressilian, 'what do you think of our example of the eternal triangle?'

Mr Treves looked discreetly blank. 'Er – what triangle?'

'Don't tell me you haven't noticed it! Nevile and his wives.'

'Oh that! The present Mrs Strange is a singularly attractive young woman.'

'So is Audrey,' said Lady Tressilian.

Mr Treves admitted: 'She has charm – yes.'

Lady Tressilian exclaimed:

'Do you mean to tell me you can understand a man leaving Audrey, who is a – a person of rare quality – for – for a *Kay*?'

Mr Treves replied calmly:

'Perfectly. It happens frequently.'

'Disgusting. I should soon grow tired of Kay if I were a man and wish I had never made such a fool of myself!'

'That also happens frequently. These sudden passionate infatuations,' said Mr Treves, looking very passionless and precise himself, 'are seldom of long duration.'

'And then what happens?' demanded Lady Tressilian.

'Usually,' said Mr Treves, 'the – er – parties adjust themselves. Quite often there is a second divorce. The man then marries a third party – someone of a sympathetic nature.'

'Nonsense! Nevile isn't a Mormon – whatever some of your clients may be!'

'The remarriage of the original parties occasionally takes place.'

Lady Tressilian shook her head.

'That *no*! Audrey has too much pride.'

'You think so?'

'I am sure of it. Do not shake your head in that aggravating fashion!'

'It has been my experience,' said Mr Treves, 'that women possess little or no pride where love affairs are concerned. Pride is a quality often on their lips, but not apparent in their actions.'

'You don't understand Audrey. She was violently in love with Nevile. Too much so, perhaps. After he left her for this girl (though I don't blame him entirely – the girl pursued him everywhere, and you know what men are!) she never wanted to see him again.'

Mr Treves coughed gently:

'And yet,' he said, 'she is here!'

'Oh well,' said Lady Tressilian, annoyed. 'I don't profess to understand these modern ideas. I imagine that Audrey is here just to show that she doesn't care, and that it doesn't matter!'

'Very likely,' Mr Treves stroked his jaw. 'She can put it to herself that way, certainly.'

'You mean,' said Lady Tressilian, 'that you think she is still hankering after Nevile and that – oh *no*! I won't believe such a thing!'

'It could be,' said Mr Treves.

'I won't have it,' said Lady Tressilian. 'I won't have it in my house.'

'You are already disturbed, are you not?' asked Mr Treves shrewdly. 'There is tension. I have felt it in the atmosphere.'

'So you feel it too?' said Lady Tressilian sharply.

'Yes, I am puzzled, I must confess. The true feelings of the parties remain obscure, but in my opinion, there is gunpowder about. The explosion may come any minute.'

'Stop talking like Guy Fawkes and tell me what to do,' said Lady Tressilian.

Mr Treves held up his hands.

'Really, I am at a loss to know what to suggest. There is, I feel sure, a focal point. If we could isolate that – but there is so much that remains obscure.'

'I have no intention of asking Audrey to leave,' said Lady Tressilian. 'As far as my observation goes, she has behaved perfectly in a very difficult situation. She has been courteous, but aloof. I consider her conduct irreproachable.'

'Oh quite,' said Mr Treves. 'Quite. But it's having a most marked effect on young Nevile Strange all the same.'

'Nevile,' said Lady Tressilian, 'is *not* behaving well. I shall speak to him about it. But I couldn't turn him out of the house for a moment. Matthew regarded him as practically his adopted son.'

'I know.'

Lady Tressilian sighed. She said in a lowered voice:

'You know that Matthew was drowned here?'

'Yes.'

'So many people have been surprised at my remaining here. Stupid of them. I have always felt Matthew near to me here. The whole house is full of him. I should feel lonely and strange anywhere else.' She paused, and went on. 'I hoped at first that it might not be very long before I joined him. Especially when my health began to fail. But it seems I am one of these creaking gates – these perpetual invalids who never die.' She thumped her pillow angrily.

'It doesn't please me, I can tell you! I always hoped that when my time came, it would come quickly – that I should meet Death face to face – not feel him creeping along behind me, always at my shoulder – gradually forcing me to sink to one indignity after another of illness. Increased helplessness – increasing dependence on other people!'

'But very devoted people, I am sure. You have a faithful maid?'

'Barrett? The one who brought you up. The comfort of my life! A grim old battleaxe, absolutely devoted. She's been with me for years.'

'And you are lucky, I should say, in having Miss Aldin.'

'You are right. I am lucky in having Mary.'

'She is a relation?'

'A distant cousin. One of those selfless creatures whose lives are continually being sacrificed to those of other people. She looked after her father – a clever man – but terribly exacting. When he died I begged her to make her home with me, and I have blessed the day she came to me. You've no idea what horrors most companions are. Futile boring creatures. Driving one mad with their inanity. They are companions because they are fit for nothing better. To have Mary, who is a well-read intelligent woman, is marvellous. She has really a first-class brain – a man's brain. She has read widely and deeply and there is nothing she cannot discuss. And she is as clever domestically as she is intellectually. She runs the house perfectly and keeps the servants happy – she eliminates all quarrels and jealousies – I don't know how she does it – just tact, I suppose.'

'She has been with you long?'

'Twelve years – no, more than that. Thirteen – fourteen – something like that. She has been a great comfort.'

Mr Treves nodded.

Lady Tressilian, watching him through half-closed lids, said suddenly:

'What's the matter? You're worried about something?'

'A trifle,' said Mr Treves. 'A mere trifle. Your eyes are sharp.'

'I like studying people,' said Lady Tressilian. 'I always knew at once if there was anything on Matthew's mind.' She sighed and leaned back on her pillows. 'I must say goodnight to you now' – it was a Queen's dismissal, nothing discourteous about it – 'I am very tired. But it has been a great, great pleasure. Come and see me again soon.'

'You may depend upon my taking advantage of those kind words. I only hope I have not talked too long.'

'Oh no. I always tire very suddenly. Ring my bell for me, will you, before you go.'

Mr Treves pulled gingerly at a large old-fashioned bellpull that ended in a huge tassel.

'Quite a survival,' he remarked.

'My bell? Yes. No new-fangled electric bells for me. Half the time they're out of order and you go on pressing away! This thing never fails. It rings in Barrett's room upstairs – the bell hangs over her bed. So there's never any delay in answering it. If there is I pull it again pretty quickly.'

As Mr Treves went out of the room he heard the bell pulled a second time and heard the tinkle of it somewhere above his head. He looked up and noticed the wires that ran along the ceiling. Barrett came hurriedly down a flight of stairs and passed him, going to her mistress.

Mr Treves went slowly downstairs, not troubling with the little lift on the downward journey. His face was drawn into a frown of uncertainty.

He found the whole party assembled in the drawing-room, and Mary Aldin at once suggested bridge, but Mr Treves refused politely on the plea that he must very shortly be starting home.

'My hotel,' he said, 'is old-fashioned. They do not expect anyone to be out after midnight.'

'It's a long time from that – only half-past ten,' said Nevile. 'They don't lock you out, I hope?'

'Oh no. In fact I doubt if the door is locked at all at night. It is shut at nine o'clock but one has only to turn the handle and walk in. People seem very haphazard down here, but I suppose they are justified in trusting to the honesty of the local people.'

'Certainly no one locks their door in the day-time here,' said Mary. 'Ours stands wide open all day long – but we do lock it up at night.'

'What's the Balmoral Court like?' asked Ted Latimer. 'It looks a queer high Victorian atrocity of a building.'

'It lives up to its name,' said Mr Treves. 'And has good solid Victorian comfort. Good beds, good cooking – roomy, Victorian wardrobes. Immense baths with mahogany surrounds.'

'Weren't you saying you were annoyed about something at first?' asked Mary.

'Ah yes. I had carefully reserved by letter two rooms on the ground floor. I have a weak heart, you know, and stairs are forbidden me. When I arrived I was vexed to find the rooms were not available. Instead I was allotted two rooms (very pleasant rooms, I must admit) on the top floor. I protested, but it seems that an old resident who had been going to Scotland this month was ill and had been unable to vacate the rooms.'

'Mr Lucan, I expect?' said Mary.

'I believe that is the name. Under the circumstances, I had to make the best of things. Fortunately there is a good automatic lift – so that I have really suffered no inconvenience.'

Kay said, 'Ted, why don't you come and stay at the Balmoral Court? You'd be much more accessible.'

'Oh, I don't think it looks my kind of place.'

'Quite right, Mr Latimer,' said Mr Treves. 'It would not be at all in your line of country.'

For some reason or other Ted Latimer flushed.

'I don't know what you mean by that,' he said.

Mary Aldin, sensing constraint, hurriedly made a remark about a newspaper sensation of the moment.

'I see they've detained a man in the Kentish Town trunk case –' she said.

'It's the second man they've detained,' said Nevile. 'I hope they've got the right one this time.'

'They may not be able to hold him even if he is,' said Mr Treves.

'Insufficient evidence?' asked Royde.

'Yes.'

'Still,' said Kay, 'I suppose they always get the evidence in the end.'

'Not always, Mrs Strange. You'd be surprised if you knew how many of the people who have committed crimes are walking about the country free and unmolested.'

'Because they've never been found out, you mean?'

'Not only that. There is a man' – he mentioned a celebrated case of two years back – 'the police know who committed those child murders – know it without a shadow of doubt – but they are powerless. That man has been given an alibi by two people, and though that alibi is false there is no proving it to be so. Therefore the murderer goes free.'

'How dreadful,' said Mary.

Thomas Royde knocked out his pipe and said in his quiet reflective voice:

'That confirms what I have always thought – that there are times when one is justified in taking the law into one's own hands.'

'What do you mean, Mr Royde?'

Thomas began to refill his pipe. He looked thoughtfully down at his hands as he spoke in jerky disconnected sentences.

'Suppose you knew – of a dirty piece of work – knew that the man who did it isn't accountable to existing laws – that he's immune from punishment. Then I hold – that one is justified in executing sentence oneself.'

Mr Treves said warmly: 'A most pernicious doctrine, Mr Royde! Such an action would be quite unjustifiable!'

'Don't see it. I'm assuming, you know, that the *facts* are proved – it's just the *law* is powerless!'

'Private action is still not to be excused.'

Thomas smiled – a very gentle smile:

'I don't agree,' he said. 'If a man ought to have his neck wrung, I wouldn't mind taking the responsibility of wringing it for him!'

'And in turn would render yourself liable to the law's penalties!'

Still smiling, Thomas said: 'I'd have to be careful, of course . . . In fact one would have to go in for a certain amount of low cunning . . .'

Audrey said in her clear voice:

'You'd be found out, Thomas.'

'Matter of fact,' said Thomas, 'I don't think I should.'

'I knew a case once,' began Mr Treves, and stopped. He said apologetically: 'Criminology is rather a hobby of mine, you know.'

'Please go on,' said Kay.

'I have had a fairly wide experience of criminal cases,' said Mr Treves. 'Only a few of them have held any real interest. Most murderers have been lamentably uninteresting and very short-sighted. However! I could tell you of one interesting example.'

'Oh do,' said Kay. 'I like murders.'

Mr Treves spoke slowly, apparently choosing his words with great deliberation and care.

'The case concerned a child. I will not mention the child's age or sex. The facts were as follows: two children were playing with bows and arrows. One child sent an arrow through the other child in a vital spot and death resulted. There was an inquest, the surviving child was completely distraught and the accident was commiserated and sympathy expressed for the unhappy author of the deed.' He paused.

'Was that all?' asked Ted Latimer.

'That was all. A regrettable accident. But there is, you see, another side to the story. A farmer, some time previously, hap-pened to have passed up a certain path in a wood nearby. There, in a little clearing, he had noticed a child practising with a bow and arrow.'

He paused – to let his meaning sink in.

'You mean,' said Mary Aldin incredulously, 'that it was *not* an accident – that it was intentional?'

'I don't know,' said Mr Treves. 'I have never known. But it was stated at the inquest that the children were unused to bows and arrows and in consequence shot wildly and ignorantly.'

'And that was not so?'

'That, in the case of *one* of the children, was certainly not so!'

'What did the farmer do?' said Audrey breathlessly.

'He did nothing. Whether he acted rightly or not, I have never been sure. It was the future of a child that was at stake. A child, he felt, ought to be given the benefit of a doubt.'

Audrey said:

'But you yourself have no doubt about what really happened?'

Mr Treves said gravely:

'Personally, I am of the opinion that it was a particularly ingenious murder – a murder committed by a child and planned down to every detail beforehand.'

Ted Latimer asked:

'Was there a reason?'

'Oh yes, there was a motive. Childish teasings, unkind words – enough to foment hatred. Children hate easily –'

Mary exclaimed: 'But the deliberation of it.'

Mr Treves nodded.

'Yes, the deliberation of it was bad. A child, keeping that murderous intention in its heart, quietly practising day after day and then the final piece of acting – the awkward shooting – the catastrophe, the pretence of grief and despair. It was all incredible – so incredible that probably it would not have been believed in court.'

'What happened to – to the child?' asked Kay curiously.

'Its name was changed, I believe,' said Mr Treves. 'After the publicity of the inquest that was deemed advisable. That child is a grown-up person today – somewhere in the world. The question is, has it still got a murderer's heart?'

He added thoughtfully:

'It was a long time ago, but I would recognize my little murderer anywhere.'

'Surely not,' objected Royde.

'Oh, yes, there was a certain physical peculiarity – well, I will not dwell on the subject. It is not a very pleasant one. I must really be on my way home.'

He rose.

Mary said, 'You will have a drink first?'

The drinks were on a table at the other end of the room. Thomas Royde, who was near them, stepped forward and took the stopper out of the whisky decanter.

'A whisky and soda, Mr Treves? Latimer, what about you?'

Nevile said to Audrey in a low voice:

'It's a lovely evening. Come out for a little.'

She had been standing by the window looking out at the moonlit terrace. He stepped past her and stood outside, waiting. She turned back into the room, shaking her head quickly.

'No, I'm tired. I – I think I'll go to bed.'

She crossed the room and went out. Kay gave a wide yawn.

'I'm sleepy too. What about you, Mary?'

'Yes, I think so. Goodnight, Mr Treves. Look after Mr Treves, Thomas.'

'Goodnight, Miss Aldin. Goodnight, Mrs Strange.'

'We'll be over for lunch tomorrow, Ted,' said Kay. 'We could bathe if it's still like this.'

'Right. I'll be looking for you. Goodnight, Miss Aldin.'

The two women left the room.

Ted Latimer said agreeably to Mr Treves:

'I'm coming your way, sir. Down to the ferry, so I pass the Hotel.'

'Thank you, Mr Latimer. I shall be glad of your escort.'

Mr Treves, although he had declared his intention of departing, seemed in no hurry. He sipped his drink with pleasant deliberation and devoted himself to the task of extracting information from Thomas Royde as to the condition of life in Malaya.

Royde was monosyllabic in his answers. The everyday details of existence might have been secrets of National importance from the difficulty with which they were dragged from him. He seemed to be lost in some abstraction of his own, out of which he roused himself with difficulty to reply to his questioner.

Ted Latimer fidgeted. He looked bored, impatient, anxious to be gone.

Suddenly interrupting, he exclaimed:

'I nearly forgot! I brought Kay over some gramophone records she wanted. They're in the hall. I'll get them. Will you tell her about them tomorrow, Royde?'

The other man nodded. Ted left the room.

'That young man has a restless nature,' murmured Mr Treves.

Royde grunted without replying.

'A friend, I think, of Mrs Strange's?' pursued the old lawyer.

'Of Kay Strange's,' said Thomas.

Mr Treves smiled.

'Yes,' he said. 'I meant that. He would hardly be a friend of the first Mrs Strange.'

Royde said emphatically:

'No, he wouldn't.'

Then, catching the other's quizzical eye, he said, flushing a little:

'What I mean is –'

'Oh, I quite understood what you meant, Mr Royde. You yourself are a friend of Mrs Audrey Strange, are you not?'

Thomas Royde slowly filled his pipe from his tobacco pouch. His eyes bent to his task, he said or rather mumbled:

'M – yes. More or less brought up together.'

'She must have been a very charming young girl?'

Thomas Royde said something that sounded like 'Um – yum.'

'A little awkward having two Mrs Stranges in the house?'

'Oh yes – yes, rather.'

'A difficult position for the original Mrs Strange.'

Thomas Royde's face flushed.

'Extremely difficult.'

Mr Treves leaned forward. His question popped out sharply:

'*Why did she come, Mr Royde?*'

'Well – I suppose –' The other's voice was indistinct. 'She – didn't like to refuse.'

'To refuse whom?'

Royde shifted awkwardly.

'Well, as a matter of fact, I believe she always comes this time of year – beginning of September.'

'And Lady Tressilian asked Nevile Strange and his new wife at the same time?' The old gentleman's voice held a nice note of polite incredulity.

'As to that, I believe Nevile asked himself.'

'He was anxious, then, for this – reunion?'

Royde shifted uneasily. He replied, avoiding the other's eye:

'I suppose so.'

'Curious,' said Mr Treves.

'Stupid sort of thing to do,' said Thomas Royde, goaded into longer speech.

'Somewhat embarrassing one would have thought,' said Mr Treves.

'Oh well – people do that sort of thing nowadays,' said Thomas Royde vaguely.

'I wondered,' said Mr Treves, 'if it had been anybody else's idea?'

Royde stared.

'Whose else's could it have been?'

Mr Treves sighed.

'There are so many kind friends about in the world – always anxious to arrange other people's lives for them – to suggest courses of action that are not in harmony –' He broke off as Nevile Strange strolled back through the french windows. At the same moment Ted Latimer entered by the door from the hall.

'Hullo, Ted, what have you got there?' asked Nevile.

'Gramophone records for Kay. She asked me to bring them over.'

'Oh did she? She didn't tell me.' There was just a moment of constraint between the two, then Nevile strolled over to the drink tray and helped himself to a whisky and soda. His face looked excited and unhappy and he was breathing deeply.

Someone in Mr Treves' hearing had referred to Nevile as 'that lucky beggar Strange – got everything in the world anyone could wish for'. Yet he did not look, at this moment, at all a happy man.

Thomas Royde, with Nevile's re-entry, seemed to feel that his duties as host were over. He left the room without attempting to say goodnight, and his walk was slightly more hurried than usual. It was almost an escape.

'A delightful evening,' said Mr Treves politely as he set down his glass. 'Most – er – instructive.'

'Instructive?' Nevile raised his eyebrows slightly.

'Information re the Malay States,' suggested Ted, smiling broadly. 'Hard work dragging answers out of Taciturn Thomas.'

'Extraordinary fellow, Royde,' said Nevile. 'I believe he's always been the same. Just smokes that awful old pipe of his and listens and says Um and Ah occasionally and looks wise like an owl.'

'Perhaps he thinks the more,' said Mr Treves. 'And now I really must take my leave.'

'Come and see Lady Tressilian again soon,' said Nevile as he accompanied the two men to the hall. 'You cheer her up enormously. She has so few contacts now with the outside world. She's wonderful, isn't she?'

'Yes, indeed. A most stimulating conversationalist.'

Mr Treves dressed himself carefully with overcoat and muffler, and after renewed goodnights he and Ted Latimer set out together.

The Balmoral Court was actually only about a hundred yards away, around one curve of the road. It loomed up prim and forbidding, the first outpost of the straggling country street.

The ferry, where Ted Latimer was bound, was two or three hundred yards farther down, at a point where the river was at its narrowest.

Mr Treves stopped at the door of the Balmoral Court and held out his hand.

'Goodnight, Mr Latimer. You are staying down here much longer?'

Ted smiled with a flash of white teeth. 'That depends, Mr Treves. I haven't had time to be bored – yet.'

'No – no, so I should imagine. I suppose like most young people nowadays, boredom is what you dread most in the world, and yet, I can assure you, there are worse things.'

'Such as?'

Ted Latimer's voice was soft and pleasant, but it held an undercurrent of something else – something not quite so easy to define.

'Oh, I leave it to your imagination, Mr Latimer. I would not presume to give you advice, you know. The advice of such elderly fogeys as myself is invariably treated with scorn. Rightly so, perhaps, who knows? But we old buffers like to think that experience has taught us something. We have noticed a good deal, you know, in the course of a lifetime.'

A cloud had come over the face of the moon. The street was very dark. Out of the darkness a man's figure came towards them walking up the hill.

It was Thomas Royde.

'Just been down to the ferry for a bit of a walk,' he said indistinctly because of the pipe clenched between his teeth.

'This your pub?' he asked Mr Treves. 'Looks as though you were locked out.'

'Oh, I don't think so,' said Mr Treves.

He turned the big brass door knob and the door swung back.

'We'll see you safely in,' said Royde.

The three of them entered the hall. It was dimly lit with only one electric light. There was no one to be seen, and an odour of bygone dinner, rather dusty velvet, and good furniture polish met their nostrils.

Suddenly Mr Treves gave an exclamation of annoyance.

On the lift in front of them hung a notice:

LIFT OUT OF ORDER

'Dear me,' said Mr Treves. 'How extremely vexing. I shall have to walk up all those stairs.'

'Too bad,' said Royde. 'Isn't there a service lift – luggage – all that?'

'I'm afraid not. This one is used for all purposes. Well I must take it slowly, that is all. Goodnight to you both.'

He started slowly up the wide staircase. Royde and Latimer wished him goodnight, then let themselves out into the dark street.

There was a moment's pause, then Royde said abruptly:

'Well, goodnight.'

'Goodnight. See you tomorrow.'

'Yes.'

Ted Latimer strode lightly down the hill towards the ferry. Thomas Royde stood looking after him for a moment, then he walked slowly in the opposite direction towards Gull's Point.

The moon came out from behind the cloud and Saltcreek was once more bathed in silvery radiance.

VII

'Just like summer,' murmured Mary Aldin.

She and Audrey were sitting on the beach just below the imposing edifice of the Easterhead Bay Hotel. Audrey wore a white swim suit and looked like a delicate ivory figure. Mary had not bathed. A little way along from them Kay lay on her face exposing her bronzed limbs and back to the sun.

'Ugh,' she sat up. 'The water's horribly cold,' she said accusingly.

'Oh well, it *is* September,' said Mary.

'It's always cold in England,' said Kay discontentedly. 'How I wish we were in the South of France. That really is hot.'

Ted Latimer from beyond her murmured:

'The sun here isn't a real sun.'

'Aren't you going in at all, Mr Latimer?' asked Mary.

Kay laughed.

'Ted never goes in the water. Just suns himself like a lizard.'

She stretched out a toe and prodded him. He sprang up.

'Come and walk, Kay. I'm cold.'

They went off together along the beach.

'Like a lizard? Rather an unfortunate comparison,' murmured Mary Aldin looking after them.

'Is that what you think of him?' asked Audrey.

Mary Aldin frowned.

'Not quite. A lizard suggests something quite tame. I don't think he is tame.'

'No,' said Audrey thoughtfully. 'I don't think so either.'

'How well they look together,' said Mary, watching the retreating pair. 'They match somehow, don't they?'

'I suppose they do.'

'They like the same things,' went on Mary. 'And have the same opinions and – and use the same language. What a thousand pities it is that –'

She stopped.

Audrey said sharply:

'That what?'

Mary said slowly:

'I suppose I was going to say what a pity it was that Nevile and she ever met.'

Audrey sat up stiffly. What Mary called to herself 'Audrey's frozen look' had come over her face. Mary said quickly:

'I'm sorry, Audrey. I shouldn't have said that.'

'I'd so much rather – not talk about it if you don't mind.'

'Of course, of course. It was very stupid of me. I – I hoped you'd got over it, I suppose.'

Audrey turned her head slowly. With a calm expressionless face she said:

'I assure you there is nothing to get over. I – I have no feeling of any kind in the matter. I hope – I hope with all my heart that Kay and Nevile will always be very happy together.'

'Well, that's very nice of you, Audrey.'

'It isn't nice. It is – just true. But I do think it is – well – unprofitable to keep on going back over the past. "It's a pity this happened – that!" It's all over now. Why take it up? We've got to go on living our lives in the present.'

'I suppose,' said Mary simply, 'that people like Kay and Ted are exciting to me because – well, they are so different from anything or anyone that I have ever come across.'

'Yes, I suppose they are.'

'Even you,' said Mary with sudden bitterness, 'have lived and had experiences that I shall probably never have. I know you've been unhappy – very unhappy – but I can't help feeling that even that is better than – well – nothing. Emptiness!'

She said the last word with a fierce emphasis.

Audrey's wide eyes looked a little startled.

'I never dreamt you ever felt like that.'

'Didn't you?' Mary Aldin laughed apologetically. 'Oh just a momentary fit of discontent, my dear. I didn't really mean it.'

'It can't be very gay for you,' said Audrey slowly. 'Just living here with Camilla – dear thing though she is. Reading to her, managing the servants, never going away.'

'I'm well fed and housed,' said Mary. 'Thousands of women aren't even that. And really, Audrey, I am quite contented. I have,' a smile played for a moment round her lips, 'my private distractions.'

'Secret vices?' asked Audrey, smiling also.

'Oh, I plan things,' said Mary vaguely. 'In my mind, you know. And I like experimenting sometimes – upon people. Just seeing, you know, if I can make them react to what I say in the way I mean.'

'You sound almost sadistic, Mary. How little I really know you!'

'Oh it's all quite harmless. Just a childish little amusement.'

Audrey asked curiously:

'Have you experimented on me?'

'No. You're the only person I have always found quite incalculable. I never know, you see, what you are thinking.'

'Perhaps,' said Audrey gravely, 'that is just as well.'

She shivered and Mary exclaimed:

'You're cold.'

'Yes. I think I will go and dress. After all, it is September.'

Mary Aldin remained alone, staring at the reflection on the water. The tide was going out. She stretched herself out on the sand, closing her eyes.

They had had a good lunch at the Hotel. It was still quite full although it was past the height of the season. A queer, mixed-looking lot of people. Oh well, it had been a day out. Something to break the monotony of day following day. It had been a relief, too, to get away from that sense of tension, that strung-up atmosphere that there had been lately at Gull's Point. It hadn't been Audrey's fault, but Nevile –

Her thoughts broke up abruptly as Ted Latimer plumped himself down on the beach beside her.

'What have you done with Kay?' Mary asked.

Ted replied briefly:

'She's been claimed by her legal owner.'

Something in his tone made Mary Aldin sit up. She glanced across the stretch of shining golden sands to where Nevile and Kay were walking by the water's edge. Then she glanced quickly at the man beside her.

She had thought of him as nerveless, as queer, as dangerous, even. Now for the first time she got a glimpse of someone young and hurt. She thought:

'He was in love with Kay – really in love with her – and then Nevile came and took her away . . .'

She said gently:

'I hope you are enjoying yourself down here.'

They were conventional words. Mary Aldin seldom used any words but conventional ones – that was her language. But her tone was an offer – for the first time – of friendliness. Ted Latimer responded to it.

'As much, probably, as I should enjoy myself anywhere.'

Mary said:

'I'm sorry.'

'But you don't care a damn, really! I'm an outsider – and what does it matter what outsiders feel and think.'

She turned her head to look at this bitter and handsome young man.

He returned her look with one of defiance.

She said slowly as one who makes a discovery:

'I see. You don't like us.'

He laughed shortly.

'Did you expect me to?'

She said thoughtfully:

'I suppose, you know, that I did expect just that. One takes, of course, too much for granted. One should be more humble. Yes, it would not have occurred to me that you would not like us. We have tried to make you welcome – as Kay's friend.'

'Yes – as Kay's friend!'

The interruption came with a quick venom.

Mary said with disarming sincerity:

'I wish you would tell me – really I wish it – just why you dislike us? What have we done? What is wrong with us?'

Ted Latimer said, with a blistering emphasis on the one word: 'Smug!'

'Smug?' Mary queried it without rancour, examining the charge with judicial appraisement.

'Yes,' she admitted. 'I see that we could seem like that.'

'You are like that. You take all the good things of life for granted. You're happy and superior in your little roped-off enclosure shut off from the common herd. You look at people like me as though I were one of the animals outside!'

'I'm sorry,' said Mary.

'It's true, isn't it?'

'No, not quite. We are stupid, perhaps, and unimaginative – but not malicious. I myself am conventional and, superficially, I dare say, what you call smug. But really, you know, I'm quite human inside. I'm very sorry, this minute, because you are unhappy, and I wish I could do something about it.'

'Well – if that's so – it's nice of you.'

There was a pause, then Mary said gently:

'Have you always been in love with Kay?'

'Pretty well.'

'And she?'

'I thought so – until Strange came along.'

Mary said gently:

'And you're still in love with her?'

'I should think that was obvious.'

After a moment or two, Mary said quietly:

'Hadn't you better go away from here?'

'Why should I?'

'Because you are only letting yourself in for more unhappiness.'

He looked at her and laughed.

'You're a nice creature,' he said. 'But you don't know much about the animals prowling about outside your little enclosure. Quite a lot of things may happen in the near future.'

'What sort of things?' said Mary sharply.

'Wait and see.'

VIII

When Audrey had dressed she went along the beach and out along a jutting point of rocks, joining Thomas Royde, who was sitting there smoking a pipe exactly opposite to Gull's Point, which stood white and serene on the opposite side of the river.

Thomas turned his head at Audrey's approach, but he did not move. She sat down beside him without speaking. They were silent with the comfortable silence of two people who know each other very well indeed.

'How near it looks,' said Audrey at last, breaking the silence.

Thomas looked across at Gull's Point.

'Yes, we could swim home.'

'Not at this tide. There was a housemaid Camilla had once. She was an enthusiastic bather, used to swim across and back whenever the tide was right. It has to be low or high – but when it's running out it sweeps you right down to the mouth of the river. It did that to her one day – only luckily she kept her head and came ashore all right on Easter Point – only very exhausted.'

'It doesn't say anything about its being dangerous here.'

'It isn't this side. The current is the other side. It's deep there under the cliffs. There was a would-be suicide last year – threw himself off Stark Head – but he was caught by a tree half-way down the cliff and the coast-guards got to him all right.'

'Poor devil,' said Thomas. 'I bet he didn't thank them. Must be sickening to have made up your mind to get out of it all and then be saved. Makes a fellow feel a fool.'

'Perhaps he's glad now,' suggested Audrey dreamily.

She wondered vaguely where the man was now and what he was doing.

Thomas puffed away at his pipe. By turning his head very slightly he could look at Audrey. He noted her grave absorbed face as she stared across the water. The long brown lashes that rested on the pure line of the cheek, the small shell-like ear.

That reminded him of something.

'Oh by the way, I've got your ear-ring – the one you lost last night.'

His fingers delved into his pocket. Audrey stretched out a hand.

'Oh good, where did you find it? On the terrace?'

'No. It was near the stairs. You must have lost it as you came down to dinner. I noticed you hadn't got it at dinner.'

'I'm glad to have it back.'

She took it. Thomas reflected that it was rather a large barbaric ear-ring for so small an ear. The ones she had on today were large, too.

He remarked:

'You wear your ear-rings even when you bathe. Aren't you afraid of losing them?'

'Oh, these are very cheap things. I hate being without ear-rings because of this.'

She touched her left ear. Thomas remembered.

'Oh yes, that time old Bouncer bit you.'

Audrey nodded.

They were silent, reliving a childish memory. Audrey Standish (as she then was), a long spindle-legged child, putting her face down on old Bouncer who had had a sore paw. A nasty bite, he had given her. She had had to have a stitch put in it. Not that there was much to show now – just the tiniest little scar.

'My dear girl,' he said, 'you can hardly see the mark. Why do you mind?'

Audrey paused before answering with evident sincerity:

'It's because – because I just can't bear a *blemish*.'

Thomas nodded. It fitted in with his knowledge of Audrey – of her instinct for perfection. She was in herself so perfectly finished an article.

He said suddenly:

'You're far more beautiful than Kay.'

She turned quickly.

'Oh no, Thomas. Kay – Kay is really lovely.'

'On the outside. Not underneath.'

'Are you referring,' said Audrey with faint amusement, 'to my beautiful soul?'

Thomas knocked out the ashes of his pipe.

'No,' he said. 'I think I mean your bones.'

Audrey laughed.

Thomas packed a new pipeful of tobacco. They were silent for quite five minutes, but Thomas glanced at Audrey more than once though he did it so unobtrusively that she was unaware of it.

He said at last quietly:

'What's wrong, Audrey?'

'Wrong? What do you mean by wrong?'

'Wrong with you. There's something.'

'No, there's nothing. Nothing at all.'

'But there is.'

She shook her head.

'Won't you tell me?'

'There's nothing to tell.'

'I suppose I'm being a chump – but I've got to say it –' He paused. 'Audrey – can't you forget about it? Can't you let it all go?'

She dug her small hands convulsively into the rock.

'You don't understand – you can't begin to understand.'

'But Audrey, my dear, I do. That's just it. I *know*.'

She turned a small doubtful face to him.

'I know exactly what you've been through. And – and what it must have meant to you.'

She was very white now, white to the lips.

'I see,' she said. 'I didn't think – anyone knew.'

'Well, I do. I – I'm not going to talk about it. But what I want to impress upon you is that it's all over – it's past and done with.'

She said in a low voice:

'Some things don't pass.'

'Look here, Audrey, it's no good brooding and remembering. Granted you've been through Hell. It does no good to go over and over a thing in your mind. Look forward – not back. You're quite young. You've got your life to live and most of that is in front of you now. Think of tomorrow, not of yesterday.'

She looked at him with a steady wide-eyed gaze that was singularly unrevealing of her real thoughts.

'And supposing,' she said, 'that I can't do that.'

'But you must.'

Audrey said gently:

'I thought you didn't understand. I'm – I'm not quite normal about – some things, I suppose.'

He broke in roughly,

'Rubbish. You –' He stopped.

'I – what?'

'I was thinking of you as you were when you were a girl – before you married Nevile. Why did you marry Nevile?'

Audrey smiled.

'Because I fell in love with him.'

'Yes, yes, I know that. But why did you fall in love with him? What attracted you to him so much?'

She crinkled her eyes as though trying to see through the eyes of a girl now dead.

'I think,' she said, 'it was because he was so "positive". He was always so much the opposite of what I was, myself. I always felt shadowy – not quite real. Nevile was very real. And so happy and sure of himself and so – everything that I was not.' She added with a smile: 'And very good-looking.'

Thomas Royde said bitterly:

'Yes, the ideal Englishman – good at sport, modest, good-looking, always the little pukka sahib – getting everything he wanted all along the line.'

Audrey sat very upright and stared at him.

'You hate him,' she said slowly. 'You hate him very much, don't you?'

He avoided her eyes, turning away to cup a match in his hands as he relit the pipe, that had gone out.

'Wouldn't be surprising if I did, would it?' he said indistinctly. 'He's got everything that I haven't. He can play games, and swim and dance, and talk. And I'm a tongue-tied oaf with a crippled arm. He's always been brilliant and successful and I've always been a dull dog. And he married the only girl I ever cared for.'

She made a faint sound. He said savagely:

'You've always known that, haven't you? You knew I cared about you ever since you were fifteen. You know that I still care –'

She stopped him.

'No. Not now.'

'What do you mean – not now?'

Audrey got up. She said in a quiet reflective voice:

'Because – now – I am different.'

'Different in what way?'

He got up too and stood facing her.

Audrey said in a quick rather breathless voice:

'If you don't know, I can't tell you . . . I'm not always sure myself. I only know –'

She broke off, and turning abruptly away she walked quickly back over the rocks towards the Hotel.

Turning a corner of the cliff she came across Nevile. He was lying full length peering into a rock pool. He looked up and grinned.

'Hullo, Audrey.'

'Hullo, Nevile.'

'I'm watching a crab. Awfully active little beggar. Look, there he is.'

She knelt down and stared where he pointed.

'See him?'

'Yes.'

'Have a cigarette?'

She accepted one and he lighted it for her. After a moment or two, during which she did not look at him, he said, nervously:

'I say, Audrey?'

'Yes.'

'It's all right, isn't it? I mean – between us.'

'Yes. Yes, of course.'

'I mean – we're friends and all that.'

'Oh yes – yes, of course.'

'I do want us to be friends.'

He looked at her anxiously. She gave him a nervous smile.

He said conversationally:

'It's been a jolly day, hasn't it? Weather good and all that?'

'Oh yes – yes.'

'Quite hot really for September.'

There was a pause.

'Audrey –'

She got up.

'Your wife wants you. She's waving to you.'

'Who – oh, Kay.'

'I said your wife.'

He scrambled to his feet and stood looking at her.

He said in a very low voice:

'You're my wife, Audrey . . .'

She turned away. Nevile ran down on to the beach and across the sand to join Kay.

IX

On their arrival back at Gull's Point, Hurstall came out into the hall and spoke to Mary.

'Would you go up at once to her ladyship, Miss? She is feeling very upset and wanted to see you as soon as you got in.'

Mary hurried up the stairs. She found Lady Tressilian looking white and shaken.

'Dear Mary, I'm so glad you have come. I am feeling most distressed. Poor Mr Treves is dead.'

'Dead?'

'Yes, isn't it terrible? So sudden. Apparently he didn't even get undressed last night. He must have collapsed as soon as he got home.'

'Oh dear, I am sorry.'

'One knows, of course, that he was delicate. A weak heart. I hope nothing happened while he was here to overstrain it? There was nothing indigestible for dinner?'

'I don't think so – no, I am sure there wasn't. He seemed quite well and in good spirits.'

'I am really very distressed. I wish, Mary, that you would go to the Balmoral Court and make a few inquiries of Mrs Rogers. Ask her if there is anything we can do. And then the funeral. For Matthew's sake I would like to do anything we could. These things are so awkward at a Hotel.'

Mary spoke firmly.

'Dear Camilla, you really must not worry. This has been a shock to you.'

'Indeed it has.'

'I will go to the Balmoral Court at once and then come back and tell you all about things.'

'Thank you, Mary dear, you are always so practical and understanding.'

'Please try and rest now. A shock of this kind is so bad for you.'

Mary Aldin left the room and came downstairs. Entering the drawing-room she exclaimed: 'Old Mr Treves is dead. He died last night after returning home.'

'Poor old boy,' exclaimed Nevile. 'What was it?'

'Heart apparently. He collapsed as soon as he got in.'

Thomas Royde said thoughtfully:

'I wonder if the stairs did him in.'

'Stairs?' Mary looked at him inquiringly.

'Yes. When Latimer and I left him he was just starting up. We told him to take it slow.'

Mary exclaimed:

'But how very foolish of him not to take the lift.'

'The lift was out of order.'

'Oh, I see. How very unfortunate. Poor old man.'

She added: 'I'm going round there now. Camilla wants to know if there is anything we can do.'

Thomas said: 'I'll come with you.'

They walked together down the road and round the corner to the Balmoral Court. Mary remarked:

'I wonder if he has any relatives who ought to be notified?'

'He didn't mention anyone.'

'No, and people usually do. They say "my niece", or "my cousin".'

'Was he married?'

'I believe not.'

They entered the open door of the Balmoral Court.

Mrs Rogers, the proprietress, was talking to a tall middle-aged man, who raised a friendly hand in greeting to Mary.

'Good afternoon, Miss Aldin.'

'Good afternoon, Dr Lazenby. This is Mr Royde. We came round with a message from Lady Tressilian to know if there is anything we can do.'

'That's very kind of you, Miss Aldin,' said the Hotel proprietress. 'Come into my room, won't you?'

They all went into the small comfortable sitting-room and Dr Lazenby said:

'Mr Treves was dining at your place last night, wasn't he?'

'Yes.'

'How did he seem? Did he show any signs of distress?'

'No, he seemed very well and cheerful.'

The doctor nodded.

'Yes, that's the worst of these heart cases. The end is nearly always sudden. I had a look at his prescriptions upstairs and it seems quite clear that he was in a very precarious state of health. I shall communicate with his London doctor, of course.'

'He was very careful of himself always,' said Mrs Rogers. 'And I'm sure he had every care here we could give him.'

'I'm sure of that, Mrs Rogers,' said the doctor tactfully. 'It was just some tiny additional strain, no doubt.'

'Such as walking upstairs,' suggested Mary.

'Yes, that might do it. In fact almost certainly would – that is, if he ever walked up those three flights – but surely he never did anything of that kind?'

'Oh no,' said Mrs Rogers. 'He always used the lift. Always. He was most particular.'

'I mean,' said Mary, 'that with the lift being out of order last night –'

Mrs Rogers was staring at her in surprise.

'But the lift wasn't out of order at all yesterday, Miss Aldin.'

Thomas Royde coughed.

'Excuse me,' he said. 'I came home with Mr Treves last night. There was a placard on the lift saying "Out of order".'

Mrs Rogers stared.

'Well, that's an odd thing. I'd have declared there was nothing wrong with the lift – in fact I'm sure there wasn't. I'd have heard about it if there was. We haven't had anything go wrong with the lift (touching wood) since – oh, not for a good eighteen months. Very reliable it is.'

'Perhaps,' suggested the doctor, 'some porter or hall boy put that notice up when he was off duty?'

'It's an automatic lift, doctor, it doesn't need anyone to work it.'

'Ah yes, so it is. I was forgetting.'

'I'll have a word with Joe,' said Mrs Rogers. She bustled out of the room calling, 'Joe – Joe.'

Dr Lazenby looked curiously at Thomas.

'Excuse me, you're quite sure, Mr – er –'

'Royde,' put in Mary.

'Quite sure,' said Thomas.

Mrs Rogers came back with the porter. Joe was emphatic that nothing whatever had been wrong with the lift on the preceding night. There was such a placard as Thomas had described – but it was tucked away under the desk and hadn't been used for over a year.

They all looked at each other and agreed it was a most mysterious thing. The doctor suggested some practical joke on the part of one of the Hotel visitors, and perforce they left it at that.

In reply to Mary's inquiries, Doctor Lazenby explained that Mr Treves' chauffeur had given him the address of Mr Treves' solicitors, and he was communicating with them and that he would come round and see Lady Tressilian and tell her what was going to be done about the funeral.

Then the busy cheerful doctor hurried off and Mary and Thomas walked slowly back to Gull's Point.

Mary said:

'You're quite sure you saw that notice, Thomas?'

'Both Latimer and I saw it.'

'What an extraordinary thing!' said Mary.

X

It was the 12th of September. 'Only two more days,' said Mary Aldin. Then she bit her lip and flushed.

Thomas Royde looked at her thoughtfully.

'Is that how you feel about it?'

'I don't know what's the matter with me,' said Mary. 'Never in all my life have I been so anxious for a visit to come to an end. And usually we enjoy having Nevile so much. And Audrey too.'

Thomas nodded.

'But this time,' went on Mary, 'one feels as though one were sitting on dynamite. At any minute the whole thing may explode. That's why I said to myself first thing this morning: "Only two days more." Audrey goes on Wednesday and Nevile and Kay on Thursday.'

'And I go on Friday,' said Thomas.

'Oh I'm not counting you. You've been a tower of strength. I don't know what I should have done without you.'

'The human buffer?'

'More than that. You've been so kind and so – so calm. That sounds rather ridiculous but it really does express what I mean.'

Thomas looked pleased though slightly embarrassed.

'I don't know why we've all been so het up,' said Mary reflectively. 'After all, if there were an – an outburst – it would be awkward and embarrassing, but nothing more.'

'But there's been more to your feeling than that.'

'Oh yes, there has. A definite feeling of apprehension. Even the servants feel it. The kitchenmaid burst into tears and gave notice this morning – for no reason at all. The cook's jumpy – Hurstall is all on edge – even Barrett, who is usually as calm as a – a battleship – has shown signs of nerves. And all because Nevile has this ridiculous idea of wanting his former and present wife to make friends and so soothe his own conscience.'

'In which ingenious idea he has singularly failed,' remarked Thomas.

'Yes. Kay is – is getting quite beside herself. And really, Thomas, I can't help sympathizing with her.' She paused. 'Did you notice the way Nevile looked after Audrey as she went up the stairs last night? He still cares about her, Thomas. The whole thing has been the most tragic mistake.'

Thomas started filling his pipe.

'He should have thought of that before,' he said in a hard voice.

'Oh I know. That's what one says. But it doesn't alter the fact that the whole thing is a tragedy. I can't help feeling sorry for Nevile.'

'People like Nevile –' began Thomas and then stopped.

'Yes.'

'People like Nevile think they can always have everything their own way – and have everything they want, too. I don't suppose Nevile has ever had a setback over anything in his life till he came up against this business of Audrey. Well, he's got it now. He can't have Audrey. She's out of his reach. No good his making a song and dance about it. He's just got to lump it.'

'I suppose you're quite right. But you do sound hard. Audrey was so much in love with Nevile when she married him – and they always got on together so well.'

'Well, she's out of love with him now.'

'I wonder,' murmured Mary under her breath.

Thomas was going on:

'And I'll tell you something else. Nevile had better look out for Kay. She's a dangerous kind of young woman – really dangerous. If she got her temper up she'd stop at nothing.'

'Oh dear,' Mary sighed and, returning to her original remarks, said hopefully: 'Well, it's only two days more.'

Things had been very difficult for the last four or five days. The death of Mr Treves had given Lady Tressilian a shock which had told adversely on her health. The funeral had taken place in London, for which Mary was thankful, since it enabled the old lady to take her mind off the sad event more quickly than she might have been able to do otherwise. The domestic side of the household had been very nervy and difficult and Mary really felt tired and dispirited this morning.

'It's partly the weather,' she said aloud. 'It's unnatural.'

It had indeed been an unusually hot and fine spell for September. On several days the thermometer had registered 70 in the shade.

Nevile strolled out of the house and joined them as she spoke.

'Blaming the weather?' he asked, with a glance up at the sky. 'It is rather incredible. Hotter than ever today. And no wind. Makes one feel jumpy somehow. However, I think we'll get rain before very long. Today is just a bit too tropical to last.'

Thomas Royde had moved very gently and aimlessly away and now disappeared round the corner of the house.

'Departure of gloomy Thomas,' said Nevile. 'Nobody could say he shows any enjoyment of my company.'

'He's rather a dear,' said Mary.

'I disagree. Narrow-minded prejudiced sort of chap.'

'He always hoped to marry Audrey, I think. And then you came along and cut him out.'

'It would have taken him about seven years to make up his mind to ask her to marry him. Did he expect the poor girl to wait while he made up his mind?'

'Perhaps,' said Mary deliberately, 'it will all come right now.'

Nevile looked at her and raised an eyebrow.

'True love rewarded? Audrey marry that wet fish? She's a lot too good for that. No, I don't see Audrey marrying gloomy Thomas.'

'I believe she is really very fond of him, Nevile.'

'What matchmakers you women always are! Can't you let Audrey enjoy her freedom for a bit?'

'If she does enjoy it, certainly.'

Nevile said quickly:

'You think she's not happy?'

'I really haven't the least idea.'

'No more have I,' said Nevile slowly. 'One never does know what Audrey is feeling.' He paused and then added, 'But Audrey is one hundred per cent thoroughbred. She's white all through.'

Then he said, more to himself than to Mary:

'God, what a damned fool I've been!'

Mary went into the house a little worried. For the third time she repeated to herself the comforting words, 'Only two days more.'

Nevile wandered restlessly about the garden and terraces.

Right at the end of the garden he found Audrey sitting on the low wall looking down at the water below. It was high tide and the river was full.

She got up at once and came towards him.

'I was just coming back to the house. It must be nearly tea-time.'

She spoke quickly and nervously without looking at him.

He walked beside her without speaking.

Only when they reached the terrace again did he say:

'Can I talk to you, Audrey?'

She said at once, her fingers gripping the edge of the balustrade: 'I think you'd better not.'

'That means you know what I want to say.'

She did not answer.

'What about it, Audrey? Can't we go back to where we were? Forget everything that has happened?'

'Including Kay?'

'Kay,' said Nevile, 'will be sensible.'

'What do you mean by sensible?'

'Simply this. I shall go to her and tell her the truth. Fling myself on her generosity. Tell her, what is true, that you are the only woman I ever loved.'

'You loved Kay when you married her.'

'My marriage to Kay was the biggest mistake I ever made. I –'

He stopped. Kay had come out of the drawing-room window. She walked towards them, and before the fury in her eyes even Nevile shrank a little.

'Sorry to interrupt this touching scene,' said Kay. 'But I think it's about time I did.'

Audrey moved away. 'I'll leave you alone,' she said.

Her face and voice were colourless.

'That's right,' said Kay. 'You've done all the mischief you wanted to do, haven't you? I'll deal with you later. Just now I'd rather have it out with Nevile.'

'Look here, Kay, Audrey has absolutely nothing to do with this. It's not her fault. Blame me if you like –'

'And I do like,' said Kay. Her eyes blazed at Nevile. 'What sort of man do you think you are?'

'A pretty poor sort of man,' said Nevile bitterly.

'You leave your wife, come bull-headed after me, get your wife to give you a divorce. Crazy about me one minute, tired of me the next! Now I suppose you want to go back to that whey-faced, mewling, double-crossing little cat –'

'Stop that, Kay!'

'Well, what do you want?'

Nevile was very white. He said:

'I'm every kind of a worm you like to call me. But it's no good,

Kay. *I can't go on.* I think – really – I must have loved Audrey all the time. My love for you was – was a kind of madness. But it's no good, my dear – you and I don't belong. I shouldn't be able to make you happy in the long run. Believe me, Kay, it's better to cut our losses. Let's try and part friends. Be generous.'

Kay said in a deceptively quiet voice:

'What exactly are you suggesting?'

Nevile did not look at her. His chin took on a dogged angle.

'We can get a divorce. You can divorce me for desertion.'

'Not for some time. You'll have to wait for it.'

'I'll wait,' said Nevile.

'And then, after three years or whatever it is, you'll ask dear sweet Audrey to marry you all over again?'

'If she'll have me.'

'She'll have you all right!' said Kay viciously. 'And where do I come in?'

'You'll be free to find a better man than I am. Naturally I shall see you're well provided for –'

'Cut out the bribes!' Her voice rose, as she lost control of herself. 'Listen to me, Nevile. You can't do this thing to me! I'll not divorce you. I married you because I loved you. I know when you started turning against me. It was after I let you know I followed you to Estoril. You wanted to think it was all Fate. It's upset your vanity to think it was *me*. Well, I'm not ashamed of what I did. You fell in love with me and married me and I'm not going to let you go back to that sly little cat who's got her hooks into you again. She meant this to happen – but she's not going to bring it off! I'll kill you first. Do you hear? I'll kill you. I'll kill her too. I'll see you both dead. I'll –'

Nevile took a step forward and caught her by the arm.

'Shut up, Kay. For goodness' sake. You can't make this kind of scene here.'

'Can't I? You'll see. I'll –'

Hurstall stepped out on the terrace. His face was quite impassive.

'Tea is served in the drawing-room,' he announced.

Kay and Nevile walked slowly towards the drawing-room window.

Hurstall stood aside to let them pass in.

Up in the sky the clouds were gathering.

XI

The rain started falling at a quarter to seven. Nevile watched it from the window of his bedroom. He had no further conversation with Kay. They had avoided each other after tea.

Dinner that evening was a stilted difficult meal. Nevile was sunk in abstraction; Kay's face had an unusual amount of make-up for her; Audrey sat like a frozen ghost. Mary Aldin did her best to keep some kind of a conversation going and was slightly annoyed with Thomas Royde for not playing up to her better.

Hurstall was nervous and his hands trembled as he handed the vegetables.

As the meal drew to a close, Nevile said with elaborate casualness: 'Think I shall go over to Easterhead after dinner and look up Latimer. We might have a game of billiards.'

'Take the latch key,' said Mary. 'In case you're back late.'

'Thanks, I will.'

They went into the drawing-room, where coffee was served.

The turning on of the wireless and the news was a welcome diversion.

Kay, who had been yawning ostentatiously ever since dinner, said she would go up to bed. She had a headache, she said.

'Have you got any aspirin?' asked Mary.

'Yes, thank you.'

Kay left the room.

Nevile turned the wireless on to a programme with music. He sat silent on the sofa for some time. He did not look once at Audrey, but sat huddled up looking like an unhappy little boy. Against her will, Mary felt quite sorry for him.

'Well,' he said, at last rousing himself, 'better be off if I'm going.'

'Are you taking your car or going by ferry?'

'Oh, ferry. No sense in going a round of fifteen miles. I shall enjoy a bit of a walk.'

'It's raining, you know.'

'I know. I've got a Burberry.' He went towards the door.

'Goodnight.'

In the hall, Hurstall came to him.

'If you please, sir, will you go up to Lady Tressilian? She wants to see you specially.'

Nevile glanced at the clock. It was already ten o'clock.

He shrugged his shoulders and went upstairs and along the corridor to Lady Tressilian's room and tapped on the door. While he waited for her to say Come in, he heard the voices of the others in the hall down below. Everybody was going to bed early tonight, it seemed.

'Come in,' said Lady Tressilian's clear voice.

Nevile went in, shutting the door behind him.

Lady Tressilian was all ready for the night. All the lights were extinguished except one reading lamp by her bed. She had been reading, but she now laid down the book. She looked at Nevile over the top of her spectacles. It was, somehow, a formidable glance.

'I want to speak to you, Nevile,' she said.

In spite of himself, Nevile smiled faintly.

'Yes, Headmaster,' he said.

Lady Tressilian did not smile.

'There are certain things, Nevile, that I will not permit in my house. I have no wish to listen to anybody's private conversations, but if you and your wife insist on shouting at each other exactly under my bedroom windows, I can hardly fail to hear what you say. I gather that you were outlining a plan whereby Kay was to divorce you and in due course you would remarry Audrey. That, Nevile, is a thing you simply cannot do and I will not hear of it for a moment.'

Nevile seemed to be making an effort to control his temper.

'I apologize for the scene,' he said, shortly. 'As for the rest of what you say, surely that is my business!'

'No, it is not. You have used my house in order to get into touch with Audrey – or else Audrey has used it –'

'She has done nothing of the sort. She –'

Lady Tressilian stopped him with upraised hand.

'Anyway, you can't do this thing, Nevile. Kay is your wife. She has certain rights of which you cannot deprive her. In this matter I am entirely on Kay's side. You have made your bed and must lie upon it. Your duty now is to Kay and I'm telling you so plainly –'

Nevile took a step forward. His voice rose:

'This is nothing whatever to do with you –'

'What is more,' Lady Tressilian swept on, regardless of his protest. 'Audrey leaves this house tomorrow –'

'You can't do that! I won't stand for it –'

'Don't shout at me, Nevile.'

'I tell you I won't have it –'

Somewhere along the passage a door shut . . .

XII

Alice Bentham, the gooseberry-eyed housemaid, came to Mrs Spicer, the cook, in some perturbation.

'Oh, Mrs Spicer, I don't rightly know what I ought to do.'

'What's the matter, Alice?'

'It's Miss Barrett. I took her in her cup of tea over an hour ago. Fast asleep she was and never woke up, but I didn't like to do much. And then, five minutes ago, I went in again because she hadn't come down and her ladyship's tea all ready and waiting for her to take in. So I went in again and she's sleeping ever so – I can't stir her.'

'Have you shaken her?'

'Yes, Mrs Spicer. I shook her head – but she just goes on lying there and she's ever such a horrid colour.'

'Goodness, she's not dead, is she?'

'Oh no, Mrs Spicer, because I can hear her breathing, but it's funny breathing. I think she's ill or something.'

'Well, I'll go up and see myself. You take in her ladyship's tea. Better make a fresh pot. She'll be wondering what's happened.'

Alice obediently did as she was told whilst Mrs Spicer went up to the second floor.

Taking the tray along the corridor, Alice knocked at Lady Tressilian's door. After knocking twice and getting no answer she went in. A moment later, there was a crash of broken crockery and a series of wild screams, and Alice came rushing out of the room and down the stairs to where Hurstall was crossing the hall to the dining-room.

'Oh, Mr Hurstall – there've been burglars and her ladyship's dead – killed – with a great hole in her head and blood everywhere . . .'

A FINE ITALIAN HAND . . .

I

Superintendent Battle had enjoyed his holiday. There were still three days of it to run and he was a little disappointed when the weather changed and the rain fell. Still, what else could you expect in England? And he'd been extremely lucky up to now.

He was breakfasting with Inspector James Leach, his nephew, when the telephone rang.

'I'll come right along, sir.' Jim put the receiver back.

'Serious?' asked Superintendent Battle. He noted the expression on his nephew's face.

'We've got a murder. Lady Tressilian. An old lady, very well known down here, an invalid. Has that house at Saltcreek that hangs right over the cliff.'

Battle nodded.

'I'm going along to see the old man' (thus disrespectfully did Leach speak of his Chief Constable). 'He's a friend of hers. We're going along together.'

As he went to the door he said pleadingly:

'You'll give me a hand, won't you, Uncle, over this? First case of this kind I've had.'

'As long as I'm here, I will. Case of robbery and housebreaking, is it?'

'I don't know yet.'

II

Half an hour later, Major Robert Mitchell, the Chief Constable, was speaking gravely to uncle and nephew.

'It's early to say as yet,' he said, 'but one thing seems clear. This wasn't an outside job. Nothing taken, no signs of breaking in. All the windows and doors found shut this morning.'

He looked directly at Battle.

'If I were to ask Scotland Yard, do you think they'd put you on the job? You're on the spot, you see. And then there's your relationship with Leach here. That is, if you're willing. It means cutting the end of your holiday.'

'That's all right,' said Battle. 'As for the other, sir, you'll have to put it up to Sir Edgar' (Sir Edgar Cotton was Assistant Commissioner) 'but I believe he's a friend of yours?'

Mitchell nodded.

'Yes, I think I can manage Edgar all right. That's settled, then! I'll get through right away.'

He spoke into the telephone: 'Get me the Yard.'

'You think it's going to be an important case, sir?' asked Battle.

Mitchell said gravely:

'It's going to be a case where we don't want the possibility of making a mistake. We want to be absolutely sure of our man – or woman, of course.'

Battle nodded. He understood quite well that there was something behind the words.

'Thinks he knows who did it,' he said to himself. 'And doesn't relish the prospect. Somebody well known and popular or I'll eat my boots!'

III

Battle and Leach stood in the doorway of the well-furnished handsome bedroom. On the floor in front of them a police officer was carefully testing for fingerprints the handle of a golf club – a heavy niblick. The head of the club was blood-stained and had one or two white hairs sticking to it.

By the bed, Dr Lazenby, who was police surgeon for the district, was bending over the body of Lady Tressilian.

He straightened up with a sigh.

'Perfectly straightforward. She was hit from in front with terrific force. First blow smashed in the bone and killed her, but the murderer struck again to make sure. I won't give you fancy terms – just the plain horse sense of it.'

'How long has she been dead?' asked Leach.

'I'd put it between ten o'clock and midnight.'

'You can't go nearer than that?'

'I'd rather not. All sorts of factors to take into account. We don't hang people on *rigor mortis* nowadays. *Not earlier than ten, not later than midnight.*'

'And she was hit with this niblick?'

The doctor glanced over at it.

'Presumably. Luck, though, that the murderer left it behind. I couldn't have deduced a niblick from the wound. As it happens the sharp edge of the club didn't touch the head – it was the angled back of the club that must have hit her.'

'Wouldn't that have been rather difficult to do?' asked Leach.

'If it had been done on purpose, yes,' agreed the doctor. 'I can only suppose, that by a rather odd chance, it just happened that way.'

Leach was raising his hands, instinctively trying to reconstruct the blow.

'Awkward,' he commented.

'Yes,' said the doctor thoughtfully. 'The whole thing was awkward. She was struck, you see, on the right temple – but whoever did it must have stood on the right-hand side of the bed – facing the head of the bed – there's no room on the left, the angle from the wall is too small.'

Leach pricked up his ears.

'Left-handed?' he queried.

'You won't get me to commit myself on that point,' said Lazenby. 'Far too many snags. I'll say, if you like, that the easiest explanation is that the murderer was left-handed – but there are other ways of accounting for it. Suppose, for instance, the old lady had turned her head slightly to the left just as the man hit. Or he may have previously moved the bed out, stood on the left of it and afterwards moved the bed back.'

'Not very likely – that last.'

'Perhaps not, but it *might* have happened. I've had some experience in these things, and I can tell you, my boy, deducing that a murderous blow was struck left-handed is full of pit-falls.'

Detective Sergeant Jones, from the floor, remarked, 'This golf club is the ordinary right-handed kind.'

Leach nodded. 'Still, it mayn't have belonged to the man who used it. It *was* a man, I suppose, doctor?'

'Not necessarily. If the weapon was that heavy niblick a woman could have landed a terrible swipe with it.'

Superintendent Battle said in his quiet voice:

'But you couldn't swear that that was the weapon, could you, doctor?'

Lazenby gave him a quick interested glance.

'No. I can only swear that it *might* have been the weapon, and that presumably it *was* the weapon. I'll analyse the blood on it, make sure that it's the same blood group – also the hairs.'

'Yes,' said Battle approvingly. 'It's always as well to be thorough.'

Lazenby asked curiously:

'Got any doubts about that golf club yourself, Superintendent?'

Battle shook his head.

'Oh no, no. I'm a simple man. Like to believe the things I see with my eyes. She was hit with something heavy – that's heavy. It has blood and hair on it, therefore presumably her blood and hair. Ergo – that was the weapon used.'

Leach asked: 'Was she awake or asleep when she was hit?'

'In my opinion, awake. There's astonishment on her face. I'd say – this is just a private personal opinion – that she didn't expect what was going to happen. There's no sign of any attempt to fight – and no horror or fear. I'd say offhand that either she had just woken up from sleep and was hazy and didn't take things in – or else she recognized her assailant as someone who could not possibly wish to harm her.'

'The bedside lamp was on and nothing else,' said Leach thoughtfully.

'Yes, that cuts either way. She may have turned it on when she was suddenly woken up by someone entering her room. Or it may have been on already.'

Detective Sergeant Jones rose to his feet. He was smiling appreciatively.

'Lovely set of prints on that club,' he said. 'Clear as anything!'

Leach gave a deep sigh.

'That ought to simplify things.'

'Obliging chap,' said Dr Lazenby. 'Left the weapon – left his fingerprints on it – wonder he didn't leave his visiting card!'

'It might be,' said Superintendent Battle, 'that he just lost his head. Some do.'

The doctor nodded.

'True enough. Well, I must go and look after my other patient.'

'What patient?' Battle sounded suddenly interested.

'I was sent for by the butler before this was discovered. Lady Tressilian's maid was found in a coma this morning.'

'What's wrong with her?'

'Heavily doped with one of the barbiturates. She's pretty bad, but she'll pull round.'

'The maid?' said Battle. His rather ox-like eyes went heavily to the big bell pull, the tassel of which rested on the pillow near the dead woman's hand.

Lazenby nodded.

'Exactly. That's the first thing Lady Tressilian would have done if she'd cause to feel alarm – pull that bell and summon the maid. Well, she could have pulled it till all was blue. The maid wouldn't have heard.'

'That was taken care of, was it?' said Battle. 'You're sure of that? She wasn't in the habit of taking sleeping draughts?'

'I'm positive she wasn't. There's no sign of such a thing in her room. And I've found out how it was given to her. Senna pods. She drank a brew of senna pods every night. The stuff was in that.'

Superintendent Battle scratched his chin.

'H'm,' he said. 'Somebody knew all about this house. You know, doctor, this is a very odd sort of murder.'

'Well,' said Lazenby, 'that's *your* business.'

'He's a good man, our doctor,' said Leach when Lazenby had left the room.

The two men were alone now. The photographs had been taken, and measurements recorded. The two police officers knew every fact that was to be known about the room where the crime had been committed.

Battle nodded in answer to his nephew's remark. He seemed to be puzzling over something.

'Do you think anyone could have handled that club – with gloves on, say – after those fingerprints were made?'

Leach shook his head.

'I don't and no more do you. You couldn't grasp that club – not *use* it, I mean, without smearing those prints. They weren't smeared. They were as clear as clear. You saw for yourself.'

Battle agreed.

'And now we ask very nicely and politely if everybody will allow us to take their fingerprints – no compulsion, of course. And everyone will say yes – and then one of two things will happen. Either none of these fingerprints will agree, or else –'

'Or else we'll have got our man?'

'I suppose so. Or our woman, perhaps.'

Leach shook his head.

'No, not a woman. Those prints on the club were a man's. Too big for a woman's. Besides, this isn't a woman's crime.'

'No.' agreed Battle. 'Quite a man's crime. Brutal, masculine, rather athletic and slightly stupid. Know anybody in the house like that?'

'I don't know anyone in the house yet. They're all together in the dining-room.'

Battle moved towards the door.

'We'll go and have a look at them.' He glanced over his shoulder at the bed, shook his head and remarked:

'I don't like that bell pull.'

'What about it?'

'It doesn't fit.'

He added as he opened the door:

'Who wanted to kill her, I wonder? A lot of cantankerous old ladies about just asking for a tap on the skull. She doesn't look that sort. I should think she was *liked*.' He paused a minute and then asked:

'Well off, wasn't she? Who gets her money?'

Leach answered the implication of the words.

'You've hit it! That will be the answer. It's one of the first things to find out.'

As they went downstairs together, Battle glanced at the list in his hand. He read out:

'Miss Aldin, Mr Royde, Mr Strange, Mrs Strange, Mrs Audrey Strange. H'm, seem a lot of the Strange family.'

'Those are his two wives, I understand.'

Battle's eyebrows rose and he murmured:

'Bluebeard, is he?'

The family were assembled round the dining-room table, where they had made a pretence of eating.

Superintendent Battle glanced keenly at the faces turned to him. He was sizing them up after his own peculiar methods. His view of them might have surprised them had they known it. It was a sternly biased view. No matter what the law pretends as to regarding people as innocent until they are proved guilty, Superintendent Battle always regarded everyone connected with a murder case as a potential murderer.

He glanced from Mary Aldin, sitting upright and pale at the head of the table, to Thomas Royde, filling a pipe beside her, to Audrey sitting with her chair pushed back, a coffee cup and saucer in her right hand, a cigarette in her left, to Nevile looking dazed and bewildered, trying with a shaking hand to light a cigarette, to Kay with her elbows on the table and the pallor of her face showing through her make-up.

These were Superintendent Battle's thoughts:

Suppose that's Miss Aldin. Cool customer – competent woman, I should say. Won't catch her off guard easily. Man next to her is a dark horse – got a groggy arm – poker face – got an inferiority complex as likely as not. That's one of these wives, I suppose – she's scared to death – yes, she's scared all right. Funny about that coffee cup. That's Strange, I've seen him before somewhere. He's got the jitters all right – nerves shot to pieces. Red-headed girl's a tartar – devil of a temper. Brains as well as temper, though.

Whilst he was thus sizing them up Inspector Leach was making a stiff little speech. Mary Aldin mentioned everyone present by name.

She ended up:

'It has been a terrible shock to us, of course, but we are anxious to help you in any way we can.'

'To begin with,' said Leach, holding it up, 'does anybody know anything about this golf club?'

With a little cry, Kay said, 'How horrible. Is that what –?' and stopped.

Nevile Strange got up and came round the table.

'Looks like one of mine. Can I just see?'

'It's quite all right *now*,' said Inspector Leach. 'You can handle it.'

That significant 'now' did not seem to produce any reaction in the onlookers. Nevile examined the club.

'I think it's one of the niblicks out of my bag,' he said. 'I can tell you for sure in a minute or two. If you will just come with me.' They followed him to a big cupboard under the stairs. He flung open the door of it and to Battle's confused eyes it seemed literally crowded with tennis racquets. At the same time, he remembered where he had seen Nevile Strange before. He said quickly:

'I've seen you play at Wimbledon, sir.'

Nevile half turned his head. 'Oh yes, have you?'

He was throwing aside some of the racquets. There were two golf bags in the cupboard leaning up against fishing tackle.

'Only my wife and I play golf,' explained Nevile. 'And that's a man's club. Yes, that's right – it's mine.'

He had taken out his bag, which contained at least fourteen clubs.

Inspector Leach thought to himself:

'These athletic chaps certainly take themselves seriously. Wouldn't like to be his caddy.'

Nevile was saying:

'It's one of Walter Hudson's niblicks from St Esbert's.'

'Thank you, Mr Strange. That settles one question.'

Nevile said: 'What beats me is that nothing was taken. And the house doesn't seem to have been broken into?' His voice was bewildered – but it was also frightened.

Battle said to himself:

'They've been thinking it out, all of them . . .'

'The servants,' said Nevile, 'are so absolutely harmless.'

'I shall talk to Miss Aldin about the servants,' said Inspector Leach smoothly. 'In the meantime I wonder if you could give me any idea who Lady Tressilian's solicitors are?'

'Askwith & Trelawny,' replied Nevile promptly. 'St Loo.'

'Thank you, Mr Strange. We shall have to find out from them all about Lady Tressilian's property.'

'Do you mean,' asked Nevile, 'who inherits her money?'

'That's right, sir. Her will, and all that.'

'I don't know about her will,' said Nevile. 'She had not very much of her own to leave so far as I know. I can tell you about the bulk of her property.'

'Yes, Mr Strange?'

'It comes to me and my wife under the will of the late

Sir Matthew Tressilian. Lady Tressilian only had a life inter-est in it.'

'Indeed, is that so?' Inspector Leach looked at Nevile with the interested attention of someone who spots a possibly valuable addition to his pet collection. The look made Nevile wince nervously. Inspector Leach went on and his voice was impos-sibly genial.

'You've no idea of the amount, Mr Strange?'

'I couldn't tell you offhand. In the neighbourhood of a hundred thousand pounds, I believe.'

'In-deed. To each of you?'

'No, divided between us.'

'I see. A very considerable sum.'

Nevile smiled. He said quietly: 'I've got plenty to live on of my own, you know, without hankering to step into dead people's shoes.'

Inspector Leach looked shocked at having such ideas attributed to him.

They went back into the dining-room and Leach said his next little piece. This was on the subject of fingerprints – a matter of routine – elimination of those of the household in the dead woman's bedroom.

Everyone expressed willingness – almost eagerness – to have their fingerprints taken. They were shepherded into the library for that purpose, where Detective Sergeant Jones was waiting for them with his little roller.

Battle and Leach began on the servants.

Nothing very much was to be got from them. Hurstall explained his system of locking up the house and swore that he had found it untouched in the morning. There were no signs of any entry by an intruder. The front door, he explained, had been left on the latch. That is to say, it was not bolted, but could be opened from outside with a key. It was left like that because Mr Nevile had gone over to Easterhead Bay and would be back late.

'Do you know what time he came in?'

'Yes, sir, I think it was about half-past two. Someone came back with him, I think. I heard voices and then a car drive away and then I heard the door close and Mr Nevile come upstairs.'

'What time did he leave here last night for Easterhead Bay?'

'About twenty past ten. I heard the door close.'

Leach nodded. There did not seem to be much more to be got from Hurstall at the moment. He interviewed the others. They were all disposed to be nervous and frightened, but no more so than was natural under the circumstances.

Leach looked questioningly at his uncle as the door closed behind the slightly hysterical kitchenmaid, who had tailed the procession.

Battle said: 'Have the housemaid back – not the popeyed one – the tall thin bit of vinegar. She knows something.'

Emma Wales was clearly uneasy. It alarmed her that this time it was the big square elderly man who took upon himself the task of questioning her.

'I'm just going to give you a bit of advice, Miss Wales,' he said pleasantly. 'It doesn't do, you know, to hold anything back from the police. Makes them look at you unfavourably, if you understand what I mean –'

Emma Wales protested indignantly but uneasily:

'I'm sure I never –'

'Now, now.' Battle held up a large square hand. 'You saw something or else you heard something – what was it?'

'I didn't exactly hear it – I mean I couldn't help hearing it – Mr Hurstall, he heard it too. And I don't think, not for a moment I don't, that it had anything to do with the murder.'

'Probably not, probably not. Just tell us what it was.'

'Well, I was going up to bed. Just after ten it was – and I'd slipped along first to put Miss Aldin's hot water bottle in her bed. Summer or winter she always has one, and so of course I had to pass right by her ladyship's door.'

'Go on,' said Battle.

'And I heard her and Mr Nevile going at it hammer and tongs. Voices right up. Shouting, he was. Oh, it was a proper quarrel!'

'Remember exactly what was said?'

'Well, I wasn't really listening as you might say.'

'No. But still you must have heard some of the words.'

'Her ladyship was saying as she wouldn't have something or other going on in her house and Mr Nevile was saying, "Don't you dare say anything against her." All worked up he was.'

Battle, with an expressionless face, tried once more, but he could get no more out of her. In the end he dismissed the woman.

He and Jim looked at each other. Leach said, after a minute or two:

'Jones ought to be able to tell us something about those prints by now.'

Battle asked:

'Who's doing the rooms?'

'Williams. He's a good man. He won't miss anything.'

'You're keeping the occupants out of them?'

'Yes, until Williams has finished.'

The door opened at that minute and young Williams put his head in.

'There's something I'd like you to see. In Mr Nevile Strange's room.'

They got up and followed him to the suite on the west side of the house.

Williams pointed to a heap on the floor. A dark blue coat, trousers and waistcoat.

Leach said sharply:

'Where did you find this?'

'Bundled down into the bottom of the wardrobe. Just look at *this*, sir.'

He picked up the coat and showed the edges of the dark blue cuffs.

'See those dark stains? That's blood, sir, or I'm a Dutchman. And see here, it's spattered all up the sleeve.'

'H'm.' Battle avoided the other's eager eyes. 'Looks bad for young Nevile, I must say. Any other suit in the room?'

'Dark grey pinstripe hanging over a chair. Lot of water on the floor here by the wash-basin.'

'Looking as though he washed the blood off himself in the devil of a hurry? Yes. It's near the open window, though, and the rain has come in a good deal.'

'Not enough to make those pools on the floor, sir. They're not dried up yet.'

Battle was silent. A picture was forming itself before his eyes. A man with blood on his hands and sleeves, flinging off his clothes, bundling the blood-stained garments into the cupboard, sluicing water furiously over his hands and bare arms.

He looked across at a door in the other wall.

Williams answered the look.

'Mrs Strange's room, sir. The door is locked.'

'Locked? On this side?'

'No. On the other.'

'On her side, eh?'

Battle was reflective for a minute or two. He said at last:

'Let's see that old butler again.'

Hurstall was nervous. Leach said crisply:

'Why didn't you tell us, Hurstall, that you overheard a quarrel between Mr Strange and Lady Tressilian last night?'

The old man blinked.

'I really didn't think twice about it, sir. I don't imagine it was what you'd call a quarrel – just an amicable difference of opinion.'

Resisting the temptation to say, 'Amicable difference of opinion my foot!' Leach went on:

'What suit was Mr Strange wearing last night at dinner?'

Hurstall hesitated. Battle said quietly:

'Dark blue suit or grey pinstripe? I dare say someone else can tell us if you don't remember.'

Hurstall broke his silence.

'I remember now, sir. It was his dark blue. The family,' he added, anxious not to lose prestige, 'have not been in the habit of changing into evening dress during the summer months. They frequently go out after dinner – sometimes in the garden, sometimes down to the quay.'

Battle nodded. Hurstall left the room. He passed Jones in the doorway. Jones looked excited.

He said:

'It's a cinch, sir. I've got all their prints. There's only one lot fills the bill. Of course I've only been able to make a rough comparison as yet, but I'll bet they're the right ones.'

'Well?' said Battle.

'The prints on that niblick, sir, *were made by Mr Nevile Strange.*'

Battle leaned back in his chair.

'Well,' he said, 'that seems to settle it, doesn't it?'

IV

They were in the Chief Constable's office – three men with grave worried faces.

Major Mitchell said with a sigh:

'Well, I suppose there's nothing to be done but arrest him?'

Leach said quietly:

'Looks like it, sir.'

Mitchell looked across at Superintendent Battle.

'Cheer up, Battle,' he said kindly. 'Your best friend isn't dead.'

Superintendent Battle sighed.

'I don't like it,' he said.

'I don't think any of us like it,' said Mitchell. 'But we've ample evidence, I think, to apply for a warrant.'

'More than ample,' said Battle.

'In fact if we don't apply for one, anybody might ask why the dickens not?'

Battle nodded an unhappy head.

'Let's go over it,' said the Chief Constable. 'You've got motive – Strange and his wife come into a considerable sum of money at the old lady's death. He's the last person known to have seen her alive – he was heard quarrelling with her. The suit he wore that night had blood-stains on it, of course, most damning of all, his fingerprints were found on the actual weapon – *and no one else's.*'

'And yet sir,' said Battle, '*you* don't like it either.'

'I'm damned if I do.'

'What is it exactly you don't like about it, sir?'

Major Mitchell rubbed his nose. 'Makes the fellow out a bit too much of a fool, perhaps?' he suggested.

'And yet, sir, they do behave like fools sometimes.'

'Oh I know – I know. Where would we be if they didn't?'

Battle said to Leach:

'What don't *you* like about it, Jim?'

Leach stirred unhappily.

'I've always liked Mr Strange. Seen him on and off down here for years. He's a nice gentleman – and he's a sportsman.'

'I don't see,' said Battle slowly, 'why a good tennis player shouldn't be a murderer as well. There's nothing against it.' He paused. 'What *I* don't like is the niblick.'

'The niblick?' asked Mitchell, slightly puzzled.

'Yes, sir, or alternatively, the bell. The bell or the niblick – not both.'

He went on in his slow careful voice.

'What do we think actually happened? Did Mr Strange go to her room, have a quarrel, lose his temper, and hit her over the head with a niblick? If so, and it was unpremeditated, how did he happen to have a niblick with him? It's not the sort of thing you carry about with you in the evenings.'

'He might have been practising swings – something like that.'

'He might – but nobody says so. Nobody saw him doing it. The last time anybody saw him with a niblick in his hand was about a week previously when he was practising sand shots down on the sands. As I look at it, you see, you can't have it both ways. Either there was a quarrel and he lost his temper – and, mind you, I've seen him on the courts, and in one of these tournament matches these tennis stars are all het up and a mass of nerves, and if their tempers fray easily it's going to show. I've never seen Mr Strange ruffled. I should say he'd got an excellent control over his temper – better than most – and yet we're suggesting that he goes berserk and hits a frail old lady over the head.'

'There's another alternative, Battle,' said the Chief Constable.

'I know, sir. The theory that it was premeditated. He wanted the old lady's money. That fits in with the bell – which entailed the doping of the maid – but it *doesn't* fit in with the niblick and the quarrel! If he'd made up his mind to do her in, he'd be very careful *not* to quarrel with her. He could dope the maid, creep into her room in the night – crack her over the head and stage a nice little robbery, wiping the niblick and putting it carefully back where it belonged! It's all wrong, sir – it's a mixture of cold premeditation and unpremeditated violence – and the two don't mix!'

'There's something in what you say, Battle – but – what's the alternative?'

'It's the niblick that takes my fancy, sir.'

'Nobody could have hit her over the head with that niblick without disturbing Nevile's prints – that's quite certain.'

'In that case,' said Superintendent Battle, 'she was hit over the head with something else.'

Major Mitchell drew a deep breath.

'That's rather a wild assumption, isn't it?'

'I think it's common sense, sir. Either Strange hit her with that niblick or nobody did. I plump for nobody. In that case that niblick was put there deliberately and blood and hair smeared on it. Dr Lazenby doesn't like the niblick much – had to accept it because it was the obvious thing and because he couldn't say definitely that it *hadn't* been used.'

Major Mitchell leaned back in his chair.

'Go on, Battle,' he said. 'I'm giving you a free hand. What's the next step?'

'Take away the niblick,' said Battle, 'and what is left? First, motive. Had Nevile Strange really got a motive for doing away with Lady Tressilian? He inherited money – a lot depends to my mind on whether he needed that money. He says not. I suggest we verify that. Find out the state of his finances. If he's in a hole financially, and needs money, then the case against him is very much strengthened. If, on the other hand, he was speaking the truth and his finances are in a good state, why then –'

'Well, what then?'

'Why then, we might have a look at the motives of the *other* people in the house.'

'You think, then, that Nevile Strange was framed?'

Superintendent Battle screwed up his eyes.

'There's a phrase I read somewhere that tickled my fancy. Something about a fine Italian hand. That's what I seem to see in this business. Ostensibly it's a blunt brutal straightforward crime, but it seems to me I catch glimpses of something else – of a fine Italian hand at work behind the scenes . . .'

There was a long pause while the Chief Constable looked at Battle. 'You may be right,' he said at last. 'Dash it all, there's *something* funny about this business. What's your idea, now, of our plan of campaign?'

Battle stroked his square jaw.

'Well, sir,' he said. 'I'm always in favour of going about things the obvious way. Everything's been set to make us suspicious of Mr Nevile Strange. Let's go on being suspicious of him. Needn't go so far as actually to arrest him, but hint at it, question him, put the wind up him – and observe everybody's reaction generally. Verify his statements, go over his movements that night with a toothcomb. In fact, show our hand as plainly as may be.'

'Quite Machiavellian,' said Major Mitchell with a twinkle. 'Imitation of a heavy-handed policeman by star actor Battle.'

The Superintendent smiled.

'I always like doing what's expected of me, sir. This time I mean to be a bit slow about it – take my time. I want to do some nosing about. Being suspicious of Mr Nevile Strange is a very good excuse for nosing about. I've an idea, you know, that something rather odd has been going on in that house.'

'Looking for the sex angle?'

'If you like to put it that way, sir.'

'Handle it your own way, Battle. You and Leach carry on between you.'

'Thank you, sir.' Battle stood up. 'Nothing suggestive from the solicitors?'

'No, I rang them up. I know Trelawny fairly well. He's sending me a copy of Sir Matthew's will and also of Lady Tressilian's. She had about five hundred a year of her own – invested in gilt-edged securities. She left a legacy to Barrett and a small one to Hurstall, the rest to Mary Aldin.'

'That's three we might keep an eye on,' said Battle.

Mitchell looked amused.

'Suspicious fellow, aren't you?'

'No use letting oneself be hypnotized by fifty thousand pounds,' said Battle stolidly. 'Many a murder has been done for less than fifty pounds. It depends on how much you want the money. Barrett got a legacy – and maybe she took the precaution to dope herself so as to avert suspicion.'

'She very nearly passed out. Lazenby hasn't let us question her yet.'

'Overdid it out of ignorance, perhaps. Then Hurstall may have been in bad need of cash for all we know. And Miss Aldin, if she's no money of her own, might have fancied a bit of life on a nice little income before she's too old to enjoy it.'

The Chief Constable looked doubtful.

'Well,' he said, 'it's up to you two. Get on with the job.'

V

Back at Gull's Point, the two police officers received Williams' and Jones' reports.

Nothing of a suspicious nature had been found in any of the bedrooms. The servants were clamouring to be allowed to get on with the housework. Should he give them the word?

'Might as well, I suppose,' said Battle. 'I'll just have a stroll myself first through the two upper floors. Rooms that haven't been done very often tell you something about their occupants that's useful to know.'

Sergeant Jones put down a small cardboard box on the table.

'From Mr Nevile Strange's dark blue coat,' he announced. 'The red hairs were on the cuff, blonde hairs on the inside of the collar and the right shoulder.'

Battle took out the two long red hairs and the half-dozen blonde ones and looked at them. He said, with a faint twinkle in his eye:

'Convenient. One blonde, one red head and one brunette in this house. So we know where we are at once. Red hair on the cuff, blonde on the collar? Mr Nevile Strange does seem to be a bit of a Bluebeard. His arm round one wife and the other one's head on his shoulder.'

'The blood on the sleeve has gone for analysis, sir. They'll ring us up as soon as they get the result.'

Leach nodded.

'What about the servants?'

'I followed your instructions, sir. None of them is under notice to leave, or seems likely to have borne a grudge against the old lady. She was strict, but well liked. In any case the management of the servants lay with Miss Aldin. She seems to have been popular with them.'

'Thought she was an efficient woman the moment I laid eyes on her,' said Battle. 'If she's our murderess, she won't be easy to hang.'

Jones looked startled.

'But those prints on that niblick, sir, were –'

'I know – I know,' said Battle. 'The singularly obliging Mr Strange's. There's a general belief that athletes aren't overburdened with brains (not at all true, by the way) but I can't believe

Nevile Strange is a complete moron. What about those senna pods of the maid's?'

'They were always on the shelf in the servants' bathroom on the second floor. She used to put 'em in to soak midday, and they stood there until the evening when she went to bed.'

'So that absolutely anybody could get at them! Anybody inside the house, that is to say.'

Leach said with conviction:

'It's an inside job all right!'

'Yes, I think so. Not that this is one of those closed circle crimes. It isn't. Anyone who had a key could have opened the front door and walked in. Nevile Strange had that key last night – but it would probably be a simple matter to have got one cut, or an old hand could do it with a bit of wire. But I don't see any outsider knowing about the bell and that Barrett took senna at night! That's local inside knowledge!

'Come along, Jim, my boy. Let's go up and see this bathroom and all the rest of it.'

They started on the top floor. First came a boxroom full of old broken furniture and junk of all kinds.

'I haven't looked through this, sir,' said Jones. 'I didn't know –'

'What you were looking for? Quite right. Only waste of time. From the dust on the floor nobody has been in here for at least six months.'

The servants' rooms were all on this floor, also two unoccupied bedrooms with a bathroom, and Battle looked into each room and gave it a cursory glance, noticing that Alice, the popeyed housemaid, slept with her window shut; that Emma, the thin one, had a great many relations, photographs of whom were crowded on her chest of drawers; and that Hurstall had one or two pieces of good, though cracked, Dresden and Crown Derby porcelain.

The cook's room was severely neat and the kitchen-maid's chaotically untidy. Battle passed on into the bathroom which was the room nearest to the head of the stairs. Williams pointed out the long shelf over the wash-basin, on which stood tooth glasses and brushes, various unguents and bottles of salts and hair lotion. A packet of senna pods stood open at one end.

'No prints on the glass or packet?'

'Only the maid's own. I got hers from her room.'

'He didn't need to handle the glass,' said Leach. 'He'd only have to drop the stuff in.'

Battle went down the stairs followed by Leach. Half-way down this top flight was a rather awkwardly placed window. A pole with a hook on the end stood in a corner.

'You draw down the top sash with that,' explained Leach. 'But there's a burglar screw. The window can be drawn down, only so far. Too narrow for anyone to get in that way.'

'I wasn't thinking of anyone getting in,' said Battle. His eyes were thoughtful.

He went in the first bedroom on the next floor, which was Audrey Strange's. It was neat and fresh, ivory brushes on the dressing table – no clothes lying about. Battle looked into the wardrobe. Two plain coats and skirts, a couple of evening dresses, one or two summer frocks. The dresses were cheap, the tailormades well cut and expensive, but not new.

Battle nodded. He stood at the writing table a minute or two, fiddling with the pen tray on the left of the blotter.

Williams said: 'Nothing of any interest on the blotting paper or in the waste paper basket.'

'Your word's good enough,' said Battle. 'Nothing to be seen here.'

They went on to the other rooms.

Thomas Royde's was untidy, with clothes lying about. Pipes and pipe ash on the tables and beside the bed, where a copy of Kipling's *Kim* lay half open.

'Used to native servants clearing up after him,' said Battle. 'Likes reading old favourites. Conservative type.'

Mary Aldin's room was small but comfortable. Battle looked at the travel books on the shelves and the old-fashioned dented silver brushes. The furnishings and colouring in the room were more modern than the rest of the house.

'She's not so conservative,' said Battle. 'No photographs either. Not one who lives in the past.'

There were three or four empty rooms, all well kept and dusted ready for occupation, and a couple of bathrooms. Then came Lady Tressilian's big double-room. After that, reached by going down three little steps, came the two rooms and bathroom occupied by the Stranges.

Battle did not waste much time in Nevile's room. He glanced out of the open casement window below which the rocks fell sheer to the sea. The view was to the west, towards Stark Head, which rose wild and forbidding out of the water.

'Gets the afternoon sun,' he murmured. 'But rather a grim morning outlook. Nasty smell of seaweed at low tide, too. And that headland has got a grim look. Don't wonder it attracts suicides!'

He passed into the larger room, the door of which had been unlocked.

Here everything was in wild confusion. Clothes lay about in heaps – filmy underwear, stockings, jumpers tried on and discarded – a patterned summer frock thrown sprawling over the back of a chair. Battle looked inside the wardrobe. It was full of furs, evening dresses, shorts, tennis frocks, playsuits.

Battle shut the doors again almost reverently.

'Expensive tastes,' he remarked. 'She must cost her husband a lot of money.'

Leach said darkly:

'Perhaps that's why –'

He left the sentence unfinished.

'Why he needed a hundred – or rather fifty thousand pounds? Maybe. We'd better see, I think, what he has to say about it.'

They went down to the library. Williams was despatched to tell the servants they could get on with the housework. The family were free to return to their rooms if they wished. They were to be informed of that fact and also that Inspector Leach would like an interview with each of them separately, starting with Mr Nevile Strange.

When Williams had gone out of the room, Battle and Leach established themselves behind a massive Victorian table. A young policeman with notebook sat in the corner of the room, his pencil poised.

Battle said:

'You carry on for a start, Jim. Make it impressive.' As the other nodded his head, Battle rubbed his chin and frowned.

'I wish I knew what keeps putting Hercule Poirot into my head.'

'You mean that old chap – the Belgian – comic little guy?'

'Comic my foot,' said Superintendent Battle. 'About as dangerous as a black mamba and a she-leopard – that's what *he* is when he starts making a mountebank of himself! I wish he was here – this sort of thing would be right up his street.'

'In what way?'

'Psychology,' said Battle. 'Real psychology – not the half-baked stuff people hand out who know nothing about it.' His memory dwelt resentfully on Miss Amphrey and his daughter Sylvia. 'No – the real genuine article – knowing just what makes the wheels go round. Keep a murderer talking – that's one of his lines. Says everyone is bound to speak what's true sooner or later – because in the end it's easier than telling lies. And so they make some little slip they don't think matters – and that's when you get them.'

'So you're going to give Nevile Strange plenty of rope?'

Battle gave an absent-minded assent. Then he added, in some annoyance and perplexity:

'But what's really worrying me is – what put Hercule Poirot into my head? Upstairs – that's where it was. Now what did I see that reminded me of that little guy?'

The conversation was put to an end by the arrival of Nevile Strange.

He looked pale and worried, but much less nervous than he had done at the breakfast table. Battle eyed him keenly. Incredible that a man who knew – and he must know if he were capable of any thought processes at all – that he had left his fingerprints on the instrument of the crime – and who had since had his fingerprints taken by the police – should show neither intense nervousness nor elaborate brazening of it out.

Nevile Strange looked quite natural – shocked, worried, grieved – and just slightly and healthily nervous.

Jim Leach was speaking in his pleasant west country voice.

'We would like you to answer certain questions, Mr Strange. Both as to your movements last night, and in reference to particular facts. At the same time I must caution you that you are not bound to answer these questions unless you like and that if you prefer to do so you may have your solicitor present.'

He leaned back to observe the effect of this.

Nevile Strange looked, quite plainly, bewildered.

'He hasn't the least idea what we're getting at, or else he's a damned good actor,' Leach thought to himself. Aloud he said, as Nevile did not answer, 'Well, Mr Strange?'

Nevile said: 'Of course, ask me anything you like.'

'You realize,' said Battle pleasantly, 'that anything you say will be taken down in writing and may subsequently be used in a court of law in evidence.'

A flash of temper showed on Strange's face. He said sharply: 'Are you threatening me?'

'No, no, Mr Strange. Warning you.'

Nevile shrugged his shoulders.

'I suppose all this is part of your routine. Go ahead.'

'You are ready to make a statement?'

'If that's what you call it.'

'Then will you tell us exactly what you did last night? From dinner onwards, shall we say?'

'Certainly. After dinner we went into the drawing-room. We had coffee. We listened to the wireless – the news and so on. Then I decided to go across to Easterhead Bay Hotel and look up a chap who is staying there – a friend of mine.'

'That friend's name is?'

'Latimer. Edward Latimer.'

'An intimate friend?'

'Oh, so-so. We've seen a good deal of him since he's been down here. He's been over to lunch and dinner and we've been over there.'

Battle said:

'Rather late, wasn't it, to go off to Easterhead Bay?'

'Oh, it's a gay spot – they keep it up till all hours.'

'But this is rather an early-to-bed household, isn't it?'

'Yes, on the whole. However, I took the latchkey with me. Nobody had to sit up.'

'Your wife didn't think of going with you?'

There was a slight change, a stiffening in Nevile's tone as he said:

'No, she had a headache. She'd already gone up to bed.'

'Please go on, Mr Strange.'

'I was just going up to change –'

Leach interrupted.

'Excuse me, Mr Strange. Change into what? Into evening dress, or out of evening dress?'

'Neither. I was wearing a blue suit – my best, as it happened, and as it was raining a bit and I proposed to take the ferry and walk the other side – it's about half a mile, as you know – I changed into an older suit – a grey pinstripe, if you want me to go into every detail.'

'We do like to get things clear,' said Leach humbly. 'Please go on.'

'I was going upstairs, as I say, when Barrett came and told me Lady Tressilian wanted to see me, so I went along and had a jaw with her for a bit.'

Battle said gently:

'You were the last person to see her alive, I think, Mr Strange?'

Nevile flushed.

'Yes – yes – I suppose I was. She was quite all right then.'

'How long were you with her?'

'About twenty minutes to half an hour, I should think, then I went to my room, changed my suit and hurried off. I took the latchkey with me.'

'What time was that?'

'About half-past ten, I should think. I hurried down the hill, just caught the ferry starting and went across to the Easterhead side. I found Latimer at the Hotel, we had a drink or two and a game of billiards. The time passed so quickly that I found I'd lost the last ferry back. It goes at one-thirty. So Latimer very decently got out his car and drove me back. That, as you know, means going all the way round by Saltington – sixteen miles. We left the Hotel at two o'clock and got back here somewhere around half-past, I should say. I thanked Ted Latimer, asked him in for a drink, but he said he'd rather get straight back, so I let myself in and went straight up to bed. I didn't see or hear anything amiss. The house seemed all asleep and peaceful. Then this morning I heard that girl screaming and –'

Leach stopped him.

'Quite, quite. Now to go back a little – to your conversation with Lady Tressilian – she was quite normal in her manner?'

'Oh, absolutely.'

'What did you talk about?'

'Oh, one thing and another.'

'Amicably?'

Nevile flushed.

'Certainly.'

'You didn't, for instance,' went on Leach smoothly, 'have a violent quarrel?'

Nevile did not answer at once. Leach said:

'You had better tell the truth, you know. I'll tell you frankly some of your conversation was overheard.'

Nevile said shortly:

'We had a bit of a disagreement. It was nothing.'

'What was the subject of the disagreement?'

With an effort Nevile recovered his temper. He smiled. 'Frankly,' he said, 'she ticked me off. That often happened. If she disapproved of anyone she let them have it straight from the shoulder. She was old-fashioned, you see, and she was inclined to be down on modern ways and modern lines of thought – divorce – all that. We had an argument and I may have got a bit heated, but we parted on perfectly friendly terms – agreeing to differ.' He added, with some heat, 'I certainly didn't bash her over the head because I lost my temper over an argument – if that's what you think!'

Leach glanced at Battle. Battle leaned forward ponderously across the table. He said:

'You recognized that niblick as your property this morning. Have you any explanation for the fact that your fingerprints were found upon it?'

Nevile stared. He said sharply:

'I – but of course they would be – it's my club – I've often handled it.'

'Any explanation, I mean, for the fact that your fingerprints show that *you were the last person to have handled it*?'

Nevile sat quite still. The colour had gone out of his face.

'That's not true,' he said at last. 'It can't be. Somebody could have handled it after me – someone wearing gloves.'

'No, Mr Strange – nobody could have handled it *in the sense you mean* – by raising it to strike – without blurring your own marks.'

There was a pause – a very long pause.

'Oh, God,' said Nevile convulsively, and gave a long shudder.

He put his hands over his eyes. The two policemen watched him.

Then he took away his hands. He sat up straight.

'It isn't true,' he said quietly. 'It simply isn't true. You think I killed her, but I didn't. I swear I didn't. There's some horrible mistake.'

'You've no explanation to offer about these fingerprints?'

'How can I have? I'm dumbfounded.'

'Have you any explanation for the fact that the sleeves and cuffs of your dark blue suit are stained with blood?'

'Blood?' It was a horror-struck whisper. 'It couldn't be!'

'You didn't, for instance, cut yourself –'

'No. No, of course I didn't!'

They waited a little while.

Nevile Strange, his forehead creased, seemed to be thinking. He looked up at them at last with frightened horror-stricken eyes.

'It's fantastic!' he said. 'Simply fantastic. It's none of it *true*.'

'Facts are true enough,' said Superintendent Battle.

'But why should I do such a thing? It's unthinkable – unbelievable! I've known Camilla all my life.'

Leach coughed.

'I believe you told us yourself, Mr Strange, that you come into a good deal of money upon Lady Tressilian's death?'

'You think that's why – But I don't want money! I don't *need* it!'

'That,' said Leach, with his little cough, 'is what you *say*, Mr Strange.'

Nevile sprang up.

'Look here, that's something I *can* prove. That I didn't need money. Let me ring up my bank manager – you can talk to him yourself.'

The call was put through. The line was clear and in a very few minutes they were through to London. Nevile spoke:

'That you, Ronaldson? Nevile Strange speaking. You know my voice. Look here, will you give the police – they're here now – all the information they want about my affairs – yes – yes, please.'

Leach took the phone. He spoke quietly. It went on, question and answer.

He replaced the phone at last.

'Well?' said Nevile eagerly.

Leach said impassively:

'You have a substantial credit balance, and the Bank have charge of all your investments and report them to be in a favourable condition.'

'So you see it's true what I said!'

'It seems so – but again, Mr Strange, you may have commitments, debts – payment of blackmail – reasons for requiring money of which we do not know.'

'But I haven't! I assure you I haven't. You won't find anything of that kind.'

Superintendent Battle shifted his heavy shoulders. He spoke in a kind, fatherly voice.

'We've sufficient evidence, as I'm sure you'll agree, Mr Strange, to ask for a warrant for your arrest. We haven't done so – *as yet.* We're giving you the benefit of the doubt, you see.'

Nevile said bitterly: 'You mean, don't you, that you've made up your minds I did it, but you want to get at the motive so as to clinch the case against me?'

Battle was silent. Leach looked at the ceiling.

Nevile said desperately:

'It's like some awful dream. There's nothing I can say or do. It's like – like being in a trap and you can't get out.'

Superintendent Battle stirred. An intelligent gleam showed between his half-closed lids.

'That's very nicely put,' he said. 'Very nicely put indeed. It gives me an idea . . .'

VI

Sergeant Jones adroitly got rid of Nevile through the hall and then brought Kay in by the french window so that husband and wife did not meet.

'He'll see all the others, though,' Leach remarked.

'All the better,' said Battle. 'It's only this one I want to deal with whilst she's still in the dark.'

The day was overcast with a sharp wind. Kay was dressed in a tweed skirt and a purple sweater, above which her hair looked like a burnished copper bowl. She looked half frightened, half excited. Her beauty and vitality bloomed against the dark Victorian background of books and saddle-back chairs.

Leach led her easily enough over her account of the previous evening.

She had had a headache and gone to bed early – about quarter-past nine, she thought. She had slept heavily and heard nothing until the next morning, when she was wakened by hearing someone screaming.

Battle took up the questioning.

'Your husband didn't come in to see how you were before he went off for the evening?'

'No.'

'You didn't see him from the time you left the drawing-room until the following morning. Is that right?'

Kay nodded.

Battle stroked his jaw.

'Mrs Strange, the door between your room and that of your husband was locked. Who locked it?'

Kay said shortly: 'I did.'

Battle said nothing – but he waited – waited like an elderly fatherly cat – for a mouse to come out of the hole he was watching.

His silence did what questions might not have accomplished. Kay burst out impetuously:

'Oh, I suppose you've got to have it all! That old doddering Hurstall must have heard us before tea and he'll tell you if I don't. He's probably told you already. Nevile and I had had a row – a flaming row! I was furious with him! I went up to bed and locked the door, because I was still in a flaming rage with him!'

'I see – I see,' said Battle, at his most sympathetic. 'And what was the trouble all about?'

'Does it matter? Oh, I don't mind telling you. Nevile has been behaving like a perfect idiot. It's all that woman's fault, though.'

'What woman?'

'His first wife. She got him to come here in the first place.'

'You mean – to meet you?'

'Yes. Nevile thinks it was all his own idea – poor innocent! But it wasn't. He never thought of such a thing until he met her in the Park one day and she got the idea into his head and made him believe he'd thought of it himself. He quite honestly thinks it was his idea, but I've seen Audrey's fine Italian hand behind it from the first.'

'Why should she do such a thing?' asked Battle.

'Because she wanted to get hold of him again,' said Kay. She spoke quickly and her breath came fast. 'She's never forgiven him for going off with me. This is her revenge. She got him to fix up that we'd all be here together and then she got to work on him. She's been doing it ever since we arrived. She's clever, you know. Knows just how to look pathetic and elusive – yes, and how to play up another man, too. She got Thomas Royde, a faithful old dog who's always adored her, to be here at the same time, and she drove Nevile mad by pretending she was going to marry him.'

She stopped, breathing angrily.

Battle said mildly:

'I should have thought he'd be glad for her to – er – find happiness with an old friend.'

'Glad? He's as jealous as Hell!'

'Then he must be very fond of her.'

'Oh, he is,' said Kay bitterly. '*She's* seen to that!'

Battle's finger still ran dubiously over his jaw.

'You might have objected to this arrangement of coming here,' he suggested.

'How could I? It would have looked as though I were jealous!'

'Well,' said Battle, 'after all, you were, weren't you?'

Kay flushed.

'Always! I've always been jealous of Audrey. Right from the beginning – or nearly the beginning. I used to feel her there in the house. It was as though it were *her* house, not mine. I changed the colour scheme and did it all up but it was no good! I'd feel her there like a grey ghost creeping about. I knew Nevile worried because he thought he'd treated her badly. He couldn't quite forget about her – she was always there – a reproachful feeling at the back of his mind. There are people, you know, who are like that. They seem rather colourless and not very interesting – but they make themselves *felt*.'

Battle nodded thoughtfully. He said:

'Well, thank you, Mrs Strange. That's all at present. We have to ask – er – a good many questions – especially with your husband inheriting so much money from Lady Tressilian – fifty thousand pounds –'

'Is it as much as that? We get it from old Sir Matthew's will, don't we?'

'You know all about it?'

'Oh yes. He left it to be divided between Nevile and Nevile's wife after Lady Tressilian's death. Not that I'm glad the old thing is dead. I'm not. I didn't like her very much – probably because she didn't like me – but it's too horrible to think of some burglar coming along and cracking her head open.'

She went out on that. Battle looked at Leach.

'What do you think of her? Good-looking bit of goods, I will say. A man could lose his head over her easy enough.'

Leach agreed.

'Doesn't seem to me quite a lady, though,' he said dubiously.

'They aren't nowadays,' said Battle. 'Shall we see No. 1? No, I think we'll have Miss Aldin next, and get an outside angle on this matrimonial business.'

Mary Aldin came in composedly and sat down. Beneath her outward calmness her eyes looked worried.

She answered Leach's questions clearly enough, confirming Nevile's account of the evening. She had come up to bed about ten o'clock.

'Mr Strange was then with Lady Tressilian?'

'Yes, I could hear them talking.'

'Talking, Miss Aldin, or quarrelling?'

She flushed but answered quietly:

'Lady Tressilian, you know, was fond of discussion. She often sounded acrimonious when she was really nothing of the kind. Also, she was inclined to be autocratic and to domineer over people – and a man doesn't take that kind of thing as easily as a woman does.'

'As you do, perhaps,' thought Battle.

He looked at her intelligent face. It was she who broke the silence.

'I don't want to be stupid – but it really seems to me incredible

– quite incredible, that you should suspect one of the people in this house. Why shouldn't it be an outsider?'

'For several reasons, Miss Aldin. For one thing, nothing was taken and no entry was forced. I needn't remind you of the geography of your own house and grounds, but just bear this in mind. On the west is a sheer cliff down to the sea, to the south are a couple of terraces with a wall and a drop to the sea, on the east the garden slopes down almost to the shore, but it is surrounded by a high wall. The only ways out are a small door leading through on to the road which was found bolted inside as usual this morning and the main door to the house, which is set on the road. I'm not saying no one could climb that wall, nor that they could not have got in by using a spare key to the front door or even a skeleton key – but I'm saying that as far as I can see no one did anything of the sort. Whoever committed this crime knew that Barrett took senna pod decoction every night, and doped it – that means someone in the house. The niblick was taken from the cupboard under the stairs. *It wasn't an outsider, Miss Aldin.*'

'It wasn't Nevile! I'm sure it wasn't Nevile!'

'Why are you so sure?'

She raised her hands hopelessly.

'It just isn't like him – that's why! He wouldn't kill a defenceless old woman in bed – *Nevile!*'

'It doesn't seem very likely,' said Battle reasonably, 'but you'd be surprised at the things people do when they've got a good enough reason. Mr Strange may have wanted money very badly.'

'I'm sure he didn't. He's not an extravagant person – he never has been.'

'No, but his wife is.'

'Kay? Yes, perhaps – but oh, it's too ridiculous. I'm sure the last thing Nevile has been thinking of lately is money.'

Superintendent Battle coughed.

'He's had other worries, I understand?'

'Kay told you, I suppose? Yes, it really has been rather difficult. Still, it's nothing to do with this dreadful business.'

'Probably not, but all the same I'd like to hear your version of the affair, Miss Aldin.'

Mary said slowly: 'Well, as I say, it has created a difficult – situation. Whosoever's idea it was to begin with –'

He interrupted her deftly.

'I understood it was Mr Nevile Strange's idea?'

'He said it was.'

'But you yourself didn't think so?'

'I – no – it isn't like Nevile somehow. I've had a feeling all along that somebody else put the idea into his head.'

'Mrs Audrey Strange, perhaps?'

'It seems incredible that Audrey should do such a thing.'

'Then who else could it have been?'

Mary raised her shoulders helplessly.

'I don't know. It's just – queer.'

'Queer,' said Battle thoughtfully. 'That's what I feel about this case. It's queer.'

'Everything's been queer. There's been a feeling – I can't describe it. Something in the air. A *menace*.'

'Everybody strung up and on edge?'

'Yes, just that . . . We've all suffered from it. Even Mr Latimer –'

She stopped.

'I was just coming to Mr Latimer. What can you tell me, Miss Aldin, about Mr Latimer? Who is Mr Latimer?'

'Well, really, I don't know much about him. He's a friend of Kay's.'

'He's Mrs Strange's friend. Known each other a long time?'

'Yes, she knew him before her marriage.'

'Mr Strange like him?'

'Quite well, I believe.'

'No – trouble there?'

Battle put it delicately. Mary replied at once and emphatically: 'Certainly not!'

'Did Lady Tressilian like Mr Latimer?'

'Not very much.'

Battle took warning from the aloof tone of her voice and changed the subject.

'This maid, now, Jane Barrett, she has been with Lady Tressilian a long time? You consider her trustworthy?'

'Oh absolutely. She was devoted to Lady Tressilian.'

Battle leaned back in his chair.

'In fact you wouldn't consider for a moment the possibility that Barrett hit Lady Tressilian over the head and then doped herself to avoid being suspected?'

'Of course not. Why on earth should she?'

'She gets a legacy, you know.'

'So do I,' said Mary Aldin.

She looked at him steadily.

'Yes,' said Battle. 'So do you. Do you know how much?'

'Mr Trelawny has just arrived. He told me.'

'You didn't know about it beforehand?'

'No. I certainly assumed, from what Lady Tressilian occasionally let fall, that she had left me something. I have very little of my own, you know. Not enough to live on without getting work of some kind. I thought that Lady Tressilian would leave me at least a hundred a year – but she has some cousins, and I did not at all know how she proposed to leave that money which was hers to dispose of. I knew, of course, that Sir Matthew's estate went to Nevile and Audrey.'

'So she didn't know what Lady Tressilian was leaving her,' Leach said when Mary Aldin had been dismissed. 'At least that's what she *says*.'

'That's what she says,' agreed Battle. 'And now for Bluebeard's first wife.'

VII

Audrey was wearing a pale grey flannel coat and skirt. In it she looked so pale and ghostlike that Battle was reminded of Kay's words, 'a grey ghost creeping about the house'.

She answered his questions simply and without any signs of emotion.

Yes, she had gone to bed at ten o'clock, the same time as Miss Aldin. She had heard nothing during the night.

'You'll excuse me butting into your private affairs,' said Battle, 'but will you explain just how it comes about that you are here in the house?'

'I always come to stay at this time. This year, my – my late husband wanted to come at the same time and asked me if I would mind.'

'It was his suggestion?'

'Oh yes.'

'Not yours?'

'Oh no.'

'But you agreed?'

'Yes, I agreed . . . I didn't feel – that I could very well refuse.'

'Why not, Mrs Strange?'

But she was vague.

'One doesn't like to be disobliging.'

'You were the injured party?'

'I beg your pardon?'

'It was you who divorced your husband?'

'Yes.'

'Do you – excuse me – feel any rancour against him?'

'No – not at all.'

'You have a very forgiving nature, Mrs Strange.'

She did not answer. He tried silence – but Audrey was not Kay, to be thus goaded into speech. She could remain silent without any hint of uneasiness. Battle acknowledged himself beaten.

'You are sure it was not your idea – this meeting?'

'Quite sure.'

'You are on friendly terms with the present Mrs Strange?'

'I don't think she likes me very much.'

'Do you like her?'

'Yes. I think she is very beautiful.'

'Well – thank you – I think that is all.'

She got up and walked towards the door. Then she hesitated and came back.

'I would just like to say –' she spoke nervously and quickly. 'You think Nevile did this – that he killed her because of the money. I'm quite sure that isn't so. Nevile has never cared much about money. I do know that. I was married to him for eight years, you know. I just can't see him killing anyone like that for money – it – it – isn't Nevile. I know my saying so isn't of any value as evidence – but I do wish you could believe it.'

She turned and hurried out of the room.

'And what do you make of *her*?' asked Leach. 'I've never seen anyone so – so devoid of emotion.'

'She didn't show any,' said Battle. 'But it's there. Some very strong emotion. And I don't know what it is . . .'

VIII

Thomas Royde came last. He sat, solemn and stiff, blinking a little like an owl.

He was home from Malaya – first time for eight years. Had been in the habit of staying at Gull's Point ever since he was a boy. Mrs Audrey Strange was a distant cousin – and had been brought up by his family from the age of nine. On the preceding night he had gone to bed just before eleven. Yes, he had heard Mr Nevile Strange leave the house but had not seen him. Nevile had left at about twenty past ten or perhaps a little later. He himself had heard nothing during the night. He was up and in the garden when the discovery of Lady Tressilian's body had been made. He was an early riser.

There was a pause.

'Miss Aldin has told us that there was a state of tension in the house. Did you notice this too?'

'I don't think so. Don't notice things much.'

'That's a lie,' thought Battle to himself. 'You notice a good deal, I should say – more than most.'

No, he didn't think Nevile Strange had been short of money in any way. He certainly had not seemed so. But he knew very little about Mr Strange's affairs.

'How well did you know the second Mrs Strange?'

'I met her here for the first time.'

Battle played his last card.

'You may know, Mr Royde, that we've found Mr Nevile Strange's fingerprints on the weapon. And we've found blood on the sleeve of the coat he wore last night.'

He paused. Royde nodded.

'He was telling us,' he muttered.

'I'm asking you frankly: *Do you think he did it?*'

Thomas Royde never liked to be hurried. He waited for a minute – which is a very long time – before he answered:

'Don't see why you ask *me*! Not my business. It's yours. Should say myself – very unlikely.'

'Can you think of anyone who seems to you more likely?'

Thomas shook his head.

'Only person I think likely, can't possibly have done it. So that's that.'

'And who is that?'

But Royde shook his head more decidedly.

'Couldn't possibly say. Only my private opinion.'

'It's your duty to assist the police.'

'Tell you any facts. This isn't facts. Just an idea. And it's impossible, anyway.'

'We didn't get much out of him,' said Leach when Royde had gone.

Battle agreed.

'No, we didn't. He's got something in his mind – something quite definite. I'd like to know what it is. This is a very peculiar sort of crime, Jim, my boy –'

The telephone rang before Leach could answer. He took up the receiver and spoke. After a minute or two of listening he said 'Good,' and slammed it down.

'Blood on the coat sleeve is human,' he announced. 'Same blood group as Lady T's. Looks as though Nevile Strange is for it –'

Battle had walked over to the window and was looking out with considerable interest.

'A beautiful young man out there,' he remarked. 'Quite beautiful and a definite wrong 'un, I should say. It's a pity Mr Latimer – for I feel that that's Mr Latimer – was over at Easterhead Bay last night. He's the type that would smash in his own grandmother's head if he thought he could get away with it and if he knew he'd make something out of it.'

'Well, there wasn't anything in it for him,' said Leach. 'Lady T's death doesn't benefit him in any way whatever.' The telephone bell rang again. 'Damn this phone, what's the matter now?'

He went to it.

'Hullo. Oh, it's you, doctor. What? Come round, has she? What? *What?*'

He turned his head. 'Uncle, just come and listen to this.'

Battle came over and took the phone. He listened, his face as usual showing no expression. He said to Leach:

'Get Nevile Strange, Jim.'

When Nevile came in, Battle was just replacing the phone on its hook.

Nevile, looking white and spent, stared curiously at the Scotland Yard superintendent, trying to read the emotion behind the wooden mask.

'Mr Strange,' said Battle. 'Do you know anyone who dislikes you very much?'

Nevile stared and shook his head.

'Sure?' Battle was impressive. 'I mean, sir, someone who does more than dislike you – someone who – frankly – hates your guts?'

Nevile sat bolt upright.

'No. No, certainly not. Nothing of the kind.'

'Think, Mr Strange. Is there no one you've injured in any way –?'

Nevile flushed.

'There's only one person I can be said to have injured and she's not the kind who bears rancour. That's my first wife, when I left her for another woman. But I can assure you that she doesn't hate me. She's – she's been an angel.'

The Superintendent leaned forward across the table.

'Let me tell you, Mr Strange; you're a very lucky man. I don't say I liked the case against you – I didn't. But it *was* a case! It would have stood up all right, and unless the jury happened to have liked your personality, *it would have hanged you*.'

'You speak,' said Nevile, 'as though all that were past?'

'It is past,' said Battle. 'You've been saved, Mr Strange, by pure chance.'

Nevile still looked inquiringly at him.

'After you left her last night,' said Battle, 'Lady Tressilian rang the bell for her maid.'

He watched whilst Nevile took it in.

'*After*. Then Barrett saw her –?'

'Yes. *Alive and well*. Barrett also saw you leave the house before she went in to her mistress.'

Nevile said:

'But the niblick – my fingerprints –'

'She wasn't hit with that niblick. Dr Lazenby didn't like it at the time. I saw that. She was killed with something else. That niblick was put there deliberately to throw suspicion on *you*. It may be by someone who overheard the quarrel and so selected you as a suitable victim, or it may be because –'

He paused, and then repeated his question:

'Who is there in this house that hates you, Mr Strange?'

IX

'I've got a question for you, doctor,' said Battle.

They were in the doctor's house after returning from the nursing home, where they had had a short interview with Jane Barrett.

Barrett was weak and exhausted but quite clear in her statement.

She had just been getting into bed after drinking her senna when Lady Tressilian's bell had rung. She had glanced at the clock and seen the time – twenty-five minutes past ten.

She had put on her dressing-gown and come down. She had heard a noise in the hall below and had looked over the banisters.

'It was Mr Nevile just going out. He was taking his raincoat down from the hook.'

'What suit was he wearing?'

'His grey pinstripe. His face was very worried and unhappy-looking. He shoved his arms into his coat as though he didn't care how he put it on. Then he went out and banged the front door behind him. I went on in to her ladyship. She was very drowsy, poor dear, and couldn't remember why she had rung for me – she couldn't always, poor lady. But I beat up her pillows and brought her a fresh glass of water and settled her comfortably.'

'She didn't seem upset or afraid of anything?'

'Just tired, that's all. I was tired myself. Yawning. I went up and went right off to sleep.'

That was Barrett's story, and it seemed impossible to doubt her genuine grief and horror at the news of her mistress's death.

They went back to Lazenby's house and it was then that Battle announced that he had a question to ask.

'Ask away,' said Lazenby.

'What time do you think Lady Tressilian died?'

'I've told you. Between ten o'clock and midnight.'

'I know that's what you said. But it wasn't my question. I asked you what you, personally, *thought*.'

'Off the record, eh?'

'Yes.'

'All right. My guess would be in the neighbourhood of eleven o'clock.'

'That's what I wanted you to say,' said Battle.

'Glad to oblige. Why?'

'Never did like the idea of her being killed before ten-twenty. Take Barrett's sleeping draught – it wouldn't have got to work by then. That sleeping draught shows that the murder was meant to be committed a good deal later – during the night. I prefer midnight, myself.'

'Could be. Eleven is only a guess.'

'But it definitely couldn't be later than midnight?'

'No.'

'It couldn't be after two-thirty?'

'Good heavens, no.'

'Well, that seems to let Strange out all right. I'll just have to check up on his movements after he left the house. If he's telling the truth he's washed out and we can go on to our other suspects.'

'The other people who inherit money?' suggested Leach.

'Maybe,' said Battle. 'But somehow, I don't think so. Someone with a kink, I'm looking for.'

'A kink?'

'A nasty kink.'

When they left the doctor's house they went on to the ferry. The ferry consisted of a rowing boat operated by two brothers, Will and George Barnes. The Barnes brothers knew everybody in Saltcreek by sight and most of the people who came over from Easterhead Bay. George said at once that Mr Strange from Gull's Point had gone across at ten-thirty on the preceding night. No, he had not brought Mr Strange back again. Last ferry had gone at one-thirty from the Easterhead side and Mr Strange wasn't on it.

Battle asked him if he knew Mr Latimer.

'Latimer? Latimer? Tall handsome young gentleman? Comes

over from the Hotel up to Gull's Point? Yes, I know him. Didn't see him at all last night, though. He's been over this morning. Went back last trip.'

They crossed on the ferry and went up to the Easterhead Bay Hotel.

Here they found Mr Latimer newly returned from the other side. He had crossed on the ferry before theirs.

Mr Latimer was very anxious to do all he could to help.

'Yes, old Nevile came over last night. Looked very blue over something. Told me he'd had a row with the old lady. I hear he'd fallen out with Kay too, but he didn't tell me that, of course. Anyway, he was a bit down in the mouth. Seemed quite glad of my company for once in a way.'

'He wasn't able to find you at once, I understand?'

Latimer said sharply:

'Don't know why. I was sitting in the lounge. Strange said he looked in and didn't see me, but he wasn't in a state to concentrate. Or I may have strolled out into the gardens for five minutes or so. Always get out when I can. Beastly smell in this Hotel. Noticed it last night in the Bar. Drains, I think! Strange mentioned it too! We both smelt it. Nasty decayed smell. Might be a dead rat under the billiard room floor.'

'You played billiards, and after your game?'

'Oh we talked a bit, had another drink or two. Then Nevile said "Hullo, I've missed the ferry," so I said I'd get out my car and drive him back, which I did. We got there about two-thirty.'

'And Mr Strange was with you all the evening?'

'Oh yes. Ask anybody. They'll tell you.'

'Thank you, Mr Latimer. We have to be so careful.'

Leach said as they left the smiling, self-possessed young man: 'What's the idea of checking up so carefully on Nevile Strange?'

Battle smiled. Leach got it suddenly.

'Good lord, it's the *other* one you're checking up on. So that's your idea.'

'It's too soon to have ideas,' said Battle. 'I've just got to know exactly where Mr Ted Latimer was last night. We know that from quarter-past eleven, say – to after midnight – he was with Nevile Strange. But where was he *before* that – when Strange arrived and couldn't find him?'

They pursued their inquiries doggedly – with bar attendants, waiters, lift boys. Latimer had been seen in the lounge between nine and ten. He had been in the bar at a quarter-past ten. But between that time and eleven-twenty he seemed to have been singularly elusive. Then one of the maids was found who declared that Mr Latimer had been 'in one of the small writing rooms with Mrs Beddoes – that's the fat North Country lady.'

Pressed as to time, she said she thought it was about eleven o'clock.

'That tears it,' said Battle gloomily. 'He was here all right. Just didn't want attention drawn to his fat (and no doubt rich) lady friend. That throws us back on those others – the servants, Kay Strange, Audrey Strange, Mary Aldin and Thomas Royde. *One* of them killed the old lady, but which? If we could find the real weapon –'

He stopped, then slapped his thigh.

'Got it, Jim, my boy! I know now what made me think of Hercule Poirot. We'll have a spot of lunch and go back to Gull's Point and I'll show you something.'

X

Mary Aldin was restless. She went in and out of the house, picked off a dead dahlia head here and there, went back into the drawing-room and shifted flower vases in an unmeaning fashion.

From the library came a vague murmur of voices. Mr Trelawny was in there with Nevile. Kay and Audrey were nowhere to be seen.

Mary went out in the garden again. Down by the wall she spied Thomas Royde placidly smoking. She went and joined him.

'Oh dear.' She sat down beside him with a deep perplexed sigh.

'Anything the matter?' Thomas asked.

Mary laughed with a slight note of hysteria in the laugh.

'Nobody but you would say a thing like that. A murder in the house and you just say "Is anything the matter?"'

Looking a little surprised, Thomas said:

'I meant anything fresh?'

'Oh, I know what you meant. It's really a wonderful relief to find anyone so gloriously just-the-same-as-usual as you are!'

'Not much good, is it, getting all het up over things?'

'No, no. You're eminently sensible. It's how you manage to do it beats me.'

'Well, I suppose I'm an outsider.'

'That's true, of course. You can't feel the relief all the rest of us do that Nevile is cleared.'

'I'm very pleased he is, of course,' said Royde.

Mary shuddered.

'It was a very near thing. If Camilla hadn't taken it into her head to ring the bell for Barrett after Nevile had left her –'

She left the sentence unfinished. Thomas finished it for her.

'Then old Nevile would have been for it all right.'

He spoke with a certain grim satisfaction, then shook his head with a slight smile, as he met Mary's reproachful gaze.

'I'm not really heartless, but now that Nevile's all right I can't help being pleased he had a bit of a shaking up. He's always so damned complacent.'

'He isn't really, Thomas.'

'Perhaps not. It's just his manner. Anyway he was looking scared as Hell this morning!'

'What a cruel streak you have!'

'Anyway it's all right now. You know, Mary, even here Nevile has had the devil's own luck. Some other poor beggar with all that evidence piled up against him mightn't have had such a break.'

Mary shivered again. 'Don't say that. I like to think the innocent are – protected.'

'Do you, my dear?' His voice was gentle.

Mary burst out suddenly:

'Thomas, I'm worried. I'm frightfully worried.'

'Yes?'

'It's about Mr Treves.'

Thomas dropped his pipe on the stones. His voice changed as he bent to pick it up.

'What about Mr Treves?'

'That night he was here – that story he told – about a little murderer! I've been wondering, Thomas . . . Was it just a story? Or did he tell it with a purpose?'

'You mean,' said Royde deliberately, 'was it aimed at someone who was in the room?'

Mary whispered, 'Yes.'

Thomas said quietly:

'I've been wondering, too. As a matter of fact that was what I was thinking about when you came along just now.'

Mary half closed her eyes.

'I've been trying to remember . . . He told it, you know, so very deliberately. He almost dragged it into the conversation. And he said he would recognize the person anywhere. He emphasized that. As though he *had* recognized him.'

'Mm,' said Thomas. 'I've been through all that.'

'But why should he do it? What was the point?'

'I suppose,' said Royde, 'it was a kind of warning. Not to try anything on.'

'You mean that Mr Treves knew then that Camilla was going to be murdered?'

'No-o. I think that's too fantastic. It may have been just a general warning.'

'What I've been wondering is, do you think we ought to tell the police?'

To that Thomas again gave his thoughtful consideration.

'I think not,' he said at last. 'I don't see that it's relevant in any way. It's not as though Treves were alive and could tell them anything.'

'No,' said Mary. 'He's dead!' She gave a quick shiver. 'It's so odd, Thomas, the way he died.'

'Heart attack. He had a bad heart.'

'I mean that curious business about the lift being out of order. *I don't like it.*'

'I don't like it very much myself,' said Thomas Royde.

XI

Superintendent Battle looked round the bedroom. The bed had been made. Otherwise the room was unchanged. It had been neat when they first looked round it. It was neat now.

'That's it,' said Superintendent Battle, pointing to the old-fashioned steel fender. 'Do you see anything odd about that fender?'

'Must take some cleaning,' said Jim Leach. 'It's well kept. Nothing odd about it that I can see, except – yes, the left-hand knob is brighter than the right-hand one.'

'That's what put Hercule Poirot into my head,' said Battle. 'You know his fad about things not being quite symmetrical – gets him all worked up. I suppose I thought unconsciously "That would worry old Poirot," and then I began talking about him. Get your fingerprint kit, Jones, we'll have a look at those two knobs.'

Jones reported presently.

'There are prints on the right-hand knob, sir, none on the left.'

'It's the left one we want, then. Those other prints are the housemaid's when she last cleaned it. That left-hand one has been cleaned twice.'

'There was a bit of screwed-up emery paper in this waste paper basket,' volunteered Jones. 'I didn't think it meant anything.'

'Because you didn't know what you were looking for, then. Gently now, I'll bet anything you like that knob unscrews – yes, I thought so.'

Presently Jones held the knob up.

'It's a good weight,' he said, weighing it in his hands.

Leach, bending over it, said:

'There's something dark – on the screw.'

'Blood, as likely as not,' said Battle. 'Cleaned the knob itself and wiped it and that little stain on the screw wasn't noticed. I'll bet anything you like that's the weapon that caved the old lady's skull in. But there's more to find. It's up to you, Jones, to search the house again. This time, you'll know exactly what you're looking for.'

He gave a few swift detailed instructions. Going to the window he put his head out.

'There's something yellow tucked into the ivy. That may be another piece of the puzzle. I rather think it is.'

XII

Crossing the hall, Superintendent Battle was waylaid by Mary Aldin.

'Can I speak to you a minute, Superintendent?'

'Certainly, Miss Aldin. Shall we come in here?'

He threw open the dining-room door. Lunch had been cleared away by Hurstall.

'I want to ask you something, Superintendent. Surely you don't, you can't still think that this – this awful crime was done by one of us? It must have been someone from outside! Some maniac!'

'You may not be far wrong there, Miss Aldin. Maniac is a word that describes this criminal very well if I'm not mistaken. But not an outsider.'

Her eyes opened very wide.

'Do you mean that someone in this house is – is *mad*?'

'You're thinking,' said the Superintendent, 'of someone foaming at the mouth and rolling their eyes. Mania isn't like that. Some of the most dangerous criminal lunatics have looked as sane as you or I. It's a question, usually, of having an obsession. One idea, preying on the mind, gradually distorting it. Pathetic, reasonable people who come up to you and explain how they're being persecuted and how everyone is spying on them – and you sometimes feel it must all be true.'

'I'm sure nobody here has any ideas of being persecuted.'

'I only gave that as an instance. There are other forms of insanity. But I believe whoever committed this crime was under the domination of one fixed idea – an idea on which they had brooded until literally nothing else mattered or had any importance.'

Mary shivered. She said:

'There's something I think you ought to know.'

Concisely and clearly she told him of Mr Treves' visit to dinner and of the story he had told. Superintendent Battle was deeply interested.

'He said he could recognize this person? Man or woman – by the way?'

'I took it that it was a boy the story was about – but it's true Mr Treves didn't actually say so – in fact I remember now – he distinctly stated he would not give any particulars as to sex or age.'

'Did he? Rather significant, perhaps. And he said there was a definite physical peculiarity by which he could be sure of knowing this child anywhere?'

'Yes.'

'A scar, perhaps – has anybody here got a scar?'

He noticed the faint hesitation before Mary Aldin replied:

'Not that I have noticed.'

'Come now, Miss Aldin,' he smiled. 'You *have* noticed something. If so, don't you think that I shall be able to notice it, too?'

She shook her head.

'I – I haven't noticed anything of the kind.'

But he saw that she was startled and upset. His words had obviously suggested a very unpleasant train of thought to her. He wished he knew just what it was, but his experience made him aware that to press her at this minute would not yield any result.

He brought the conversation back to old Mr Treves.

Mary told him of the tragic sequel to the evening.

Battle questioned her at some length. Then he said quietly:

'That's a new one on me. Never came across that before.'

'What do you mean?'

'I've never come across a murder committed by the simple expedient of hanging a placard on a lift.'

She looked horrified.

'You don't really think –?'

'That it was murder? Of course it was! Quick, resourceful murder. It might not have come off, of course – but it *did* come off.'

'Just because Mr Treves knew –?'

'Yes. Because he would have been able to direct our attention to one particular person in this house. As it is, we've started in the dark. But we've got a glimmer of light now, and every minute the case is getting clearer. I'll tell you this, Miss Aldin – this murder was very carefully planned beforehand down to the smallest detail. And I want to impress one thing on your mind – don't let anybody know that you've told me what you have. That is important. Don't tell *anyone*, mind.'

Mary nodded. She was still looking dazed.

Superintendent Battle went out of the room and proceeded to do what he had been about to do when Mary Aldin intercepted him. He was a methodical man. He wanted certain information, and a new and promising hare did not distract him from the orderly performance of his duties, however tempting this new hare might be.

He tapped on the library door, and Nevile Strange's voice called 'Come in.'

Battle was introduced to Mr Trelawny, a tall distinguished-looking man with a keen dark eye.

'Sorry if I am butting in,' said Superintendent Battle apologetically. 'But there's something I haven't got clear. You, Mr Strange, inherit half the late Sir Matthew's estate, but who inherits the other half?'

Nevile looked surprised.

'I told you. My wife.'

'Yes. But –' Battle coughed in a deprecating manner, 'which wife, Mr Strange?'

'Oh, I see. Yes, I expressed myself badly. The money goes to Audrey, who was my wife at the time the will was made. That's right, Mr Trelawny?'

The lawyer assented.

'The bequest is quite clearly worded. The estate is to be divided between Sir Matthew's ward, Nevile Henry Strange, and his wife, Audrey Elizabeth Strange, née Standish. The subsequent divorce makes no difference whatever.'

'That's clear, then,' said Battle. 'I take it Mrs Audrey Strange is fully aware of these facts?'

'Certainly,' said Mr Trelawny.

'And the present Mrs Strange?'

'Kay?' Nevile looked slightly surprised. 'Oh, I suppose so. At least – I've never talked much about it with her –'

'I think you'll find,' said Battle, 'that she's under a misapprehension. She thinks that the money on Lady Tressilian's death comes to you and your *present* wife. At least, that's what she gave me to understand this morning. That's why I came along to find out how the position really lay.'

'How extraordinary,' said Nevile. 'Still, I suppose it might have happened quite easily. She has said once or twice, now that I think about it, "We come into that money when Camilla dies," but I suppose I assumed that she was just associating herself with me in my share of it.'

'It's extraordinary,' said Battle, 'the amount of misunderstandings there are even between two people who discuss a thing quite often – both of them assuming different things and neither of them discovering the discrepancy.'

'I suppose so,' said Nevile, not sounding very interested. 'It doesn't matter much in this case, anyway. It's not as though we're short of money at all. I'm very glad for Audrey. She has been very hard up and this will make a big difference to her.'

Battle said bluntly: 'But surely, sir, at the time of the divorce, she was entitled to an allowance from you?'

Nevile flushed. He said in a constrained voice:

'There is such a thing as – as pride, Superintendent. Audrey has always persistently refused to touch a penny of the allowance I wished to make her.'

'A very generous allowance,' put in Mr Trelawny. 'But Mrs Audrey Strange has always returned it and refused to accept it.'

'Very interesting,' said Battle, and went out before anyone could ask him to elaborate that comment.

He went out and found his nephew.

'On its face value,' he said, 'there's a nice monetary motive for nearly everybody in this case. Nevile Strange and Audrey Strange get a cool fifty thousand each. Kay Strange thinks she's entitled to fifty thousand. Mary Aldin gets an income that frees her from having to earn her living. Thomas Royde, I'm bound to say, doesn't gain. But we can include Hurstall and even Barrett if we admit that she'd take the risk of finishing herself off to avoid suspicion. Yes, as I say, there are no lack of money motives. And yet, if I'm right, money doesn't enter into this at all. If there's such a thing as murder for pure hate, this is it. And if no one comes along and throws a spanner into the works, I'm going to get the person who did it!'

XIII

Angus MacWhirter sat on the terrace of the Easterhead Bay Hotel and stared across the river to the frowning height of Stark Head opposite.

He was engaged at the moment in a careful stocktaking of his thoughts and emotions.

He hardly knew what it was that had made him choose to spend his last few days of leisure where he now was. Yet something had drawn him there. Perhaps the wish to test himself – to see if there remained in his heart any of the old despair.

Mona? How little he cared now. She was married to the other man. He had passed her in the street one day without feeling any emotion. He could remember his grief and bitterness when she left him, but they were past now and gone.

He was recalled from these thoughts by an impact of wet dog and the frenzied appeal of a newly made friend, Miss Diana Brinton, aged thirteen.

'Oh come away, Don. Come *away*. Isn't it awful? He's rolled on some fish or something down on the beach. You can smell him yards away. The fish was awfully dead, you know!'

MacWhirter's nose confirmed this assumption.

'In a sort of crevice on the rocks,' said Miss Brinton. 'I took him into the sea and tried to wash it off, but it doesn't seem to have done much good.'

MacWhirter agreed. Don, a wire-haired terrier of amiable and loving disposition, was looking hurt by the tendency of his friends to keep him firmly at arm's length.

'Sea water's no good,' said MacWhirter. 'Hot water and soap's the only thing.'

'I know. But that's not so jolly easy in a Hotel. We haven't got a private bath.'

In the end MacWhirter and Diana surreptitiously entered by the side door with Don on a lead, and smuggling him up to MacWhirter's bathroom, a thorough cleansing took place and both MacWhirter and Diana got very wet. Don was very sad when it was all over. That disgusting smell of soap again – just when he had found a really nice perfume such as any other dog would envy. Oh well, it was always the same with humans – they had no decent sense of smell.

The little incident had left MacWhirter in a more cheerful mood. He took the bus into Saltington, where he had left a suit to be cleaned.

The girl in charge of the 24-Hour Cleaners looked at him vacantly.

'MacWhirter, did you say? I'm afraid it isn't ready yet.'

'It should be.' He had been promised that suit the day before, and even that would have been 48 and not 24 hours. A woman might have said all this. MacWhirter merely scowled.

'There's not been time yet,' said the girl, smiling indifferently.

'Nonsense.'

The girl stopped smiling. She snapped,

'Anyway, it's not done,' she said.

'Then I'll take it away as it is,' said MacWhirter.

'Nothing's been done to it,' the girl warned him.

'I'll take it away.'

'I dare say we might get it done by tomorrow – as a special favour.'

'I'm not in the habit of asking for special favours. Just give me the suit, please.'

Giving him a bad-tempered look, the girl went into the back room. She returned with a clumsily done up parcel which she pushed across the counter.

MacWhirter took it and went out.

He felt, quite ridiculously, as though he had won a victory. Actually it merely meant that he would have to have the suit cleaned elsewhere!

He threw the parcel on his bed when he returned to the Hotel and looked at it with annoyance. Perhaps he could get it sponged and pressed in the Hotel. It was not really too bad – perhaps it didn't actually need cleaning?

He undid the parcel and gave vent to an expression of annoyance. Really, the 24-Hour Cleaners were too inefficient for words. This wasn't his suit. It wasn't even the same colour. It had been a dark blue suit he had left with them. Impertinent, inefficient muddlers.

He glanced irritably at the label. It had the name MacWhirter all right. Another MacWhirter? Or some stupid interchange of labels?

Staring down vexedly at the crumpled heap, he suddenly sniffed.

Surely he knew that smell – a particularly unpleasant smell . . . connected somehow with a dog. Yes, that was it. Diana and her dog. Absolutely and literally stinking fish!

He bent down and examined the suit. There it was, a discoloured patch on the shoulder of the coat. On the *shoulder* –

Now that, thought MacWhirter, is really very curious . . .

Anyway, next day, he would have a few grim words with the girl at the 24-Hour Cleaners. Gross mismanagement!

XIV

After dinner he strolled out of the Hotel and down the road to the Ferry. It was a clear night, but cold, with a sharp foretaste of winter. Summer was over.

MacWhirter crossed in the ferry to the Saltcreek side. It was the second time that he was revisiting Stark Head. The place had a fascination for him. He walked slowly up the hill, passing the Balmoral Court Hotel and then a big house set on the point of a cliff. Gull's Point – he read the name on the painted door. Of course, that was where the old lady had been murdered. There had been a lot of talk in the Hotel about it, his chambermaid had insisted on telling him all about it and the newspapers had given it a prominence which had annoyed MacWhirter, who preferred to read of world-wide affairs and who was not interested in crime.

He went on, downhill again to skirt a small beach and some old-fashioned fishing cottages that had been modernized. Then up again till the road ended and petered out into the track that led up on Stark Head.

It was grim and forbidding on Stark Head. MacWhirter stood on the cliff edge looking down to the sea. So he had stood on that other night. He tried to recapture some of the feeling he had had then – the desperation, anger, weariness – the longing to be out of it all. But there was nothing to recapture. All that had gone. There was instead a cold anger. Caught on that tree, rescued by coast-guards, fussed over like a naughty child in hospital, a series of indignities and affronts. Why couldn't he have been *let alone*? He would rather, a thousand times rather, be out of it all. He still felt that. The only thing he had lost was the necessary impetus.

How it had hurt him then to think of Mona! He could think of her quite calmly now. She had always been rather a fool. Easily taken by anyone who flattered her or played up to her idea of herself. Very pretty. Yes, very pretty – but no mind, not the kind of woman he had once dreamed about.

But that was beauty, of course – some vague fancied picture of a woman flying through the night with white draperies streaming

out behind her . . . Something like the figure-head of a ship –
only not so solid . . . not nearly so solid . . .

And then, with dramatic suddenness, the incredible happened!
Out of the night came a flying figure. One minute she was not
there, the next minute she was – a white figure running –
running – to the cliff's edge. A figure, beautiful and desperate,
driven to destruction by pursuing Furies! Running with a terrible
desperation . . . He knew that desperation. He knew what it
meant . . .

He came with a rush out of the shadows and caught her just
as she was about to go over the edge!

He said fiercely: 'No you don't . . .'

It was just like holding a bird. She struggled – struggled silently,
and then, again like a bird, was suddenly dead still.

He said urgently:

'Don't throw yourself over! Nothing's worth it. *Nothing*. Even
if you are desperately unhappy –'

She made a sound. It was, perhaps, a far-off ghost of a
laugh.

He said sharply:

'You're not unhappy? What is it then?'

She answered him at once with the low softly-breathed word:
'*Afraid*.'

'Afraid?' He was so astonished that he let her go, standing back
a pace to see her better.

He realized then the truth of her words. It was fear that had
lent that urgency to her footsteps. It was fear that made her
small white intelligent face blank and stupid. Fear that dilated
those wide-apart eyes.

He said incredulously: 'What are you afraid of?'

She replied so low that he hardly heard it.

'*I'm afraid of being hanged* . . .'

Yes, she had said just that. He stared and stared. He looked
from her to the cliff's edge.

'So that's why?'

'Yes. A quick death instead of –' She closed her eyes and
shivered. She went on shivering.

MacWhirter was piecing things together logically in his mind.
He said at last:

'Lady Tressilian? The old lady who was murdered?' Then, accusingly: 'You'll be Mrs Strange – the first Mrs Strange.'

Still shivering she nodded her head.

MacWhirter went on in his slow careful voice, trying to remember all that he had heard. Rumour had been incorporated with fact.

'They detained your husband – that's right, isn't it? A lot of evidence against him – and then they found that that evidence had been faked by someone . . .'

He stopped and looked at her. She wasn't shivering any longer. She was standing looking at him like a docile child. He found her attitude unendurably affecting.

His voice went on:

'I see . . . Yes, I see how it was . . . He left you for another woman, didn't he? And you loved him . . . That's why –' He broke off. He said, 'I understand. My wife left me for another man . . .'

She flung out her arms. She began stammering wildly, hopelessly:

'It's n-n-not – it's n-n-not l-like that. N-not at all –'

He cut her short. His voice was stern and commanding.

'Go home. *You needn't be afraid any longer.* D'you hear? I'll see that you're not hanged!'

XV

Mary Aldin was lying on the drawing-room sofa. Her head ached and her whole body felt worn out.

The inquest had taken place the day before and, after formal evidence of identification, had been adjourned for a week.

Lady Tressilian's funeral was to take place on the morrow. Audrey and Kay had gone into Saltington in the car to get some black clothes. Ted Latimer had gone with them. Nevile and Thomas Royde had gone for a walk, so except for the servants, Mary was alone in the house.

Superintendent Battle and Inspector Leach had been absent today, and that, too, was a relief. It seemed to Mary that with their absence a shadow had been lifted. They had been polite, quite pleasant, in fact, but the ceaseless questions, that quiet deliberate probing and sifting of every fact was the sort of thing that wore hardly on the nerves. By now that wooden-faced Superintendent must have learned of every incident, every word, every gesture, even, of the past ten days.

Now, with their going, there was peace. Mary let herself relax. She would forget everything – everything. Just lie back and rest.

'Excuse me, Madam –'

It was Hurstall in the doorway, looking apologetic.

'Yes, Hurstall?'

'A gentleman wishes to see you. I have put him in the study.'

Mary looked at him in astonishment and some annoyance.

'Who is it?'

'He gave his name as Mr MacWhirter, Miss.'

'I've never heard of him.'

'No, Miss.'

'He must be a reporter. You shouldn't have let him in, Hurstall.'

Hurstall coughed.

'I don't think he is a reporter, Miss. I think he is a friend of Miss Audrey's.'

'Oh, that's different.'

Smoothing her hair, Mary went wearily across the hall and into the small study. She was, somehow, a little surprised as the tall man standing by the window turned. He did not look in the least like a friend of Audrey's.

However, she said pleasantly:

'I'm sorry Mrs Strange is out. You wanted to see her?'

He looked at her in a thoughtful, considering way.

'You'll be Miss Aldin?' he said.

'Yes.'

'I dare say you can help me just as well. I want to find some rope.'

'Rope?' said Mary in lively amazement.

'Yes, rope. Where would you be likely to keep a piece of rope?'

Afterwards Mary considered that she had been half-hypnotized. If this strange man had volunteered any explanation she might have resisted. But Angus MacWhirter, unable to think of a plausible explanation, decided very wisely to do without one. He just stated quite simply what he wanted. She found herself, semi-dazed, leading MacWhirter in search of rope.

'What kind of rope?' she had asked.

And he had replied: 'Any rope will do.'

She said doubtfully: 'Perhaps in the potting shed –'

'Shall we go there?'

She led the way. There was twine and an odd bit of cord, but MacWhirter shook his head.

He wanted rope – a good-sized coil of rope.

'There's the boxroom,' said Mary hesitatingly.

'Ay, that might be the place.'

They went indoors and upstairs. Mary threw open the boxroom door. MacWhirter stood in the doorway looking in. He gave a curious sigh of contentment.

'There it is,' he said.

There was a big coil of rope lying on a chest just inside the door in company with old fishing tackle and some moth-eaten cushions. He laid a hand on her arm and impelled Mary gently forward until they stood looking down on the rope. He touched it and said:

'I'd like you to charge your memory with this, Miss Aldin. You'll notice that everything round about is covered with dust. *There's no dust on this rope.* Just feel it.'

She said:

'It feels slightly damp,' in a surprised tone.

'Just so.'

He turned to go out again.

'But the rope? I thought you wanted it?' said Mary in surprise.

MacWhirter smiled.

'I just wanted to know it was there. That's all. Perhaps you wouldn't mind locking this door, Miss Aldin – and taking the key out? Yes. I'd be obliged if you'd hand the key to Superintendent Battle or Inspector Leach. It would be best in their keeping.'

As they went downstairs, Mary made an effort to rally herself. She protested as they reached the main hall:

'But really, I don't understand.'

MacWhirter said firmly:

'There's no need for you to understand.' He took her hand and shook it heartily. 'I'm very much obliged to you for your co-operation.'

Whereupon he went straight out of the front door. Mary wondered if she had been dreaming!

Nevile and Thomas came in presently and the car arrived back shortly afterwards and Mary Aldin found herself envying Kay and Ted for being able to look quite cheerful. They were laughing and joking together. After all, why not? she thought. Camilla Tressilian had been nothing to Kay. All this tragic business was very hard on a bright young creature.

They had just finished lunch when the police came. There was something scared in Hurstall's voice as he announced that Superintendent Battle and Inspector Leach were in the drawing-room.

Superintendent Battle's face was quite genial as he greeted them.

'Hope I haven't disturbed you all,' he said apologetically. 'But there are one or two things I'd like to know about. This glove, for instance, who does it belong to?'

He held it out, a small yellow chamois leather glove.

He addressed Audrey.

'Is it yours, Mrs Strange?'

She shook her head.

'No – no, it isn't mine.'

'Miss Aldin?'

'I don't think so. I have none of that colour.'

'May I see?' Kay held out her hand. 'No.'

'Perhaps you'd just slip it on.'

Kay tried, but the glove was too small.

'Miss Aldin?'

Mary tried in her turn.

'It's too small for you also,' said Battle. He turned back to Audrey. 'I think you'll find it fits you all right. Your hand is smaller than either of the other ladies'.'

Audrey took it from him and slipped it on over her right hand.

Nevile Strange said sharply:

'She's already told you, Battle, that it isn't her glove.'

'Ah well,' said Battle, 'perhaps she made a mistake. Or forgot.'

Audrey said: 'It may be mine – gloves are so alike, aren't they?'

Battle said:

'At any rate it was found outside your window, Mrs Strange, pushed down into the ivy – *with its fellow*.'

There was a pause. Audrey opened her mouth to speak, then closed it up again. Her eyes fell before the Superintendent's steady gaze.

Nevile sprang forward. 'Look here, Superintendent –'

'Perhaps we might have a word with you, Mr Strange, privately?' Battle said gravely.

'Certainly, Superintendent. Come into the library.'

He led the way and the two police officers followed him.

As soon as the door had closed Nevile said sharply:

'What's this ridiculous story about gloves outside my wife's window?'

Battle said quietly: 'Mr Strange, we've found some very curious things in this house.'

Nevile frowned.

'Curious? What do you mean by curious?'

'I'll show you.'

In obedience to a nod, Leach left the room and came back holding a very strange implement.

Battle said:

'This consists, as you see, sir, of a steel ball taken from a Victorian fender – a heavy steel ball. Then the head has been sawed off a tennis racquet and the ball has been screwed into the handle of the racquet.' He paused. 'I think there can be no doubt that this is what was used to kill Lady Tressilian.'

'Horrible!' said Nevile with a shudder. 'But where did you find this – this nightmare?'

'The ball had been cleaned and put back on the fender. The murderer had, however, neglected to clean the screw. We found a trace of blood on that. In the same way the handle and the head of the racquet were joined together again by means of adhesive surgical plaster. It was then thrown carelessly back into the cupboard under the stairs, where it would probably have remained quite unnoticed amongst so many others if we hadn't happened to be looking for something of that kind.'

'Smart of you, Superintendent.'

'Just a matter of routine.'

'No fingerprints, I suppose?'

'That racquet which belongs by its weight, I should say, to Mrs Kay Strange, had been handled by her and also by you and both your prints are on it. *But it also shows unmistakable signs that someone wearing gloves handled it after you did.* There was just one fingerprint – left this time in inadvertence, I think. That was on the surgical strapping that had been applied to bind the racquet together again. I'm not going for the moment to say whose print that was. I've got some other points to mention first.'

Battle paused, then he said:

'I want you to prepare yourself for a shock, Mr Strange. And first I want to ask you something. Are you quite sure that it was your own idea to have this meeting here and that it was not actually suggested to you by Mrs Audrey Strange?'

'Audrey did nothing of the sort, Audrey –'

The door opened and Thomas Royde came in.

'Sorry to butt in,' he said, 'but I thought I'd like to be in on this.'

Nevile turned a harassed face towards him.

'Do you mind, old fellow? This is all rather private.'

'I'm afraid I don't care about that. You see, I heard a name outside.' He paused. 'Audrey's name.'

'And what the Hell has Audrey's name got to do with you?' demanded Nevile, his temper rising.

'Well, what has it to do with you if it comes to that? I haven't said anything definite to Audrey, but I came here meaning to ask her to marry me, and I think she knows it. What's more, I mean to marry her.'

Superintendent Battle coughed. Nevile turned to him with a start.

'Sorry, Superintendent. This interruption –'

Battle said:

'It doesn't matter to me, Mr Strange. I've got one more question to ask you. That dark blue coat you wore at dinner the night of the murder, it's got fair hairs inside the collar and on the shoulders? Do you know how they got there?'

'I suppose they're my hairs.'

'Oh no, they're not yours, sir. They're a lady's hairs, and there's a red hair on the sleeve.'

'I suppose that's my wife's – Kay's. The others, you are suggesting, are Audrey's. Very likely they are. I caught my cuff button in her hair one night outside on the terrace, I remember.'

'In that case,' murmured Inspector Leach, 'the fair hair would be on the cuff.'

'What the devil are you suggesting?' cried Nevile.

'There's a trace of powder, too, inside the coat collar,' said Battle. 'Primavera Naturelle No. 1 – a very pleasant-scented powder and expensive – but it's no good telling me that you use it, Mr Strange, because I shan't believe you. And Mrs Strange uses Orchid Sun Kiss. Mrs Audrey Strange does use Primavera Naturelle No. 1.'

'What are you suggesting?' repeated Nevile.

Battle leaned forward.

'I'm suggesting that – on some occasion *Mrs Audrey Strange wore that coat*. It's the only reasonable way the hair and the powder could get where it did. Then you've seen that glove I produced just now? It's her glove all right. That was the right hand, *here's the left*.' He drew it out of his pocket and put it down on the table. It was crumpled and stained with rusty brown patches.

Nevile said with a note of fear in his voice: 'What's that on it?'

'Blood, Mr Strange,' said Battle firmly. 'And you'll note this, it's the *left* hand. Now Mrs Audrey Strange is left-handed. I noted that first thing when I saw her sitting with her coffee cup in her right hand and her cigarette in her left at the breakfast table. And the pen tray on her writing table had been shifted to the left-hand side. It all fits in. The knob from her grate, the gloves outside her window, the hair and powder on the coat. Lady Tressilian was struck on the right temple – but the position of the bed made it impossible for anyone to have stood on the other side of it. It follows that to strike Lady Tressilian a blow with the right hand would be a very awkward thing to do – but it's the natural way to strike for a *left-handed* person . . .'

Nevile laughed scornfully.

'Are you suggesting that Audrey – *Audrey* would make all these elaborate preparations and strike down an old lady whom she had known for years in order to get her hands on that old lady's money?'

Battle shook his head.

'I'm suggesting nothing of the sort. I'm sorry, Mr Strange, you've got to understand just how things are. This crime, first, last, and all the time was directed against *you*. Ever since you left her, Audrey Strange has been brooding over the possibilities of revenge. In the end she has become mentally unbalanced. Perhaps she was never mentally very strong. She thought, perhaps, of killing you but that wasn't enough. She thought at last of getting you hanged for murder. She chose an evening when she knew you had quarrelled with Lady Tressilian. She took the coat from your bedroom and wore it when she struck the old lady down so that it should be blood-stained. She put your niblick on the floor, knowing we would find your fingerprints on it, and smeared blood and hair on the head of the club. It was she who instilled into your mind the idea of coming here when she was here. And the thing that saved you was the one thing she couldn't count on – the fact that Lady Tressilian rang her bell for Barrett and that Barrett saw you leave the house.'

Nevile had buried his face in his hands. He said now:

'It's not true. It's not true! Audrey's never borne a grudge against me. You've got the whole thing wrong. She's the straightest, truest creature – without thought of evil in her heart.'

Battle sighed.

'It's not my business to argue with you, Mr Strange. I only wanted to prepare you. I shall caution Mrs Strange and ask her to accompany me. I've got the warrant. You'd better see about getting a solicitor for her.'

'It's preposterous. Absolutely preposterous.'

'Love turns to hate more easily than you think, Mr Strange.'

'I tell you it's all wrong – preposterous.'

Thomas Royde broke in. His voice was quiet and pleasant.

'Do stop repeating that it's preposterous, Nevile. Pull yourself together. Don't you see that the only thing that can help Audrey now is for you to give up all your ideas of chivalry and come out with the truth?'

'The truth? You mean –?'

'I mean the truth about Audrey and Adrian.' Royde turned to

the police officers. 'You see, Superintendent, you've got the facts wrong. Nevile didn't leave Audrey. She left him. She ran away with my brother Adrian. Then Adrian was killed in a car accident. Nevile behaved with the utmost chivalry to Audrey. He arranged that she should divorce him and that he would take the blame.'

'Didn't want her name dragged through the mud,' muttered Nevile sulkily. 'Didn't know anyone knew.'

'Adrian wrote out to me, just before,' explained Thomas briefly. He went on: 'Don't you see, Superintendent, that knocks your motive out! Audrey has no cause to hate Nevile. On the contrary, she has every reason to be grateful to him. He's tried to get her to accept an allowance which she wouldn't do. Naturally when he wanted her to come and meet Kay she didn't feel she could refuse.'

'You see,' Nevile put in eagerly. 'That cuts out her motive. Thomas is right.'

Battle's wooden face was immovable.

'Motive's only one thing,' he said. 'I may have been wrong about that. But facts are another. All the facts show that she's guilty.'

Nevile said meaningly:

'All the facts showed that *I* was guilty two days ago!'

Battle seemed a little taken aback.

'That's true enough. But look here, Mr Strange, at what you're asking me to believe. You're asking me to believe that there's someone who hates both of you – someone who, if the plot against you failed, had laid a second trail to lead to Audrey Strange. Now can you think of anyone, Mr Strange, who hates both you *and* your former wife?'

Nevile's head had dropped into his hands again.

'When you say it like that you make it all sound fantastic!'

'Because it *is* fantastic. I've got to go by the facts. If Mrs Strange has any explanations to offer –'

'Did I have any explanation?' asked Nevile.

'It's no good, Mr Strange. I've got to do my duty.'

Battle got up abruptly. He and Leach left the room first. Nevile and Royde came close behind them.

They went on across the hall into the drawing-room. There they stopped.

Audrey Strange got up. She walked forward to meet them. She looked straight at Battle, her lips parted in what was very nearly a smile.

She said very softly:

'You want me, don't you?'

Battle became very official.

'Mrs Strange, I have a warrant here for your arrest on the charge of murdering Camilla Tressilian on Monday last, September 12th. I must caution you that anything you say will be written down and may be used in evidence at your trial.'

Audrey gave a sigh. Her small clear-cut face was peaceful and pure as a cameo.

'It's almost a relief. I'm glad it's – over!'

Nevile sprang forward.

'Audrey – don't say anything – don't speak at all.'

She smiled at him.

'But why not, Nevile? It's all true – and I'm so tired.'

Leach drew a deep breath. Well, that was that. Mad as a hatter, of course, but it would save a lot of worry! He wondered what had happened to his uncle. The old boy was looking as though he had seen a ghost. Staring at the poor demented creature as though he couldn't believe his eyes. Oh, well, it had been an interesting case, Leach thought comfortably.

And then, an almost grotesque anticlimax, Hurstall opened the drawing-room door and announced: 'Mr MacWhirter.'

MacWhirter strode in purposefully. He went straight up to Battle. 'Are you the police officer in charge of the Tressilian case?' he asked.

'I am.'

'Then I have an important statement to make. I am sorry not to have come forward before, but the importance of something I happened to see on the night of Monday last has only just dawned on me.' He gave a quick glance round the room. 'If I can speak to you somewhere?'

Battle turned to Leach.

'Will you stay here with Mrs Strange?'

Leach said officially: 'Yes, sir.'

Then he leaned forward and whispered something into the other's ear.

Battle turned to MacWhirter. 'Come this way.'

He led the way into the library.

'Now then, what's all this? My colleague tells me that he's seen you before – last winter?'

'Quite right,' said MacWhirter. 'Attempted suicide. That's part of my story.'

'Go on, Mr MacWhirter.'

'Last January I attempted to kill myself by throwing myself off Stark Head. This year the fancy took me to revisit the spot. I walked up there on Monday night. I stood there for some time. I looked down at the sea and across to Easterhead Bay and I then looked to my left. That is to say I looked across towards this house. I could see it quite plainly in the moonlight.'

'Yes.'

'Until today I had not realized *that that was the night when a murder was committed.*'

He leant forward. 'I'll tell you what I saw.'

XVI

It was really only about five minutes before Battle returned to the drawing-room, but to those there it seemed much longer.

Kay had suddenly lost control of herself. She had cried out to Audrey.

'I knew it was you. I always knew it was you. I knew you were up to something –'

Mary Aldin said quickly:

'Please, Kay.'

Nevile said sharply:

'Shut up, Kay, for God's sake.'

Ted Latimer came over to Kay, who had begun to cry.

'Get a grip on yourself,' he said kindly.

He said to Nevile angrily:

'You don't seem to realize that Kay has been under a lot of strain! Why don't you look after her a bit, Strange?'

'I'm all right,' said Kay.

'For two pins,' said Ted, 'I'd take you away from the lot of them!'

Inspector Leach cleared his throat. A lot of injudicious things were said at times like these, as he well knew. The unfortunate part was that they were usually remembered most inconveniently afterwards.

Battle came back into the room. His face was expressionless.

He said: 'Will you put one or two things together, Mrs Strange? I'm afraid Inspector Leach must come upstairs with you.'

Mary Aldin said: 'I'll come too.'

When the two women had left the room with the Inspector, Nevile said anxiously: 'Well, what did that chap want?'

Battle said slowly:

'Mr MacWhirter tells a very odd story.'

'Does it help Audrey? Are you still determined to arrest her?'

'I've told you, Mr Strange. I've got to do my duty.'

Nevile turned away, the eagerness dying out of his face.

He said:

'I'd better telephone Trelawny, I suppose.'

'There's no immediate hurry for that, Mr Strange. There's a certain experiment I want to make first as a result of Mr MacWhirter's statement. I'll just see that Mrs Strange gets off first.'

Audrey was coming down the stairs, Inspector Leach beside her. Her face still had that remote detached composure.

Nevile came towards her, his hands outstretched.

'Audrey —'

Her colourless glance swept over him. She said:

'It's all right, Nevile. I don't mind. I don't mind anything.'

Thomas Royde stood by the front door, almost as though he would bar the way out.

A very faint smile came to her lips.

'"True Thomas",' she murmured.

He mumbled: 'If there's anything I can do —'

'No one can do anything,' said Audrey.

She went out with her head high. A police car was waiting outside with Sergeant Jones in it. Audrey and Leach got in.

Ted Latimer murmured appreciatively:

'Lovely exit!'

Nevile turned on him furiously. Superintendent Battle dexterously interposed his bulk and raised a soothing voice:

'As I said, I've got an experiment to make. Mr MacWhirter is waiting down at the ferry. We're to join him there in ten minutes' time. We shall be going out in a motor launch, so the ladies had better wrap up warmly. In ten minutes, please.'

He might have been a stage manager ordering a company on to the stage. He took no notice at all of their puzzled faces.

ZERO HOUR

I

It was chilly on the water and Kay hugged the little fur jacket she was wearing closer round her.

The launch chugged down the river below Gull's Point, and then swung round into the little bay that divided Gull's Point from the frowning mass of Stark Head.

Once or twice a question began to be asked, but each time Superintendent Battle held up a large hand rather like a cardboard ham, intimating that the time had not come yet. So the silence was unbroken save for the rushing of the water past them. Kay and Ted stood together looking down into the water. Nevile was slumped down, his legs stuck out. Mary Aldin and Thomas Royde sat up in the bows. And one and all glanced from time to time curiously at the tall aloof figure of MacWhirter by the stern. He looked at none of them, but stood with his back turned and his shoulders hunched up.

Not until they were under the frowning shadow of Stark Head did Battle throttle down the engine and begin to speak his piece. He spoke without self-consciousness and in a tone that was more reflective than anything else.

'This has been a very odd case – one of the oddest I've ever known, and I'd like to say something on the subject of murder generally. What I'm going to say is not original – actually I overheard young Mr Daniels, the KC, say something of the kind, and I wouldn't be surprised if *he'd* got it from someone else – he's a trick of doing that!

'It's this! When you read the account of a murder – or say, a fiction story based on murder, you usually begin with the murder itself. That's all wrong. The murder begins a *long time beforehand*. A murder is the culmination of a lot of different circumstances, all converging at a given moment at a given point. People are brought into it from different parts of the globe and for unforeseen reasons. Mr Royde is here from Malaya. Mr MacWhirter is here because he wanted to revisit a spot where he once tried to commit suicide. The murder itself is the end of the story. It's Zero Hour.'

He paused.

'*It's Zero Hour now.*'

Five faces were turned to him – only five, for MacWhirter did not turn his head. Five puzzled faces.

Mary Aldin said:

'You mean that Lady Tressilian's death was the culmination of a long train of circumstances?'

'No, Miss Aldin, not Lady Tressilian's death. Lady Tressilian's death was only incidental to the main object of the murderer. The murder I am talking of *is the murder of Audrey Strange.*'

He listened to the sharp indrawing of breath. He wondered if, suddenly, someone was afraid . . .

'This crime was planned quite a long time ago – probably as early as last winter. It was planned down to the smallest detail. It had one object, and one object only: that Audrey Strange should be hanged by the neck till she was dead . . .

'It was cunningly planned by someone who thought themselves very clever. Murderers are usually vain. There was first the superficial unsatisfactory evidence against Nevile Strange which we were meant to see through. But having been presented with one lot of faked evidence, it was not considered likely that we should consider a *second edition of the same thing.* And yet, if you come to look at it, all the evidence against Audrey Strange *could* be faked. The weapon taken from her fireplace, her gloves – the left-hand glove dipped in blood – hidden in the ivy outside her window. The powder she uses dusted on the inside of a coat collar, and a few hairs placed there too. Her own fingerprint, occurring quite naturally on a roll of adhesive plaster taken from her room. Even the left-handed nature of the blow.

'And there was the final damning evidence of Mrs Strange herself – I don't believe there's one of you (except the one who *knows*) who can credit her innocence after the way she behaved when we took her into custody. Practically admitted her guilt, didn't she? I mightn't have believed in her being innocent myself if it hadn't been for a private experience of my own . . . Struck me right between the eyes it did, when I saw and heard her – because, you see, I'd known another girl who did that very same thing, who admitted guilt when she wasn't guilty – and Audrey Strange was looking at me *with that other girl's eyes* . . .

'I'd got to do my duty. I knew that. We police officers have to act on evidence – not on what we feel and think. But I can tell you that at that minute I prayed for a miracle – because I didn't see that anything but a miracle was going to help that poor lady.

'Well, I got my miracle. Got it right away!

'Mr MacWhirter, here, turned up with his story.'

He paused.

'Mr MacWhirter, will you repeat what you told me up at the house?'

MacWhirter turned. He spoke in short sharp sentences that carried conviction just because of their conciseness.

He told of his rescue from the cliff the preceding January and of his wish to revisit the scene. He went on:

'I went up there on Monday night. I stood there lost in my own thoughts. It must have been, I suppose, in the neighbourhood of eleven o'clock. I looked across at that house on the point – Gull's Point, as I know it now to be.'

He paused and then went on.

'There was a rope hanging from a window of that house into the sea. I saw a man climbing up that rope . . .'

Just a moment elapsed before they took it in. Mary Aldin cried out:

'Then it *was* an outsider after all? It was nothing to do with any of us. It was an ordinary burglar!'

'Not quite so fast,' said Battle. 'It was someone who came from the other side of the river, yes, since he swam across. But someone in the house had to have the rope ready for him, therefore *someone inside* must have been concerned.'

He went on slowly:

'And we know of someone who was on the other side of the river that night – someone who wasn't seen between ten-thirty and a quarter-past eleven, and who might have been swimming over and back. Someone who might have had a friend on this side of the water.'

He added: 'Eh, Mr Latimer?'

Ted took a step backward. He cried out shrilly:

'But I can't swim! Everybody knows I can't swim. Kay, tell them I can't swim.'

'Of course Ted can't swim!' Kay said.

'Is that so?' asked Battle pleasantly.

He moved along the boat as Ted moved in the other direction. There was some clumsy movement and a splash.

'Dear me,' said Superintendent Battle in deep concern. 'Mr Latimer's gone overboard.'

His hand closed like a vice on Nevile's arm as the latter was preparing to jump in after him.

'No, no, Mr Strange. No need for you to get yourself wet. There are two of my men handy – fishing in the dinghy there.' He peered over the side of the boat. 'It's quite true,' he said with interest. 'He can't swim. It's all right. They've got him. I'll apologize presently, but really there's only one way to make sure that a person can't swim and that's to throw them in and watch. You see, Mr Strange, I like to be thorough. I had to eliminate Mr Latimer first. Mr Royde here has got a groggy arm, he couldn't do any rope climbing.'

Battle's voice took on a purring quality.

'So that brings us to *you*, doesn't it, Mr Strange? A good athlete, a mountain climber, a swimmer and all that. You went over on the ten-thirty ferry all right but no one can swear to seeing you at the Easterhead Hotel until a quarter-past eleven in spite of your story of having been looking for Mr Latimer then.'

Nevile jerked his arm away. He threw back his head and laughed.

'You suggest that *I* swam across the river and climbed up a rope –'

'Which you had left ready hanging from your window,' said Battle.

'Killed Lady Tressilian and swam back again? Why should I do such a fantastic thing? And who laid all those clues against me? I suppose *I* laid them against *myself*?'

'Exactly,' said Battle. 'And not half a bad idea either.'

'And why should I want to kill Camilla Tressilian?'

'You didn't,' said Battle. 'But you did want to hang the woman who left you for another man. You're a bit unhinged mentally, you know. Have been ever since you were a child – I've looked up that old bow and arrow case, by the way. Anyone who does you an injury has to be punished – and death doesn't seem to you an excessive penalty for them to pay. Death by itself wasn't enough for Audrey – *your* Audrey whom you loved – oh, yes, you loved her all right before your love turned to hate. You had to think of some special kind of death, some long drawn out specialized death. And when you'd thought of it, the fact that it entailed the killing of a woman who had been something like a mother to you didn't worry you in the least . . .'

Nevile said, and his voice was quite gentle:

'All lies! All lies! And I'm not mad. I'm *not* mad.'

Battle said contemptuously:

'Flicked you on the raw, didn't she, when she went off and left you for another man? Hurt your vanity! To think *she* should walk out on *you*. You salved your pride by pretending to the world at large that *you'd* left *her* and you married another girl who was in love with you just to bolster up that belief. But underneath you planned what you'd do to Audrey. You couldn't think of anything worse than this – to get her hanged. A fine idea – pity you hadn't the brains to carry it out better!'

Nevile's tweed-coated shoulders moved, a queer, wriggling movement.

Battle went on:

'Childish – all that niblick stuff! Those crude trails pointing to you! Audrey must have known what you were after! She must have laughed up her sleeve! Thinking *I* didn't suspect you! You murderers are funny little fellows! So puffed up. Always thinking you've been clever and resourceful and really being quite pitifully childish . . .'

It was a strange queer scream that came from Nevile.

'It *was* a clever idea – it *was*. You'd never have guessed. Never! Not if it hadn't been for this interfering jackanapes, this pompous Scotch fool. I'd thought out every detail – every *detail*! I can't help what went wrong. How was I to know Royde knew the truth about Audrey and Adrian? Audrey and Adrian . . . Curse Audrey – she *shall* hang – you've *got* to hang her – I want her to die afraid – to die – to die . . . I hate her. I tell you I want her to die . . .'

The high whinnying voice died away. Nevile slumped down and began to cry quietly.

'Oh God,' said Mary Aldin. She was white to the lips.

Battle said gently, in a low voice:

'I'm sorry, but I had to push him over the edge . . . There was precious little evidence, you know.'

Nevile was still whimpering. His voice was like a child's.

'*I want her to be hanged. I do want her to be hanged . . .*'

Mary Aldin shuddered and turned to Thomas Royde.

He took her hands in his.

II

'I was always frightened,' said Audrey.

They were sitting on the terrace. Audrey sat close to Superintendent Battle. Battle had resumed his holiday and was at Gull's Point as a friend.

'Always frightened – all the time,' said Audrey.

Battle said, nodding his head:

'I knew you were dead scared first moment I saw you. And you'd got that colourless reserved way people have who are holding some very strong emotion in check. It might have been love or hate, but actually it was *fear*, wasn't it?'

She nodded.

'I began to be afraid of Nevile soon after we were married. But the awful thing is, you see, that I didn't know *why*. I began to think that *I* was mad.'

'It wasn't you,' said Battle.

'Nevile seemed to me when I married him so particularly sane and normal – always delightfully good-tempered and pleasant.'

'Interesting,' said Battle. 'He played the part of the good sportsman, you know. That's why he could keep his temper so well at tennis. His role as a good sportsman was more important to him than winning matches. But it put a strain upon him, of course; playing a part always does. He got worse underneath.'

'Underneath,' whispered Audrey with a shudder. 'Always *underneath*. Nothing you could get hold of. Just sometimes a word or a look and then I'd fancy I'd imagined it . . . Something queer. And then, as I say, I thought *I* must be queer. And I went on getting more and more afraid – the kind of unreasoning fear, you know, that makes you *sick*!

'I told myself I was going mad – but I couldn't help it. I felt I'd do anything in the world to get away! And then Adrian came and told me he loved me, and I thought it would be wonderful to go away with him, and he said . . .'

She stopped.

'You know what happened? I went off to meet Adrian – he never came . . . he was killed . . . I felt as though Nevile had managed it somehow.'

'Perhaps he did,' said Battle.

Audrey turned a startled face to him.

'Oh, do you think so?'

'We'll never know now. Motor accidents can be arranged. Don't brood on it, though, Mrs Strange. As likely as not, it just happened naturally.'

'I – I was all broken up. I went back to the Rectory – Adrian's home. We were going to have written to his mother, but as she didn't know about us, I thought I wouldn't tell her and give her pain. And Nevile came almost at once. He was very nice – and – kind – and all the time I talked to him I was quite sick with fear! He said no one need know about Adrian, that I could divorce him on evidence he would send me and that he was going to remarry afterwards. I felt so thankful. I knew he had thought Kay attractive and I hoped that everything would turn out right and that I should get over this queer obsession of mine. I still thought it must be *me*.

'But I couldn't get rid of it – quite. I never felt I'd really escaped. And then I met Nevile in the Park one day and he explained that he did so want me and Kay to be friends and suggested that we should all come here in September. I couldn't refuse, how could I? After all the kind things he'd done.'

'"Will you walk into my parlour? said the spider to the fly",' remarked Superintendent Battle.

Audrey shivered.

'Yes, just that . . .'

'Very clever he was about that,' said Battle. 'Protested so loudly to everyone that it was *his* idea, that everyone at once got the impression that it wasn't.'

Audrey said:

'And then I got here – and it was like a kind of nightmare. I *knew* something awful was going to happen – I *knew* Nevile meant it to happen – and that it was to happen to *me. But I didn't know what it was*. I think, you know, that I nearly *did* go off my head! I was just paralysed with fright – like you are in a dream when something's going to happen and you can't move . . .'

'I've always thought,' said Superintendent Battle, 'that I'd like to have seen a snake fascinate a bird so that it can't fly away – but now I'm not so sure.'

Audrey went on:

'Even when Lady Tressilian was killed, I didn't realize what it *meant*. I was puzzled. I didn't even suspect Nevile. I knew he didn't care about money – it was absurd to think he'd kill her in order to inherit fifty thousand pounds.

'I thought over and over again about Mr Treves and the story he had told that evening. Even then I didn't connect it with Nevile. Treves had mentioned some physical peculiarity by which he could recognize the child of long ago. I've got a scar on my ear but I don't think anyone else has any sign that you'd notice.'

Battle said: 'Miss Aldin has a lock of white hair. Thomas Royde has a stiff arm which might not have been only the result of an earthquake. Mr Ted Latimer has rather an odd-shaped skull. And Nevile Strange –' He paused.

'Surely there was no physical peculiarity about Nevile?'

'Oh yes, there was. His left-hand little finger is shorter than his right. That's very unusual, Mrs Strange – very unusual indeed.'

'So *that* was it?'

'That was it.'

'And Nevile hung that sign on the lift?'

'Yes. Nipped down there and back whilst Royde and Latimer were giving the old boy drinks. Clever and simple – doubt if we could ever prove *that* was murder.'

Audrey shivered again.

'Now, now,' said Battle. 'It's all over now, my dear. Go on talking.'

'You're very clever . . . I haven't talked so much for years!'

'No! That's what's been wrong. When did it first dawn on you what Master Nevile's game was?'

'I don't know exactly. It came to me all at once. He himself had been cleared and that left all of *us*. And then, suddenly, I saw him looking at me – a sort of gloating look. And I *knew*! That was when –'

She stopped abruptly.

'That was when what –?'

Audrey said slowly:

'When I thought a quick way out would be – best.'

Superintendent Battle shook his head.

'Never give in. That's my motto.'

'Oh, you're quite right. But you don't know what it does to you being so afraid for so long. It paralyses you – you can't think – you can't plan – you just wait for something awful to happen. And then, when it does happen' – she gave a sudden quick smile – 'you'd be surprised at the *relief*! No more waiting and fearing – it's *come*. You'll think I'm quite demented, I suppose, if I tell you that when you came to arrest me for murder I didn't mind at all. Nevile had done his worst and it was over. I felt so safe going off with Inspector Leach.'

'That's partly why we did it,' said Battle. 'I wanted you out of that madman's reach. And besides, if I wanted to break him down I wanted to be able to count on the shock of the reaction. He'd seen his plan come off, as he thought – so the jolt would be all the greater.'

Audrey said in a low voice:

'If he hadn't broken down would there have been any evidence?'

'Not too much. There was MacWhirter's story of seeing a man climb up a rope in the moonlight. And there was the rope itself confirming his story, coiled up in the attic and still faintly damp. It was raining that night, you know.'

He paused and stared hard at Audrey as though he were expecting her to say something.

As she merely looked interested he went on:

'And there was the pinstripe suit. He stripped, of course, in the dark at that rocky point on the Easterhead Bay side, and thrust his suit into a niche in the rock. As it happened he put it down on a decayed bit of fish washed up by the flood tide. It made a stained patch on the shoulder – and it smelt. There was some talk, I found out, about the drains being wrong in the Hotel. Nevile himself put that story about. He'd got his raincoat on over his suit, but the smell was a pervasive one. Then he got the wind up about that suit afterwards and at the first opportunity he took it off to the cleaners and like a fool, didn't give his own name. Took a name at random, actually one he'd seen in the Hotel register. That's how your friend got hold of it and, having a good head on him, he linked it up with the man climbing up the rope. You *step* on decayed fish but you don't put your *shoulder* down on it *unless you have taken your clothes off to bathe at night*, and no one would bathe for pleasure on a wet night in September. He fitted the whole thing together. Very ingenious man, Mr MacWhirter.'

'More than ingenious,' said Audrey.

'Mm, well, perhaps. Like to know about him? I can tell you something of his history.'

Audrey listened attentively. Battle found her a good listener. She said:

'I owe a lot to him – and to you.'

'Don't owe very much to me,' said Superintendent Battle. 'If I hadn't been a fool I'd have seen the point of that bell.'

'Bell? What bell?'

'The bell in Lady Tressilian's room. Always did feel there was something wrong about that bell. I nearly got it, too, when I came down the stairs from the top floor and saw one of those poles you open windows with.

'That was the whole point of the bell, see – to give Nevile Strange an alibi. Lady T didn't remember what she had rung for – of course she didn't, because *she hadn't rung at all*! Nevile rang the bell from outside in the passage with that long pole, the wires ran along the ceiling. So down comes Barrett and sees Mr Nevile Strange go downstairs and out, and she finds Lady Tressilian alive and well. The whole business of the maid was fishy. What's the good of doping her for a murder *that's going to be committed before midnight*? Ten to one she won't have gone off properly by then. But it fixes the murder as an inside job, and it allows a little time for Nevile to play his role of first suspect – then Barrett speaks and Nevile is so triumphantly cleared that no one is going to inquire very closely as to exactly what time he got to the Hotel. We know he didn't cross back by ferry, and no boats had been taken. There remained the possibility of swimming. He was a powerful swimmer, but even then the time must have been short. Up the rope he's left hanging into his bedroom and a good deal of water on the floor as we noticed (but without seeing the point, I'm sorry to say). Then into his blue coat and trousers, along to Lady Tressilian's room – we won't go into that – wouldn't have taken more than a couple of minutes, he'd fixed that steel ball beforehand – then back, out of his clothes, down the rope and back to Easterhead.'

'Suppose Kay had come in?'

'She'd been mildly doped, I'll bet. She was yawning from dinner on, so they tell me. Besides, he'd taken care to have a quarrel with her so that she'd lock her door and keep out of his way.'

'I'm trying to think if I noticed the ball was gone from the fender. I don't think I did. When did he put it back?'

'Next morning when all the hullaballoo arose. Once he got back in Ted Latimer's car, he had all night to clear up his traces and fix things, mend the tennis racquet, etc. By the way, he hit the old lady *backhanded*, you know. That's why the crime appeared to be left-handed. Strange's backhand was always his strong point, remember!'

'Don't – *don't* –' Audrey put up her hands. 'I can't bear any more.'

He smiled at her.

'All the same it's done you good to talk it all out. Mrs Strange, may I be impertinent and give you some advice?'

'Yes, please.'

'You lived for eight years with a criminal lunatic – that's enough to sap any woman's nerves. *But you've got to snap out of it now, Mrs Strange.* You don't need to be afraid any more – and you've got to make yourself realize that.'

Audrey smiled at him. The frozen look had gone from her face; it was a sweet, rather timid, but confiding face, with the wide-apart eyes full of gratitude.

She said, hesitating a little: 'You told the others there was a girl – a girl who acted as I did?'

Battle slowly nodded his head.

'My own daughter,' he said. 'So you see, my dear, that miracle *had* to happen. These things are sent to teach us!'

III

Angus MacWhirter was packing.

He laid three shirts carefully in his suitcase, and then that dark blue suit which he had remembered to fetch from the cleaners. Two suits left by two different MacWhirters had been too much for the girl in charge.

There was a tap on the door and he called 'Come in.'

Audrey Strange walked in. She said:

'I've come to thank you – are you packing?'

'Yes. I'm leaving here tonight. And sailing the day after tomorrow.'

'For South America?'

'For Chile.'

She said:

'I'll pack for you.'

He protested, but she overbore him. He watched her as she worked deftly and methodically.

'There,' she said when she had finished.

'You did that well,' said MacWhirter.

There was a silence. Then Audrey said:

'You saved my life. If you hadn't happened to see what you did see –'

She broke off.

Then she said: 'Did you realize at once, that night on the cliff when you – you stopped me going over – when you said "Go home, I'll see that you're not hanged" – did you realize *then* that you'd got some important evidence?'

'Not precisely,' said MacWhirter. 'I had to think it out.'

'Then how could you say – what you did say?'

MacWhirter always felt annoyed when he had to explain the intense simplicity of his thought processes.

'I meant just precisely that – that I intended to prevent you from being hanged.'

The colour came up in Audrey's cheeks.

'Supposing I had done it?'

'That would have made no difference.'

'Did you think I *had* done it, then?'

'I didn't speculate on the matter overmuch. I was inclined to believe you were innocent, but it would have made no difference to my course of action.'

'And then you remembered the man on the rope?'

MacWhirter was silent for a few moments. then he cleared his throat.

'You may as well know, I suppose. I did not actually see a man climbing up a rope – indeed I could not have done so, for I was up on Stark Head on Sunday night, not on Monday. I deduced what must have happened from the evidence of the suit and my suppositions were confirmed by the findings of a wet rope in the attic.'

From red Audrey had gone white. She said incredulously:

'Your story was all a lie?'

'Deductions would not have carried weight with the police. I had to say I saw what happened.'

'But – you might have had to swear to it at my trial.'

'Yes.'

'You would have done that?'

'I would.'

Audrey cried incredulously: 'And you – you are the man who lost his job and came down to throwing himself off a cliff because he wouldn't tamper with the truth!'

'I have a great regard for the truth. But I've discovered there are things that matter more.'

'Such as?'

'You,' said MacWhirter.

Audrey's eyes dropped. MacWhirter cleared his throat in an embarrassed manner.

'There's no need for you to feel under a great obligation or anything of that kind. You'll never hear of me again after today. The police have got Strange's confession and they'll not need my evidence. In any case I hear he's so bad he'll maybe not live to come to trial.'

'I'm glad of that,' said Audrey.

'You were fond of him once?'

'Of the man I thought he was.'

MacWhirter nodded. 'We've all felt that way, maybe.' He went on: 'Everything's turned out well. Superintendent Battle was able to act upon my story and break down the man –'

Audrey interrupted. She said:

'He worked upon your story, yes. But I don't believe you fooled him. He deliberately shut his eyes.'

'Why do you say that?'

'When he was talking to me he mentioned it was lucky you saw what you did in the moonlight, and then added something – a sentence or two later – about its being a *rainy night.*'

MacWhirter was taken aback. 'That's true. On Monday night I doubt if I'd have seen anything at all.'

'It doesn't matter,' said Audrey.

'He knew that what you pretended to have seen was what had really happened. But it explains why he worked on Nevile to break him down. He suspected Nevile as soon as Thomas told him about me and Adrian. He knew then that if he was right about the kind of crime – he had fixed on the wrong person – what he wanted was some kind of evidence to use on Nevile. He wanted, as he said, a miracle – you were Superintendent Battle's answer to prayer.'

'That's a curious thing for him to say,' said MacWhirter dryly.

'So you see,' said Audrey, 'you are a miracle. My special miracle.'

MacWhirter said earnestly:

'I'd not like you to feel you're under an obligation to me. I'm going right out of your life –'

'Must you?' said Audrey.

He stared at her. The colour came up, flooding her ears and temples.

She said:

'Won't you take me with you?'

'You don't know what you're saying!'

'Yes, I do. I'm doing something very difficult – but that matters to me more than life or death. I know the time is very short. By the way, I'm conventional, I should like to be married before we go!'

'Naturally,' said MacWhirter, deeply shocked. 'You don't imagine I'd suggest anything else.'

'I'm sure you wouldn't,' said Audrey.

MacWhirter said:

'I'm not your kind. I thought you'd marry that quiet fellow who's cared for you so long.'

'Thomas? Dear True Thomas. He's too true. He's faithful to the image of a girl he loved years ago. But the person he really cares for is Mary Aldin, though he doesn't know it yet himself.'

MacWhirter took a step towards her. He spoke sternly.

'Do you mean what you're saying?'

'Yes . . . I want to be with you always, never to leave you. If you go I shall never find anybody like you, and I shall go lonely all my days.'

MacWhirter sighed. He took out his wallet and carefully examined its contents.

He murmured:

'A special licence comes expensive. I'll need to go to the Bank first thing tomorrow.'

'I could lend you some money,' murmured Audrey.

'You'll do nothing of the kind. If I marry a woman, I pay for the licence. You understand?'

'You needn't,' said Audrey softly, 'look so stern.'

He said gently as he came towards her:

'Last time I had my hands on you, you felt like a bird – struggling to escape. You'll never escape now . . .'

She said:

'I shall never want to escape.'

•

SPARKLING CYANIDE

•

Six people were thinking of Rosemary Barton who
had died nearly a year ago . . .

BOOK I • ROSEMARY

'What can I do to drive away remembrances
from mine eyes?'

CHAPTER I

IRIS MARLE

I

Iris Marle was thinking about her sister, Rosemary.

For nearly a year she had deliberately tried to put the thought of Rosemary away from her. She hadn't wanted to remember.

It was too painful – too horrible!

The blue cyanosed face, the convulsed clutching fingers . . .

The contrast between that and the gay lovely Rosemary of the day before . . . Well, perhaps not exactly *gay*. She had had 'flu – she had been depressed, run down . . . All that had been brought out at the inquest. Iris herself had laid stress on it. It accounted, didn't it, for Rosemary's suicide?

Once the inquest was over, Iris had deliberately tried to put the whole thing out of her mind. Of what good was remembrance? Forget it all! Forget the whole horrible business.

But now, she realized, she had got to remember. She had got to think back into the past . . . To remember carefully every slight unimportant seeming incident . . .

That extraordinary interview with George last night necessitated remembrance.

It had been so unexpected, so frightening. Wait – *had* it been so unexpected? Hadn't there been indications beforehand? George's growing absorption, his absentmindedness, his unaccountable actions – his – well, *queerness* was the only word for it! All leading up to that moment last night when he had called her into the study and taken the letters from the drawer of the desk.

So now there was no help for it. She had got to think about Rosemary – to *remember*.

Rosemary – her sister . . .

With a shock Iris realized suddenly that it was the first time in her life she had ever thought about Rosemary. Thought about her, that is, objectively, as a *person*.

She had always accepted Rosemary without thinking about her. You didn't think about your mother or your father or your sister or your aunt. They just existed, unquestioned, in those relationships.

You didn't think about them as *people*. You didn't ask yourself, even, what they were *like*.

What had Rosemary been like?

That might be very important now. A lot might depend upon it. Iris cast her mind back into the past. Herself and Rosemary as children . . .

Rosemary had been the elder by six years.

II

Glimpses of the past came back – brief flashes – short scenes. Herself as a small child eating bread and milk, and Rosemary, important in pig tails, 'doing lessons' at a table.

The seaside one summer – Iris envying Rosemary who was a 'big girl' and could swim!

Rosemary going to boarding school – coming home for the holidays. Then she herself at school, and Rosemary being 'finished' in Paris. Schoolgirl Rosemary; clumsy, all arms and legs. 'Finished' Rosemary coming back from Paris with a strange new frightening elegance, soft voiced, graceful, with a swaying undulating figure, with red gold chestnut hair and big black fringed dark blue eyes. A disturbing beautiful creature – grown up – in a different world!

From then on they had seen very little of each other, the six-year gap had been at its widest.

Iris had been still at school, Rosemary in the full swing of a 'season.' Even when Iris came home, the gap remained. Rosemary's life was one of late mornings in bed, fork luncheons with other débutantes, dances most evenings of the week. Iris had been in the schoolroom with Mademoiselle, had gone for walks in the Park, had had supper at nine o'clock and gone to bed at ten. The intercourse between the sisters had been limited to such brief interchanges as:

'Hullo, Iris, telephone for a taxi for me, there's a lamb, I'm going to be devastatingly late,' or

'I don't like that new frock, Rosemary. It doesn't suit you. It's all bunch and fuss.'

Then had come Rosemary's engagement to George Barton. Excitement, shopping, streams of parcels, bridesmaids' dresses.

The wedding. Walking up the aisles behind Rosemary, hearing whispers:

'What a *beautiful* bride she makes . . .'

Why had Rosemary married George? Even at the time Iris had been vaguely surprised. There had been so many exciting young men, ringing Rosemary up, taking her out. Why choose George Barton, fifteen years older than herself, kindly, pleasant, but definitely dull?

George was well off, but it wasn't money. Rosemary had her own money, a great deal of it.

Uncle Paul's money . . .

Iris searched her mind carefully, seeking to differentiate between what she knew now and what she had known then: Uncle Paul, for instance?

He wasn't really an uncle, she had always known that. Without ever having been definitely told them she knew certain facts. Paul Bennett had been in love with their mother. She had preferred another and a poorer man. Paul Bennett had taken his defeat in a romantic spirit. He had remained the family friend, adopted an attitude of romantic platonic devotion. He had become Uncle Paul, had stood godfather to the first-born child, Rosemary. When he died, it was found that he had left his entire fortune to his little god-daughter, then a child of thirteen.

Rosemary, besides her beauty, had been an heiress. And she had married nice dull George Barton.

Why? Iris had wondered then. She wondered now. Iris didn't believe that Rosemary had ever been in love with him. But she had seemed very happy with him and she had been fond of him – yes, definitely fond of him. Iris had good opportunities for knowing, for a year after the marriage, their mother, lovely delicate Viola Marle, had died, and Iris, a girl of seventeen, had gone to live with Rosemary Barton and her husband.

A girl of seventeen. Iris pondered over the picture of herself. What had she been like? What had she felt, thought, seen?

She came to the conclusion that that young Iris Marle had been slow of development – unthinking, acquiescing in things as they were. Had she resented, for instance, her mother's earlier absorption in Rosemary? On the whole she thought not. She had accepted, unhesitatingly, the fact that Rosemary was the important one. Rosemary was 'out' – naturally her mother was occupied as far as her health permitted with her elder daughter. That had been natural enough. Her own turn would come some day. Viola Marle had always been a somewhat remote mother, preoccupied mainly with her own health, relegating her children to nurses, governesses, schools, but invariably charming to them in those brief moments when she came across them. Hector Marle had died when Iris was five years old. The knowledge that he drank more than was good for him had permeated so subtly that she had not the least idea how it had actually come to her.

Seventeen-year-old Iris Marle had accepted life as it came, had duly mourned for her mother, had worn black clothes, had gone to live with her sister and her sister's husband at their house in Elvaston Square.

Sometimes it had been rather dull in that house. Iris wasn't to come out, officially, until the following year. In the meantime she took French and German lessons three times a week, and also attended domestic science classes. There were times when she had nothing much to do and nobody to talk to. George was kind, invariably affectionate and brotherly. His attitude had never varied. He was the same now.

And Rosemary? Iris had seen very little of Rosemary. Rosemary had been out a good deal. Dressmakers, cocktail parties, bridge . . .

What did she really *know* about Rosemary when she came to think of it? Of her tastes, of her hopes, of her fears? Frightening, really, how little you might know of a person after living in the same house with them! There had been little or no intimacy between the sisters.

But she'd got to think now. She'd got to remember. It might be important.

Certainly Rosemary had *seemed* happy enough . . .

III

Until that day – a week before it happened.

She, Iris, would never forget that day. It stood out crystal clear – each detail, each word. The shining mahogany table, the pushed back chair, the hurried characteristic writing . . .

Iris closed her eyes and let the scene come back . . .

Her own entry into Rosemary's sitting-room, her sudden stop.

It had startled her so; what she saw! Rosemary, sitting at the writing table, her head laid down on her outstretched arms. Rosemary weeping with a deep abanoned sobbing. She'd never seen Rosemary cry before – and this bitter, violent weeping frightened her.

True, Rosemary had had a bad go of 'flu. She'd only been up a day or two. And everyone knew that 'flu *did* leave you depressed. Still –

Iris had cried out, her voice childish, startled:

'Oh, Rosemary, what is it?'

Rosemary sat up, swept the hair back from her disfigured face. She struggled to regain command of herself. She said quickly:

'It's nothing – nothing – don't stare at me like that!'

She got up and passing her sister, she ran out of the room.

Puzzled, upset, Iris went farther into the room. Her eyes, drawn wonderingly to the writing table, caught sight of her own name in her sister's handwriting. Had Rosemary been writing to her then?

She drew nearer, looked down on the sheet of blue notepaper with the big characteristic sprawling writing, even more sprawling than usual owing to the haste and agitation behind the hand that held the pen.

Darling Iris,

There isn't any point in my making a will because my money goes to you anyway, but I'd like certain of my things to be given to certain people.

To George, the jewellery he's given me, and the little enamel casket we bought together when we were engaged.

To Gloria King, my platinum cigarette case.

To Maisie, my Chinese Pottery horse that she's always admired –

It stopped there, with a frantic scrawl of the pen as Rosemary had dashed it down and given way to uncontrollable weeping.

Iris stood as though turned to stone.

What did it mean? Rosemary wasn't going to *die*, was she? She'd been very ill with influenza, but she was all right now. And anyway people didn't die of 'flu – at least sometimes they did, but Rosemary hadn't. She was quite well now, only weak and run down.

Iris's eyes went over the words again and this time a phrase stood out with startling effect:

'. . . *my money goes to you anyway . . .*'

It was the first intimation she had had of the terms of Paul Bennett's will. She had known since she was a child that Rosemary had inherited Uncle Paul's money, that Rosemary was rich whilst she herself was comparatively poor. But until this moment she had never questioned what would happen to that money on Rosemary's death.

If she had been asked, she would have replied that she supposed it would go to George as Rosemary's husband, but would have added that it seemed absurd to think of Rosemary dying before George!

But here it was, set down in black and white, in Rosemary's own hand. At Rosemary's death the money came to her, Iris. But surely that wasn't legal? A husband or wife got any money, not a *sister*. Unless, of course, Paul Bennett had left it that way in his will. Yes, that must be it. Uncle Paul had said the money was to go to her if Rosemary died. That did make it rather less unfair –

Unfair? She was startled as the word leapt to her thoughts. Had she been thinking that it was unfair for Rosemary to get *all* Uncle Paul's money? She supposed that, deep down, she must have been feeling just that. It *was* unfair. They were sisters, she and Rosemary. They were both her mother's children. Why should Uncle Paul give it all to Rosemary?

Rosemary always had everything!

Parties and frocks and young men in love with her and an adoring husband.

The only unpleasant thing that ever happened to Rosemary was having an attack of 'flu! And even *that* hadn't lasted longer than a week!

Iris hesitated, standing by the desk. That sheet of paper – would Rosemary want it left about for the servants to see?

After a minute's hesitation she picked it up, folded it in two and slipped it into one of the drawers of the desk.

It was found there after the fatal birthday party, and provided an additional proof, if proof was necessary, that Rosemary had been in a depressed and unhappy state of mind after her illness, and had possibly been thinking of suicide even then.

Depression after influenza. That was the motive brought forward at the inquest, the motive that Iris's evidence helped to establish. An inadequate motive, perhaps, but the only one available, and consequently accepted. It had been a bad type of influenza that year.

Neither Iris nor George Barton could have suggested any other motive – *then*.

Now, thinking back over the incident in the attic, Iris wondered that she could have been so blind.

The whole thing must have been going on under her eyes! And she had seen nothing, noticed nothing!

Her mind took a quick leap over the tragedy of the birthday party. No need to think of *that*! That was over – done with. Put away the horror of that and the inquest and George's twitching face and bloodshot eyes. Go straight on to the incident of the trunk in the attic.

IV

That had been about six months after Rosemary's death.

Iris had continued to live at the house in Elvaston Square. After the funeral the Marle family solicitor, a courtly old gentleman with a shining bald head and unexpectedly shrewd eyes, had had an interview with Iris. He had explained with admirable clarity that under the will of Paul Bennett, Rosemary had inherited his estate in trust to pass at her death to any children she might have. If Rosemary died childless, the estate was to go to Iris absolutely. It was, the solicitor explained, a very large fortune which would belong to her absolutely upon attaining the age of twenty-one or on her marriage.

In the meantime, the first thing to settle was her place of residence. Mr George Barton had shown himself anxious for her to continue living with him and had suggested that her father's sister, Mrs Drake, who was in impoverished circumstances owing to the financial claims of a son (the black sheep of the Marle family), should make her home with them and chaperon Iris in society. Did Iris approve of this plan?

Iris had been quite willing, thankful not to have to make new plans. Aunt Lucilla she remembered as an amiable friendly sheep with little will of her own.

So the matter had been settled. George Barton had been touchingly pleased to have his wife's sister still with him and treated her affectionately as a younger sister. Mrs Drake, if not a stimulating companion, was completely subservient to Iris's wishes. The household settled down amicably.

It was nearly six months later that Iris made her discovery in the attic.

The attics of the Elvaston Square house were used as storage rooms for odds and ends of furniture, and a number of trunks and suitcases.

Iris had gone up there one day after an unsuccessful hunt for an old red pullover for which she had an affection. George had begged her not to wear mourning for Rosemary, Rosemary had always been opposed to the idea, he said. This, Iris knew, was true, so she acquiesced and continued to wear ordinary clothes, somewhat to the disapproval of Lucilla Drake, who was old-fashioned and liked what she called 'the decencies' to be observed. Mrs Drake herself was still inclined to wear crêpe for a husband deceased some twenty-odd years ago.

Various unwanted clothes, Iris knew, had been packed away in a trunk upstairs. She started hunting through it for her pullover, coming across, as she did so, various forgotten belongings, a grey coat and skirt, a pile of stockings, her skiing kit and one or two old bathing dresses.

It was then that she came across an old dressing-gown that had belonged to Rosemary and which had somehow or other escaped being given away with the rest of Rosemary's things. It was a mannish affair of spotted silk with big pockets.

Iris shook it out, noting that it was in perfectly good condition. Then she folded it carefully and returned it to the trunk. As she did so, her hand felt something crackle in one of the pockets. She thrust in her hand and drew out a crumpled-up piece of paper. It was in Rosemary's handwriting and she smoothed it out and read it.

Leopard darling, you can't mean it . . . You can't – you can't . . . We love each other! We belong together! You must know that just as I know it! We can't just say goodbye and go on coolly with our own lives. You know that's impossible, darling – quite impossible. You and I belong together – for ever and ever. I'm not a conventional woman – I don't mind about what people say. Love matters more to me than anything else. We'll go away together – and be happy – I'll make you happy. You said to me once that life without me was dust and ashes to you – do you remember, Leopard darling? And now you write calmly that all this had better end – that it's only fair to me. Fair to me? But I can't live without you! I'm sorry about George – he's always been sweet to me – but he'll understand. He'll want to give me my freedom. It isn't right to live together if you don't love each other any more. God meant us for each other, darling – I know He did. We're going to be wonderfully happy – but we must be brave. I shall tell George myself – I want to be quite straight about the whole thing – but not until after my birthday.

I know I'm doing what's right, Leopard darling – and I can't live without you – can't, can't – CAN'T. How stupid it is of me to write all this. Two lines would have done. Just 'I love you. I'm never going to let you go.' Oh darling –

The letter broke off.

Iris stood motionless, staring down at it.

How little one knew of one's own sister!

So Rosemary had had a lover – had written him passionate love letters – had planned to go away with him?

What had happened? Rosemary had never sent the letter after all. What letter had she sent? What had been finally decided between Rosemary and this unknown man?

('Leopard!' What extraordinary fancies people had when they were in love. So silly. *Leopard* indeed!)

Who was this man? Did he love Rosemary as much as she loved him? Surely he must have done. Rosemary was so unbelievably lovely. And yet, according to Rosemary's letter, he had suggested 'ending it all'. That suggested – what? Caution? He had evidently said that the break was for Rosemary's sake. That it was only fair to her. Yes, but didn't men say that sort of thing to save their faces? Didn't it really mean that the man, whoever he was, was tired of it all? Perhaps it had been to him a mere passing distraction. Perhaps he had never really cared. Somehow Iris got the impression that the unknown man had been very determined to break with Rosemary finally . . .

But Rosemary had thought differently. Rosemary wasn't going to count the cost. Rosemary had been determined, too . . .

Iris shivered.

And she, Iris, hadn't known a thing about it! Hadn't even guessed! Had taken it for granted that Rosemary was happy and contented and that she and George were quite satisfied with one another. Blind! She must have been blind not to know a thing like that about her own sister.

But who was the man?

She cast her mind back, thinking, remembering. There had been so many men about, admiring Rosemary, taking her out, ringing her up. There had been no one special. But there must have been – the rest of the bunch were mere camouflage for the one, the only one, that mattered. Iris frowned perplexedly, sorting her remembrances carefully.

Two names stood out. It must, yes, positively it must, be one or the other. Stephen Farraday? It must be Stephen Farraday. What could Rosemary have seen in him? A stiff pompous young man – and not so very young either. Of course people did say he was brilliant. A rising politician, an under-secretaryship prophesied in the near future, and all the weight of the influential Kidderminster connection behind him. A possible future Prime Minister! Was that what had given him glamour in Rosemary's eyes? Surely she couldn't care so desperately for the man himself – such a cold self-contained creature? But they said that his own wife was passionately in love with him, that she had gone against all the wishes of her powerful family in marrying him – a mere nobody with political ambitions! If one woman felt like that about him, another woman might also. Yes, it *must* be Stephen Farraday.

Because, if it wasn't Stephen Farraday, it must be Anthony Browne.

And Iris didn't want it to be Anthony Browne.

True, he'd been very much Rosemary's slave, constantly at her beck and call, his dark good-looking face expressing a kind of humorous desperation. But surely that devotion had been too open, too freely declared to go really deep?

Odd the way he had disappeared after Rosemary's death. They had none of them seen him since.

Still not so odd really – he was a man who travelled a lot. He had talked about the Argentine and Canada and Uganda and the U.S.A. She had an idea that he was actually an American or a Canadian, though he had hardly any accent. No, it wasn't really strange that they shouldn't have seen anything of him since.

It was Rosemary who had been his friend. There was no reason why he should go on coming to see the rest of them. He had been Rosemary's friend. But not Rosemary's lover! She didn't want him to have been Rosemary's lover. That would hurt – that would hurt terribly . . .

She looked down at the letter in her hand. She crumpled it up. She'd throw it away, burn it . . .

It was sheer instinct that stopped her.

Some day it might be important to produce that letter . . .

She smoothed it out, took it down with her and locked it away in her jewel case.

It might be important, some day, to show why Rosemary took her own life.

V

'And the next thing, please?'

The ridiculous phrase came unbidden into Iris's mind and twisted her lips into a wry smile. The glib shopkeeper's question seemed to represent so exactly her own carefully directed mental processes.

Was not that exactly what she was trying to do in her survey of the past? She had dealt with the surprising discovery in the attic. And now – on to 'the next thing, please!' What was the next thing?

Surely the increasingly odd behaviour of George. That dated back for a long time. Little things that had puzzled her became clear now in the light of the surprising interview last night.

Disconnected remarks and actions took their proper place in the course of events.

And there was the reappearance of Anthony Browne. Yes, perhaps that ought to come next in sequence, since it had followed the finding of the letter by just one week.

Iris couldn't recall her sensations exactly . . .

Rosemary had died in November. In the following May, Iris, under the wing of Lucilla Drake, had started her social young girl's life. She had gone to luncheons and teas and dances without, however, enjoying them very much. She had felt listless and unsatisfied. It was at a somewhat dull dance towards the end of June that she heard a voice say behind her:

'It *is* Iris Marle, isn't it?'

She had turned, flushing, to look into Anthony's – Tony's – dark quizzical face.

He said:

'I don't expect you to remember me, but –'

She interrupted.

'Oh, but I do remember you. Of course I do!'

'Splendid. I was afraid you'd have forgotten me. It's such a long time since I saw you.'

'I know. Not since Rosemary's birthday par –'

She stopped. The words had come gaily, unthinkingly, to her lips. Now the colour rushed away from her cheeks, leaving them white and drained of blood. Her lips quivered. Her eyes were suddenly wide and dismayed.

Anthony Browne said quickly:

'I'm terribly sorry. I'm a brute to have reminded you.'

Iris swallowed. She said:

'It's all right.'

(Not since the night of Rosemary's birthday party. Not since the night of Rosemary's suicide. She wouldn't think of it. She would *not* think of it!)

Anthony Browne said again:

'I'm terribly sorry. Please forgive me. Shall we dance?'

She nodded. Although already engaged for the dance that was just beginning, she had floated on to the floor in his arms. She saw her partner, a blushing immature young man whose collar seemed too big for him, peering about for her. The sort of partner, she thought scornfully, that debs have to put up with. Not like this man – Rosemary's friend.

A sharp pang went through her. *Rosemary's friend*. That letter. Had it been written to this man she was dancing with now? Something in the easy feline grace with which he danced lent substance to the nickname 'Leopard'. Had he and Rosemary –

She said sharply:

'Where have you been all this time?'

He held her a little way from him, looking down into her face. He was unsmiling now, his voice held coldness.

'I've been travelling – on business.'

'I see.' She went on uncontrollably, 'Why have you come back?'

He smiled then. He said lightly:

'Perhaps – to see you, Iris Marle.'

And suddenly gathering her up a little closer, he executed a long daring glide through the dancers, a miracle of timing and steering. Iris wondered why, with a sensation that was almost wholly pleasure, she should feel afraid.

Since then Anthony had definitely become part of her life. She saw him at least once a week.

She met him in the Park, at various dances, found him put next to her at dinner.

The only place he never came to was the house in Elvaston Square. It was some time before she noticed this, so adroitly did he manage to evade or refuse invitations there. When she did realize it she began to wonder why. Was it because he and Rosemary –

Then, to her astonishment, George, easy-going, non-interfering George, spoke to her about him.

'Who's this fellow, Anthony Browne, you're going about with? What do you know about him?'

She stared at him.

'Know about him? Why, he was a friend of Rosemary's!'

George's face twitched. He blinked. He said in a dull heavy voice:

'Yes, of course, so he was.'

Iris cried remorsefully:

'I'm sorry. I shouldn't have reminded you.'

George Barton shook his head. He said gently:

'No, no, I don't want her forgotten. Never that. After all,' he spoke awkwardly, his eyes averted, 'that's what her name means. Rosemary – remembrance.' He looked full at her. 'I don't want you to forget your sister, Iris.'

She caught her breath.

'I never shall.'

George went on:

'But about this young fellow, Anthony Browne. Rosemary may have liked him, but I don't believe she knew much about him. You know, you've got to be careful, Iris. You're a very rich young woman.'

A kind of burning anger swept over her.

'Tony – Anthony – has plenty of money himself. Why, he stays at Claridge's when he's in London.'

George Barton smiled a little. He murmured:

'Eminently respectable – as well as costly. All the same, my dear, nobody seems to know much about this fellow.'

'He's an American.'

'Perhaps. If so, it's odd he isn't sponsored more by his own Embassy. He doesn't come much to this house, does he?'

'No. And I can see why, if you're so horrid about him!'

George shook his head.

'Seem to have put my foot in it. Oh well. Only wanted to give you a timely warning. I'll have a word with Lucilla.'

'Lucilla!' said Iris scornfully.

George said anxiously:

'Is everything all right? I mean, does Lucilla see to it that you get the sort of time you ought to have? Parties – all that sort of thing?'

'Yes, indeed, she works like a beaver . . .'

'Because, if not, you've only got to say, you know, child. We could get hold of someone else. Someone younger and more up to date. I want you to enjoy yourself.'

'I do, George. Oh, George, I do.'

He said rather heavily:

'Then that's all right. I'm not much hand at these shows myself – never was. But see to it you get everything you want. There's no need to stint expense.'

That was George all over – kind, awkward, blundering.

True to his promise, or threat, he 'had a word' with Mrs Drake on the subject of Anthony Browne, but as Fate would have it the moment was unpropitious for gaining Lucilla's full attention.

She had just had a cable from that ne'er-do-well son who was the apple of her eye and who knew, only too well, how to wring the maternal heartstrings to his own financial advantage.

'Can you send me two hundred pounds. Desperate. Life or death. Victor.'

'Victor is so honourable. He knows how straitened my circumstances are and he'd never apply to me except in the last resource. He never has. I'm always so afraid he'll shoot himself.'

'Not he,' said George Barton unfeelingly.

'You don't know him. I'm his mother and naturally I know what my own son is like. I should never forgive myself if I didn't do what he asked. I could manage by selling out those shares.'

George sighed.

'Look here, Lucilla. I'll get full information by cable from one of my correspondents out there. We'll find out just exactly what sort of a jam Victor's in. But my advice to you is to let him stew in his own juice. He'll never make good until you do.'

'You're so hard, George. The poor boy has always been unlucky –'

George repressed his opinions on that point. Never any good arguing with women.

He merely said:

'I'll get Ruth on to it at once. We should hear by tomorrow.'

Lucilla was partially appeased. The two hundred was eventually cut down to fifty, but that amount Lucilla firmly insisted on sending.

George, Iris knew, provided the amount himself though pretending to Lucilla that he was selling her shares. Iris admired George very much for his generosity and said so. His answer was simple.

'Way I look at it – always some black sheep in the family.

Always someone who's got to be kept. Someone or other will have to fork out for Victor until he dies.'

'But it needn't be you. He's not *your* family.'

'Rosemary's family's *mine*.'

'You're a darling, George. But couldn't *I* do it? You're always telling me I'm rolling.'

He grinned at her.

'Can't do anything of that kind until you're twenty-one, young woman. And if you're wise you won't do it then. But I'll give you one tip. When a fellow wires that he'll end everything unless he gets a couple of hundred by return, you'll usually find that twenty pounds will be ample . . . I daresay a tenner would do! You can't stop a mother coughing up, but you can reduce the amount – remember that. Of course Victor Drake would never do away with himself, not he! These people who threaten suicide never do it.'

Never? Iris thought of Rosemary. Then she pushed the thought away. George wasn't thinking of Rosemary. He was thinking of an unscrupulous, plausible young man in Rio de Janeiro.

The net gain from Iris's point of view was that Lucilla's maternal preoccupations kept her from paying full attention to Iris's friendship with Anthony Browne.

So – on to the 'next thing, Madam.' The change in George! Iris couldn't put it off any longer. When had that begun? What was the cause of it?

Even now, thinking back, Iris could not put her finger definitely on the moment when it began. Ever since Rosemary's death George had been abstracted, had had fits of inattention and brooding. He had seemed older, heavier. That was all natural enough. But when exactly had his abstraction become something more than natural?

It was, she thought, after their clash over Anthony Browne, that she had first noticed him staring at her in a bemused, perplexed manner. Then he formed a new habit of coming home early from business and shutting himself up in his study. He didn't seem to be doing anything there. She had gone in once and found him sitting at his desk staring straight ahead of him. He looked at her when she came in with dull lack-lustre eyes. He behaved like a man who has had a shock, but to her question as to what was the matter, he replied briefly, 'Nothing.'

As the days went on, he went about with the careworn look of a man who has some definite worry upon his mind.

Nobody had paid very much attention. Iris certainly hadn't. Worries were always conveniently 'Business'.

Then, at odd intervals, and with no seeming reason, he began to ask questions. It was then that she began to put his manner down as definitely 'queer'.

'Look here, Iris, did Rosemary ever talk to you much?'

Iris stared at him.

'Why, of course, George. At least – well, about what?'

'Oh, herself – her friends – how things were going with her. Whether she was happy or unhappy. That sort of thing.'

She thought she saw what was in his mind. He must have got wind of Rosemary's unhappy love affair.

She said slowly:

'She never said much. I mean – she was always busy – doing things.'

'And you were only a kid, of course. Yes, I know. All the same, I thought she might have said something.'

He looked at her inquiringly – rather like a hopeful dog.

She didn't want George to be hurt. And anyway Rosemary never *had* said anything. She shook her head.

George sighed. He said heavily:

'Oh, well, it doesn't matter.'

Another day he asked her suddenly who Rosemary's best women friends had been.

Iris reflected.

'Gloria King. Mrs Atwell – Maisie Atwell. Jean Raymond.'

'How intimate was she with them?'

'Well, I don't know exactly.'

'I mean, do you think she might have confided in any of them?'

'I don't really know . . . I don't think it's awfully likely . . . What sort of confidence do you mean?'

Immediately she wished she hadn't asked that last question, but George's response to it surprised her.

'Did Rosemary ever say she was afraid of anybody?'

'Afraid?' Iris stared.

'What I'm trying to get at is, did Rosemary have any enemies?'

'Amongst other women?'

'No, no, not that kind of thing. Real enemies. There wasn't anyone – that you knew of – who – who might have had it in for her?'

Iris's frank stare seemed to upset him. He reddened, muttered:

'Sounds silly, I know. Melodramatic, but I just wondered.'

It was a day or two after that that he started asking about the Farradays.

How much had Rosemary seen of the Farradays?

Iris was doubtful.

'I really don't know, George.'

'Did she ever talk about them?'

'No, I don't think so.'

'Were they intimate at all?'

'Rosemary was very interested in politics.'

'Yes. After she met the Farradays in Switzerland. Never cared a button about politics before that.'

'No. I think Stephen Farraday interested her in them. He used to lend her pamphlets and things.'

George said:

'What did Sandra Farraday think about it?'

'About what?'

'About her husband lending Rosemary pamphlets.'

Iris said uncomfortably:

'I don't know.'

George said, 'She's a very reserved woman. Looks cold as ice. But they say she's crazy about Farraday. Sort of woman who might resent his having a friendship with another woman.'

'Perhaps.'

'How did Rosemary and Farraday's wife get on?'

Iris said slowly:

'I don't think they did. Rosemary laughed at Sandra. Said she was one of those stuffed political women like a rocking horse. (She is rather like a horse, you know.) Rosemary used to say that "if you pricked her sawdust would ooze out."'

George grunted.

Then he said:

'Still seeing a good deal of Anthony Browne?'

'A fair amount.' Iris's voice was cold, but George did not repeat his warnings. Instead he seemed interested.

'Knocked about a good deal, hasn't he? Must have had an interesting life. Does he ever talk to you about it?'

'Not much. He's travelled a lot, of course.'

'Business, I suppose.'

'I suppose so.'

'What is his business?'

'I don't know.'

'Something to do with armament firms, isn't it?'

'He's never said.'

'Well, needn't mention I asked. I just wondered. He was about a lot last Autumn with Dewsbury, who's chairman of the United Arms Ltd . . . Rosemary saw rather a lot of Anthony Browne, didn't she?'

'Yes – yes, she did.'

'But she hadn't known him very long – he was more or less of a casual acquaintance? Used to take her dancing, didn't he?'

'Yes.'

'I was rather surprised, you know, that she wanted him at her birthday party. Didn't realize she knew him so well.'

Iris said quietly:

'He dances very well . . .'

'Yes – yes, of course . . .'

Without wishing to, Iris unwillingly let a picture of that evening flit across her mind.

The round table at the Luxembourg, the shaded lights, the flowers. The dance band with its insistent rhythm. The seven people round the table, herself, Anthony Browne, Rosemary, Stephen Farraday, Ruth Lessing, George, and on George's right, Stephen Farraday's wife, Lady Alexandra Farraday with her pale straight hair and those slightly arched nostrils and her clear arrogant voice. Such a gay party it had been, or hadn't it?

And in the middle of it, Rosemary – *No, no, better not think about that*. Better only to remember herself sitting next to Tony – that was the first time she had really met him. Before that he had been only a name, a shadow in the hall, a back accompanying Rosemary down the steps in front of the house to a waiting taxi.

Tony –

She came back with a start. George was repeating a question.

'Funny he cleared off so soon after. Where did he go, do you know?'

She said vaguely, 'Oh, Ceylon, I think, or India.'

'Never mentioned it that night.'

Iris said sharply:

'Why should he? And have we got to talk about – that night?'

His face crimsoned over.

'No, no, of course not. Sorry, old thing. By the way, ask Browne to dinner one night. I'd like to meet him again.'

Iris was delighted. George was coming round. The invitation was duly given and accepted, but at the last minute Anthony had to go North on business and couldn't come.

One day at the end of July, George startled both Lucilla and Iris by announcing that he had bought a house in the country.

'Bought a *house*?' Iris was incredulous. 'But I thought we were going to rent that house at Goring for two months?'

'Nicer to have a place of one's own – eh? Can go down for weekends all through the year.'

'Where is it? On the river?'

'Not exactly. In fact, not at all. Sussex. Marlingham. Little Priors, it's called. Twelve acres – small Georgian house.'

'Do you mean you've bought it without us even seeing it?'

'Rather a chance. Just came into the market. Snapped it up.'

Mrs Drake said:

'I suppose it will need a lot of doing up and redecorating.'

George said in an off-hand way:

'Oh, that's all right. Ruth has seen to all that.'

They received the mention of Ruth Lessing, George's capable secretary, in respectful silence. Ruth was an institution – practically one of the family. Good looking in a severe black-and-white kind of way, she was the essence of efficiency combined with tact . . .

During Rosemary's lifetime, it had been usual for Rosemary to say, 'Let's get Ruth to see to it. She's marvellous. Oh, leave it to Ruth.'

Every difficulty could always be smoothed out by Miss

Lessing's capable fingers. Smiling, pleasant, aloof, she surmounted all obstacles. She ran George's office and, it was suspected, ran George as well. He was devoted to her and leaned upon her judgement in every way. She seemed to have no needs, no desires of her own.

Nevertheless on this occasion Lucilla Drake was annoyed.

'My dear George, capable as Ruth is, well, I mean – the women of a family do like to arrange the colour scheme of their own drawing-room! Iris should have been consulted. I say nothing about myself. *I* do not count. But it is annoying for Iris.'

George looked conscience-stricken.

'I wanted it to be a surprise!'

Lucilla had to smile.

'What a boy you are, George.'

Iris said:

'I don't mind about colour schemes. I'm sure Ruth will have made it perfect. She's so clever. What shall we do down there? There's a tennis court, I suppose.'

'Yes, and golf links six miles away, and it's only about fourteen miles to the sea. What's more we shall have neighbours. Always wise to go to a part of the world where you know somebody, I think.'

'What neighbours?' asked Iris sharply.

George did not meet her eyes.

'The Farradays,' he said. 'They live about a mile and a half away just across the park.'

Iris stared at him. In a minute she leapt to the conviction that the whole of this elaborate business, the purchasing and equipping of a country house, had been undertaken with one object only – to bring George into close relationship with Stephen and Sandra Farraday. Near neighbours in the country, with adjoining estates, the two families were bound to be on intimate terms. Either that or a deliberate coolness!

But why? Why this persistent harping on the Farradays? Why this costly method of achieving an incomprehensible aim?

Did George suspect that Rosemary and Stephen Farraday had been something more than friends? Was this a strange manifestation of post-mortem jealousy? Surely that was a thought too far-fetched for words!

But what *did* George want from the Farradays? What was the point of all the odd questions he was continually shooting at her, Iris? Wasn't there something very queer about George lately?

The odd fuddled look he had in the evenings! Lucilla attributed it to a glass or so too much of port. Lucilla would!

No, there was something queer about George lately. He seemed to be labouring under a mixture of excitement interlarded with great spaces of complete apathy when he sunk in a coma.

Most of that August they spent in the country at Little Priors. Horrible house! Iris shivered. She hated it. A gracious well-built house, harmoniously furnished and decorated (Ruth Lessing was never at fault!). And curiously, frighteningly *vacant*. They didn't live there. They *occupied* it. As soldiers, in a war, occupied some look-out post.

What made it horrible was the overlay of ordinary normal summer living. People down for weekends, tennis parties, informal dinners with the Farradays. Sandra Farraday had been charming to them – the perfect manner to neighbours who were already friends. She introduced them to the county, advised George and Iris about horses, was prettily deferential to Lucilla as an older woman.

And behind the mask of her pale smiling face no one could know what she was thinking. A woman like a sphinx.

Of Stephen they had seen less. He was very busy, often absent on political business. To Iris it seemed certain that he deliberately avoided meeting the Little Priors party more than he could help.

So August had passed and September, and it was decided that in October they should go back to the London house.

Iris had drawn a deep breath of relief. Perhaps, once they were back George would return to his normal self.

And then, last night, she had been roused by a low tapping on her door. She switched on the light and glanced at the time. Only one o'clock. She had gone to bed at half-past ten and it had seemed to her it was much later.

She threw on a dressing-gown and went to the door. Somehow that seemed more natural than just to shout 'Come in.'

George was standing outside. He had not been to bed and was still in his evening clothes. His breath was coming unevenly and his face was a curious blue colour.

He said:

'Come down to the study, Iris. I've got to talk to you. I've got to talk to someone.'

Wondering, still dazed with sleep, she obeyed.

Inside the study, he shut the door and motioned her to sit opposite him at the desk. He pushed the cigarette box across to her, at the same time taking one and lighting it, after one or two attempts, with a shaking hand.

She said, 'Is anything the matter, George?'

She was really alarmed now. He looked ghastly.

George spoke between small gasps, like a man who has been running.

'I can't go on by myself. I can't keep it any longer. You've got to tell me what you think – whether it's true – whether it's *possible* –'

'But what is it you're talking about, George?'

'You must have noticed something, seen something. There must have been something she *said*. There must have been a *reason* –'

She stared at him.

He passed his hand over his forehead.

'You don't understand what I'm talking about. I can see that. Don't look so scared, little girl. You've got to help me. You've got to remember every damned thing you can. Now, now, I know I sound a bit incoherent, but you'll understand in a minute – when I've shown you the letters.'

He unlocked one of the drawers at the side of the desk and took out two single sheets of paper.

They were of a pale innocuous blue, with words printed on them in small prim letters.

'Read that,' said George.

Iris stared down at the paper. What it said was quite clear and devoid of circumlocution:

'*YOU THINK YOUR WIFE COMMITTED SUICIDE. SHE DIDN'T. SHE WAS KILLED.*'

The second ran:

'*YOUR WIFE ROSEMARY DIDN'T KILL HERSELF. SHE WAS MURDERED.*'

As Iris stayed staring at the words, George went on:

'They came about three months ago. At first I thought it was a joke – a cruel rotten sort of joke. Then I began to think. Why *should* Rosemary have killed herself?'

Iris said in a mechanical voice:

'Depression after influenza.'

'Yes, but really when you come to think of it, that's rather piffle, isn't it? I mean lots of people have influenza and feel a bit depressed afterwards – what?'

Iris said with an effort:

'She might – have been unhappy?'

'Yes, I suppose she might.' George considered the point quite calmly. 'But all the same I don't see Rosemary putting an end to herself because she was unhappy. She might threaten to, but I don't think she would really do it when it came to the point.'

'But she *must* have done, George! What other explanation could there be? Why, they even found the stuff in her handbag.'

'I know. It all hangs together. But ever since these came,' he tapped the anonymous letters with his finger-nail, 'I've been turning things over in my mind. And the more I've thought about it the more I feel sure there's something in it. That's why I've asked you all those questions – about Rosemary ever making any enemies. About anything she'd ever said that sounded as though she were afraid of someone. Whoever killed her must have had a *reason* –'

'But, George, you're crazy –'

'Sometimes I think I am. Other times I know that I'm on the right track. But I've got to *know*. I've got to find out. You've got to help me, Iris. You've got to *think*. You've got to remember. That's it – *remember*. Go back over that night again and again. Because you do see, don't you, that if she was killed, it *must have been some-one who was at the table that night?* You do see that, don't you?'

Yes, she had seen that. There was no pushing aside the remembrance of that scene any longer. She must remember it all. The music, the roll of drums, the lowered lights, the cabaret and the lights going up again and Rosemary sprawled forward on the table, her face blue and convulsed.

Iris shivered. She was frightened now – horribly frightened . . .

She must think – go back – remember.

Rosemary, that's for remembrance.
There was to be no oblivion.

CHAPTER 2

RUTH LESSING

Ruth Lessing, during a momentary lull in her busy day, was remembering her employer's wife, Rosemary Barton.

She had disliked Rosemary Barton a good deal. She had never known quite how much until that November morning when she had first talked with Victor Drake.

That interview with Victor had been the beginning of it all, had set the whole train in motion. Before then, the things she had felt and thought had been so far below the stream of her consciousness that she hadn't really known about them.

She was devoted to George Barton. She always had been. When she had first come to him, a cool, competent young woman of twenty-three, she had seen that he needed taking charge of. She had taken charge of him. She had saved him time, money and worry. She had chosen his friends for him, and directed him to suitable hobbies. She had restrained him from ill-advised business adventures, and encouraged him to take judicious risks on occasions. Never once in their long association had George suspected her of being anything other than subservient, attentive and entirely directed by himself. He took a distinct pleasure in her appearance, the neat shining dark head, the smart tailor-mades and crisp shirts, the small pearls in her well-shaped ears, the pale discreetly powdered face and the faint restrained rose shade of her lipstick.

Ruth, he felt, was absolutely right.

He liked her detached impersonal manner, her complete absence of sentiment or familiarity. In consequence he talked to her a good deal about his private affairs and she listened sympathetically and always put in a useful word of advice.

She had nothing to do, however, with his marriage. She did not like it. However, she accepted it and was invaluable in helping with the wedding arrangements, relieving Mrs Marle of a great deal of work.

For a time after the marriage, Ruth was on slightly less confidential terms with her employer. She confined herself strictly to the office affairs. George left a good deal in her hands.

Nevertheless such was her efficiency that Rosemary soon found that George's Miss Lessing was an invaluable aid in all sorts of ways. Miss Lessing was always pleasant, smiling and polite.

George, Rosemary and Iris all called her Ruth and she often came to Elvaston Square to lunch. She was now twenty-nine and looked exactly the same as she had looked at twenty-three.

Without an intimate word ever passing between them, she was always perfectly aware of George's slightest emotional reactions. She knew when the first elation of his married life passed into an ecstatic content, she was aware when that content gave way to something else that was not so easy to define. A certain inattention to detail shown by him at this time was corrected by her own forethought.

However distrait George might be, Ruth Lessing never seemed to be aware of it. He was grateful to her for that.

It was on a November morning that he spoke to her of Victor Drake.

'I want you to do a rather unpleasant job for me, Ruth?'

She looked at him inquiringly. No need to say that certainly she would do it. That was understood.

'Every family's got a black sheep,' said George.

She nodded comprehendingly.

'This is a cousin of my wife's – a thorough bad hat, I'm afraid. He's half ruined his mother – a fatuous sentimental soul who has sold out most of what few shares she has on his behalf. He started by forging a cheque at Oxford – they got that hushed up and since then he's been shipped about the world – never making good anywhere.'

Ruth listened without much interest. She was familiar with the type. They grew oranges, started chicken farms, went as jackaroos to Australian stations, got jobs with meat-freezing concerns in New Zealand. They never made good, never stayed anywhere long, and invariably got through any money that had been invested on their behalf. They had never interested her much. She preferred success.

'He's turned up now in London and I find he's been worrying

my wife. She hadn't set eyes on him since she was a schoolgirl, but he's a plausible sort of scoundrel and he's been writing to her for money, and I'm not going to stand for that. I've made an appointment with him for twelve o'clock this morning at his hotel. I want you to deal with it for me. The fact is I don't want to get into contact with the fellow. I've never met him and I never want to and I don't want Rosemary to meet him. I think the whole thing can be kept absolutely businesslike if it's fixed up through a third party.'

'Yes, that is always a good plan. What is the arrangement to be?'

'A hundred pounds cash and a ticket to Buenos Aires. The money to be given to him actually on board the boat.'

Ruth smiled.

'Quite so. You want to be sure he actually sails!'

'I see you understand.'

'It's not an uncommon case,' she said indifferently.

'No, plenty of that type about.' He hesitated. 'Are you sure you don't mind doing this?'

'Of course not.' She was a little amused. 'I can assure you I am quite capable of dealing with the matter.'

'You're capable of anything.'

'What about booking his passage? What's his name, by the way?'

'Victor Drake. The ticket's here. I rang up the steamship company yesterday. It's the *San Cristobal,* sails from Tilbury tomorrow.'

Ruth took the ticket, glanced over it to make sure of its correctness and put it into her handbag.

'That's settled. I'll see to it. Twelve o'clock. What address?'

'The Rupert, off Russell Square.'

She made a note of it.

'Ruth, my dear, I don't know what I should do without you –' He put a hand on her shoulder affectionately; it was the first time he had ever done such a thing. 'You're my right hand, my other self.'

She flushed, pleased.

'I've never been able to say much – I've taken all you do for granted – but it's not really like that. You don't know how much

I rely on you for everything –' he repeated: '*everything*. You're the kindest, dearest, most helpful girl in the world!'

Ruth said, laughing to hide her pleasure and embarrassment, 'You'll spoil me saying such nice things.'

'Oh, but I mean them. You're part of the firm, Ruth. Life without you would be unthinkable.'

She went out feeling a warm glow at his words. It was still with her when she arrived at the Rupert Hotel on her errand.

Ruth felt no embarrassment at what lay before her. She was quite confident of her powers to deal with any situation. Hard-luck stories and people never appealed to her. She was prepared to take Victor Drake as all in the day's work.

He was very much as she had pictured him, though perhaps definitely more attractive. She made no mistake in her estimate of his character. There was not much good in Victor Drake. As cold-hearted and calculating a personality as could exist, well masked behind an agreeable devilry. What she had not allowed for was his power of reading other people's souls, and the practised ease with which he could play on the emotions. Perhaps, too, she had underestimated her own resistance to his charm. For he had charm.

He greeted her with an air of delighted surprise.

'George's emissary? But how wonderful. What a surprise!'

In dry even tones, she set out George's terms. Victor agreed to them in the most amiable manner.

'A hundred pounds? Not bad at all. Poor old George. I'd have taken sixty – but don't tell him so! Conditions: – "Do not worry lovely Cousin Rosemary – do not contaminate innocent Cousin Iris – do not embarrass worthy Cousin George." All agreed to! Who is coming to see me off on the *San Cristobal*? You are, my dear Miss Lessing? Delightful.' He wrinkled up his nose, his dark eyes twinkled sympathetically. He had a lean brown face and there was a suggestion about him of a toreador – romantic conception! He was attractive to women and knew it!

'You've been with Barton some time, haven't you, Miss Lessing?'

'Six years.'

'And he wouldn't know what to do without you. Oh yes, I know all about it. And I know all about you, Miss Lessing.'

'How do you know?' asked Ruth sharply.

Victor grinned. 'Rosemary told me.'

'Rosemary? But –'

'That's all right. I don't propose to worry Rosemary any further. She's already been very nice to me – quite sympathetic. I got a hundred out of her, as a matter of fact.'

'You –'

Ruth stopped and Victor laughed. His laugh was infectious. She found herself laughing too.

'That's too bad of you, Mr Drake.'

'I'm a very accomplished sponger. Highly finished technique. The mater, for instance, will always come across if I send a wire hinting at imminent suicide.'

'You ought to be ashamed of yourself.'

'I disapprove of myself very deeply. I'm a bad lot, Miss Lessing. I'd like *you* to know just how bad.'

'Why?' She was curious.

'I don't know. You're different. I couldn't play up the usual technique to you. Those clear eyes of yours – you wouldn't fall for it. No, "More sinned against than sinning, poor fellow," wouldn't cut any ice with you. You've no pity in you.'

Her face hardened.

'I despise pity.'

'In spite of your name? Ruth *is* your name, isn't it? Piquant that. Ruth the ruthless.'

She said, 'I've no sympathy with weakness!'

'Who said I was weak? No, no, you're wrong there, my dear. Wicked, perhaps. But there's one thing to be said for me.'

Her lip curled a little. The inevitable excuse.

'Yes?'

'I enjoy myself. Yes,' he nodded, 'I enjoy myself immensely. I've seen a good deal of life, Ruth. I've done almost everything. I've been an actor and a storekeeper and a waiter and an odd job man, and a luggage porter, and a property man in a circus! I've sailed before the mast in a tramp steamer. I've been in the running for President in a South American Republic. I've been in prison! There are only two things I've never done, an honest day's work, or paid my own way.'

He looked at her, laughing. She ought, she felt, to have been revolted. But the strength of Victor Drake was the strength of the devil. He could make evil seem amusing. He was looking at her now with that uncanny penetration.

'You needn't look so smug, Ruth! You haven't as many morals as you think you have! Success is your fetish. You're the kind of girl who ends up by marrying the boss. That's what you ought to have done with George. George oughtn't to have married that little ass Rosemary. He ought to have married *you*. He'd have done a damned sight better for himself if he had.'

'I think you're rather insulting.'

'Rosemary's a damned fool, always has been. Lovely as paradise and dumb as a rabbit. She's the kind men fall for but never stick to. Now you – you're different. My God, if a man fell in love with you – he'd never tire.'

He had reached the vulnerable spot. She said with sudden raw sincerity:

'If! But he wouldn't fall in love with me!'

'You mean George didn't? Don't fool yourself, Ruth. If anything happened to Rosemary, George would marry you like a shot.'

(Yes, that was it. That was the beginning of it all.)

Victor said, watching her:

'But you know that as well as I do.'

(George's hand on hers, his voice affectionate, warm – Yes, surely it was true . . . He turned to her, depended on her . . .)

Victor said gently: 'You ought to have more confidence in yourself, my dear girl. You could twist George round your little finger. Rosemary's only a silly little fool.'

'It's true,' Ruth thought. 'If it weren't for Rosemary, I could make George ask me to marry him. I'd be good to him. I'd look after him well.'

She felt a sudden blind anger, an uprushing of passionate resentment. Victor Drake was watching her with a good deal of amusement. He liked putting ideas into people's heads. Or, as in this case, showing them the ideas that were already there . . .

Yes, that was how it started – that chance meeting with the man who was going to the other side of the globe on the following day. The Ruth who came back to the office was not quite the same

Ruth who had left it, though no one could have noticed anything different in her manner or appearance.

Shortly after she had returned to the office Rosemary Barton rang up on the telephone.

'Mr Barton has just gone out to lunch. Can I do anything?'

'Oh, Ruth, would you? That tiresome Colonel Race has sent a telegram to say he won't be back in time for my party. Ask George who he'd like to ask instead. We really ought to have another man. There are four women – Iris is coming as a treat and Sandra Farraday and – who on earth's the other? I can't remember.'

'I'm the fourth, I think. You very kindly asked me.'

'Oh, of course. I'd forgotten all about you!'

Rosemary's laugh came light and tinkling. She could not see the sudden flush, the hard line of Ruth Lessing's jaw.

Asked to Rosemary's party as a favour – a concession to George! 'Oh, yes, we'll have your Ruth Lessing. After all she'll be pleased to be asked, and she is awfully useful. She looks quite presentable too.'

In that moment Ruth Lessing knew that she hated Rosemary Barton.

Hated her for being rich and beautiful and careless and brainless. No routine hard work in an office for Rosemary – everything handed to her on a golden platter. Love affairs, a doting husband – no need to work or plan –

Hateful, condescending, stuck-up, frivolous beauty . . .

'I wish you were dead,' said Ruth Lessing in a low voice to the silent telephone.

Her own words startled her. They were so unlike her. She had never been passionate, never vehement, never been anything but cool and controlled and efficient.

She said to herself: 'What's happening to me?'

She had hated Rosemary Barton that afternoon. She still hated Rosemary Barton on this day a year later.

Some day, perhaps, she would be able to forget Rosemary Barton. But not yet.

She deliberately sent her mind back to those November days.

Sitting looking at the telephone – feeling hatred surge up in her heart . . .

Giving Rosemary's message to George in her pleasant controlled voice. Suggesting that she herself should not come so as to leave the number even. George had quickly over-ridden *that*!

Coming in to report next morning on the sailing of the *San Cristobal*. George's relief and gratitude.

'So he's sailed on her all right?'

'Yes. I handed him the money just before the gangway was taken up.' She hesitated and said, 'He waved his hand as the boat backed away from the quay and called out "Love and kisses to George and tell him I'll drink his health tonight."'

'Impudence!' said George. He asked curiously, 'What did you think of him, Ruth?'

Her voice was deliberately colourless as she replied:

'Oh – much as I expected. A weak type.'

And George saw nothing, noticed nothing! She felt like crying out: 'Why did you send me to see him? Didn't you know what he might do to me? Don't you realize that I'm a different person since yesterday? Can't you see that I'm *dangerous*? That there's no knowing what I may do?'

Instead she said in her businesslike voice, 'About that San Paulo letter –'

She was the competent efficient secretary . . .

Five more days.

Rosemary's birthday.

A quiet day at the office – a visit to the hairdresser – the putting on of a new black frock, a touch of make-up skilfully applied. A face looking at her in the glass that was not quite her own face. A pale, determined, bitter face.

It was true what Victor Drake had said. There was no pity in her.

Later, when she was staring across the table at Rosemary Barton's blue convulsed face, she still felt no pity.

Now, eleven months later, thinking of Rosemary Barton, she felt suddenly afraid . . .

CHAPTER 3

ANTHONY BROWNE

Anthony Browne was frowning into the middle distance as he thought about Rosemary Barton.

A damned fool he had been ever to get mixed up with her. Though a man might be excused for that! Certainly she was easy upon the eyes. That evening at the Dorchester he'd been able to look at nothing else. As beautiful as a houri – and probably just about as intelligent!

Still he'd fallen for her rather badly. Used up a lot of energy trying to find someone who would introduce him. Quite unforgivable really when he ought to have been attending strictly to business. After all, he wasn't idling his days away at Claridge's for pleasure.

But Rosemary Barton was lovely enough in all conscience to excuse any momentary lapse from duty. All very well to kick himself now and wonder why he'd been such a fool. Fortunately there was nothing to regret. Almost as soon as he spoke to her the charm had faded a little. Things resumed their normal proportions. This wasn't love – nor yet infatuation. A good time was to be had by all, no more, no less.

Well, he'd enjoyed it. And Rosemary had enjoyed it too. She danced like an angel and wherever he took her men turned round to stare at her. It gave a fellow a pleasant feeling. So long as you didn't expect her to talk. He thanked his stars he wasn't married to her. Once you got used to all that perfection of face and form where would you be? She couldn't even listen intelligently. The sort of girl who would expect you to tell her every morning at the breakfast table that you loved her passionately!

Oh, all very well to think those things now.

He'd fallen for her all right, hadn't he?

Danced attendance on her. Rung her up, taken her out, danced with her, kissed her in the taxi. Been in a fair way to making rather a fool of himself over her until that startling, that incredible day.

He could remember just how she had looked, the piece of chestnut hair that had fallen loose over one ear, the lowered lashes and the gleam of her dark blue eyes through them. The pout of the soft red lips.

'Anthony Browne. It's a nice name!'

He said lightly:

'Eminently well established and respectable. There was a chamberlain to Henry the Eighth called Anthony Browne.'

'An ancestor, I suppose?'

'I wouldn't swear to that.'

'You'd better not!'

He raised his eyebrows.

'I'm the Colonial branch.'

'Not the Italian one?'

'Oh,' he laughed. 'My olive complexion? I had a Spanish mother.'

'That explains it.'

'Explains what?'

'A great deal, Mr Anthony Browne.'

'You're very fond of my name.'

'I said so. It's a nice name.'

And then quickly like a bolt from the blue: 'Nicer than Tony Morelli.'

For a moment he could hardly believe his ears! It was incredible! Impossible!

He caught her by the arm. In the harshness of his grip she winced away.

'Oh, you're hurting me!'

'Where did you get hold of that name?'

His voice was harsh, menacing.

She laughed, delighted with the effect she had produced. The incredible little fool!

'Who told you?'

'Someone who recognized you.'

'Who was it? This is serious, Rosemary. I've got to know.'

She shot a sideways glance at him.

'A disreputable cousin of mine, Victor Drake.'

'I've never met anyone of that name.'

'I imagine he wasn't using that name at the time you knew him. Saving the family feelings.'

Anthony said slowly. 'I see. It was – in prison?'

'Yes. I was reading Victor the riot act – telling him he was a disgrace to us all. He didn't care, of course. Then he grinned and said, "You aren't always so particular yourself, sweetheart. I saw you the other night dancing with an ex-gaol-bird – one of your best boy friends, in fact. Calls himself Anthony Browne, I hear, but in stir he was Tony Morelli."'

Anthony said in a light voice:

'I must renew my acquaintance with this friend of my youth. We old prison ties must stick together.'

Rosemary shook her head. 'Too late. He's been shipped off to South America. He sailed yesterday.'

'I see.' Anthony drew a deep breath. 'So you're the only person who knows my guilty secret?'

She nodded. 'I won't tell on you.'

'You'd better not.' His voice grew stern. 'Look here, Rosemary, this is dangerous. You don't want your lovely face carved up, do you? There are people who don't stick at a little thing like ruining a girl's beauty. And there's such a thing as being bumped off. It doesn't only happen in books and films. It happens in real life, too.'

'Are you threatening me, Tony?'

'Warning you.'

Would she take the warning? Did she realize that he was in deadly earnest? Silly little fool. No sense in that lovely empty head. You couldn't rely on her to keep her mouth shut. All the same he'd have to try and ram his meaning home.

'Forget you've ever heard the name of Tony Morelli, do you understand?'

'But I don't mind a bit, Tony. I'm quite broad-minded. It's quite a thrill for me to meet a criminal. You needn't feel ashamed of it.'

The absurd little idiot. He looked at her coldly. He wondered in that moment how he could ever have fancied he cared. He'd never been able to suffer fools gladly – not even fools with pretty faces.

'Forget about Tony Morelli,' he said grimly. 'I mean it. Never mention that name again.'

He'd have to get out. That was the only thing to do. There was no relying on this girl's silence. She'd talk whenever she felt inclined.

She was smiling at him – an enchanting smile, but it left him unmoved.

'Don't be so fierce. Take me to the Jarrows' dance next week.'

'I shan't be here. I'm going away.'

'Not before my birthday party. You can't let me down. I'm counting on you. Now don't say no. I've been miserably ill with that horrid 'flu and I'm still feeling terribly weak. I musn't be crossed. You've got to come.'

He might have stood firm. He might have chucked it all – gone right away.

Instead, through an open door, he saw Iris coming down the stairs. Iris, very straight and slim, with her pale face and black hair and grey eyes. Iris with much less than Rosemary's beauty and with all the character that Rosemary would never have.

In that moment he hated himself for having fallen a victim, in however small a degree, to Rosemary's facile charm. He felt as Romeo felt remembering Rosaline when he had first seen Juliet.

Anthony Browne changed his mind.

In the flash of a second he committed himself to a totally different course of action.

CHAPTER 4

STEPHEN FARRADAY

Stephen Farraday was thinking of Rosemary – thinking of her with that incredulous amazement that her image always aroused in him. Usually he banished all thoughts of her from his mind as promptly as they arose – but there were times when, persistent in death as she had been in life, she refused to be thus arbitrarily dismissed.

His first reaction was always the same, a quick irresponsible shudder as he remembered the scene in the restaurant. At least he need not think again of *that*. His thoughts turned further back, to Rosemary alive, Rosemary smiling, breathing, gazing into his eyes . . .

What a fool – what an incredible fool he had been!

And amazement held him, sheer bewildered amazement. How

had it all come about? He simply could not understand it. It was as though his life were divided into two parts, one, the larger part, a sane well-balanced orderly progression, the other a brief uncharacteristic madness. The two parts simply did not fit.

For with all his ability and his clever, shrewd intellect, Stephen had not the inner perception to see that actually they fitted only too well.

Sometimes he looked back over his life, appraising it coldly and without undue emotion, but with a certain priggish self-congratulation. From a very early age he had been determined to succeed in life, and in spite of difficulties and certain initial disadvantages he *had* succeeded.

He had always had a certain simplicity of belief and outlook. He believed in the Will. What a man willed, that he could do!

Little Stephen Farraday had steadfastly cultivated his Will. He could look for little help in life save that which he got by his own efforts. A small pale boy of seven, with a good forehead and a determined chin, he meant to rise – and rise high. His parents, he already knew, would be of no use to him. His mother had married beneath her station in life – and regretted it. His father, a small builder, shrewd, cunning and cheese-paring, was despised by his wife and also by his son . . . For his mother, vague, aimless, and given to extraordinary variations of mood, Stephen felt only a puzzled incomprehension until the day he found her slumped down on the corner of a table with an empty eau-de-Cologne bottle fallen from her hand. He had never thought of drink as an explanation of his mother's moods. She never drank spirits or beer, and he had never realized that her passion for eau-de-Cologne had had any other origin than her vague explanation of headaches.

He realized in that moment that he had little affection for his parents. He suspected shrewdly that they had not much for him. He was small for his age, quiet, with a tendency to stammer. Namby-pamby his father called him. A well-behaved child, little trouble in the house. His father would have preferred a more rumbustious type. 'Always getting into mischief *I* was, at his age.' Sometimes, looking at Stephen, he felt uneasily his own social inferiority to his wife. Stephen took after her folk.

Quietly, with growing determination, Stephen mapped out

his own life. He was going to succeed. As a first test of will, he determined to master his stammer. He practised speaking slowly, with a slight hesitation between every word. And in time his efforts were crowned with success. He no longer stammered. In school he applied himself to his lessons. He intended to have education. Education got you somewhere. Soon his teachers became interested, encouraged him. He won a scholarship. His parents were approached by the educational authorities – the boy had promise. Mr Farraday, doing well out of a row of jerry-built houses, was persuaded to invest money in his son's education.

At twenty-two Stephen came down from Oxford with a good degree, a reputation as a good and witty speaker, and a knack of writing articles. He had also made some useful friends. Politics were what attracted him. He had learnt to overcome his natural shyness and to cultivate an admirable social manner – modest, friendly, and with that touch of brilliance that led people to say, 'That young man will go far.' Though by predilection a Liberal, Stephen realized that for the moment, at least, the Liberal Party was dead. He joined the ranks of the Labour Party. His name soon became known as that of a 'coming' young man. But the Labour Party did not satisfy Stephen. He found it less open to new ideas, more hidebound by tradition than its great and powerful rival. The Conservatives, on the other hand, were on the look-out for promising young talent.

They approved of Stephen Farraday – he was just the type they wanted. He contested a fairly solid Labour constituency and won it by a very narrow majority. It was with a feeling of triumph that Stephen took his seat in the House of Commons. His career had begun and this was the right career he had chosen. Into this he could put all his ability, all his ambition. He felt in him the ability to govern, and to govern well. He had a talent for handling people, for knowing when to flatter and when to oppose. One day, he swore it, he would be in the Cabinet.

Nevertheless, once the excitement of actually being in the House had subsided, he experienced swift disillusionment. The hardly fought election had put him in the limelight, now he was down in the rut, a mere insignificant unit of the rank and file, subservient to the party whips, and kept in his place. It was not easy here to rise out of obscurity. Youth here was looked upon with suspicion. One needed something above ability. One needed influence.

There were certain interests. Certain families. You had to be sponsored.

He considered marriage. Up to now he had thought very little about the subject. He had a dim picture in the back of his mind of some handsome creature who would stand hand in hand with him sharing his life and his ambitions; who would give him children and to whom he could unburden his thoughts and perplexities. Some woman who felt as he did and who would be eager for his success and proud of him when he achieved it.

Then one day he went to one of the big receptions at Kidderminster House. The Kidderminster connection was the most powerful in England. They were, and always had been, a great political family. Lord Kidderminster, with his little Imperial, his tall, distinguished figure, was known by sight everywhere. Lady Kidderminster's large rocking-horse face was familiar on public platforms and on committees all over England. They had five daughters, three of them beautiful, and one son still at Eton.

The Kidderminsters made a point of encouraging likely young members of the Party. Hence Farraday's invitation.

He did not know many people there and he was standing alone near a window about twenty minutes after his arrival. The crowd by the tea table was thinning out and passing into the other rooms when Stephen noticed a tall girl in black standing alone by the table looking for a moment slightly at a loss.

Stephen Farraday had a very good eye for faces. He had picked up that very morning in the Tube a 'Home Gossip' discarded by a woman traveller and glanced over it with slight amusement. There had been a rather smudgy reproduction of Lady Alexandra Hayle, third daughter of the Earl of Kidderminster, and below a gossipy little extract about her – '. . . always been of a shy and retiring disposition – devoted to animals – Lady Alexandra has taken a course in Domestic Science as Lady Kidderminster believes in her daughters being thoroughly grounded in all domestic subjects.'

That was Lady Alexandra Hayle standing there, and with the unerring perception of a shy person, Stephen knew that she, too, was shy. The plainest of the five daughters, Alexandra had always suffered under a sense of inferiority. Given the same education and upbringing as her sisters, she had never quite attained their *savoir faire*, which annoyed her mother considerably. Sandra must make an effort – it was absurd to appear so awkward, so *gauche*.

Stephen did not know that, but he knew that the girl was ill at ease and unhappy. And suddenly a rush of conviction came to him. This was his chance! *'Take it, you fool, take it! It's now or never!'*

He crossed the room to the long buffet. Standing beside the girl he picked up a sandwich. Then, turning, and speaking nervously and with an effort (no acting, that – he *was* nervous!) he said:

'I say, do you mind if I speak to you? I don't know many people here and I can see you don't either. Don't snub me. As a matter of fact I'm awfully s-s-shy' (his stammer of years ago came back at a most opportune moment) 'and – and I think you're s-s-shy too, aren't you?'

The girl flushed – her mouth opened. But as he had guessed, she could not say it. Too difficult to find words to say 'I'm the daughter of the house.' Instead she admitted quietly:

'As a matter of fact, I – I am shy. I always have been.'

Stephen went on quickly:

'It's a horrible feeling. I don't know whether one ever gets over it. Sometimes I feel absolutely tongue-tied.'

'So do I.'

He went on – talking rather quickly, stammering a little – his manner was boyish, appealing. It was a manner that had been natural to him a few years ago and which was now consciously retained and cultivated. It was young, naïve, disarming.

He led the conversation soon to the subject of plays, mentioned one that was running which had attracted a good deal of interest. Sandra had seen it. They discussed it. It had dealt with some point of the social services and they were soon deep in a discussion of these measures.

Stephen did not overdo things. He saw Lady Kidderminster entering the room, her eyes in search of her daughter. It was no part of his plan to be introduced now. He murmured a goodbye.

'I have enjoyed talking to you. I was simply hating the whole show till I found you. Thank you.'

He left Kidderminster House with a feeling of exhilaration. He had taken his chance. Now to consolidate what he had started.

For several days after that he haunted the neighbourhood of Kidderminster House. Once Sandra came out with one of her sisters. Once she left the house alone, but with a hurried step. He shook his head. That would not do, she was obviously en route to some particular appointment. Then, about a week after the party, his patience was rewarded. She came out one morning with a small black Scottie dog and she turned with a leisurely step in the direction of the Park.

Five minutes later, a young man walking rapidly in the opposite direction pulled up short and stopped in front of Sandra. He exclaimed blithely:

'I say, what luck! I wondered if I'd ever see you again.'

His tone was so delighted that she blushed just a little.

He stooped to the dog.

'What a jolly little fellow. What's his name?'

'MacTavish.'

'Oh, very Scotch.'

They talked dog for some moments. Then Stephen said, with a trace of embarrassment:

'I never told you my name the other day. It's Farraday. Stephen Farraday. I'm an obscure M.P.'

He looked inquiringly and saw the colour come up in her cheeks again as she said: 'I'm Alexandra Hayle.'

He responded to that very well. He might have been back in the O.U.D.S. Surprise, recognition, dismay, embarrassment!

'Oh, you're – you're Lady Alexandra Hayle – you – my goodness! *What* a stupid fool you must have thought me the other day!'

Her answering move was inevitable. She was bound both by her breeding and her natural kindliness to do all she could to put him at his ease, to reassure him.

'I ought to have told you at the time.'

'I ought to have known. What an oaf you must think me!'

'How should you have known? What does it matter anyway? Please, Mr Farraday, don't look so upset. Let's walk to the Serpentine. Look, MacTavish is simply pulling.'

After that, he met her several times in the Park. He told her his ambitions. Together they discussed political topics. He found her intelligent, well-informed and sympathetic. She had good brains and a singularly unbiased mind. They were friends now.

The next advance came when he was asked to dinner at Kidderminster House and to go on to a dance. A man had fallen through at the last moment. When Lady Kidderminster was racking her brains Sandra said quietly:

'What about Stephen Farraday?'

'Stephen Farraday?'

'Yes, he was at your party the other day and I've met him once or twice since.'

Lord Kidderminster was consulted and was all in favour of encouraging the young hopefuls of the political world.

'Brilliant young fellow – quite brilliant. Never heard of his people, but he'll make a name for himself one of these days.'

Stephen came and acquitted himself well.

'A useful young man to know,' said Lady Kidderminster with unconscious arrogance.

Two months later Stephen put his fortunes to the test. They were by the Serpentine and MacTavish sat with his head on Sandra's foot.

'Sandra, you know – you must know that I love you. I want you to marry me. I wouldn't ask you if I didn't believe that I shall make a name for myself one day. I do believe it. You shan't be ashamed of your choice. I swear it.'

She said, 'I'm not ashamed.'

'Then you do care?'

'Didn't you know?'

'I hoped – but I couldn't be sure. Do you know that I've loved you since that very first moment when I saw you across the room and took my courage in both hands and came to speak to you. I was never more terrified in my life.'

She said, 'I think I loved you then, too . . .'

It was not all plain sailing. Sandra's quiet announcement that she was going to marry Stephen Farraday sent her family into immediate protests. Who was he? What did they know about him?

To Lord Kidderminster Stephen was quite frank about his family and origin. He spared a fleeting thought that it was just as well for his prospects that his parents were now both dead.

To his wife, Lord Kidderminster said, 'H'm, it might be worse.'

He knew his daughter fairly well, knew that her quiet manner hid inflexible purpose. If she meant to have the fellow she would have him. She'd never give in!

'The fellow's got a career ahead of him. With a bit of backing he'll go far. Heaven knows we could do with some young blood. He seems a decent chap, too.'

Lady Kidderminster assented grudgingly. It was not at all her idea of a good match for her daughter. Still, Sandra was certainly the most difficult of the family. Susan had been a beauty and Esther had brains. Diana, clever child, had married the young Duke of Harwich – the *parti* of the season. Sandra had certainly less charm – there was her shyness – and if this young man had a future as everyone seemed to think . . .

She capitulated, murmuring:

'But, of course, one will have to use *influence* . . .'

So Alexandra Catherine Hayle took Stephen Leonard Farraday for better and for worse, in white satin and Brussels lace, with six bridesmaids and two minute pages and all the accessories of a fashionable wedding. They went to Italy for the honeymoon and came back to a small charming house in Westminster, and a short time afterwards Sandra's godmother died and left her a very delightful small Queen Anne Manor house in the country. Everything went well for the young married pair. Stephen plunged into Parliamentary life with renewed ardour, Sandra aided and abetted him in every way, identifying herself heart and soul with his ambitions. Sometimes, Stephen would think with an almost incredulous realization of how Fortune had favoured him! His alliance with the powerful Kidderminster faction assured him of rapid rise in his career. His own ability and brilliance would consolidate the position that opportunity made for him. He believed honestly in his own powers and was prepared to work unsparingly for the good of his country.

Often, looking across the table at his wife, he felt gladly what a perfect helpmate she was – just what he had always imagined. He liked the lovely clean lines of her head and neck, the direct hazel eyes under their level brows, the rather high white forehead and the faint arrogance of her aquiline nose. She looked, he thought, rather like a racehorse – so well groomed, so instinct with breeding, so proud. He found her an ideal companion, their minds raced alike to the same quick conclusions. Yes, he thought, Stephen Farraday, that little disconsolate boy, had done very well for himself. His life was shaping exactly as he had meant it to be. He was only a year or two over thirty and already success lay in the hollow of his hand.

And in that mood of triumphant satisfaction, he went with his wife for a fortnight to St Moritz, and looking across the hotel lounge saw Rosemary Barton.

What happened to him at that moment he never understood. By a kind of poetic revenge the words he had spoken to another woman came true. Across a room he fell in love. Deeply, overwhelmingly, crazily in love. It was the kind of desperate, headlong, adolescent calf love that he should have experienced years ago and got over.

He had always assumed that he was not a passionate type of man. One or two ephemeral affairs, a mild flirtation – that, so far as he knew, was all that 'love' meant to him. Sensual pleasures simply did not appeal to him. He told himself that he was too fastidious for that sort of thing.

If he had been asked if he loved his wife, he would have replied 'Certainly' – yet he knew, well enough, that he would not have dreamed of marrying her if she had been, say, the daughter of a penniless country gentleman. He liked her, admired her and felt a deep affection for her and also a very real gratitude for what her position had brought him.

That he could fall in love with the abandon and misery of a callow boy was a revelation. He could think of nothing but Rosemary. Her lovely laughing face, the rich chestnut of her hair, her swaying voluptuous figure. He couldn't eat – he couldn't sleep. They went ski-ing together. He danced with her. And as he held her to him he knew that he wanted her more than anything on earth. So this, this misery, this aching longing agony – this was love!

Even in his preoccupation he blessed Fate for having given him a naturally imperturbable manner. No one must guess, no one must know, what he was feeling – except Rosemary herself.

The Bartons left a week earlier than the Farradays. Stephen said to Sandra that St Moritz was not very amusing. Should they cut their time short and go back to London? She agreed very amiably. Two weeks after their return, he became Rosemary's lover.

A strange ecstatic hectic period – feverish, unreal. It lasted – how long? Six months at most. Six months during which Stephen went about his work as usual, visited his constituency, asked questions in the House, spoke at various meetings, discussed politics with Sandra and thought of one thing only – Rosemary.

Their secret meetings in the little flat, her beauty, the passionate endearments he showered on her, her clinging passionate embraces. A dream. A sensual infatuated dream.

And after the dream – the awakening.

It seemed to happen quite suddenly.

Like coming out of a tunnel into the daylight.

One day he was a bemused lover, the next day he was Stephen Farraday again thinking that perhaps he ought not to see Rosemary quite so often. Dash it all, they had been taking some terrific risks. If Sandra was ever to suspect – He stole a look at her down the breakfast table. Thank goodness, she didn't suspect. She hadn't an idea. Yet some of his excuses for absence lately had been pretty thin. Some women would have begun to smell a rat. Thank goodness Sandra wasn't a suspicious woman.

He took a deep breath. Really he and Rosemary had been very reckless! It was a wonder her husband hadn't got wise to things. One of those foolish unsuspecting chaps – years older than she was.

What a lovely creature she was . . .

He thought suddenly of golf links. Fresh air blowing over sand dunes, tramping round with clubs – swinging a driver – a nice clean shot off the tee – a little chip with a mashie. Men. Men in plus fours smoking pipes. And no women allowed on the links!

He said suddenly to Sandra:

'Couldn't we go down to Fairhaven?'

She looked up, surprised.

'Do you want to? Can you get away?'

'Might take the inside of a week, I'd like to get some golf. I feel stale.'

'We could go tomorrow if you like. It will mean putting off the Astleys, and I must cancel that meeting on Tuesday. But what about the Lovats?'

'Oh, let's cancel that too. We can think of some excuse. I want to get away.'

It had been peaceful at Fairhaven with Sandra and the dogs on the terrace and in the old walled garden, and with golf at Sandley Heath, and pottering down to the farm in the evening with MacTavish at his heels.

He had felt rather like someone who is recovering from an illness.

He had frowned when he saw Rosemary's writing. He'd told her not to write. It was too dangerous. Not that Sandra ever asked him who his letters were from, but all the same it was unwise. Servants weren't always to be trusted.

He ripped open the envelope with some annoyance, having taken the letter into his study. Pages. Simply pages.

As he read, the old enchantment swept over him again. She adored him, she loved him more than ever, she couldn't endure not seeing him for five whole days. Was he feeling the same? Did the Leopard miss his Ethiopian?

He half-smiled, half-sighed. That ridiculous joke – born when he had bought her a man's spotted dressing-gown that she had admired. The Leopard changing his spots, and he had said, 'But you mustn't change your skin, darling.' And after that she had called him Leopard and he had called her his Black Beauty.

Damned silly, really. Yes, damned silly. Rather sweet of her to have written such pages and pages. But still she shouldn't have done it. Dash it all, they'd got to be *careful*! Sandra wasn't the sort of woman who would stand for anything of that kind. If she once got an inkling – Writing letters was dangerous. He'd told Rosemary so. Why couldn't she wait until he got back to town? Dash it all, he'd see her in another two or three days.

There was another letter on the breakfast table the following morning. This time Stephen swore inwardly. He thought Sandra's eyes rested on it for a couple of seconds. But she didn't say anything. Thank goodness she wasn't the sort of woman who asked questions about a man's correspondence.

After breakfast he took the car over the market town eight miles away. Wouldn't do to put through a call from the village. He got Rosemary on the phone.

'Hullo – that you, Rosemary? Don't write any more letters.'

'Stephen, darling, how lovely to hear your voice!'

'Be careful, can anyone overhear you?'

'Of course not. Oh, angel, I have missed you. Have you missed me?'

'Yes, of course. But don't write. It's much too risky.'

'Did you like my letter? Did it make you feel I was with you? Darling, I want to be with you every minute. Do you feel that too?'

'Yes – but not on the phone, old thing.'

'You're so ridiculously cautious. What does it matter?'

'I'm thinking of you, too, Rosemary. I couldn't bear any trouble to come to you through me.'

'I don't care what happens to me. You know that.'

'Well, I care, sweetheart.'

'When are you coming back?'

'Tuesday.'

'And we'll meet at the flat, Wednesday.'

'Yes – er, yes.'

'Darling, I can hardly bear to wait. Can't you make some excuse and come up today? Oh, Stephen, you *could*! Politics or something stupid like that?'

'I'm afraid it's out of the question.'

'I don't believe you miss me half as much as I miss you.'

'Nonsense, of course I do.'

When he rang off he felt tired. Why should women insist on being so damned reckless? Rosemary and he must be more careful in future. They'd have to meet less often.

Things after that became difficult. He was busy – very busy. It was quite impossible to give as much time to Rosemary – and the trying thing was she didn't seem able to understand. He explained but she just wouldn't listen.

'Oh, your stupid old politics – as though *they* were important!'

'But they *are* –'

She didn't realize. She didn't care. She took no interest in his work, in his ambitions, in his career. All she wanted was to hear him reiterate again and again that he loved her. 'Just as much as ever? Tell me again that you *really* love me?'

Surely, he thought, she might take that for granted by this time! She was a lovely creature, lovely – but the trouble was that you couldn't *talk* to her.

The trouble was they'd been seeing too much of each other. You couldn't keep up an affair at fever heat. They must meet less often – slacken off a bit.

But that made her resentful – very resentful. She was always reproaching him now.

'You don't love me as you used to do.'

And then he'd have to reassure her, to swear that of course he did. And she *would* constantly resurrect everything he had ever said to her.

'Do you remember when you said it would be lovely if we died together? Fell asleep for ever in each other's arms? Do you remember when you said we'd take a caravan and go off into the desert? Just the stars and the camels – and how we'd forget everything in the world?'

What damned silly things one said when one was in love! They hadn't seemed fatuous at the time, but to have them hashed up in cold blood! Why couldn't women let things decently alone? A man didn't want to be continually reminded what an ass he'd made of himself.

She came out with sudden unreasonable demands. Couldn't he go abroad to the South of France and she'd meet him there? Or go to Sicily or Corsica – one of those places where you never saw anyone you knew? Stephen said grimly that there was no such place in the world. At the most unlikely spots you always met some dear old school friend that you'd never seen for years.

And then she said something that frightened him.

'Well, but it wouldn't really matter, would it?'

He was alert, watchful, suddenly cold within.

'What do you mean?'

She was smiling up at him, that same enchanting smile that had once made his heart turn over and his bones ache with longing. Now it made him merely impatient.

'Leopard, darling, I've thought sometimes that we're stupid to go on trying to carry on this hole-and-corner business. It's not worthy, somehow. Let's go away together. Let's stop pretending. George will divorce me and your wife will divorce you and then we can get married.'

Just like that! Disaster! Ruin! And she couldn't see it!

'I wouldn't let you do such a thing.'

'But, darling, I don't care. I'm not really very conventional.'

'But I am. But I am,' thought Stephen.

'I do feel that love is the most important thing in the world. It doesn't matter what people think of us.'

'It would matter to me, my dear. An open scandal of that kind would be the end of my career.'

'But would that really matter? There are hundreds of other things that you could do.'

'Don't be silly.'

'Why have you got to do anything anyway? I've got lots of money, you know. Of my own, I mean, not George's. We could wander about all over the world, going to the most enchanting out-of-the-way places – places, perhaps, where nobody else has ever been. Or to some island in the Pacific – think of it, the hot sun and the blue sea and the coral reefs.'

He did think of it. A South Sea Island! Of all the idiotic ideas. What sort of a man did she think he was – a beachcomber?

He looked at her with eyes from which the last traces of scales had fallen. A lovely creature with the brains of a hen! He'd been mad – utterly and completely mad. But he was sane again now. And he'd got to get out of this fix. Unless he was careful she'd ruin his whole life.

He said all the things that hundreds of men had said before him. They must end it all – so he wrote. It was only fair to her. He couldn't risk bringing unhappiness on her. She didn't understand – and so on and so on.

It was all over – he must make her understand that.

But that was just what she refused to understand. It wasn't to be as easy as that. She adored him, she loved him more than ever, she couldn't live without him! The only honest thing was for her to tell her husband, and for Stephen to tell his wife the truth! He remembered how cold he had felt as he sat holding her letter. The little fool! The silly clinging fool! She'd go and blab the whole thing to George Barton and then George would divorce her and cite him as co-respondent. And Sandra would perforce divorce him too. He hadn't any doubt of that. She had spoken once of a friend, had said with faint surprise, 'But of course when she found out he was having an affair with another woman, what else could she do but divorce him?' That was what Sandra would feel. She was proud. She would never share a man.

And then he would be done, finished – the influential Kidderminster backing would be withdrawn. It would be the kind of scandal that he would not be able to live down, even though public opinion was broader-minded than it used to be. But not in a flagrant case like this! Goodbye to his dreams, his ambitions. Everything wrecked, broken – all because of a crazy infatuation for a silly woman. Calf love, that was all it had been. Calf love contracted at the wrong time of life.

He'd lose everything he'd staked. Failure! Ignominy!

He'd lose Sandra . . .

And suddenly, with a shock of surprise he realized that it was that that he would mind most. *He'd lose Sandra.* Sandra with her square white forehead and her clear hazel eyes. Sandra, his dear friend and companion, his arrogant, proud, loyal Sandra. No, he couldn't lose Sandra – he couldn't . . . Anything but that.

The perspiration broke out on his forehead.

Somehow he *must* get out of this mess.

Somehow he must make Rosemary listen to reason . . . But would she? Rosemary and reason didn't go together. Supposing he were to tell her that, after all, he loved his wife? No. She simply wouldn't believe it. She was such a stupid woman. Empty-headed, clinging, possessive. And she loved him still – that was the mischief of it.

A kind of blind rage rose up in him. How on earth was he to keep her quiet? To shut her mouth? Nothing short of a dose of poison would do that, he thought bitterly.

A wasp was buzzing close at hand. He stared abstractedly. It had got inside a cut-glass jampot and was trying to get out.

Like me, he thought, entrapped by sweetness and now – he can't get out, poor devil.

But he, Stephen Farraday, was going to get out somehow. Time, he must play for time.

Rosemary was down with 'flu at the moment. He'd sent conventional inquiries – a big sheaf of flowers. It gave him a respite. Next week Sandra and he were dining with the Bartons – a birthday party for Rosemary. Rosemary had said, 'I shan't do anything until after my birthday – it would be too cruel to George. He's making such a fuss about it. He's such a dear. After it's all over we'll come to an understanding.'

Supposing he were to tell her brutally that it was all over, that he no longer cared? He shivered. No, he dare not do that. She might go to George in hysterics. She might even come to Sandra. He could hear her tearful, bewildered voice.

'He says he doesn't care any more, but I *know* it's not true. He's trying to be loyal – to play the game with *you* – but I know you'll agree with me that when people love each other honesty is the *only* way. That's why I'm asking you to give him his freedom.'

That was just the sort of nauseating stuff she would pour out. And Sandra, her face proud and disdainful, would say, 'He can have his freedom!'

She wouldn't believe – how could she believe? If Rosemary were to bring out those letters – the letters he'd been asinine enough to write to her. Heaven knew what he had said in them. Enough and more than enough to convince Sandra – letters such as he had never written to *her* –

He must think of something – some way of keeping Rosemary quiet. 'It's a pity,' he thought grimly, 'that we don't live in the days of the Borgias . . .'

A glass of poisoned champagne was about the only thing that would keep Rosemary quiet.

Yes, he had actually thought that.

Cyanide of potassium in her champagne glass, cyanide of potassium in her evening bag. Depression after influenza.

And across the table, Sandra's eyes meeting his.

Nearly a year ago – and he couldn't forget.

CHAPTER 5
··
ALEXANDRA FARRADAY

Sandra Farraday had not forgotten Rosemary Barton.

She was thinking of her at this very minute – thinking of her slumped forward across the table in the restaurant that night.

She remembered her own sharp indrawn breath and how then, looking up, she had found Stephen watching her . . .

Had he read the truth in her eyes? Had he seen the hate, the mingling of horror and triumph?

Nearly a year ago now – and as fresh in her mind as if it had been yesterday! *Rosemary, that's for remembrance.* How horribly true that was. It was no good a person being dead if they lived on in your mind. That was what Rosemary had done. In Sandra's mind – and in Stephen's, too? She didn't know, but she thought it probable.

The Luxembourg – that hateful place with its excellent food, its deft swift service, its luxurious *décor* and setting. An impossible place to avoid, people were always asking you there.

She would have liked to forget – but everything conspired to make her remember. Even Fairhaven was no longer exempt now that George Barton had come to live at Little Priors.

It was really rather extraordinary of him. George Barton was altogether an odd man. Not at all the kind of neighbour she liked to have. His presence at Little Priors spoiled for her the charm and peace of Fairhaven. Always, up to this summer, it had been a place of healing and rest, a place where she and Stephen had been happy – that is, if they ever had been happy?

Her lips pressed thinly together. Yes, a thousand times, yes! They could have been happy but for Rosemary. It was Rosemary who had shattered the delicate edifice of mutual trust and tenderness that she and Stephen were beginning to build. Something, some instinct, had bade her hide from Stephen her own passion, her single-hearted devotion. She had loved him from the moment he came across the room to her that day at Kidderminster House, pretending to be shy, pretending not to know who she was.

For he *had* known. She could not say when she had first accepted that fact. Some time after their marriage, one day when he was expounding some neat piece of political manipulation necessary to the passing of some Bill.

The thought had flashed across her mind then: 'This reminds me of something. What?' Later she realized that it was, in essence, the same tactics he had used that day at Kidderminster House. She accepted the knowledge without surprise, as though it were something of which she had long been aware, but which had only just risen to the surface of her mind.

From the day of their marriage she had realized that he did not love her in the same way as she loved him. But she thought it possible that he was actually incapable of such a love. That power of loving was her own unhappy heritage. To care with a desperation, an intensity that was, she knew, unusual among women! She would have died for him willingly; she was ready to lie for him, scheme for him, suffer for him! Instead she accepted with pride and reserve the place he wanted her to fill. He wanted her co-operation, her sympathy, her active and intellectual help. He wanted of her, not her heart, but her brains, and those material advantages which birth had given her.

One thing she would never do, embarrass him by the expression of a devotion to which he could make no adequate return. And she did believe honestly that he liked her, that he took pleasure in her company. She foresaw a future in which her burden would be immeasurably lightened – a future of tenderness and friendship.

In his way, she thought, he loved her.

And then Rosemary came.

She wondered sometimes, with a wry painful twist of the lips, how it was that he could imagine that she did not know. She had known from the first minute – up there at St Moritz – when she had first seen the way he looked at the woman.

She had known the very day the woman became his mistress. She knew the scent the creature used . . .

She could read in Stephen's polite face, with eyes abstracted, just what his memories were, what he was thinking about – that woman – the woman he had just left!

It was difficult, she thought dispassionately, to assess the suffering she had been through. Enduring, day after day, the tortures of the damned, with nothing to carry her through but her belief in courage – her own natural pride. She would not show, she would never show, what she was feeling. She lost weight, grew thinner and paler, the bones of her head and shoulders showing more distinctly with the flesh stretched tightly over them. She forced herself to eat, but could not force herself to sleep. She lay long nights, with dry eyes, staring into darkness. She despised the taking of drugs as weakness. She would hang on. To show herself hurt, to plead, to protest – all these things were abhorrent to her.

She had one crumb of comfort, a meagre one – Stephen did not wish to leave her. Granted that that was for the sake of his career, not out of fondness for her, still the fact remained. He did not want to leave her.

Some day, perhaps, the infatuation would pass . . .

What could he, after all, see in the girl? She was attractive, beautiful – but so were other women. What did he find in Rosemary Barton that infatuated him?

She was brainless – silly – and not – she clung to this point especially – not even particularly amusing. If she had had wit, charm and provocation of manner – those were the things that held men. Sandra clung to the belief that the thing would end – that Stephen would tire of it.

She was convinced that the main interest in his life was his work. He was marked out for great things and he knew it. He had a fine statesmanlike brain and he delighted in using it. It was his appointed task in life. Surely once the infatuation began to wane he would realize that fact?

Never for one minute did Sandra consider leaving him. The idea never even came to her. She was his, body and soul, to take or discard. He was her life, her existence. Love burned in her with a medieval force.

There was a moment when she had hope. They went down to Fairhaven. Stephen seemed more his normal self. She felt suddenly a renewal of the old sympathy between them. Hope rose in her heart. He wanted her still, he enjoyed her company, he relied on her judgement. For the moment, he had escaped from the clutches of that woman.

He looked happier, more like his own self.

Nothing was irretrievably ruined. He was getting over it. If only he could make up his mind to break with her . . .

Then they went back to London and Stephen relapsed. He looked haggard, worried, ill. He began to be unable to fix his mind on his work.

She thought she knew the cause. Rosemary wanted him to go away with her . . . He was making up his mind to take the step – to break with everything he cared about most. Folly! Madness! He was the type of man with whom his work would always come first – a very English type. He must know that himself, deep down – Yes, but Rosemary was very lovely – and very stupid. Stephen would not be the first man who had thrown away his career for a woman and been sorry afterwards!

Sandra caught a few words – a phrase one day at a cocktail party.

'. . . Telling George – got to make up our minds.'

It was soon after that that Rosemary went down with 'flu.

A little hope rose in Sandra's heart. Suppose she were to get pneumonia – people did after 'flu – a young friend of hers had died that way only last winter. If Rosemary were to die –

She did not try to repress the thought – she was not horrified at herself. She was medieval enough to hate with a steady and untroubled mind.

She hated Rosemary Barton. If thoughts could kill, she would have killed her.

But thoughts do not kill –

Thoughts are not enough . . .

How beautiful Rosemary had looked that night at the Luxembourg with her pale fox furs slipping off her shoulders in the ladies' cloak-room. Thinner, paler since her illness – an air of delicacy made her beauty more ethereal. She had stood in front of the glass touching up her face . . .

Sandra, behind her, looked at their joint reflection in the mirror. Her own face like something sculptured, cold, lifeless. No feeling there, you would have said – a cold hard woman.

And then Rosemary said: 'Oh, Sandra, am I taking all the glass? I've finished now. This horrid 'flu has pulled me down a lot. I look a sight. And I feel quite weak still and headachy.'

Sandra had asked with quiet polite concern:

'Have you got a headache tonight?'

'Just a bit of one. You haven't got an aspirin, have you?'

'I've got a Cachet Faivre.'

She had opened her handbag, taken out the cachet. Rosemary had accepted it. 'I'll take it in my bag in case.'

That competent dark-haired girl, Barton's secretary, had watched the little transaction. She came in turn to the mirror, and just put on a slight dusting of powder. A nice-looking girl, almost handsome. Sandra had the impression that she didn't like Rosemary.

Then they had gone out of the cloak-room, Sandra first, then Rosemary, then Miss Lessing – oh, and of course, the girl Iris, Rosemary's sister, she had been there. Very excited, with big grey eyes, and a schoolgirlish white dress.

They had gone out and joined the men in the hall.

And the head waiter had come bustling forward and showed them to their table. They had passed in under the great domed arch and there had been nothing, absolutely nothing, to warn one of them that she would never come out through that door again alive . . .

CHAPTER 6

GEORGE BARTON

Rosemary . . .

George Barton lowered his glass and stared rather owlishly into the fire.

He had drunk just enough to feel maudlin with self-pity.

What a lovely girl she had been. He'd always been crazy about her. She knew it, but he'd always supposed she'd only laugh at him.

Even when he first asked her to marry him, he hadn't done it with any conviction.

Mowed and mumbled. Acted like a blithering fool.

'You know, old girl, any time – you've only got to say. I know it's no good. You wouldn't look at me. I've always been the most awful fool. Got a bit of a corporation, too. But you do know what I feel, don't you, eh? I mean – I'm always there. Know I haven't got an earthly chance, but thought I'd just mention it.'

And Rosemary had laughed and kissed the top of his head.

'You're sweet, George, and I'll remember the kind offer, but I'm not marrying anyone just at present.'

And he had said seriously: 'Quite right. Take plenty of time to look around. You can take your pick.'

He'd never had any hope – not any real hope.

That's why he had been so incredulous, so dazed when Rosemary had said she was going to marry him.

She wasn't in love with him, of course. He knew that quite well. In fact, she admitted as much.

'You do understand, don't you? I want to feel settled down and happy and safe. I shall with you. I'm so sick of being in love. It always goes wrong somehow and ends in a mess. I like you, George. You're nice and funny and sweet and you think I'm wonderful. That's what I want.'

He had answered rather incoherently:

'Steady does it. We'll be as happy as kings.'

Well, that hadn't been far wrong. They had been happy. He'd always felt humble in his own mind. He'd always told himself that there were bound to be snags. Rosemary wasn't going to be satisfied with a dull kind of chap like himself. There would be *incidents*! He'd schooled himself to accept – incidents! He would hold firm to the belief that they wouldn't be lasting! Rosemary would always come back to him. Once let him accept that view and all would be well.

For she was fond of him. Her affection for him was constant and unvarying. It existed quite apart from her flirtations and her love affairs.

He had schooled himself to accept those. He had told himself that they were inevitable with someone of Rosemary's susceptible temperament and unusual beauty. What he had not bargained for were his own reactions.

Flirtations with this young man and that were nothing, but when he first got an inkling of a serious affair –

He'd known quick enough, sensed the difference in her. The rising excitement, the added beauty, the whole glowing radiance. And then what his instinct told him was confirmed by ugly concrete facts.

There was that day when he'd come into her sitting-room and she had instinctively covered with her hand the page of the letter she was writing. He'd known then. She was writing to her lover.

Presently, when she went out of the room, he went across to the blotter. She had taken the letter with her, but the blotting sheet was nearly fresh. He'd taken it across the room and held it up to the glass – seen the words in Rosemary's dashing script, 'My own beloved darling . . .'

His blood had sung in his ears. He understood in that moment just what Othello had felt. Wise resolutions? Pah! Only the natural man counted. He'd like to choke the life out of her! He'd like to murder the fellow in cold blood. Who was it? That fellow Browne? Or that stick Stephen Farraday? They'd both of them been making sheep's eyes at her.

He caught sight of his face in the glass. His eyes were suffused with blood. He looked as though he were going to have a fit.

As he remembered that moment, George Barton let his glass fall from his hand. Once again he felt the choking sensation, the beating blood in his ears. Even now –

With an effort he pushed remembrance away. Mustn't go over that again. It was past – done with. He wouldn't ever suffer like that again. Rosemary was dead. Dead and at peace. And he was at peace too. No more suffering . . .

Funny to think that that was what her death had meant to him. Peace . . .

He'd never told even Ruth that. Good girl, Ruth. A good headpiece on her. Really, he didn't know what he would do without her. The way she helped. The way she sympathized. And never a hint of sex. Not man mad like Rosemary . . .

Rosemary . . . Rosemary sitting at the round table in the restaurant. A little thin in the face after 'flu – a little pulled down – but lovely, so lovely. And only an hour later –

No, he wouldn't think of that. Not just now. His plan. He would think of The Plan.

He'd speak to Race first. He'd show Race the letters. What would Race make of these letters? Iris had been dumbfounded. She evidently hadn't had the slightest idea.

Well, he was in charge of the situation now. He'd got it all taped.

The Plan. All worked out. The date. The place.

Nov. 2nd. *All Souls' Day.* That was a good touch. The Luxembourg, of course. He'd try to get the same table.

And the same guests. Anthony Browne, Stephen Farraday, Sandra Farraday. Then, of course, Ruth and Iris and himself. And as the odd, the seventh guest he'd get Race. Race who was originally to have been at the dinner.

And there would be one empty place.

It would be splendid!

Dramatic!

A repetition of the crime.

Well, not quite a repetition . . .

His mind went back . . .

Rosemary's birthday . . .

Rosemary, sprawled forward on that table – dead . . .

BOOK 2 • ALL SOULS' DAY

'There's Rosemary, that's for remembrance.'

Lucilla Drake was twittering. That was the term always used in the family and it was really a very apt description of the sounds that issued from Lucilla's kindly lips.

She was concerned on this particular morning with many things – so many that she found it hard to pin her attention down to one at a time. There was the imminence of the move back to town and the household problems involved in that move. Servants, housekeeping, winter storage, a thousand minor details – all these contended with a concern over Iris's looks.

'Really, dear, I feel quite anxious about you – you look so white and washed out – as though you hadn't slept – did you sleep? If not, there's that nice sleeping preparation of Dr Wylie's or was it Dr Gaskell's? – which reminds me – I shall have to go and speak to the grocer *myself* – either the maids have been ordering things in on their own, or else it's deliberate swindling on his part. Packets and packets of soap flakes – and I never allow more than three a week. But perhaps a tonic would be better? Eaton's syrup, they used to give when I was a girl. And spinach, of course. I'll tell cook to have spinach for lunch today.'

Iris was too languid and too used to Mrs Drake's discursive style to inquire why the mention of Dr Gaskell should have reminded her aunt of the local grocer, though had she done so, she would have received the immediate response: 'Because the grocer's name is Cranford, my dear.' Aunt Lucilla's reasoning was always crystal clear to herself.

Iris merely said with what energy she could command, 'I'm perfectly well, Aunt Lucilla.'

'Black under the eyes,' said Mrs Drake. 'You've been doing too much.'

'I've done nothing at all – for weeks.'

'So you think, dear. But too much tennis is overtiring for young girls. And I think the air down here is inclined to be enervating. This place is in a hollow. If George had consulted *me* instead of that girl.'

'Girl?'

'That Miss Lessing he thinks so much of. All very well in the office, I daresay – but a great mistake to take her out of her place. Encourage her to think herself one of the family. Not that she needs any encouragement, I should say.'

'Oh, well, Aunt Lucilla, Ruth *is* practically one of the family.'

Mrs Drake sniffed. 'She means to be – that's quite clear. Poor George – really an infant in arms where women are concerned. But it won't do, Iris. George must be protected from himself and if I were you I should make it very clear that nice as Miss Lessing is, any idea of marriage is out of the question.'

Iris was startled for a moment out of her apathy.

'I never thought of George marrying Ruth.'

'You don't see what goes on under your nose, child. Of course you haven't had my experience of life.' Iris smiled in spite of herself. Aunt Lucilla was really very funny sometimes. 'That young woman is out for matrimony.'

'Would it matter?' asked Iris.

'Matter? Of course it would matter.'

'Wouldn't it really be rather nice?' Her aunt stared at her. 'Nice for George, I mean. I think you're right about her, you know. I think she is fond of him. And she'd be an awfully good wife to him and look after him.'

Mrs Drake snorted and an almost indignant expression appeared on her rather sheep-like amiable face.

'George is very well looked after at present. What more can he want, I should like to know? Excellent meals and his mending seen to. Very pleasant for him to have an attractive young girl like you about the house and when you marry some day I should hope I was still capable of seeing to his comfort and looking after his health. Just as well or better than a young woman out of an office could do – what does she know about housekeeping? Figures and ledgers and shorthand and typing – what good is that in a man's home?'

Iris smiled and shook her head, but she did not argue the point. She was thinking of the smooth dark satin of Ruth's head, of the clear complexion and the figure so well set off by the severe tailor-made clothes that Ruth affected. Poor Aunt Lucilla, all her mind on comfort and housekeeping, with romance so very far behind her that she had probably forgotten what it meant – if indeed, thought Iris, remembering her uncle by marriage, it had ever meant much.

Lucilla Drake had been Hector Marle's half-sister, the child of an earlier marriage. She had played the little mother to a very much younger brother when his own mother died. Housekeeping for her father, she had stiffened into a pronounced spinsterhood. She was close on forty when she met the Rev Caleb Drake, he himself a man of over fifty. Her married life had been short, a mere two years, then she had been left a widow with an infant son. Motherhood, coming late and unexpectedly, had been the supreme experience of Lucilla Drake's life. Her son had turned out an anxiety, a source of grief and a constant financial drain – but never a disappointment. Mrs Drake refused to recognize anything in her son Victor except an amiable weakness of character. Victor was too trusting – too easily led astray by bad companions because of his own belief in them. Victor was unlucky. Victor was deceived. Victor was swindled. He was the cat's-paw of wicked men who exploited his innocence. The pleasant, rather silly sheep's face hardened into obstinacy when criticism of Victor was to the fore. She knew her own son. He was a dear boy, full of high spirits, and his so-called friends took advantage of him. She knew, none better, how Victor hated having to ask her for money. But when the poor boy was really in such a terrible situation, what else could he do? It wasn't as though he had anyone but her to go to.

All the same, as she admitted, George's invitation to come and live in the house and look after Iris, had come as a god-send, at a moment when she really had been in desperate straits of genteel poverty. She had been very happy and comfortable this last year and it was not in human nature to look kindly on the possibility of being superseded by an upstart young woman, all modern efficiency and capability, who in any case, so she persuaded herself, would only be marrying George for his money. Of course that was what she was after! A good home and a rich indulgent husband. You couldn't tell Aunt Lucilla, at her age, that any young woman really *liked* working for her living! Girls were the same as they always had been – if they could get a man to keep them in comfort, they much preferred it. This Ruth Lessing was clever, worming her way into a position of confidence, advising George about house furnishing, making herself indispensable – but, thank goodness, there was *one* person at least who saw what she was up to!

Lucilla Drake nodded her head several times, causing her soft double chins to quiver, raised her eyebrows with an air of superb human sapience, and abandoned the subject for one equally interesting and possibly even more pressing.

'It's the blankets I can't make up my mind about, dear. You see, I can't get it clearly laid down whether we shan't be coming down again until next spring or whether George means to run down for weekends. He won't say.'

'I suppose he doesn't really know.' Iris tried to give her attention to a point that seemed completely unimportant. 'If it was nice weather it might be fun to come down occasionally. Though I don't think I want to particularly. Still the house will be here if we do want to come.'

'Yes, dear, but one wants to *know*. Because, you see, if we aren't coming down until next year, then the blankets ought to be put away with moth balls. But if we *are* coming down, that wouldn't be necessary, because the blankets would be *used* – and the smell of moth balls is so unpleasant.'

'Well, don't use them.'

'Yes, but it's been such a hot summer there are a lot of moths about. Everyone says it's a bad year for moths. And for wasps, of course. Hawkins told me yesterday he's taken thirty wasps' nests this summer – thirty – just fancy –'

Iris thought of Hawkins – stalking out at dusk – cyanide in hand – *Cyanide* – *Rosemary* – Why did everything lead back to that –?

The thin trickle of sound that was Aunt Lucilla's voice was going on – it had reached by now a different point –

'– and whether one ought to send the silver to the bank or not? Lady Alexandra was saying so many burglaries – though of course we do have good shutters – I don't like the way she does her hair myself – it makes her face look so hard – but I should think she was a hard woman. And nervy, too. Everyone is nervy nowadays. When I was a girl people didn't know what nerves were. Which reminds me that I didn't like the look of George lately – I wonder if he could be going to have 'flu? I've wondered once or twice whether he was feverish. But perhaps it is some business worry. He looks to me, you know, as though he has got something on his mind.'

Iris shivered, and Lucilla Drake exclaimed triumphantly: 'There, I said you had a chill.'

CHAPTER 2

'How I wish they had never come here.'

Sandra Farraday uttered the words with such unusual bitterness that her husband turned to look at her in surprise. It was as though his own thoughts had been put into words – the thoughts that he had been trying so hard to conceal. So Sandra, too, felt as he did? She, too, had felt that Fairhaven was spoiled, its peace impaired, by these new neighbours a mile away across the Park. He said, voicing his surprise impulsively:

'I didn't know you felt like that about them, too.'

Immediately, or so it seemed to him, she withdrew into herself.

'Neighbours are so important in the country. One has either to be rude or friendly; one can't, as in London, just keep people as amiable acquaintances.'

'No,' said Stephen, 'one can't do that.'

'And now we're committed to this extraordinary party.'

They were both silent, running over in their minds the scene at lunch. George Barton had been friendly, even exuberant in manner, with a kind of undercurrent of excitement of which they had both been conscious. George Barton was really very odd these days. Stephen had never noticed him much in the time preceding Rosemary's death. George had just been there in the background, the kindly dull husband of a young and beautiful wife. Stephen had never even felt a pang of disquiet over the betrayal of George. George had been the kind of husband who was born to be betrayed. So much older – so devoid of the attractions necessary to hold an attractive and capricious woman. Had George himself been deceived? Stephen did not think so. George, he thought, knew Rosemary very well. He loved her, and he was the kind of man who was humble about his own powers of holding a wife's interest.

All the same, George must have suffered . . .

Stephen began to wonder just what George had felt when Rosemary died.

He and Sandra had seen little of him in the months following the tragedy. It was not until he had suddenly appeared as a near neighbour at Little Priors that he had reentered their lives and at once, so Stephen thought, he had seemed different.

More alive, more positive. And – yes, decidedly *odd*.

He had been odd today. That suddenly blurted out invitation. A party for Iris's eighteenth birthday. He did so hope Stephen and Sandra would both come. Stephen and Sandra had been so kind to them down here.

Sandra had said quickly; of course, it would be delightful. Naturally Stephen would be rather tied when they got back to London and she herself had a great many tiresome engagements, but she did hope they would be able to manage it.

'Then let's settle a day now, shall we?'

George's face – florid, smiling, insistent.

'I thought perhaps one day the week after next – Wednesday or Thursday? Thursday is November 2nd. Would that be all right? But we'll arrange any day that suits you both.'

It had been the kind of invitation that pinned you down – there was a certain lack of social *savoir-faire*. Stephen noticed that Iris Marle had gone red and looked embarrassed. Sandra had been perfect. She had smilingly surrendered to the inevitable and said that Thursday, November 2nd, would suit them very well.

Suddenly voicing his thoughts, Stephen said sharply, 'We needn't go.'

Sandra turned her face slightly towards him. It wore a thoughtful considering air.

'You think not?'

'It's easy to make some excuse.'

'He'll only insist on us coming some other time – or change the day. He – he seems very set on our coming.'

'I can't think why. It's Iris's party – and I can't believe she is so particularly anxious for our company.'

'No – no –' Sandra sounded thoughtful.

Then she said:

'You know where this party is to be?'

'No.'

'The Luxembourg.'

The shock nearly deprived him of speech. He felt the colour ebbing out of his cheeks. He pulled himself together and met her eyes. Was it his fancy or was there meaning in the level gaze?

'But it's preposterous,' he exclaimed, blustering a little in his attempt to conceal his own personal emotion. 'The Luxembourg where – to revive all that. The man must be mad.'

'I thought of that,' said Sandra.

'But then we shall certainly refuse to go. The – the whole thing was terribly unpleasant. You remember all the publicity – the pictures in the papers.'

'I remember the unpleasantness,' said Sandra.

'Doesn't he realize how disagreeable it would be for us?'

'He has a reason, you know, Stephen. A reason that he gave me.'

'What was it?'

He felt thankful that she was looking away from him when she spoke.

'He took me aside after lunch. He said he wanted to explain. He told me that the girl – Iris – had never recovered properly from the shock of her sister's death.'

She paused and Stephen said unwillingly:

Well, I daresay that may be true enough – she looks far from well. I thought at lunch how ill she was looking.'

'Yes, I noticed it too – although she has seemed in good health and spirits on the whole lately. But I am telling you what George Barton said. He told me that Iris has consistently avoided the Luxembourg ever since as far as she was able.'

'I don't wonder.'

'But according to him that is all wrong. It seems he consulted a nerve specialist on the subject – one of these modern men – and his advice is that after a shock of any kind, the trouble must be faced, not avoided. The principle, I gather, is like that of sending up an airman again immediately after a crash.'

'Does the specialist suggest another suicide?'

Sandra replied quietly, 'He suggests that the associations of the restaurant must be overcome. It is, after all, just a restaurant. He proposed an ordinary pleasant party with, as far as possible, the same people present.'

'Delightful for the people!'

'Do you mind so much, Stephen?'

A swift pang of alarm shot through him. He said quickly: 'Of course I don't mind. I just thought it rather a gruesome idea. Personally *I* shouldn't mind in the least . . . I was really thinking of *you*. If you don't mind –'

She interrupted him.

'I do mind. Very much. But the way George Barton put it made it very difficult to refuse. After all, I have frequently been to the Luxembourg since – so have you. One is constantly being asked there.'

'But not under these circumstances.'

'No.'

Stephen said:

'As you say, it is difficult to refuse – and if we put it off the invitation will be renewed. But there's no reason, Sandra, why *you* should have to endure it. I'll go and you can cry off at the last minute – a headache, chill – something of that kind.'

He saw her chin go up.

'That would be cowardly. No, Stephen, if you go, I go. After all,' she laid her hand on his arm, 'however little our marriage means, it should at least mean sharing our difficulties.'

But he was staring at her – rendered dumb by one poignant phrase which had escaped her so easily, as though it voiced a long familiar and not very important fact.

Recovering himself he said, 'Why do you say that? *However little our marriage means?*'

She looked at him steadily, her eyes wide and honest.

'Isn't it true?'

'No, a thousand times no. Our marriage means everything to me.'

She smiled.

'I suppose it does – in a way. We're a good team, Stephen. We pull together with a satisfactory result.'

'I didn't mean that.' He found his breath was coming unevenly. He took her hand in both of his, holding it very closely – 'Sandra, don't you know that you mean all the world to me?'

And suddenly she did know it. It was incredible – unforeseen, but it was so.

She was in his arms and he was holding her close, kissing her, stammering out incoherent words.

'Sandra – Sandra – darling. I love you . . . I've been so afraid – so afraid I'd lose you.'

She heard herself saying:

'Because of Rosemary?'

'Yes.' He let go of her, stepped back, his face was ludicrous in its dismay.

'You knew – about Rosemary?'

'Of course – all the time.'

'And you understand?'

She shook her head.

'No, I don't understand. I don't think I ever should. You loved her?'

'Not really. It was you I loved.'

A surge of bitterness swept over her. She quoted: 'From the first moment you saw me across the room? Don't repeat that lie – for it was a lie!'

He was not taken aback by that sudden attack. He seemed to consider her words thoughtfully.

'Yes, it was a lie – and yet in a queer way it wasn't. I'm beginning to believe that it was true. Oh, try and *understand*, Sandra. You know the people who always have a noble and good reason to mask their meaner actions? The people who "have to be honest" when they want to be unkind, who "thought it their duty to repeat so and so," who are such hypocrites to themselves that they go through to their life's end convinced that every mean and beastly action was done in a spirit of unselfishness! Try and realize that the opposite of those people can exist too. People who are so cynical, so distrustful of themselves and of life that they only believe in their bad motives. You were the woman I needed. That, at least, is true. And I do honestly believe, now, looking back on it, that if it hadn't been true, I should never have gone through with it.'

She said bitterly:

'You were not in love with me.'

'No. I'd never been in love. I was a starved, sexless creature who prided himself – yes, I did – on the fastidious coldness of his nature! And then I did fall in love "across a room" – a silly violent puppy love. A thing like a midsummer thunderstorm, brief, unreal, quickly over.' He added bitterly: 'Indeed a "tale told by an idiot, full of sound and fury, signifying nothing."'

He paused, and then went on:

'It was here, at Fairhaven, that I woke up and realized the truth.'

'The truth?'

'The only thing in life that mattered to me was you – and keeping your love.'

'If I had only known . . .'

'What did you think?'

'I thought you were planning to go away with her.'

'With Rosemary?' He gave a short laugh. 'That would indeed have been penal servitude for life!'

'Didn't she want you to go away with her?'

'Yes, she did.'

'What happened?'

Stephen drew a deep breath. They were back again. Facing once more that intangible menace. He said:

'The Luxembourg happened.'

They were both silent, seeing, they both knew, the same thing. The blue cyanosed face of a once lovely woman.

Staring at a dead woman, and then – looking up to meet each other's eyes . . .

Stephen said:

'Forget it, Sandra, for God's sake, let us forget it!'

'It's no use forgetting. We're not going to be allowed to forget.'

There was a pause. Then Sandra said:

'What are we going to do?'

'What you said just now. Face things – together. Go to this horrible party whatever the reason for it may be.'

'You don't believe what George Barton said about Iris?'

'No. Do you?'

'It could be true. But even if it is, it's not the real reason.'

'What do you think the real reason is?'

'I don't know, Stephen. But I'm afraid.'

'Of George Barton?'

'Yes, I think he – knows.'

Stephen said sharply:

'Knows what?'

She turned her head slowly until her eyes met his.

She said in a whisper:

'We mustn't be afraid. We must have courage – all the courage in the world. You're going to be a great man, Stephen – a man the world needs – and nothing shall interfere with that. I'm your wife and I love you.'

'What do you think this party is, Sandra?'

'I think it's a trap.'

He said slowly, 'And we walk into it?'

'We can't afford to show we know it's a trap.'

'No, that's true.'

Suddenly Sandra threw back her head and laughed. She said: 'Do your worst, Rosemary. You won't win.'

He gripped her shoulder.

'Be quiet, Sandra. Rosemary's dead.'

'Is she? Sometimes – she feels very much alive . . .'

CHAPTER 3

Halfway across the Park Iris said:

'Do you mind if I don't come back with you, George? I feel like a walk. I thought I'd go up over Friar's Hill and come down through the wood. I've had an awful headache all day.'

'My poor child. Do go. I won't come with you – I'm expecting a fellow along some time this afternoon and I'm not quite sure when he'll turn up.'

'Right. Goodbye till tea-time.'

She turned abruptly and made off at right angles to where a belt of larches showed on the hillside.

When she came out on the brow of the hill she drew a deep breath. It was one of those close humid days common in October. A dank moisture coated the leaves of the trees and the grey cloud hung low overhead promising yet more rain shortly. There was not really much more air up here on the hill than there had been in the valley, but Iris felt nevertheless as though she could breathe more freely.

She sat down on the trunk of a fallen tree and stared down into the valley to where Little Priors nestled demurely in its wooded hollow. Farther to the left, Fairhaven Manor showed a glimpse of rose red on brick.

Iris stared out sombrely over the landscape, her chin cupped in her hand.

The slight rustle behind her was hardly louder than the drip of the leaves, but she turned her head sharply as the branches parted and Anthony Browne came through them.

She cried half angrily: 'Tony! Why do you always have to arrive like – like a demon in a pantomime?'

Anthony dropped to the ground beside her. He took out his cigarette case, offered her one and when she shook her head took one himself and lighted it. Then inhaling the first puff he replied:

'It's because I'm what the papers call a Mystery Man. I *like* appearing from nowhere.'

'How did you know where I was?'

'An excellent pair of bird glasses. I heard you were lunching with the Farradays and spied on you from the hillside when you left.'

'Why don't you come to the house like an ordinary person?'

'I'm not an ordinary person,' said Anthony in a shocked tone. 'I'm very extraordinary.'

'I think you are.'

He looked at her quickly. Then he said:

'Is anything the matter?'

'No, of course not. At least –'

She paused. Anthony said interrogatively:

'At least?'

She drew a deep breath.

'I'm tired of being down here. I hate it. I want to go back to London.'

'You're going soon, aren't you?'

'Next week.'

'So this was a farewell party at the Farradays'?'

'It wasn't a party. Just them and one old cousin.'

'Do you like the Farradays, Iris?'

'I don't know. I don't think I do very much – although I shouldn't say that because they've really been very nice to us.'

'Do you think they like you?'

'No, I don't. I think they hate us.'

'Interesting.'

'Is it?'

'Oh, not the hatred – if true. I meant the use of the word "us". My question referred to you personally.'

'Oh, I see . . . I think they like *me* quite well in a negative sort of way. I think it's us as a family living next door that they mind about. We weren't particular friends of theirs – they were Rosemary's friends.'

'Yes,' said Anthony, 'as you say they were Rosemary's friends – not that I should imagine Sandra Farraday and Rosemary were ever bosom friends, eh?'

'No,' said Iris. She looked faintly apprehensive but Anthony smoked peacefully. Presently he said:

'Do you know what strikes me most about the Farradays?'

'What?'

'Just that – that they are the Farradays. I always think of them like that – not as Stephen and Sandra, two individuals linked by the State and the Established Church – but as a definite dual entity – the Farradays. That is rarer than you would think. They are two people with a common aim, a common way of life, identical hopes and fears and beliefs. And the odd part of it is that they are actually very dissimilar in character. Stephen Farraday, I should say, is a man of very wide intellectual scope, extremely sensitive to outside opinion, horribly diffident about himself and somewhat lacking in moral courage. Sandra, on the other hand, has a narrow medieval mind, is capable of fanatical devotion, and is courageous to the point of recklessness.'

'He always seems to me,' said Iris, 'rather pompous and stupid.'

'He's not at all stupid. He's just one of the usual unhappy successes.'

'Unhappy?'

'Most successes are unhappy. That's why they are successes – they have to reassure themselves about themselves by achieving something that the world will notice.'

'What extraordinary ideas you have, Anthony.'

'You'll find they're quite true if you only examine them. The happy people are failures because they are on such good terms with themselves that they don't give a damn. Like me. They are also usually agreeable to get on with – again like me.'

'You have a very good opinion of yourself.'

'I am just drawing attention to my good points in case you mayn't have noticed them.'

Iris laughed. Her spirits had risen. The dull depression and fear had lifted from her mind. She glanced down at her watch.

'Come home and have tea, and give a few more people the benefit of your unusually agreeable society.'

Anthony shook his head.

'Not today. I must be getting back.'

Iris turned sharply on him.

'Why will you never come to the house? There must be a reason.'

Anthony shrugged his shoulders.

'Put it that I'm rather peculiar in my ideas of accepting hospitality. Your brother-in-law doesn't like me – he's made that quite clear.'

'Oh, don't bother about George. If Aunt Lucilla and I ask you – she's an old dear – you'd like her.'

'I'm sure I should – but my objection holds.'

'You used to come in Rosemary's time.'

'That,' said Anthony, 'was rather different.'

A faint cold hand touched Iris's heart. She said, 'What made you come down here today? Had you business in this part of the world?'

'Very important business – with you. I came here to ask you a question, Iris.'

The cold hand vanished. Instead there came a faint flutter, that throb of excitement that women have known from time immemorial. And with it Iris's face adopted that same look of blank inquiry that her great-grandmother might have worn prior to saying a few minutes later, 'Oh, Mr X, this is so sudden!'

'Yes?' She turned that impossibly innocent face towards Anthony. He was looking at her, his eyes were grave, almost stern.

'Answer me truthfully, Iris. This is my question. Do you trust me?'

It took her aback. It was not what she had expected. He saw that.

'You didn't think that that was what I was going to say? But it is a very important question, Iris. The most important question in the world to me. I ask it again. Do you trust me?'

She hesitated, a bare second, then she answered, her eyes falling: 'Yes.'

'Then I'll go on and ask you something else. Will you come up to London and marry me without telling anybody about it?'

She stared.

'But I couldn't! I simply couldn't.'

'You couldn't marry me?'

'Not in that way.'

'And yet you love me. You do love me, don't you?'

She heard herself saying:

'Yes, I love you, Anthony.'

'But you won't come and marry me at the Church of Saint Elfrida, Bloomsbury, in the parish of which I have resided for some weeks and where I can consequently get married by licence at any time?'

'How can I do a thing like that? George would be terribly hurt and Aunt Lucilla would never forgive me. And anyway I'm not of age. I'm only eighteen.'

'You'd have to lie about your age. I don't know what penalties I should incur for marrying a minor without her guardian's consent. Who is your guardian, by the way?'

'George. He's my trustee as well.'

'As I was saying, whatever penalties I incurred, they couldn't unmarry us and that is really all I care about.'

Iris shook her head. 'I couldn't do it. I couldn't be so unkind. And in any case, *why*? What's the point of it?'

Anthony said: 'That's why I asked you first if you could trust me. You'd have to take my reasons on trust. Let's say that it is the simplest way. But never mind.'

Iris said timidly:

'If George only got to know you a little better. Come back now with me. It will be only he and Aunt Lucilla.'

'Are you sure? I thought –' he paused. 'As I struck up the hill I saw a man going up your drive – and the funny thing is that I believe I recognized him as a man I' – he hesitated – 'had met.'

'Of course – I forgot – George said he was expecting someone.'

'The man I thought I saw was a man called Race – Colonel Race.'

'Very likely,' Iris agreed. 'George does know a Colonel Race. He was coming to dinner on that night when Rosemary –'

She stopped, her voice quivering. Anthony gripped her hand.

'Don't go on remembering it, darling. It was beastly, I know.'

She shook her head.

'I can't help it. Anthony –'

'Yes?'

'Did it ever occur to you – did you ever think –' she found a difficulty in putting her meaning into words.

'Did it ever strike you that – that Rosemary might not have committed suicide? That she might have been – *killed*?'

'Good God, Iris, what put that idea into your head?'

She did not reply – merely persisted: 'That idea never occurred to you?'

'Certainly not. Of course Rosemary committed suicide.'

Iris said nothing.

'Who's been suggesting these things to you?'

For a moment she was tempted to tell him George's incredible story, but she refrained. She said slowly:

'It was just an idea.'

'Forget it, darling idiot.' He pulled her to her feet and kissed her cheek lightly. 'Darling morbid idiot. Forget Rosemary. Only think of me.'

CHAPTER 4

Puffing at his pipe, Colonel Race looked speculatively at George Barton.

He had known George Barton ever since the latter's boyhood. Barton's uncle had been a country neighbour of the Races. There was a difference of over twenty years between the two men. Race was over sixty, a tall, erect, military figure, with sunburnt face, closely cropped iron-grey hair, and shrewd dark eyes.

There had never been any particular intimacy between the two men – but Barton remained to Race 'young George' – one of the many vague figures associated with earlier days.

He was thinking at this moment that he had really no idea what 'young George' was like. On the brief occasions when they had met in later years, they had found little in common. Race was an out-of-door man, essentially of the Empire-builder type – most of his life had been spent abroad. George was emphatically the city gentleman. Their interests were dissimilar and when they met it was to exchange rather lukewarm reminiscences of 'the old days,' after which an embarrassed silence was apt to occur. Colonel Race was not good at small talk and might indeed have posed as the model of a strong silent man so beloved by an earlier generation of novelists.

Silent at this moment, he was wondering just why 'young George' had been so insistent on this meeting. Thinking, too, that there was some subtle change in the man since he had last seen him a year ago. George Barton had always struck him as the essence of stodginess – cautious, practical, unimaginative.

There was, he thought, something very wrong with the fellow. Jumpy as a cat. He'd already re-lit his cigar three times – and that wasn't like Barton at all.

He took his pipe out of his mouth.

'Well, young George, what's the trouble?'

'You're right, Race, it is trouble. I want your advice badly – and your help.'

The colonel nodded and waited.

'Nearly a year ago you were coming to dine with us in London – at the Luxembourg. You had to go abroad at the last minute.'

Again Race nodded.

'South Africa.'

'At that dinner party my wife died.'

Race stirred uncomfortably in his chair.

'I know. Read about it. Didn't mention it now or offer you sympathy because I didn't want to stir up things again. But I'm sorry, old man, you know that.'

'Oh, yes, yes. That's not the point. My wife was supposed to have committed suicide.'

Race fastened on the key word. His eyebrows rose.

'*Supposed?*'

'Read these.'

He thrust the two letters into the other's hand. Race's eyebrows rose still higher.

'Anonymous letters?'

'Yes. And I believe them.'

Race shook his head slowly.

'That's a dangerous thing to do. You'd be surprised how many lying spiteful letters get written after any event that's been given any sort of publicity in the Press.'

'I know that. But these weren't written at the time – they weren't written until six months afterwards.'

Race nodded.

'That's a point. Who do you think wrote them?'

'I don't know. I don't care. The point is that I believe what they say is true. My wife was murdered.'

Race laid down his pipe. He sat up a little straighter in his chair.

'Now just why do you think that? Had you any suspicion at the time. Had the police?'

'I was dazed when it happened – completely bowled over. I just accepted the verdict at the inquest. My wife had had 'flu, was run down. No suspicion of anything but suicide arose. The stuff was in her handbag, you see.'

'What was the stuff?'

'Cyanide.'

'I remember. She took it in champagne.'

'Yes. It seemed, at the time, all quite straightforward.'

'Had she ever threatened to commit suicide?'

'No, never. Rosemary,' said George Barton, 'loved life.'

Race nodded. He had only met George's wife once. He had thought her a singularly lovely nit-wit – but certainly not a melancholic type.

'What about the medical evidence as to state of mind, etcetera?'

'Rosemary's own doctor – an elderly man who has attended the Marle family since they were young children – was away on a sea voyage. His partner, a young man, attended Rosemary when she had 'flu. All he said, I remember, was that the type of 'flu about was inclined to leave serious depression.'

George paused and went on.

'It wasn't until after I got these letters that I talked with Rosemary's own doctor. I said nothing of the letters, of course – just discussed what had happened. He told me then that he was very surprised at what had happened. He would never have believed it, he said. Rosemary was not at all a suicidal type. It showed, he said, how even a patient one knew well might act in a thoroughly uncharacteristic manner.'

Again George paused and then went on:

'It was after talking to him that I realized how absolutely unconvincing to *me* Rosemary's suicide was. After all, I knew her very well. She was a person who was capable of violent fits of unhappiness. She could get very worked up over things, and she would on occasions take very rash and unconsidered action, but I have never known her in the frame of mind that "wanted to get out of it all."'

Race murmured in a slightly embarrassed manner:

'Could she have had a motive for suicide apart from mere depression? Was she, I mean, definitely unhappy about anything?'

'I – no – she was perhaps rather nervy.'

Avoiding looking at his friend, Race said:

'Was she at all a melodramatic person? I only saw her once, you know. But there is a type that – well – might get a kick out of attempted suicide – usually if they've quarrelled with someone. The rather childish motive of – "I'll make them sorry!"'

'Rosemary and I hadn't quarrelled.'

'No. And I must say that the fact of cyanide having been used rather rules that possibility out. It's not the kind of thing you can monkey about with safely – and everybody knows it.'

'That's another point. If by any chance Rosemary *had* contemplated doing away with herself, surely she'd never do it that way? Painful and – and ugly. An overdose of some sleeping stuff would be far more likely.'

'I agree. Was there any evidence as to her purchasing or getting hold of the cyanide?'

'No. But she had been staying with friends in the country and they had taken a wasps' nest one day. It was suggested that she might have taken a handful of potassium cyanide crystals then.'

'Yes – it's not a difficult thing to get hold of. Most gardeners keep a stock of it.'

He paused and then said:

'Let me summarize the position. There was no positive evidence as to a disposition to suicide, or to any preparation for it. The whole thing was negative. But there can also have been no positive evidence pointing to murder, or the police would have got hold of it. They're quite wide awake, you know.'

'The mere idea of murder would have seemed fantastic.'

'But it didn't seem fantastic to you six months later?'

George said slowly:

'I think I must have been unsatisfied all along. I think I must have been subconsciously preparing myself so that when I saw the thing written down in black and white I accepted it without doubt.'

'Yes.' Race nodded. 'Well, then, let's have it. Who do you suspect?'

George leaned forward – his face twitching.

'That's what is so terrible. *If* Rosemary was killed, one of those people round the table, one of our friends, must have done it. No one else came near the table.'

'Waiters? Who poured out the wine?'

'Charles, the head waiter at the Luxembourg. You know Charles?'

Race assented. Everybody knew Charles. It seemed quite impossible to imagine that Charles could have deliberately poisoned a client.

'And the waiter who looked after us was Giuseppe. We know

Giuseppe well. I've known him for years. He always looks after me there. He's a delightful cheery little fellow.'

'So we come to the dinner party. Who was there?'

'Stephen Farraday, the M.P. His wife, Lady Alexandra Farraday. My secretary, Ruth Lessing. A fellow called Anthony Browne. Rosemary's sister, Iris, and myself. Seven in all. We should have been eight if you had come. When you dropped out we couldn't think of anybody suitable to ask at the last minute.'

'I see. Well, Barton, who do you think did it?'

George cried out: 'I don't know – I tell you I don't know. If I had any idea –'

'All right – all right. I just thought you might have a definite suspicion. Well, it oughtn't to be difficult. How did you sit – starting with yourself?'

'I had Sandra Farraday on my right, of course. Next to her, Anthony Browne. Then Rosemary. Then Stephen Farraday, then Iris, then Ruth Lessing who sat on my left.'

'I see. And your wife had drunk champagne earlier in the evening?'

'Yes. The glasses had been filled up several times. It – it happened while the cabaret show was on. There was a lot of noise – it was one of those negro shows and we were all watching it. She slumped forward on the table just before the lights went up. She may have cried out – or gasped – but nobody heard anything. The doctor said that death must have been practically instantaneous. Thank God for that.'

'Yes, indeed. Well, Barton – on the face of it, it seems fairly obvious.'

'You mean?'

'Stephen Farraday of course. He was on her right hand. Her champagne glass would be close to his left hand. Easiest thing in the world to put the stuff in as soon as the lights were lowered and general attention went to the raised stage. I can't see that anybody else had anything like as good an opportunity. I know those Luxembourg tables. There's plenty of room round them – I doubt very much if anybody could have leaned across the table, for instance, without being noticed even if the lights were down. The same thing applies to the fellow on Rosemary's left. He would have had to lean across her to put anything in her glass.

There *is* one other possibility, but we'll take the obvious person first. Any reason why Stephen Farraday, M.P., should want to do away with your wife?'

George said in a stifled voice:

'They – they had been rather close friends. If – if Rosemary had turned him down, for instance, he might have wanted revenge.'

'Sounds highly melodramatic. That is the only motive you can suggest?'

'Yes,' said George. His face was very red. Race gave him the most fleeting of glances. Then he went on:

'We'll examine possibility No. 2. One of the women.'

'Why the women?'

'My dear George, has it escaped your notice that in a party of seven, four women and three men, there will probably be one or two periods during the evening when three couples are dancing and one woman is sitting alone at the table? You did all dance?'

'Oh, yes.'

'Good. Now before the cabaret, can you remember who was sitting alone at any moment?'

George thought a minute.

'I think – yes, Iris was odd man out last, and Ruth the time before.'

'You don't remember when your wife drank champagne last?'

'Let me see, she had been dancing with Browne. I remember her coming back and saying that had been pretty strenuous – he's rather a fancy dancer. She drank up the wine in her glass then. A few minutes later they played a waltz and she – she danced with me. She knew a waltz is the only dance I'm really any good at. Farraday danced with Ruth and Lady Alexandra with Browne. Iris sat out. Immediately after that, they had the cabaret.'

'Then let's consider your wife's sister. Did she come into any money on your wife's death?'

George began to splutter.

'My dear Race – don't be absurd. Iris was a mere child, a schoolgirl.'

'I've known two schoolgirls who committed murder.'

'But Iris! She was devoted to Rosemary.'

'Never mind, Barton. She had opportunity. I want to know if she had motive. Your wife, I believe, was a rich woman. Where did her money go – to you?'

'No, it went to Iris – a trust fund.'

He explained the position, to which Race listened attentively.

'Rather a curious position. The rich sister and the poor sister. Some girls might have resented that.'

'I'm sure Iris never did.'

'Maybe not – but she had a motive all right. We'll try that tack now. Who else had a motive?'

'Nobody – nobody at all. Rosemary hadn't an enemy in the world, I'm sure. I've been looking into all that – asking questions – trying to find out. I've even taken this house near the Farradays' so as to –'

He stopped. Race took up his pipe and began to scratch at its interior.

'Hadn't you better tell me everything, young George?'

'What do you mean?'

'You're keeping something back – it sticks out a mile. You can sit there defending your wife's reputation – or you can try and find out if she was murdered or not – but if the latter matters most to you, you'll have to come clean.'

There was a silence.

'All right then,' said George in a stifled voice. 'You win.'

'You'd reason to believe your wife had a lover, is that it?'

'Yes.'

'Stephen Farraday?'

'I don't know! I swear to you I don't know! It might have been him or it might have been the other fellow, Browne. I couldn't make up my mind. It was hell.'

'Tell me what you know about this Anthony Browne? Funny, I seem to have heard the name.'

'I don't know anything about him. Nobody does. He's a good-looking, amusing sort of chap – but nobody knows the first thing about him. He's supposed to be an American but he's got no accent to speak of.'

'Oh, well, perhaps the Embassy will know something about him. You've no idea – which?'

'No – no, I haven't. I'll tell you, Race. She was writing a letter

– I – I examined the blotting-paper afterwards. It – it was a love letter all right – but there was no name.'

Race turned his eyes away carefully.

'Well, that gives us a bit more to go on. Lady Alexandra, for instance – she comes into it, if her husband was having an affair with your wife. She's the kind of woman, you know, who feels things rather intensely. The quiet, deep type. It's a type that will do murder at a pinch. We're getting on. There's Mystery Browne and Farraday and his wife, and young Iris Marle. What about this other woman, Ruth Lessing?'

'Ruth couldn't have had anything to do with it. She at least had no earthly motive.'

'Your secretary, you say? What sort of a girl is she?'

'The dearest girl in the world.' George spoke with enthusiasm. 'She's practically one of the family. She's my right hand – I don't know anyone I think more highly of, or have more absolute faith in.'

'You're fond of her,' said Race, watching him thoughtfully.

'I'm devoted to her. That girl, Race, is an absolute trump. I depend upon her in every way. She's the truest, dearest creature in the world.'

Race murmured something that sounded liked 'Umhum' and left the subject. There was nothing in his manner to indicate to George that he had mentally chalked down a very definite motive to the unknown Ruth Lessing. He could imagine that this 'dearest girl in the world' might have a very decided reason for wanting the removal of Mrs George Barton to another world. It might be a mercenary motive – she might have envisaged herself as the second Mrs Barton. It might be that she was genuinely in love with her employer. But the motive for Rosemary's death was there.

Instead he said gently: 'I suppose it's occurred to you, George, that you had a pretty good motive yourself.'

'I?' George looked flabbergasted.

'Well, remember Othello and Desdemona.'

'I see what you mean. But – but it wasn't like that between me and Rosemary. I adored her, of course, but I always knew that there would be things that – that I'd have to endure. Not that she wasn't fond of me – she was. She was very fond of me and sweet to me always. But of course I'm a dull stick, no getting away from it. Not romantic, you know. Anyway, I'd made up my mind when I married her that it wasn't going to be all beer and skittles. She as good as warned me. It hurt, of course, when it happened – but to suggest that I'd have touched a hair of her head –'

He stopped, and then went on in a different tone:

'Anyway, if I'd done it, why on earth should I go raking it all up? I mean, after a verdict of suicide, and everything all settled and over. It would be madness.'

'Absolutely. That's why I don't seriously suspect you, my dear fellow. If you were a successful murderer and got a couple of letters like these, you'd put them quietly in the fire and say nothing at all about it. And that brings me to what I think is the one really interesting feature of the whole thing. Who wrote those letters?'

'Eh?' George looked rather startled. 'I haven't the least idea.'

'The point doesn't seem to have interested you. It interests me. It's the first question I asked you. We can assume, I take it, that they weren't written by the murderer. Why should he queer his own pitch when, as you say, everything had settled down and suicide was universally accepted? Then who wrote them? Who is it who is interested in stirring the whole thing up again?'

'Servants?' hazarded George vaguely.

'Possibly. If so, what servants, and what do they know? Did Rosemary have a confidential maid?'

George shook his head.

'No. At the time we had a cook – Mrs Pound – we've still got her, and a couple of maids. I think they've both left. They weren't with us very long.'

'Well, Barton, if you want my advice, which I gather you do, I should think the matter over very carefully. On one side there's the fact that Rosemary is dead. You can't bring her back to life whatever you do. If the evidence for suicide isn't particularly good, neither is the evidence for murder. Let us say, for the sake of argument, that Rosemary *was* murdered. Do you really wish to rake up the whole thing? It may mean a lot of unpleasant publicity, a lot of washing of dirty linen in public, your wife's love affairs becoming public property –'

George Barton winced. He said violently:

'Do you really advise me to let some swine get away with it? That stick Farraday, with his pompous speeches, and his precious career – and all the time, perhaps, a cowardly murderer.'

'I only want you to be clear what it involves.'

'I want to get at the truth.'

'Very well. In that case, I should go to the police with these letters. They'll probably be able to find out fairly easily who wrote them and if the writer knows anything. Only remember that once you've started them on the trail, you won't be able to call them off.'

'I'm not going to the police. That's why I wanted to see you. I'm going to set a trap for the murderer.'

'What on earth do you mean?'

'Listen, Race. I'm going to have a party at the Luxembourg. I want you to come. The same people, the Farradays, Anthony Browne, Ruth, Iris, myself. I've got it all worked out.'

'What are you going to do?'

George gave a faint laugh.

'That's my secret. It would spoil it if I told anyone beforehand – even you. I want you to come with an unbiased mind and – see what happens.'

Race leant forward. His voice was suddenly sharp.

'I don't like it, George. These melodramatic ideas out of books don't work. Go to the police – there's no better body of men. They know how to deal with these problems. They're professionals. Amateur shows in crime aren't advisable.'

'That's why I want you there. You're not an amateur.'

'My dear fellow. Because I once did work for M.I.5? And anyway you propose to keep me in the dark.'

'That's necessary.'

Race shook his head.

'I'm sorry. I refuse. I don't like your plan and I won't be a party to it. Give it up, George, there's a good fellow.'

'I'm not going to give it up. I've got it all worked out.'

'Don't be so damned obstinate. I know a bit more about these shows than you do. I don't like the idea. It won't work. It may even be dangerous. Have you thought of that?'

'It will be dangerous for somebody all right.'

Race sighed.

'You don't know what you're doing. Oh, well, don't say I haven't warned you. For the last time I beg you to give up this crack-brained idea of yours.'

George Barton only shook his head.

CHAPTER 5

The morning of November 2nd dawned wet and gloomy. It was so dark in the dining-room of the house in Elvaston Square that they had to have the lights on for breakfast.

Iris, contrary to her habit, had come down instead of having her coffee and toast sent up to her and sat there white and ghostlike pushing uneaten food about her plate. George rustled his *Times* with a nervy hand and at the other end of the table Lucilla Drake wept copiously into a handkerchief.

'I know the dear boy will do something dreadful. He's so sensitive – and he wouldn't say it was a matter of life and death if it wasn't.'

Rustling his paper, George said sharply:

'Please don't worry, Lucilla. I've said I'll see to it.'

'I know, dear George, you are always so kind. But I do feel any delay might be fatal. All these inquiries you speak of making – they will all take *time*.'

'No, no, we'll hurry them through.'

'He says: "without fail by the 3rd" and tomorrow *is* the 3rd. I should never forgive myself if anything happened to the darling boy.'

'It won't.' George took a long drink of coffee.

'And there is still that Conversion Loan of mine –'

'Look here, Lucilla, you leave it all to me.'

'Don't worry, Aunt Lucilla,' put in Iris. 'George will be able to arrange it all. After all, this has happened before.'

'Not for a long time' ('Three months,' said George), 'not since the poor boy was deceived by those dreadful swindling friends of his on that horrid ranch.'

George wiped his moustache on his napkin, got up, patted Mrs Drake kindly on the back as he made his way out of the room.

'Now do cheer up, my dear. I'll get Ruth to cable right away.'

As he went out in the hall, Iris followed him.

'George, don't you think we ought to put off the party tonight? Aunt Lucilla is so upset. Hadn't we better stay at home with her?'

'Certainly not!' George's pink face went purple. 'Why should that damned swindling young crook upset our whole lives? It's blackmail – sheer blackmail, that's what it is. If I had my way, he shouldn't get a penny.'

'Aunt Lucilla would never agree to that.'

'Lucilla's a fool – always has been. These women who have children when they're over forty never seem to learn any sense. Spoil the brats from the cradle by giving them every damned thing they want. If young Victor had once been told to get out of this mess by himself it might have been the making of him. Now don't argue, Iris. I'll get something fixed up before tonight so that Lucilla can go to bed happy. If necessary we'll take her along with us.'

'Oh, no, she hates restaurants – and gets so sleepy, poor darling. And she dislikes the heat and the smoky air gives her asthma.'

'I know. I wasn't serious. Go and cheer her up, Iris. Tell her everything will be all right.'

He turned away and out of the front door. Iris turned slowly back towards the dining-room. The telephone rang and she went to answer it.

'Hallo – who?' Her face changed, its white hopelessness dissolved into pleasure. 'Anthony!'

'Anthony himself. I rang you up yesterday but couldn't get you. Have you been putting in a spot of work with George?'

'What do you mean?'

'Well, George was so pressing over his invitation to your party tonight. Quite unlike his usual style of "hands off my lovely ward"! Absolutely insistent that I should come. I thought perhaps it was the result of some tactful work on your part.'

'No – no – it's nothing to do with me.'

'A change of heart all on his own?'

'Not exactly. It's –'

'Hallo – have you gone away?'

'No, I'm here.'

'You were saying something. What's the matter, darling? I can hear you sighing through the telephone. Is anything the matter?'

'No – nothing. I shall be all right tomorrow. Everything will be all right tomorrow.'

'What touching faith. Don't they say "tomorrow never comes"?'

'Don't.'

'Iris – something *is* the matter?'

'No, nothing. I can't tell you. I promised, you see.'

'Tell me, my sweet.'

'No – I can't really. Anthony, will you tell *me* something?'

'If I can.'

'Were you – ever in love with Rosemary?'

A momentary pause and then a laugh.

'So that's it. Yes, Iris, I was a bit in love with Rosemary. She was very lovely, you know. And then one day I was talking to her and I saw you coming down the staircase – and in a minute it was all over, blown away. There was nobody but you in the world. That's the cold sober truth. Don't brood over a thing like that. Even Romeo, you know, had his Rosaline before he was bowled over for good and all by Juliet.'

'Thank you, Anthony. I'm glad.'

'See you tonight. It's your birthday, isn't it?'

'Actually not for a week – it's my birthday party though.'

'You don't sound very enthusiastic about it.'

'I'm not.'

'I suppose George knows what he's doing, but it seems to me a crazy idea to have it at the same place where –'

'Oh, I've been to the Luxembourg several times since – since Rosemary – I mean, one can't avoid it.'

'No, and it's just as well. I've got a birthday present for you, Iris. I hope you'll like it. *Au revoir.*'

He rang off.

Iris went back to Lucilla Drake, to argue, persuade and reassure.

George, on his arrival at his office, sent at once for Ruth Lessing.

His worried frown relaxed a little as she entered, calm and smiling, in her neat black coat and skirt.

'Good morning.'

'Good morning, Ruth. Trouble again. Look at this.'

She took the cable he held out.

'Victor Drake again!'

'Yes, curse him.'

She was silent a minute, holding the cable. A lean, brown face wrinkling up round the nose when he laughed. A mocking voice saying, 'the sort of girl who ought to marry the Boss . . .' How vividly it all came back.

She thought:

'It might have been yesterday . . .'

George's voice recalled her.

'Wasn't it about a year ago that we shipped him out there?'

She reflected.

'I think so, yes. Actually I believe it was October 27th.'

'What an amazing girl you are. What a memory!'

She thought to herself that she had a better reason for remembering than he knew. It was fresh from Victor Drake's influence that she had listened to Rosemary's careless voice over the phone and decided that she hated her employer's wife.

'I suppose we're lucky,' said George, 'that he's lasted as long as he has out there. Even if it did cost us fifty pounds three months ago.'

'Three hundred pounds now seems a lot.'

'Oh, yes. He won't get as much as that. We'll have to make the usual investigations.'

'I'd better communicate with Mr Ogilvie.'

Alexander Ogilvie was their agent in Buenos Aires – a sober, hard-headed Scotsman.

'Yes. Cable at once. His mother is in a state, as usual. Practically hysterical. Makes it very difficult with the party tonight.'

'Would you like me to stay with her?'

'No.' He negatived the idea emphatically. 'No, indeed. You're the one person who's got to be there. I need you, Ruth.' He took her hand. 'You're too unselfish.'

'I'm not unselfish at all.'

She smiled and suggested:

'Would it be worth trying telephonic communication with Mr Ogilvie? We might get the whole thing cleared up by tonight.'

'A good idea. Well worth the expense.'

'I'll get busy at once.'

Very gently she disengaged her hand from his and went out.

George dealt with various matters awaiting his attention.

At half-past twelve he went out and took a taxi to the Luxembourg.

Charles, the notorious and popular head waiter, came towards him, bending his stately head and smiling in welcome.

'Good morning, Mr Barton.'

'Good morning, Charles. Everything all right for tonight?'

'I think you will be satisfied, sir.'

'The same table?'

'The middle one in the alcove, that is right, is it not?'

'Yes – and you understand about the extra place?'

'It is all arranged.'

'And you've got the – the rosemary?'

'Yes, Mr Barton. I'm afraid it won't be very decorative. You wouldn't like some red berries incorporated – or say a few chrysanthemums?'

'No, no, only the rosemary.'

'Very good, sir. You would like to see the menu. Guiseppe.'

With a flick of the thumb Charles produced a smiling little middle-aged Italian.

'The menu for Mr Barton.'

It was produced.

Oysters, Clear Soup, Sole Luxembourg, Grouse, Poires Hélène, Chicken Livers in Bacon.

George cast an indifferent eye over it.

'Yes, yes, quite all right.'

He handed it back. Charles accompanied him to the door. Sinking his voice a little, he murmured:

'May I just mention how appreciative we are, Mr Barton, that you are – er – coming back to us?'

A smile, rather a ghastly smile, showed on George's face. He said:

'We've got to forget the past – can't dwell on the past. All that is over and done with.'

'Very true, Mr Barton. You know how shocked and grieved we were at the time. I'm sure I hope that Mademoiselle will have a very happy birthday party and that everything will be as you like it.'

Gracefully bowing, Charles withdrew and darted like an angry dragon-fly on some very inferior grade of waiter who was doing the wrong thing at a table near the window.

George went out with a wry smile on his lips. He was not an imaginative enough man to feel a pang of sympathy for the Luxembourg. It was not, after all, the fault of the Luxembourg that Rosemary had decided to commit suicide there or that someone had decided to murder her there. It had been decidedly hard on the Luxembourg. But like most people with an idea, George thought only of that idea.

He lunched at his club and went afterwards to a directors' meeting.

On his way back to the office, he put through a phone call to a Maida Vale number from a public call box. He came out with a sigh of relief. Everything was set according to schedule.

He went back to the office.

Ruth came to him at once.

'About Victor Drake.'

'Yes?'

'I'm afraid it's rather a bad business. A possibility of criminal prosecution. He's been helping himself to the firm's money over a considerable period.'

'Did Ogilvie say so?'

'Yes. I got through to him this morning and he got a call through to us this afternoon ten minutes ago. He says Victor was quite brazen about the whole thing.'

'He would be!'

'But he insists that they won't prosecute if the money is refunded. Mr Ogilvie saw the senior partner and that seems to be correct. The actual sum in question is one hundred and sixty-five pounds.'

'So that Master Victor was hoping to pocket a clear hundred and thirty-five on the transaction?'

'I'm afraid so.'

'Well, we've scotched that, at any rate,' said George with grim satisfaction.

'I told Mr Ogilvie to go ahead and settle the business. Was that right?'

'Personally I should be delighted to see that young crook go to prison – but one has to think of his mother. A fool – but a dear soul. So Master Victor scores as usual.'

'How good you are,' said Ruth.

'Me?'

'I think you're the best man in the world.'

He was touched. He felt pleased and embarrassed at the same time. On an impulse he picked up her hand and kissed it.

'Dearest Ruth. My dearest and best of friends. What would I have done without you?'

They stood very close together.

She thought: 'I could have been happy with him. I could have made him happy. If only –'

He thought: 'Shall I take Race's advice? Shall I give it all up? Wouldn't that really be the best thing?'

Indecision hovered over him and passed. He said:

'9.30 at the Luxembourg.'

CHAPTER 6

They had all come.

George breathed a sigh of relief. Up to the last moment he had feared some last minute defection – but they were all here. Stephen Farraday, tall and stiff, a little pompous in manner. Sandra Farraday in a severe black velvet gown wearing emeralds around her neck. The woman had breeding, not a doubt of it. Her manner was completely natural, possibly a little more gracious than usual. Ruth also in black with no ornament save one jewelled clip. Her raven black hair smooth and lying close to her head, her neck and arms very white – whiter than those of the other women. Ruth was a working girl, she had no long leisured ease in which to acquire sun tan. His eyes met hers and, as though she saw the anxiety in his, she smiled reassurance. His heart lifted. Loyal Ruth. Beside him Iris was unusually silent. She alone showed consciousness of this being an unusual party. She was pale but in some way it suited her, gave her a grave steadfast beauty. She wore a straight simple frock of leaf-green. Anthony Browne came last, and to George's mind, he came with the quick stealthy step of a wild creature – a panther, perhaps, or a leopard. The fellow wasn't really quite civilized.

They were all there – all safe in George's trap. Now, the play could begin . . .

Cocktails were drained. They got up and passed through the open arch into the restaurant proper.

Dancing couples, soft negro music, deft hurrying waiters.

Charles came forward and smilingly piloted them to their table. It was at the far end of the room, a shallow arched alcove which held three tables – a big one in the middle and two small ones for two people either side of it. A middle-aged sallow foreigner and a blonde lovely were at one, a slip of a boy and a girl at the other. The middle table was reserved for the Barton party.

George genially assigned them to their places.

'Sandra, will you sit here, on my right. Browne next to her. Iris, my dear, it's your party. I must have you here next to me, and you beyond her, Farraday. Then you, Ruth –'

He paused – between Ruth and Anthony was a vacant chair – the table had been laid for seven.

'My friend Race may be a bit late. He said we weren't to wait for him. He'll be along some time. I'd like you all to know him – he's a splendid fellow, knocked about all over the world and can tell you some good yarns.'

Iris was conscious of a feeling of anger as she seated herself. George had done it on purpose – separated her from Anthony. Ruth ought to have been sitting where she was, next to her host. So George still disliked and mistrusted Anthony.

She stole a glance across the table. Anthony was frowning. He did not look across at her. Once he directed a sharp sideways glance at the empty chair beside him. He said:

'Glad you've got another man, Barton. There's just a chance I may have to go off early. Quite unavoidable. But I ran into a man here I know.'

George said smilingly:

'Running business into pleasure hours? You're too young for that, Browne. Not that I've ever known exactly what your business is?'

By chance there was a lull in the conversation. Anthony's reply came deliberately and coolly.

'Organized crime, Barton, that's what I always say when I'm asked. Robberies arranged. Larcenies a feature. Families waited upon at their private addresses.'

Sandra Farraday laughed as she said:

'You're something to do with armaments, aren't you, Mr Browne? An armament king is always the villain of the piece nowadays.'

Iris saw Anthony's eyes momentarily widen in a stare of quick surprise. He said lightly:

'You mustn't give me away, Lady Alexandra, it's all very hush-hush. The spies of a foreign power are everywhere. Careless talk.'

He shook his head with mock solemnity.

The waiter took away the oyster plates. Stephen asked Iris if she would like to dance.

Soon they were all dancing. The atmosphere lightened.

Presently Iris's turn came to dance with Anthony.

She said: 'Mean of George not to let us sit together.'

'Kind of him. This way I can look at you all the time across the table.'

'You won't really have to go early?'

'I might.'

Presently he said:

'Did you know that Colonel Race was coming?'

'No, I hadn't the least idea.'

'Rather odd, that.'

'Do you know him? Oh, yes, you said so, the other day.'

She added:

'What sort of a man is he?'

'Nobody quite knows.'

They went back to the table. The evening wore on. Slowly the tension, which had relaxed, seemed to close again. There was an atmosphere of taut nerves about the table. Only the host seemed genial and unconcerned.

Iris saw him glance at his watch.

Suddenly there was a roll of drums – the lights went down. A stage rose in the room. Chairs were pushed a little back, turned sideways. Three men and three girls took the floor, dancing. They were followed by a man who could make noises. Trains, steam rollers, aeroplanes, sewing machines, cows coughing. He was a success. Lenny and Flo followed in an exhibition dance which was more of a trapeze act than a dance. More applause. Then another ensemble by the Luxembourg Six. The lights went up.

Everyone blinked.

At the same time a wave of sudden freedom from restraint seemed to pass over the party at the table. It was as though they had been subconsciously expecting something that had failed to happen. For on an earlier occasion the going up of the lights had coincided with the discovery of a dead body lying across the table. It was as though now the past was definitely past – vanished into oblivion. The shadow of a bygone tragedy had lifted.

Sandra turned to Anthony in an animated way. Stephen made an observation to Iris and Ruth leaned forward to join in. Only George sat in his chair staring – staring, his eyes fixed on the empty chair opposite him. The place in front of it was laid. There was champagne in the glass. At any moment, someone might come, might sit down there –

A nudge from Iris recalled him:

'Wake up, George. Come and dance. You haven't danced with me yet.'

He roused himself. Smiling at her he lifted his glass.

'We'll drink a toast first – to the young lady whose birthday we're celebrating. Iris Marle, may her shadow never grow less!'

They drank it laughing, then they all got up to dance, George and Iris, Stephen and Ruth, Anthony and Sandra.

It was a gay jazz melody.

They all came back together, laughing and talking. They sat down.

Then suddenly George leaned forward.

'I've something I want to ask you all. A year ago, more or less, we were here before on an evening that ended tragically. I don't want to recall past sadness, but it's just that I don't want to feel that Rosemary is completely forgotten. I'll ask you to drink to her memory – for Remembrance sake.'

He raised his glass. Everyone else obediently raised theirs. Their faces were polite masks.

George said:

'*To Rosemary for remembrance.*'

The glasses were raised to their lips. They drank.

There was a pause – then George swayed forward and slumped down in his chair, his hands rising frenziedly to his neck, his face turning purple as he fought for breath.

It took him a minute and a half to die.

BOOK 3 • IRIS

'For I thought that the dead had peace
But it is not so . . .'

Colonel Race turned into the doorway of New Scotland Yard. He filled in the form that was brought forward and a very few minutes later he was shaking hands with Chief Inspector Kemp in the latter's room.

The two men were well acquainted. Kemp was slightly reminiscent of that grand old veteran, Battle, in type. Indeed, since he had worked under Battle for many years, he had perhaps unconsciously copied a good many of the older man's mannerisms. He bore about him the same suggestion of being carved all in one piece – but whereas Battle had suggested some wood such as teak or oak, Chief Inspector Kemp suggested a somewhat more showy wood – mahogany, say, or good old-fashioned rosewood.

'It was good of you to ring us, colonel,' said Kemp. 'We shall want all the help we can get on this case.'

'It seems to have got us into exalted hands,' said Race.

Kemp did not make modest disclaimers. He accepted quite simply the indubitable fact that only cases of extreme delicacy, wide publicity or supreme importance came his way. He said seriously:

'It's the Kidderminster connection. You can imagine that means careful going.'

Race nodded. He had met Lady Alexandra Farraday several times. One of those quiet women of unassailable position whom it seems fantastic to associate with sensational publicity. He had heard her speak on public platforms – without eloquence, but clearly and competently, with a good grasp of her subject, and with an excellent delivery.

The kind of woman whose public life was in all the papers, and whose private life was practically non-existent except as a bland domestic background.

Nevertheless, he thought, such women *have* a private life. They know despair, and love, and the agonies of jealousy. They can lose control and risk life itself on a passionate gamble.

He said curiously:

'Suppose she "done it," Kemp?'

'Lady Alexandra? Do you think she did, sir?'

'I've no idea. But suppose she did. Or her husband – who comes under the Kidderminster mantle.'

The steady sea-green eyes of Chief Inspector Kemp looked in an untroubled way into Race's dark ones.

'If either of them did murder, we'll do our level best to hang him or her. *You* know that. There's no fear and no favour for murderers in this country. But we'll have to be absolutely sure of our evidence – the public prosecutor will insist on that.'

Race nodded.

Then he said, 'Let's have the doings.'

'George Barton died of cyanide poisoning – same thing as his wife a year ago. You said you were actually in the restaurant?'

'Yes. Barton had asked me to join his party. I refused. I didn't like what he was doing. I protested against it and urged him, if he had doubts about his wife's death, to go to the proper people – to you.'

Kemp nodded.

'That's what he ought to have done.'

'Instead he persisted in an idea of his own – setting a trap for the murderer. He wouldn't tell me what that trap was. I was uneasy about the whole business – so much so that I went to the Luxembourg last night so as to keep an eye on things. My table, necessarily, was some distance away – I didn't want to be spotted too obviously. Unfortunately I can tell you nothing. I saw nothing in the least suspicious. The waiters and his own party were the only people who approached the table.'

'Yes,' said Kemp, 'it narrows it down, doesn't it? It was one of them, or it was the waiter, Giuseppe Bolsano. I've got him on the mat again this morning – thought you might like to see him – but I can't believe he had anything to do with it. Been at the Luxembourg for twelve years – good reputation, married, three children, good record behind him. Gets on well with all the clients.'

'Which leaves us with the guests.'

'Yes. The same party as was present when Mrs Barton – died.'

'What about that business, Kemp?'

'I've been going into it since it seems pretty obvious that the two hang together. Adams handled it. It wasn't what we call a clear case of suicide, but suicide was the most probable solution and in the absence of any direct evidence suggesting murder, one had to let it go as suicide. Couldn't do anything else. We've a good many cases like that in our records, as you know. Suicide with a query mark. The public doesn't know about the query mark – but we keep it in mind. Sometimes we go on quite a bit hunting about quietly.

'Sometimes something crops up – sometimes it doesn't. In this case it didn't.'

'Until now.'

'Until now. Somebody tipped Mr Barton off to the fact that his wife had been murdered. He got busy on his own – he as good as announced that he was on the right track – whether he was or not I don't know – but the murderer must have thought so – so the murderer gets rattled and bumps off Mr Barton. That seems the way of it as far as I can see – I hope you agree?'

'Oh, yes – that part of it seems straightforward enough. God knows what the "trap" was – I noticed that there was an empty chair at the table. Perhaps it was waiting for some unexpected witness. Anyhow it accomplished rather more than it was meant to do. It alarmed the guilty person so much that he or she didn't wait for the trap to be sprung.'

'Well,' said Kemp, 'we've got five suspects. And we've got the first case to go on – Mrs Barton.'

'You're definitely of the opinion now that it was *not* suicide?'

'This murder seems to prove that it wasn't. Though I don't think you can blame us at the time for accepting the suicide theory as the most probable. There was some evidence for it.'

'Depression after influenza?'

Kemp's wooden face showed a ripple of a smile.

'That was for the coroner's court. Agreed with the medical

evidence and saved everybody's feelings. That's done every day. And there was a half-finished letter to the sister directing how her personal belongings were to be given away – showed she'd had the idea of doing away with herself in her mind. She was depressed all right, I don't doubt, poor lady – but nine times out of ten, with women, it's a love affair. With men it's mostly money worries.'

'So you knew Mrs Barton had a love affair.'

'Yes, we soon found that out. It had been discreet – but it didn't take much finding.'

'Stephen Farraday?'

'Yes. They used to meet in a little flat out Earl's Court way. It had been going on for over six months. Say they'd had a quarrel – or possibly he was getting tired of her – well, she wouldn't be the first woman to take her life in a fit of desperation.'

'By potassium cyanide in a public restaurant?'

'Yes – if she wanted to be dramatic about it – with him looking on and all. Some people have a feeling for the spectacular. From what I could find out she hadn't much feeling for the conventions – all the precautions were on his side.'

'Any evidence as to whether his wife knew what was going on?'

'As far as we could learn she knew nothing about it.'

'She may have, for all that, Kemp. Not the kind of woman to wear her heart on her sleeve.'

'Oh, quite so. Count them both in as possibles. She for jealousy. He for his career. Divorce would have dished that. Not that divorce means as much as it used to, but in his case it would have meant the antagonism of the Kidderminster clan.'

'What about the secretary girl?'

'She's a possible. Might have been sweet on George Barton. They were pretty thick at the office and there's an idea there that she was keen on him. Actually yesterday afternoon one of the telephone girls was giving an imitation of Barton holding Ruth Lessing's hand and saying he couldn't do without her, and Miss Lessing came out and caught them and sacked the girl there and then – gave her a month's money and told her to go. Looks as though she was sensitive about it all. Then the sister came into a peck of money – one's got to remember that. Looked a nice kid, but you can never tell. And there was Mrs Barton's other boy friend.'

'I'm rather anxious to hear what you know about him?'

Kemp said slowly:

'Remarkably little – but what there is isn't too good. His passport's in order. He's an American citizen about whom we can't find anything, detrimental or otherwise. He came over here, stayed at Claridge's and managed to strike up an acquaintance with Lord Dewsbury.'

'Confidence man?'

'Might be. Dewsbury seems to have fallen for him – asked him to stay. Rather a critical time just then.'

'Armaments,' said Race. 'There was that trouble about the new tank trials in Dewsbury's works.'

'Yes. This fellow Browne represented himself as interested in armaments. It was soon after he'd been up there that they discovered that sabotage business – just in the nick of time. Browne met a good many cronies of Dewsbury – he seemed to have cultivated all the ones who were connected with the armament firms. As a result he's been shown a lot of stuff that in my opinion he ought never to have seen – and in one or two cases there's been serious trouble in the works not long after he's been in the neighbourhood.'

'An interesting person, Mr Anthony Browne?'

'Yes. He's got a lot of charm, apparently, and plays it for all he's worth.'

'And where did Mrs Barton come in? George Barton hasn't anything to do with the armament world?'

'No. But they seem to have been fairly intimate. He may have let out something to her. *You* know, colonel, none better, what a pretty woman can get out of a man.'

Race nodded, taking the chief inspector's words, as meant, to refer to the Counter-Espionage Department which he had once controlled and not – as some ignorant person might have thought – to some personal indiscretions of his own.

He said after a minute or two:

'Have you had a go at those letters that George Barton received?'

'Yes. Found them in his desk at his house last night. Miss Marle found them for me.'

'You know I'm interested in those letters, Kemp. What's the expert opinion on them?'

'Cheap paper, ordinary ink – fingerprints show George Barton and Iris Marle handled them – and a horde of unidentified dabs on the envelope, postal employees, etc. They were printed and the experts say by someone of good education in normal health.'

'Good education. Not a servant?'

'Presumably not.'

'That makes it more interesting still.'

'It means that somebody else had suspicions, at least.'

'Someone who didn't go to the police. Someone who was prepared to arouse George's suspicions but who didn't follow the business up. There's something odd there, Kemp. He couldn't have written them himself, could he?'

'He could have. But why?'

'As a preliminary to suicide – a suicide which he intended to look like murder.'

'With Stephen Farraday booked for the hangman's rope? It's an idea – but he'd have made quite sure that everything pointed to Farraday as the murderer. As it is we've nothing against Farraday at all.'

'What about cyanide? Was there any container found?'

'Yes. A small white paper packet under the table. Traces of cyanide crystals inside. No fingerprints on it. In a detective story, of course, it would be some special kind of paper or folded in some special way. I'd like to give these detective story writers a course of routine work. They'd soon learn how most things are untraceable and nobody ever notices anything anywhere!'

Race smiled.

'Almost too sweeping a statement. Did anybody notice anything last night?'

'Actually that's what I'm starting on today. I took a brief statement from everyone last night and I went back to Elvaston Square with Miss Marle and had a look through Barton's desk and papers. I shall get fuller statements from them all today – also statements from the people sitting at the other two tables in the alcove –' He rustled through some papers – 'Yes, here they are. Gerald Tollington, Grenadier Guards, and the Hon. Patricia Brice-Woodworth. Young engaged couple. I'll bet they didn't see anything but each other. And Mr Pedro Morales –

nasty bit of goods from Mexico – even the whites of his eyes are yellow – and Miss Christine Shannon – a gold-digging blonde lovely – I'll bet she didn't see anything – dumber than you'd believe possible except where money is concerned. It's a hundred to one chance that any of them saw anything, but I took their names and addresses on the off chance. We'll start off with the waiter chap, Giuseppe. He's here now. I'll have him sent in.'

CHAPTER 2

Giuseppe Bolsano was a middle-aged man, slight with a rather monkey-like intelligent face. He was nervous, but not unduly so. His English was fluent since he had, he explained, been in the country since he was sixteen and had married an English wife.

Kemp treated him sympathetically.

'Now then, Giuseppe, let's hear whether anything more has occurred to you about this.'

'It is for me very unpleasant. It is I who serve that table. I who pour out the wine. People will say that I am off my head, that I put poison into the wine glasses. It is not so, but that is what people will say. Already, Mr Goldstein says it is better that I take a week away from work – so that people do not ask me questions there and point me out. He is a fair man, and just, and he knows it is not my fault, and that I have been there for many years, so he does not dismiss me as some restaurant owners would do. M. Charles, too, he has been kind, but all the same it is a great misfortune for me – and it makes me afraid. Have I an enemy, I ask myself?'

'Well,' said Kemp at his most wooden, 'have you?'

The sad monkey-face twitched into laughter. Giuseppe stretched out his arms.

'I? I have not an enemy in the world. Many good friends but no enemies.'

Kemp grunted.

'Now about last night. Tell me about the champagne.'

'It was Clicquot, 1928 – very good and expensive wine. Mr

Barton was like that – he liked good food and drink – the best.'

'Had he ordered the wine beforehand?'

'Yes. He had arranged everything with Charles.'

'What about the vacant place at the table?'

'That, too, he had arranged for. He told Charles and he told me. A young lady would occupy it later in the evening.'

'A young lady?' Race and Kemp looked at each other. 'Do you know who the young lady was?'

Giuseppe shook his head.

'No, I know nothing about that. She was to come later, that is all I heard.'

'Go on about the wine. How many bottles?'

'Two bottles and a third to be ready if needed. The first bottle was finished quite quickly. The second I open not long before the cabaret. I fill up the glasses and put the bottle in the ice bucket.'

'When did you last notice Mr Barton drinking from his glass?'

'Let me see, when the cabaret was over, they drink the young lady's health. It is her birthday so I understand. Then they go and dance. It is after that, when they come back, that Mr Barton drinks and in a minute, like *that*! he is dead.'

'Had you filled up the glasses during the time they were dancing?'

'No, monsieur. They were full when they drank to mademoiselle and they did not drink much, only a few mouthfuls. There was plenty left in the glasses.'

'Did anyone – *anyone* at all – come near the table whilst they were dancing?'

'No one at all, sir. I am sure of that.'

'Did they all go to dance at the same time?'

'Yes.'

'And came back at the same time?'

Giuseppe screwed up his eyes in an effort of memory.

'Mr Barton he came back first – with the young lady. He was stouter than the rest – he did not dance quite so long, you comprehend. Then came the fair gentleman, Mr Farraday, and the young lady in black. Lady Alexandra Farraday and the dark gentleman came last.'

'You know Mr Farraday and Lady Alexandra?'

'Yes, sir. I have seen them in the Luxembourg often. They are very distinguished.'

'Now, Giuseppe, would you have seen if one of those people had put something in Mr Barton's glass?'

'That I cannot say, sir. I have my service, the other two tables in the alcove, and two more in the main restaurant. There are dishes to serve. I do not watch at Mr Barton's table. After the cabaret everyone nearly gets up and dances, so at that time I am standing still – and that is why I can be sure that no one approached the table then. But as soon as people sit down, I am at once very busy.'

Kemp nodded.

'But I think,' Giuseppe continued, 'that it would be very difficult to do without being observed. It seems to me that only Mr Barton himself could do it. But you do not think so, no?'

He looked inquiringly at the police officer.

'So that's your idea, is it?'

'Naturally I know nothing – but I wonder. Just a year ago that beautiful lady, Mrs Barton, she kills herself. Could it not be that Mr Barton he grieves so much that he too decides to kill himself the same way? It would be poetic. Of course it is not good for the restaurant – but a gentleman who is going to kill himself would not think of that.'

He looked eagerly from one to the other of the two men.

Kemp shook his head.

'I doubt if it's as easy as that,' he said.

He asked a few more questions, then Giuseppe was dismissed.

As the door closed behind Giuseppe, Race said:

'I wonder if that's what we are meant to think?'

'Grieving husband kills himself on anniversary of wife's death? Not that it was the anniversary – but near enough.'

'It was All Soul's Day,' said Race.

'True. Yes, it's possible that *was* the idea – but if so, whoever it was can't have known about those letters being kept and that Mr Barton had consulted you and shown them to Iris Marle.'

He glanced at his watch.

'I'm due at Kidderminster House at 12.30. We've time before

that to go and see those people at the other two tables – some of them at any rate. Come with me, won't you, colonel?'

CHAPTER 3

Mr Morales was staying at the Ritz. He was hardly a pretty sight at this hour in the morning, still unshaven, the whites of his eyes bloodshot and with every sign of a severe hangover.

Mr Morales was an American subject and spoke a variant of the American language. Though professing himself willing to remember anything he could, his recollections of the previous evening were of the vaguest description.

'Went with Chrissie – that baby is sure hard-boiled! She said it was a good joint. Honey pie, I said, we'll go just where you say. It was a classy joint, that I'll admit – and do they know how to charge you! Set me back the best part of thirty dollars. But the band was punk – they just couldn't seem to swing it.'

Diverted from his recollections of his own evening, Mr Morales was pressed to remember the table in the middle of the alcove. Here he was not very helpful.

'Sure there was a table and some people at it. I don't remember what they looked like, though. Didn't take much account of them till the guy there croaked. Thought at first he couldn't hold his liquor. Say now, I remember one of the dames. Dark hair and she had what it takes, I should say.'

'You mean the girl in the green velvet dress?'

'No, not that one. She was skinny. This baby was in black with some good curves.'

It was Ruth Lessing who had taken Mr Morales' roving eye.

He wrinkled up his nose appreciatively.

'I watched her dancing – and say, could that baby dance! I gave her the high sign once or twice, but she had a frozen eye – just looked through me in your British way.'

Nothing more of value could be extracted from Mr Morales and he admitted frankly that his alcoholic condition was already well advanced by the time the cabaret was on.

Kemp thanked him and prepared to take his leave.

'I'm sailing for New York tomorrow,' said Morales. 'You wouldn't,' he asked wistfully, 'care for me to stay on?'

'Thank you, but I don't think your evidence will be needed at the inquest.'

'You see I'm enjoying it right here – and if it was police business the firm couldn't kick. When the police tell you to stay put, you've got to stay put. Maybe I *could* remember something if I thought hard enough?'

But Kemp declined to rise to this wistful bait, and he and Race drove to Brook Street where they were greeted by a choleric gentleman, the father of the Hon. Patricia Brice-Woodworth.

General Lord Woodworth received them with a good deal of outspoken comment.

What on earth was the idea of suggesting that his daughter – *his* daughter! – was mixed up in this sort of thing? If a girl couldn't go out with her fiancé to dine in a restaurant without being subjected to annoyance by detectives and Scotland Yard, what was England coming to? She didn't even know these people what was their name – Hubbard – Barton? Some City fellow or other! Showed you couldn't be too careful where you went – Luxembourg was always supposed to be all right – but apparently this was the second time a thing of this sort had happened there. Gerald must be a fool to have taken Pat there – these young men thought they knew everything. But in any case he wasn't going to have his daughter badgered and bullied and cross-questioned – not without a solicitor's say so. He'd ring up old Anderson in Lincoln's Inn and ask him –

Here the general paused abruptly and staring at Race said, 'Seen you somewhere. Now where –?'

Race's answer was immediate and came with a smile.

'Badderpore. 1923.'

'By Jove,' said the general. 'If it isn't Johnny Race! What are you doing mixed up in this show?'

Race smiled.

'I was with Chief Inspector Kemp when the question of interviewing your daughter came up. I suggested it would be much pleasanter for her if Inspector Kemp came round here than if she had to come down to Scotland Yard, and I thought I'd come along too.'

'Oh – er – well, very decent, of you, Race.'

'We naturally wanted to upset the young lady as little as possible,' put in Chief Inspector Kemp.

But at this moment the door opened and Miss Patricia Brice-Woodworth walked in and took charge of the situation with the coolness and detachment of the very young.

'Hallo,' she said. 'You're from Scotland Yard, aren't you? About last night? I've been longing for you to come. Is father being tiresome? Now don't, daddy – you know what the doctor said about your blood pressure. Why you want to get into such states about everything, I can't think. I'll just take the inspectors or superintendents or whatever they are into my room and I'll send Walters to you with a whisky and soda.'

The general had a choleric desire to express himself in several blistering ways at once, but only succeeded in saying, 'Old friend of mine, Major Race,' at which introduction, Patricia lost interest in Race and bent a beatific smile on Chief Inspector Kemp.

With cool generalship, she shepherded them out of the room and into her own sitting-room, firmly shutting her father in his study.

'Poor daddy,' she observed. 'He *will* fuss. But he's quite easy to manage really.'

The conversation then proceeded on most amicable lines but with very little result.

'It's maddening really,' said Patricia. 'Probably the only chance in my life that I shall ever have of being right on the spot when a murder was done – it is a murder, isn't it? The papers were very cautious and vague, but I said to Gerry on the telephone that it must be murder. Think of it, a murder done right close by me and I wasn't even looking!'

The regret in her voice was unmistakable.

It was evident enough that, as the chief inspector had gloomily prognosticated, the two young people who had got engaged only a week previously had had eyes only for each other.

With the best will in the world, a few personalities were all that Patricia Brice-Woodworth could muster.

'Sandra Farraday was looking very smart, but then she always does. That was a Schiaparelli model she had on.'

'You know her?' Race asked.

Patricia shook her head.

'Only by sight. He looks rather a bore, I always think. So pompous, like most politicians.'

'Did you know any of the others by sight?'

She shook her head.

'No, I'd never seen any of them before – at least I don't think so. In fact, I don't suppose I would have noticed Sandra Farraday if it hadn't been for the Schiaparelli.'

'And you'll find,' said Chief Inspector Kemp grimly as they left the house, 'that Master Tollington will be exactly the same – only there won't even have been a Skipper – skipper what – sounds like a sardine – to attract his attention.'

'I don't suppose,' agreed Race, 'that the cut of Stephen Farraday's dress suit will have caused him any heart pangs.'

'Oh, well,' said the inspector. 'Let's try Christine Shannon. Then we'll have finished with the outside chances.'

Miss Shannon was, as Chief Inspector Kemp had stated, a blonde lovely. The bleached hair, carefully arranged, swept back from a soft vacant baby-like countenance. Miss Shannon might be as Inspector Kemp had affirmed, dumb – but she was eminently easy to look at, and a certain shrewdness in the large baby-blue eyes indicated that her dumbness only extended in intellectual directions and that where horse sense and a knowledge of finance were indicated, Christine Shannon was right on the spot.

She received the two men with the utmost sweetness, pressing drinks upon them and when these were refused, urging cigarettes. Her flat was small and cheaply modernistic.

'I'd just love to be able to help you, chief inspector. Do ask me any questions you like.'

Kemp led off with a few conventional questions about the bearing and demeanour of the party at the centre table.

At once Christine showed herself to be an unusually keen and shrewd observer.

'The party wasn't going well – you could see that. Stiff as stiff could be. I felt quite sorry for the old boy – the one who was giving it. Going all out he was to try and make things go – and just as nervous as a cat on wires – but all he could do didn't seem to cut any ice. The tall woman he'd got on his right was as stiff as though she'd swallowed the poker and the kid on his left was just mad, you could see, because she wasn't sitting next to the nice-looking dark boy opposite. As for the tall fair fellow next to her he looked as though his tummy was out of order, ate his food as though he thought it would choke him. The woman next to him was doing her best, she pegged away at him, but she looked rather as though she had the jumps herself.'

'You seem to have been able to notice a great deal, Miss Shannon,' said Colonel Race.

'I'll let you into a secret. I wasn't being so much amused myself. I'd been out with that boy friend of mine three nights running, and was I getting tired of him! He was all out for seeing London – especially what he called the classy spots – and I will say for him he wasn't mean. Champagne every time. We went to the Compradour and the Mille Fleurs and finally the Luxembourg, and I'll say he enjoyed himself. In a way it was kind of pathetic. But his conversation wasn't what you'd call interesting. Just long histories of business deals he'd put through in Mexico and most of those I heard three times – and going on to all the dames he'd known and how mad they were about him. A girl gets kind of tired listening after a while and you'll admit that Pedro is nothing much to look at – so I just concentrated on the eats and let my eyes roam round.'

'Well, that's excellent from our point of view, Miss Shannon,' said the chief inspector. 'And I can only hope that you will have seen something that may help us solve our problem.'

Christine shook her blonde head.

'I've no idea who bumped the old boy off – no idea at all. He just took a drink of champagne, went purple in the face and sort of collapsed.'

'Do you remember when he had last drunk from his glass before that?'

The girl reflected.

'Why – yes – it was just after the cabaret. The lights went up and he picked up his glass and said something and the others did it too. Seemed to me it was a toast of some kind.'

The chief inspector nodded.

'And then?'

'Then the music began and they all got up and went off to dance, pushing their chairs back and laughing. Seemed to get warmed up for the first time. Wonderful what champagne will do for the stickiest parties.'

'They all went together – leaving the table empty?'

'Yes.'

'And no one touched Mr Barton's glass.'

'No one at all.' Her reply came promptly. 'I'm perfectly certain of that.'

'And no one – no one at all came near the table while they were away.'

'No one – except the waiter, of course.'

'A waiter? Which waiter?'

'One of the half-fledged ones with an apron, round about sixteen. Not the real waiter. He was an obliging little fellow rather like a monkey – Italian I guess he was.'

Chief Inspector Kemp acknowledged this description of Giuseppe Bolsano with a nod of the head.

'And what did he do, this young waiter? He filled up the glasses?'

Christine shook her head.

'Oh, no. He didn't touch anything on the table. He just picked up an evening bag that one of the girls had dropped when they all got up.'

'Whose bag was it?'

Christine took a minute or two to think. Then she said:

'That's right. It was the kid's bag – a green and gold thing. The other two women had black bags.'

'What did the waiter do with the bag?'

Christine looked surprised.

'He just put it back on the table, that's all.'

'You're quite sure he didn't touch any of the glasses?'

'Oh, no. He just dropped the bag down very quick and ran off because one of the real waiters was hissing at him to go somewhere or get something and everything was going to be his fault!'

'And that's the only time anyone went near the table?'

'That's right.'

'But of course someone might have gone to the table without your noticing?'

But Christine shook her head very determinedly.

'No, I'm quite sure they didn't. You see Pedro had been called to the telephone and hadn't got back yet, so I had nothing to do but look around and feel bored. I'm pretty good at noticing things and from where I was sitting there wasn't much else to see but the empty table next to us.'

Race asked:

'Who came back first to the table?'

'The girl in green and the old boy. They sat down and then the fair man and the girl in black came back and after them the haughty piece of goods and the good-looking dark boy. Some dancer, he was. When they were all back and the waiter was warming up a dish like mad on the spirit lamp, the old boy leaned forward and made a kind of speech and then they all picked up their glasses again. And then it happened.' Christine paused and added brightly, 'Awful, wasn't it? Of course I thought it was a stroke. My aunt had a stroke and she went down just like that. Pedro came back just then and I said, "Look, Pedro, that man's had a stroke." And all Pedro would say was, "Just passing out – just passing out – that's all" which was about what *he* was doing. I had to keep my eye on him. They don't like you passing out at a place like the Luxembourg. That's why I don't like Dagoes. When they've drunk too much they're not a bit refined any more – a girl never knows what unpleasantness she may be let in for.' She brooded for a moment and then glancing at a showy looking bracelet on her right wrist, she added, 'Still, I must say they're generous enough.'

Gently distracting her from the trials and compensations of a girl's existence Kemp took her through her story once more.

'That's our last chance of outside help gone,' he said to Race when they had left Miss Shannon's flat. 'And it would have been a good chance if it had come off. That girl's the right kind of witness. Sees things and remembers them accurately. If there had been anything to see, she'd have seen it. So the answer is that there wasn't anything to see. It's incredible. It's a conjuring trick! George Barton drinks champagne and goes and dances. He comes back, drinks from the same glass that no one has touched and Hey Presto it's full of cyanide. It's crazy – I tell you – it couldn't have happened except that it did.'

He stopped a minute.

'That waiter. The little boy. Giuseppe never mentioned him.

I might look into that. After all, he's the one person who was near the table whilst they were all away dancing. There *might* be something in it.'

Race shook his head.

'If he'd put anything in Barton's glass, that girl would have seen him. She's a born observer of detail. Nothing to think about inside her head and so she uses her eyes. No, Kemp, there must be some quite simple explanation if only we could get it.'

'Yes, there's one. He dropped it in himself.'

'I'm beginning to believe that that *is* what happened – that it's the only thing that can have happened. But if so, Kemp, I'm convinced he didn't know it was cyanide.'

'You mean someone gave it to him? Told him it was for indigestion or blood pressure – something like that?'

'It could be.'

'Then who was the someone? Not either of the Farradays.'

'That would certainly seem unlikely.'

'And I'd say Mr Anthony Browne is equally unlikely. That leaves us two people – an affectionate sister-in-law –'

'And a devoted secretary.'

Kemp looked at him.

'Yes – she could have planted something of the kind on him – I'm due now to go to Kidderminster House – What about you? Going round to see Miss Marle?'

'I think I'll go and see the other one – at the office. Condolences of an old friend. I might take her out to lunch.'

'So that *is* what you think.'

'I don't think anything yet. I'm casting about for spoor.'

'You ought to see Iris Marle, all the same.'

'I'm going to see her – but I'd rather go to the house first when she isn't there. Do you know why, Kemp?'

'I'm sure I couldn't say.'

'Because there's someone there who twitters – twitters like a little bird . . . A little bird told me – was a saying of my youth. It's very true, Kemp – these twitterers can tell one a lot if one just lets them – twitter!'

CHAPTER 4

The two men parted. Race halted a taxi and was driven to George Barton's office in the city. Chief Inspector Kemp, mindful of his expense account, took a bus to within a stone's throw of Kidderminster House.

The inspector's face was rather grim as he mounted the steps and pushed the bell. He was, he knew, on difficult ground. The Kidderminster faction had immense political influence and its ramifications spread out like a network throughout the country. Chief Inspector Kemp had full belief in the impartiality of British justice. If Stephen or Alexandra Farraday had been concerned in the death of Rosemary Barton or in that of George Barton no 'pull' or 'influence' would enable them to escape the consequences. But if they were guiltless, or the evidence against them was too vague to ensure conviction, then the responsible officer must be careful how he trod or he would be liable to get a rap over the knuckles from his superiors. In these circumstances it can be understood that the chief inspector did not much relish what lay before him. It seemed to him highly probable that the Kidderminsters would, as he phrased it to himself, 'cut up rough'.

Kemp soon found, however, that he had been somewhat naïve in his assumption. Lord Kidderminster was far too experienced a diplomat to resort to crudities.

On stating his business, Chief Inspector Kemp was taken at once by a pontifical butler to a dim book-lined room at the back of the house where he found Lord Kidderminster and his daughter and son-in-law awaiting him.

Coming forward, Lord Kidderminster shook hands and said courteously:

'You are exactly on time, chief inspector. May I say that I much appreciate your courtesy in coming here instead of demanding that my daughter and her husband should come to Scotland Yard which, of course, they would have been quite prepared to do if necessary – that goes without saying – but they appreciate your kindness.'

Sandra said in a quiet voice:

'Yes, indeed, inspector.'

She was wearing a dress of some soft dark red material, and sitting as she was with the light from the long narrow window behind her, she reminded Kemp of a stained glass figure he had once seen in a cathedral abroad. The long oval of her face and the slight angularity of her shoulders helped the illusion. Saint Somebody or other, they had told him – but Lady Alexandra Farraday was no saint – not by a long way. And yet some of these old saints had been funny people from his point of view, not kindly ordinary decent Christian folk, but intolerant, fanatical, cruel to themselves and others.

Stephen Farraday stood close by his wife. His face expressed no emotion whatever. He looked correct and formal, an appointed legislator of the people. The natural man was well buried. But the natural man was there, as the chief inspector knew.

Lord Kidderminster was speaking, directing with a good deal of ability the trend of the interview.

'I won't disguise from you, chief inspector, that this is a very painful and disagreeable business for us all. This is the second time that my daughter and son-in-law have been connected with a violent death in a public place – the same restaurant and two members of the same family. Publicity of such a kind is always harmful to a man in the public eye. Publicity, of course, cannot be avoided. We all realize that, and both my daughter and Mr Farraday are anxious to give you all the help they can in the hope that the matter may be cleared up speedily and public interest in it die down.'

'Thank you, Lord Kidderminster. I much appreciate the attitude you have taken up. It certainly makes things easier for us.'

Sandra Farraday said:

'Please ask us any questions you like, chief inspector.'

'Thank you, Lady Alexandra.'

'Just one point, chief inspector,' said Lord Kidderminster. 'You have, of course, your own sources of information and I gather from my friend the Commissioner that this man Barton's death is regarded as murder rather than suicide, though on the face of it, to the outside public, suicide would seem a more likely explanation. *You* thought it was suicide, didn't you, Sandra, my dear?'

The Gothic figure bowed its head slightly. Sandra said in a thoughtful voice.

'It seemed to me so obvious last night. We were there in the same restaurant and actually at the same table where poor Rosemary Barton poisoned herself last year. We have seen something of Mr Barton during the summer in the country and he has really been very odd – quite unlike himself – and we all thought that his wife's death was preying on his mind. He was very fond of her, you know, and I don't think he ever got over her death. So that the idea of suicide seemed, if not natural, at least possible – whereas I can't imagine why *anyone* should want to murder George Barton.'

Stephen Farraday said quickly:

'No more can I. Barton was an excellent fellow. I'm sure he hadn't got an enemy in the world.'

Chief Inspector Kemp looked at the three inquiring faces turned towards him and reflected a moment before speaking. 'Better let 'em have it,' he thought to himself.

'What you say is quite correct, I am sure, Lady Alexandra. But you see there are a few things that you probably don't know yet.'

Lord Kidderminster interposed quickly:

'We mustn't force the chief inspector's hand. It is entirely in his discretion what facts he makes public.'

'Thanks, m'lord, but there's no reason I shouldn't explain things a little more clearly. I'll boil it down to this. George Barton, before his death, expressed to two people his belief that his wife had not, as was believed, committed suicide, but had instead been poisoned by some third party. He also thought that he was on the track of that third party, and the dinner and celebration last night, ostensibly in honour of Miss Marle's birthday, was really some part of a plan he had made for finding out the identity of his wife's murderer.'

There was a moment's silence – and in that silence Chief Inspector Kemp, who was a sensitive man in spite of his wooden appearance, felt the presence of something that he classified as dismay. It was not apparent on any face, but he could have sworn that it was there.

Lord Kidderminster was the first to recover himself. He said:

'But surely – that belief in itself might point to the fact that poor Barton was not quite – er – himself? Brooding over his wife's death might have slightly unhinged him mentally.'

'Quite so, Lord Kidderminster, but it at least shows that his frame of mind was definitely not suicidal.'

'Yes – yes, I take your point.'

And again there was silence. Then Stephen Farraday said sharply:

'But how did Barton get such an idea into his head? After all, Mrs Barton *did* commit suicide.'

Chief Inspector Kemp transferred a placid gaze to him.

'Mr Barton didn't think so.'

Lord Kidderminster interposed.

'But the police were satisfied? There was no suggestion of anything but suicide at the time?'

Chief Inspector Kemp said quietly:

'The facts were compatible with suicide. There was no evidence that her death was due to any other agency.'

He knew that a man of Lord Kidderminster's calibre would seize on the exact meaning of that.

Becoming slightly more official, Kemp said, 'I would like to ask you some questions now, if I may, Lady Alexandra?'

'Certainly.' She turned her head slightly towards him.

'You had no suspicions at the time of Mr Barton's death that it might be murder, not suicide?'

'Certainly not. I was quite sure it was suicide.' She added, 'I still am.'

Kemp let that pass. He said:

'Have you received any anonymous letters in the past year, Lady Alexandra?'

The calm of her manner seemed broken by pure astonishment.

'Anonymous letters? Oh, no.'

'You're quite sure? Such letters are very unpleasant things and people usually prefer to ignore them, but they may be particularly important in this case, and that is why I want to stress that if you did receive any such letters it is most essential that I should know about them.'

'I see. But I can only assure you, chief inspector, that I have received nothing of the kind.'

'Very well. Now you say Mr Barton's manner has been odd this summer. In what way?'

She considered a minute.

'Well, he was jumpy, nervous. It seemed difficult for him to focus his attention on what was said to him.' She turned her head towards her husband. 'Was that how it struck you, Stephen?'

'Yes, I should say that was a very fair description. The man looked physically ill, too. He had lost weight.'

'Did you notice any difference in his attitude towards you and your husband? Any less cordiality, for instance?'

'No. On the contrary. He had bought a house, you know, quite close to us, and he seemed very grateful for what we were able to do for him – in the way of local introductions, I mean, and all that. Of course we were only too pleased to do everything we could in that line, both for him and for Iris Marle who is a charming girl.'

'Was the late Mrs Barton a great friend of yours, Lady Alexandra?'

'No, we were not very intimate.' She gave a light laugh. 'She was really mostly Stephen's friend. She became interested in politics and he helped to – well, educate her politically – which I'm sure he enjoyed. She was a very charming and attractive woman, you know.'

'And you're a very clever one,' thought Chief Inspector Kemp to himself appreciatively. 'I wonder how much you know about those two – a good deal, I shouldn't wonder.'

He went on:

'Mr Barton never expressed to *you* the view that his wife did not commit suicide?'

'No, indeed. That was why I was so startled just now.'

'And Miss Marle? She never talked about her sister's death, either?'

'No.'

'Any idea what made George Barton buy a house in the country? Did you or your husband suggest the idea to him?'

'No. It was quite a surprise.'

'And his manner to you was always friendly?'

'Very friendly indeed.'

'And what do you know about Mr Anthony Browne, Lady Alexandra?'

'I really know nothing at all. I have met him occasionally and that is all.'

'What about you, Mr Farraday?'

'I think I know probably less about Browne than my wife does. She at any rate has danced with him. He seems a likeable chap – American, I believe.'

'Would you say from observation at the time that he was on special terms of intimacy with Mrs Barton?'

'I have absolutely no knowledge on that point, chief inspector.'

'I am simply asking you for your impression, Mr Farraday.'

Stephen frowned.

'They were friendly – that is all I can say.'

'And you, Lady Alexandra?'

'Simply my impression, chief inspector?'

'Simply your impression.'

'Then, for what it is worth, I did form the impression that they knew each other well and were on intimate terms. Simply, you understand, from the way they looked at each other – I have no concrete evidence.'

'Ladies have often very good judgement on these matters,' said Kemp. That somewhat fatuous smile with which he delivered this remark would have amused Colonel Race if he had been present. 'Now, what about Miss Lessing, Lady Alexandra?'

'Miss Lessing, I understand, was Mr Barton's secretary. I met her for the first time on the evening that Mrs Barton died. After that I met her once when she was staying down in the country, and last night.'

'If I may ask you another informal question, did you form the impression that she was in love with George Barton?'

'I really haven't the least idea.'

'Then we'll come to the events of last night.'

He questioned both Stephen and his wife minutely on the course of the tragic evening. He had not hoped for much from this, and all he got was confirmation of what he had already been told. All accounts agreed on the important points – Barton had proposed a toast to Iris, had drunk it and immediately afterwards had got up to dance. They had all left the table together and George and Iris had been the first to return to it. Neither of them had any explanation to offer as to the empty chair except that George Barton had distinctly said that he was expecting a friend of his, a Colonel Race, to occupy it later in the evening – a statement which, as the inspector knew, could not possibly be the truth. Sandra Farraday said, and her husband agreed, that when the lights went up after the cabaret, George had stared at the empty chair in a peculiar manner and had for some moments seemed so absent-minded as not to hear what was said to him – then he had rallied himself and proposed Iris's health.

The only item that the chief inspector could count as an addition to his knowledge, was Sandra's account of her conversation with George at Fairhaven – and his plea that she and her husband would collaborate with him over this party for Iris's sake.

It was a reasonably plausible pretext, the chief inspector thought, though not the true one. Closing his notebook in which he had jotted down one or two hieroglyphics, he rose to his feet.

'I'm very grateful to you, my lord, and to Mr Farraday and Lady Alexandra for your help and collaboration.'

'Will my daughter's presence be required at the inquest?'

'The proceedings will be purely formal on this occasion. Evidence of identification and the medical evidence will be taken and the inquest will then be adjourned for a week. By then,' said the chief inspector, his tone changing slightly, 'we shall, I hope, be further on.'

He turned to Stephen Farraday:

'By the way, Mr Farraday, there are one or two small points where I think you could help me. No need to trouble Lady Alexandra. If you will give me a ring at the Yard, we can settle a time that will suit you. You are, I know, a busy man.'

It was pleasantly said, with an air of casualness, but on three pairs of ears the words fell with deliberate meaning.

With an air of friendly co-operation Stephen managed to say:

'Certainly, chief inspector.' Then he looked at his watch and murmured: 'I must go along to the House.'

When Stephen had hurried off, and the chief inspector had likewise departed, Lord Kidderminster turned to his daughter and asked a question with no beating about the bush.

'Had Stephen been having an affair with that woman?'

There was a split second of a pause before his daughter answered.

'Of course not. I should have known it if he had. And anyway, Stephen's not that kind.'

'Now, look here, my dear, no good laying your ears back and digging your hoofs in. These things are bound to come out. We want to know where we are in this business.'

'Rosemary Barton was a friend of that man, Anthony Browne. They went about everywhere together.'

'Well,' said Lord Kidderminster slowly. 'You should know.'

He did not believe his daughter. His face, as he went slowly out of the room, was grey and perplexed. He went upstairs to his wife's sitting-room. He had vetoed her presence in the library, knowing too well that her arrogant methods were apt to arouse antagonism and at this juncture he felt it vital that relations with the official police should be harmonious.

'Well?' said Lady Kidderminster. 'How did it go off?'

'Quite well on the face of it,' said Lord Kidderminster slowly. 'Kemp is a courteous fellow – very pleasant in his manner – he handled the whole thing with tact – just a little too much tact for my fancy.'

'It's serious, then?'

'Yes, it's serious. We should never have let Sandra marry that fellow, Vicky.'

'That's what I said.'

'Yes – yes . . .' He acknowledged her claim. 'You were right – and I was wrong. But, mind you, she would have had him anyway. You can't turn Sandra when her mind is fixed on a thing. Her meeting Farraday was a disaster – a man of whose antecedents and ancestors we know nothing. When a crisis comes how does one know how a man like that will react?'

'I see,' said Lady Kidderminster. 'You think we've taken a murderer into the family?'

'I don't know. I don't want to condemn the fellow off-hand – but it's what the police think – and they're pretty shrewd. He had an affair with this Barton woman – that's plain enough. Either she committed suicide on his account, or else he – Well, whatever happened, Barton got wise to it and was heading for an exposé and scandal. I suppose Stephen simply couldn't take it – and –'

'Poisoned him?'

'Yes.'

Lady Kidderminster shook her head.

'I don't agree with you.'

'I hope you're right. But somebody poisoned him.'

'If you ask me,' said Lady Kidderminster, 'Stephen simply wouldn't have the nerve to do a thing like that.'

'He's in deadly earnest about his career – he's got great gifts, you know, and the makings of a true statesman. You can't say what anyone will do when they're forced into a corner.'

His wife still shook her head.

'I still say he hasn't got the nerve. You want someone who's a gambler and capable of being reckless. I'm afraid, William, I'm horribly afraid.'

He stared at her. 'Are you suggesting that Sandra – *Sandra* –?'

'I hate even to suggest such a thing – but it's no use being cowardly and refusing to face possibilities. She's besotted about that man – she always has been – and there's a queer streak in Sandra. I've never really understood her – but I've always been afraid for her. She'd risk anything – *anything* – for Stephen. Without counting the cost. And if she's been mad enough and wicked enough to do this thing, she's got to be protected.'

'Protected? What do you mean – protected?'

'By you. We've got to do something about our own daughter, haven't we? Mercifully you can pull any amount of strings.'

Lord Kidderminster was staring at her. Though he had thought he knew his wife's character well, he was nevertheless appalled at the force and courage of her realism – at her refusal to blink at unpalatable facts – and also at her unscrupulousness.

'If my daughter's a murderess, do you suggest that I should use my official position to rescue her from the consequences of her act?'

'Of course,' said Lady Kidderminster.

'My dear Vicky! You don't understand! One can't do things like that. It would be a breach of – of honour.'

'Rubbish!' said Lady Kidderminster.

They looked at each other – so far divided that neither could see the other's point of view. So might Agamemnon and Clytemnestra have stared at each other with the word Iphigenia on their lips.

'You could bring government pressure to bear on the police so that the whole thing is dropped and a verdict of suicide brought in. It has been done before – don't pretend.'

'That has been when it was a matter of public policy – in the interests of the State. This is a personal and private matter. I doubt very much whether I could do such a thing.'

'You can if you have sufficient determination.'

Lord Kidderminster flushed angrily.

'If I could, I wouldn't! It would be abusing my public position.'

'If Sandra were arrested and tried, wouldn't you employ the best counsel and do everything possible to get her off however guilty she was?'

'Of course, of course. That's entirely different. You women never grasp these things.'

Lady Kidderminster was silent, unperturbed by the thrust. Sandra was the least dear to her of her children – nevertheless she was at this moment a mother, and a mother only – willing to defend her young by any means, honourable or dishonourable. She would fight with tooth and claw for Sandra.

'In any case,' said Lord Kidderminster, 'Sandra will not be charged unless there is an absolutely convincing case against her. And I, for one, refuse to believe that a daughter of mine is a murderess. I'm astonished at you, Vicky, for entertaining such an idea for a moment.'

His wife said nothing, and Lord Kidderminster went uneasily out of the room. To think that Vicky – *Vicky* – whom he had known intimately for so many years – should prove to have such unsuspected and really very disturbing depths in her!

CHAPTER 5

Race found Ruth Lessing busy with papers at a large desk. She was dressed in a black coat and skirt and a white blouse and he was impressed by her quiet unhurried efficiency. He noticed the dark circles under her eyes and the unhappy set line of her mouth, but her grief, if it was grief, was as well controlled as all her other emotions.

Race explained his visit and she responded at once.

'It is very good of you to come. Of course I know who you are. Mr Barton was expecting you to join us last night, was he not? I remember his saying so.'

'Did he mention that before the evening itself?'

She thought for a moment.

'No. It was when we were actually taking our seats round the table. I remember that I was a little surprised –' She paused and flushed slightly. 'Not, of course, at his inviting you. You are an old friend, I know. And you were to have been at the other party a year ago. All I meant was that I was surprised, if you were coming, that Mr Barton hadn't invited another woman to balance the numbers – but of course if you were going to be late and might perhaps not come at all –' She broke off. 'How stupid I am. Why go over all these petty things that don't matter? I *am* stupid this morning.'

'But you have come to work as usual?'

'Of course.' She looked surprised – almost shocked. 'It is my job. There is so much to clear up and arrange.'

'George always told me how much he relied upon you,' said Race gently.

She turned away. He saw her swallow quickly and blink her eyes. Her absence of any display of emotion almost convinced him of her entire innocence. Almost, but not quite. He had met women who were good actresses before now, women whose reddened eyelids and the black circles underneath whose eyes had been due to art and not to natural causes.

Reserving judgement, he said to himself:

'At any rate she's a cool customer.'

Ruth turned back to the desk and in answer to his last remark she said quietly:

'I was with him for many years – it will be eight years next April – and I knew his ways, and I think he – trusted me.'

'I'm sure of that.'

He went on: 'It is nearly lunch-time. I hoped you would come out and lunch quietly with me somewhere? There is a good deal I would like to say to you.'

'Thank you. I should like to very much.'

He took her to a small restaurant that he knew of, where the tables were set far apart and where a quiet conversation was possible.

He ordered, and when the waiter had gone, looked across the table at his companion.

She was a good-looking girl, he decided, with her sleek dark head and her firm mouth and chin.

He talked a little on desultory topics until the food was brought, and she followed his lead, showing herself intelligent and sensible.

Presently, after a pause, she said:

'You want to talk to me about last night? Please don't hesitate to do so. The whole thing is so incredible that I would like to talk about it. Except that it happened and I saw it happen, I would not have believed it.'

'You've seen Chief Inspector Kemp, of course?'

'Yes, last night. He seems intelligent and experienced.' She paused. 'Was it really *murder*, Colonel Race?'

'Did Kemp tell you so?'

'He didn't volunteer any information, but his questions made it plain enough what he had in mind.'

'*Your* opinion as to whether or not it was suicide should be as good as anyone's, Miss Lessing. You knew Barton well and you were with him most of yesterday, I imagine. How did he seem? Much as usual? Or was he disturbed – upset – excited?'

She hesitated.

'It's difficult. He was upset and disturbed – but then there was a reason for that.'

She explained the situation that had arisen in regard to Victor Drake and gave a brief sketch of that young man's career.

'H'm,' said Race. 'The inevitable black sheep. And Barton was upset about him?'

Ruth said slowly:

'It's difficult to explain. I knew Mr Barton so well, you see. He was annoyed and bothered about the business – and I gather Mrs Drake had been very tearful and upset, as she always was on these occasions – so of course he wanted to straighten it all out. But I had the impression –'

'Yes, Miss Lessing? I'm sure your impressions will be accurate.'

'Well, then, I fancied that his annoyance was not quite the usual annoyance, if I may put it like that. Because we had had this same business before, in one form or another. Last year Victor Drake was in this country and in trouble, and we had to ship him off to South America, and only last June he cabled home for money. So you see I was familiar with Mr Barton's reactions. And it seemed to me this time that his annoyance was principally at the cable having arrived just at this moment when he was entirely preoccupied with the arrangements for the party he was giving. He seemed so taken up by the preparations for it that he grudged any other preoccupation arising.'

'Did it strike you that there was anything odd about this party of his, Miss Lessing?'

'Yes, it did. Mr Barton was really most peculiar about it. He was excited – like a child might have been.'

'Did it occur to you that there might have been a special purpose for such a party?'

'You mean that it was a replica of the party a year ago when Mrs Barton committed suicide?'

'Yes.'

'Frankly, I thought it a most extraordinary idea.'

'But George didn't volunteer any explanation – or confide in you in any way?'

She shook her head.

'Tell me, Miss Lessing, has there ever been any doubt in your mind as to Mrs Barton's having committed suicide?'

She looked astonished. 'Oh, no.'

'George Barton didn't tell you that he believed his wife had been murdered?'

She stared at him.

'George believed *that*?'

'I see that is news to you. Yes, Miss Lessing. George had received anonymous letters stating that his wife had not committed suicide but had been killed.'

'So that is why he became so odd this summer? I couldn't think what was the matter with him.'

'You knew nothing about these anonymous letters?'

'Nothing. Were there many of them?'

'He showed me two.'

'And I knew nothing about them!'

There was a note of bitter hurt in her voice.

He watched her for a moment or two, then he said:

'Well, Miss Lessing, what do you say? Is it possible, in your opinion, for George to have committed suicide?'

She shook her head.

'No – oh, no.'

'But you said he was excited – upset?'

'Yes, but he had been like that for some time. I see why now. And I see why he was so excited about last night's party. He must have had some special idea in his head – he must have hoped that by reproducing the conditions, he would gain some additional knowledge – poor George, he must have been so muddled about it all.'

'And what about Rosemary Barton, Miss Lessing? Do you still think her death was suicide?'

She frowned.

'I've never dreamt of it being anything else. It seemed so natural.'

'Depression after influenza?'

'Well, rather more than that, perhaps. She was definitely very unhappy. One could see that.'

'And guess the cause?'

'Well – yes. At least I did. Of course I may have been wrong. But women like Mrs Barton are very transparent – they don't trouble to hide their feelings. Mercifully I don't think Mr Barton knew anything . . . Oh, yes, she was very unhappy. And I know she had a bad headache that night besides being run down with 'flu.'

'How did you know she had a headache?'

'I heard her telling Lady Alexandra so – in the cloakroom when we were taking off our wraps. She was wishing she had a Cachet Faivre and luckily Lady Alexandra had one with her and gave it to her.'

Colonel Race's hand stopped with a glass in mid air.

'And she took it?'

'Yes.'

He put his glass down untasted and looked across the table. The girl looked placid and unaware of any significance in what she had said. But it *was* significant. It meant that Sandra who, from her position at table, would have had the most difficulty in putting anything unseen in Rosemary's glass, had had another opportunity of administering the poison. She could have given it to Rosemary in a cachet. Ordinarily a cachet would take only a few minutes to dissolve, but possibly this had been a special kind of cachet, it might have had a lining of gelatine or some other substance. Or Rosemary might possibly not have swallowed it then but later.

He said abruptly:

'Did you see her take it?'

'I beg your pardon?'

He saw by her puzzled face that her mind had gone on elsewhere.

'Did you see Rosemary Barton swallow that cachet?'

Ruth looked a little startled.

'I – well, no, I didn't actually see her. She just thanked Lady Alexandra.'

So Rosemary might have slipped the cachet in her bag and then, during the cabaret, with a headache increasing, she might have dropped it into her champagne glass and let it dissolve. Assumption – pure assumption – but a possibility.

Ruth said:

'Why do you ask me that?'

Her eyes were suddenly alert, full of questions. He watched, so it seemed to him, her intelligence working.

Then she said:

'Oh, I see. I see why George took that house down there near the Farradays. And I see why he didn't tell me about those letters. It seemed to me so extraordinary that he hadn't. But of course if he believed them, it meant that one of us, one of those five people round the table must have killed her. It might – it might even have been *me*!'

Race said in a very gentle voice:

'Had you any reason for killing Rosemary Barton?'

He thought at first that she hadn't heard the question. She sat so very still with her eyes cast down.

But suddenly with a sigh, she raised them and looked straight at him.

'It is not the sort of thing one cares to talk about,' she said. 'But I think you had better know. I was in love with George Barton. I was in love with him before he even met Rosemary. I don't think he ever knew – certainly he didn't care. He was fond of me – very fond of me – but I suppose never in that way. And yet I used to think that I would have made him a good wife – that I could have made him happy. He loved Rosemary, but he wasn't happy with her.'

Race said gently:

'And you disliked Rosemary?'

'Yes, I did. Oh! She was very lovely and very attractive and could be very charming in her way. She never bothered to be charming to me! I disliked her a good deal. I was shocked when she died – and at the way she died, but I wasn't really sorry. I'm afraid I was rather glad.'

She paused.

'Please, shall we talk about something else?'

Race responded quickly:

'I'd like you to tell me exactly, in detail, everything you can remember about yesterday – from the morning onwards – especially anything George did or said.'

Ruth replied promptly, going over the events of the morning – George's annoyance over Victor's importunity, her own telephone calls to South America and the arrangements made and George's pleasure when the matter was settled. She then described her arrival at the Luxembourg and George's flurried excited bearing as host. She carried her narrative up to the final moment of the tragedy. Her account tallied in every respect with those he had already heard.

With a worried frown, Ruth voiced his own perplexity.

'It wasn't suicide – I'm sure it wasn't suicide – but how can it have been murder? I mean, how can it have been done? The answer is, it couldn't, not by one of us! Then was it someone who slipped the poison into George's glass while we were away dancing? But if so, who could it have been? It doesn't seem to make sense.'

'The evidence is that *no one* went near the table while you were dancing.'

'Then it really doesn't make sense! Cyanide doesn't get into a glass by itself!'

'Have you absolutely no idea – no suspicion, even, who might have put the cyanide in the glass? Think back over last night. Is there nothing, no small incident, that awakens your suspicions in any degree, however small?'

He saw her face change, saw for a moment uncertainty come into her eyes. There was a tiny, almost infinitesimal pause before she answered 'Nothing.'

But there *had* been something. He was sure of that. Something she had seen or heard or noticed that, for some reason or other, she had decided not to tell.

He did not press her. He knew that with a girl of Ruth's type that would be no good. If, for some reason, she had made up her mind to keep silence, she would not, he felt sure, change her mind.

But there had been *something*. That knowledge cheered him and gave him fresh assurance. It was the first sign of a crevice in the blank wall that confronted him.

He took leave of Ruth after lunch and drove to Elvaston Square thinking of the woman he had just left.

Was it possible that Ruth Lessing was guilty? On the whole, he was prepossessed in her favour. She had seemed entirely frank and straightforward.

Was she capable of murder? Most people were, if you came to it. Capable not of murder in general, but of one particular individual murder. That was what made it so difficult to weed anyone out. There was a certain quality of ruthlessness about that young woman. And she had a motive – or rather a choice of motives. By removing Rosemary she had a very good chance of becoming Mrs George Barton. Whether it was a question of marrying a rich man, or of marrying the man she had loved, the removal of Rosemary was the first essential.

Race was inclined to think that marrying a rich man was not enough. Ruth Lessing was too cool-headed and cautious to risk her neck for mere comfortable living as a rich man's wife. Love? Perhaps. For all her cool and detached manner, he suspected her of being one of those women who can be kindled to unlikely passion by one particular man. Given love of George and hate of Rosemary, she might have coolly planned and executed Rosemary's death. The fact that it had gone off without a hitch, and that suicide had been universally accepted without demur, proved her inherent capability.

And then George had received anonymous letters (From whom? Why? That was the teasing vexing problem that never ceased to nag at him) and had grown suspicious. He had planned a trap. And Ruth had silenced him.

No, that wasn't right. That didn't ring true. That spelt panic – and Ruth Lessing was not the kind of woman who panicked. She had better brains than George and could have avoided any trap that he was likely to set with the greatest of ease.

It looked as though Ruth didn't add up after all.

CHAPTER 6

Lucilla Drake was delighted to see Colonel Race.

The blinds were all down and Lucilla came into the room draped in black and with a handkerchief to her eyes and explained, as she advanced a tremulous hand to meet his, how of course she couldn't have seen anyone – anyone at all – except such an old friend of dear, *dear* George's – and it was so dreadful to have no man in the house! Really without a man in the house one didn't know how to tackle *anything*. Just herself, a poor lonely widow, and Iris, just a helpless young girl, and George had always looked after everything. So kind of dear Colonel Race and really she was so grateful – no idea what they ought to do. Of course Miss Lessing would attend to all business matters – and the funeral to arrange for – but how about the inquest? and so dreadful having the police – actually in the house – plain clothes, of course, and really very considerate. But she was so bewildered and the whole thing was such an absolute tragedy and didn't Colonel Race think it must be all due to *suggestion* – that was what the psychoanalyst said, wasn't it, that everything is *suggestion*? And poor George at that horrid place, the Luxembourg, and practically the same party and remembering how poor Rosemary had died there – and it must have come over him quite suddenly, only if he'd listened to what she, Lucilla, had said, and taken that excellent tonic of dear Dr Gaskell's – run down, all the summer – yes, thoroughly run down.

Whereupon Lucilla herself ran down temporarily, and Race had a chance to speak.

He said how deeply he sympathized and how Mrs Drake must count upon him in every way.

Whereupon Lucilla started off again and said it was indeed kind of him, and it was the shock that had been so terrible – here today, and gone tomorrow, as it said in the Bible, cometh up like grass and cut down in the evening – only that wasn't quite right, but Colonel Race would know what she meant, and it was so nice to feel there was someone on whom they could rely. Miss Lessing meant well, of course, and was very efficient, but rather an unsympathetic manner and sometimes took things upon herself a little too much, and in her, Lucilla's, opinion, George had always relied upon her *far too much*, and at one time she had been really afraid that he might do something foolish which would have been a great pity and probably she would have bullied him unmercifully once they were married. Of course she, Lucilla, had seen what was in the wind. Dear Iris was so unworldly, and it was nice, didn't Colonel Race think, for young girls to be unspoilt and simple? Iris had really always been very young for her age and very quiet – one didn't know half the time what she was thinking about. Rosemary being so pretty and so gay had been out a great deal, and Iris had mooned about the house which wasn't really right for a young girl – they should go to classes – cooking and perhaps dressmaking. It occupied their minds and one never knew when it might come in useful. It had really been a mercy that she, Lucilla, had been free to come and live here after poor Rosemary's death – that horrid 'flu, quite an unusual kind of 'flu, Dr Gaskell had said. Such a clever man and such a nice, breezy manner.

She had wanted Iris to see him this summer. The girl had looked so white and pulled down. 'But really, Colonel Race, I think it was the situation of the house. *Low*, you know, and *damp*, with quite a *miasma* in the evenings.' Poor George had gone off and bought it all by himself without asking anyone's advice – such a pity. He had said he wanted it to be a surprise, but really it would have been better if he had taken some older woman's advice. Men knew nothing about houses. George might have realized that she, Lucilla, would have been willing to take any *amount* of trouble. For, after all, what was her life now? Her dear husband dead many years ago, and Victor, her dear boy, far away in the Argentine – she meant

Brazil, or was it the Argentine? Such an affectionate, handsome boy.

Colonel Race said he had heard she had a son abroad.

For the next quarter of an hour, he was regaled with a full account of Victor's multitudinous activities. Such a spirited boy, willing to turn his hand to anything – here followed a list of Victor's varied occupations. Never unkind, or bearing malice to anyone. 'He's always been unlucky, Colonel Race. He was misjudged by his house-master and I consider the authorities at Oxford behaved quite disgracefully. People don't seem to understand that a clever boy with a taste for drawing would think it an excellent joke to imitate someone's handwriting. He did it for the fun of the thing, not for money.' But he'd always been a good son to his mother, and he never failed to let her know when he was in trouble which showed, didn't it, that he trusted her? Only it did seem curious, didn't it, that the jobs people found for him so often seemed to take him out of England. She couldn't help feeling that if only he could be given a nice job, in the Bank of England say, he would settle down much better. He might perhaps live a little out of London and have a little car.

It was quite twenty minutes before Colonel Race, having heard all Victor's perfections and misfortunes, was able to switch Lucilla from the subject of sons to that of servants.

Yes, it was very true what he said, the old-fashioned type of servant didn't exist any longer. Really the trouble people had nowadays! Not that she ought to complain, for really they had been very lucky. Mrs Pound, though she had the misfortune to be slightly deaf, was an excellent woman. Her pastry sometimes a little heavy and a tendency to over-pepper the soup, but really on the whole most reliable – and economical too. She had been there ever since George married and she had made no fuss about going to the country this year, though there had been trouble with the others over that and the parlourmaid had left – but that really was all for the best – an impertinent girl who answered back – besides breaking six of the best wineglasses, not one by one at odd times which might happen to *anybody*, but all at once which really meant gross carelessness, didn't Colonel Race think so?

'Very careless indeed.'

'That is what I told her. And I said to her that I should be obliged to say so in her reference – for I really feel one has a *duty*, Colonel Race. I mean, one should not mislead. Faults should be mentioned as well as good qualities. But the girl was – really – well, quite *insolent* and said that at any rate she hoped that in her next place she wouldn't be in the kind of house where people got bumped off – a dreadful common expression, acquired at the cinema, I believe, and ludicrously inappropriate since poor dear Rosemary took her own life – though not at the time responsible for her actions as the coroner very rightly pointed out – and that dreadful expression refers, I believe, to gangsters executing each other with tómmy-guns. I am so thankful that we have nothing of that kind in England. And so, as I say, I put in her reference that Betty Archdale thoroughly understood her duties as parlourmaid and was sober and honest, but that she was inclined to have too many breakages and was not always respectful in her manner. And personally, if *I* had been Mrs Rees-Talbot, I should have read between the lines and not engaged her. But people nowadays just jump at anything they can get, and will sometimes take a girl who has only stayed her month in three places running.'

Whilst Mrs Drake paused to take breath, Colonel Race asked quickly whether that was Mrs Richard Rees-Talbot? If so, he had known her, he said, in India.

'I really couldn't say. Cadogan Square was the address.'

'Then it *is* my friends.'

Lucilla said that the world was such a small place, wasn't it? And that there were no friends like old friends. Friendship was a wonderful thing. She had always thought it had been so romantic about Viola and Paul. Dear Viola, she had been a lovely girl, and so many men in love with her, but, oh dear, Colonel Race wouldn't even know who she was talking about. One did so tend to re-live the past.

Colonel Race begged her to go on and in return for this politeness received the life history of Hector Marle, of his upbringing by his sister, of his peculiarities and his weaknesses and finally, when Colonel Race had almost forgotten her, of his marriage to the beautiful Viola. 'She was an orphan, you know, and a ward in Chancery.' He heard how Paul Bennett, conquering his disappointment at Viola's refusal, had transformed himself from lover to family friend, and of his fondness for his godchild,

Rosemary, and of his death and the terms of his will. 'Which I have always felt *most* romantic – such an enormous fortune! Not of course that money is everything – no, indeed. One has only to think of poor Rosemary's tragic death. And even dear Iris I am not quite happy about!'

Race gave her an inquiring look.

'I find the responsibility most worrying. The fact that she is a great heiress is of course well known. I keep a very sharp eye on the undesirable type of young man, but what can one do, Colonel Race? One can't look after girls nowadays as one used to do. Iris has friends I know next to nothing about. "Ask them to the house, dear," is what I always say – but I gather that some of these young men simply will *not* be brought. Poor George was worried, too. About a young man called Browne. I myself have never seen him, but it seems that he and Iris have been seeing a good deal of each other. And one does feel that she could do better. George didn't like him – I'm quite sure of that. And I always think, Colonel Race, that men are so much better judges of other men. I remember thinking Colonel Pusey, one of our churchwardens, such a charming man, but my husband always preserved a very distant attitude towards him and enjoined on me to do the same – and sure enough one Sunday when he was handing round the offertory plate, he fell right down – completely intoxicated, it seems. And of course afterwards – one always hears these things *afterwards*, so much better if one heard them *before* – we found out that dozens of empty brandy bottles were taken out of the house every week! It was very sad really, because he was truly religious, though inclined to be Evangelical in his views. He and my husband had a terrific battle over the details of the service on All Saints' Day. Oh, dear, All Saints' Day. To think that yesterday was All Souls' Day.'

A faint sound made Race look over Lucilla's head at the open doorway. He had seen Iris before – at Little Priors. Nevertheless he felt that he was seeing her now for the first time. He was struck by the extraordinary tension behind her stillness and her wide eyes met his with something in their expression that he felt he ought to recognize, yet failed to do so.

In her turn, Lucilla Drake turned her head.

'Iris, dear, I didn't hear you come in. You know Colonel Race? He is being so very kind.'

Iris came and shook hands with him gravely, the black dress she wore made her look thinner and paler than he remembered her.

'I came to see if I could be of any help to you,' said Race.

'Thank you. That was kind of you.'

She had had a bad shock, that was evident, and was still suffering from the effects of it. But had she been so fond of George that his death could affect her so powerfully?

She turned her eyes to her aunt and Race realized that they were watchful eyes. She said:

'What were you talking about – just now, as I came in?'

Lucilla became pink and flustered. Race guessed that she was anxious to avoid any mention of the young man, Anthony Browne. She exclaimed:

'Now let me see – oh, yes, All Saints' Day – and yesterday being All Souls'. All Souls' – that seems to me such an *odd* thing – one of those coincidences one never believes in in real life.'

'Do you mean,' said Iris, 'that Rosemary came back yesterday to fetch George?'

Lucilla gave a little scream.

'Iris, dear, don't. What a terrible thought – so un-Christian.'

'Why un-Christian? It's the Day of the Dead. In Paris people used to go and put flowers on the graves.'

'Oh, I know, dear, but then they are Catholics, aren't they?'

A faint smile twisted Iris's lips. Then she said directly:

'I thought, perhaps, you were talking of Anthony – Anthony Browne.'

'Well,' Lucilla's twitter became very high and birdlike, 'as a matter of fact we did just *mention* him. I happened to say, you know, that we know *nothing about* him –'

Iris interrupted, her voice hard:

'Why should you know anything about him?'

'No, dear, of course not. At least, I mean, well, it would be rather nice, wouldn't it, if we did?'

'You'll have every chance of doing so in future,' said Iris, 'because I'm going to marry him.'

'Oh, Iris!' It was halfway between a wail and a bleat. 'You

mustn't do anything rash – I mean nothing can be settled at present.'

'It *is* settled, Aunt Lucilla.'

'No, dear, one can't talk about things like marriage when the funeral hasn't even taken place yet. It wouldn't be decent. And this dreadful inquest and everything. And really, Iris, I don't think dear George would have approved. He didn't like this Mr Browne.'

'No,' said Iris, 'George wouldn't have liked it and he didn't like Anthony, but that doesn't make any difference. It's my life, not George's – and anyway George is dead . . .'

Mrs Drake gave another wail.

'Iris, Iris. What has come over you? Really that was a most unfeeling thing to say.'

'I'm sorry, Aunt Lucilla.' The girl spoke wearily. 'I know it must have sounded like that but I didn't mean it that way. I only meant that George is at peace somewhere and hasn't got to worry about me and my future any more. I must decide things for myself.'

'Nonsense, dear, nothing can be decided at a time like this – it would be most unfitting. The question simply doesn't arise.'

Iris gave a sudden short laugh.

'But it has arisen. Anthony asked me to marry him before we left Little Priors. He wanted me to come up to London and marry him the next day without telling anyone. I wish now that I had.'

'Surely that was a very curious request,' said Colonel Race gently.

She turned defiant eyes to him.

'No, it wasn't. It would have saved a lot of fuss. Why couldn't I trust him? He asked me to trust him and I didn't. Anyway, I'll marry him now as soon as he likes.'

Lucilla burst out in a stream of incoherent protest. Her plump cheeks quivered and her eyes filled.

Colonel Race took rapid charge of the situation.

'Miss Marle, might I have a word with you before I go? On a strictly business matter?'

Rather startled, the girl murmured 'Yes,' and found herself moving to the door. As she passed through, Race took a couple of strides back to Mrs Drake.

'Don't upset yourself, Mrs Drake. Least said, you know, soonest mended. We'll see what we can do.'

Leaving her slightly comforted he followed Iris who led him across the hall and into a small room giving out on the back of the house where a melancholy plane-tree was shedding its last leaves.

Race spoke in a business-like tone.

'All I had to say, Miss Marle, was that Chief Inspector Kemp is a personal friend of mine, and that I am sure you will find him most helpful and kindly. His duty is an unpleasant one, but I'm sure he will do it with the utmost consideration possible.'

She looked at him for a moment or two without speaking, then she said abruptly:

'Why didn't you come and join us last night as George expected you to do?'

He shook his head.

'George didn't expect me.'

'But he said he did.'

'He may have said so, but it wasn't true. George knew perfectly well that I wasn't coming.'

She said: 'But that empty chair . . . Who was it for?'

'Not for me.'

Her eyes half-closed and her face went very white. She whispered:

'It was for Rosemary . . . I see . . . It was for Rosemary . . .'

He thought she was going to fall. He came quickly to her and steadied her, then forced her to sit down.

'Take it easy . . .'

She said in a low breathless voice:

'I'm all right . . . But I don't know what to do . . . I don't know what to do.'

'Can I help you?'

She raised her eyes to his face. They were wistful and sombre.

Then she said: 'I must get things clear. I must get them' – she made a groping gesture with her hands – 'in sequence. First of all, George believed Rosemary didn't kill herself – but was killed. He believed that because of those letters. Colonel Race, who wrote those letters?'

'I don't know. Nobody knows. Have you yourself any idea?'

'I simply can't imagine. Anyway, George believed what they

said, and he arranged this party last night, and he had an empty chair and it was All Souls' Day . . . that's the Day of the Dead – and it was a day when Rosemary's spirit could have come back and – and told him the truth.'

'You mustn't be too imaginative.'

'But I've felt her myself – felt her quite near sometimes – I'm her sister – and I think she's trying to tell me something.'

'Take it easy, Iris.'

'I *must* talk about it. George drank Rosemary's health and he – died. Perhaps – she came and took him.'

'The spirits of the dead don't put potassium cyanide in a champagne glass, my dear.'

The words seemed to restore her balance. She said in a more normal tone:

'But it's so incredible. George was killed – yes, *killed*. That's what the police think and it must be true. Because there isn't any other alternative. But it doesn't make sense.'

'Don't you think it does? If Rosemary was killed, and George was beginning to suspect by whom –'

She interrupted him.

'Yes, but Rosemary *wasn't* killed. That's why it doesn't make sense. George believed those stupid letters partly because depression after influenza isn't a very convincing reason for killing yourself. But Rosemary *had* a reason. Look, I'll show you.'

She ran out of the room and returned a few moments later with a folded letter in her hand. She thrust it on him.

'Read it. See for yourself.'

He unfolded the slightly crumpled sheet.

'*Leopard darling . . .*'

He read it twice before handing it back.

The girl said eagerly:

'You see? She was unhappy – broken-hearted. She didn't want to go on living.'

'Do you know to whom that letter was written?'

Iris nodded.

'Stephen Farraday. It wasn't Anthony. She was in love with

Stephen and he was cruel to her. So she took the stuff with her to the restaurant and drank it there where he could see her die. Perhaps she hoped he'd be sorry then.'

Race nodded thoughtfully, but said nothing. After a moment or two he said:

'When did you find this?'

'About six months ago. It was in the pocket of an old dressing-gown.'

'You didn't show it to George?'

Iris cried passionately:

'How could I? How could I? Rosemary was my sister. How could I give her away to George? He was so sure that she loved him. How could I show him this after she was dead? He'd got it all wrong, but I couldn't tell *him* so. But what I want to know is, what am I to do *now*? I've shown it to you because you were George's friend. Has Inspector Kemp got to see it?'

'Yes. Kemp must have it. It's evidence, you see.'

'But then they'll – they might read it out in court?'

'Not necessarily. That doesn't follow. It's George's death that is being investigated. Nothing will be made public that is not strictly relevant. You had better let me take this now.'

'Very well.'

She went with him to the front door. As he opened it she said abruptly:

'It does show, doesn't it, that Rosemary's death *was* suicide?'

Race said:

'It certainly shows that she had a motive for taking her own life.'

She gave a deep sigh. He went down the steps. Glancing back once, he saw her standing framed in the open doorway, watching him walk away across the square.

CHAPTER 7

Mary Rees-Talbot greeted Colonel Race with a positive shriek of unbelief.

'My dear, I haven't seen you since you disappeared so mysteriously from Allahabad that time. And why are you here now? It isn't to see me, I'm quite sure. You never pay social calls. Come on now, own up, you needn't be diplomatic about it.'

'Diplomatic methods would be a waste of time with you, Mary. I always have appreciated your X-ray mind.'

'Cut the cackle and come to the horses, my pet.'

Race smiled.

'Is the maid who let me in Betty Archdale?' he inquired.

'So that's it! Now don't tell me that the girl, a pure Cockney if ever there was one, is a well-known European spy because I simply don't believe it.'

'No, no, nothing of the kind.'

'And don't tell me she's one of our counter-espionage either, because I don't believe that.'

'Quite right. The girl is simply a parlourmaid.'

'And since when have you been interested in simple parlourmaids – not that Betty is simple – an artful dodger is more like it.'

'I think,' said Colonel Race, 'that she might be able to tell me something.'

'If you asked her nicely? I shouldn't be surprised if you're right. She has the close-to-the-door-when-there's-anything-interesting-going-on technique very highly developed. What does M. do?'

'M. very kindly offers me a drink and rings for Betty and orders it.'

'And when Betty brings it?'

'By then M. has very kindly gone away.'

'To do some listening outside the door herself?'

'If she likes.'

'And after that I shall be bursting with Inside Information about the latest European crisis?'

'I'm afraid not. There is no political situation involved in this.'

'What a disappointment! All right. I'll play!'

Mrs Rees-Talbot, who was a lively near-brunette of forty-nine, rang the bell and directed her good-looking parlourmaid to bring Colonel Race a whisky and soda.

When Betty Archdale returned, with a salver and the drink upon it, Mrs Rees-Talbot, was standing by the far door into her own sitting-room.

'Colonel Race has some questions to ask you,' she said and went out.

Betty turned her impudent eyes on the tall grey-haired soldier with some alarm in their depths. He took the glass from the tray and smiled.

'Seen the papers today?' he asked.

'Yes, sir.' Betty eyed him warily.

'Did you see that Mr George Barton died last night at the Luxembourg Restaurant?'

'Oh, yes, sir.' Betty's eyes sparkled with the pleasure of public disaster. 'Wasn't it dreadful?'

'You were in service there, weren't you?'

'Yes, sir. I left last winter, soon after Mrs Barton died.'

'She died at the Luxembourg, too.'

Betty nodded. 'Sort of funny, that, isn't it, sir?'

Race did not think it funny, but he knew what the words were intended to convey. He said gravely:

'I see you've got brains. You can put two and two together.'

Betty clasped her hands and cast discretion to the winds.

'Was he done in, too? The papers didn't say exactly.'

'Why do you say "too"? Mrs Barton's death was brought in by the coroner's jury as suicide.'

She gave him a quick look out of the corner of her eye. Ever so old, she thought, but he's nice looking. That quiet kind. A real gentleman. Sort of gentleman who'd have given you a gold sovereign when he was young. Funny, I don't even know what a sovereign looks like! What's he after, exactly?

She said demurely: 'Yes, sir.'

'But perhaps you never thought it *was* suicide?'

'Well, no, sir. I didn't – not really.'

'That's very interesting – very interesting indeed. Why didn't you think so?'

She hesitated, her fingers began pleating her apron.

So nicely he said that, so gravely. Made you feel important and as though you wanted to help him. And anyway she *had* been smart over Rosemary Barton's death. Never been taken in, she hadn't!

'She was done in, sir, wasn't she?'

'It seems possible that it may be so. But how did you come to think so?'

'Well,' Betty hesitated. 'It was something I heard one day.'

'Yes?'

His tone was quietly encouraging.

'The door wasn't shut or anything. I mean I'd never go and listen at a door. I don't like that sort of thing,' said Betty virtuously. 'But I was going through the hall to the dining-room and carrying the silver on a tray and they were speaking quite loud. Saying something she was – Mrs Barton I mean – about Anthony Browne not being his name. And then he got really nasty, Mr Browne did. I wouldn't have thought he had it in him – so nice-looking and so pleasant spoken as he was as a rule. Said something about carving up her face – ooh! and then he said if she didn't do what he told her he'd bump her off. Just like that! I didn't hear any more because Miss Iris was coming down the stairs, and of course I didn't think very much of it at the time, but after there was all the fuss about her committing suicide at that party and I heard he'd been there at the time – well, it gave me shivers all down my back – it did indeed!'

'But you didn't say anything?'

The girl shook her head.

'I didn't want to get mixed up with the police – and anyway I didn't know anything – not really. And perhaps if I had said anything I'd have been bumped off too. Or taken for a ride as they call it.'

'I see.' Race paused a moment and then said in his gentlest voice: 'So you just wrote an anonymous letter to Mr George Barton?'

She stared at him. He detected no uneasy guilt – nothing but pure astonishment.

'Me? Write to Mr Barton? Never.'

'Now don't be afraid to tell about it. It was really a very good idea. It warned him without your having to give yourself away. It was very clever of you.'

'But I didn't, sir. I never thought of such a thing. You mean write to Mr Barton and say that his wife had been done in? Why, the idea never came into my head!'

She was so earnest in her denial that, in spite of himself, Race was shaken. But it all fitted in so well – it could all be explained so naturally if only the girl had written the letters. But she persisted in her denials, not vehemently or uneasily, but soberly and without undue protestation. He found himself reluctantly believing her.

He shifted his ground.

'Whom did you tell about this?'

She shook her head.

'I didn't tell anyone. I'll tell you honest, sir, I was scared. I thought I'd better keep my mouth shut. I tried to forget it. I only brought it up once – that was when I gave Mrs Drake my notice – fussing terribly she'd been, more than a girl could stand, and now wanting me to go and bury myself in the dead of the country and not even a bus route! And then she turned nasty about my reference, saying I broke things, and I said sarcastic-like that at any rate I'd find a place where people didn't get bumped off – and I felt scared when I'd said it, but she didn't pay any real attention. Perhaps I ought to have spoken out at the time, but I couldn't really tell. I mean the whole thing might have been a joke. People do say all sorts of things, and Mr Browne was ever so nice really, and quite a one for joking, so I couldn't tell, sir, could I?'

Race agreed that she couldn't. Then he said:

'Mrs Barton spoke of Browne not being his real name. Did she mention what his real name was?'

'Yes, she did. Because he said, "Forget about Tony" – now what was it? Tony something . . . Reminded me of the cherry jam cook had been making.'

'Tony Cheriton? Cherable.'

She shook her head.

'More of a fancy name than that. Began with an M. And sounded foreign.'

'Don't worry. It will come back to you, perhaps. If so, let me know. Here is my card with my address. If you remember the name write to me at that address.'

He handed her the card and a treasury note.

'I will, sir, thank you, sir.'

A gentleman, she thought, as she ran downstairs. A pound note, not ten shillings. It must have been nice when there were gold sovereigns . . .

Mary Rees-Talbot came back into the room.

'Well, successful?'

'Yes, but there's still one snag to surmount. Can your ingenuity help me? Can you think of a name that would remind you of cherry jam?'

'What an extraordinary proposition.'

'Think Mary. I'm not a domestic man. Concentrate on jam making, cherry jam in particular.'

'One doesn't often make cherry jam.'

'Why not?'

'Well, it's inclined to go sugary – unless you use cooking cherries, Morello cherries.'

Race gave an exclamation.

'That's it – I bet that's it. Goodbye, Mary, I'm endlessly grateful. Do you mind if I ring that bell so that the girl comes and shows me out?'

Mrs Rees-Talbot called after him as he hurried out of the room:

'Of all the ungrateful wretches! Aren't you going to tell me what it's all about?'

He called back:

'I'll come and tell you the whole story later.'

'Sez you,' murmured Mrs Rees-Talbot.

Downstairs, Betty waited with Race's hat and stick.

He thanked her and passed out. On the doorstep he paused.

'By the way,' he said, 'was the name Morelli?'

Betty's face lighted up.

'Quite right, sir. That was it. Tony Morelli that's the name he told her to forget. And he said he'd been in prison, too.'

Race walked down the steps smiling.

From the nearest call-box he put through a call to Kemp.

Their interchange was brief but satisfactory. Kemp said:

'I'll send off a cable at once. We ought to hear by return. I must say it will be a great relief if you're right.'

'I think I'm right. The sequence is pretty clear.'

CHAPTER 8

Chief Inspector Kemp was not in a very good humour.

For the last half-hour he had been interviewing a frightened white rabbit of sixteen who, by virtue of his uncle Charles's great position, was aspiring to be a waiter of the class required by the Luxembourg. In the meantime, he was one of six harried underlings who ran about with aprons round their waists to distinguish them from the superior article, and whose duty it was to bear the blame for everything, fetch and carry, provide rolls and pats of butter and be occasionally and unceasingly hissed at in French, Italian and occasionally English. Charles, as befitted a great man, so far from showing favour to a blood relation, hissed, cursed and swore at him even more than he did at the others. Nevertheless Pierre aspired in his heart to be no less than the head waiter of a *chic* restaurant himself one day in the far future.

At the moment, however, his career had received a check, and he gathered that he was suspected of no less than murder.

Kemp turned the lad inside out and disgustedly convinced himself that the boy had done no less and no more than what he had said – namely, picked up a lady's bag from the floor and replaced it by her plate.

'It is as I am hurrying with sauce to M. Robert and already he is impatient, and the young lady sweeps her bag off the table as she goes to dance, so I pick it up and put it on the table, and then I hurry on, for already M. Robert he is making the signs frantically to me. That is all, monsieur.'

And that *was* all. Kemp disgustedly let him go, feeling strongly tempted to add, 'But don't let me catch you doing that sort of thing again.'

Sergeant Pollock made a distraction by announcing that they had telephoned up to say that a young lady was asking for him or rather for the officer in charge of the Luxembourg case.

'Who is she?'

'Her name is Miss Chloe West.'

'Let's have her up,' said Kemp resignedly. 'I can give her ten minutes. Mr Farraday's due after that. Oh, well, won't do any harm to keep *him* waiting a few minutes. Makes them jittery, that does.'

When Miss Chloe West walked into the room, Kemp was at once assailed by the impression that he recognized her. But a minute later he abandoned that impression. No, he had never seen this girl before, he was sure of that. Nevertheless the vague haunting sense of familiarity remained to plague him.

Miss West was about twenty-five, tall, brown-haired and very pretty. Her voice was rather conscious of its diction and she seemed decidedly nervous.

'Well, Miss West, what can I do for you?'

Kemp spoke briskly.

'I read in the paper about the Luxembourg – the man who died there.'

'Mr George Barton? Yes? Did you know him?'

'Well, no, not exactly. I mean I didn't really *know* him.'

Kemp looked at her carefully and discarded his first deduction.

Chloe West was looking extremely refined and virtuous – severely so. He said pleasantly:

'Can I have your exact name and address first, please, so that we know where we are?'

'Chloe Elizabeth West. 15 Merryvale Court, Maida Vale. I'm an actress.'

Kemp looked at her again out of the corner of his eye, and decided that that was what she really was. Repertory, he fancied – in spite of her looks she was the earnest kind.

'Yes, Miss West?'

'When I read about Mr Barton's death and that the – the police were inquiring into it, I thought perhaps I ought to come and tell you something. I spoke to my friend about it and she seemed to think so. I don't suppose it's really anything to do with it, but –'

Miss West paused.

'We'll be the judge of that,' said Kemp pleasantly. 'Just tell me about it.'

'I'm not acting just at the moment,' explained Miss West.

Inspector Kemp nearly said 'Resting' to show that he knew the proper terms, but restrained himself.

'But my name is down at the agencies and my picture in *Spotlight* . . . That, I understand, is where Mr Barton saw it. He got into touch with me and explained what he wanted me to do.'

'Yes?'

'He told me he was having a dinner party at the Luxembourg and that he wanted to spring a surprise on his guests. He showed me a photograph and told me that he wanted me to make up as the original. I was very much the same colouring, he said.'

Illumination flashed across Kemp's mind. The photograph of Rosemary he had seen on the desk in George's room in Elvaston Square. That was who the girl reminded him of. She *was* like Rosemary Barton – not perhaps startlingly so – but the general type and cast of features was the same.

'He also brought me a dress to wear – I've brought it with me. A greyish green silk. I was to do my hair like the photograph (it was a coloured one) and accentuate the resemblance with make-up. Then I was to come to the Luxembourg and go into the restaurant during the first cabaret show and sit down at Mr Barton's table where there would be a vacant place. He took me to lunch there and showed me where the table would be.'

'And why didn't you keep the appointment, Miss West?'

'Because about eight o'clock that night – someone – Mr Barton – rang up and said the whole thing had been put off. He said he'd let me know next day when it was coming off. Then, the next morning, I saw his death in the papers.'

'And very sensibly you came along to us,' said Kemp pleasantly. 'Well, thank you very much, Miss West. You've cleared up one mystery – the mystery of the vacant place. By the way, you said just now – "someone" – and then, "Mr Barton". Why is that?'

'Because at first I didn't think it *was* Mr Barton. His voice sounded different.'

'It was a man's voice?'

'Oh, yes, I think so – at least – it was rather husky as though he had a cold.'

'And that's all he said?'

'That's all.'

Kemp questioned her a little longer, but got no further.

When she had gone, he said to the sergeant:

'So that was George Barton's famous "plan". I see now why they all said he stared at the empty chair after the cabaret and looked queer and absent-minded. His precious plan had gone wrong.'

'You don't think it was he who put her off?'

'Not on your life. And I'm not so sure it was a man's voice, either. Huskiness is a good disguise through the telephone. Oh, well, we're getting on. Send in Mr Farraday if he's here.'

CHAPTER 9

I

Outwardly cool and unperturbed, Stephen Farraday had turned into Great Scotland Yard full of inner shrinking. An intolerable weight burdened his spirits. It had seemed that morning as though things were going so well. Why had Inspector Kemp asked for his presence here with such significance? What did he know or suspect? It *could* be only vague suspicion. The thing to do was to keep one's head and admit nothing.

He felt strangely bereft and lonely without Sandra. It was as though when the two faced a peril together it lost half its terrors. Together they had strength, courage, power. Alone, he was nothing, less than nothing. And Sandra, did she feel the same? Was she sitting now in Kidderminster House, silent, reserved, proud and inwardly feeling horribly vulnerable?

Inspector Kemp received him pleasantly but gravely. There was a uniformed man sitting at a table with a pencil and a pad of paper. Having asked Stephen to sit down, Kemp spoke in a strongly formal manner.

'I propose, Mr Farraday, to take a statement from you. That statement will be written down and you will be asked to read it over and sign it before you leave. At the same time it is my duty to tell you that you are at liberty to refuse to make such a statement and that you are entitled to have your solicitor present if you so desire.'

Stephen was taken aback but did not show it. He forced a wintry smile. 'That sounds very formidable, chief inspector.'

'We like everything to be clearly understood, Mr Farraday.'

'Anything I say may be used against me, is that it?'

'We don't use the word against. Anything you say will be liable to be used in evidence.'

Stephen said quietly:

'I understand, but I cannot imagine, inspector, why you should need any further statement from me? You heard all I had to say this morning.'

'That was a rather informal session – useful as a preliminary starting-off point. And also, Mr Farraday, there are certain facts which I imagined you would prefer to discuss with me here. Anything irrelevant to the case we try to be as discreet about as is compatible with the attainment of justice. I daresay you understand what I am driving at.'

'I'm afraid I don't.'

Chief Inspector Kemp sighed.

'Just this. You were on very intimate terms with the late Mrs Rosemary Barton –'

Stephen interrupted him.

'Who says so?'

Kemp leaned forward and took a typewritten document from his desk.

'This is a copy of a letter found amongst the late Mrs Barton's belongings. The original is filed here and was handed to us by Miss Iris Marle, who recognizes the writing as that of her sister.'

Stephen read:

'*Leopard darling –*'

A wave of sickness passed over him. Rosemary's voice . . . speaking – pleading . . . Would the past never die – never consent to be buried?

He pulled himself together and looked at Kemp.

'You may be correct in thinking Mrs Barton wrote this letter – but there is nothing to indicate that it was written to me.'

'Do you deny that you paid the rent of 21 Malland Mansions, Earl's Court?'

So they knew! He wondered if they had known all the time. He shrugged his shoulders.

'You seem very well informed. May I ask why my private affairs should be dragged into the limelight?'

'They will not unless they prove to be relevant to the death of George Barton.'

'I see. You are suggesting that I first made love to his wife, and then murdered him.'

'Come, Mr Farraday, I'll be frank with you. You and Mrs Barton were very close friends – you parted by your wish, not the lady's. She was proposing, as this letter shows, to make trouble. Very conveniently, she died.'

'She committed suicide. I daresay I may have been partly to blame. I may reproach myself, but it is no concern of the law's.'

'It may have been suicide – it may not. George Barton thought not. He started to investigate – and he died. The sequence is rather suggestive.'

'I do not see why you should – well, pitch on me.'

'You admit that Mrs Barton's death came at a very convenient moment for you? A scandal, Mr Farraday, would have been highly prejudicial to your career.'

'There would have been no scandal. Mrs Barton would have seen reason.'

'I wonder! Did your wife know about this affair, Mr Farraday?'

'Certainly not.'

'You are quite sure of that statement?'

'Yes, I am. My wife has no idea that there was anything but friendship between myself and Mrs Barton. I hope she will never learn otherwise.'

'Is your wife a jealous woman, Mr Farraday?'

'Not at all. She has never displayed the least jealousy where I am concerned. She is far too sensible.'

The inspector did not comment on that. Instead he said:

'Have you at any time in the past year had cyanide in your possession, Mr Farraday?'

'No.'

'But you keep a supply of cyanide at your country property?'

'The gardener may. I know nothing about it.'

'You have never purchased any yourself at a chemist's or for photography?'

'I know nothing of photography, and I repeat that I have never purchased cyanide.'

Kemp pressed him a little further before he finally let him go.

To his subordinate he said thoughtfully, 'He was very quick denying that his wife knew about his affair with the Barton woman. Why was that, I wonder?'

'Daresay he's in a funk in case she should get to hear of it, sir.'

'That may be, but I should have thought he'd got the brains to see that if his wife was in ignorance, and would cut up rough, that gives him an additional motive for wanting to silence Rosemary Barton. To save his skin his line ought to have been that his wife more or less knew about the affair but was content to ignore it.'

'I daresay he hadn't thought of that, sir.'

Kemp shook his head. Stephen Farraday was not a fool. He had a clear and astute brain. And he had been passionately keen to impress on the inspector that Sandra knew nothing.

'Well,' said Kemp, 'Colonel Race seems pleased with the line he's dug up and if he's right, the Farradays are out – both of them. I shall be glad if they are. I like this chap. And personally I don't think he's a murderer.'

II

Opening the door of their sitting-room, Stephen said, 'Sandra?'

She came to him out of the darkness, suddenly holding him, her hands on his shoulders.

'Stephen?'

'Why are you all in the dark?'

'I couldn't bear the light. Tell me.'

He said:

'They know.'

'About Rosemary?'

'Yes.'

'And what do they think?'

'They see, of course, that I had a motive. . . . Oh, my darling, see what I've dragged you into. It's all my fault. If only I'd cut loose after Rosemary's death – gone away – left you free – so that at any rate *you* shouldn't be mixed up in all this horrible business.'

'No, not that . . . Never leave me . . . never leave me.'

She clung to him – she was crying, the tears coursing down her cheeks. He felt her shudder.

'You're my life, Stephen, all my life – never leave me . . .'

'Do you care so much, Sandra? I never knew . . .'

'I didn't want you to know. But now –'

'Yes, now . . . We're in this together, Sandra . . . we'll face it together . . . whatever comes, together!'

Strength came to them as they stood there, clasped together in the darkness.

Sandra said with determination:

'This shall *not* wreck our lives! It shall not. It shall not!'

CHAPTER 10

Anthony Browne looked at the card the little page was holding out to him.

He frowned, then shrugged his shoulders. He said to the boy: 'All right, show him up.'

When Colonel Race came in, Anthony was standing by the window with the bright sun striking obliquely over his shoulder.

He saw a tall soldierly man with a lined bronze face and iron-grey hair – a man whom he had seen before, but not for some years, and a man whom he knew a great deal about.

Race saw a dark graceful figure and the outline of a well-shaped head. A pleasant indolent voice said:

'Colonel Race? You were a friend of George Barton's, I know. He talked about you on that last evening. Have a cigarette.'

'Thank you, I will.'

Anthony said as he held a match:

'You were the unexpected guest that night who did not turn up – just as well for you.'

'You are wrong there. That empty place was not for me.'

Anthony's eyebrows went up.

'Really? Barton said –'

Race cut in.

'George Barton may have said so. His plans were quite different. That chair, Mr Browne, was intended to be occupied when the lights went down by an actress called Chloe West.'

Anthony stared.

'Chloe West? Never heard of her. Who is she?'

'A young actress not very well known but who possesses a certain superficial resemblance to Rosemary Barton.'

Anthony whistled.

'I begin to see.'

'She had been given a photograph of Rosemary so that she could copy the style of hairdressing and she also had the dress which Rosemary wore the night she died.'

'So that was George's plan? Up go the lights – Hey Presto, gasps of supernatural dread! *Rosemary has come back.* The guilty party gasps out: "It's true – it's true – I dunnit."' He paused and added: 'Rotten – even for an ass like poor old George.'

'I'm not sure I understand you.'

Anthony grinned.

'Oh, come now, sir – a hardened criminal isn't going to behave like a hysterical schoolgirl. If somebody poisoned Rosemary Barton in cold blood, and was preparing to administer the same fatal dose of cyanide to George Barton, that person had a certain amount of nerve. It would take more than an actress dressed up as Rosemary to make him or her spill the beans.'

'Macbeth, remember, a decidedly hardened criminal, went to pieces when he saw the ghost of Banquo at the feast.'

'Ah, but what Macbeth saw really *was* a ghost! It wasn't a ham actor wearing Banquo's duds! I'm prepared to admit that a real ghost might bring its own atmosphere from another world. In fact I am willing to admit that I believe in ghosts – have believed in them for the last six months – one ghost in particular.'

'Really – and whose ghost is that?'

'Rosemary Barton's. You can laugh if you like. I've not seen her – but I've felt her presence. For some reason or other Rosemary, poor soul, can't stay dead.'

'I could suggest a reason.'

'Because she was murdered?'

'To put it in another idiom, because she was bumped off. *How about that, Mr Tony Morelli?*'

There was a silence. Anthony sat down, chucked his cigarette into the grate and lighted another one.

Then he said:

'How did you find out?'

'You admit that you are Tony Morelli?'

'I shouldn't dream of wasting time by denying it. You've obviously cabled to America and got all the dope.'

'And you admit that when Rosemary Barton discovered your identity you threatened to bump her off unless she held her tongue.'

'I did everything I could think of to scare her into holding her tongue,' agreed Tony pleasantly.

A strange feeling stole over Colonel Race. This interview was not going as it should. He stared at the figure in front of him lounging back in its chair – and an odd sense of familiarity came to him.

'Shall I recapitulate what I know about you, Morelli?'

'It might be amusing.'

'You were convicted in the States of attempted sabotage in the Ericsen aeroplane works and were sentenced to a term of imprisonment. After serving your sentence, you came out and the authorities lost sight of you. You were next heard of in London staying at Claridge's and calling yourself Anthony Browne. There you scraped acquaintance with Lord Dewsbury and through him you met certain other prominent armaments manufacturers. You stayed in Lord Dewsbury's house and by means of your position as his guest you were shown things which you ought never to have seen! It is curious coincidence, Morelli, that a trail of unaccountable accidents and some very near escapes from disaster on a large scale followed very closely after your visits to various important works and factories.'

'Coincidences,' said Anthony, 'are certainly extraordinary things.'

'Finally, after another lapse of time, you reappeared in London and renewed your acquaintance with Iris Marle, making excuses not to visit her home, so that her family should not realize how intimate you were becoming. Finally you tried to induce her to marry you secretly.'

'You know,' said Anthony, 'it's really extraordinary the way you have found out all these things – I don't mean the armaments business – I mean my threats to Rosemary, and the tender nothings I whispered to Iris. Surely those don't come within the province of M.I.5?'

Race looked sharply at him.

'You've got a good deal to explain, Morelli.'

'Not at all. Granted your facts are all correct, what of them? I've served my prison sentence. I've made some interesting friends. I've fallen in love with a very charming girl and am naturally impatient to marry her.'

'So impatient that you would prefer the wedding to take place before her family have the chance of finding out anything about your antecedents. Iris Marle is a very rich young woman.'

Anthony nodded his head agreeably.

'I know. When there's money, families are inclined to be abominably nosy. And Iris, you see, doesn't know anything about my murky past. Frankly, I'd rather she didn't.'

'I'm afraid she is going to know all about it.'

'A pity,' said Anthony.

'Possibly you don't realize –'

Anthony cut in with a laugh.

'Oh! I can dot the i's and cross the t's. Rosemary Barton knew my criminal past, so I killed her. George Barton was growing suspicious of me, so I killed him! Now I'm after Iris's money! It's all very agreeable and it hangs together nicely, but you haven't got a mite of proof.'

Race looked at him attentively for some minutes. Then he got up.

'Everything I have said is true,' he said. '*And it's all wrong.*'

Anthony watched him narrowly.

'What's wrong?'

'You're wrong.' Race walked slowly up and down the room. 'It hung together all right until I saw you – but now I've seen you, *it won't do. You're not a crook.* And if you're not a crook, you're one of *our* kind. I'm right, aren't I?'

Anthony looked at him in silence while a smile slowly broadened on his face. Then he hummed softly under his breath.

'"*For the Colonel's lady and Judy O'Grady are sisters under the skin.*" Yes, funny how one knows one's own kind. That's why I've tried to avoid meeting you. I was afraid you'd spot me for what I am. It was important then that nobody should know – important up to yesterday. Now, thank goodness, the balloon's gone up! We've swept our gang of international saboteurs into the net. I've been working on this assignment for three years. Frequenting certain meetings, agitating among workmen, getting myself the right reputation. Finally it was fixed that I pulled an important job and got sentenced. The business had to be genuine if I was to establish my *bona fides*.

'When I came out, things began to move. Little by little I got further into the centre of things – a great international net run from Central Europe. It was as *their* agent I came to London and went to Claridge's. I had orders to get on friendly terms with Lord Dewsbury – that was my lay, the social butterfly! I got to know Rosemary Barton in my character of attractive young man about town. Suddenly, to my horror, I found that she knew I had been in prison in America as Tony Morelli. I was terrified for *her*! The people I was working with would have had her killed without a moment's hesitation if they had thought she knew that. I did my best to scare her into keeping her mouth shut, but I wasn't very hopeful. Rosemary was born to be indiscreet. I thought the best thing I could do was to sheer off – and then I saw Iris coming down a staircase, and I swore that after my job was done I would come back and marry her.

'When the active part of my work was over, I turned up again and got into touch with Iris, but I kept aloof from the house and her people for I knew they'd want to make inquiries about me and I had to keep under cover for a bit longer. But I got worried about her. She looked ill and afraid – and George Barton seemed to be behaving in a very odd fashion. I urged her to come away and marry me. Well, she refused. Perhaps she was right. And then I was roped in for this party. It was as we sat down to dinner that George mentioned *you* were to be there. I said rather quickly that I'd met a man I knew and might have to leave early. Actually I *had* seen a fellow I knew in America – Monkey Coleman – though he didn't remember me – but I really wanted to avoid meeting you. I was still on my job.

'You know what happened next – George died. I had nothing to do with his death or with Rosemary's. I don't know now who did kill them.'

'Not even an idea?'

'It must have been either the waiter or one of the five people round the table. I don't think it was the waiter. It wasn't me and it wasn't Iris. It could have been Sandra Farraday or it could have been Stephen Farraday, or it could have been both of them together. But the best bet, in my opinion, is Ruth Lessing.'

'Have you anything to support that belief?'

'No. She seems to me the most likely person – but I don't see in the least how she did it! In both tragedies she was so placed at the table that it would be practically impossible for her to tamper with the champagne glass – and the more I think over what happened the other night, the more it seems to me impossible that George could have been poisoned at all – and yet he was!' Anthony paused. 'And there's another thing that gets me – have you found out who wrote those anonymous letters that started him on the track?'

Race shook his head.

'No. I thought I had – but I was wrong.'

'Because the interesting thing is that it means that there is *someone, somewhere*, who knows that Rosemary was murdered, so that, unless you're careful – that person will be murdered next!'

CHAPTER 11

From information received over the telephone Anthony knew that Lucilla Drake was going out at five o'clock to drink a cup of tea with a dear old friend. Allowing for possible contingencies (returing for a purse, determination after all to take an umbrella just in case, and last-minute chats on the doorstep) Anthony timed his own arrival at Elvaston Square at precisely twenty-five minutes past five. It was Iris he wanted to see, not her aunt. And by all accounts once shown into Lucilla's presence, he would have had very little chance of uninterrupted conversation with his lady.

He was told by the parlourmaid (a girl lacking the impudent polish of Betty Archdale) that Miss Iris had just come in and was in the study.

Anthony said with a smile, 'Don't bother. I'll find my way,' and went past her and along to the study door.

Iris spun round at his entrance with a nervous start.

'Oh, it's you.'

He came over to her swiftly.

'What's the matter, darling?'

'Nothing.' She paused, then said quickly, 'Nothing. Only I was nearly run over. Oh, my own fault, I expect I was thinking so hard and mooning across the road without looking, and the car came tearing round a corner and just missed me.'

He gave her a gentle little shake.

'You mustn't do that sort of thing, Iris. I'm worried about you – oh! not about your miraculous escape from under the wheels of a car, but about the reason that lets you moon about in the midst of traffic. What is it, darling? There's something special, isn't there?'

She nodded. Her eyes, raised mournfully to his, were large and dark with fear. He recognized their message even before she said very low and quick:

'*I'm afraid.*'

Anthony recovered his calm smiling poise. He sat down beside Iris on a wide settee.

'Come on,' he said, 'let's have it.'

'I don't think I want to tell you, Anthony.'

'Now then, funny, don't be like the heroines of third-rate thrillers who start in the very first chapter by having something they can't possibly tell for no real reason except to gum up the hero and make the book spin itself out for another fifty thousand words.'

She gave a faint pale smile.

'I want to tell you, Anthony, but I don't know what you'd think – I don't know if you'd believe –'

Anthony raised a hand and began to check off the fingers.

'One, an illegitimate baby. Two, a blackmailing lover. Three –'

She interrupted him indignantly:

'Of course not. Nothing of *that* kind.'

'You relieve my mind,' said Anthony. 'Come on, little idiot.'
Iris's face clouded over again.

'It's nothing to laugh at. It's – it's about the other night.'

'Yes?' His voice sharpened.

Iris said:

'You were at the inquest this morning – you heard –'
She paused.

'Very little,' said Anthony. 'The police surgeon being technical about cyanides generally and the effect of potassium cyanide on George, and the police evidence as given by that first inspector, not Kemp, the one with the smart moustache who arrived first at the Luxembourg and took charge. Identification of the body by George's chief clerk. The inquest was then adjourned for a week by a properly docile coroner.'

'It's the inspector I mean,' said Iris. 'He described finding a small paper packet under the table containing traces of potassium cyanide.'

Anthony looked interested.

'Yes. Obviously whoever slipped that stuff into George's glass just dropped the paper that had contained it under the table. Simplest thing to do. Couldn't risk having it found on him – or her.'

To his surprise Iris began to tremble violently.

'Oh, no, Anthony. Oh, no, it wasn't like that.'

'What do you mean, darling? What do you know about it?'

Iris said, '*I* dropped that packet under the table.'

He turned astonished eyes upon her.

'Listen, Anthony. You remember how George drank off that champagne and then it happened?'

He nodded.

'It was awful – like a bad dream. Coming just when everything had seemed to be all right. I mean that, after the cabaret, when the lights went up – I felt so relieved. Because it was *then*, you know, that we found Rosemary dead – and somehow, I don't know why, I felt I'd see it all happen again . . . I felt she was there, dead, at the table . . .'

'Darling . . .'

'Oh, I know. It was just nerves. But anyway, there we were, and there was nothing awful and suddenly it seemed the whole thing was really done with at last and one could – I don't know how to explain it – *begin again*. And so I danced with George and really felt I was enjoying myself at last, and we came back to the table. And then George suddenly talked about Rosemary and asked us to drink to her memory and then *he* died and all the nightmare had come back.

'I just felt paralysed I think. I stood there, shaking. You came round to look at him, and I moved back a little, and the waiters came and someone asked for a doctor. And all the time I was standing there frozen. Then suddenly a big lump came in my throat and tears began to run down my cheeks and I jerked open my bag to get my handkerchief. I just fumbled in it, not seeing properly, and got out my handkerchief, but there was something caught up inside the handkerchief – a folded stiff bit of white paper, like the kind you get powders in from the chemist. Only, you see, Anthony, *it hadn't been in my bag when I started from home.* I hadn't had anything like that! I'd put the things in myself when the bag was quite empty – a powder compact, a lip-stick, my handkerchief, my evening comb in its case and a shilling and a couple of sixpences. *Somebody had put that packet in my bag* – they must have done. And I remembered how they'd found a packet like that in Rosemary's bag after she died and how it had had cyanide in it. I was frightened, Anthony, I was horribly frightened. My fingers went limp and the packet fluttered down from my handkerchief under the table. I let it go. And I didn't say anything. I was too frightened. Somebody meant it to look as though *I* had killed George, and I *didn't*.'

Anthony gave vent to a long and prolonged whistle.

'And nobody saw you?' he said.

Iris hesitated.

'I'm not sure,' she said slowly. 'I believe Ruth noticed. But she was looking so dazed that I don't know whether she really *noticed* – or if she was just staring at me blankly.'

Anthony gave another whistle.

'This,' he remarked, 'is a pretty kettle of fish.'

Iris said:

'It's got worse and worse. I've been so afraid they'd find out.'

'Why weren't your fingerprints on it, I wonder? The first thing they'd do would be to fingerprint it.'

'I suppose it was because I was holding it through the handkerchief.'

Anthony nodded.

'Yes, you had luck there.'

'But who could have put it in my bag? I had my bag with me all the evening.'

'That's not so impossible as you think. When you went to dance after the cabaret, you left your bag on the table. Somebody may have tampered with it then. And there are the women. Could you get up and give me an imitation of just how a woman behaves in the ladies' cloakroom? It's the sort of thing I wouldn't know. Do you congregate and chat or do you drift off to different mirrors?'

Iris considered.

'We all went to the same table – a great long glass-topped one. And we put our bags down and looked at our faces, you know.'

'Actually I don't. Go on.'

'Ruth powdered her nose and Sandra patted her hair and pushed a hairpin in and I took off my fox cape and gave it to the woman and then I saw I'd got some dirt on my hand – a smear of mud and I went over to the washbasins.'

'Leaving your bag on the glass table?'

'Yes. And I washed my hands. Ruth was still fixing her face I think and Sandra went and gave up her cloak and then she went back to the glass and Ruth came and washed her hands and I went back to the table and just fixed my hair a little.'

'So either of those two could have put something in your bag without your seeing?'

'Yes, but I can't believe either Ruth or Sandra would do such a thing.'

'You think too highly of people. Sandra is the kind of Gothic creature who would have burned her enemies at the stake in the Middle Ages – and Ruth would make the most devastatingly practical poisoner that ever stepped this earth.'

'If it was Ruth why didn't she say she saw me drop it?'

'You have me there. If Ruth deliberately planted cyanide on you, she'd take jolly good care you didn't get rid of it. So it looks as though it wasn't Ruth. In fact the waiter is far and away the best bet. The waiter, the waiter! If only we had a strange waiter, a peculiar waiter, a waiter hired for that evening only. But instead we have Giuseppe and Pierre and they just don't fit . . .'

Iris sighed.

'I'm glad I've told you. No one will ever know now, will they? Only you and I?'

Anthony looked at her with a rather embarrassed expression.

'It's not going to be just like that, Iris. In fact you're coming with me now in a taxi to old man Kemp. We can't keep this under our hats.'

'Oh, no, Anthony. They'll think I killed George.'

They'll certainly think so if they find out later that you sat tight and said nothing about all this! Your explanation will then sound extremely thin. If you volunteer it now there's a likelihood of its being believed.'

'Please, Anthony.'

'Look here, Iris, you're in a tight place. But apart from anything else, there's such a thing as *truth*. You can't play safe and take care of your own skin when it's a question of justice.'

'Oh, Anthony, must you be so grand?'

'That,' said Anthony, 'was a very shrewd blow! But all the same we're going to Kemp! Now!'

Unwillingly she came with him out into the hall. Her coat was lying tossed on a chair and he took it and held it out for her to put on.

There was both mutiny and fear in her eyes, but Anthony showed no sign of relenting. He said:

'We'll pick up a taxi at the end of the Square.'

As they went towards the hall door the bell was pressed and they heard it ringing in the basement below.

Iris gave an exclamation.

'I forgot. It's Ruth. She was coming here when she left the office to settle about the funeral arrangements. It's to be the day after tomorrow. I thought we could settle things better while Aunt Lucilla was out. She does confuse things so.'

Anthony stepped forward and opened the door, forestalling the parlourmaid who came running up the stairs from below.

'It's all right, Evans,' said Iris, and the girl went down again.

Ruth was looking tired and rather dishevelled. She was carrying a large-sized attaché case.

'I'm sorry I'm late, but the tube was so terribly crowded tonight and then I had to wait for three buses and not a taxi in sight.'

It was, thought Anthony, unlike the efficient Ruth to apologize. Another sign that George's death had succeeded in shattering that almost inhuman efficiency.

Iris said:

'I can't come with you now, Anthony. Ruth and I must settle things.'

Anthony said firmly:

'I'm afraid this is more important . . . I'm awfully sorry, Miss Lessing, to drag Iris off like this, but it really *is* important.'

Ruth said quickly:

'That's quite all right, Mr Browne. I can arrange everything with Mrs Drake when she comes in.' She smiled faintly. 'I can really manage her quite well, you know.'

'I'm sure you could manage anyone, Miss Lessing,' said Anthony admiringly.

'Perhaps, Iris, if you can tell me any special points?'

'There aren't any. I suggested our arranging this together simply because Aunt Lucilla changes her mind about everything every two minutes, and I thought it would be rather hard on you. You've had so much to do. But I really don't care what sort of funeral it is! Aunt Lucilla *likes* funerals, but I hate them. You've got to bury people, but I hate making a fuss about it. It can't matter to the people themselves. They've got away from it all. The dead don't come back.'

Ruth did not answer, and Iris repeated with a strange defiant insistence: 'The dead don't come back!'

'Come on,' said Anthony, and pulled her out through the open door.

A cruising taxi was coming slowly along the Square. Anthony hailed it and helped Iris in.

'Tell me, beautiful,' he said, after he had directed the driver to go to Scotland Yard. 'Who exactly did you feel was there in the hall when you found it so necessary to affirm that the dead are dead? Was it George or Rosemary?'

'Nobody! Nobody at all! I just hate funerals, I tell you.'

Anthony sighed.

'Definitely,' he said. 'I must be psychic!'

CHAPTER 12

Three men sat at a small round marble-topped table.

Colonel Race and Chief Inspector Kemp were drinking cups of dark brown tea, rich in tannin. Anthony was drinking an English café's idea of a nice cup of coffee. It was not Anthony's idea, but he endured it for the sake of being admitted on equal terms to the other two men's conference. Chief Inspector Kemp, having painstakingly verified Anthony's credentials, had consented to recognize him as a colleague.

'If you ask me,' said the chief inspector, dropping several lumps of sugar into his black brew and stirring it, 'this case will never be brought to trial. We'll never get the evidence.'

'You think not?' asked Race.

Kemp shook his head and took an approving sip of his tea.

'The only hope was to get evidence concerning the actual purchasing or handling of cyanide by one of those five. I've drawn a blank everywhere. It'll be one of those cases where you *know* who did it, and can't ever prove it.'

'So you know who did it?' Anthony regarded him with interest.

'Well, I'm pretty certain in my own mind. Lady Alexandra Farraday.'

'So that's your bet,' said Race. 'Reasons?'

'You shall have 'em. I'd say she's the type that's madly jealous. And autocratic, too. Like that queen in history – Eleanor of Something, that followed the clue to Fair Rosamund's Bower and offered her the choice of a dagger or a cup of poison.'

'Only in this case,' said Anthony, 'she didn't offer Fair Rosemary any choice.'

Chief Inspector Kemp went on:

'Someone tips Mr Barton off. He becomes suspicious – and I should say his suspicions were pretty definite. He wouldn't have gone so far as actually buying a house in the country unless he wanted to keep an eye on the Farradays. He must have made it pretty plain to her – harping on this party and urging them to come to it. She's not the kind to Wait and See. Autocratic again, she finished him off! That, you say so far, is all theory and based on character. But I'll say that the *only* person who could have had any chance whatever of dropping something into Mr Barton's glass just before he drank would be the lady on his right.'

'And nobody saw her do it?' said Anthony.

'Quite. They might have – but they didn't. Say, if you like, she was pretty adroit.'

'A positive conjurer.'

Race coughed. He took out his pipe and began stuffing the bowl.

'Just one minor point. Granted Lady Alexandra is autocratic, jealous and passionately devoted to her husband, granted that she'd not stick at murder, do you think she is the type to slip incriminating evidence into a girl's handbag? A perfectly innocent girl, mind, who has never harmed her in any way? Is that in the Kidderminster tradition?'

Inspector Kemp squirmed uneasily in his seat and peered into his teacup.

'Women don't play cricket,' he said. 'If that's what you mean.'

'Actually, a lot of them do,' said Race, smiling. 'But I'm glad to see you look uncomfortable.'

Kemp escaped from his dilemma by turning to Anthony with an air of gracious patronage.

'By the way, Mr Browne (I'll still call you that, if you don't mind), I want to say that I'm very much obliged to you for the prompt way you brought Miss Marle along this evening to tell that story of hers.'

'I had to do it promptly,' said Anthony. 'If I'd waited I should probably not have brought her along at all.'

'She didn't want to come, of course,' said Colonel Race.

'She's got the wind up badly, poor kid,' said Anthony. 'Quite natural, I think.'

'Very natural,' said the inspector and poured himself out another cup of tea. Anthony took a gingerly sip of coffee.

'Well,' said Kemp. 'I think we relieved her mind – she went off home quite happily.'

'After the funeral,' said Anthony, 'I hope she'll get away to the country for a bit. Twenty-four hours' peace and quiet away from Auntie Lucilla's non-stop tongue will do her good, I think.'

'Aunt Lucilla's tongue has its uses,' said Race.

'You're welcome to it,' said Kemp. 'Lucky I didn't think it

necessary to have a shorthand report made when I took her statement. If I had, the poor fellow would have been in hospital with writer's cramp.'

'Well,' said Anthony. 'I daresay you're right, chief inspector, in saying that the case will never come to trial – but that's a very unsatisfactory finish – and there's one thing we still don't know – who wrote those letters to George Barton telling him his wife was murdered? We haven't the least idea who that person is.'

Race said: 'Your suspicions still the same, Browne?'

'Ruth Lessing? Yes, I stick to her as my candidate. You told me that she admitted to you she was in love with George. Rosemary by all accounts was pretty poisonous to her. Say she saw suddenly a good chance of getting rid of Rosemary, and was fairly convinced that with Rosemary out of the way, she could marry George out of hand.'

'I grant you all that,' said Race. 'I'll admit that Ruth Lessing has the calm practical efficiency that can contemplate and carry out murder, and that she perhaps lacks that quality of pity which is essentially a product of imagination. Yes, I give you the first murder. But I simply can't see her committing the second one. I simply cannot see her panicking and poisoning the man she loved and wanted to marry! Another point that rules her out – why did she hold her tongue when she saw Iris throw the cyanide packet under the table?'

'Perhaps she didn't see her do it,' suggested Anthony, rather doubtfully.

'I'm fairly sure she did,' said Race. 'When I was questioning her, I had the impression that she was keeping something back. And Iris Marle herself thought Ruth Lessing saw her.'

'Come now, colonel,' said Kemp. 'Let's have your "spot". You've got one, I suppose?'

Race nodded.

'Out with it. Fair's fair. You've listened to ours – *and* raised objections.'

Race's eyes went thoughtfully from Kemp's face to Anthony and rested there.

Anthony's eyebrows rose.

'Don't say you still think I am the villain of the piece?'

Slowly Race shook his head.

'I can imagine no possible reason why you should kill George Barton. I think I know who did kill him – and Rosemary Barton too.'

'Who is it?'

Race said musingly:

'Curious how we have all selected women as suspects. I suspect a woman, too.' He paused and said quietly: 'I think the guilty person is Iris Marle.'

With a crash Anthony pushed his chair back. For a moment his face went dark crimson – then with an effort, he regained command of himself. His voice, when he spoke, had a slight tremor but was deliberately as light and mocking as ever.

'By all means let us discuss the possibility,' he said. 'Why Iris Marle? And if so, why should she, of her own accord, tell me about dropping the cyanide paper under the table?'

'Because,' said Race, 'she knew that Ruth Lessing had seen her do it.'

Anthony considered the reply, his head on one side. Finally he nodded.

'Passed,' he said. 'Go on. Why did you suspect her in the first place?'

'Motive,' said Race. 'An enormous fortune had been left to Rosemary in which Iris was not to participate. For all we know she may have struggled for years with a sense of unfairness. She was aware that if Rosemary died childless, all that money came to her. And Rosemary was depressed, unhappy, run down after 'flu, just the mood when a verdict of suicide would be accepted without question.'

'That's right, make the girl out a monster!' said Anthony.

'Not a monster,' said Race. 'There is another reason why I suspected her – a far-fetched one, it may seem to you – Victor Drake.'

'Victor Drake?' Anthony stared.

'Bad blood. You see, I didn't listen to Lucilla Drake for nothing. I know all about the Marle family. Victor Drake – not so much weak as positively evil. His mother, feeble in intellect and incapable of concentration. Hector Marle, weak, vicious and a drunkard. Rosemary, emotionally unstable. A family history of weakness, vice and instability. Predisposing causes.'

Anthony lit a cigarette. His hands trembled.

'Don't you believe that there may be a sound blossom on a weak or even a bad stock?'

'Of course there may. But I am not sure that Iris Marle *is* a sound blossom.'

'And my word doesn't count,' said Anthony slowly, 'because I'm in love with her. George showed her those letters, and she got in a funk and killed him? That's how it goes on, is it?'

'Yes. Panic *would* obtain in her case.'

'And how did she get the stuff into George's champagne glass?'

'That, I confess, I do not know.'

'I'm thankful there's something you don't know.' Anthony tilted his chair back and then forward. His eyes were angry and dangerous. 'You've got a nerve saying all this to me.'

Race replied quietly:

'I know. But I consider it had to be said.'

Kemp watched them both with interest, but he did not speak. He stirred his tea round and round absent-mindedly.

'Very well.' Anthony sat upright. 'Things have changed. It's no longer a question of sitting round a table, drinking disgusting fluids, and airing academic theories. This case has *got* to be solved. We've *got* to resolve all the difficulties and get at the truth. That's got to be my job – and I'll do it somehow. I've got to hammer at the things we don't know – because when we do know them, the whole thing will be clear.

'I'll re-state the problem. Who knew that Rosemary had been murdered? Who wrote to George telling him so? Why did they write to him?

'And now the murders themselves. Wash out the first one. It's too long ago, and we don't know exactly what happened. But the second murder took place in front of my eyes. I *saw* it happen. Therefore I ought to know *how* it happened. The ideal time to put the cyanide in George's glass was during the cabaret – but it couldn't have been put in then because he drank from his glass immediately afterwards. I *saw* him drink. After he drank, nobody put anything in his glass. Nobody touched his glass, nevertheless next time he drank, it was full of cyanide. He *couldn't* have been poisoned – but he was! There was cyanide in his glass – *but nobody could have put it there!* Are we getting on?'

'No,' said Chief Inspector Kemp.

'Yes,' said Anthony. 'The thing has now entered into the realm of a conjuring trick. Or a spirit manifestation. I will now outline my psychic theory. Whilst we were dancing, the ghost of Rosemary hovers near George's glass and drops in some cleverly materialized cyanide – any spirit can make cyanide out of ectoplasm. George comes back and drinks her health and – oh, *Lord*!'

The other two stared curiously at him. His hands were holding his head. He rocked to and fro in apparent mental agony. He said:

'That's it . . . that's it . . . the bag . . . the waiter . . .'

'The waiter?' Kemp was alert.

Anthony shook his head.

'No, no. I don't mean what you mean. I did think once that what we needed was a waiter who was not a waiter but a conjurer – a waiter who had been engaged the day before. Instead we had a waiter who had always been a waiter – and a little waiter who was of the royal line of waiters – a cherubic waiter – a waiter above suspicion. And he's still above suspicion – but he played his part! Oh, Lord, yes, he played a star part.'

He stared at them.

'Don't you see it? *A* waiter could have poisoned the champagne but *the* waiter didn't. Nobody touched George's glass but George was poisoned. *A*, indefinite article. *The*, definite article. George's glass! George! Two separate things. And the money – lots and lots of money! And who knows – perhaps love as well? Don't look at me as though I'm mad. Come on, I'll show you.'

Thrusting his chair back he sprang to his feet and caught Kemp by the arm.

'Come with me.'

Kemp cast a regretful glance at his half-full cup.

'Got to pay,' he muttered.

'No, no, we'll be back in a moment. Come on. I must show you outside. Come on, Race.'

Pushing the table aside, he swept them away with him to the vestibule.

'You see that telephone box there?'

'Yes?'

Anthony felt in his pockets.

'Damn, I haven't got twopence. Never mind. On second thoughts I'd rather not do it that way. Come back.'

They went back into the café, Kemp first, Race following with Anthony's hand on his arm.

Kemp had a frown on his face as he sat down and picked up his pipe. He blew down it carefully and began to operate on it with a hairpin which he brought out of his waistcoat pocket.

Race was frowning at Anthony with a puzzled face. He leaned back and picked up his cup, draining the remaining fluid in it.

'Damn,' he said violently. 'It's got sugar in it!'

He looked across the table to meet Anthony's slowly widening smile.

'Hallo,' said Kemp, as he took a sip from his cup. 'What the hell's this?'

'Coffee,' said Anthony. 'And I don't think you'll like it. I didn't.'

<hr />

CHAPTER 13

Anthony had the pleasure of seeing instant comprehension flash into the eyes of both his companions.

His satisfaction was short-lived, for another thought struck him with the force of a physical blow.

He ejaculated out loud:

'My God – that *car!*'

He sprang up.

'Fool that I was – idiot! She told me that a car had nearly run her down – and I hardly listened. Come on, quick!'

Kemp said:

'She said she was going straight home when she left the Yard.'

'Yes. Why didn't I go with her?'

'Who's at the house?' asked Race.

'Ruth Lessing was there, waiting for Mrs Drake. It's possible that they're both discussing the funeral still!'

'Discussing everything else as well if I know Mrs Drake,' said Race. He added abruptly, 'Has Iris Marle any other relations?'

'Not that I know of.'

'I think I see the direction in which your thoughts, ideas, are leading you. But – is it physically possible?'

'I think so. Consider for yourself how much has been taken for granted *on one person's word.*'

Kemp was paying the check. The three men hurried out as Kemp said:

'You think the danger is acute? To Miss Marle?'

'Yes, I do.'

Anthony swore under his breath and hailed a taxi. The three men got in and the driver was told to go to Elvaston Square as quickly as possible.

Kemp said slowly:

'I've only got the general idea as yet. It washes the Farradays right out.'

'Yes.'

'Thank goodness for that. But surely there wouldn't be another attempt – so soon?'

'The sooner the better,' said Race. 'Before there's any chance of our minds running on the right track. Third time lucky – that will be the idea.' He added: 'Iris Marle told me, in front of Mrs Drake, that she would marry you as soon as you wanted her to.'

They spoke in spasmodic jerks, for the taxi-driver was taking their directions literally and was hurtling round corners and cutting through traffic with immense enthusiasm.

Turning with a final spurt into Elvaston Square, he drew up with a terrific jerk in front of the house.

Elvaston Square had never looked more peaceful.

Anthony, with an effort regained his usual cool manner, murmured:

'Quite like the movies. Makes one feel rather a fool, somehow.'

But he was on the top step ringing the bell while Race paid off the taxi and Kemp followed up the steps.

The parlourmaid opened the door.

Anthony said sharply:

'Has Miss Iris got back?'

Evans looked a little surprised.

'Oh, yes, sir. She came in half an hour ago.'

Anthony breathed a sigh of relief. Everything in the house was so calm and normal that he felt ashamed of his recent melodramatic fears.

'Where is she?'

'I expect she's in the drawing-room with Mrs Drake.'

Anthony nodded and took the stairs in easy strides, Race and Kemp close behind him.

In the drawing-room, placid under its shaded electric lights, Lucilla Drake was hunting through the pigeon holes of the desk with the hopeful absorption of a terrier and murmuring audibly:

'Dear, dear, now where *did* I put Mrs Marsham's letter? Now, let me see . . .'

'Where's Iris?' demanded Anthony abruptly.

Lucilla turned and stared.

'Iris? She – I beg your pardon!' She drew herself up. 'May I ask who you *are?*'

Race came forward from behind him and Lucilla's face cleared. She did not yet see Chief Inspector Kemp who was the third to enter the room.

'Oh, dear, Colonel Race! How kind of you to come! But I do wish you could have been here a little earlier – I *should* have liked to consult you about the funeral arrangements – a man's advice, so valuable – and really I was feeling so upset, as I said to Miss Lessing, that really I couldn't even *think* – and I must say that Miss Lessing was really very sympathetic for once and offered to do everything she could to take the burden off my shoulders – only, as she put it very reasonably, naturally *I* should be the person most likely to know what were George's favourite hymns – not that I actually *did*, because I'm afraid George didn't very often go to church – but naturally, as a clergyman's wife – I mean widow – I do know what is *suitable* –'

Race took advantage of a momentary pause to slip in his question: 'Where is Miss Marle?'

'Iris? She came in some time ago. She said she had a headache and was going straight up to her room. Young girls, you know, do not seem to me to have very much stamina nowadays – they don't eat enough spinach – and she seems positively to dislike talking about the funeral arrangements, but after all, *someone* has to do these things – and one does want to feel that everything has been done for the best, and proper respect shown to the dead – not that I have ever thought motor hearses really *reverent* – if you know what I mean – not like· horses with their long black tails – but, of course, I said at once that it was quite all right, and Ruth – I called her Ruth and not Miss Lessing – and I were managing splendidly, and she could leave everything to us.'

Kemp asked:

'Miss Lessing has gone?'

'Yes, we settled everything, and Miss Lessing left about ten minutes ago. She took the announcements for the papers with her. No flowers, under the circumstances – and Canon Westbury to take the service –'

As the flow went on, Anthony edged gently out of the door. He had left the room before Lucilla, suddenly interrupting her narrative, paused to say: 'Who *was* that young man who came with you? I didn't realize at first that *you* had brought him. I thought possibly he might have been one of those dreadful reporters. We have had such *trouble* with them.'

Anthony was running lightly up the stairs. Hearing footsteps behind him, he turned his head, and grinned at Chief Inspector Kemp.

'You deserted too? Poor old Race!'

Kemp muttered.

'He does these things so nicely. I'm not popular in that quarter.'

They were on the second floor and just preparing to start up the third when Anthony heard a light footstep descending. He pulled Kemp inside an adjacent bathroom door.

The footsteps went on down the stairs.

Anthony emerged and ran up the next flight of stairs. Iris's room, he knew, was the small one at the back. He rapped lightly on the door.

'Hi – Iris.' There was no reply – and he knocked and called again. Then he tried the handle but found the door locked.

With real urgency now he beat upon it.

'Iris – Iris –'

After a second or two, he stopped and glanced down. He was standing on one of those woolly old-fashioned rugs made to fit outside doors to obviate draughts. This one was close up against the door. Anthony kicked it away. The space under the door at the bottom was quite wide – sometime, he deduced, it had been cut to clear a fitted carpet instead of stained boards.

He stooped to the keyhole but could see nothing, but suddenly he raised his head and sniffed. Then he lay down flat and pressed his nose against the crack under the door.

Springing up, he shouted: 'Kemp!'

There was no sign of the chief inspector. Anthony shouted again.

It was Colonel Race, however, who came running up the stairs. Anthony gave him no chance to speak. He said:

'Gas – pouring out! We'll have to break the door down.'

Race had a powerful physique. He and Anthony made short shrift of the obstacle. With a splintering, cracking noise, the lock gave.

They fell back for a moment, then Race said:

'She's there by the fireplace. I'll dash in and break the window. You get her.'

Iris Marle was lying by the gas fire – her mouth and nose lying on the wide open gas jet.

A minute or two later, choking and spluttering, Anthony and Race laid the unconscious girl on the landing floor in the draught of the passage window.

Race said:

'I'll work on her. You get a doctor quickly.'

Anthony swung down the stairs. Race called after him:

'Don't worry. I think she'll be all right. We got here in time.'

In the hall Anthony dialled and spoke into the mouthpiece, hampered by a background of exclamations from Lucilla Drake.

He turned at last from the telephone to say with a sigh of relief:

'Caught him. He lives just across the Square. He'll be here in a couple of minutes.'

'– but I must know what has *happened*! Is Iris ill?'

It was a final wail from Lucilla.

Anthony said:

'She was in her room. Door locked. Her head in the gas fire and the gas full on.'

'Iris?' Mrs Drake gave a piercing shriek. 'Iris has committed *suicide*? I can't believe it. I *don't* believe it!'

A faint ghost of Anthony's grin returned to him.

'You don't need to believe it,' he said. 'It isn't true.'

CHAPTER 14

'And now, please, Tony, will you tell me all about it?'

Iris was lying on a sofa, and the valiant November sunshine was making a brave show outside the windows of Little Priors.

Anthony looked across at Colonel Race who was sitting on the window-sill, and grinned engagingly:

'I don't mind admitting, Iris, that I've been waiting for this moment. If I don't explain to someone soon how clever I've been, I shall burst. There will be no modesty in this recital. It will be shameless blowing of my own trumpet with suitable pauses to enable you to say "Anthony, how clever of you" or "Tony, how wonderful" or some phrase of a like nature. Ahem! The performance will now begin. Here we go.

'The thing as a whole *looked* simple enough. What I mean is, that it looked like a clear case of cause and effect. Rosemary's death, accepted at the time as suicide, was not suicide. George became suspicious, started investigating, was presumably getting near the truth, and before he could unmask the murderer was, in his turn, murdered. The sequence, if I may put it that way, seems perfectly clear.

'But almost at once we came across some apparent contradictions. Such as: A. George could not be poisoned. B. George *was* poisoned. And: A. Nobody touched George's glass. B. George's glass was tampered with.

'Actually I was overlooking a very significant fact – the varied use of the possessive case. George's ear is George's ear indisputably because it is attached to his head and cannot be removed without a surgical operation! But by George's watch, I only mean the watch that George is wearing – the question might arise whether it is his or maybe one lent him by someone else.

And when I come to George's glass, or George's teacup, I begin to realize that I mean something very vague indeed. All I actually mean is the glass or cup out of which George has lately been drinking – and which has nothing to distinguish it from several other cups and glasses of the same pattern.

'To illustrate this, I tried an experiment. Race was drinking tea without sugar, Kemp was drinking tea with sugar, and I was drinking coffee. In appearance the three fluids were of much the same colour. We were sitting round a small marble-topped table among several other round marble-topped tables. On the pretext of an urgent brainwave I urged the other two out of their seats and out into the vestibule, pushing the chairs aside as we went, and also managing to move Kemp's pipe which was lying by his plate to a similar position by my plate but without letting him see me do it. As soon as we were outside I made an excuse and we returned, Kemp slightly ahead. He pulled the chair to the table and sat down opposite the plate that was marked by the pipe he had left behind him. Race sat on his right as before and I on his left – *but mark what had happened* – a new A. and B. contradiction! A. Kemp's cup has sugared tea in it. B. Kemp's cup has coffee in it. Two conflicting statements that *cannot* both be true – But they *are* both true. The misleading term is *Kemp's* cup. Kemp's cup when he *left* the table and Kemp's cup when he *returned* to the table are *not the same.*

'And that, Iris, *is what happened at the Luxembourg that night.* After the cabaret, when you all went to dance, you dropped your bag. A waiter picked it up – not *the* waiter, the waiter attending on that table who knew just where you had been sitting – but *a* waiter, an anxious hurried little waiter with everybody bullying him, running along with a sauce, and who quickly stooped, picked up the bag and placed it by a plate – actually by the plate one place to the left of where you had been sitting. You and George came back first and you went without a thought straight to the place marked by your bag – just as Kemp did to the place marked by his pipe. George sat down in what he thought to be his place, on your right. And when he proposed his toast in memory of Rosemary, he drank from what he thought was *his* glass but was in reality *your glass* – the glass that can quite easily have been poisoned without needing a conjuring trick to explain it, because the only person who did *not* drink after the cabaret, was necessarily the *person whose health was being drunk!*

'Now go over the whole business again and the set-up is entirely different! *You* are the intended victim, not George! So it looks, doesn't it, as though George is being *used.* What, if things had not gone wrong, would have been the story as the world would see it? A repetition of the party a year ago – and a repetition of – suicide! Clearly, people would say, a suicidal streak in that family! Bit of paper which has contained cyanide found in your bag. Clear case! Poor girl has been brooding over her sister's death. Very sad – but these rich girls are sometimes very neurotic!'

Iris interrupted him. She cried out:

'But why should anyone want to kill me? Why? *Why?*'

'All that lovely money, angel. Money, money, money! Rosemary's money went to you on her death. Now suppose you were to die – unmarried. What would happen to that money? The answer was it would go to your next of kin – to your aunt, Lucilla Drake. Now from all accounts of the dear lady, I could hardly see Lucilla Drake as First Murderess. But is there anyone else who would benefit? Yes, indeed. Victor Drake. If Lucilla has money, it will be exactly the same as Victor having it – Victor will see to that! He has always been able to do what he likes with his mother. And there is nothing difficult about seeing Victor as First Murderer. All along, from the very start of the case, there have been references to Victor, mentions of Victor. He has been in the offing, a shadowy, unsubstantial, evil figure.'

'But Victor's in the Argentine! He's been in South America for over a year.'

'Has he? We're coming now to what has been said to be the fundamental plot of every story. "Girl meets Boy!" When Victor met Ruth Lessing, this particular story started. He got hold of her. I think she must have fallen for him pretty badly. Those quiet, level-headed, law-abiding women are the kind that often fall for a real bad lot.

'Think a minute and you'll realize that all the evidence for Victor's being in South America depends on Ruth's word. None of it was verified because it was never a main issue! *Ruth* said that she had seen Victor off on the S.S. *Cristobal* before Rosemary's death! It was *Ruth* who suggested putting a call through to

Buenos Aires on the day of George's death – and later sacked the telephone girl who might have inadvertently let out that she did no such thing.

'Of course it's been easy to check up now! Victor Drake arrived in Buenos Aires by a boat leaving England the day *after* Rosemary's death a year ago. Ogilvie, in Buenos Aires, had no telephone conversation with Ruth on the subject of Victor Drake on the day of George's death. *And Victor Drake left Buenos Aires for New York some weeks ago*. Easy enough for him to arrange for a cable to be sent off in his name on a certain day – one of those well-known cables asking for money that seemed proof positive that he was many thousands of miles away. Instead of which –'

'Yes, Anthony?'

'Instead of which,' said Anthony, leading up to his climax with intense pleasure, 'he was sitting at the next table to ours at the Luxembourg with a not so dumb blonde!'

'Not that awful looking man?'

'A yellow blotchy complexion and bloodshot eyes are easy things to assume, and they make a lot of difference to a man. Actually, of our party, *I* was the only person (apart from Ruth Lessing) who had ever seen Victor Drake – and I had never known him under *that name*! In any case I was sitting with my back to him. I did think I recognized, in the cocktail lounge outside, as we came in, a man I had known in my prison days – Monkey Coleman. But as I was now leading a highly respectable life I was not too anxious that he should recognize me. I never for one moment suspected that Monkey Coleman had had anything to do with the crime – much less that he and Victor Drake were one and the same.'

'But I don't see now how he did it?'

Colonel Race took up the tale.

'In the easiest way in the world. During the cabaret he went out to telephone, passing our table. Drake had been an actor and he had been something more important – a *waiter*. To assume the make-up and play the part of Pedro Morales was child's play to an actor, but to move deftly round a table, with the step and gait of a waiter, filling up the champagne glasses, needed the definite knowledge and technique of a man who had actually *been* a waiter. A clumsy action or movement would have drawn your attention to him, but as a *bona fide* waiter none of you noticed or saw him. You were looking at the Cabaret, not noticing that portion of the restaurant's furnishings – the waiter!'

Iris said in a hesitating voice:

'And Ruth?'

Anthony said:

'It was Ruth, of course, who put the cyanide paper in your bag – probably in the cloak-room at the beginning of the evening. The same technique she had adopted a year ago – with Rosemary.'

'I always thought it odd,' said Iris, 'that George hadn't told Ruth about those letters. He consulted her about everything.'

Anthony gave a short laugh.

'Of course he told her – first thing. She knew he would. That's why she wrote them. Then she arranged all his "plan" for him – having first got him well worked up. And so she had the stage set – all nicely arranged for suicide No. 2 – and if George chose to believe that you had killed Rosemary and were committing suicide out of remorse or panic – well, that wouldn't make any difference to Ruth!'

'And to think I liked her – liked her very much! And actually wanted her to marry George.'

'She'd probably have made him a very good wife, if she hadn't come across Victor,' said Anthony. 'Moral: every murderess was a nice girl once.'

Iris shivered. 'All that for money!'

'You innocent, money is what these things are done for! Victor certainly did it for money. Ruth partly for money, partly for Victor, and partly, I think, because she hated Rosemary. Yes, she'd travelled a long way by the time she deliberately tried to run you down in a car, and still further when she left Lucilla in the drawing-room, banged the front door and then ran up to your bedroom. What did she seem like? Excited at all?'

Iris considered.

'I don't think so. She just tapped on the door, came in and said everything was fixed up and she hoped I was feeling all right. I said yes, I was just a bit tired. And then she picked up my big rubber-covered torch and said what a nice torch that was and after that I don't seem to remember anything.'

'No, dear,' said Anthony. 'Because she hit you a nice little crack, not too hard, on the back of the neck with your nice torch. Then she arranged you artistically by the gas fire, shut the windows tight, turned on the gas, went out, locking the door and passing the key underneath it, pushed the woolly mat close up against the crack so as to shut out any draught and tripped gently down the stairs. Kemp and I just got into the bathroom in time. I raced on up to you and Kemp followed Miss Ruth Lessing unbeknownst to where she had left that car parked – you know, I felt at the time there was something fishy and uncharacteristic about the way Ruth tried to force it on our minds that she had come by bus and tube!'

Iris gave a shudder.

'It's horrible – to think anyone was as determined to kill me as all that. Did she hate me too by then?'

'Oh, I shouldn't think so. But Miss Ruth Lessing is a very efficient young woman. She'd already been an accessory in two murders and she didn't fancy having risked her neck for nothing. I've no doubt Lucilla Drake bleated out your decision to marry me at a moment's notice, and in that case there was no time to lose. Once married, I should be your next of kin and not Lucilla.'

'Poor Lucilla. I'm so terribly sorry for her.'

'I think we all are. She's a harmless, kindly soul.'

'Is he really arrested?'

Anthony looked at Race, who nodded and said:

'This morning, when he landed in New York.'

'Was he going to marry Ruth – afterwards?'

'That was Ruth's idea. I think she would have brought it off too.'

'Anthony – I don't think I like my money very much.'

'All right, sweet – we'll do something noble with it if you like. I've got enough money to live on – and to keep a wife in reasonable comfort. We'll give it all away if you like – endow homes for children, or provide free tobacco for old men, or – how about a campaign for serving better coffee all over England?'

'I shall keep a little,' said Iris. 'So that if I ever wanted to, I could be grand and walk out and leave you.'

'I don't think, Iris, that is the right spirit in which to enter upon married life. And, by the way, you didn't once say "Tony, how wonderful" or "Anthony, how clever of you"!'

Colonel Race smiled and got up.

'Going over to the Farradays for tea,' he exclaimed. There was a faint twinkle in his eye as he said to Anthony: 'Don't suppose you're coming?'

Anthony shook his head and Race went out of the room. He paused in the doorway to say, over his shoulder:

'Good show.'

'That,' said Anthony as the door closed behind him, 'denotes supreme British approval.'

Iris asked in a calm voice:

'He thought I'd done it, didn't he?'

'You mustn't hold that against him,' said Anthony. 'You see, he's known so many beautiful spies, all stealing secret formulas and wheedling secrets out of major-generals, that it's soured his nature and warped his judgement. He thinks it's just got to be the beautiful girl in the case!'

'Why did you know I hadn't, Tony?'

'Just love, I suppose,' said Anthony lightly.

Then his face changed, grew suddenly serious. He touched a little vase by Iris's side in which was a single sprig of grey-green with a mauve-flower.

'What's that doing in flower at this time of year?'

'It does sometimes – just an odd sprig – if it's a mild autumn.'

Anthony took it out of the glass and held it for a moment against his cheek. He half-closed his eyes and saw rich chestnut hair, laughing blue eyes and a red passionate mouth . . .

He said in a quiet conversational tone:

'She's not around now any longer, is she?'

'Who do you mean?'

'You know who I mean. Rosemary . . . I think she knew, Iris, that you were in danger.'

He touched the sprig of fragrant green with his lips and threw it lightly out of the window.

'Good-bye, Rosemary, thank you . . .'

Iris said softly:

'*That's for remembrance . . .*'

And more softly still:

'*Pray love remember . . .*'

CROOKED HOUSE

AUTHOR'S FOREWORD

This book is one of my own special favourites. I saved it up for years, thinking about it, working it out, saying to myself: 'One day, when I've plenty of time, and want to really enjoy myself – I'll begin it!' I should say that of one's output, five books are work to one that is real pleasure. *Crooked House* was pure pleasure. I often wonder whether people who read a book can know if it has been hard work or a pleasure to write? Again and again someone says to me: '*How* you must have enjoyed writing so and so!' This about a book that obstinately refused to come out the way you wished, whose characters are sticky, the plot needlessly involved, and the dialogue stilted – or so you think yourself. But perhaps the author isn't the best judge of his or her own work. However, practically everybody has liked *Crooked House*, so I am justified in my own belief that it is one of my best.

I don't know what put the Leonides family into my head – they just came. Then, like Topsy 'they growed'.

I feel that I myself was only their scribe.

Agatha Christie

I first came to know Sophia Leonides in Egypt towards the end of the war. She held a fairly high administrative post in one of the Foreign Office departments out there. I knew her first in an official capacity, and I soon appreciated the efficiency that had brought her to the position she held, in spite of her youth (she was at that time just twenty-two).

Besides being extremely easy to look at, she had a clear mind and a dry sense of humour that I found very delightful. We became friends. She was a person whom it was extraordinarily easy to talk to and we enjoyed our dinners and occasional dances very much.

All this I knew; it was not until I was ordered East at the close of the European war that I knew something else – that I loved Sophia and that I wanted to marry her.

We were dining at Shepheard's when I made this discovery. It did not come to me with any shock of surprise, but more as the recognition of a fact with which I had been long familiar. I looked at her with new eyes – but I saw what I had already known for a long time. I liked everything I saw. The dark crisp hair that sprang up proudly from her forehead, the vivid blue eyes, the small square fighting chin, and the straight nose. I liked the well-cut light-grey tailor-made, and the crisp white shirt. She looked refreshingly English and that appealed to me strongly after three years without seeing my native land. Nobody, I thought, could be more English – and even as I was thinking exactly that, I suddenly wondered if, in fact, she was, or indeed could be, as English as she looked. Does the real thing ever have the perfection of a stage performance?

I realized that much and freely as we had talked together, discussing ideas, our likes and dislikes, the future, our immediate friends and acquaintances – Sophia had never mentioned her home or her family. She knew all about me (she was, as I have indicated, a good listener) but about her I knew nothing. She had, I supposed, the usual background, but she had never talked about it. And until this moment I had never realized the fact.

Sophia asked me what I was thinking about.

I replied truthfully: 'You.'

'I see,' she said. And she sounded as though she did see.

'We may not meet again for a couple of years,' I said. 'I don't know when I shall get back to England. But as soon as I do get back, the first thing I shall do will be to come and see you and ask you to marry me.'

She took it without batting an eyelash. She sat there, smoking, not looking at me.

For a moment or two I was nervous that she might not understand.

'Listen,' I said. 'The one thing I'm determined *not* to do, is to ask you to marry me now. That wouldn't work out anyway. First you might turn me down, and then I'd go off miserable and probably tie up with some ghastly woman just to restore my vanity. And if you didn't turn me down what could we do about it? Get married and part at once? Get engaged and settle down to a long waiting period? I couldn't stand your doing that. You might meet someone else and feel bound to be "loyal" to me. We've been living in a queer hectic get-on-with-it-quickly atmosphere. Marriages and love affairs making and breaking all round us. I'd like to feel you'd gone home, free and independent, to look round you and size up the new post-war world and decide what you want out of it. What is between you and me, Sophia, has got to be *permanent*. I've no use for any other kind of marriage.'

'No more have I,' said Sophia.

'On the other hand,' I said, 'I think I'm entitled to let you know how I – well – how I feel.'

'But without undue lyrical expression?' murmured Sophia.

'Darling – don't you understand? I've tried *not* to say I love you –'

She stopped me.

'I do understand, Charles. And I like your funny way of doing things. And you may come and see me when you come back – if you still want to –'

It was my turn to interrupt.

'There's no doubt about that.'

'There's always a doubt about everything, Charles. There may always be some incalculable factor that upsets the apple-cart. For one thing, you don't know much about me, do you?'

'I don't even know where you live in England.'

'I live at Swinly Dean.'

I nodded at the mention of the well-known outer suburb of London which boasts three excellent golf courses for the city financier.

She added softly in a musing voice: '*In a little crooked house . . .*'

I must have looked slightly startled, for she seemed amused, and explained by elaborating the quotation. '*"And they all lived together in a little crooked house."* That's us. Not really such a little house either. But definitely crooked – running to gables and half-timbering!'

'Are you one of a large family? Brothers and sisters?'

'One brother, one sister, a mother, a father, an uncle, an aunt by marriage, a grandfather, a great-aunt, and a step-grandmother.'

'Good gracious!' I exclaimed, slightly overwhelmed.

She laughed.

'Of course we don't normally all live together. The war and blitzes have brought that about – but I don't know' – she frowned reflectively – 'perhaps spiritually the family has always lived together – under my grandfather's eye and protection. He's rather a Person, my grandfather. He's over eighty, about four-foot ten, and everybody else looks rather dim beside him.'

'He sounds interesting,' I said.

'He is interesting. He's a Greek from Smyrna. Aristide Leonides.' She added, with a twinkle, 'He's extremely rich.'

'Will anybody be rich after this is over?'

'My grandfather will,' said Sophia with assurance. 'No soak-the-rich tactics would have any effect on him. He'd just soak the soakers.

'I wonder,' she added, 'if you'll like him?'

'Do you?' I asked.

'Better than anyone in the world,' said Sophia.

CHAPTER 2

It was over two years before I returned to England. They were not easy years. I wrote to Sophia and heard from her fairly frequently. Her letters, like mine, were not love letters. They were letters written to each other by close friends – they dealt with ideas and thoughts and with comments on the daily trend of life. Yet I know that as far as I was concerned, and I believed as far as Sophia was concerned too, our feelings for each other grew and strengthened.

I returned to England on a soft grey day in September. The leaves on the trees were golden in the evening light. There were playful gusts of wind. From the airfield I sent a telegram to Sophia.

'*Just arrived back. Will you dine this evening Mario's nine o'clock Charles.*'

A couple of hours later I was sitting reading the *Times*; and scanning the Births, Marriages and Deaths column my eye was caught by the name Leonides:

On Sept. 19th, at Three Gables, Swinly Dean, Aristide Leonides, beloved husband of Brenda Leonides, in his eighty-eighth year. Deeply regretted.

There was another announcement immediately below:

LEONIDES – Suddenly, at his residence, Three Gables, Swinly Dean, Aristide Leonides. Deeply mourned by his loving children and grandchildren. Flowers to St Eldred's Church, Swinly Dean.

I found the two announcements rather curious. There seemed to have been some faulty staff work resulting in overlapping. But my main preoccupation was Sophia. I hastily sent her a second telegram:

'*Just seen news of your grandfather's death. Very sorry. Let me know when I can see you. Charles.*'

A telegram from Sophia reached me at six o'clock at my father's house. It said:

'Will be at Mario's nine o'clock. Sophia.'

The thought of meeting Sophia again made me both nervous and excited. The time crept by with maddening slowness. I was at Mario's waiting twenty minutes too early. Sophia herself was only five minutes late.

It is always a shock to meet again someone whom you have not seen for a long time but who has been very much present in your mind during that period. When at last Sophia came through the swing doors our meeting seemed completely unreal. She was wearing black, and that, in some curious way, startled me. Most other women were wearing black, but I got it into my head that it was definitely mourning – and it surprised me that Sophia should be the kind of person who did wear black – even for a near relative.

We had cocktails – then went and found our table. We talked rather fast and feverishly – asking after old friends of the Cairo days. It was artificial conversation, but it tided us over the first awkwardness. I expressed commiseration for her grandfather's death and Sophia said quietly that it had been 'very sudden'. Then we started off again reminiscing. I began to feel, uneasily, that something was the matter – something, I mean, other than the first natural awkwardness of meeting again. There was something wrong, definitely wrong, with Sophia herself. Was she, perhaps, going to tell me that she had found some other man whom she cared for more than she did for me? That her feeling for me had been 'all a mistake'?

Somehow I didn't think it was that – I didn't know what it was. Meanwhile we continued our artificial talk.

Then, quite suddenly, as the waiter placed coffee on the table and retired bowing, everything swung into focus. Here were Sophia and I sitting together as so often before at a small table in a restaurant. The years of our separation might never have been.

'*Sophia*,' I said.

And immediately she said, 'Charles!'

I drew a deep breath of relief.

'Thank goodness that's over,' I said. 'What's been the matter with us?'

'Probably my fault. I was stupid.'

'But it's all right now?'

'Yes, it's all right now.'

We smiled at each other.

'Darling!' I said. And then: 'How soon will you marry me?'

Her smile died. The something, whatever it was, was back.

'I don't know,' she said. 'I'm not sure, Charles, that I can ever marry you.'

'But, Sophia! Why not? Is it because you feel I'm a stranger? Do you want time to get used to me again? Is there someone else? No —' I broke off. 'I'm a fool. It's none of those things.'

'No, it isn't.' She shook her head. I waited. She said in a low voice:

'It's my grandfather's death.'

'Your grandfather's death? But why? What earthly difference can that make? You don't mean — surely you can't imagine — is it money? Hasn't he left any? But surely, dearest —'

'It isn't money.' She gave a fleeting smile. 'I think you'd be quite willing to "take me in my shift", as the old saying goes. And grandfather never lost any money in his life.'

'Then what is it?'

'It's just his death — you see, I think, Charles, that he didn't just — die. I think he may have been — killed . . .'

I stared at her.

'But — what a fantastic idea. What made you think of it?'

'*I* didn't think of it. The doctor was queer to begin with. He wouldn't sign a certificate. They're going to have a post-mortem. It's quite clear that they suspect something is wrong.'

I didn't dispute that with her. Sophia had plenty of brains; any conclusions she had drawn could be relied upon.

Instead I said earnestly:

'Their suspicions may be quite unjustified. But putting that aside, supposing that they are justified, how does that affect you and me?'

'It might under certain circumstances. You're in the Diplomatic Service. They're rather particular about wives. No — please don't say all the things that you're bursting to say. You're bound to say them – and I believe you really think them – and theoretically I quite agree with them. But I'm proud – I'm devilishly proud. I want our marriage to be a good thing for everyone – I don't want to represent one-half of a sacrifice for love! And, as I say, it *may* be all right . . .'

'You mean the doctor – may have made a mistake?'

'Even if he hasn't made a mistake, it won't matter – so long as the right person killed him.'

'What *do* you mean, Sophia?'

'It was a beastly thing to say. But, after all, one might as well be honest.'

She forestalled my next words.

'No, Charles, I'm not going to say any more. I've probably said too much already. But I was determined to come and meet you tonight – to see you myself and make you understand. We can't settle anything until this is cleared up.'

'At least tell me about it.'

She shook her head.

'I don't want to.'

'But – Sophia –'

'No, Charles. I don't want you to see us from *my* angle. I want you to see us unbiased from the outside point of view.'

'And how am I to do that?'

She looked at me, a queer light in her brilliant blue eyes.

'You'll get that from your father,' she said.

I had told Sophia in Cairo that my father was Assistant Commissioner of Scotland Yard. He still held that office. At her words, I felt a cold weight settling down on me.

'It's as bad as that, then?'

'I think so. Do you see a man sitting at a table by the door all alone – rather a nice-looking stolid ex-Army type?'

'Yes.'

'He was on Swinly Dean platform this evening when I got into the train.'

'You mean he's followed you here?'

'Yes. I think we're all – how does one put it? – under observation. They more or less hinted that we'd all better not leave the house. But I was determined to see you.' Her small square chin shot out pugnaciously. 'I got out of the bathroom window and shinned down the water-pipe.'

'Darling!'

'But the police are very efficient. And of course there was the telegram I sent you. Well – never mind – we're here – together . . . But from now on, we've both got to play a lone hand.'

She paused and then added:

'Unfortunately – there's no doubt – about our loving each other.'

'No doubt at all,' I said. 'And don't say unfortunately. You and I have survived a world war, we've had plenty of near escapes from sudden death – and I don't see why the sudden death of just one old man – how old was he, by the way?'

'Eighty-seven.'

'Of course. It was in the *Times*. If you ask me, he just died of old age, and any self-respecting GP would accept the fact.'

'If you'd known my grandfather,' said Sophia, 'you'd have been surprised at his dying of *anything*!'

CHAPTER 3

I'd always taken a certain amount of interest in my father's police work, but nothing had prepared me for the moment when I should come to take a direct and personal interest in it.

I had not yet seen the Old Man. He had been out when I arrived, and after a bath, a shave, and change I had gone out to meet Sophia. When I returned to the house, however, Glover told me that he was in his study.

He was at his desk, frowning over a lot of papers. He jumped up when I came in.

'Charles! Well, well, it's been a long time.'

Our meeting, after five years of war, would have disappointed a Frenchman. Actually all the emotion of reunion was there all right. The Old Man and I are very fond of each other, and we understand each other pretty well.

'I've got some whisky,' he said. 'Say when. Sorry I was out when you got here. I'm up to the ears in work. Hell of a case just unfolding.'

I leaned back in my chair and lit a cigarette.

'Aristide Leonides?' I asked.

His brows came down quickly over his eyes. He shot me a quick appraising glance. His voice was polite and steely.

'Now what makes you say that, Charles?'

'I'm right then?'

'How did you know about this?'

'Information received.'

The Old Man waited.

'My information,' I said, 'came from the stable itself.'

'Come on, Charles, let's have it.'

'You mayn't like it,' I said. 'I met Sophia Leonides out in Cairo. I fell in love with her. I'm going to marry her. I met her tonight. She dined with me.'

'Dined with you? In London? I wonder just how she managed to do that! The family was asked – oh, quite politely, to stay put.'

'Quite so. She shinned down a pipe from the bathroom window.'

The Old Man's lips twitched for a moment into a smile.

'She seems,' he said, 'to be a young lady of some resource.'

'But your police force is fully efficient,' I said. 'A nice Army type tracked her to Mario's. I shall figure in the reports you get. Five foot eleven, brown hair, brown eyes, dark-blue pin-stripe suit, etc.'

The Old Man looked at me hard.

'Is this – serious?' he asked.

'Yes,' I said. 'It's serious, Dad.'

There was a moment's silence.

'Do you mind?' I asked.

'I shouldn't have minded – a week ago. They're a well-established family – the girl will have money – and I know you. You don't lose your head easily. As it is –'

'Yes, Dad?'

'It may be all right, if –'

'If what?'

'If the right person did it.'

It was the second time that night I had heard that phrase. I began to be interested.

'Just who *is* the right person?'

He threw a sharp glance at me.

'How much do you know about it all?'

'Nothing.'

'Nothing?' He looked surprised. 'Didn't the girl tell you?'

'No. She said she'd rather I saw it all – from an outside point of view.'

'Now I wonder why that was?'

'Isn't it rather obvious?'

'No, Charles. I don't think it is.'

He walked up and down frowning. He had lit a cigar and the cigar had gone out. That showed me just how disturbed the old boy was.

'How much do you know about the family?' he shot at me.

'Damn all! I know there was the old man and a lot of sons and grandchildren and in-laws. I haven't got the ramifications clear.' I paused and then said, 'You'd better put me in the picture, Dad.'

'Yes.' He sat down. 'Very well then – I'll begin at the beginning – with Aristide Leonides. He arrived in England when he was twenty-four.'

'A Greek from Smyrna.'

'You do know that much?'

'Yes, but it's about all I do know.'

The door opened and Glover came in to say that Chief-Inspector Taverner was here.

'He's in charge of the case,' said my father. 'We'd better have him in. He's been checking up on the family. Knows more about them than I do.'

I asked if the local police had called in the Yard.

'It's in our jurisdiction. Swinly Dean is Greater London.'

I nodded as Chief-Inspector Taverner came into the room. I knew Taverner from many years back. He greeted me warmly and congratulated me on my safe return.

'I'm putting Charles in the picture,' said the Old Man. 'Correct me if I go wrong, Taverner. Leonides came to London in 1884. He started up a little restaurant in Soho. It paid. He started up another. Soon he owned seven or eight of them. They all paid hand over fist.'

'Never made any mistakes in anything he handled,' said Chief-Inspector Taverner.

'He'd got a natural flair,' said my father. 'In the end he was behind most of the well-known restaurants in London. Then he went into the catering business in a big way.'

'He was behind a lot of other businesses as well,' said Taverner. 'Second-hand clothes trade, cheap jewellery stores, lots of things. Of course,' he added thoughtfully, 'he was always a twister.'

'You mean he was a crook?' I asked.

Taverner shook his head.

'No, I don't mean that. Crooked, yes – but not a crook. Never anything outside the law. But he was the sort of chap that thought up all the ways you can get round the law. He's cleaned up a packet that way even in this last war, and old as he was. Nothing he did was ever illegal – but as soon as he'd got on to it, you had to have a law about it, if you know what I mean. But by that time he'd gone on to the next thing.'

'He doesn't sound a very attractive character,' I said.

'Funnily enough, he was attractive. He'd got personality, you know. You could feel it. Nothing much to look at. Just a gnome – ugly little fellow – but magnetic – women always fell for him.'

'He made a rather astonishing marriage,' said my father. 'Married the daughter of a country squire – an MFH.'

I raised my eyebrows. 'Money?'

The Old Man shook his head.

'No, it was a love match. She met him over some catering arrangements for a friend's wedding – and she fell for him. Her parents cut up rough, but she was determined to have him. I tell you, the man had charm – there was something exotic and dynamic about him that appealed to her. She was bored stiff with her own kind.'

'And the marriage was happy?'

'It was very happy, oddly enough. Of course their respective friends didn't mix (those were the days before money swept aside all class distinctions) but that didn't seem to worry them. They did without friends. He built a rather preposterous house at Swinly Dean and they lived there and had eight children.'

'This is indeed a family chronicle.'

'Old Leonides was rather clever to choose Swinly Dean. It

was only beginning to be fashionable then. The second and third golf courses hadn't been made. There was a mixture of Old Inhabitants who were passionately fond of their gardens and who liked Mrs Leonides, and rich City men who wanted to be in with Leonides, so they could take their choice of acquaintances. They were perfectly happy, I believe, until she died of pneumonia in 1905.'

'Leaving him with eight children?'

'One died in infancy. Two of the sons were killed in the last war. One daughter married and went to Australia and died there. An unmarried daughter was killed in a motor accident. Another died a year or two ago. There are two still living – the eldest son, Roger, who is married but has no children, and Philip, who married a well-known actress and has three children. Your Sophia, Eustace, and Josephine.'

'And they are all living at – what is it? – Three Gables?'

'Yes. The Roger Leonides were bombed out early in the war. Philip and his family have lived there since 1937. And there's an elderly aunt, Miss de Haviland, sister of the first Mrs Leonides. She always loathed her brother-in-law apparently, but when her sister died she considered it her duty to accept her brother-in-law's invitation to live with him and bring up the children.'

'She's very hot on duty,' said Inspector Taverner. 'But she's not the kind that changes her mind about people. She always disapproved of Leonides and his methods –'

'Well,' I said, 'it seems a pretty good houseful. Who do you think killed him?'

Taverner shook his head.

'Early days,' he said, 'early days to say that.'

'Come on, Taverner,' I said. 'I bet you think you know who did it. We're not in court, man.'

'No,' said Taverner gloomily. 'And we may never be.'

'You mean he may not have been murdered?'

'Oh, he was murdered all right. Poisoned. But you know what these poisoning cases are like. It's very tricky getting the evidence. Very tricky. All the possibilities may point one way –'

'That's what I'm trying to get at. You've got it all taped out in your mind, haven't you?'

'It's a case of very strong probability. It's one of those obvious things. The perfect set-up. But I don't know, I'm sure. It's tricky.'

I looked appealingly at the Old Man.

He said slowly: 'In murder cases, as you know, Charles, the obvious is usually the right solution. Old Leonides married again, ten years ago.'

'When he was seventy-seven?'

'Yes, he married a young woman of twenty-four.'

I whistled.

'What sort of a young woman?'

'A young woman out of a tea-shop. A perfectly respectable young woman – good-looking in an anæmic, apathetic sort of way.'

'And she's the strong probability?'

'I ask you, sir,' said Taverner. 'She's only thirty-four now – and that's a dangerous age. She likes living soft. And there's a young man in the house. Tutor to the grandchildren. Not been in the war – got a bad heart or something. They're as thick as thieves.'

I looked at him thoughtfully. It was, certainly, an old and familiar pattern. The mixture as before. And the second Mrs Leonides was, my father had emphasized, very respectable. In the name of respectability many murders had been committed.

'What was it?' I asked. 'Arsenic?'

'No. We haven't got the analyst's report yet – but the doctor thinks it's eserine.'

'That's a little unusual, isn't it? Surely easy to trace the purchaser.'

'Not this thing. It was his own stuff, you see. Eye-drops.'

'Leonides suffered from diabetes,' said my father. 'He had regular injections of insulin. Insulin is given out in small bottles with a rubber cap. A hypodermic needle is pressed down through the rubber cap and the injection drawn up.'

I guessed the next bit.

'And it wasn't insulin in the bottle, but eserine?'

'Exactly.'

'And who gave him the injection?' I asked.

'His wife.'

I understood now what Sophia meant by the 'right person'.

I asked: 'Does the family get on well with the second Mrs Leonides?'

'No. I gather they are hardly on speaking terms.'

It all seemed clearer and clearer. Nevertheless, Inspector Taverner was clearly not happy about it.

'What don't you like about it?' I asked him.

'If she did it, Mr Charles, it would have been so easy for her to substitute a bona fide bottle of insulin afterwards. In fact, if she is guilty, I can't imagine why on earth she didn't do just that.'

'Yes, it does seem indicated. Plenty of insulin about?'

'Oh yes, full bottles and empty ones. And if she'd done that, ten to one the doctor wouldn't have spotted it. Very little is known of the post-mortem appearances in human poisoning by eserine. But as it was he checked up on the insulin (in case it was the wrong strength or something like that) and so, of course, he soon spotted that it *wasn't* insulin.'

'So it seems,' I said thoughtfully, 'that Mrs Leonides was either very stupid – or possibly very clever.'

'You mean –'

'That she may be gambling on your coming to the conclusion that nobody could have been as stupid as she appears to have been. What are the alternatives? Any other – suspects?'

The Old Man said quietly:

'Practically anyone in the house could have done it. There was always a good store of insulin – at least a fortnight's supply. One of the phials could have been tampered with, and replaced in the knowledge that it would be used in due course.'

'And anybody, more or less, had access to them?'

'They weren't locked away. They were kept on a special shelf in the medicine cupboard in the bathroom of his part of the house. Everybody in the house came and went freely.'

'Any strong motive?'

My father sighed.

'My dear Charles. Aristide Leonides was enormously rich. He has made over a good deal of his money to his family, it is true, but it may be that somebody wanted more.'

'But the one that wanted it most would be the present widow. Has her young man any money?'

'No. Poor as a church mouse.'

Something clicked in my brain. I remembered Sophia's quotation. I suddenly remembered the whole verse of the nursery rhyme:

> *There was a crooked man and he went a crooked mile.*
> *He found a crooked sixpence beside a crooked stile.*
> *He had a crooked cat which caught a crooked mouse,*
> *And they all lived together in a little crooked house.*

I said to Taverner:

'How does she strike you – Mrs Leonides? What do you think of her?'

He replied slowly:

'It's hard to say – very hard to say. She's not easy. Very quiet – so you don't know what she's thinking. But she likes living soft – that I'll swear I'm right about. Puts me in mind, you know, of a cat, a big purring lazy cat ... Not that I've anything against cats. Cats are all right ...'

He sighed.

'What we want,' he said, 'is *evidence*.'

Yes, I thought, we *all* wanted evidence that Mrs Leonides had poisoned her husband. Sophia wanted it, and I wanted it, and Chief-Inspector Taverner wanted it.

Then everything in the garden would be lovely!

But Sophia wasn't sure, and I wasn't sure, and I didn't think Chief-Inspector Taverner was sure either.

CHAPTER 4

On the following day I went down to Three Gables with Taverner.

My position was a curious one. It was, to say the least of it, quite unorthodox. But the Old Man has never been highly orthodox.

I had a certain standing. I had worked with the Special Branch at the Yard during the early days of the war.

This, of course, was entirely different – but my earlier performances had given me, so to speak, a certain official standing.

My father said:

'If we're ever going to solve this case, we've got to get some inside dope. We've got to know all about the people in that house. We've got to know them from the *inside* – not the outside. You're the man who can get that for us.'

I didn't like that. I threw my cigarette end into the grate as I said:

'I'm a police spy? Is that it? I'm to get the inside dope from Sophia whom I love and who both loves and trusts me, or so I believe.'

The Old Man became quite irritable. He said sharply:

'For heaven's sake don't take the commonplace view. To begin with, you don't believe, do you, that your young woman murdered her grandfather?'

'Of course not. The idea's absolutely absurd.'

'Very well – we don't think so either. She's been away for some years, she has always been on perfectly amicable terms with him. She has a very generous income and he would have been, I should say, delighted to hear of her engagement to you and would probably have made a handsome marriage settlement on her. We don't suspect her. Why should we? But you can make quite sure of one thing. If this thing isn't cleared up, that girl won't marry you. From what you've told me I'm fairly sure of that. And mark this, it's the kind of crime that may *never* be cleared up. We may be reasonably sure that the wife and her young man were in cahoots over it – but proving it will be another matter. There's not even a case to put up to the DPP so far. And unless we get definite evidence against her, there'll always be a nasty doubt. You see that, don't you?'

Yes, I saw that.

The Old Man then said quietly:

'Why not put it to her?'

'You mean – ask Sophia if I –' I stopped.

The Old Man was nodding his head vigorously.

'Yes, yes. I'm not asking you to worm your way in without telling the girl what you're up to. See what she has to say about it.'

And so it came about that the following day I drove down with Chief-Inspector Taverner and Detective-Sergeant Lamb to Swinly Dean.

A little way beyond the golf course, we turned in at a gateway where I imagined that before the war there had been an imposing pair of gates. Patriotism or ruthless requisitioning had swept these away. We drove up a long curving drive flanked with rhododendrons and came out on a gravelled sweep in front of the house.

It was incredible! I wondered why it had been called *Three* Gables. Eleven Gables would have been more apposite! The curious thing was that it had a strange air of being distorted – and I thought I knew why. It was the type, really, of a cottage, it was a cottage swollen out of all proportion. It was like looking at a country cottage through a gigantic magnifying-glass. The slant-wise beams, the half-timbering, the gables – it was a little crooked house that had grown like a mushroom in the night!

Yet I got the idea. It was a Greek restaurateur's idea of something English. It was meant to be an Englishman's home – built the size of a castle! I wondered what the first Mrs Leonides had thought of it. She had not, I fancied, been consulted or shown the plans. It was, most probably, her exotic husband's little surprise. I wondered if she had shuddered or smiled.

Apparently she had lived there quite happily.

'Bit overwhelming, isn't it?' said Inspector Taverner. 'Of course, the old gentleman built on to it a good deal – making it into three separate houses, so to speak, with kitchens and everything. It's all tip-top inside, fitted up like a luxury hotel.'

Sophia came out of the front door. She was hatless and wore a green shirt and a tweed skirt.

She stopped dead when she saw me.

'*You?*' she exclaimed.

I said:

'Sophia, I've got to talk to you. Where can we go?'

For a moment I thought she was going to demur, then she turned and said: 'This way.'

We walked down across the lawn. There was a fine view across Swinly Dean's No. 1 course – away to a clump of pine trees on a hill, and beyond it, to the dimness of hazy countryside.

Sophia led me to a rock-garden, now somewhat neglected, where there was a rustic wooden seat of great discomfort, and we sat down.

'Well?' she said.

Her voice was not encouraging.

I said my piece – all of it.

She listened very attentively. Her face gave little indication of what she was thinking, but when I came at last to a full stop, she sighed. It was a deep sigh.

'Your father,' she said, 'is a very clever man.'

'The Old Man has his points. I think it's a rotten idea myself – but –'

She interrupted me.

'Oh no,' she said. 'It isn't a rotten idea at all. It's the only thing that might be any good. Your father, Charles, knows exactly what's been going on in my mind. He knows better than you do.'

With a sudden almost despairing vehemence, she drove one clenched hand into the palm of the other.

'I've *got* to have the truth. I've got to *know*.'

'Because of us? But, dearest –'

'Not only because of us, Charles. I've got to know for my own peace of mind. You see, Charles, I didn't tell you last night – but the truth is – I'm afraid.'

'Afraid?'

'Yes – afraid – afraid – afraid. The police think, your father thinks, you think, everybody thinks – that it was Brenda.'

'The probabilities –'

'Oh yes, it's quite probable. It's possible. But when I say, "Brenda probably did it," I'm quite conscious that it's only wishful thinking. Because, you see, I *don't really think so*.'

'You *don't* think so?' I said slowly.

'I don't *know*. You've heard about it all from the outside as I wanted you to. Now I'll show it you from the inside. I simply don't feel that Brenda is that kind of a person – she's not the sort of person, I feel, who would ever do anything that might involve her in any danger. She's far too careful of herself.'

'How about this young man? Laurence Brown.'

'Laurence is a complete rabbit. He wouldn't have the guts.'

'I wonder.'

'Yes, we don't really know, do we? I mean, people are capable of surprising one frightfully. One gets an idea of them into one's head, and sometimes it's absolutely wrong. Not always – but sometimes. But all the same, Brenda' – she shook her head – 'she's always acted so completely in character. She's what I call the harem type. Likes sitting about and eating sweets and having nice clothes and jewellery and reading cheap novels and going to the cinema. And it's a queer thing to say, when one remembers that he was eighty-seven, but I really think she was rather thrilled by grandfather. He had a power, you know. I should imagine he could make a woman feel – oh – rather like a queen – the sultan's favourite! I think – I've always thought – that he made Brenda feel as though she were an exciting, romantic person. He's been clever with women all his life – and that kind of thing is a sort of art – you don't lose the knack of it, however old you are.'

I left the problem of Brenda for the moment and harked back to a phrase of Sophia's which had disturbed me.

'Why did you say,' I asked, 'that you were afraid?'

Sophia shivered a little and pressed her hands together.

'Because it's true,' she said in a low voice. 'It's very important, Charles, that I should make you understand this. You see, we're a very queer family . . . There's a lot of *ruthlessness* in us – and – different kinds of ruthlessness. That's what's so disturbing. The different kinds.'

She must have seen incomprehension in my face. She went on, speaking energetically.

'I'll try and make what I mean clear. Grandfather, for instance. Once when he was telling us about his boyhood in Smyrna, he mentioned, quite casually, that he had stabbed two men. It was some kind of a brawl – there had been some unforgivable insult – I don't know – but it was just a thing that had happened quite naturally. He'd really practically forgotten about it. But it was, somehow, such a queer thing to hear about, quite casually, in *England.*' I nodded.

'That's one kind of ruthlessness,' went on Sophia, 'and then there was my grandmother. I only just remember her, but I've heard a good deal about her. I think she might have had the ruthlessness that comes from having no imagination whatever. All those fox-hunting forebears – and the old Generals, the shoot-'em-down type. Full of rectitude and arrogance, and not a bit afraid of taking responsibility in matters of life and death.'

'Isn't that a bit far-fetched?'

'Yes, I dare say – but I'm always rather afraid of that type. It's full of rectitude but it *is* ruthless. And then there's my own mother – she's an actress – she's a darling, but she's got absolutely *no* sense of proportion. She's one of those unconscious egoists who can only see things in relation to how it affects *them*. That's rather frightening, sometimes, you know. And there's Clemency, Uncle Roger's wife. She's a scientist – she's doing some kind of very important research – she's ruthless too, in a kind of cold-blooded impersonal way. Uncle Roger's the exact opposite – he's the kindest and most lovable person in the world, but he's got a really terrific temper. Things make his blood boil and then he hardly knows what he's doing. And there's father –'

She made a long pause.

'Father,' she said slowly, 'is almost too well controlled. You never know what he's thinking. He never shows any emotion at all. It's probably a kind of unconscious self-defence against mother's absolute orgies of emotion, but sometimes – it worries me a little.'

'My dear child,' I said, 'you're working yourself up unnecessarily. What it comes to in the end is that everybody, perhaps, is capable of murder.'

'I suppose that's true. Even me.'

'Not you!'

'Oh yes, Charles, you can't make me an exception. I suppose I *could* murder someone . . .' She was silent a moment or two, then added, 'But if so, it would have to be for something really worth while!'

I laughed then. I couldn't help it. And Sophia smiled.

'Perhaps I'm a fool,' she said, 'but we've got to find out the truth about grandfather's death. We've got to. If only it *was* Brenda . . .'

I felt suddenly rather sorry for Brenda Leonides.

CHAPTER 5

Along the path towards us came a tall figure walking briskly. It had on a battered old felt hat, a shapeless skirt, and a rather cumbersome jersey.

'Aunt Edith,' said Sophia.

The figure paused once or twice, stooping to the flower borders, then it advanced upon us. I rose to my feet.

'This is Charles Hayward, Aunt Edith. My aunt, Miss de Haviland.'

Edith de Haviland was a woman of about seventy. She had a mass of untidy grey hair, a weather-beaten face and a shrewd and piercing glance.

'How d'ye do?' she said. 'I've heard about you. Back from the East. How's your father?'

Rather surprised, I said he was very well.

'Knew him when he was a boy,' said Miss de Haviland. 'Knew his mother very well. You look rather like her. Have you come to help us – or the other thing?'

'I hope to help,' I said rather uncomfortably.

She nodded.

'We could do with some help. Place swarming with policemen. Pop out at you all over the place. Don't like some of the types. A boy who's been to a decent school oughtn't to go into the police. Saw Moyra Kinoul's boy the other day holding up the traffic at Marble Arch. Makes you feel you don't know where you are!'

She turned to Sophia.

'Nannie's asking for you, Sophia. Fish.'

'Bother,' said Sophia. 'I'll go and telephone about it.'

She walked briskly towards the house. Miss de Haviland turned and walked slowly in the same directon. I fell into step beside her.

'Don't know what we'd all do without nannies,' said Miss de Haviland. 'Nearly everybody's got an old nannie. They come back and wash and iron and cook and do housework. Faithful. Chose this one myself – years ago.'

She stopped and pulled viciously at an entangling twining bit of green.

'Hateful stuff – bindweed! Worst weed there is! Choking, entangling – and you can't get at it properly, runs along underground.'

With her heel she ground the handful of greenstuff viciously underfoot.

'This is a bad business, Charles Hayward,' she said. She was looking towards the house. 'What do the police think about it? Suppose I mustn't ask you that. Seems odd to think of Aristide being poisoned. For that matter it seems odd to think of him being dead. I never liked him – never! But I can't get used to the idea of his being dead . . . Makes the house seem so – empty.'

I said nothing. For all her curt way of speech, Edith de Haviland seemed in a reminiscent mood.

'Was thinking this morning – I've lived here a long time. Over forty years. Came here when my sister died. *He* asked me to. Seven children – and the youngest only a year old . . . Couldn't leave 'em to be brought up by a dago, could I? An impossible marriage, of course. I always felt Marcia must have been – well – bewitched. Ugly common little foreigner! He gave me a free hand – I will say that. Nurses, governesses, school. And proper wholesome nursery food – not those queer spiced rice dishes *he* used to eat.'

'And you've been here ever since?' I murmured.

'Yes. Queer in a way . . . I *could* have left, I suppose, when the children grew up and married . . . I suppose, really, I'd got interested in the garden. And then there was Philip. If a man marries an actress he can't expect to have any home life. Don't know why actresses have children. As soon as a baby's born they rush off and play in Repertory in Edinburgh or somewhere as remote as possible. Philip did the sensible thing – moved in here with his books.'

'What does Philip Leonides do?'

'Writes books. Can't think why. Nobody wants to read them. All about obscure historical details. You've never even heard of them, have you?'

I admitted it.

'Too much money, that's what he's had,' said Miss de Haviland. 'Most people have to stop being cranks and earn a living.'

'Don't his books pay?'

'Of course not. He's supposed to be a great authority on certain periods and all that. But he doesn't have to make his books pay – Aristide settled something like a hundred thousand pounds – something quite fantastic – on him! To avoid death duties! Aristide made them all financially independent. Roger runs Associated Catering – Sophia has a very handsome allowance. The children's money is in trust for them.'

'So no one gains particularly by his death?'

She threw me a strange glance.

'Yes, they do. They all get more money. But they could probably have had it, if they asked for it, anyway.'

'Have you any idea who poisoned him, Miss de Haviland?'

She replied characteristically:

'No, indeed I haven't. It's upset me very much. Not nice to think one has a Borgia sort of person loose about the house. I suppose the police will fasten on poor Brenda.'

'You don't think they'll be right in doing so?'

'I simply can't tell. She's always seemed to me a singularly stupid and commonplace young woman – rather conventional. Not my idea of a poisoner. Still, after all, if a young woman of twenty-four marries a man close on eighty, it's fairly obvious that she's marrying him for his money. In the normal course of events she could have expected to become a rich widow fairly soon. But Aristide was a singularly tough old man. His diabetes wasn't getting any worse. He really looked like living to be a hundred. I suppose she got tired of waiting . . .'

'In that case,' I said, and stopped.

'In that case,' said Miss de Haviland briskly, 'it will be more or less all right. Annoying publicity, of course. But after all, she isn't one of the family.'

'You've no other ideas?' I asked.

'What other ideas should I have?'

I wondered. I had a suspicion that there might be more going on under the battered felt hat than I knew.

Behind the perky, almost disconnected utterance, there was, I thought, a very shrewd brain at work. Just for a moment I even wondered whether Miss de Haviland had poisoned Aristide Leonides herself . . .

It did not seem an impossible idea. At the back of my mind

was the way she had ground the bindweed into the soil with her heel with a kind of vindictive thoroughness.

I remembered the word Sophia had used. *Ruthlessness.*

I stole a sideways glance at Edith de Haviland.

Given good and sufficient reason . . . But what exactly would seem to Edith de Haviland good and sufficient reason?

To answer that, I should have to know her better.

CHAPTER 6

The front door was open. We passed through it into a rather surprisingly spacious hall. It was furnished with restraint – well-polished dark oak and gleaming brass. At the back, where the staircase would normally appear, was a white panelled wall with a door in it.

'My brother-in-law's part of the house,' said Miss de Haviland. 'The ground floor is Philip and Magda's.'

We went through a doorway on the left into a large drawing-room. It had pale-blue panelled walls, furniture covered in heavy brocade, and on every available table and on the walls were hung photographs and pictures of actors, dancers, and stage scenes and designs. A Degas of ballet dancers hung over the mantelpiece. There were masses of flowers, enormous brown chrysanthemums and great vases of carnations.

'I suppose,' said Miss de Haviland, 'that you want to see Philip?'

Did I want to see Philip? I had no idea. All I had wanted to do was to see Sophia. That I had done. She had given emphatic encouragement to the Old Man's plan – but she had now receded from the scene and was presumably somewhere telephoning about fish, having given me no indication of how to proceed. Was I to approach Philip Leonides as a young man anxious to marry his daughter, or as a casual friend who had dropped in (surely not at such a moment!) or as an associate of the police?

Miss de Haviland gave me no time to consider her question. It was, indeed, not a question at all, but more an assertion. Miss de Haviland, I judged, was more inclined to assert than to question.

'We'll go to the library,' she said.

She led me out of the drawing-room, along a corridor and in through another door.

It was a big room, full of books. The books did not confine themselves to the bookcases that reached up to the ceiling. They were on chairs and tables and even on the floor. And yet there was no sense of disarray about them.

The room was cold. There was some smell absent in it that I was conscious of having expected. It smelt of the mustiness of old books and just a little beeswax. In a second or two I realized what I missed. It was the scent of tobacco. Philip Leonides was not a smoker.

He got up from behind his table as we entered – a tall man, aged somewhere around fifty, an extraordinarily handsome man. Everyone had laid so much emphasis on the ugliness of Aristide Leonides, that for some reason I expected his son to be ugly too. Certainly I was not prepared for this perfection of feature the straight nose, the flawless line of jaw, the fair hair touched with grey that swept back from a well-shaped forehead.

'This is Charles Hayward, Philip,' said Edith de Haviland.

'Ah, how do you do?'

I could not tell if he had ever heard of me. The hand he gave me was cold. His face was quite incurious. It made me rather nervous. He stood there, patient and uninterested.

'Where are those awful policemen?' demanded Miss de Haviland. 'Have they been in here?'

'I believe Chief-Inspector' – (he glanced down at a card on the desk) – 'er – Taverner is coming to talk to me presently.'

'Where is he now?'

'I've no idea, Aunt Edith. Upstairs, I suppose.'

'With Brenda?'

'I really don't know.'

Looking at Philip Leonides, it seemed quite impossible that a murder could have been committed anywhere in his vicinity.

'Is Magda up yet?'

'I don't know. She's not usually up before eleven.'

'That sounds like her,' said Edith de Haviland.

What sounded like Mrs Philip Leonides was a high voice talking very rapidly and approaching fast. The door behind me burst open and a woman came in. I don't know how she managed to give the impression of its being three women rather than one who entered.

She was smoking a cigarette in a long holder and was wearing a peach satin *négligé* which she was holding up with one hand. A cascade of Titian hair rippled down her back. Her face had that almost shocking air of nudity that a woman's has nowadays when it is not made up at all. Her eyes were blue and enormous and she was talking very rapidly in a husky, rather attractive voice with a very clear enunciation.

'Darling, I can't stand it – I simply can't stand it – just think of the notices – it isn't in the papers yet, but of course it will be – and I simply can't make up my mind what I ought to wear at the inquest – very, very subdued – not black though, perhaps dark purple – and I simply haven't got a coupon left – I've lost the address of that dreadful man who sells them to me – you know, the garage somewhere near Shaftesbury Avenue – and if I went up there in the car the police would follow me, and they might ask the most awkward questions, mightn't they? I mean, what could one say? How calm you are, Philip! How can you be so calm? Don't you realize we can leave this awful house now? Freedom – freedom! Oh, how unkind – the poor old Sweetie – of course we'd never have left him while he was alive. He really did dote on us, didn't he – in spite of all the trouble that woman upstairs tried to make between us. I'm quite sure that if we had gone away and left him to her, he'd have cut us right out of everything. Horrible creature! After all, poor old Sweetie Pie was just on ninety – all the family feeling in the world couldn't have stood up against a dreadful woman who was on the spot. You know, Philip, I really believe that this would be a wonderful opportunity to put on the Edith Thompson play. This murder would give us a lot of advance publicity. Bildenstein said he could get the Thespian – that dreary play in verse about miners is coming off any minute – it's a wonderful part – wonderful. I know they say I must always play comedy because of my nose – but you know there's quite a lot of comedy to be got out of Edith Thompson – I don't think the author realized that – comedy always heightens the suspense. I know just how I'd play it – commonplace, silly, make-believe up to the last minute and then –'

She cast out an arm – the cigarette fell out of the holder on to the polished mahogany of Philip's desk and began to burn it. Impassively he reached for it and dropped it into the wastepaper basket.

'And then,' whispered Magda Leonides, her eyes suddenly widening, her face stiffening, 'just *terror* . . .'

The stark fear stayed on her face for about twenty seconds, then her face relaxed, crumpled, a bewildered child was about to burst into tears.

Suddenly all emotion was wiped away as though by a sponge and, turning to me, she asked in a businesslike tone:

'Don't you think that would be the way to play Edith Thompson?'

I said I thought that would be exactly the way to play Edith Thompson. At the moment I could only remember very vaguely who Edith Thompson was, but I was anxious to start off well with Sophia's mother.

'Rather like Brenda, really, wasn't she?' said Magda. 'D'you know, I never thought of that. It's very interesting. Shall I point that out to the inspector?'

The man behind the desk frowned very slightly.

'There's really no need, Magda,' he said, 'for you to see him at all. I can tell him anything he wants to know.'

'Not see him?' Her voice went up. 'But *of course* I must see him! Darling, darling, you're so terribly unimaginative! You don't realize the importance of *details*. He'll want to know exactly how and when everything happened, all the little things one noticed and wondered about at the time –'

'Mother,' said Sophia, coming through the open door, 'you're not to tell the inspector a lot of lies.'

'Sophia – *darling* . . .'

'I know, precious, that you've got it all set and that you're ready to give a most beautiful performance. But you've got it wrong. Quite wrong.'

'Nonsense. You don't know –'

'I do know. You've got to play it quite differently, darling. Subdued – saying very little – holding it all back – on your guard – protecting the family.'

Magda Leonides' face showed the naïve perplexity of a child.

'Darling,' she said, 'do you really think –'

'Yes, I do. Throw it away. That's the idea.'

Sophia added, as a little pleased smile began to show on her mother's face:

'I've made you some chocolate. It's in the drawing-room.'

'Oh – good – I'm starving –'

She paused in the doorway.

'You don't know,' she said, and the words appeared to be addressed either to me or to the bookshelf behind my head, 'how lovely it is to have a daughter!'

On this exit line she went out.

'God knows,' said Miss de Haviland, 'what she will say to the police!'

'She'll be all right,' said Sophia.

'She might say *anything*.'

'Don't worry,' said Sophia. 'She'll play it the way the producer says. *I'm* the producer!'

She went out after her mother, then wheeled back to say:

'Here's Chief-Inspector Taverner to see you, Father. You don't mind if Charles stays, do you?'

I thought that a very faint air of bewilderment showed on Philip Leonides' face. It well might! But his incurious habit served me in good stead. He murmured:

'Oh certainly – certainly,' in a rather vague voice.

Chief-Inspector Taverner came in, solid, dependable, and with an air of businesslike promptitude that was somehow soothing.

'Just a little unpleasantness,' his manner seemed to say, 'and then we shall be out of the house for good – and nobody will be more pleased than I shall. *We* don't want to hang about, I can assure you . . .'

I don't know how he managed, without any words at all, but merely by drawing up a chair to the desk, to convey what he did, but it worked. I sat down unobtrusively a little way off.

'Yes, Chief-Inspector?' said Philip.

Miss de Haviland said abruptly:

'You don't want me, Chief-Inspector?'

'Not just at the moment, Miss de Haviland. Later, if I might have a few words with you –'

'Of course. I shall be upstairs.'

She went out, shutting the door behind her.

'Well, Chief-Inspector?' Philip repeated.

'I know you're a very busy gentleman and I don't want to disturb you for long. But I may mention to you in confidence that our suspicions are confirmed. Your father did not die a natural death. His death was the result of an overdose of physostigmine – more usually known as eserine.'

Philip bowed his head. He showed no particular emotion.

'I don't know whether that suggests anything to you?' Taverner went on.

'What should it suggest? My own view is that my father must have taken the poison by accident.'

'You really think so, Mr Leonides?'

'Yes, it seems to me perfectly possible. He was close on ninety, remember, and with very imperfect eyesight.'

'So he emptied the contents of his eyedrop bottle into an insulin bottle. Does that really seem to you a credible suggestion, Mr Leonides?'

Philip did not reply. His face became even more impassive.

Taverner went on:

'We have found the eyedrop bottle, empty – in the dustbin, with no fingerprints on it. That in itself is curious. In the normal way there should have been fingerprints. Certainly your father's, possibly his wife's, or the valet . . .'

Philip Leonides looked up.

'What about the valet?' he said. 'What about Johnson?'

'You are suggesting Johnson as the possible criminal? He certainly had opportunity. But when we come to motive it is different. It was your father's custom to pay him a bonus every year – each year the bonus was increased. Your father made it clear to him that this was in lieu of any sum that he might otherwise have left him in his will. The bonus now, after seven years' service, has reached a very considerable sum every year and is still rising. It was obviously to Johnson's interest that your father should live as long as possible. Moreover, they were on excellent terms, and Johnson's record of past service is unimpeachable – he is a thoroughly skilled and faithful valet attendant.' He paused. 'We do not suspect Johnson.'

Philip replied tonelessly: 'I see.'

'Now, Mr Leonides, perhaps you will give me a detailed

account of your own movements on the day of your father's death?'

'Certainly, Chief-Inspector. I was here, in this room, all that day – with the exception of meals, of course.'

'Did you see your father at all?'

'I said good morning to him after breakfast as was my custom.'

'Were you alone with him then?'

'My – er – stepmother was in the room.'

'Did he seem quite as usual?'

With a slight hint of irony, Philip replied:

'He showed no foreknowledge that he was to be murdered that day.'

'Is your father's portion of the house entirely separate from this?'

'Yes, the only access to it is through the door in the hall.'

'Is that door kept locked?'

'No.'

'Never?'

'I have never known it to be so.'

'Anyone could go freely between that part of the house and this?'

'Certainly. It was only separate from the point of view of domestic convenience.'

'How did you first hear of your father's death?'

'My brother Roger, who occupies the west wing of the floor above, came rushing down to tell me that my father had had a sudden seizure. He had difficulty in breathing and seemed very ill.'

'What did you do?'

'I telephoned through to the doctor, which nobody seemed to have thought of doing. The doctor was out – but I left a message for him to come as soon as possible. I then went upstairs.'

'And then?'

'My father was clearly very ill. He died before the doctor came.'

There was no emotion in Philip's voice. It was a simple statement of fact.

'Where was the rest of your family?'

'My wife was in London. She returned shortly afterwards. Sophia was also absent, I believe. The two younger ones, Eustace and Josephine, were at home.'

'I hope you won't misunderstand me, Mr Leonides, if I ask you exactly how your father's death will affect your financial position.'

'I quite appreciate that you want to know all the facts. My father made us financially independent a great many years ago. My brother he made Chairman and principal shareholder of Associated Catering – his largest company, and put the management of it entirely in his hands. He made over to me what he considered an equivalent sum – actually I think it was a hundred and fifty thousand pounds in various bonds and securities – so that I could use the capital as I chose. He also settled very generous amounts on my two sisters, who have since died.'

'But he left himself still a very rich man?'

'No, actually he only retained for himself a comparatively modest income. He said it would give him an interest in life. Since that time' – for the first time a faint smile creased Philip's lips – 'he has become, as the result of various undertakings, an even richer man than he was before.'

'Your brother and yourself came here to live. That was not the result of any financial – difficulties?'

'Certainly not. It was a mere matter of convenience. My father always told us that we were welcome to make a home with him. For various domestic reasons this was a convenient thing for me to do.

'I was also,' added Philip deliberately, 'extremely fond of my father. I came here with my family in 1937. I pay no rent, but I pay my proportion of the rates.'

'And your brother?'

'My brother came here as a result of the blitz, when his house in London was bombed in 1943.'

'Now, Mr Leonides, have you any idea what your father's testamentary dispositions are?'

'A very clear idea. He re-made his will in 1946. My father was not a secretive man. He had a great sense of family. He held a family conclave at which his solicitor was also present and who, at his request, made clear to us the terms of the will. These terms I expect you already know. Mr Gaitskill will doubtless have informed you. Roughly, a sum of a hundred thousand pounds free of duty was left to my stepmother in addition to her already very generous marriage settlement. The residue of his property was divided into three portions, one to myself, one to my brother, and a third in trust for the three grandchildren. The estate is a large one, but the death duties, of course, will be very heavy.'

'Any bequests to servants or to charity?'

'No bequests of any kind. The wages paid to servants were increased annually if they remained in his service.'

'You are not – you will excuse my asking – in actual need of money, Mr Leonides?'

'Income tax, as you know, is somewhat heavy, Chief-Inspector – but my income amply suffices for my needs – and for my wife's. Moreover, my father frequently made us all very generous gifts, and had any emergency arisen, he would have come to the rescue immediately.'

Philip added coldly and clearly:

'I can assure you that I had no financial reason for desiring my father's death, Chief-Inspector.'

'I am very sorry, Mr Leonides, if you think I suggested anything of the kind. But we have to get at all the facts. Now I'm afraid I must ask you some rather delicate questions. They refer to the relations between your father and his wife. Were they on happy terms together?'

'As far as I know, perfectly.'

'No quarrels?'

'I do not think so.'

'There was a – great disparity in age?'

'There was.'

'Did you – excuse me – approve of your father's second marriage.'

'My approval was not asked.'

'That is not an answer, Mr Leonides.'

'Since you press the point, I will say that I considered the marriage unwise.'

'Did you remonstrate with your father about it.'

'When I heard of it, it was an accomplished fact.'

'Rather a shock to you – eh?'

Philip did not reply.

'Was there any bad feeling about the matter?'

'My father was at perfect liberty to do as he pleased.'

'Your relations with Mrs Leonides have been amicable?'

'Perfectly.'

'You are on friendly terms with her?'

'We very seldom meet.'

Chief-Inspector Taverner shifted his ground.

'Can you tell me something about Mr Laurence Brown?'

'I'm afraid I can't. He was engaged by my father.'

'But he was engaged to teach your children, Mr Leonides.'

'True. My son was a sufferer from infantile paralysis – fortunately a light case – and it was considered not advisable to send him to a public school. My father suggested that he and my young daughter Josephine should have a private tutor – the choice at the time was rather limited – since the tutor in question must be ineligible for military service. This young man's credentials were satisfactory, my father and my aunt (who has always looked after the children's welfare) were satisfied, and I acquiesced. I may add that I have no fault to find with his teaching, which has been conscientious and adequate.'

'His living quarters are in your father's part of the house, not here?'

'There was more room up there.'

'Have you ever noticed – I am sorry to ask this – any signs of intimacy between Laurence Brown and your stepmother?'

'I have had no opportunity of observing anything of the kind.'

'Have you heard any gossip or tittle-tattle on the subject?'

'I don't listen to gossip or tittle-tattle, Chief-Inspector.'

'Very creditable,' said Inspector Taverner. 'So you've seen no evil, heard no evil, and aren't speaking any evil?'

'If you like to put it that way, Chief-Inspector.'

Inspector Taverner got up.

'Well,' he said, 'thank you very much, Mr Leonides.'

I followed him unobtrusively out of the room.

'Whew,' said Taverner, 'he's a cold fish!'

CHAPTER 7

'And now,' said Taverner, 'we'll go and have a word with Mrs Philip. Magda West, her stage name is.'

'Is she any good?' I asked. 'I know her name, and I believe I've seen her in various shows, but I can't remember when and where.'

'She's one of those Near Successes,' said Taverner. 'She's starred once or twice in the West End, she's made quite a name for herself in Repertory – she plays a lot for the little highbrow theatres and the Sunday clubs. The truth is, I think, she's been handicapped by not having to earn her living at it. She's been able to pick and choose, and to go where she likes and occasionally to put up the money and finance a show where she's fancied a certain part – usually the last part in the world to suit her. Result is, she's receded a bit into the amateur class rather than the professional. She's good, mind you, especially in comedy – but managers don't like her much – they say she's too independent, and she's a troublemaker – foments rows and enjoys a bit of mischief-making. I don't know how much of it is true – but she's not too popular amongst her fellow artists.'

Sophia came out of the drawing-room and said: 'My mother is in here, Chief-Inspector.'

I followed Taverner into the big drawing-room. For a moment I hardly recognized the woman who sat on the brocaded settee.

The Titian hair was piled high on her head in an Edwardian coiffure, and she was dressed in a well-cut dark-grey coat and skirt with a delicately pleated pale mauve shirt fastened at the neck by a small cameo brooch. For the first time I was aware of the charm of her delightfully tip-tilted nose. I was faintly reminded of Athene Seyler – and it seemed quite impossible to believe that this was the tempestuous creature in the peach *négligé*.

'Inspector Taverner?' she said. '*Do* come in and sit down. Will you smoke? This is a most terrible business. I simply feel at the moment that I just can't take it in.'

Her voice was low and emotionless, the voice of a person determined at all costs to display self-control. She went on:

'Please tell me if I can help you in any way.'

'Thank you, Mrs Leonides. Where were you at the time of the tragedy?'

'I suppose I must have been driving down from London. I'd lunched that day at the Ivy with a friend. Then we'd gone to a dress show. We had a drink with some other friends at the Berkeley. Then I started home. When I got here everything was in commotion. It seemed my father-in-law had had a sudden seizure. He was – dead.' Her voice trembled just a little.

'You were fond of your father-in-law?'

'I was devoted –'

Her voice rose. Sophia adjusted, very slightly, the angle of the Degas picture. Magda's voice dropped to its former subdued tone.

'I was very fond of him,' she said in a quiet voice. 'We all were. He was – very good to us.'

'Did you get on well with Mrs Leonides?'

'We didn't see very much of Brenda.'

'Why was that?'

'Well, we hadn't much in common. Poor dear Brenda. Life must have been hard for her sometimes.'

Again Sophia fiddled with the Degas.

'Indeed? In what way?'

'Oh, I don't know.' Magda shook her head, with a sad little smile.

'Was Mrs Leonides happy with her husband?'

'Oh, I think so.'

'No quarrels?'

Again the slight smiling shake of the head.

'I really don't know, Inspector. Their part of the house is quite separate.'

'She and Mr Laurence Brown were very friendly, were they not?'

Magda Leonides stiffened. Her eyes opened reproachfully at Taverner.

'I don't think,' she said with dignity, 'that you ought to ask me things like that. Brenda was quite friendly to *everyone*. She is really a very amiable sort of person.'

'Do you like Mr Laurence Brown?'

'He's very quiet. Quite nice, but you hardly know he's there. I haven't really seen very much of him.'

'Is his teaching satisfactory?'

'I suppose so. I really wouldn't know. Philip seems quite satisfied.'

Taverner essayed some shock tactics.

'I'm sorry to ask you this, but in your opinion was there anything in the nature of a love affair between Mr Brown and Mrs Brenda Leonides?'

Magda got up. She was very much the *grande dame*.

'I have never seen any evidence of anything of that kind,' she said. 'I don't think really, Inspector, that that is a question you ought to ask me. She was my father-in-law's wife.'

I almost applauded.

The Chief-Inspector also rose.

'More a question for the servants?' he suggested.

Magda did not answer.

'Thank you, Mrs Leonides,' said the Inspector and went out.

'You did that beautifully, darling,' said Sophia to her mother warmly.

Magda twisted up a curl reflectively behind her right ear and looked at herself in the glass.

'Ye-es,' she said, 'I *think* it was the right way to play it.'

Sophia looked at me.

'Oughtn't you,' she asked, 'to go with the Inspector?'

'Look here, Sophia, what am I supposed –'

I stopped. I could not very well ask outright in front of Sophia's mother exactly what my role was supposed to be. Magda Leonides had so far evinced no interest in my presence at all, except as a useful recipient of an exit line on daughters. I might be a reporter, her daughter's fiancé, or an obscure hanger-on of the police force, or even an undertaker – to Magda Leonides they would one and all come under the general heading of audience.

Looking down at her feet, Mrs Leonides said with dissatis-faction:

'These shoes are wrong. Frivolous.'

Obeying Sophia's imperious wave of the head, I hurried after Taverner. I caught him up in the outer hall just going through the door to the stairway.

'Just going up to see the elder brother,' he explained.

I put my problem to him without more ado.

'Look here, Taverner, who am I supposed to *be*?'

He looked surprised.

'Who are you supposed to be?'

'Yes, what am I doing here in this house? If anyone asks me, what do I say?'

'Oh I see.' He considered for a moment. Then he smiled. 'Has anybody asked you?'

'Well – no.'

'Then why not leave it at that. *Never explain.* That's a very good motto. Especially in a house upset like this house is. Everyone is far too full of their own private worries and fears to be in a questioning mood. They'll take you for granted so long as you just seem sure of yourself. It's a great mistake ever to say anything when you needn't. H'm, now we go through this door and up the stairs. Nothing locked. Of course you realize, I expect, that these questions I'm asking are all a lot of hooey! Doesn't matter a hoot who was in the house and who wasn't, or where they all were on that particular day –'

'Then why –'

He went on: 'Because it at least gives me a chance to look at them all, and size them up, and hear what they've got to say, and to hope that, quite by chance, somebody might give me a useful pointer.' He was silent a moment and then murmured: 'I bet Mrs Magda Leonides could spill a mouthful if she chose.'

'Would it be reliable?' I asked.

'Oh no,' said Taverner, 'it wouldn't be reliable. But it might start a possible line of inquiry. Everybody in the damned house had means and opportunity. What I want is a motive.'

At the top of the stairs, a door barred off the right-hand corridor. There was a brass knocker on it and Inspector Taverner duly knocked.

It was opened with startling suddenness by a man who must have been standing just inside. He was a clumsy giant of a man, with powerful shoulders, dark rumpled hair, and an exceedingly ugly but at the same time rather pleasant face. His eyes looked at us and then quickly away in that furtive, embarrassed manner which shy but honest people often adopt.

'Oh, I say,' he said. 'Come in. Yes, do. I was going – but it doesn't matter. Come into the sitting-room. I'll get Clemency – oh, you're there, darling. It's Chief-Inspector Taverner. He – are there any cigarettes? Just wait a minute. If you don't mind.' He collided with a screen, said 'I beg your pardon' to it in a flustered manner, and went out of the room.

It was rather like the exit of a bumble-bee and left a noticeable silence behind it.

Mrs Roger Leonides was standing up by the window. I was intrigued at once by her personality and by the atmosphere of the room in which we stood.

The walls were painted white – really white, not an ivory or a pale cream which is what one usually means when one says 'white' in house decoration. They had no pictures on them except one over the mantelpiece, a geometrical fantasia in triangles of dark grey and battleship blue. There was hardly any furniture – only mere utilitarian necessities, three or four chairs, a glass-topped table, one small bookshelf. There were no ornaments. There was light and space and air. It was as different from the big brocaded and flowered drawing-room on the floor below as chalk from cheese. And Mrs Roger Leonides was as different from Mrs Philip Leonides as one woman could be from another. Whilst one felt that Magda Leonides could be, and often was, at least half a dozen different women, Clemency Leonides, I was sure, could never be anyone but herself. She was a woman of very sharp and definite personality.

She was about fifty, I suppose; her hair was grey, cut very short in what was almost an Eton crop but which grew so beautifully on her small well-shaped head that it had none of the ugliness I have always associated with that particular cut. She had an intelligent, sensitive face, with light-grey eyes of a peculiar and searching intensity. She had on a simple dark-red woollen frock that fitted her slenderness perfectly.

She was, I felt at once, rather an alarming woman . . . I think, because I judged that the standards by which she lived might not be those of an ordinary woman. I understood at once why Sophia had used the word ruthlessness in connection with her. The room was cold and I shivered a little.

Clemency Leonides said in a quiet, well-bred voice:

'Do sit down, Chief-Inspector. Is there any further news?'

'Death was due to eserine, Mrs Leonides.'

She said thoughtfully:

'So that makes it murder. It couldn't have been an accident of any kind, could it?'

'No, Mrs Leonides.'

'Please be very gentle with my husband, Chief-Inspector. This will affect him very much. He worshipped his father and he feels things very acutely. He is an emotional person.'

'You were on good terms with your father-in-law, Mrs Leonides?'

'Yes, on quite good terms.' She added quietly: 'I did not like him very much.'

'Why was that?'

'I disliked his objectives in life – and his methods of attaining them.'

'And Mrs Brenda Leonides?'

'Brenda? I never saw very much of her.'

'Do you think it possible that there was anything between her and Mr Laurence Brown?'

'You mean – some kind of a love affair? I shouldn't think so. But I really wouldn't know anything about it.'

Her voice sounded completely uninterested.

Roger Leonides came back with a rush, and the same bumble-bee effect.

'I got held up,' he said. 'Telephone. Well, Inspector? Well? Have you got news? What caused my father's death?'

'Death was due to eserine poisoning.'

'It was? My God! Then it was that woman! She couldn't wait! He took her more or less out of the gutter and this is his reward. She murdered him in cold blood! God, it makes my blood boil to think of it.'

'Have you any particular reason for thinking that?' Taverner asked.

Roger was pacing up and down, tugging at his hair with both hands.

'Reason? Why, who else could it be? I've never trusted her – never liked her! We've none of us liked her. Philip and I were both appalled when Dad came home one day and told us what he had done! At his age! It was madness – *madness*. My father was an amazing man, Inspector. In intellect he was as young and fresh as a man of forty. Everything I have in the world I owe to him. He did everything for me – never failed me. It was I who failed *him* – when I think of it –'

He dropped heavily on to a chair. His wife came quietly to his side.

'Now, Roger, that's enough. Don't work yourself up.'

'I know, dearest – I know,' he took her hand. 'But how can I keep calm – how can I help feeling –'

'But we must all keep calm, Roger. Chief-Inspector Taverner wants our help.'

'That is right, Mrs Leonides.'

Roger cried:

'Do you know what I'd like to do? I'd like to strangle that woman with my own hands. Grudging that dear old man a few extra years of life. If I had her here –' He sprang up. He was shaking with rage. He held out convulsive hands. 'Yes, I'd wring her neck, wring her neck . . .'

'Roger!' said Clemency sharply.

He looked at her, abashed.

'Sorry, dearest.' He turned to us. 'I do apologize. My feelings get the better of me. I – excuse me –'

He went out of the room again. Clemency Leonides said with a very faint smile:

'Really, you know, he wouldn't hurt a fly.'

Taverner accepted her remark politely.

Then he started on his so-called routine questions.

Clemency Leonides replied concisely and accurately.

Roger Leonides had been in London on the day of his father's death at Box House, the headquarters of the Associated Catering. He had returned early in the afternoon and had spent some time with his father as was his custom. She herself had been, as usual, at the Lambert Institute in Gower Street where she worked. She had returned to the house just before six o'clock.

'Did you see your father-in-law?'

'No. The last time I saw him was on the day before. We had coffee with him after dinner.'

'But you did not see him on the day of his death?'

'No. I actually went over to his part of the house because Roger thought he had left his pipe there – a very precious pipe, but as it happened he had left it on the hall table there, so I did not need to disturb the old man. He often dozed off about six.'

'When did you hear of his illness?'

'Brenda came rushing over. That was just a minute or two after half-past six.'

These questions, as I knew, were unimportant, but I was aware how keen was Inspector Taverner's scrutiny of the woman who answered them. He asked her a few questions about the nature of her work in London. She said that it had to do with the radiation effects of atomic disintegration.

'You work on the atom bomb, in fact?'

'The work has nothing destructive about it. The Institute is carrying out experiments on the therapeutic effects.'

When Taverner got up, he expressed a wish to look round their part of the house. She seemed a little surprised, but showed him its extent readily enough. The bedroom with its twin beds and white coverlets and its simplified toilet appliances reminded me again of a hospital or some monastic cell. The bathroom, too, was severely plain with no special luxury fitting and no array of cosmetics. The kitchen was bare, spotlessly clean, and well equipped with labour-saving devices of a practical kind. Then we came to a door which Clemency opened, saying: 'This is my husband's special room.'

'Come in,' said Roger. 'Come in.'

I drew a faint breath of relief. Something in the spotless austerity elsewhere had been getting me down. This was an intensely personal room. There was a large roll-top desk untidily covered with papers, old pipes, and tobacco ash. There were big shabby easy-chairs. Persian rugs covered the floor. On the walls were groups, their photography somewhat faded. School groups, cricket groups, military groups. Water-colour sketches of deserts and minarets, and of sailing-boats and sea effects and sunsets. It was, somehow, a pleasant room, the room of a lovable, friendly, companionable man.

Roger, clumsily, was pouring out drinks from a tantalus, sweeping books and papers off one of the chairs.

'Place is in a mess. I was turning out. Clearing up old papers. Say when.' The inspector declined a drink. I accepted. 'You must forgive me just now,' went on Roger. He brought my drink over to me, turning his head to speak to Taverner as he did so. 'My feelings ran away with me.'

He looked round almost guiltily, but Clemency Leonides had not accompanied us into the room.

'She's so wonderful,' he said. 'My wife, I mean. All through this, she's been splendid – *splendid!* I can't tell you how I admire that woman. And she's had such a hard time – a terrible time. I'd like to tell you about it. Before we were married, I mean. Her first husband was a fine chap – fine mind, I mean – but terribly delicate – tubercular as a matter of fact. He was doing very valuable research work on crystallography, I believe. Poorly paid and very exacting, but he wouldn't give up. She slaved for him, practically kept him, knowing all the time that he was dying. And never a complaint – never a murmur of weariness. She always said she was happy. Then he died, and she was terribly cut up. At last she agreed to marry me. I was so glad to be able to give her some rest, some happiness, I wished she would stop working, but of course she felt it her duty in wartime, and she still seems to feel she should go on. But she's been a wonderful wife – the most wonderful wife a man ever had. Gosh, I've been lucky! I'd do anything for her.'

Taverner made a suitable rejoinder. Then he embarked once more on the familiar routine questions. When had he first heard of his father's illness?

'Brenda had rushed over to call me. My father was ill – she said he had had a seizure of some sort.

'I'd been sitting with the dear old boy only about half an hour earlier. He'd been perfectly all right then. I rushed over. He was blue in the face, gasping. I dashed down to Philip. He rang up the doctor. I – we couldn't do anything. Of course I never dreamed for a moment then that there had been any funny business. Funny? Did I say funny? God, what a word to use.'

With a little difficulty, Taverner and I disentangled ourselves from the emotional atmosphere of Roger Leonides' room and found ourselves outside the door, once more at the top of the stairs.

'Whew!' said Taverner. 'What a contrast from the other brother.' He added, rather inconsequently: 'Curious things, rooms. Tell you quite a lot about the people who live in them.'

I agreed and he went on:

'Curious the people who marry each other, too, isn't it?'

I was not quite sure if he was referring to Clemency and Roger, or to Philip and Magda. His words applied equally well to either. Yet it seemed to me that both the marriages might be classed as happy ones. Roger's and Clemency's certainly was.

'I shouldn't say he was a poisoner, would you?' asked Taverner. 'Not off-hand, I wouldn't. Of course you never know. Now she's more the type. Remorseless sort of woman. Might be a bit mad.'

Again I agreed. 'But I don't suppose,' I said, 'that she'd murder anyone just because she didn't approve of their aims and mode of life. Perhaps, if she really hated the old man – but are any murders committed just out of pure hate?'

'Precious few,' said Taverner. 'I've never come across one myself. No, I think we're a good deal safer to stick to Mrs Brenda. But God knows if we'll ever get any evidence.'

CHAPTER 8

A parlourmaid opened the door of the opposite wing to us. She looked scared but slightly contemptuous when she saw Taverner.

'You want to see the mistress?'

'Yes, please.'

She showed us into a big drawing-room and went out.

Its proportions were the same as the drawing-room on the ground floor below. There were coloured cretonnes, very gay in colour, and striped silk curtains. Over the mantelpiece was a portrait that held my gaze riveted – not only because of the master hand that had painted it, but also because of the arresting face of the subject.

It was the portrait of a little old man with dark, piercing eyes. He wore a black velvet skull cap and his head was sunk down in his shoulders, but the vitality and power of the man radiated forth from the canvas. The twinkling eyes seemed to hold mine.

'That's him,' said Chief-Inspector Taverner ungrammatically. 'Painted by Augustus John. Got a personality, hasn't he?'

'Yes,' I said, and felt the monosyllable was inadequate.

I understood now just what Edith de Haviland had meant when she said the house seemed so empty without him. This was the Original Crooked Little Man who had built the Crooked Little House – and without him the Crooked Little House had lost its meaning.

'That's his first wife over there, painted by Sargent,' said Taverner.

I examined the picture on the wall between the windows. It had a certain cruelty like many of Sargent's portraits. The length of the face was exaggerated, I thought – so was the faint suggestion of horsiness – the indisputable correctness. It was a portrait of a typical English Lady – in Country (not Smart) Society. Handsome, but rather lifeless. A most unlikely wife for the grinning, powerful little despot over the mantelpiece.

The door opened and Sergeant Lamb stepped in.

'I've done what I could with the servants, sir,' he said. 'Didn't get anything.'

Taverner sighed.

Sergeant Lamb took out his notebook and retreated to the far end of the room, where he seated himself unobtrusively.

The door opened again and Aristide Leonide's second wife came into the room.

She wore black – very expensive black and a good deal of it. It swathed her up to the neck and down to the wrists. She moved easily and indolently, and black certainly suited her. Her face was mildly pretty, and she had rather nice brown hair arranged in somewhat too elaborate style. Her face was well powdered and she had on lipstick and rouge, but she had clearly been crying. She was wearing a string of very large pearls and she had a big emerald ring on one hand and an enormous ruby on the other.

There was one other thing I noticed about her. She looked frightened.

'Good morning, Mrs Leonides,' said Taverner easily. 'I'm sorry to have to trouble you again.'

She said in a flat voice:

'I suppose it can't be helped.'

'You understand, don't you, Mrs Leonides, that if you wish your solicitor to be present, that is perfectly in order?'

I wondered if she did understand the significance of those words. Apparently not. She merely said rather sulkily:

'I don't like Mr Gaitskill. I don't want him.'

'You could have your own solicitor, Mrs Leonides.'

'Must I? I don't like solicitors. They confuse me.'

'It's entirely for you to decide,' said Taverner, producing an automatic smile. 'Shall we go on, then?'

Sergeant Lamb licked his pencil. Brenda Leonides sat down on a sofa facing Taverner.

'Have you found out anything?' she asked.

I noticed her fingers nervously twisting and untwisting a pleat of the chiffon of her dress.

'We can state definitely now that your husband died as a result of eserine poisoning.'

'You mean those eyedrops killed him?'

'It seems quite certain that when you gave Mr Leonides that last injection, it was eserine that you injected and not insulin.'

'But I didn't know that. I didn't have anything to do with it. Really I didn't, Inspector.'

'Then somebody must have deliberately replaced the insulin by the eyedrops.'

'What a wicked thing to do!'

'Yes, Mrs Leonides.'

'Do you think – someone did it on purpose? Or by accident? It couldn't have been a – a joke, could it?'

Taverner said smoothly:

'We don't think it was a joke, Mrs Leonides.'

'It must have been one of the servants.'

Taverner did not answer.

'It must. I don't see who else could have done it.'

'Are you sure? Think, Mrs Leonides. Haven't you any ideas at all? There's been no ill-feeling anywhere? No quarrel? No grudge?'

She still stared at him with large defiant eyes.

'I've no idea at all,' she said.

'You had been at the cinema that afternoon, you said?'

'Yes – I came in at half-past six – it was time for the insulin – I – I – gave him the injection just the same as usual and then he – he went all queer. I was terrified – I rushed over to Roger – I've told you all this before. Have I got to go over it again and again?' Her voice rose hysterically.

'I'm sorry, Mrs Leonides. Now can I speak to Mr Brown?'

'To Laurence? Why? He doesn't know anything about it.'

'I'd like to speak to him all the same.'

She stared at him suspiciously.

'Eustace is doing Latin with him in the schoolroom. Do you want him to come here?'

'No – we'll go to him.'

Taverner went quickly out of the room. The sergeant and I followed.

'You've put the wind up her, sir,' said Sergeant Lamb.

Taverner grunted. He led the way up a short flight of steps and along a passage into a big room looking over the garden. There a fair-haired young man of about thirty and a handsome, dark boy of sixteen were sitting at a table.

They looked up at our entrance. Sophia's brother Eustace looked at me, Laurence Brown fixed an agonized gaze on Chief-Inspector Taverner.

I have never seen a man look so completely paralysed with fright. He stood up, then sat down again. He said, and his voice was almost a squeak:

'Oh – er – good morning, Inspector.'

'Good morning.' Taverner was curt. 'Can I have a word with you?'

'Yes, of course. Only too pleased. At least –'

Eustace got up.

'Do you want me to go away, Chief-Inspector?' His voice was pleasant with a faintly arrogant note.

'We – we can continue our studies later,' said the tutor.

Eustace strolled negligently towards the door. He walked rather stiffly. Just as he went through the door he caught my eye, drew a forefinger across the front of his throat and grinned. Then he shut the door behind him.

'Well, Mr Brown,' said Taverner. 'The analysis is quite definite. It was eserine that caused Mr Leonides' death.'

'I – you mean – Mr Leonides was really poisoned? I have been hoping –'

'He was poisoned,' said Taverner curtly. 'Someone substituted eserine eyedrops for insulin.'

'I can't believe it . . . It's incredible.'

'The question is, who had a motive?'

'Nobody. Nobody at all!' The young man's voice rose excitedly.

'You wouldn't like to have your solicitor present, would you?' inquired Taverner.

'I haven't got a solicitor. I don't want one. I have nothing to hide – nothing . . .'

'And you quite understand that what you say is about to be taken down?'

'I'm innocent – I assure you, I'm innocent.'

'I have not suggested anything else.' Taverner paused. 'Mrs Leonides was a good deal younger than her husband, was she not?'

'I – I suppose so – I mean, well, yes.'

'She must have felt lonely sometimes?'

Laurence Brown did not answer. He passed his tongue over his dry lips.

'To have a companion of more or less her own age living here must have been agreeable to her?'

'I – no, not at all – I mean – I don't know.'

'It seems to me quite natural that an attachment should have sprung up between you.'

The young man protested vehemently.

'It didn't! It wasn't! Nothing of the kind! I know what you're thinking, but it wasn't so! Mrs Leonides was very kind to me always and I had the greatest – the greatest respect for her – but nothing more – nothing more, I do assure you. It's monstrous to suggest things of that kind! Monstrous! I wouldn't kill *anybody* – or tamper with bottles – or anything like that. I'm very sensitive and highly strung. I – the very idea of killing is a *nightmare* to me – they quite understood that at the tribunal – I have religious objections to killing. I did hospital work instead – stoking boilers – terribly heavy work – I couldn't go on with it – but they let me take up educational work. I have done my best here with Eustace and with Josephine – a very intelligent child, but difficult. And everybody has been most kind to me – Mr Leonides and Mrs Leonides and Miss de Haviland. And now this awful thing happens . . . And you suspect me – *me* – of murder!'

Inspector Taverner looked at him with a slow, appraising interest.

'I haven't said so,' he remarked.

'But you think so! I know you think so! They all think so! They look at me. I – I can't go on talking to you. I'm not well.'

He hurried out of the room. Taverner turned his head slowly to look at me.

'Well, what do you think of him?'

'He's scared stiff.'

'Yes, I know, but is he a murderer?'

'If you ask me,' said Sergeant Lamb, 'he'd never have had the nerve.'

'He'd never have bashed anyone on the head, or shot off a pistol,' agreed the Chief-Inspector. 'But in this particular crime what is there to do? Just monkey about with a couple of bottles . . . Just help a very old man out of the world in a comparatively painless manner.'

'Practically euthanasia,' said the sergeant.

'And then, perhaps, after a decent interval, marriage with a woman who inherits a hundred thousand pounds free of legacy duty, who already has about the same amount settled upon her, and who has in addition pearls and rubies and emeralds the size of what's-its-name eggs!'

'Ah, well –' Taverner sighed. 'It's all theory and conjecture! I managed to scare him all right, but that doesn't prove anything. He's just as likely to be scared if he's innocent. And anyway, I rather doubt if he *was* the one actually to do it. More likely to have been the woman – only why on earth didn't she throw away the insulin bottle, or rinse it out?' He turned to the sergeant. 'No evidence from the servants about any goings on?'

'The parlourmaid says they're sweet on each other.'

'What grounds?'

'The way he looks at her when she pours out his coffee.'

'Fat lot of good that would be in a court of law! Definitely no carryings on?'

'Not that anybody's seen.'

'I bet they would have seen, too, if there had been anything to see. You know I'm beginning to believe there really is nothing between them.' He looked at me. 'Go back and talk to her. I'd like your impression of her.'

I went, half-reluctantly, yet I was interested.

CHAPTER 9

I found Brenda Leonides sitting exactly where I had left her. She looked up sharply as I entered.

'Where's Inspector Taverner? Is he coming back?'

'Not just yet.'

'Who are you?'

At last I had been asked the question that I had been expecting all the morning.

I answered it with reasonable truth.

'I'm connected with the police, but I'm also a friend of the family.'

'The family! Beasts! I hate them all.'

She looked at me, her mouth working. She looked sullen and frightened and angry.

'They've been beastly to me always – always. From the very first. Why shouldn't I marry their precious father? What did it matter to *them*? They'd all got loads of money. *He* gave it to them. They wouldn't have had the brains to make any for themselves!'

She went on:

'Why shouldn't a man marry again – even if he is a bit old? And he wasn't really old at all – not in himself. I was very fond of him. I *was* fond of him.' She looked at me defiantly.

'I see,' I said. 'I see.'

'I suppose you don't believe that – but it's true. I was sick of men. I wanted to have a home – I wanted someone to make a fuss of me and say nice things to me. Aristide said lovely things to me – and he could make you laugh – and he was clever. He thought up all sorts of smart ways to get round all these silly regulations. He was very, very clever. I'm not glad he's dead. I'm sorry.'

She leaned back on the sofa. She had rather a wide mouth; it curled up sideways in a queer, sleepy smile.

'I've been happy here. I've been safe. I went to all those posh dressmakers – the ones I'd read about. I was as good as anybody. And Aristide gave me lovely things.' She stretched out a hand, looking at the ruby on it.

Just for a moment I saw the hand and arm like an outstretched cat's claw, and heard her voice as a purr. She was still smiling to herself.

'What's wrong with that?' she demanded. 'I was nice to him. I made him happy.' She leaned forward. 'Do you know how I met him?'

She went on without waiting for an answer.

'It was in the Gay Shamrock. He'd ordered scrambled eggs on toast and when I brought them to him I was crying. "Sit down," he said, "and tell me what's the matter." "Oh, I couldn't," I said. "I'd get the sack if I did a thing like that." "No, you won't," he said, "I own this place." I looked at him then. Such an odd little man he was, I thought at first – but he'd got a sort of power. I told him all about it . . . You'll have heard about it all from *them*, I expect – making out I was a regular bad lot – but I wasn't. I was brought up very carefully. We had a shop – a very high-class shop – art needlework. I was never the sort of girl who had a lot of boy friends or made herself cheap. But Terry was different. He was Irish – and he was going overseas . . . He never wrote or anything – I suppose I was a fool. So there it was, you see. I was in trouble – just like some dreadful little servant girl . . .'

Her voice was disdainful in its snobbery.

'Aristide was wonderful. He said everything would be all right. He said he was lonely. We'd be married at once, he said. It was like a dream. And then I found out he was the great Mr Leonides. He owned masses of shops and restaurants and night clubs. It was quite like a fairy tale, wasn't it?'

'One kind of a fairy tale,' I said drily.

'We were married at a little church in the City – and then we went abroad.'

She looked at me with eyes that came back from a long distance.

'There wasn't a child after all. It was all a mistake.'

She smiled, the curled-up sideways, crooked smile.

'I vowed to myself that I'd be a really good wife to him, and I *was*. I ordered all the kinds of food he liked, and wore the colours he fancied and I did all I could to please him. And he was happy. But we never got rid of that family of his. Always coming and sponging and living in his pocket. Old Miss de Haviland – I think she ought to have gone away when he got married. I said so. But Aristide said, "She's been here so long. It's her home now." The truth is he liked to have them all about and underfoot. They were beastly to *me*, but he never seemed to notice that or to mind about it. Roger hates me – have you seen Roger? He's always hated me. He's jealous. And Philip's so stuck up he never speaks to me. And now they're trying to pretend I murdered him – and I didn't – I *didn't*!' She leaned towards me. 'Please believe I didn't.'

I found her very pathetic. The contemptuous way the Leonides family had spoken of her, their eagerness to believe that she had committed the crime – now, at this moment, it all seemed positively inhuman conduct. She was alone, defenceless, hunted down.

'And if it's not me, they think it's Laurence,' she went on.

'What about Laurence?' I asked.

'I'm terribly sorry for Laurence. He's delicate and he couldn't go and fight. It's not because he was a coward. It's because he's sensitive. I've tried to cheer him up and to make him feel happy. He has to teach those horrible children. Eustace is always sneering at him, and Josephine – well, you've seen Josephine. You know what she's like.'

I said I hadn't met Josephine yet.

'Sometimes I think that child isn't right in her head. She has horrible sneaky ways, and she looks queer . . . She gives me the shivers sometimes.'

I didn't want to talk about Josephine. I harked back to Laurence Brown.

'Who is he?' I asked. 'Where does he come from?'

I had phrased it clumsily. She flushed.

'He isn't anybody particular. He's just like me . . . What chance have we got against all of *them*?'

'Don't you think you're being a little hysterical?'

'No, I don't. They want to make out that Laurence did it – or that I did. They've got that policeman on their side. What chance have I got?'

'You mustn't work yourself up,' I said.

'Why shouldn't it be one of them who killed him? Or someone from outside? Or one of the servants?'

'There's a certain lack of motive.'

'Oh, *motive*! What motive had *I* got? Or Laurence?'

I felt rather uncomfortable as I said:

'They might think, I suppose, that you and – er – Laurence – are in love with each other – that you wanted to marry.'

She sat bolt upright.

'That's a wicked thing to suggest! And it's not true! We've never said a word of that kind to each other. I've just been sorry for him and tried to cheer him up. We've been friends, that's all. You do believe me, don't you?'

I did believe her. That is, I believed that she and Laurence were, as she put it, only friends. But I also believed that, possibly unknown to herself, she was actually in love with the young man.

It was with that thought in my mind that I went downstairs in search of Sophia.

As I was about to go into the drawing-room, Sophia poked her head out of a door farther along the passage.

'Hallo,' she said. 'I'm helping Nannie with lunch.'

I would have joined her, but she came out into the passage, shut the door behind her, and taking my arm led me into the drawing-room, which was empty.

'Well,' she said, 'did you see Brenda? What did you think of her?'

'Frankly,' I said, 'I was sorry for her.'

Sophia looked amused.

'I see,' she said. 'So she got you.'

I felt slightly irritated.

'The point is,' I said, 'that I can see her side of it. Apparently you can't.'

'Her side of what?'

'Honestly, Sophia, have any of the family ever been nice to her, or even fairly decent to her, since she came here?'

'No, we haven't been nice to her. Why should we be?'

'Just ordinary Christian kindliness, if nothing else.'

'What a very high moral tone you're taking, Charles. Brenda must have done her stuff pretty well.'

'Really, Sophia, you seem – I don't know what's come over you.'

'I'm just being honest and not pretending. You've seen Brenda's side of it, so you say. Now take a look at my side. I don't like the type of young woman who makes up a hard-luck story and marries a very rich old man on the strength of it. I've a perfect right not to like that type of young woman, and there is no earthly reason why I should pretend I do. And if the facts were written down in cold blood on paper, *you* wouldn't like that young woman either.'

'Was it a made-up story?' I asked.

'About the child? I don't know. Personally, I think so.'

'And you resent the fact that your grandfather was taken in by it?'

'Oh, grandfather wasn't taken in.' Sophia laughed. 'Grandfather was never taken in by anybody. He wanted Brenda. He wanted to play Cophetua to her beggar-maid. He knew just what he was doing and it worked out beautifully according to plan. From grandfather's point of view the marriage was a complete success – like all his other operations.'

'Was engaging Laurence Brown as tutor another of your grandfather's successes?' I asked ironically.

Sophia frowned.

'Do you know, I'm not sure that it wasn't. He wanted to keep Brenda happy and amused. He may have thought that jewels and clothes weren't enough. He may have thought she wanted a mild romance in her life. He may have calculated that someone like Laurence Brown, somebody really *tame*, if you know what I mean, would just do the trick. A beautiful soulful friendship tinged with melancholy that would stop Brenda from having a real affair with someone outside. I wouldn't put it past grandfather to have worked out something on those lines. He was rather an old devil, you know.'

'He must have been,' I said.

'He couldn't, of course, have visualized that it would lead to murder . . . And that,' said Sophia, speaking with such vehemence, 'is really why I don't, much as I would like to, really believe that she did it. If she'd planned to murder him – or if she and Laurence had planned it together – grandfather would have known about it. I dare say that seems a bit far-fetched to you –'

'I must confess it does,' I said.

'But then you didn't know grandfather. He certainly wouldn't have connived at his own murder! So there you are! Up against a blank wall.'

'She's frightened, Sophia,' I said. 'She's very frightened.'

'Chief-Inspector Taverner and his merry, merry men? Yes, I dare say they are rather alarming. Laurence, I suppose, is in hysterics?'

'Practically. He made, I thought, a disgusting exhibition of himself. I don't understand what a woman can see in a man like that.'

'Don't you, Charles? Actually Laurence has a lot of sex appeal.'

'A weakling like that,' I said incredulously.

'Why do men always think that a caveman must necessarily be the only type of person attractive to the opposite sex? Laurence has got sex appeal all right – but I wouldn't expect you to be aware of it.' She looked at me. 'Brenda got her hooks into you all right.'

'Don't be absurd. She's not even really good-looking. And she certainly didn't –'

'Display allure? No, she just made you sorry for her. She's not actually beautiful, she's not in the least clever – but she's got one very outstanding characteristic. She can make trouble. She's made trouble, already, between you and me.'

'Sophia!' I cried aghast.

Sophia went to the door.

'Forget it, Charles. I must get on with lunch.'

'I'll come and help.'

'No, you stay here. It will rattle Nannie to have "a gentleman in the kitchen".'

'Sophia,' I called as she went out.

'Yes, what is it?'

'Just a servant problem. Why haven't you got any servants

down here and upstairs something in an apron and a cap opened the door to us?'

'Grandfather had a cook, housemaid, parlourmaid, and valet-attendant. He liked servants. He paid them the earth, of course, and he got them. Clemency and Roger just have a daily woman who comes in and cleans. They don't like servants – or rather Clemency doesn't. If Roger didn't get a square meal in the City every day, he'd starve. Clemency's idea of a meal is lettuce, tomatoes, and raw carrot. We sometimes have servants, and then mother throws one of her temperaments and they leave, and we have dailies for a bit and then start again. We're in the daily period. Nannie is the permanency and copes in emergencies. Now you know.'

Sophia went out. I sank down in one of the large brocaded chairs and gave myself up to speculation.

Upstairs I had seen Brenda's side of it. Here and now I had been shown Sophia's side of it. I realized completely the justice of Sophia's point of view – what might be called the Leonides family's point of view. They resented a stranger within the gates who had obtained admission by what they regarded as ignoble means. They were entirely within their rights. As Sophia had said: on paper it wouldn't look well . . .

But there was the human side of it – the side that I saw and that they didn't. They were, they always had been, rich and well established. They had no conception of the temptations of the underdog. Brenda Leonides had wanted wealth, and pretty things and safety – and a home. She had claimed that in exchange she had made her old husband happy. I had sympathy with her. Certainly, while I was talking with her, I had had sympathy for her . . . Had I got as much sympathy now?

Two sides to the question – different angles of vision – which was the true angle . . . the true angle . . .

I had slept very little the night before. I had been up early to accompany Taverner. Now, in the warm, flower-scented atmosphere of Magda Leonides' drawing-room, my body relaxed in the cushioned embrace of the big chair and my eyelids dropped . . .

Thinking of Brenda, of Sophia, of an old man's picture, my thoughts slid together into a pleasant haze.

I slept . . .

CHAPTER 10

I returned to consciousness so gradually that I didn't at first realize that I had been asleep.

The scent of the flowers was in my nose. In front of me a round white blob appeared to float in space. It was some few seconds before I realized that it was a human face I was looking at – a face suspended in the air about a foot or two away from me. As my faculties returned, my vision became more precise. The face still had its goblin suggestion – it was round with a bulging brow, combed-back hair and small, rather beady, black eyes. But it was definitely attached to a body – a small skinny body. It was regarding me very earnestly.

'Hallo,' it said.

'Hallo,' I replied, blinking.

'I'm Josephine.'

I had already deduced that. Sophia's sister, Josephine, was, I judged, about eleven or twelve years of age. She was a fantastically ugly child with a very distinct likeness to her grandfather. It seemed to me possible that she also had his brains.

'You're Sophia's young man,' said Josephine.

I acknowledged the correctness of this remark.

'But you came down here with Chief-Inspector Taverner. Why did you come with Chief-Inspector Taverner?'

'He's a friend of mine.'

'Is he? I don't like him. I shan't tell him things.'

'What sort of things?'

'The things I know. I know a lot of things. I like knowing things.'

She sat down on the arm of the chair and continued her searching scrutiny of my face. I began to feel quite uncomfortable.

'Grandfather's been murdered. Did you know?'

'Yes,' I said. 'I knew.'

'He was poisoned. With es-er-ine.' She pronounced the word very carefully. 'It's interesting, isn't it?'

'I suppose it is.'

'Eustace and I are very interested. We like detective stories.

I've always wanted to be a detective. I'm being one now. I'm collecting clues.'

She was, I felt, rather a ghoulish child.

She returned to the charge.

'The man who came with Chief-Inspector Taverner is a detective too, isn't he? In books it says you can always know plain-clothes detectives by their boots. But this detective was wearing suede shoes.'

'The old order changeth,' I said.

Josephine interpreted this remark according to her own ideas.

'Yes,' she said, 'there will be a lot of changes here now, I expect. We shall go and live in a house in London on the Embankment. Mother has wanted to for a long time. She'll be very pleased. I don't expect father will mind if his books go, too. He couldn't afford it before. He lost an awful lot of money over *Jezebel*.'

'Jezebel?' I queried.

'Yes, didn't you see it?'

'Oh, it was a play? No, I didn't. I've been abroad.'

'It didn't run very long. Actually it was the most awful flop. I don't think mother's really the type to play Jezebel, do you?'

I balanced my impressions of Magda. Neither in the peach-coloured *négligé* nor in the tailored suit had she conveyed any suggestion of Jezebel, but I was willing to believe that there were other Magdas that I had not yet seen.

'Perhaps not,' I said cautiously.

'Grandfather always said it would be a flop. He said he wouldn't put up any money for one of those historical religious plays. He said it would never be a box-office success. But mother was frightfully keen. I didn't like it much myself. It wasn't really a bit like the story in the Bible. I mean, Jezebel wasn't wicked like she is in the Bible. She was all patriotic and really quite nice. That made it dull. Still, the end was all right. They threw her out of the window. Only no dogs came and ate her. I think that was a pity, don't you? I like the part about the dogs eating her best. Mother says you can't have dogs on the stage but I don't see why. You could have performing dogs.' She quoted with gusto: '"*And they ate her all but the palms of her hands.*" Why didn't they eat the palms of her hands?'

'I've really no idea,' I said.

'You wouldn't think, would you, that dogs were so particular. Our dogs aren't. They eat simply *anything*.'

Josephine brooded on this Biblical mystery for some seconds.

'I'm sorry the play was a flop,' I said.

'Yes. Mother was terribly upset. The notices were simply frightful. When she read them, she burst into tears and cried all day and she threw her breakfast tray at Gladys, and Gladys gave notice. It was rather fun.'

'I perceive that you like drama, Josephine,' I said.

'They did a post-mortem on grandfather,' said Josephine. 'To find out what he had died of. A P.M., they call it, but I think that's rather confusing, don't you? Because P.M. stands for Prime Minister too. And for afternoon,' she added thoughtfully.

'Are you sorry your grandfather is dead?' I asked.

'Not particularly. I didn't like him much. He stopped me learning to be a ballet dancer.'

'Did you want to learn ballet dancing?'

'Yes, and mother was willing for me to learn, and father didn't mind, but grandfather said I'd be no good.'

She slipped off the arm of the chair, kicked off her shoes and endeavoured to get on to what are called technically, I believe, her points.

'You have to have the proper shoes, of course,' she explained, 'and even then you get frightful abscesses sometimes on the ends of your toes.' She resumed her shoes and inquired casually:

'Do you like this house?'

'I'm not quite sure,' I said.

'I suppose it will be sold now. Unless Brenda goes on living in it. And I suppose Uncle Roger and Aunt Clemency won't be going away now.'

'Were they going away?' I asked with a faint stirring of interest.

'Yes. They were going on Tuesday. Abroad somewhere. They were going by air. Aunt Clemency bought one of those new featherweight cases.'

'I hadn't heard they were going abroad,' I said.

'No,' said Josephine. 'Nobody knew. It was a secret. They

weren't going to tell anyone until after they'd gone. They were going to leave a note behind for grandfather.'

She added:

'Not pinned to the pin-cushion. That's only in very old-fashioned books and wives do it when they leave their husbands. But it would be silly now because nobody has pin-cushions any more.'

'Of course they don't. Josephine, do you know why your Uncle Roger was – going away?'

She shot me a cunning sideways glance.

'I think I do. It was something to do with Uncle Roger's office in London. I rather think – but I'm not sure – that he'd *embezzled* something.'

'What makes you think that?'

Josephine came nearer and breathed heavily in my face.

'The day that grandfather was poisoned Uncle Roger was shut up in his room with him ever so long. They were talking and talking. And Uncle Roger was saying that he'd never been any good, and that he'd let grandfather down – and that it wasn't the money so much – it was the feeling he'd been unworthy of trust. He was in an awful state.'

I looked at Josephine with mixed feelings.

'Josephine,' I said, 'hasn't anybody ever told you that it's not nice to listen at doors?'

Josephine nodded her head vigorously.

'Of course they have. But if you want to find things out, you *have* to listen at doors. I bet Chief-Inspector Taverner does, don't you?'

I considered the point. Josephine went on vehemently:

'And anyway, if *he* doesn't, the other one does, the one with the suede shoes. And they look in people's desks and read all their letters, and find out all their secrets. Only they're stupid! They don't know where to look!'

Josephine spoke with cold superiority. I was stupid enough to let the inference escape me. The unpleasant child went on:

'Eustace and I know lots of things – but I know more than Eustace does. And I shan't tell him. He says women can't ever be great detectives. But I say they can. I'm going to write down everything in a notebook and then, when the police are completely baffled, I shall come forward and say, "*I* can tell you who did it."'

'Do you read a lot of detective stories, Josephine?'

'Masses.'

'I suppose you think you know who killed your grandfather?'

'Well, I *think* so – but I shall have to find a few more clues.' She paused and added: 'Chief-Inspector Taverner thinks that Brenda did it, doesn't he? Or Brenda and Laurence together because they're in love with each other.'

'You shouldn't say things like that, Josephine.'

'Why not? They are in love with each other.'

'You can't possibly judge.'

'Yes, I can. They write to each other. Love letters.'

'Josephine! How do you know that?'

'Because I've read them. Awfully soppy letters. But Laurence is soppy. He was too frightened to fight in the war. He went into basements, and stoked boilers. When the flying-bombs went over here, he used to turn green – really green. It made Eustace and me laugh a lot.'

What I would have said next I do not know, for at that moment a car drew up outside. In a flash Josephine was at the window, her snub nose pressed to the pane.

'Who is it?' I asked.

'It's Mr Gaitskill, grandfather's lawyer. I expect he's come about the will.'

Breathing excitedly, she hurried from the room, doubtless to resume her sleuthing activities.

Magda Leonides came into the room, and to my surprise came across to me and took my hands in hers.

'My dear,' she said, 'thank goodness you're still here. One *needs* a man so badly.'

She dropped my hands, crossed to a high-backed chair, altered its position a little, glanced at herself in a mirror, then, picking up a small Battersea enamel box from a table, she stood pensively opening and shutting it.

It was an attractive pose.

Sophia put her head in at the door and said in an admonitory whisper, 'Gaitskill!'

'I know,' said Magda.

A few moments later Sophia entered the room, accompanied by a small elderly man, and Magda put down her enamel box and came forward to meet him.

'Good morning, Mrs Philip. I'm on my way upstairs. It seems there's some misunderstanding about the will. Your husband wrote to me with the impression that the will was in my keeping. I understood from Mr Leonides himself that it was at his vault. You don't know anything about it, I suppose?'

'About poor Sweetie's will?' Magda opened astonished eyes. 'No, of course not. Don't tell me that wicked woman upstairs has destroyed it?'

'Now, Mrs Philip,' – he shook an admonitory finger at her – 'no wild surmises. It's just a question of where your father-in-law kept it.'

'But he sent it to you – surely he did – after signing it. He actually told us he had.'

'The police, I understand, have been through Mr Leonides' private papers,' said Mr Gaitskill. 'I'll just have a word with Chief-Inspector Taverner.'

He left the room.

'Darling,' cried Magda. 'She *has* destroyed it. I know I'm right.'

'Nonsense, Mother, she wouldn't do a stupid thing like that.'

'It wouldn't be stupid at all. If there's no will she'll get everything.'

'Ssh – here's Gaitskill back again.'

The lawyer re-entered the room. Chief-Inspector Taverner was with him and behind Taverner came Philip.

'I understood from Mr Leonides,' Gaitskill was saying, 'that he had placed his will with the Bank for safe keeping.'

Taverner shook his head.

'I've been in communication with the Bank. They have no private papers belonging to Mr Leonides beyond certain securities which they held for him.'

Philip said:

'I wonder if Roger – or Aunt Edith . . . Perhaps, Sophia, you'd ask them to come down here.'

But Roger Leonides, summoned with the others to the conclave, could give no assistance.

'But it's nonsense – absolute nonsense,' he declared. 'Father signed the will and said distinctly that he was posting it to Mr Gaitskill on the following day.'

'If my memory serves me,' said Mr Gaitskill, leaning back and half-closing his eyes, 'it was on November 24th of last year that I forwarded a draft drawn up according to Mr Leonides' instructions. He approved the draft, returned it to me, and in due course I sent him the will for signature. After a lapse of a week, I ventured to remind him that I had not yet received the will duly signed and attested, and asking him if there was anything he wished altered. He replied that he was perfectly satisfied, and added that after signing the will he had sent it to his bank.'

'That's quite right,' said Roger eagerly. 'It was about the end of November last year – you remember, Philip? Father had us all up one evening and read the will to us.'

Taverner turned towards Philip Leonides.

'That agrees with your recollection, Mr Leonides?'

'Yes,' said Philip.

'It was rather like the Voysey Inheritance,' said Magda. She sighed pleasurably. 'I always think there's something so dramatic about a will.'

'Miss Sophia?'

'Yes,' said Sophia. 'I remember perfectly.'

'And the provisions of that will?' asked Taverner.

Mr Gaitskill was about to reply in his precise fashion, but Roger Leonides got ahead of him.

'It was a perfectly simple will. Electra and Joyce had died and their share of the settlements had returned to father. Joyce's son, William, had been killed in action in Burma, and the money he left went to his father. Philip and I and the children were the only relatives left. Father explained that. He left fifty thousand pounds free of duty to Aunt Edith, a hundred thousand pounds free of duty to Brenda, this house to Brenda, or else a suitable house in London to be purchased for her, whichever she preferred. The residue to be divided into three portions, one to myself, one to Philip, the third to be divided between Sophia, Eustace, and Josephine, the portions of the last two to be held in trust until they should come of age. I think that's right, isn't it, Mr Gaitskill?'

'Those are – roughly stated – the provisions of the document I drew up,' agreed Mr Gaitskill, displaying some slight acerbity at not having been allowed to speak for himself.

'Father read it out to us,' said Roger. 'He asked if there was any comment we might like to make. Of course there was none.'

'Brenda made a comment,' said Miss de Haviland.

'Yes,' said Magda with zest. 'She said she couldn't bear her darling old Aristide to talk about death. It "gave her the creeps", she said. And after he was dead she didn't want any of the horrid money!'

'That,' said Miss de Haviland, 'was a conventional protest, typical of her class.'

It was a cruel and biting little remark. I realized suddenly how much Edith de Haviland disliked Brenda.

'A very fair and reasonable disposal of his estate,' said Mr Gaitskill.

'And after reading it what happened?' asked Inspector Taverner.

'After reading it,' said Roger, 'he signed it.'

Taverner leaned forward.

'Just how and when did he sign it?'

Roger looked round at his wife in an appealing way. Clemency spoke in answer to that look. The rest of the family seemed content for her to do so.

'You want to know exactly what took place?'

'If you please, Mrs Roger.'

'My father-in-law laid the will down on his desk and requested one of us – Roger, I think – to ring the bell. Roger did so. When Johnson came in answer to the bell, my father-in-law requested him to fetch Janet Wolmer, the parlourmaid. When they were both there, he signed the will and requested them to sign their own names beneath his signature.'

'The correct procedure,' said Mr Gaitskill. 'A will must be signed by the testator in the presence of two witnesses who must affix their own signatures at the same time and place.'

'And after that?' asked Taverner.

'My father-in-law thanked them, and they went out. My father-in-law picked up the will, put it in a long envelope and mentioned that he would send it to Mr Gaitskill on the following day.'

'You all agree,' said Inspector Taverner, looking round, 'that this is an accurate account of what happened?'

There were murmurs of agreement.

'The will was on the desk, you said. How near were any of you to that desk?'

'Not very near. Five or six yards, perhaps, would be the nearest.'

'When Mr Leonides read you the will was he himself sitting at the desk?'

'Yes.'

'Did he get up, or leave the desk, after reading the will and before signing it?'

'No.'

'Could the servants read the document when they signed their names?'

'No,' said Clemency. 'My father-in-law placed a sheet of paper across the upper part of the document.'

'Quite properly,' said Philip. 'The contents of the will were no business of the servants.'

'I see,' said Taverner. 'At least – I don't see.'

With a brisk movement he produced a long envelope and leaned forward to hand it to the lawyer.

'Have a look at that,' he said. 'And tell me what it is.'

Mr Gaitskill drew a folded document out of the envelope. He looked at it with lively astonishment, turning it round and round in his hands.

'This,' he said, 'is somewhat surprising. I do not understand it at all. Where was this, if I may ask?'

'In the safe, amongst Mr Leonides' other papers.'

'But what is it?' demanded Roger. 'What's all the fuss about?'

'This is the will I prepared for your father's signature, Roger – but – I can't understand it after what you have all said – it is not signed.'

'What? Well, I suppose it is just a draft.'

'No,' said the lawyer. 'Mr Leonides returned me the original draft. I then drew up the will – *this* will,' he tapped it with his finger – 'and sent it to him for signature. According to your evidence he signed the will in front of you all – and two witnesses also appended their signatures – and yet this will is unsigned.'

'But that's impossible,' exclaimed Philip Leonides, speaking with more animation than I had yet heard from him.

Taverner asked: 'How good was your father's eyesight?'

'He suffered from glaucoma. He used strong glasses, of course, for reading.'

'He had those glasses on that evening?'

'Certainly. He didn't take his glasses off until after he had signed. I think I am right.'

'Quite right,' said Clemency.

'And nobody – you are all sure of that – went near the desk before the signing of the will?'

'I wonder now,' said Magda, screwing up her eyes. 'If one could only visualize it all again.'

'Nobody went near the desk,' said Sophia. 'And grandfather sat at it all the time.'

'The desk was in the position it is now? It was not near a door, or a window, or any drapery?'

'It was where it is now.'

'I am trying to see how a substitution of some kind could be effected,' said Taverner. 'Some kind of substitution there must have been. Mr Leonides was under the impression that he was signing the document he had just read aloud.'

'Couldn't the signatures have been erased?' Roger demanded.

'No, Mr Leonides. Not without leaving signs of erasion. There is one other possibility. That this is not the document sent to Mr Leonides by Mr Gaitskill and which he signed in your presence.'

'On the contrary,' said Mr Gaitskill. 'I could swear to this being the original document. There is a small flaw in the paper – at the top left-hand corner – it resembles, by a stretch of fancy, an aeroplane. I noticed it at the time.'

The family looked blankly at one another.

'A most curious set of circumstances,' said Mr Gaitskill. 'Quite without precedent in my experience.'

'The whole thing's impossible,' said Roger. 'We were all there. It simply couldn't have happened.'

Miss de Haviland gave a dry cough.

'Never any good wasting breath saying something that has happened couldn't have happened,' she remarked. 'What's the position now? That's what I'd like to know.'

Gaitskill immediately became the cautious lawyer.

'The position will have to be examined very carefully,' he said. 'This document, of course, revokes all former wills and testaments. There are a large number of witnesses who saw Mr Leonides sign what he certainly believed to be this will in perfectly good faith. Hum. Very interesting. Quite a little legal problem.'

Taverner glanced at his watch.

'I'm afraid,' he said, 'I've been keeping you from your lunch.'

'Won't you stay and lunch with us, Chief-Inspector?' asked Philip.

'Thank you, Mr Leonides, but I am meeting Dr Gray in Swinly Dean.'

Philip turned to the lawyer.

'You'll lunch with us, Gaitskill?'

'Thank you, Philip.'

Everybody stood up. I edged unobtrusively towards Sophia.

'Do I go or stay?' I murmured. It sounded ridiculously like the title of a Victorian song.

'Go, I think,' said Sophia.

I slipped quietly out of the room in pursuit of Taverner. Josephine was swinging to and fro on a baize door leading to the back quarters. She appeared to be highly amused about something.

'The police are stupid,' she observed.

Sophia came out of the drawing-room.

'What have you been doing, Josephine?'

'Helping Nannie.'

'I believe you've been listening outside the door.'

Josephine made a face at her and retreated.

'That child,' said Sophia, 'is a bit of a problem.'

CHAPTER 11

I

I came into the AC's room at the Yard to find Taverner finishing the recital of what had apparently been a tale of woe.

'And there you are,' he was saying. 'I've turned the lot of them inside out – and what do I get – nothing at all! No motives. None of them hard up. And all that we've got against the wife and her young man is that he made sheep's eyes at her when she poured him out his coffee!'

'Come, come, Taverner,' I said. 'I can do a little better than that for you.'

'You can, can you? Well, Mr Charles, what did *you* get?'

I sat down, lit a cigarette, leaned back and let them have it.

'Roger Leonides and his wife were planning a getaway abroad next Tuesday. Roger and his father had a stormy interview on the day of the old man's death. Old Leonides had found out something was wrong, and Roger was admitting culpability.'

Taverner went purple in the face.

'Where the hell did you get all that from?' he demanded. 'If you got it from the servants –'

'I didn't get it from the servants. I got it,' I said, 'from a private inquiry agent.'

'What do you mean?'

'And I must say that, in accordance with the canons of the best detective stories, he, or rather she – or perhaps I'd better say *it* – has licked the police hollow!

'I also think,' I went on, 'that my private detective has a few more things up his, her or its sleeve.'

Taverner opened his mouth and shut it again. He wanted to ask so many questions at once that he found it hard to begin.

'Roger!' he said. 'So Roger's a wrong 'un, is he?'

I felt a slight reluctance as I unburdened myself. I had liked Roger Leonides. Remembering his comfortable, friendly room, and the man's own friendly charm, I disliked setting the hounds of justice on his track. It was possible, of course, that all Josephine's information would be unreliable, but I did not really think so.

'So the kid told you?' said Taverner. 'She seems to be wise to everything that goes on in that house.'

'Children usually are,' said my father drily.

This information, if true, altered the whole position. If Roger had been, as Josephine confidently suggested, 'embezzling' the funds of Associated Catering and if the old man had found it out, it might have been vital to silence old Leonides and to leave England before the truth came out. Possibly Roger had rendered himself liable to criminal prosecution.

It was agreed that inquiries should be made without delay into the affairs of Associated Catering.

'It will be an almighty crash, if that goes,' my father remarked. 'It's a huge concern. There are millions involved.'

'If it's really in Queer Street, it gives us what we want,' said Taverner. 'Father summons Roger. Roger breaks down and confesses. Brenda Leonides was out at a cinema. Roger has only got to leave his father's room, walk into the bathroom, empty out an insulin phial and replace it with the strong solution of eserine and there you are. Or his wife may have done it. She went over to the other wing after she came home that day – says she went to fetch a pipe Roger had left there. But she could have gone over to switch the stuff before Brenda came home and gave him his injection. She'd be quite cool and capable about it.'

I nodded. 'Yes, I fancy her as the actual doer of the deed. She's cool enough for anything! And I don't really think that Roger Leonides would think of poison as a means – that trick with the insulin has something feminine about it.'

'Plenty of men poisoners,' said my father drily.

'Oh, I know, sir,' said Taverner. 'Don't I know!' he added with feeling.

'All the same I shouldn't have said Roger was the type.'

'Pritchard,' the Old Man reminded him, 'was a good mixer.'

'Let's say they were in it together.'

'With the accent on Lady Macbeth,' said my father, as Taverner departed. 'Is that how she strikes you, Charles?'

I visualized the slight, graceful figure standing by the window in that austere room.

'Not quite,' I said. 'Lady Macbeth was essentially a greedy woman. I don't think Clemency Leonides is. I don't think she wants or cares for possessions.'

'But she might care, desperately, about her husband's safety?'

'That, yes. And she could certainly be – well, ruthless.'

'*Different kinds of ruthlessness* . . .' That was what Sophia had said.

I looked up to see the Old Man watching me.

'What's in your mind, Charles?'

But I didn't tell him then.

II

I was summoned on the following day and found Taverner and my father together.

Taverner was looking pleased with himself and slightly excited.

'Associated Catering is on the rocks,' said my father.

'Due to crash at any minute,' said Taverner.

'I saw there had been a sharp fall in the shares last night,' I said. 'But they seem to have recovered this morning.'

'We've had to go about it very cautiously,' said Taverner. 'No direct inquiries. Nothing to cause a panic – or to put the wind up our absconding gentleman. But we've got certain private sources of information and the information is fairly definite. Associated Catering is on the verge of a crash. It can't possibly meet its commitments. The truth seems to be that it's been grossly mismanaged for years.'

'By Roger Leonides?'

'Yes. He's had supreme power, you know.'

'And he's helped himself to money –'

'No,' said Taverner. 'We don't think he has. To put it bluntly, he may be a murderer, but we don't think he's a swindler. Quite frankly he's just been – a fool. He doesn't seem to have had any kind of judgement. He's launched out where he ought to have held in – he's hesitated and retreated where he ought to have launched out. He's delegated power to the last sort of people he ought to have delegated it to. He's a trustful sort of chap, and he's trusted the wrong people. At every time, and on every occasion, he's done the wrong thing.'

'There are people like that,' said my father. 'And they're not really stupid either. They're bad judges of men, that's all. And they're enthusiastic at the wrong time.'

'A man like that oughtn't to be in business at all,' said Taverner.

'He probably wouldn't be,' said my father, 'except for the accident of being Aristide Leonides' son.'

'That show was absolutely blooming when the old man handed

it over to him. It ought to have been a gold mine! You'd think he could have just sat back and let the show run itself.'

'No,' my father shook his head. 'No show runs itself. There are always decisions to be made – a man sacked here – a man appointed there – small questions of policy. And with Roger Leonides the answer seems to have been always wrong.'

'That's right,' said Taverner. 'He's a loyal sort of chap, for one thing. He kept on the most frightful duds – just because he had an affection for them – or because they'd been there a long time. And then he sometimes had wild impractical ideas and insisted on trying them out in spite of the enormous outlay involved.'

'But nothing criminal?' my father insisted.

'No, nothing criminal.'

'Then why murder?' I asked.

'He may have been a fool and not a knave,' said Taverner. 'But the result was the same – or nearly the same. The only thing that could save Associated Catering from the smash was a really colossal sum of money by next' (he consulted a notebook) 'by next Wednesday at the latest.'

'Such a sum as he would inherit, or thought he would have inherited, under his father's will?'

'Exactly.'

'But he wouldn't be able to have got that sum in cash.'

'No. But he'd have got credit. It's the same thing.'

The Old Man nodded.

'Wouldn't it have been simpler to go to old Leonides and ask for help?' he suggested.

'I think he did,' said Taverner. 'I think that's what the kid overheard. The old boy refused point blank, I should imagine, to throw good money after bad. He would, you know.'

I thought that Taverner was right there. Aristide Leonides had refused the backing for Magda's play – he had said that it would not be a box-office success. Events had proved him correct. He was a generous man to his family, but he was not a man to waste money in unprofitable enterprises. And Associated Catering ran to thousands, or probably hundreds of thousands. He had refused point blank, and the only way for Roger to avoid financial ruin was for his father to die.

Yes, there was certainly a motive there all right.

My father looked at his watch.

'I've asked him to come here,' he said. 'He'll be here any minute now.'

'Roger?'

'Yes.'

'Will you walk into my parlour, said the spider to the fly?' I murmured.

Taverner looked at me in a shocked way.

'We shall give him all the proper cautions,' he said severely.

The stage was set, the shorthand writer established. Presently the buzzer sounded, and a few minutes later Roger Leonides entered the room.

He came in eagerly – and rather clumsily – he stumbled over a chair. I was reminded as before of a large friendly dog. At the same time I decided quite definitely that it was not he who had carried out the actual process of transferring eserine to an insulin bottle. He would have broken it, spilled it, or muffed the operation in some way or the other. No, Clemency's, I decided, had been the actual hand, though Roger had been privy to the deed.

Words rushed from him.

'You wanted to see me? You've found out something? Hallo, Charles. I didn't see you. Nice of you to come along. But please tell me, Sir Arthur –'

Such a nice fellow – really such a nice fellow. But lots of murderers had been nice fellows – so their astonished friends had said afterwards. Feeling rather like Judas, I smiled a greeting.

My father was deliberate, coldly official. The glib phrases were uttered. Statement . . . taken down . . . no compulsion . . . solicitor . . .

Roger Leonides brushed them all aside with the same characteristic eager impatience.

I saw the faint sardonic smile on Chief-Inspector Taverner's face, and read from it the thought in his mind.

'*Always sure of themselves, these chaps*. They can't make a mistake. They're far too clever!'

I sat down unobtrusively in a corner and listened.

'I have asked you to come here, Mr Leonides,' my father said, 'not to give you fresh information, but to ask for some information from you – information that you have previously withheld.'

Roger Leonides looked bewildered.

'Withheld? But I've told you everything – absolutely everything!'

'I think not. You had a conversation with the deceased on the afternoon of his death?'

'Yes, yes, I had tea with him. I told you so.'

'You told us that, yes, but you did not tell us about your conversation.'

'We – just – talked.'

'What about?'

'Daily happenings, the house, Sophia –'

'What about Associated Catering? Was that mentioned?'

I think I had hoped up to then that Josephine had been inventing the whole story; but if so, that hope was quickly quenched.

Roger's face changed. It changed in a moment from eagerness to something that was recognizably close to despair.

'Oh, my God,' he said. He dropped into a chair and buried his face in his hands.

Taverner smiled like a contented cat.

'You admit, Mr Leonides, that you have not been frank with us?'

'How did you get to know about that? I thought nobody knew – I don't see how anybody *could* know.'

'We have means of finding out these things, Mr Leonides.' There was a majestic pause. 'I think you will see now that you had better tell us the truth.'

'Yes, yes, of course. I'll tell you. What do you want to know?'

'Is it true that Associated Catering is on the verge of collapse?'

'Yes. It can't be staved off now. The crash is bound to come. If only my father could have died without ever knowing. I feel so ashamed – so disgraced –'

'There is a possibility of criminal prosecution?'

Roger sat up sharply.

'No, indeed. It will be bankruptcy – but an honourable bankruptcy. Creditors will be paid twenty shillings in the pound if I throw in my personal assets, which I shall do. No, the disgrace I feel is to have failed my father. He trusted me. He made over to me this, his largest concern – and his pet concern. He never interfered, he never asked what I was doing. He just – trusted me . . . And I let him down.'

My father said drily:

'You say there was no likelihood of criminal prosecution? Why then had you and your wife planned to go abroad without telling anybody of your intention?'

'You know that too?'

'Yes, Mr Leonides.'

'But don't you see?' He leaned forward eagerly. 'I couldn't face him with the truth. It would have looked, you see, as if I was asking for money. As though I wanted him to set me on my feet again. He – he was very fond of me. He would have wanted to help. But I couldn't – I couldn't go on – it would have meant making a mess of things all over again – I'm no good. I haven't got the ability. I'm not the man my father was. I've always known it. I've tried. But it's no good. I've been so miserable – God! you don't know how miserable I've been! Trying to get out of the muddle, hoping I'd just get square, hoping the dear old man would never need to hear about it. And then it came – no more hope of avoiding the crash. Clemency – my wife – she understood, she agreed with me. We thought out this plan. Say nothing to anyone. Go away. And then let the storm break. I'd leave a letter for my father, telling him all about it – telling him how ashamed I was and begging him to forgive me. He's been so good to me always – you don't know! But it would be too late then for him to do anything. That's what I wanted. Not to ask him – or even to seem to ask him for help. Start again on my own somewhere. Live simply and humbly. Grow things. Coffee – fruit. Just have the bare necessities of life – hard on Clemency, but she swore she didn't mind. She's wonderful – absolutely wonderful.'

'I see.' My father's voice was dry. 'And what made you change your mind?'

'Change my mind?'

'Yes. What made you decide to go to your father and ask for financial help after all?'

Roger stared at him.

'But I didn't!'

'Come now, Mr Leonides.'

'You've got it all wrong. I didn't go to him. *He* sent for *me*.

He'd heard, somehow, in the City. A rumour, I suppose. But he always knew things. Someone had told him. He tackled me with it. Then, of course, I broke down . . . I told him everything. I said it wasn't so much the money – it was the feeling I'd let him down after he'd trusted me.'

Roger swallowed convulsively.

'The dear old man,' he said. 'You can't imagine how good he was to me. No reproaches. Just kindness. I told him I didn't want help, that I preferred not to have it – that I'd rather go away as I'd planned to do. But he wouldn't listen. He insisted on coming to the rescue – on putting Associated Catering on its legs again.'

Taverner said sharply:

'You are asking us to believe that your father intended to come to your assistance financially?'

'Certainly he did. He wrote to his brokers then and there, giving them instructions.'

I suppose he saw the incredulity on the two men's faces. He flushed.

'Look here,' he said, 'I've still got the letter. I was to post it. But of course later – with – with the shock and confusion, I forgot. I've probably got it in my pocket now.'

He drew out his wallet and started hunting through it. Finally he found what he wanted. It was a creased envelope with a stamp on it. It was addressed, as I saw by leaning forward, to Messrs Greatorex and Hanbury.

'Read it for yourselves,' he said, 'if you don't believe me.'

My father tore open the letter. Taverner went round behind him. I did not see the letter then, but I saw it later. It instructed Messrs Greatorex and Hanbury to realize certain investments and asked for a member of the firm to be sent down on the following day to take certain instructions *re* the affairs of Associated Catering. Some of it was unintelligible to me, but its purpose was clear enough. Aristide Leonides was preparing to put Associated Catering on its feet again.

Taverner said:

'We will give you a receipt for this, Mr Leonides.'

Roger took the receipt. He got up and said:

'Is that all? You do see how it all was, don't you?'

Taverner said:

'Mr Leonides gave you this letter and then you left him? What did you do next?'

'I rushed back to my own part of the house. My wife had just come in. I told her what my father proposed to do. How wonderful he had been! I – really, I hardly knew what I was doing.'

'And your father was taken ill – how long after that?'

'Let me see – half an hour, perhaps, or an hour. Brenda came rushing in. She was frightened. She said he looked queer. I – I rushed over with her. But I've told you all this before.'

'During your former visit, did you go into the bathroom adjoining your father's room at all?'

'I don't think so. No – no, I am sure I didn't. Why, you can't possibly think that I –'

My father quelled the sudden indignation. He got up and shook hands.

'Thank you, Mr Leonides,' he said. 'You have been very helpful. But you should have told us all this before.'

The door closed behind Roger. I got up and came to look at the letter lying on my father's table.

'It *could* be a forgery,' said Taverner hopefully.

'It could be,' said my father, 'but I don't think it is. I think we'll have to accept it exactly as it stands. Old Leonides was prepared to get his son out of this mess. It could have been done more efficiently by him alive than it could by Roger after his death – especially as it now transpires that no will is to be found and that in consequence Roger's actual amount of inheritance is open to question. That means delays – and difficulties. As things now stand, the crash is bound to come. No, Taverner, Roger Leonides and his wife had no motive for getting the old man out of the way. On the contrary –'

He stopped and repeated thoughtfully as though a sudden thought had occurred to him: 'On the contrary . . .'

'What's on your mind, sir?' Taverner asked.

The Old Man said slowly:

'If Aristide Leonides had lived only another twenty-four hours, Roger would have been all right. But he didn't live twenty-four hours. He died suddenly and dramatically within little more than an hour.'

'H'm,' said Taverner. 'Do you think somebody in the house

wanted Roger to go broke? Someone who had an opposing financial interest? Doesn't seem likely.'

'What's the position as regards the will?' my father asked. 'Who actually gets old Leonides' money?'

Taverner heaved an exasperated sigh.

'You know what lawyers are. Can't get a straight answer out of them. There's a former will. Made when he married the second Mrs Leonides. That leaves the same sum to her, rather less to Miss de Haviland, and the remainder between Philip and Roger. I should have thought that if this will isn't signed, then the old one would operate, but it seems it isn't so simple as that. First the making of the new will revoked the former one and there are witnesses to the signing of it, and the "testator's intention". It seems to be a toss-up if it turns out that he died intestate. Then the widow apparently gets the lot – or a life interest at any rate.'

'So if the will's disappeared Brenda Leonides is the most likely person to profit by it?'

'Yes. If there's been any hocus-pocus, it seems probable that she's at the bottom of it. And there obviously *has* been hocus-pocus, but I'm dashed if I see how it was done.'

I didn't see, either. I suppose we were really incredibly stupid. But we were looking at it, of course, from the wrong angle.

CHAPTER 12

There was a short silence after Taverner had gone out.

Then I said:

'Dad, what are murderers like?'

The Old Man looked at me thoughtfully. We understand each other so well that he knew exactly what was in my mind when I put that question. And he answered it very seriously.

'Yes,' he said. 'That's important now – very important, for you . . . Murder's come close to you. You can't go on looking at it from the outside.'

I had always been interested, in an amateurish kind of way, in some of the more spectacular 'cases' with which the CID had dealt, but, as my father said, I had been interested from the outside – looking in, as it were, through the shop window. But now, as Sophia had seen much more quickly than I did, murder had become a dominant factor in my life.

The Old Man went on:

'I don't know if I'm the right person to ask. I could put you on to a couple of the tame psychiatrists who do jobs for us. They've got it all cut and dried. Or Taverner could give you all the inside dope. But you want, I take it, to hear what I, personally, as the result of my experience of criminals, think about it?'

'That's what I want,' I said gratefully.

My father traced a little circle with his finger on the desk-top.

'What are murderers like? Some of them' – a faint rather melancholy smile showed on his face – 'have been thoroughly nice chaps.'

I think I looked a little startled.

'Oh yes, they have,' he said. 'Nice ordinary fellows like you and me – or like that chap who went out just now – Roger Leonides. Murder, you see, is an amateur crime. I'm speaking of course of the kind of murder you have in mind – not gangster stuff. One feels, very often, as though these nice ordinary chaps had been overtaken, as it were, by murder, almost accidentally. They've been in a tight place, or they've wanted something very badly, money or a woman – and they've killed to get it. The brake that operates with most of us doesn't operate with them. A child, you know, translates desire into action without compunction. A child is angry with its kitten, says "I'll kill you," and hits it on the head with a hammer – and then breaks its heart because the kitten doesn't come alive again! Lots of kids try to take a baby out of a pram and "drown it", because it usurps attention – or interferes with their pleasures. They get – very early – to a stage when they know that that is "wrong" – that is, that it will be punished. Later, they get to *feel* that it is wrong. But some people, I suspect, remain morally immature. They continue to be aware that murder is wrong, but they do not feel it. I don't think, in my experience, that any murderer has really felt remorse . . . And that, perhaps, is the mark of Cain. Murderers are set apart, they are "different" – murder is wrong – but not for *them* – for them it is necessary – the victim has "asked for it", it was "the only way".'

'Do you think,' I asked, 'that if someone hated old Leonides, had hated him, say, for a very long time, that that would be a reason?'

'Pure hate? Very unlikely, I should say.' My father looked at me curiously. 'When you say hate, I presume you mean dislike carried to excess. A jealous hate is different – that rises out of affection and frustration. Constance Kent, everybody said, was very fond of the baby brother she killed. But she wanted, one supposes, the attention and the love that was bestowed on him. I think people more often kill those they love than those they hate. Possibly because only the people you love can really make life unendurable to you.

'But all this doesn't help you much, does it?' he went on. 'What you want, if I read you correctly, is some token, some universal sign that will help you to pick out a murderer from a household of apparently normal and pleasant people?'

'Yes, that's it.'

'Is there a common denominator? I wonder. You know,' he paused in thought, 'if there is, I should be inclined to say it is vanity.'

'Vanity?'

'Yes, I've never met a murderer who wasn't vain . . . It's their vanity that leads to their undoing, nine times out of ten. They may be frightened of being caught, but they can't help strutting and boasting and usually they're sure they've been far too clever to be caught.' He added: 'And here's another thing, a murderer wants to *talk*.'

'To talk?'

'Yes; you see, having committed a murder puts you in a position of great loneliness. You'd like to tell somebody all about it – and you never can. And that makes you want to all the more. And so – if you can't talk about how you did it, you can at least talk about the murder itself – discuss it, advance theories – go over it.

'If I were you, Charles, I should look out for that. Go down there again, mix with them all, and get them to talk. Of course it won't be plain sailing. Guilty or innocent, they'll be glad of the chance to talk to a stranger, because they can say things to you that they couldn't say to each other. But it's possible, I think, that you might spot a difference. A person who has something to hide can't really afford to talk *at all*. The blokes knew that in Intelligence during the war. If you were captured, your name, rank, and number, but *nothing more*. People who attempt to give false information nearly always slip up. Get that household talking, Charles, and watch out for a slip or for some flash of self-revelation.'

I told him then what Sophia had said about the ruthlessness in the family – the different kinds of ruthlessness. He was interested.

'Yes,' he said. 'Your young woman has got something there. Most families have got a defect, a chink in their armour. Most people can deal with one weakness – but they mightn't be able to deal with two weaknesses of a different kind. Interesting thing, heredity. Take the de Haviland ruthlessness, and what we might call the Leonides unscrupulousness – the de Havilands are all right because they're not unscrupulous, and the Leonides are all right because, though unscrupulous, they are kindly – but get a descendant who inherited both of those traits – see what I mean?'

I had not thought of it quite in those terms. My father said:

'But I shouldn't worry your head about heredity. It's much too tricky and complicated a subject. No, my boy, go down there and *let them talk to you*. Your Sophia is quite right about one thing. Nothing but the truth is going to be any good to her or to you. You've got to *know*.'

He added as I went out of the room:

'And be careful of the child.'

'Josephine? You mean don't let on to her what I'm up to.'

'No, I didn't mean that. I meant – look after her. We don't want anything to happen to her.'

I stared at him.

'Come, come, Charles. There's a cold-blooded killer somewhere in that household. The child Josephine appears to know most of what goes on.'

'She certainly knew all about Roger – even if she did leap to the conclusion that he was a swindler. Her account of what she overheard seems to have been quite accurate.'

'Yes, yes. Child's evidence is always the best evidence there is. I'd rely on it every time. No good in court, of course. Children can't stand being asked direct questions. They mumble or else look idiotic and say they don't know. They're at their best when they're showing off. That's what the child was doing to you. Showing off. You'll get more out of her in the same way. Don't go asking her questions. Pretend you think she doesn't know anything. That'll fetch her.'

He added:

'But take care of her. She may know a little too much for somebody's safety.'

CHAPTER 13

I went down to the Crooked House (as I called it in my own mind) with a slightly guilty feeling. Though I had repeated to Taverner Josephine's confidences about Roger, I had said nothing about her statement that Brenda and Laurence Brown wrote love letters to each other.

I excused myself by pretending that it was mere romancing, and that there was no reason to believe that it was true. But actually I had felt a strange reluctance to pile up additional evidence against Brenda Leonides. I had been affected by the pathos of her position in the house – surrounded by a hostile family united solidly against her. If such letters existed doubtless Taverner and his myrmidons would find them. I disliked to be the means of bringing fresh suspicion on a woman in a difficult position. Moreover, she had assured me solemnly that there was nothing of that kind between her and Laurence and I felt more inclined to believe her than to believe that malicious gnome Josephine. Had not Brenda said herself that Josephine was 'not all there'?

I stifled an uneasy certainty that Josephine was very much all there. I remembered the intelligence of her beady black eyes.

I had rung up Sophia and asked if I might come down again.

'Please do, Charles.'

'How are things going?'

'I don't know. All right. They keep on searching the house. What are they looking for?'

'I've no idea.'

'We're all getting very nervy. Come as soon as you can. I shall go crazy if I can't talk to someone.'

I said I would come down straight away.

There was no one in sight as I drove up to the front door. I paid the taxi and it drove away. I felt uncertain whether to ring the bell or to walk in. The front door was open.

As I stood there, hesitating, I heard a slight sound behind me. I turned my head sharply. Josephine, her face partially obscured by a very large apple, was standing in the opening of the yew hedge looking at me.

As I turned my head, she turned away.

'Hallo, Josephine.'

She did not answer, but disappeared behind the hedge. I crossed the drive and followed her. She was seated on the uncomfortable rustic bench by the goldfish pond swinging her legs to and fro and biting into her apple. Above its rosy circumference her eyes regarded me sombrely and with what I could not but feel was hostility.

'I've come down again, Josephine,' I said.

It was a feeble opening, but I found Josephine's silence and her unblinking gaze rather unnerving.

With excellent strategic sense, she still did not reply.

'Is that a good apple?' I asked.

This time Josephine did condescend to reply. Her reply consisted of one word.

'Woolly.'

'A pity,' I said. 'I don't like woolly apples.'

Josephine replied scornfully:

'Nobody does.'

'Why wouldn't you speak to me when I said hallo?'

'I didn't want to.'

'Why not?'

Josephine removed the apple from her face to assist in the clearness of her denunciation.

'You went and sneaked to the police,' she said.

'Oh!' I was rather taken aback. 'You mean – about –'

'About Uncle Roger.'

'But it's all right, Josephine,' I assured her. 'Quite all right.

They know he didn't do anything wrong – I mean, he hadn't embezzled any money or anything of that kind.'

Josephine threw me an exasperated glance.

'How stupid you are.'

'I'm sorry.'

'I wasn't worrying about Uncle Roger. It's simply that that's not the way to do detective work. Don't you know that you *never* tell the police until the very end?'

'Oh, I see,' I said. 'I'm sorry, Josephine. I'm really very sorry.'

'So you should be.' She added reproachfully: 'I trusted you.'

I said I was sorry for the third time. Josephine appeared a little mollified. She took another couple of bites of apple.

'But the police would have been bound to find out about all this,' I said. 'You – I – we couldn't have kept it a secret.'

'You mean because he's going bankrupt?'

As usual Josephine was well informed.

'I suppose it will come to that.'

'They're going to talk about it tonight,' said Josephine. 'Father and Mother and Uncle Roger and Aunt Edith. Aunt Edith would give him her money – only she hasn't got it yet – but I don't think father will. He says if Roger has got in a jam he's only got himself to blame and what's the good of throwing good money after bad, and Mother won't hear of giving him any because she wants Father to put up the money for Edith Thompson. Do you know about Edith Thompson? She was married, but she didn't like her husband. She was in love with a young man called Bywaters who came off a ship and he went down a different street after the theatre and stabbed him in the back.'

I marvelled once more at the range and completeness of Josephine's knowledge; and also at the dramatic sense which, only slightly obscured by hazy pronouns, had presented all the salient facts in a nutshell.

'It sounds all right,' said Josephine, 'but I don't suppose the play will be like that at all. It will be like *Jezebel* again.' She sighed. 'I wish I knew *why* the dogs wouldn't eat the palms of her hands.'

'Josephine,' I said. 'You told me that you were almost sure who the murderer was?'

'Well?'

'Who is it?'

She gave me a look of scorn.

'I see,' I said. 'Not till the last chapter? Not even if I promise not to tell Inspector Taverner?'

'I want just a few more clues,' said Josephine.

'Anyway,' she added, throwing the core of the apple into the goldfish pool, 'I wouldn't tell *you*. If you're anyone, you're Watson.'

I stomached this insult.

'OK,' I said. 'I'm Watson. But even Watson was given the data.'

'The what?'

'The facts. And then he made the wrong deductions from them. Wouldn't it be a lot of fun for you to see me making the wrong deductions?'

For a moment Josephine was tempted. Then she shook her head.

'No,' she said, and added: 'Anyway, I'm not very keen on Sherlock Holmes. It's awfully old-fashioned. They drive about in dog-carts.'

'What about those letters?' I asked.

'What letters?'

'The letters you said Laurence Brown and Brenda wrote to each other.'

'I made that up,' said Josephine.

'I don't believe you.'

'Yes, I did. I often make things up. It amuses me.'

I stared at her. She stared back.

'Look here, Josephine. I know a man at the British Museum who knows a lot about the Bible. If I find out from him why the dogs didn't eat the palms of Jezebel's hands, will you tell me about those letters?'

This time Josephine really hesitated.

Somewhere, not very far away, a twig snapped with a sharp cracking noise. Josephine said flatly:

'No, I won't.'

I accepted defeat. Rather late in the day, I remembered my father's advice.

'Oh well,' I said, 'it's only a game. Of course you don't really know anything.'

Josephine's eyes snapped, but she resisted the bait.

I got up. 'I must go in now,' I said, 'and find Sophia. Come along.'

'I shall stop here,' said Josephine.

'No, you won't,' I said. 'You're coming in with me.'

Unceremoniously I yanked her to her feet. She seemed surprised and inclined to protest, but yielded with a fairly good grace – partly, no doubt, because she wished to observe the reactions of the household to my presence.

Why I was so anxious for her to accompany me I could not at that moment have said. It only came to me as we were passing through the front door.

It was because of the sudden snapping of a twig.

CHAPTER 14

There was a murmur of voices from the big drawing-room. I hesitated but did not go in. I wandered down the passage and, led by some impulse, I pushed open a baize door. The passage beyond was dark, but suddenly a door opened showing a big lighted kitchen. In the doorway stood an old woman – a rather bulky old woman. She had a very clean white apron tied round her ample waist and the moment I saw her I knew that everything was all right. It is the feeling that a good Nannie can always give you. I am thirty-five, but I felt just like a reassured little boy of four.

As far as I knew, Nannie had never seen me, but she said at once:

'It's Mr Charles, isn't it? Come into the kitchen and let me give you a cup of tea.'

It was a big happy-feeling kitchen. I sat down by the centre table and Nannie brought me a cup of tea and two sweet biscuits on a plate. I felt more than ever that I was in the nursery again. Everything was all right – and the terrors of the dark and the unknown were no more with me.

'Miss Sophia will be glad you've come,' said Nannie. 'She's been getting rather over-excited.' She added disapprovingly: 'They're all over-excited.'

I looked over my shoulder.

'Where's Josephine? She came in with me.'

Nannie made a disapproving clacking noise with her tongue.

'Listening at doors and writing down things in that silly little book she carries about with her,' she said. 'She ought to have gone to school and had children of her own age to play with. I've said so to Miss Edith and she agrees – but the master would have it that she was best here in her home.'

'I suppose he's very fond of her,' I said.

'He was, sir. He was fond of them all.'

I looked slightly astonished, wondering why Philip's affection for his offspring was put so definitely in the past. Nannie saw my expression and flushing slightly, she said:

'When I said the master, it was old Mr Leonides I meant.'

Before I could respond to that, the door opened with a rush and Sophia came in.

'Oh, Charles,' she said, and then quickly: 'Oh, Nannie, I'm so glad he's come.'

'I know you are, love.'

Nannie gathered up a lot of pots and pans and went off into a scullery with them. She shut the door behind her.

I got up from the table and went over to Sophia. I put my arms round her and held her to me.

'Dearest,' I said. 'You're trembling. What is it?'

Sophia said:

'I'm frightened, Charles. I'm frightened.'

'I love you,' I said. 'If I could take you away –'

She drew apart and shook her head.

'No, that's impossible. We've got to see this through. But you know, Charles, I don't like it. I don't like the feeling that someone – someone in this house – someone I see and speak to every day is a cold-blooded, calculating poisoner . . .'

And I didn't know how to answer that. To someone like Sophia one can give no easy meaningless reassurances.

She said: 'If only one *knew* –'

'That must be the worst of it,' I agreed.

'You know what really frightens me?' she whispered. 'It's that we may *never* know . . .'

I could visualize easily what a nightmare that would be . . . And it seemed to me highly probable that it never might be known who had killed old Leonides.

But it also reminded me of a question I had meant to put to Sophia on a point that had interested me.

'Tell me, Sophia,' I said. 'How many people in this house knew about the eserine eyedrops – I mean (a) that your grandfather had them, and (b) that they were poisonous and what would be a fatal dose?'

'I see what you're getting at, Charles. But it won't work. You see, we all knew.'

'Well, yes, vaguely, I suppose, but specifically –'

'We knew specifically. We were all up with grandfather one day for coffee after lunch. He liked all the family round him, you know. And his eyes had been giving him a lot of trouble. And Brenda got the eserine to put a drop in each eye, and Josephine, who always asks questions about everything, said: "Why does it say *Eyedrops – not to be taken* on the bottle?" And grandfather smiled and said: "If Brenda were to make a mistake and inject eyedrops into me one day instead of insulin – I suspect I should give a big gasp, and go rather blue in the face and then die, because you see, my heart isn't very strong." And Josephine said: "Oo," and grandfather went on: "So we must be careful that Brenda does not give me an injection of eserine instead of insulin, mustn't we?"' Sophia paused and then said: 'We were all there listening. You see? We all heard!'

I did see. I had some faint idea in my mind that just a little specialized knowledge would have been needed. But now it was borne in upon me that old Leonides had actually supplied the blueprint for his own murder. The murderer had not had to think out a scheme, or to plan or devise anything. A simple easy method of causing death had been supplied by the victim himself.

I drew a deep breath. Sophia, catching my thought, said: 'Yes, it's rather horrible, isn't it?'

'You know, Sophia,' I said slowly. 'There's just one thing does strike me.'

'Yes?'

'That you're right, and that it couldn't have been Brenda. She couldn't do it exactly that way – when you'd all listened – when you'd all remember.'

'I don't know about that. She is rather dumb in some ways, you know.'

'Not as dumb as all that,' I said. 'No, it couldn't have been Brenda.'

Sophia moved away from me.

'You don't want it to be Brenda, do you?' she asked.

And what could I say? I couldn't – no, I couldn't – say flatly: 'Yes, I hope it *is* Brenda.'

Why couldn't I? Just the feeling that Brenda was all alone on one side, and the concentrated animosity of the powerful Leonides family was arrayed against her on the other side. Chivalry? A feeling for the weaker? For the defenceless? I remembered her sitting on the sofa in her expensive rich mourning, the hopelessness in her voice – the fear in her eyes.

Nannie came back rather opportunely from the scullery. I don't know whether she sensed a certain strain between myself and Sophia.

She said disapprovingly:

'Talking murders and such-like. Forget about it, that's what I say. Leave it to the police. It's their nasty business, not yours.'

'Oh, Nannie – don't you realize that someone in this house is a murderer –'

'Nonsense, Miss Sophia, I've no patience with you. Isn't the front door open all the time – all the doors open, nothing locked – asking for thieves and burglars?'

'But it couldn't have been a burglar, nothing was stolen. Besides, why should a burglar come in and poison somebody?'

'I didn't say it was a burglar, Miss Sophia. I only said all the doors were open. Anyone could have got in. If you ask me it was the Communists.'

Nannie nodded her head in a satisfied way.

'Why on earth should Communists want to murder poor grandfather?'

'Well, everyone says that they're at the bottom of everything that goes on. But if it wasn't the Communists, mark my word, it was the Catholics. The Scarlet Woman of Babylon, that's what they are.'

With the air of one saying the last word, Nannie disappeared again into the scullery.

Sophia and I laughed.

'A good old Black Protestant,' I said.

'Yes, isn't she? Come on, Charles, come into the drawing-room. There's a kind of family conclave going on. It was scheduled for this evening – but it's started prematurely.'

'I'd better not butt in, Sophia.'

'If you're ever going to marry into the family, you'd better see just what it's like when it has the gloves off.'

'What's it all about?'

'Roger's affairs. You seem to have been mixed up in them already. But you're crazy to think that Roger would ever have killed grandfather. Why, Roger adored him.'

'I didn't really think Roger had. I thought Clemency might have.'

'Only because I put it into your head. But you're wrong there too. I don't think Clemency will mind a bit if Roger loses all his money. I think she'll actually be rather pleased. She's got a queer kind of passion for *not* having things. Come on.'

When Sophia and I entered the drawing-room, the voices that were speaking stopped abruptly. Everybody looked at us.

They were all there. Philip sitting in a big crimson brocaded arm-chair between the windows, his beautiful face set in a cold, stern mask. He looked like a judge about to pronounce sentence. Roger was astride a big pouffe by the fireplace. He had ruffled up his hair between his fingers until it stood up all over his head. His left trouser leg was rucked up and his tie askew. He looked flushed and argumentative. Clemency sat beyond him, her slight form seemed too slender for the big stuffed chair. She was looking away from the others and seemed to be studying the wall panels with a dispassionate gaze. Edith sat in a grandfather chair, bolt upright. She was knitting with incredible energy, her lips pressed tightly together. The most beautiful thing in the room to look at was Magda and Eustace. They looked like a portrait by Gainsborough. They sat together on the sofa – the dark, handsome boy with a sullen expression on his face, and beside him, one arm thrust out along the back of the sofa, sat Magda, the Duchess of Three Gables in a picture gown of taffetas with one small foot in a brocaded slipper thrust out in front of her.

Philip frowned.

'Sophia,' he said, 'I'm sorry, but we are discussing family matters which are of a private nature.'

Miss de Haviland's needles clicked. I prepared to apologize and retreat. Sophia forestalled me. Her voice was clear and determined.

'Charles and I,' she said, 'hope to get married. I want Charles to be here.'

'And why on earth not?' cried Roger, springing up from his pouffe with explosive energy. 'I keep telling you, Philip, there's nothing *private* about this! The whole world is going to know tomorrow or the day after. Anyway, my dear boy,' he came and put a friendly hand on my shoulder, '*you* know all about it. You were there this morning.'

'Do tell me,' cried Magda, leaning forward. 'What is it like at Scotland Yard? One always wonders. A table? A desk? Chairs? What kind of curtains? No flowers, I suppose? A dictaphone?'

'Put a sock in it, Mother,' said Sophia. 'And anyway, you told Vavasour Jones to cut that Scotland Yard scene. You said it was an anti-climax.'

'It makes it too like a detective play,' said Magda. 'Edith Thompson is definitely a psychological drama – or psychological thriller – which do you think sounds best?'

'You were there this morning?' Philip asked me sharply. 'Why? Oh, of course – your father –'

He frowned. I realized more clearly than ever that my presence was unwelcome, but Sophia's hand was clenched on my arm.

Clemency moved a chair forward.

'Do sit down,' she said.

I gave her a grateful glance and accepted.

'You may say what you like,' said Miss de Haviland, apparently going on from where they had all left off, 'but I do think we ought to respect Aristide's wishes. When this will business is straightened out, as far as I am concerned, my legacy is entirely at your disposal, Roger.'

Roger tugged his hair in a frenzy.

'No Aunt Edith. *No!*' he cried.

'I wish I could say the same,' said Philip, 'but one has to take every factor into consideration –'

'Dear old Phil, don't you understand? I'm not going to take a penny from *anyone.*'

'Of course he can't!' snapped Clemency.

'Anyway, Edith,' said Magda. '*If* the will is straightened out, he'll have his own legacy.'

'But it can't possibly be straightened out in time, can it?' asked Eustace.

'You don't know anything about it, Eustace,' said Philip.

'The boy's absolutely right,' cried Roger. 'He's put his finger on the spot. Nothing can avert the crash. Nothing.'

He spoke with a kind of relish.

'There is really nothing to discuss,' said Clemency.

'Anyway,' said Roger, 'what does it matter?'

'I should have thought it mattered a good deal,' said Philip, pressing his lips together.

'No,' said Roger. '*No!* Does anything matter compared with the fact that father is dead? Father is *dead*! And we sit here discussing mere money matters!'

A faint colour rose in Philip's pale cheeks.

'We are only trying to help,' he said stiffly.

'I know, Phil, old boy, I know. But there's nothing anyone can do. So let's call it a day.'

'I suppose,' said Philip, 'that I *could* raise a certain amount of money. Securities have gone down a good deal and some of my capital is tied up in such a way that I can't touch it: Magda's settlement and so on – but –'

Magda said quickly:

'Of course you can't raise the money, darling. It would be absurd to try – and not very fair on the children.'

'I tell you I'm not asking anyone for *anything*!' shouted Roger. 'I'm *hoarse* with telling you so. I'm quite content that things should take their course.'

'It's a question of prestige,' said Philip. 'Father's. Ours.'

'It wasn't a family business. It was solely *my* concern.'

'Yes,' said Philip, looking at him. 'It was entirely your concern.'

Edith de Haviland got up and said: 'I think we've discussed this enough.'

There was in her voice that authentic note of authority that never fails to produce its effect.

Philip and Magda got up. Eustace lounged out of the room and I noticed the stiffness of his gait. He was not exactly lame, but his walk was a halting one.

Roger linked his arm in Philip's and said:

'You've been a brick, Phil, even to think of such a thing!' The brothers went out together.

Magda murmured, 'Such a fuss!' as she followed them, and Sophia said that she must see about my room.

Edith de Haviland stood rolling up her knitting. She looked towards me and I thought she was going to speak to me. There was something almost like appeal in her glance. However, she changed her mind, sighed, and went out after the others.

Clemency had moved over to the window and stood looking out into the garden. I went over and stood beside her. She turned her head slightly towards me.

'Thank goodness that's over,' she said – and added with distaste: 'What a preposterous room this is!'

'Don't you like it?'

'I can't breathe in it. There's always a smell of half-dead flowers and dust.'

I thought she was unjust to the room. But I knew what she meant. It was very definitely an interior.

It was a woman's room, exotic, soft, shut away from the rude blasts of outside weather. It was not a room that a man would be happy in for long. It was not a room where you could relax and read the newspaper and smoke a pipe and put up your feet. Nevertheless I preferred it to Clemency's own abstract expression of herself upstairs. On the whole I prefer a boudoir to an operating theatre.

She said, looking round:

'It's just a stage set. A background for Magda to play her scenes against.' She looked at me. 'You realize, don't you, what we've just been doing? Act II – the family conclave. Magda arranged it. It didn't mean a thing. There was nothing to talk about, nothing to discuss. It's all settled – finished.'

There was no sadness in her voice. Rather there was satisfaction. She caught my glance.

'Oh, don't you understand?' she said impatiently. 'We're *free* – at last! Don't you understand that Roger's been miserable –

absolutely *miserable* – for years? He never had any aptitude for business. He likes things like horses and cows and pottering round in the country. But he adored his father – they all did. That's what's wrong with this house – too much family. I don't mean that the old man was a tyrant, or preyed upon them, or bullied them. He didn't. He gave them money and freedom. He was devoted to them. And they kept on being devoted to him.'

'Is there anything wrong in that?'

'I think there is. I think, when your children have grown up, that you should cut away from them, efface yourself, slink away, *force* them to forget you.'

'Force them? That's rather drastic, isn't it? Isn't coercion as bad one way as another?'

'If he hadn't made himself such a personality –'

'You can't make yourself a personality,' I said. 'He *was* a personality.'

'He was too much of a personality for Roger. Roger worshipped him. He wanted to do everything his father wanted him to do, he wanted to be the kind of son his father wanted. And he couldn't. His father made over Associated Catering to him – it was the old man's particular joy and pride, and Roger tried hard to carry on in his father's footsteps. But he hadn't got that kind of ability. In business matters Roger is – yes, I'll say it plainly – a fool. And it nearly broke his heart. He's been miserable for years, struggling, seeing the whole thing go down the hill, having sudden wonderful "ideas" and "schemes" which always went wrong and made it worse than ever. It's a terrible thing to feel you're a failure year after year. You don't know how unhappy he's been. I do.'

Again she turned and faced me.

'You thought, you actually suggested to the police, that Roger would have killed his father – for money! You don't know how – how absolutely *ridiculous* that is!'

'I do know it now,' I said humbly.

'When Roger knew he couldn't stave it off any more – that the crash was bound to come, he was actually relieved. Yes, he was. He worried about his father's knowing – but not about anything else. He was looking forward to the new life we were going to live.'

Her face quivered a little and her voice softened.

'Where were you going?' I asked.

'To Barbados. A distant cousin of mine died a short time ago and left me a tiny estate out there – oh, nothing much. But it was somewhere to go. We'd have been desperately poor, but we'd have scratched a living – it costs very little just to live. We'd have been together – unworried, away from them all.'

She sighed.

'Roger is a ridiculous person. He would worry about *me* – about *my* being poor. I suppose he's got the Leonides' attitude to money too firmly in his mind. When my first husband was alive, we were terribly poor – and Roger thinks it was so brave and wonderful of me! He doesn't realize that I was *happy* – really happy! I've never been so happy since. And yet – I never loved Richard as I love Roger.'

Her eyes half-closed. I was aware of the intensity of her feeling.

She opened her eyes, looked at me and said:

'So you see, I would never have killed anyone for money. I don't *like* money.'

I was quite sure that she meant exactly what she said. Clemency Leonides was one of those rare people to whom money does not appeal. They dislike luxury, prefer austerity and are suspicious of possessions.

Still, there are many to whom money has no personal appeal, but who can be tempted by the power it confers.

I said: 'You mightn't want money for yourself – but wisely directed, money can do a lot of interesting things. It can endow research, for example.'

I had suspected that Clemency might be a fanatic about her work, but she merely said:

'I doubt if endowments ever do much good. They're usually spent in the wrong way. The things that are worth while are usually accomplished by someone with enthusiasm and drive – and with natural vision. Expensive equipment and training and experiment never does what you'd imagine it might do. The spending of it usually gets into the wrong hands.'

'Will you mind giving up your work when you go to Barbados?' I asked. 'You're still going, I presume?'

'Oh, yes, as soon as the police will let us. No, I shan't mind giving up my work at all. Why should I? I wouldn't like to be idle, but I shan't be idle in Barbados.'

She added impatiently:

'Oh, if only this could all be cleared up *quickly* and we could get away.'

'Clemency,' I said, 'have you any idea at all who did do this? Granting that you and Roger had no hand in it (and really I can't see any reason to think you had), surely, with your intelligence, you must have *some* idea of who did?'

She gave me a rather peculiar look, a darting, sideways glance. When she spoke her voice had lost its spontaneity. It was awkward, rather embarrassed.

'One can't make guesses, it's unscientific,' she said. 'One can only say that Brenda and Laurence are the obvious suspects.'

'So you think they did it?'

Clemency shrugged her shoulders.

She stood for a moment as though listening, then she went out of the room, passing Edith de Haviland in the doorway.

Edith came straight over to me.

'I want to talk to you,' she said.

My father's words leapt into my mind. Was this –

But Edith de Haviland was going on:

'I hope you didn't get the wrong impression,' she said. 'About Philip, I mean. Philip is rather difficult to understand. He may seem to you reserved and cold, but that is not so at all. It's just a manner. He can't help it.'

'I really hadn't thought –' I began.

But she swept on:

'Just now – about Roger. It isn't really that he's grudging. He's never been mean about money. And he's really a dear – he's always been a dear – but he needs understanding.'

I looked at her with the air, I hope, of one who was willing to understand. She went on:

'It's partly, I think, from having been the second of the family. There's often something about a second child – they start handicapped. He adored his father, you see. Of course, all the children adored Aristide and he adored them. But Roger was his especial pride and joy. Being the eldest – the first. And I think Philip felt it. He drew back right into himself. He began to like books and the past and things that were well divorced from everyday life. I think he suffered – children do suffer . . .'

She paused and went on:

'What I really mean, I suppose, is that he's always been jealous of Roger. I think perhaps he doesn't know it himself. But I think the fact that Roger has come a cropper – oh, it seems an odious thing to say and really I'm sure he doesn't realize it himself – but I think perhaps Philip isn't as sorry about it as he ought to be.'

'You mean really that he's rather pleased Roger has made a fool of himself.'

'Yes,' said Miss de Haviland. 'I mean just exactly that.'

She added, frowning a little:

'It distressed me, you know, that he didn't at once offer to help his brother.'

'Why should he?' I said. 'After all, Roger *has* made a muck of things. He's a grown man. There are no children to consider. If he were ill or in real want, of course his family would help – but I've no doubt Roger would really much prefer to start afresh entirely on his own.'

'Oh! he would. It's only Clemency he minds about. And Clemency is an extraordinary creature. She really likes being uncomfortable and having only one utility teacup to drink out of. Modern, I suppose. She's no sense of the past, no sense of beauty.'

I felt her shrewd eyes looking me up and down.

'This is a dreadful ordeal for Sophia,' she said. 'I am so sorry her youth should be dimmed by it. I love them all, you know. Roger and Philip, and now Sophia and Eustace and Josephine. All the dear children. Marcia's children. Yes, I love them dearly.' She paused and then added sharply: 'But, mind you, this side idolatry.'

She turned abruptly and went. I had the feeling that she had meant something by her last remark that I did not quite understand.

CHAPTER 15

'Your room's ready,' said Sophia.

She stood by my side looking out at the garden. It looked bleak and grey now with the half-denuded trees swaying in the wind.

Sophia echoed my thoughts as she said:

'How desolate it looks . . .'

As we watched, a figure, and then presently another came through the yew hedge from the rock garden. They both looked grey and unsubstantial in the fading light.

Brenda Leonides was the first. She was wrapped in a grey chinchilla coat and there was something catlike and stealthy in the way she moved. She slipped through the twilight with a kind of eerie grace.

I saw her face as she passed the window. There was a half-smile on it, the curving, crooked smile I had noticed upstairs. A few minutes later Laurence Brown, looking slender and shrunken, also slipped through the twilight. I can only put it that way. They did not seem like two people walking, two people who had been out for a stroll. There was something furtive and unsubstantial about them like two ghosts.

I wondered if it was under Brenda's or Laurence's foot a twig had snapped.

By a natural association of ideas, I asked:

'Where's Josephine?'

'Probably with Eustace up in the schoolroom.' She frowned. 'I'm worried about Eustace, Charles.'

'Why?'

'He's so moody and odd. He's been so different ever since that wretched paralysis. I can't make out what's going on in his mind. Sometimes he seems to hate us all.'

'He'll probably grow out of all that. It's just a phase.'

'Yes, I suppose so. But I do get worried, Charles.'

'Why, dear heart?'

'Really, I suppose, because mother and father never worry. They're not like a mother and father.'

'That may be all for the best. More children suffer from interference than from non-interference.'

'That's true. You know, I never thought about it until I came back from abroad, but they really are a queer couple. Father living determinedly in a world of obscure historical by-paths and mother having a lovely time creating scenes. That tomfoolery this evening was all mother. There was no need for it. She just wanted to play a family conclave scene. She gets bored, you know, down here and has to try and work up a drama.'

For the moment I had a fantastic vision of Sophia's mother poisoning her elderly father-in-law in a light-hearted manner in order to observe a murder drama at first-hand with herself in the leading role.

An amusing thought! I dismissed it as such – but it left me a little uneasy.

'Mother,' said Sophia, 'has to be looked after the whole time. You never know *what* she's up to!'

'Forget your family, Sophia,' I said firmly.

'I shall be only too delighted to, but it's a little difficult at the present moment. But I *was* happy out in Cairo when I had forgotten them all.'

I remembered how Sophia had never mentioned her home or her people.

'Is that why you never talked about them?' I asked. 'Because you wanted to forget them?'

'I think so. We've always, all of us, lived too much in each other's pockets. We're – we're all too fond of each other. We're not like some families where they all hate each other like poison. That must be pretty bad, but it's almost worse to live all tangled up in conflicting affections.'

She added:

'I think that's what I mean when I said we all lived together in a little crooked house. I didn't mean that it was crooked in the dishonest sense. I think what I meant was that we hadn't been able to grow up independent, standing by ourselves, upright. We're all a bit twisted and twining.'

I saw Edith de Haviland's heel grinding a weed into the path as Sophia added:

'Like bindweed . . .'

And then suddenly Magda was with us – flinging open the door – crying out:

'Darlings, why don't you have the lights on? It's almost dark.'

And she pressed the switches and the lights sprang up on the walls and on the tables, and she and Sophia and I pulled the heavy rose curtains, and there we were in the flower-scented interior, and Magda flinging herself on the sofa, cried:

'What an incredible scene it was, wasn't it? How cross Eustace was! He told me he thought it was all positively indecent. How funny boys are!'

She sighed.

'Roger's rather a pet. I love him when he rumples his hair and starts knocking things over. Wasn't it sweet of Edith to offer her legacy to him? She really meant it, you know, it wasn't just a gesture. But it was terribly stupid – it might have made Philip think he ought to do it too! Of course Edith would do *anything* for the family! There's something very pathetic in the love of a spinster for her sister's children. Some day I shall play one of those devoted spinster aunts. Inquisitive and obstinate and devoted.'

'It must have been hard for her after her sister died,' I said, refusing to be side-tracked into discussion of another of Magda's roles. 'I mean if she disliked old Leonides so much.'

Magda interrupted me.

'Disliked him? Who told you that? Nonsense. She was in love with him.'

'Mother!' said Sophia.

'Now don't try and contradict me, Sophia. Naturally at your age, you think love is all two good-looking young people in the moonlight.'

'She told me,' I said, 'that she had always disliked him.'

'Probably she did when she first came. She'd been angry with her sister for marrying him. I dare say there was always some antagonism – but she was in love with him all right! Darling, I do know what I'm talking about! Of course, with deceased wife's sister and all that, he couldn't have married her, and I dare say he never thought of it – and quite probably she didn't either. She was quite happy mothering the children, and having fights with him. But she didn't like it when he married Brenda. She didn't like it a *bit!*'

'No more did you and father,' said Sophia.

'No, of course we hated it! Naturally! But Edith hated it most. Darling, the way I've seen her *look* at Brenda!'

'Now, Mother,' said Sophia.

Magda threw her an affectionate and half-guilty glance, the glance of a mischieveous, spoilt child.

She went on, with no apparent realization of any lack of continuity:

'I've decided Josephine really must go to school.'

'Josephine? To school?'

'Yes. To Switzerland. I'm going to see about it tomorrow. I really think we might get her off *at once*. It's so bad for her to be mixed up in a horrid business like this. She's getting quite morbid about it. What she needs is other children of her own age. School life. I've always thought so.'

'Grandfather didn't want her to go to school,' said Sophia slowly. 'He was very much against it.'

'Darling old Sweetie Pie liked us all here under his eye. Very old people are often selfish in that way. A child ought to be amongst other children. And Switzerland is so healthy – all the winter sports, and the air, and so much, much better food than we get here!'

'It will be difficult to arrange for Switzerland now with all the currency regulations, won't it?' I asked.

'Nonsense, Charles. There's some kind of educational racket – or you exchange with a Swiss child – there are all sorts of ways. Rudolph Alstir's in Lausanne. I shall wire him tomorrow to arrange *everything*. We can get her off by the end of the week!'

Magda punched a cushion, smiled at us, went to the door, stood a moment looking back at us in a quite enchanting fashion.

'It's only the young who count,' she said. As she said it, it was a lovely line. 'They must always come first. And, darlings – think of the flowers – the blue gentians, the narcissus . . .'

'In October?' asked Sophia, but Magda had gone.

Sophia heaved an exasperated sigh.

'Really,' she said. 'Mother is too trying! She gets these sudden ideas, and she sends thousands of telegrams and everything has to be arranged at a moment's notice. Why should Josephine be hustled off to Switzerland all in a flurry?'

'There's probably something in the idea of school. I think children of her own age would be a good thing for Josephine.'

'Grandfather didn't think so,' said Sophia obstinately.

I felt slightly irritated.

'My dear Sophia, do you really think an old gentleman of over eighty is the best judge of a child's welfare?'

'He was about the best judge of anybody in this house,' said Sophia.

'Better than your Aunt Edith?'

'No, perhaps not. She did rather favour school. I admit Josephine's got into rather difficult ways – she's got a horrible habit of snooping. But I really think it's just because she's playing detectives.'

Was it only the concern for Josephine's welfare which had occasioned Magda's sudden decision? I wondered. Josephine was remarkably well-informed about all sorts of things that had happened prior to the murder and which had been certainly no business of hers. A healthy school life with plenty of games would probably do her a world of good. But I did rather wonder at the suddenness and urgency of Magda's decision – Switzerland was a long way off.

CHAPTER 16

The Old Man had said:

'Let them talk to you.'

As I shaved the following morning, I considered just how far that had taken me.

Edith de Haviland had talked to me – she had sought me out for that especial purpose. Clemency had talked to me (or had I talked to her?). Magda had talked to me in a sense – that is, I had formed part of the audience to one of her broadcasts. Sophia naturally had talked to me. Even Nannie had talked to me. Was I any the wiser for what I had learned from them all? Was there any significant word or phrase? More, was there any evidence of that abnormal vanity on which my father had laid stress? I couldn't see that there was.

The only person who had shown absolutely no desire to talk

to me in any way, or on any subject, was Philip. Was not that, in a way, rather abnormal? He must know by now that I wanted to marry his daughter. Yet he continued to act as though I was not in the house at all. Presumably he resented my presence there. Edith de Haviland had apologized for him. She had said it was just 'manner'. She had shown herself concerned about Philip. Why?

I considered Sophia's father. He was in every sense a repressed individual. He had been an unhappy jealous child. He had been forced back into himself. He had taken refuge in the world of books – in the historical past. That studied coldness and reserve of his might conceal a good deal of passionate feeling. The inadequate motive of financial gain by his father's death was unconvincing – I did not think for a moment that Philip Leonides would kill his father because he himself had not quite as much money as he would like to have. But there might be some deep psychological reason for his desiring his father's death. Philip had come back to his father's house to live, and later, as a result of the Blitz, Roger had come – and Philip had been obliged to see day by day that Roger was his father's favourite . . . Might things have come to such a pass in his tortured mind that the only relief possible was his father's death? And supposing that death should incriminate his elder brother? Roger was short of money – on the verge of a crash. Knowing nothing of that last interview between Roger and his father and the latter's offer of assistance, might not Philip have believed that the motive would seem so powerful that Roger would be at once suspected? Was Philip's mental balance sufficiently disturbed to lead him to do murder?

I cut my chin with the razor and swore.

What the hell was I trying to do? Fasten murder on Sophia's father? That was a nice thing to try and do! That wasn't what Sophia had wanted me to come down here for.

Or – was it? There was something, had been something all along, behind Sophia's appeal. If there was any lingering suspicion in her mind that her father was the killer, then she would never consent to marry me – in case that suspicion might be true. And since she was Sophia, clear-eyed and brave, she wanted the truth, since uncertainty would be an eternal and perpetual barrier between us. Hadn't she been in effect saying to me, 'Prove that this dreadful thing I am imagining is not true – but if it *is* true, then prove its truth to me – so that I can know the worst and face it!'

Did Edith de Haviland know, or suspect, that Philip was guilty. What had she meant by 'this side idolatry'?

And what had Clemency meant by that peculiar look she had thrown at me when I had asked her who she suspected and she had answered: 'Laurence and Brenda are the obvious suspects, aren't they?'

The whole family wanted it to be Brenda and Laurence, hoped it might be Brenda and Laurence, but didn't really believe it was Brenda and Laurence . . .

And of course, the whole family might be wrong, and it might really be Laurence and Brenda after all.

Or, it might be Laurence, and not Brenda . . .

That would be a much better solution.

I finished dabbing my cut chin and went down to breakfast filled with the determination to have an interview with Laurence Brown as soon as possible.

It was only as I drank my second cup of coffee that it occurred to me that the Crooked House was having its effect on me also. I, too, wanted to find, not the true solution, but the solution that suited *me* best.

After breakfast I went through the hall and up the stairs. Sophia had told me that I should find Laurence giving instruction to Eustace and Josephine in the schoolroom.

I hesitated on the landing outside Brenda's front door. Did I ring and knock, or did I walk right in? I decided to treat the house as an integral Leonides home and not as Brenda's private residence.

I opened the door and passed inside. Everything was quiet, there seemed no one about. On my left the door into the big drawing-room was closed. On my right two open doors showed a bedroom and adjoining bathroom. This I knew was the bathroom adjoining Aristide Leonides' bedroom where the eserine and the insulin had been kept.

The police had finished with it now. I pushed the door open and slipped inside. I realized then how easy it would have been for anyone in the house (or from outside the house for the matter of that!) to come up here and into the bathroom unseen.

I stood in the bathroom looking round. It was sumptuously appointed with gleaming tiles and a sunken bath. At one side were various electric appliances; a hot plate and grill under, an electric kettle – a small electric saucepan, a toaster – everything that a valet attendant to an old gentleman might need. On the wall was a white enamelled cupboard. I opened it. Inside were medical appliances, two medicine glasses, eye-bath, eye dropper, and a few labelled bottles. Aspirin, boracic powder, iodine. Elastoplast bandages, etc. On a separate shelf were the stacked supply of insulin, two hypodermic needles, and a bottle of surgical spirit. On a third shelf was a bottle marked *'The Tablets – one or two to be taken at night as ordered.'* On this shelf, no doubt, had stood the bottle of eyedrops. It was all clear, well arranged, easy for anyone to get at if needed, and equally easy to get at for murder.

I could do what I liked with the bottles and then go softly out and downstairs again and nobody would ever know I had been there. All this was, of course, nothing new, but it brought home to me how difficult the task of the police was.

Only from the guilty party or parties could one find out what one needed.

'Rattle 'em,' Taverner had said to me. 'Get 'em on the run. Make 'em think we're on to something. Keep ourselves well in the limelight. Sooner or later, if we do, our criminal will stop leaving well alone and try to be smarter still – and then – we've got him.'

Well, the criminal hadn't reacted to this treatment so far.

I came out of the bathroom. Still no one about. I went on along the corridor. I passed the dining-room on the left, and Brenda's bedroom and bathroom on the right. In the latter, one of the maids was moving about. The dining-room door was closed. From a room beyond that, I heard Edith de Haviland's voice telephoning to the inevitable fishmonger. A spiral flight of stairs led to the floor above. I went up them. Edith's bedroom and sitting-room were here, I knew, and two more bathrooms and Laurence Brown's room. Beyond that again the short flight of steps down to the big room built out over the servants' quarters at the back which was used as a schoolroom.

Outside the door I paused. Laurence Brown's voice could be heard, slightly raised, from inside.

I think Josephine's habit of snooping must have been catching. Quite unashamedly I leaned against the door jamb and listened.

It was a history lesson that was in progress, and the period in question was the French *Directoire*.

As I listened astonishment opened my eyes. It was a considerable surprise to me to discover that Laurence Brown was a magnificent teacher.

I don't know why it should have surprised me so much. After all, Aristide Leonides had always been a good picker of men. For all his mouselike exterior, Laurence had that supreme gift of being able to rouse enthusiasm and imagination in his pupils. The drama of Thermidor, the decree of outlawry against the Robespierrists, the magnificence of Barras, the cunning of Fouché – Napoleon the half-starved young gunner lieutenant – all these were real and living.

Suddenly Laurence stopped, he asked Eustace and Josephine a question, he made them put themselves in the place of first one and then another figure in the drama. Though he didn't get much result from Josephine, whose voice sounded as though she had a cold in the head, Eustace sounded quite different from his usual moody self. He showed brains and intelligence and the keen historical sense which he had doubtless inherited from his father.

Then I heard the chairs being pushed back and scraped across the floor. I retreated up the steps and was apparently just coming down them when the door opened.

Eustace and Josephine came out.

'Hallo,' I said.

Eustace looked surprised to see me.

'Do you want anything?' he asked politely.

Josephine, taking no interest in my presence, slipped past me.

'I just wanted to see the schoolroom,' I said rather feebly.

'You saw it the other day, didn't you? It's just a kid's place really. Used to be the nursery. It's still got a lot of toys in it.'

He held open the door for me and I went in.

Laurence Brown stood by the table. He looked up, flushed,

murmured something in answer to my good morning and went hurriedly out.

'You've scared him,' said Eustace. 'He's very easily scared.'

'Do you like him, Eustace?'

'Oh! he's all right. An awful ass, of course.'

'But not a bad teacher?'

'No, as a matter of fact he's quite interesting. He knows an awful lot. He makes you see things from a different angle. I never knew that Henry the Eighth wrote poetry – to Ann Boleyn, of course – jolly decent poetry.'

We talked for a few moments on such subjects as *The Ancient Mariner*, Chaucer, the political implications behind the Crusades, the medieval approach to life, and the, to Eustace, surprising fact that Oliver Cromwell had prohibited the celebration of Christmas Day. Behind Eustace's scornful and rather ill-tempered manner there was, I perceived, an inquiring and able mind.

Very soon, I began to realize the source of his ill humour. His illness had not only been a frightening ordeal, it had also been a frustration and a setback, just at a moment when he had been enjoying life.

'I was to have been in the eleven next term – and I'd got my house colours. It's pretty thick to have to stop at home and do lessons with a rotten kid like Josephine. Why, she's only twelve.'

'Yes, but you don't have the same studies, do you?'

'No, of course she doesn't do advanced maths – or Latin. But you don't want to have to share a tutor with a *girl*.'

I tried to soothe his injured male pride by remarking that Josephine was quite an intelligent girl for her age.

'D'you think so? I think she's awfully wet. She's mad keen on this detecting stuff – goes round poking her nose in everywhere and writing things down in a little black book and pretending that she's finding out a lot. Just a silly kid, that's all she is,' said Eustace loftily.

'Anyway,' he added, 'girls can't be detectives. I told her so. I think mother's quite right and the sooner Jo's packed off to Switzerland the better.'

'Wouldn't you miss her?'

'Miss a kid of that age?' said Eustace haughtily. 'Of course not. My goodness, this house is the absolute limit! Mother always haring up and down to London and bullying tame dramatists to rewrite plays for her, and making frightful fusses about nothing at all. And father shut up with his books and sometimes not hearing you if you speak to him. I don't see why I should have to be burdened with such peculiar parents. Then there's Uncle Roger – always so hearty that it makes you shudder. Aunt Clemency's all right, she doesn't bother you, but I sometimes think she's a bit batty. Aunt Edith's not too bad, but she's old. Things have been a bit more cheerful since Sophia came back – though she can be pretty sharp sometimes. But it is a queer household, don't you think so? Having a step-grandmother young enough to be your aunt or your older sister. I mean, it makes you feel an awful ass!'

I had some comprehension of his feelings. I remembered (very dimly) my own supersensitiveness at Eustace's age. My horror of appearing in any way unusual or of my near relatives departing from the normal.

'What about your grandfather?' I said. 'Were you fond of him?'

A curious expression flitted across Eustace's face.

'Grandfather,' he said, 'was definitely anti-social!'

'In what way?'

'He thought of nothing but the profit motive. Laurence says that's completely wrong. And he was a great individualist. All that sort of thing has got to go, don't you think so?'

'Well,' I said, rather brutally, 'he has gone.'

'A good thing, really,' said Eustace. 'I don't want to be callous, but you can't really *enjoy* life at that age!'

'Didn't he?'

'He couldn't have. Anyway, it was time he went. He –'

Eustace broke off as Laurence Brown came back into the schoolroom.

Laurence began fussing about with some books, but I thought that he was watching me out of the corner of his eye.

He looked at his wrist-watch and said:

'Please be back here sharp at eleven, Eustace. We've wasted too much time the last few days.'

'OK, sir.'

Eustace lounged towards the door and went out whistling.

Laurence Brown darted another sharp glance at me. He moistened his lips once or twice. I was convinced that he had come back into the schoolroom solely in order to talk to me.

Presently, after a little aimless stacking and unstacking of books and a pretence of looking for a book that was missing, he spoke:

'Er – How are they getting on?' he said.

'They?'

'The police.'

His nose twitched. A mouse in a trap, I thought, a mouse in a trap.

'They don't take me into their confidence,' I said.

'Oh. I thought your father was the Assistant Commissioner.'

'He is,' I said. 'But naturally he would not betray official secrets.'

I made my voice purposely pompous.

'Then you don't know how – what – if –' His voice trailed off. 'They're not going to make an arrest, are they?'

'Not so far as I know. But then, as I say, I mightn't know.'

Get 'em on the run, Inspector Taverner had said. Get 'em rattled. Well, Laurence Brown was rattled all right.

He began talking quickly and nervously.

'You don't know what it's like . . . The strain . . . Not knowing what – I mean, they just come and go – Asking questions . . . Questions that don't seem to have anything to do with the case . . .'

He broke off. I waited. He wanted to talk – well, then, let him talk.

'You were there when the Chief Inspector made that monstrous suggestion the other day? About Mrs Leonides and myself . . . It *was* monstrous. It makes one feel so helpless. One is powerless to prevent people *thinking* things! And it is all so wickedly untrue. Just because she is – was – so many years younger than her husband. People have dreadful minds – dreadful minds. I feel – I can't help feeling, that it is all a *plot*.'

'A plot? That's interesting.'

It was interesting, though not quite in the way he took it.

'The family, you know; Mr Leonides' family, have never been

sympathetic to me. They were always aloof. I always felt that they despised me.'

His hands had begun to shake.

'Just because they have always been rich and – powerful. They looked down on me. What was I to them? Only the tutor. Only a wretched conscientious objector. And my objections *were* conscientious. They were indeed!'

I said nothing.

'All right then,' he burst out. 'What if I was – afraid? Afraid I'd make a mess of it. Afraid that when I had to pull a trigger – I mightn't be able to bring myself to do it. How can you be sure it's a Nazi you're going to kill? It might be some decent lad – some village boy – with no political leanings, just called up for his country's service. I believe war is *wrong*, do you understand? I believe it is *wrong*.'

I was still silent. I believed that my silence was achieving more than any arguments or agreements could do. Laurence Brown was arguing with himself, and in so doing was revealing a good deal of himself.

'Everyone's always laughed at me.' His voice shook. 'I seem to have a knack of making myself ridiculous. It isn't that I really lack courage – but I always do the thing wrong. I went into a burning house to rescue a woman they said was trapped there. But I lost the way at once, and the smoke made me unconscious, and it gave a lot of trouble to the firemen finding me. I heard them say, "Why couldn't the silly chump leave it to us?" It's no good my trying, everyone's against me. Whoever killed Mr Leonides arranged it so that I would be suspected. Someone killed him so as to ruin *me*.'

'What about Mrs Leonides?' I asked.

He flushed. He became less of a mouse and more like a man.

'Mrs Leonides is an angel,' he said, 'an angel. Her sweetness, her kindness to her elderly husband were wonderful. To think of her in connection with poison is laughable – laughable! And that thick-headed Inspector can't see it!'

'He's prejudiced,' I said, 'by the number of cases on his files where elderly husbands have been poisoned by sweet young wives.'

'The insufferable dolt,' said Laurence Brown angrily.

He went over to a bookcase in the corner and began rummaging the books in it. I didn't think I should get anything more out of him. I went slowly out of the room.

As I was going along the passage, a door on my left opened and Josephine almost fell on top of me. Her appearance had the suddenness of a demon in an old-fashioned pantomime.

Her face and hands were filthy and a large cobweb floated from one ear.

'Where have you been, Josephine?'

I peered through the half-open door. A couple of steps led up into an attic-like rectangular space in the gloom of which several large tanks could be seen.

'In the cistern room.'

'Why in the cistern room?'

Josephine replied in a brief businesslike way:

'Detecting.'

'What on earth is there to detect among the cisterns?'

To this, Josephine merely replied:

'I must wash.'

'I should say most decidedly.'

Josephine disappeared through the nearest bathroom door. She looked back to say:

'I should say it's about time for the next murder, wouldn't you?'

'What do you mean – the next murder?'

'Well, in books there's always a second murder about now. Someone who knows something is bumped off before they can tell what they know.'

'You read too many detective stories, Josephine. Real life isn't like that. And if anybody in this house knows something the last thing they seem to want to do is to talk about it.'

Josephine's reply came to me rather obscurely by the gushing of water from a tap.

'Sometimes it's something that they don't know that they do know.'

I blinked as I tried to think this out. Then, leaving Josephine to her ablutions, I went down to the floor below.

Just as I was going out through the front door to the staircase, Brenda came with a soft rush through the drawing-room door.

She came close to me and laid her hand on my arm, looking up in my face.

'Well?' she asked.

It was the same demand for information that Laurence had made, only it was phrased differently. And her one word was far more effective.

I shook my head.

'Nothing,' I said.

She gave a long sigh.

'I'm so frightened,' she said. 'Charles, I'm so frightened . . .'

Her fear was very real. It communicated itself to me there in that narrow space. I wanted to reassure her, to help her. I had once more that poignant sense of her as terribly alone in hostile surroundings.

She might well have cried out: '*Who is on my side?*'

And what would the answer have been? Laurence Brown? And what, after all, was Laurence Brown? No tower of strength in a time of trouble. One of the weaker vessels. I remembered the two of them drifting in from the garden the night before.

I wanted to help her. I badly wanted to help her. But there was nothing much I could say or do. And I had at the bottom of my mind an embarrassed guilty feeling, as though Sophia's scornful eyes were watching me. I remembered Sophia's voice saying: 'So she got you.'

And Sophia did not see, did not want to see, Brenda's side of it. Alone, suspected of murder, with no one to stand by her.

'The inquest is tomorrow,' Brenda said. 'What – what will happen?'

There I could reassure her.

'Nothing,' I said. 'You needn't worry about that. It will be adjourned for the police to make inquiries. It will probably set the Press loose, though. So far, there's been no indication in the papers that it wasn't a natural death. The Leonides have got a good deal of influence. But with an adjourned inquest – well, the fun will start.'

(What extraordinary things one said! The *fun*! Why must I choose that particular word?)

'Will – will they be very dreadful?'

'I shouldn't give any interviews if I were you. You know,

Brenda, you ought to have a lawyer –' She recoiled with a terrific gasp of dismay. 'No – no – not the way you mean. But someone to look after your interests and advise you as to procedure, and what to say and do, and what not to say and do.

'You see,' I added, 'you're very much alone.'

Her hand pressed my arm more closely.

'Yes,' she said. 'You do understand that. You've helped, Charles, you have helped . . .'

I went down the stairs with a feeling of warmth, of satisfaction . . . Then I saw Sophia standing by the front door. Her voice was cold and rather dry.

'What a long time you've been,' she said. 'They rang up for you from London. Your father wants you.'

'At the Yard?'

'Yes.'

'I wonder what they want me for. They didn't say?'

Sophia shook her head. Her eyes were anxious. I drew her to me.

'Don't worry, darling,' I said, 'I'll soon be back.'

CHAPTER 17

There was something strained in the atmosphere of my father's room. The Old Man sat behind his table, Chief-Inspector Taverner leaned against the window frame. In the visitors' chair sat Mr Gaitskill, looking ruffled.

'– extraordinary want of confidence,' he was saying acidly.

'Of course, of course.' My father spoke soothingly. 'Ah, hallo, Charles, you've made good time. Rather a surprising development has occurred.'

'Unprecedented,' Mr Gaitskill said.

Something had clearly ruffled the little lawyer to the core. Behind him, Chief-Inspector Taverner grinned at me.

'If I may recapitulate?' my father said. 'Mr Gaitskill received a somewhat surprising communication this morning, Charles. It was from a Mr Agrodopolous, proprietor of the Delphos Restaurant. He is a very old man, a Greek by birth, and when he was a young man he was helped and befriended by Aristide

Leonides. He has always remained deeply grateful to his friend and benefactor and it seems that Aristide Leonides placed great reliance and trust in him.'

'I would never have believed Leonides was of such a suspicious and secretive nature,' said Mr Gaitskill. 'Of course, he was of advanced years – practically in his dotage, one might say.'

'Nationality tells,' said my father gently. 'You see, Gaitskill, when you are very old your mind dwells a good deal on the days of your youth and the friends of your youth.'

'But Leonides' affairs had been in my hands for well over forty years,' said Mr Gaitskill. 'Forty-three years and six months to be precise.'

Taverner grinned again.

'What happened?' I asked.

Mr Gaitskill opened his mouth, but my father fore-stalled him.

'Mr Agrodopolous stated in his communication that he was obeying certain instructions given him by his friend Aristide Leonides. Briefly, about a year ago he had been entrusted by Mr Leonides with a sealed envelope which Mr Agrodopolous was to forward to Mr Gaitskill immediately after Mr Leonides' death. In the event of Mr Agrodopolous dying first, his son, a godson of Mr Leonides, was to carry out the same instructions. Mr Agrodopolous apologizes for the delay, but explains that he has been ill with pneumonia and only learned of his old friend's death yesterday afternoon.'

'The whole business is most unprofessional,' said Mr Gaitskill.

'When Mr Gaitskill had opened the sealed envelope and made himself acquainted with its contents, he decided that it was his duty –'

'Under the circumstances,' said Mr Gaitskill.

'To let us see the enclosures. They consist of a will, duly signed and attested, and a covering letter.'

'So the will has turned up at last?' I said.

Mr Gaitskill turned a bright purple.

'It is not the same will,' he barked. 'This is not the document I drew up at Mr Leonides' request. This has been written out in his own hand, a most dangerous thing for any layman to do. It seems to have been Mr Leonides' intention to make me look a complete fool.'

Chief-Inspector Taverner endeavoured to inject a little balm into the prevailing bitterness.

'He was a very old gentleman, Mr Gaitskill,' he said. 'They're inclined to be cranky when they get old, you know – not barmy, of course, but just a little eccentric.'

Mr Gaitskill sniffed.

'Mr Gaitskill rang us up,' my father said, 'and apprised us of the main contents of the will and I asked him to come round and bring the two documents with him. I also rang you up, Charles.'

I did not quite see why I had been rung up. It seemed to me singularly unorthodox procedure on both my father's and Taverner's part. I should have learnt about the will in due course, and it was really not my business at all how old Leonides had left his money.

'Is it a different will?' I asked. 'I mean, does it dispose of his estate in a different way?'

'It does indeed,' said Mr Gaitskill.

My father was looking at me. Chief-Inspector Taverner was very carefully not looking at me. In some way, I felt vaguely uneasy . . .

Something was going on in both their minds – and it was a something to which I had no clue.

I looked inquiringly at Gaitskill.

'It's none of my business,' I said. 'But –'

He responded.

'Mr Leonides' testamentary dispositions are not, of course, a secret,' he said. 'I conceived it to be my duty to lay the facts before the police authorities first, and to be guided by them in my subsequent procedure. I understand,' he paused, 'that there is an – understanding, shall we say – between you and Miss Sophia Leonides?'

'I hope to marry her,' I said, 'but she will not consent to an engagement at the present time.'

'Very proper,' said Mr Gaitskill.

I disagreed with him. But this was no time for argument.

'By this will,' said Mr Gaitskill, 'dated November the 29th of last year, Mr Leonides, after a bequest to his wife of one hundred thousand pounds, leaves his entire estate, real and personal, to his granddaughter, Sophia Katherine Leonides absolutely.'

I gasped. Whatever I had expected, it was not this.

'He left the whole caboodle to Sophia,' I said. 'What an extraordinary thing. Any reason?'

'He set out his reasons very clearly in the covering letter,' said my father. He picked up a sheet of paper from the desk in front of him. 'You have no objection to Charles reading this, Mr Gaitskill?'

'I am in your hands,' said Mr Gaitskill coldly. 'The letter does at least offer an explanation – and possibly (though I am doubtful as to this) an excuse for Mr Leonides' extraordinary conduct.'

The Old Man handed me the letter. It was written in a small crabbed handwriting in very black ink. The handwriting showed character and individuality. It was not at all like the careful forming of the letters, more characteristic of a bygone period, when literacy was something painstakingly acquired and correspondingly valued.

Dear Gaitskill [it ran],

You will be astonished to get this, and probably offended. But I have my own reasons for behaving in what may seem to you an unnecessarily secretive manner. I have long been a believer in the individual. In a family (this I have observed in my boyhood and never forgotten) there is always one strong character and it usually falls to this one person to care for, and bear the burden of, the rest of the family. In my family I was that person. I came to London, established myself there, supported my mother and my aged grandparents in Smyrna, extricated one of my brothers from the grip of the law, secured the freedom of my sister from an unhappy marriage and so on. God has been pleased to grant me a long life, and I have been able to watch over and care for my own children and their children. Many have been taken from me by death; the rest, I am happy to say, are under my roof. When I die, the burden I have carried must descend on someone else. I have debated whether to divide my fortune as equally as possible amongst my dear ones – but to do so would not eventually result in a proper equality. Men are not born equal – to offset the natural inequality of Nature one must redress the balance. In other words, someone must be my successor, must take upon him or herself the burden of responsibility for the rest of the family. After close observation

I do not consider either of my sons fit for this responsibility. My dearly loved son Roger has no business sense, and though of a lovable nature is too impulsive to have good judgement. My son Philip is too unsure of himself to do anything but retreat from life. Eustace, my grandson, is very young and I do not think he has the qualities of sense and judgement necessary. He is indolent and very easily influenced by the ideas of anyone whom he meets. Only my granddaughter Sophia seems to me to have the positive qualities required. She has brains, judgement, courage, a fair and unbiased mind and, I think, generosity of spirit. To her I commit the family welfare – and the welfare of my kind sister-in-law Edith de Haviland, for whose life-long devotion to the family I am deeply grateful.

This explains the enclosed document. What will be harder to explain – or rather to explain to you, my old friend – is the deception that I have employed. I thought it wise not to raise speculation about the disposal of my money, and I have no intention of letting my family know that Sophia is to be my heir. Since my two sons have already had considerable fortunes settled upon them, I do not feel that my testamentary dispositions will place them in a humiliating position.

To stifle curiosity and surmise, I asked you to draw me up a will. This will I read aloud to my assembled family. I laid it on my desk, placed a sheet of blotting paper over it and asked for two servants to be summoned. When they came I slid the blotting paper up a little, exposing the bottom of a document, signed my name and caused them to sign theirs. I need hardly say that what I and they signed was the will which I now enclose and not the one drafted by you which I had read aloud.

I cannot hope that you will understand what prompted me to execute this trick. I will merely ask you to forgive me for keeping you in the dark. A very old man likes to keep his little secrets.

Thank you, my dear friend, for the assiduity with which you have always attended to my affairs. Give Sophia my dear love. Ask her to watch over the family well and shield them from harm.

Yours very sincerely,
Aristide Leonides.

I read this very remarkable document with intense interest.

'Extraordinary,' I said.

'Most extraordinary,' said Mr Gaitskill, rising. 'I repeat, I think my old friend Mr Leonides might have trusted *me*.'

'No, Gaitskill,' said my father. 'He was a natural twister. He liked, if I may put it so, doing things the crooked way.'

'That's right, sir,' said Chief-Inspector Taverner. 'He was a twister if there ever was one!'

He spoke with feeling.

Gaitskill stalked out unmollified. He had been wounded to the depths of his professional nature.

'It's hit him hard,' said Taverner. 'Very respectable firm, Gaitskill, Callum & Gaitskill. No hanky panky with them. When old Leonides put through a doubtful deal, he never put it through with Gaitskill, Callum & Gaitskill. He had half a dozen different firms of solicitors who acted for him. Oh, he was a twister!'

'And never more so than when making his will,' said my father.

'We were fools,' said Taverner. 'When you come to think of it, the only person who *could* have played tricks with that will was the old boy himself. It just never occurred to us that he could want to!'

I remembered Josephine's superior smile as she had said:

'Aren't the police *stupid*?'

But Josephine had not been present on the occasion of the will. And even if she had been listening outside the door (which I was fully prepared to believe!) she could hardly have guessed what her grandfather was doing. Why, then, the superior air? What did she know that made her say the police were stupid? Or was it, again, just showing off?

Struck by the silence in the room I looked up sharply – both my father and Taverner were watching me. I don't know what there was in their manner that compelled me to blurt out defiantly:

'Sophia knew nothing about this! Nothing at all.'

'No?' said my father.

I didn't quite know whether it was an agreement or a question.

'She'll be absolutely astounded!'

'Yes?'

'Astounded!'

There was a pause. Then, with what seemed sudden harshness, the telephone on my father's desk rang.

'Yes?' He lifted the receiver – listened and then said: 'Put her through.'

He looked at me.

'It's your young woman,' he said. 'She wants to speak to us. It's urgent.'

I took the receiver from him.

'Sophia?'

'Charles? Is that you? It's – Josephine!' Her voice broke slightly.

'What about Josephine?'

'She's been hit on the head. Concussion. She's – she's pretty bad . . . They say she may not recover . . .'

I turned to the other two.

'Josephine's been knocked out,' I said.

My father took the receiver from me. He said sharply as he did so:

'I told you to keep an eye on that child . . .'

CHAPTER 18

In next to no time Taverner and I were racing in a fast police car in the direction of Swinly Dean.

I remembered Josephine emerging, from among the cisterns, and her airy remark that it was 'about time for the second murder'. The poor child had had no idea that she herself was likely to be the victim of the 'second murder'.

I accepted fully the blame that my father had tacitly ascribed to me. Of course I ought to have kept an eye on Josephine. Though neither Taverner nor I had any real clue to the poisoner of old Leonides, it was highly possible that Josephine had. What I had taken for childish nonsense and 'showing off' might very well have been something quite different. Josephine, in her favourite sports of snooping and prying, might have become aware of some piece of information that she herself could not assess at its proper value.

I remembered the twig that had cracked in the garden.

I had had an inkling then that danger was about. I had acted upon it at the moment, and afterwards it had seemed to me that my suspicions had been melodramatic and unreal. On the contrary, I should have realized that this was murder, that whoever had committed murder had endangered their neck, and that consequently that same person would not hesitate to repeat the crime if by that way safety could be assured.

Perhaps Magda, by some obscure maternal instinct, had recognized that Josephine was in peril, and that may have been what occasioned her sudden feverish haste to get the child sent to Switzerland.

Sophia came out to meet us as we arrived. Josephine, she said, had been taken by ambulance to Market Basing General Hospital. Dr Gray would let them know as soon as possible the result of the X-ray.

'How did it happen?' asked Taverner.

Sophia led the way round to the back of the house and through a door in a small disused yard. In one corner a door stood ajar.

'It's a kind of wash-house,' Sophia explained. 'There's a cat hole cut in the bottom of the door, and Josephine used to stand on it and swing to and fro.'

I remembered swinging on doors in my own youth.

The wash-house was small and rather dark. There were wooden boxes in it, some old hose pipe, a few derelict garden implements, and some broken furniture. Just inside the door was a marble lion door-stop.

'It's the door-stopper from the front door,' Sophia explained. 'It must have been balanced on top of the door.'

Taverner reached up a hand to the top of the door. It was a low door, the top of it only about a foot above his head.

'A booby trap,' he said.

He swung the door experimentally to and fro. Then he stooped to the block of marble but he did not touch it.

'Has anyone handled this?'

'No,' said Sophia. 'I wouldn't let anyone touch it.'

'Quite right. Who found her?'

'I did. She didn't come in for her dinner at one o'clock. Nannie was calling her. She'd passed through the kitchen and out into the stable yard about a quarter of an hour before. Nannie said,

"She'll be bouncing her ball or swinging on that door again." I said I'd fetch her in.'

Sophia paused.

'She had a habit of playing in that way, you said? Who knew about that?'

Sophia shrugged her shoulders.

'Pretty well everybody in the house, I should think.'

'Who else used the wash-house? Gardeners?'

Sophia shook her head.

'Hardly anyone ever goes into it.'

'And this little yard isn't overlooked from the house?' Taverner summed it up. 'Anyone could have slipped out from the house or round the front and fixed up that trap ready. But it would be chancy . . .'

He broke off, looking at the door, and swinging it gently to and fro.

'Nothing certain about it. Hit or miss. And likelier miss than hit. But she was unlucky. With her it was hit.'

Sophia shivered.

He peered at the floor. There were various dents on it.

'Looks as though someone experimented first . . . to see just how it would fall . . . The sound wouldn't carry to the house.'

'No, we didn't hear anything. We'd no idea anything was wrong until I came out and found her lying face down – all sprawled out.' Sophia's voice broke a little. 'There was blood on her hair.'

'That her scarf?' Taverner pointed to a checked woollen muffler lying on the floor.

'Yes.'

Using the scarf he picked up the block of marble carefully.

'There may be fingerprints,' he said, but he spoke without much hope. 'But I rather think whoever did it was – careful.' He said to me: 'What are you looking at?'

I was looking at a broken-backed wooden kitchen chair which was among the derelicts. On the seat of it were a few fragments of earth.

'Curious,' said Taverner. 'Someone stood on that chair with muddy feet. Now why was that?'

He shook his head.

'What time was it when you found her, Miss Leonides?'

'It must have been five minutes past one.'

'And your Nannie saw her going out about twenty minutes earlier. Who was the last person before that known to have been in the wash-house?'

'I've no idea. Probably Josephine herself. Josephine was swinging on the door this morning after breakfast, I know.'

Taverner nodded.

'So between then and a quarter to one *someone set the trap.* You say that bit of marble is the door-stop you use for the front door? Any idea when that was missing?'

Sophia shook her head.

'The door hasn't been propped open all to-day. It's been too cold.'

'Any idea where everyone was all the morning?'

'I went out for a walk. Eustace and Josephine did lessons until half-past twelve – with a break at half-past ten. Father, I think, has been in the library all the morning.'

'Your mother?'

'She was just coming out of her bedroom when I came in from my walk – that was about a quarter-past twelve. She doesn't get up very early.'

We re-entered the house. I followed Sophia to the library. Philip, looking white and haggard, sat in his usual chair. Magda crouched against his knees, crying quietly. Sophia asked:

'Have they telephoned yet from the hospital?'

Philip shook his head.

Magda sobbed.

'Why wouldn't they let me go with her? My baby – my funny ugly baby. And I used to call her a changeling and make her so angry. How could I be so cruel? And now she'll die. I know she'll die.'

'Hush, my dear,' said Philip. 'Hush.'

I felt that I had no place in this family scene of anxiety and grief. I withdrew quietly and went to find Nannie. She was sitting in the kitchen crying quietly.

'It's a judgement on me, Mr Charles, for the hard things I've been thinking. A judgement, that's what it is.'

I did not try and fathom her meaning.

'There's wickedness in this house. That's what there is. I didn't wish to see it or believe it. But seeing's believing. Somebody killed the master and the same somebody must have tried to kill Josephine.'

'Why should they try and kill Josephine?'

Nannie removed a corner of her handkerchief from her eye and gave me a shrewd glance.

'You know well enough what she was like, Mr Charles. She liked to know things. She was always like that, even as a tiny thing. Used to hide under the dinner table and listen to the maids talking and then she'd hold it over them. Made her feel important. You see, she was passed over, as it were, by the mistress. She wasn't a handsome child, like the other two. She was always a plain little thing. A changeling, the mistress used to call her. I blame the mistress for that, for it's my belief it turned the child sour. But in a funny sort of way she got her own back by finding out things about people and letting them know she knew them. But it isn't safe to do that when there's a poisoner about!'

No, it hadn't been safe. And that brought something else to my mind. I asked Nannie: 'Do you know where she kept a little black book – a note-book of some kind where she used to write down things?'

'I know what you mean, Mr Charles. Very sly about it, she was. I've seen her sucking her pencil and writing in the book and sucking her pencil again. And "don't do that", I'd say, "you'll get lead poisoning" and "oh no, I shan't,", she said, "because it isn't really lead in a pencil. It's carbon", though I don't see how *that* could be so for if you call a thing a lead pencil it stands to reason that that's because there's lead in it.'

'You'd think so,' I agreed. 'But as a matter of fact she was right.' (Josephine was always right!) 'What about this note-book? Do you know where she kept it?'

'I've no idea at all, sir. It was one of the things she was sly about.'

'She hadn't got it with her when she was found?'

'Oh no, Mr Charles, there was no note-book.'

Had someone taken the note-book? Or had she hidden it in her own room? The idea came to me to look and see. I was not sure which Josephine's room was, but as I stood hesitating in the passage Taverner's voice called me:

'Come in here,' he said. 'I'm in the kid's room. Did you ever see such a sight?'

I stepped over the threshold and stopped dead.

The small room looked as though it had been visited by a tornado. The drawers of the chest of drawers were pulled out and their contents scattered on the floor. The mattress and bedding had been pulled from the small bed. The rugs were tossed into heaps. The chairs had been turned upside down, the pictures taken down from the wall, the photographs wrenched out of their frames.

'Good Lord,' I exclaimed. 'What was the big idea?'

'What do you think?'

'Someone was looking for something.'

'Exactly.'

I looked round and whistled.

'But who on earth – surely nobody could come in here and do all this and not be heard – or seen?'

'Why not? Mrs Leonides spends the morning in her bedroom doing her nails and ringing up her friends on the telephone and playing with her clothes. Philip sits in the library browsing over books. The nurse woman is in the kitchen peeling potatoes and stringing beans. In a family that knows each other's habits it would be easy enough. And I'll tell you this. Anyone in the house could have done our little job – could have set the trap for the child and wrecked her room. But it was someone in a hurry, someone who hadn't the time to search quietly.'

'Anyone in the house, you say?'

'Yes, I've checked up. Everyone has some time or other unaccounted for. Philip, Magda, the nurse, your girl. The same upstairs. Brenda spent most of the morning alone. Laurence and Eustace had a half hour break – from ten-thirty to eleven – you were with them part of that time – but not all of it. Miss de Haviland was in the garden alone. Roger was in his study.'

'Only Clemency was in London at her job.'

'No, even she isn't out of it. She stayed at home today with a headache – she was alone in her room having that headache. Any of them – any blinking one of them! And I don't know which! I've no idea. If I knew what they were looking for in here –'

His eyes went round the wrecked room . . .

'And if I knew whether they'd found it . . .'

Something stirred in my brain – a memory . . .

Taverner clinched it by asking me:

'What was the kid doing when you last saw her?'

'Wait,' I said.

I dashed out of the room and up the stairs. I passed through the left-hand door and went up to the top floor. I pushed open the door of the cistern room, mounted the two steps and bending my head, since the ceiling was low and sloping, I looked round me.

Josephine had said when I asked her what she was doing there that she was 'detecting'.

I didn't see what there could be to detect in a cobwebby attic full of water tanks. But such an attic would make a good hiding-place. I considered it probable that Josephine had been hiding something there, something that she knew quite well she had no business to have. If so, it oughtn't to take long to find it.

It took me just three minutes. Tucked away behind the largest tank, from the interior of which a sibilant hissing added an eerie note to the atmosphere, I found a packet of letters wrapped in a torn piece of brown paper.

I read the first letter.

Oh Laurence – my darling, my own dear love . . . It was wonderful last night when you quoted that verse of poetry. I knew it was meant for me, though you didn't look at me. Aristide said, 'You read verse well.' He didn't guess what we were both feeling. My darling, I feel convinced that soon everything will come right. We shall be glad that he never knew, that he died happy. He's been good to me. I don't want him to suffer. But I don't really think that it can be any pleasure to live after you're eighty. I shouldn't want to! Soon we shall be together for always. How wonderful it will be when I can say to you: 'My dear dear husband . . .' Dearest, we were made for each other. I love you, love you, love you – I can see no end to our love, I –

There was a good deal more, but I had no wish to go on.

Grimly I went downstairs and thrust my parcel into Taverner's hands.

'It's possible,' I said, 'that that's what our unknown friend was looking for.'

Taverner read a few passages, whistled and shuffled through the various letters.

Then he looked at me with the expression of a cat who has been fed with the best cream.

'Well,' he said softly. 'This pretty well cooks Mrs Brenda Leonides' goose. *And* Mr Laurence Brown's. So it *was* them, all the time . . .'

CHAPTER 19

It seems odd to me, looking back, how suddenly and completely my pity and sympathy for Brenda Leonides vanished with the discovery of her letters, the letters she had written to Laurence Brown. Was my vanity unable to stand up to the revelation that she loved Laurence Brown with a doting and sugary infatuation and had deliberately lied to me? I don't know. I'm not a psychologist. I prefer to believe that it was the thought of the child Josephine, struck down in ruthless self-preservation, that dried up the springs of my sympathy.

'Brown fixed that booby trap, if you ask me,' said Taverner, 'and it explains what puzzled me about it.'

'What did puzzle you?'

'Well, it was such a sappy thing to do. Look here, say the kid's got hold of these letters – letters that are absolutely damning! The first thing to do is to try and get them back (after all, if the kid talks about them, but has got nothing to show, it can be put down as mere romancing), but you can't get them back because you can't find them. Then the only thing to do is to put the kid out of action for good. You've done one murder and you're not squeamish about doing another. You know she's fond of swinging on a door in a disused yard. The ideal thing to do is wait behind the door and lay her out as she comes through with a poker, or an iron bar, or a nice bit of hose-pipe. They're all there ready to hand. Why fiddle about with a marble lion perched on top of a door which is as likely as not to miss her altogether and which even if it *does* fall on her may not do the job properly (which actually is how it turns out). I ask you – *why*?'

'Well,' I said, 'what's the answer?'

'The only idea I got to begin with was that it was intended to tie in with someone's alibi. Somebody would have a nice fat alibi for the time when Josephine was being slugged. But that doesn't wash because, to begin with, nobody seems to have any kind of alibi, and second, someone's bound to look for the child at lunch time, and they'll find the booby trap and the marble block, the whole *modus operandi* will be quite plain to see. Of course, *if* the murderer had removed the block before the child was found, then we might have been puzzled. But as it is the whole thing just doesn't make sense.'

He stretched out his hands.

'And what's your present explanation?'

'The personal element. Personal idiosyncrasy. Laurence Brown's idiosyncrasy. *He doesn't like violence – he can't force himself to do physical violence. He* literally *couldn't* have stood behind the door and socked the kid on the head. He *could* rig up a booby trap and go away and not see it happen.'

'Yes, I see,' I said slowly. 'It's the eserine in the insulin bottle all over again?'

'Exactly.'

'Do you think he did that without Brenda's knowing?'

'It would explain why she didn't throw away the insulin bottle. Of course, they may have fixed it up between them – or she may have thought up the poison trick all by herself – a nice easy death for her tired old husband and all for the best in the best possible worlds! But I bet she didn't fix the booby trap. Women never have any faith in mechanical things working properly. And they are right. I think myself the eserine was her idea, but that she made her besotted slave do the switch. She's the kind that usually manages to avoid doing anything equivocal themselves. Then they keep a nice happy conscience.'

He paused, then went on:

'With these letters I think the DPP will say we have a case. They'll take a bit of explaining away! Then, if the kid gets through all right everything in the garden will be lovely.' He gave me a sideways glance. 'How does it feel to be engaged to about a million pounds sterling?'

I winced. In the excitement of the last few hours, I had forgotten the developments about the will.

'Sophia doesn't know yet,' I said. 'Do you want me to tell her?'

'I understand Gaitskill is going to break the sad (or glad) news after the inquest tomorrow.' Taverner paused and looked at me thoughtfully.

'I wonder,' he said, 'what the reactions will be from the family?'

CHAPTER 20

The inquest went off much as I had prophesied. It was adjourned at the request of the police.

We were in good spirits, for news had come through the night before from the hospital that Josephine's injuries were much less serious than had been feared and that her recovery would be rapid. For the moment, Dr Gray said, she was to be allowed no visitors – not even her mother.

'Particularly not her mother,' Sophia murmured to me. 'I made that quite clear to Dr Gray. Anyway, he knows mother.'

I must have looked rather doubtful, for Sophia said sharply: 'Why the disapproving look?'

'Well – surely a mother –'

'I'm glad you've got a few nice old-fashioned ideas, Charles. But you don't quite know what my mother is capable of yet. The darling can't help it, but there would simply have to be a grand dramatic scene. And dramatic scenes aren't the best things for anyone recovering from head injuries.'

'You do think of everything, don't you, my sweet.'

'Well, somebody's got to do the thinking now that grandfather's gone.'

I looked at her speculatively. I saw that old Leonides' acumen had not deserted him. The mantle of his responsibilities was already on Sophia's shoulders.

After the inquest, Gaitskill accompanied us back to Three Gables. He cleared his throat and said pontifically:

'There is an announcement it is my duty to make to you all.'

For this purpose the family assembled in Magda's drawing-room. I had on this occasion the rather pleasurable sensations of the man behind the scenes. I knew in advance what Gaitskill had to say.

I prepared myself to observe the reactions of everyone.

Gaitskill was brief and dry. Any signs of personal feeling and annoyance were well held in check. He read first Aristide Leonides' letter and then the will itself.

It was very interesting to watch. I only wished my eyes could be everywhere at once.

I did not pay much attention to Brenda and Laurence. The provision for Brenda in this will was the same. I watched primarily Roger and Philip, and after them Magda and Clemency.

My first impression was that they all behaved very well.

Philip's lips were pressed closely together, his handsome head was thrown back against the tall chair in which he was sitting. He did not speak.

Magda, on the contrary, burst into speech as soon as Mr Gaitskill finished, her rich voice surging over his thin tones like an incoming tide drowning a rivulet.

'Darling Sophia – how extraordinary – how *romantic*. Fancy old Sweetie Pie being so cunning and deceitful – just like a dear old baby. Didn't he trust us? Did he think we'd be cross? He never seemed to be fonder of Sophia than the rest of us. But really, it's most dramatic.'

Suddenly Magda jumped lightly to her feet, danced over to Sophia and swept her a very grand court curtsey.

'Madame Sophia, your penniless and broken-down-old mother begs you for alms.' Her voice took on a Cockney whine. 'Spare us a copper, old dear. Your Ma wants to go to the pictures.'

Her hand, crooked into a claw, twitched urgently at Sophia.

Philip, without moving, said through stiff lips:

'Please, Magda, there's no call for any unnecessary clowning.'

'Oh, but Roger,' cried Magda, suddenly turning to Roger. 'Poor darling Roger. Sweetie was going to come to the rescue and then, before he could do it, he died. And now Roger doesn't get *anything*. Sophia,' she turned imperiously, 'you simply must do something about Roger.'

'No,' said Clemency. She had moved forward a step. Her face was defiant. 'Nothing. Nothing at all.'

Roger came shambling over to Sophia like a large amiable bear.

He took her hands affectionately.

'I don't want a penny, my dear girl. As soon as this business is cleared up – or has died down, which is more what it looks like – then Clemency and I are off to the West Indies and the simple life. If I'm ever in extremis I'll apply to the head of the family' – he grinned at her engagingly – 'but until then I don't want a penny. I'm a very simple person really, my dear – you ask Clemency if I'm not.'

An unexpected voice broke in. It was Edith de Haviland's.

'That's all very well,' she said. 'But you've got to pay some attention to the look of the thing. If you go bankrupt, Roger, and then slink off to the ends of the earth without Sophia's holding out a helping hand, there will be a good deal of ill-natured talk that will not be pleasant for Sophia.'

'What does public opinion matter?' asked Clemency scornfully.

'We know it doesn't to you, Clemency,' said Edith de Haviland sharply, 'but Sophia lives in *this* world. She's a girl with good brains and a good heart, and I've no doubt that Aristide was quite right in his selection of her to hold the family fortunes – though to pass over your two sons in their lifetime seems odd to our English ideas – but I think it would be very unfortunate if it got about that she behaved greedily over this – and had let Roger crash without trying to help him.'

Roger went over to his aunt. He put his arms round her and hugged her.

'Aunt Edith,' he said. 'You are a darling – and a stubborn fighter, but you don't begin to understand. Clemency and I know what we want – and what we don't want!'

Clemency, a sudden spot of colour showing in each thin cheek, stood defiantly facing them.

'None of you,' she said, 'understand Roger. You never have! I don't suppose you ever will! Come on, Roger.'

They left the room as Mr Gaitskill began clearing his throat and arranging his papers. His countenance was one of deep disapprobation. He had disliked the foregoing scenes very much. That was clear.

My eyes came at last to Sophia herself. She stood straight and handsome by the fireplace, her chin up, her eyes steady. She had just been left an immense fortune, but my principal thought was how alone she had suddenly become. Between her and her family a barrier had been erected. Henceforth she was divided from them, and I fancied that she already knew and faced that fact. Old Leonides had laid a burden upon her shoulders – he had been aware of that and she knew it herself. He had believed that her shoulders were strong enough to bear it, but just at this moment I felt unutterably sorry for her.

So far she had not spoken – indeed she had been given no chance, but very soon now speech would be forced from her. Already, beneath the affection of her family, I could sense latent hostility. Even in Magda's graceful play-acting there had been, I fancied, a subtle malice. And there were other darker undercurrents that had not yet come to the surface.

Mr Gaitskill's throat clearings gave way to precise and measured speech.

'Allow me to congratulate you, Sophia,' he said. 'You are a very wealthy woman. I should not advise any – er – precipitate action. I can advance you what ready money is needed for current expenses. If you wish to discuss future arrangements I shall be happy to give you the best advice in my power. Make an appointment with me at Lincoln's Inn when you have had plenty of time to think things over.'

'Roger,' began Edith de Haviland obstinately.

Mr Gaitskill snapped in quickly.

'Roger,' he said, 'must fend for himself. He's a grown man – er, fifty-four, I believe. And Aristide Leonides was quite right, you know. He isn't a business man. Never will be.' He looked at Sophia. 'If you put Associated Catering on its legs again, don't be under any illusions that Roger can run it successfully.'

'I shouldn't dream of putting Associated Catering on its legs again,' said Sophia.

It was the first time she had spoken. Her voice was crisp and businesslike.

'It would be an idiotic thing to do,' she added.

Gaitskill shot a glance at her from under his brows, and smiled to himself. Then he wished everyone goodbye and went out.

There were a few moments of silence, a realization that the family circle was alone with itself.

Then Philip got up stiffly.

'I must get back to the library,' he said. 'I have lost a lot of time.'

'Father –' Sophia spoke uncertainly, almost pleadingly.

I felt her quiver and draw back as Philip turned cold hostile eyes on her.

'You must forgive me not congratulating you,' he said. 'But this has been rather a shock to me. I would not have believed that my father would have so humiliated me – that he would have disregarded my lifetime's devotion – yes – devotion.'

For the first time, the natural man broke through the crust of icy restraint.

'My God,' he cried. 'How could he do this to me? He was always unfair to me – always.'

'Oh no, Philip, no, you mustn't think that,' cried Edith de Haviland. 'Don't regard this as another slight. It isn't. When people get old, they turn naturally to a younger generation . . . I assure you it's only that . . . and besides, Aristide had a very keen business sense. I've often heard him say that two lots of death duties –'

'He never cared for me,' said Philip. His voice was low and hoarse. 'It was always Roger – Roger. Well, at least' – an extraordinary expression of spite suddenly marred his handsome features – 'father realized that Roger was a fool and a failure. He cut Roger out, too.'

'What about me?' said Eustace.

I had hardly noticed Eustace until now, but I perceived that he was trembling with some violent emotion. His face was crimson, there were, I thought, tears in his eyes. His voice shook as it rose hysterically.

'It's a shame!' said Eustace. 'It's a damned shame! How dare grandfather do this to me? How dare he? I was his only grandson.

How dare he pass me over for Sophia? It's not fair. I hate him. I hate him. I'll never forgive him as long as I live. Beastly tyrannical old man. I wanted him to die. I wanted to get out of this house. I wanted to be my own master. And now I've got to be bullied and messed around by Sophia, and be made to look a fool. I wish I was dead . . .'

His voice broke and he rushed out of the room.

Edith de Haviland gave a sharp click of her tongue.

'No self-control,' she murmured.

'I know just how he feels,' cried Magda.

'I'm sure you do,' said Edith with acidity in her tone.

'The poor sweet! I must go after him.'

'Now, Magda –' Edith hurried after her.

Their voices died away. Sophia remained looking at Philip. There was, I think, a certain pleading in her glance. If so, it got no response. He looked at her coldly, quite in control of himself once more.

'You played your cards very well, Sophia,' he said and went out of the room.

'That was a cruel thing to say,' I cried. 'Sophia –'

She stretched out her hands to me. I took her in my arms.

'This is too much for you, my sweet.'

'I know just how they feel,' said Sophia.

'That old devil, your grandfather, shouldn't have let you in for this.'

She straightened her shoulders.

'He believed I could take it. And so I can. I wish – I wish Eustace didn't mind so much.'

'He'll get over it.'

'Will he? I wonder. He's the kind that broods terribly. And I hate father being hurt.'

'Your mother's all right.'

'She minds a bit. It goes against the grain to have to come and ask your daughter for money to put on plays. She'll be after me to put on the Edith Thompson one before you can turn round.'

'And what will you say? If it keeps her happy . . .'

Sophia pulled herself right out of my arms, her head went back.

'I shall say *No*! It's a rotten play and mother couldn't play the part. It would be throwing the money away.'

I laughed softly. I couldn't help it.

'What is it?' Sophia demanded suspiciously.

'I'm beginning to understand why your grandfather left you his money. You're a chip off the old block, Sophia.'

CHAPTER 21

My one feeling of regret at this time was that Josephine was out of it all. She would have enjoyed it all so much.

Her recovery was rapid and she was expected to be back any day now, but nevertheless she missed another event of importance.

I was in the rock garden one morning with Sophia and Brenda when a car drew up to the front door. Taverner and Sergeant Lamb got out of it. They went up the steps and into the house.

Brenda stood still, staring at the car.

'It's those men,' she said. 'They've come back, and I thought they'd given up – I thought it was all over.'

I saw her shiver.

She had joined us about ten minutes before. Wrapped in her chinchilla coat, she had said: 'If I don't get some air and exercise, I shall go mad. If I go outside the gate there's always a reporter waiting to pounce on me. It's like being besieged. Will it go on for ever?'

Sophia said that she supposed the reporters would soon get tired of it.

'You can go out in the car,' she added.

'I tell you I want to get some exercise.'

Then she said abruptly:

'You're giving Laurence the sack, Sophia. Why?'

Sophia answered quietly:

'We're making other arrangements for Eustace. And Josephine is going to Switzerland.'

'Well, you've upset Laurence very much. He feels you don't trust him.'

Sophia did not reply and it was at that moment that Taverner's car had arrived.

Standing there, shivering in the moist autumn air, Brenda muttered: 'What do they want? Why have they come?'

I thought I knew why they had come. I said nothing to Sophia of the letters I had found by the cistern, but I knew that they had gone to the Director of Public Prosecutions.

Taverner came out of the house again. He walked across the drive and the lawn towards us. Brenda shivered more violently.

'What does he want?' she repeated nervously. 'What does he want?'

Then Taverner was with us. He spoke curtly in his official voice, using the official phrases.

'I have a warrant here for your arrest – you are charged with administering eserine to Aristide Leonides on September 19th last. I must warn you that anything you say may be used in evidence at your trial.'

And then Brenda went to pieces. She screamed. She clung to me. She cried out, 'No, no, no, it isn't true! Charles, tell them it isn't true! I didn't do it. I didn't know anything about it. It's all a plot. Don't let them take me away. It isn't true, I tell you . . . It *isn't true* . . . I haven't done anything . . .'

It was horrible – unbelievably horrible. I tried to soothe her, I unfastened her fingers from my arm. I told her that I would arrange for a lawyer for her – that she was to keep calm – that a lawyer would arrange everything –

Taverner took her gently under the elbow.

'Come along, Mrs Leonides,' he said. 'You don't want a hat, do you? No? Then we'll go off right away.'

She pulled back, staring at him with enormous cat's eyes.

'Laurence,' she said. 'What have you done to Laurence?'

'Mr Laurence Brown is also under arrest,' said Taverner.

She wilted then. Her body seemed to collapse and shrink. The tears poured down her face. She went away quietly with Taverner across the lawn to the car. I saw Laurence Brown and Sergeant Lamb come out of the house. They all got into the car. The car drove away.

I drew a deep breath and turned to Sophia. She was very pale and there was a look of distress on her face.

'It's horrible, Charles,' she said. 'It's quite horrible.'

'I know.'

'You must get her a really first-class solicitor – the best there is. She – she must have all the help possible.'

'One doesn't realize,' I said, 'what these things are like. I've never seen anyone arrested before.'

'I know. One has no idea.'

We were both silent. I was thinking of the desperate terror on Brenda's face. It had seemed familiar to me and suddenly I realized why. It was the same expression that I had seen on Magda Leonides' face the first day I had come to the Crooked House when she had been talking about the Edith Thompson play.

'And then,' she had said, *'sheer terror,* don't you think so?'

Sheer terror – that was what had been on Brenda's face. Brenda was not a fighter. I wondered that she had ever had the nerve to do murder. But possibly she had not. Possibly it had been Laurence Brown, with his persecution mania, his unstable personality, who had put the contents of one little bottle into another little bottle – a simple easy act – to free the woman he loved.

'So it's over,' said Sophia.

She sighed deeply, then asked:

'But why arrest them now? I thought there wasn't enough evidence.'

'A certain amount of evidence has come to light. Letters.'

'You mean love letters between them?'

'Yes.'

'What fools people are to keep these things!'

Yes, indeed. Fools. The kind of folly which never seemed to profit by the experience of others. You couldn't open a daily newspaper without coming across some instance of that folly – the passion to keep the written word, the written assurance of love.

'It's quite beastly, Sophia,' I said. 'But it's no good minding about it. After all, it's what we've been hoping all along, isn't it? It's what you said that first night at Mario's. You said it would be all right if the right person had killed your grandfather. Brenda was the right person, wasn't she? Brenda or Laurence?'

'Don't, Charles, you make me feel awful.'

'But we must be sensible. We can marry now, Sophia. You can't hold me off any longer. The Leonides family are out of it.'

She stared at me. I had never realized before the vivid blue of her eyes.

'Yes,' she said. 'I suppose we're out of it now. We *are* out of it, aren't we. You're sure?'

'My dear girl, none of you ever really had a shadow of motive.'

Her face went suddenly white.

'Except me, Charles. *I* had a motive.'

'Yes, of course –' I was taken aback. 'But not really. You didn't know, you see, about the will.'

'But I did, Charles,' she whispered.

'What?' I stared at her. I felt suddenly cold.

'I knew all the time that grandfather had left his money to me.'

'But how?'

'He told me. About a fortnight before he was killed. He said to me quite suddenly: "I've left all my money to you, Sophia. You must look after the family when I've gone."'

I stared.

'You never told me.'

'No. You see, when they all explained about the will and his signing it, I thought perhaps he had made a mistake – that he was just imagining that he had left it to me. Or that if he had made a will leaving it to me, then it had got lost and would never turn up. I didn't want it to turn up – I was afraid.'

'Afraid? Why?'

'I suppose – because of murder.'

I remembered the look of terror on Brenda's face – the wild unreasoning panic. I remembered the sheer panic that Magda had conjured up at will when she considered playing the part of a murderess. There would be no panic in Sophia's mind, but she was a realist, and she could see clearly enough that Leonides' will made her a suspect. I understood better now (or thought I did) her refusal to become engaged to me and her insistence that I should find out the truth. Nothing but the truth, she had said, was any good to her. I remembered the passion, the earnestness with which she had said it.

We had turned to walk towards the house and suddenly, at a certain spot, I remembered something else she had said.

She had said that she supposed she could murder some-one, but if so, she had added, it must be for something really worth while.

CHAPTER 22

Round a turn of the rock garden Roger and Clemency came walk-ing briskly towards us. Roger's flapping tweeds suited him better than his City clothes. He looked eager and excited. Clemency was frowning.

'Hallo, you two,' said Roger. 'At last! I thought they were never going to arrest that foul woman. What they've been waiting for, I don't know. Well, they've pinched her now, and her miserable boyfriend – and I hope they hang them both.'

Clemency's frown increased. She said:

'Don't be so uncivilized, Roger.'

'Uncivilized? Bosh! Deliberate cold-blooded poisoning of a helpless trusting old man – and when I'm glad the murderers are caught and will pay the penalty you say I'm uncivilized! I tell you I'd willingly strangle that woman myself.'

He added:

'She was with you, wasn't she, when the police came for her? How did she take it?'

'It was horrible,' said Sophia in a low voice. 'She was scared out of her wits.'

'Serve her right.'

'Don't be vindictive,' said Clemency.

'Oh, I know, dearest, but you can't understand. It wasn't your father. I *loved* my father. Don't you understand? I *loved* him!'

'I should understand by now,' said Clemency.

Roger said to her, half-jokingly:

'You've no imagination, Clemency. Suppose it had been I who had been poisoned –?'

I saw the quick droop of her lids, her half-clenched hands. She said sharply: 'Don't say things like that even in fun.'

'Never mind, darling, we'll soon be away from all this.'

We moved towards the house. Roger and Sophia walked ahead and Clemency and I brought up the rear. She said:

'I suppose now – they'll let us go?'

'Are you so anxious to get off?' I asked.

'It's wearing me out.'

I looked at her in surprise. She met my glance with a faint desperate smile and a nod of the head.

'Haven't you seen, Charles, that I'm fighting all the time? Fighting for my happiness. For Roger's. I've been so afraid the family would persuade him to stop in England. That we'd go on tangled up in the midst of them, stifled with family ties. I was afraid Sophia would offer him an income and that he'd stay in England because it would mean greater comfort and amenities for me. The trouble with Roger is that he will *not* listen. He gets ideas in his head – and they're never the right ideas. He doesn't know *anything*. And he's enough of a Leonides to think that happiness for a woman is bound up with comfort and money. But I will fight for my happiness – I will. I will get Roger away and give him the life that suits him where he won't feel a failure. I want him to myself – away from them all – right away –'

She had spoken in a low hurried voice with a kind of desperation that startled me. I had not realized how much on edge she was. I had not realized, either, quite how desperate and possessive was her feeling for Roger.

It brought back to my mind that odd quotation of Edith de Haviland's. She had quoted the line 'this side idolatry' with a peculiar intonation. I wondered if she had been thinking of Clemency.

Roger, I thought, had loved his father better than he would ever love anyone else, better even than his wife, devoted though he was to her. I realized for the first time how urgent was Clemency's desire to get her husband to herself. Love for Roger, I saw, made up her entire existence. He was her child, as well as her husband and her lover.

A car drove up to the front door.

'Hallo,' I said. 'Here's Josephine back.'

Josephine and Magda got out of the car. Josephine had a bandage round her head but otherwise looked remarkably well.

She said at once:

'I want to see my goldfish,' and started towards us and the pond.

'Darling,' cried Magda, 'you'd better come in first and lie down a little, and perhaps have a little nourishing soup.'

'Don't fuss, Mother,' said Josephine. 'I'm quite all right, and I hate nourishing soup.'

Magda looked irresolute. I knew that Josephine had really been fit to depart from the hospital for some days, and that it was only a hint from Taverner that had kept her there. He was taking no chances on Josephine's safety until his suspects were safe under lock and key.

I said to Magda:

'I dare say fresh air will do her good. I'll go and keep an eye on her.'

I caught Josephine up before she got to the pond.

'All sorts of things have been happening while you've been away,' I said.

Josephine did not reply. She peered with her short-sighted eyes into the pond.

'I don't see Ferdinand,' she said.

'Which is Ferdinand?'

'The one with four tails.'

'That kind is rather amusing. I like that bright gold one.'

'It's quite a common one.'

'I don't much care for that moth-eaten white one.'

Josephine cast me a scornful glance.

'That's a shebunkin. They cost a lot – far more than goldfish.'

'Don't you want to hear what's been happening, Josephine?'

'I expect I know about it.'

'Did you know that another will has been found and that your grandfather left all his money to Sophia?'

Josephine nodded in a bored kind of way.

'Mother told me. Anyway, I knew it already.'

'Do you mean you heard it in hospital?'

'No, I mean I knew that grandfather had left his money to Sophia. I heard him tell her so.'

'Were you listening again?'

'Yes. I like listening.'

'It's a disgraceful thing to do, and remember this, listeners hear no good of themselves.'

Josephine gave me a peculiar glance.

'I heard what he said about me to her, if that's what you mean.'

She added:

'Nannie gets wild if she catches me listening at doors. She says it's not the sort of thing a little lady does.'

'She's quite right.'

'Pooh,' said Josephine. 'Nobody's a lady nowadays. They said so on the Brains Trust. They said it was ob-so-lete.' She pronounced the word carefully.

I changed the subject.

'You've got home a bit late for the big event,' I said. 'Chief-Inspector Taverner has arrested Brenda and Laurence.'

I expected that Josephine, in her character of young detective, would be thrilled by this information, but she merely repeated in her maddening bored fashion:

'Yes, I know.'

'You can't know. It's only just happened.'

'The car passed us on the road. Inspector Taverner and the detective with the suede shoes were inside with Brenda and Laurence, so of course I knew they must have been arrested. I hope he gave them the proper caution. You have to, you know.'

I assured her that Taverner had acted strictly according to etiquette.

'I had to tell him about the letters,' I said apologetically. 'I found them behind the cistern. I'd have let you tell him only you were knocked out.'

Josephine's hand went gingerly to her head.

'I ought to have been killed,' she said with complacency. 'I told you it was about time for the second murder. The cistern was a rotten place to hide those letters. I guessed at once when I saw Laurence coming out of there one day. I mean he's not a useful kind of man who does things with ball taps, or pipes or fuses, so I knew he must have been hiding something.'

'But I thought –' I broke off as Edith de Haviland's voice called authoritatively:

'Josephine, Josephine, come here at once.'

Josephine sighed.

'More fuss,' she said. 'But I'd better go. You have to, if it's Aunt Edith.'

She ran across the lawn. I followed more slowly.

After a brief interchange of words Josephine went into the house. I joined Edith de Haviland on the terrace.

This morning she looked fully her age. I was startled by the lines of weariness and suffering on her face. She looked exhausted and defeated. She saw the concern in my face and tried to smile.

'That child seems none the worse for her adventure,' she said. 'We must look after her better in future. Still – I suppose now it won't be necessary?'

She sighed and said:

'I'm glad it's over. But what an exhibition! If you *are* arrested for murder, you might at least have some dignity. I've no patience with people like Brenda who go to pieces and squeal. No guts, these people. Laurence Brown looked like a cornered rabbit.'

An obscure instinct of pity rose in me.

'Poor devils,' I said.

'Yes – poor devils. She'll have the sense to look after herself, I suppose? I mean the right lawyers – all that sort of thing.'

It was queer, I thought, the dislike they all had for Brenda, and their scrupulous care for her to have all the advantages for defence.

Edith de Haviland went on:

'How long will it be? How long will the whole thing take?'

I said I didn't know exactly. They would be charged at the police court and presumably sent for trial. Three or four months, I estimated – and if convicted, there would be the appeal.

'Do you think they will be convicted?' she asked.

'I don't know. I don't know exactly how much evidence the police have. There are letters.'

'Love letters – They *were* lovers then?'

'They were in love with each other.'

Her face grew grimmer.

'I'm not happy about this, Charles. I don't like Brenda. In the past, I've disliked her very much. I've said sharp things about her. But now – I do feel that I want her to have every chance – every possible chance. Aristide would have wished that. I feel it's up to me to see that – that Brenda gets a square deal.'

'And Laurence?'

'Oh, Laurence!' she shrugged her shoulders impatiently. 'Men must look after themselves. But Aristide would never forgive us if −' She left the sentence unfinished.

Then she said:

'It must be almost lunch time. We'd better go in.'

I explained that I was going up to London.

'In your car?'

'Yes.'

'H'm. I wonder if you'd take me with you. I gather we're allowed off the lead now.'

'Of course I will, but I believe Magda and Sophia are going up after lunch. You'll be more comfortable with them than in my two-seater.'

'I don't want to go with them. Take me with you, and don't say much about it.'

I was surprised, but I did as she asked. We did not speak much on the way to town. I asked her where I should put her down.

'Harley Street.'

I felt some faint apprehension, but I didn't like to say anything. She continued:

'No, it's too early. Drop me at Debenhams. I can have some lunch there and go to Harley Street afterwards.'

'I hope −' I began and stopped.

'That's why I didn't want to go up with Magda. She dramatizes things. Lots of fuss.'

'I'm very sorry,' I said.

'You needn't be. I've had a good life. A very good life.' She gave a sudden grin. 'And it's not over yet.'

CHAPTER 23

I had not seen my father for some days. I found him busy with things other than the Leonides case, and I went in search of Taverner.

Taverner was enjoying a short spell of leisure and was willing to come out and have a drink with me. I congratulated him on having cleared up the case and he accepted my congratulation, but his manner remained far from jubilant.

'Well, that's over,' he said. 'We've got a case. Nobody can deny we've got a case.'

'Do you think you'll get a conviction?'

'Impossible to say. The evidence is circumstantial – it nearly always is in a murder case – bound to be. A lot depends on the impression they make on the jury.'

'How far do the letters go?'

'At first sight, Charles, they're pretty damning. There are references to their life together when her husband's dead. Phrases like – "it won't be long now". Mind you, defence counsel will try and twist it the other way – the husband was so old that of course they could reasonably expect him to die. There's no actual mention of poisoning – not down in black and white – but there are some passages that could mean that. It depends what judge we get. If it's old Carberry he'll be down on them all through. He's always very righteous about illicit love. I suppose they'll have Eagles or Humphrey Kerr for the defence – Humphrey is magnificent in these cases – but he likes a gallant war record or something of that kind to help him do his stuff. A conscientious objector is going to cramp his style. The question is going to be will the jury like them? You can never tell with juries. You know, Charles, those two are not really sympathetic characters. She's a good-looking woman who married a very old man for his money, and Brown is a neurotic conscientious objector. The crime is so familiar – so according to pattern that you really believe they didn't do it. Of course, they may decide that he did it and she knew nothing about it – or alternately that she did it, and he didn't know about it – or they may decide that they were both in it together.'

'And what do you yourself think?' I asked.

He looked at me with a wooden expressionless face.

'I don't think anything. I've turned in the facts and they went to the DPP and it was decided that there was a case. That's all. I've done my duty and I'm out of it. So now you know, Charles.'

But I didn't know. I saw that for some reason Taverner was unhappy.

It was not until three days later that I unburdened myself to my father. He himself had never mentioned the case to me. There had been a kind of restraint between us – and I thought I knew the reason for it. But I had to break down that barrier.

'We've got to have this out,' I said. 'Taverner's not satisfied that those two did it – and you're not satisfied either.'

My father shook his head. He said what Taverner had said: 'It's out of our hands. There is a case to answer. No question about that.'

'But you don't – Taverner doesn't – think that they're guilty?'

'That's for a jury to decide.'

'For God's sake,' I said, 'don't put me off with technical terms. What do you think – both of you – *personally*?'

'My personal opinion is no better than yours, Charles.'

'Yes, it is. You've more experience.'

'Then I'll be honest with you. I just – don't know!'

'They *could* be guilty?'

'Oh, yes.'

'But you don't feel sure that they are?'

My father shrugged his shoulders.

'How can one be sure?'

'Don't fence with me, Dad. You've been sure other times, haven't you? Dead sure? No doubt in your mind at all?'

'Sometimes, yes. Not always.'

'I wish to God you were sure this time.'

'So do I.'

We were silent. I was thinking of those two figures drifting in from the garden in the dusk. Lonely and haunted and afraid. They had been afraid from the start. Didn't that show a guilty conscience?

But I answered myself: 'Not necessarily.' Both Brenda and Laurence were afraid of life – they had no confidence in themselves, in their ability to avoid danger and defeat, and they could see, only too clearly, the pattern of illicit love leading to murder which might involve them at any moment.

My father spoke, and his voice was grave and kind:

'Come, Charles,' he said, 'let's face it. You've still got it in your mind, haven't you, that one of the Leonides family is the real culprit?'

'Not really. I only wonder –'

'You do think so. You may be wrong, but you do think so.'

'Yes,' I said.

'Why?'

'Because' – I thought about it, trying to see clearly – to bring my wits to bear – 'because' (yes, that was it), 'because they think so themselves.'

'They think so themselves? That's interesting. That's very interesting. Do you mean that they all suspect each other, or that they know, actually, who did do it?'

'I'm not sure,' I said. 'It's all very nebulous and confused. I think – on the whole – that they try to cover up the knowledge from themselves.'

My father nodded.

'Not Roger,' I said. 'Roger wholeheartedly believes it was Brenda and he wholeheartedly wants her hanged. It's – it's a relief to be with Roger, because he's simple and positive, and hasn't any reservations in the back of his mind.

'But the others are apologetic, they're uneasy – they urge me to be sure that Brenda has the best defence – that every possible advantage is given her – why?'

My father answered: 'Because they don't really, in their hearts, believe she is guilty . . . Yes, that's sound.'

Then he asked quietly:

'Who *could* have done it? You've talked to them all? Who's the best bet?'

'I don't know,' I said. 'And it's driving me frantic. None of them fits your "sketch of a murderer" and yet I feel – I do feel – that one of them *is* a murderer.'

'Sophia?'

'No. Good God, no!'

'The possibility's in your mind, Charles – yes, it is, don't deny it. All the more potently because you won't acknowledge it. What about the others? Philip?'

'Only for the most fantastic motive.'

'Motives can be fantastic – or they can be absurdly slight. What's his motive?'

'He is bitterly jealous of Roger – always has been all his life. His father's preference for Roger drove Philip in upon himself. Roger was about to crash, then the old man heard of it. He promised to put Roger on his feet again. Supposing Philip learnt that. If the old man died that night there would be no assistance for Roger. Roger would be down and out. Oh! I know it's absurd –'

'Oh no, it isn't. It's abnormal, but it happens. It's human. What about Magda?'

'She's rather childish. She – she gets things out of proportion. But I would never have thought twice about her being involved if it hadn't been for the sudden way she wanted to pack Josephine off to Switzerland. I couldn't help feeling she was afraid of something that Josephine knew or might say –'

'And then Josephine was conked on the head?'

'Well, that couldn't be her mother!'

'Why not?'

'But Dad, a mother wouldn't –'

'Charles, Charles, don't you ever read the police news? Again and again a mother takes a dislike to one of her children. Only one – she may be devoted to the others. There's some association, some reason, but it's often hard to get at. But when it exists, it's an unreasoning aversion, and it's very strong.'

'She called Josephine a changeling,' I admitted unwillingly.

'Did the child mind?'

'I don't think so.'

'Who else is there? Roger?'

'Roger didn't kill his father. I'm quite sure of that.'

'Wash out Roger then. His wife – what's her name – Clemency?'

'Yes,' I said. 'If she killed old Leonides it was for a very odd reason.'

I told him of my conversation with Clemency. I said I thought it possible that in her passion to get Roger away from England she might have deliberately poisoned the old man.

'She persuaded Roger to go without telling his father. Then the old man found out. He was going to back up Associated Catering. All Clemency's hopes and plans were frustrated. And she really does care desperately for Roger – beyond idolatry.'

'You're repeating what Edith de Haviland said!'

'Yes. And Edith's another whom I think – might have done it. But I don't know why. I can only believe that for what she considered a good and sufficient reason she might take the law into her own hands. She's that kind of person.'

'And she also was very anxious that Brenda should be adequately defended?'

'Yes. That, I suppose, might be conscience. I don't think for a moment that if she did do it, she intended them to be accused of the crime.'

'Probably not. But would she knock out the child, Josephine?'

'No,' I said slowly. 'I can't believe that. Which reminds me that there's something that Josephine said to me that keeps nagging at my mind, and I can't remember what it is. It's slipped my memory. But it's something that doesn't fit in where it should. If only I could remember –'

'Never mind. It will come back. Anything or anyone else on your mind?'

'Yes,' I said. 'Very much so. How much do you know about infantile paralysis. Its after-effects on character, I mean?'

'Eustace?'

'Yes. The more I think about it, the more it seems to me that Eustace might fit the bill. His dislike and resentment against his grandfather. His queerness and moodiness. He's not normal.

'He's the only one of the family who I can see knocking out Josephine quite callously if she knew something about him – and she's quite likely to know. That child knows everything. She writes it down in a little book –'

I stopped.

'Good Lord,' I said. 'What a fool I am.'

'What's the matter?'

'I know now what was wrong. We assumed, Taverner and I, that the wrecking of Josephine's room, the frantic search, was for those letters. I thought that she'd got hold of them and that she'd hidden them up in the cistern room. But when she was talking to me the other day she made it quite clear that it was *Laurence* who had hidden them there. She saw him coming out of the cistern room and went snooping around and found the letters. Then, of course, she read them. She would! But she left them where they were.'

'Well?'

'Don't you see? *It couldn't have been the letters someone was looking for in Josephine's room.* It must have been something else.'

'And that something –'

'Was the little black book she writes down her "detection" in. That's what someone was looking for! I think, too, that whoever it was didn't find it. I think Josephine still has it. But if so –'

I half rose.

'If so,' said my father, 'she still isn't safe. Is that what you were going to say?'

'Yes. She won't be out of danger until she's actually started for Switzerland. They're planning to send her there, you know.'

'Does she want to go?'

I considered.

'I don't think she does.'

'Then she probably hasn't gone,' said my father, drily. 'But I think you're right about the danger. You'd better go down there.'

'Eustace?' I cried desperately. 'Clemency?'

My father said gently:

'To my mind the facts point clearly in one direction . . . I wonder you don't see it yourself. I . . .'

Glover opened the door.

'Beg pardon, Mr Charles, the telephone. Miss Leonides speaking from Swinly Dean. It's urgent.'

It seemed like a horrible repetition. Had Josephine again fallen a victim. And had the murderer this time made no mistake . . . ?

I hurried to the telephone.

'Sophia? It's Charles here.'

Sophia's voice came with a kind of hard desperation in it. 'Charles, it isn't all over. The murderer is still here.'

'What on earth do you mean? What is wrong? Is it – Josephine?'

'It's not Josephine. It's Nannie.'

'*Nannie?*'

'Yes, there was some cocoa – Josephine's cocoa, she didn't drink it. She left it on the table. Nannie thought it was a pity to waste it. So she drank it.'

'Poor Nannie. Is she very bad?'

Sophia's voice broke.

'Oh, Charles, she's *dead*.'

CHAPTER 24

We were back again in the nightmare.

That is what I thought as Taverner and I drove out of London. It was a repetition of our former journey.

At intervals, Taverner swore.

As for me, I repeated from time to time, stupidly, unprofitably: 'So it wasn't Brenda and Laurence. It wasn't Brenda and Laurence.'

Had I really thought it was? I had been so glad to think it. So glad to escape from other, more sinister, possibilities . . .

They had fallen in love with each other. They had written silly sentimental romantic letters to each other. They had indulged in hopes that Brenda's old husband might soon die peacefully and happily – but I wondered really if they had even acutely desired his death. I had a feeling that the despairs and longings of an unhappy love affair suited them as well or better than commonplace married life together. I didn't think Brenda was really passionate. She was too anaemic, too apathetic. It was romance she craved for. And I thought Laurence, too, was the type to enjoy frustration and vague future dreams of bliss rather than the concrete satisfaction of the flesh.

They had been caught in a trap and, terrified, they had not had the wit to find their way out. Laurence, with incredible stupidity, had not even destroyed Brenda's letters. Presumably Brenda had destroyed his, since they had not been found. And it was not Laurence who had balanced the marble doorstop on the wash-house door. It was someone else whose face was still hidden behind a mask.

We drove up to the door. Taverner got out and I followed him. There was a plain clothes man in the hall whom I didn't know. He saluted Taverner and Taverner drew him aside.

My attention was taken by a pile of luggage in the hall. It was labelled and ready for departure. As I looked at it Clemency came down the stairs and through the open door at the bottom. She was dressed in her same red dress with a tweed coat over it and a red felt hat.

'You're in time to say goodbye, Charles,' she said.

'You're leaving?'

'We go to London tonight. Our plane goes early tomorrow morning.'

She was quiet and smiling, but I thought her eyes were watchful.

'But surely you can't go now?'

'Why not?' Her voice was hard.

'With this death –'

'Nannie's death has nothing to do with us.'

'Perhaps not. But all the same –'

'Why do you say "perhaps not"? It *has* nothing to do with us. Roger and I have been upstairs, finishing packing up. We did not come down at all during the time that the cocoa was left on the hall table.'

'Can you prove that?'

'I can answer for Roger. And Roger can answer for me.'

'No more than that . . . You're man and wife, remember.'

Her anger flamed out.

'You're impossible, Charles! Roger and I are going away – to lead our own life. Why on earth should we want to poison a nice stupid old woman who had never done us any harm?'

'It mightn't have been her you meant to poison.'

'Still less are we likely to poison a child.'

'It depends rather on the child, doesn't it?'

'What do you mean?'

'Josephine isn't quite the ordinary child. She knows a good deal about people. She –'

I broke off. Josephine had emerged from the door leading to the drawing-room. She was eating the inevitable apple, and over its round rosiness her eyes sparkled with a kind of ghoulish enjoyment.

'Nannie's been poisoned,' she said. 'Just like grandfather. It's awfully exciting, isn't it?'

'Aren't you at all upset about it?' I demanded severely. 'You were fond of her, weren't you?'

'Not particularly. She was always scolding me about something or other. She fussed.'

'Are you fond of anybody, Josephine?' asked Clemency.

Josephine turned her ghoulish eyes towards Clemency.

'I love Aunt Edith,' she said. 'I love Aunt Edith very much. And I could love Eustace, only he's always such a beast to me and won't be interested in finding out who did all this.'

'You'd better stop finding things out, Josephine,' I said. 'It isn't very safe.'

'I don't need to find out any more,' said Josephine. 'I know.'

There was a moment's silence. Josephine's eyes, solemn and unwinking, were fixed on Clemency. A sound like a long sigh reached my ears. I swung sharply round. Edith de Haviland stood half-way down the staircase – but I did not think it was she who had sighed. The sound had come from behind the door through which Josephine had just come.

I stepped sharply across to it and yanked it open. There was no one to be seen.

Nevertheless I was seriously disturbed. Someone had stood just within that door and had heard those words of Josephine's. I went back and took Josephine by the arm. She was eating her apple and staring stolidly at Clemency. Behind the solemnity there was, I thought, a certain malignant satisfaction.

'Come on, Josephine,' I said. 'We're going to have a little talk.'

I think Josephine might have protested, but I was not standing any nonsense. I ran her along forcibly into her own part of the house. There was a small unused morning room where we could be reasonably sure of being undisturbed. I took her in there, closed the door firmly, and made her sit on a chair. I took another chair and drew it forward so that I faced her. 'Now, Josephine,' I said, 'we're going to have a showdown. What exactly do you know?'

'Lots of things.'

'That I have no doubt about. That noddle of yours is probably crammed to overflowing with relevant and irrelevant information. But you know perfectly what I mean. Don't you?'

'Of course I do. *I'm* not stupid.'

I didn't know whether the disparagement was for me or the police, but I paid no attention to it and went on:

'You know who put something in your cocoa?'

Josephine nodded.

'You know who poisoned your grandfather?'

Josephine nodded again.

'And who knocked you on the head?'

Again Josephine nodded.

'Then you're going to come across with what you know. You're going to tell me all about it – now.'

'Shan't.'

'You've got to. Every bit of information you've got or ferret out has got to be given to the police.'

'I won't tell the police anything. They're stupid. They thought Brenda had done it – or Laurence. I wasn't stupid like that. I knew jolly well they hadn't done it. I've had an idea who it was all along, and then I made a kind of test – and now I know I'm right.'

She finished on a triumphant note.

I prayed to Heaven for patience and started again.

'Listen, Josephine, I dare say you're extremely clever –' Josephine looked gratified. 'But it won't be much good to you to be clever if you're not alive to enjoy the fact. Don't you see, you little fool, that as long as you keep your secrets in this silly way you're in imminent danger?'

Josephine nodded approvingly. 'Of course I am.'

'Already you've had two very narrow escapes. One attempt nearly did for you. The other has cost somebody else their life. Don't you see if you go on strutting about the house and proclaiming at the top of your voice that you know who the killer is, there will be more attempts made – and that either you'll die or somebody else will?'

'In some books person after person is killed,' Josephine informed me with gusto. 'You end by spotting the murderer because he or she is practically the only person left.'

'This isn't a detective story. This is Three Gables, Swinly Dean, and you're a silly little girl who's read more than is good for her. I'll make you tell me what you know if I have to shake you till your teeth rattle.'

'I could always tell you something that wasn't true.'

'You could, but you won't. What are you waiting for, anyway?'

'You don't understand,' said Josephine. 'Perhaps I may never tell. You see, I might – be fond of the person.'

She paused as though to let this sink in.

'And if I do tell,' she went on, 'I shall do it properly. I shall have everybody sitting round, and then I'll go over it all – with the clues, and then I shall say, quite suddenly:

'"And it was *you* . . ."'

She thrust out a dramatic forefinger just as Edith de Haviland entered the room.

'Put that core in the waste-paper basket, Josephine,' said Edith. 'Have you got a handkerchief? Your fingers are sticky. I'm taking you out in the car.' Her eyes met mine with significance as she said: 'You'll be safer out here for the next hour or so.' As Josephine looked mutinous, Edith added: 'We'll go into Longbridge and have an ice cream soda.'

Josephine's eyes brightened and she said: 'Two.'

'Perhaps,' said Edith. 'Now go and get your hat and coat on and your dark blue scarf. It's cold out today. Charles, you had better go with her while she gets them. Don't leave her. I have just a couple of notes to write.'

She sat down at the desk, and I escorted Josephine out of the room. Even without Edith's warning, I would have stuck to Josephine like a leech.

I was convinced that there was danger to the child very near at hand.

As I finished superintending Josephine's toilet, Sophia came into the room. She seemed rather astonished to see me.

'Why, Charles, have you turned nursemaid? I didn't know you were here.'

'I'm going in to Longbridge with Aunt Edith,' said Josephine importantly. 'We're going to have ice creams.'

'Brrr, on a day like this?'

'Ice cream sodas are always lovely,' said Josephine. 'When you're cold inside, it makes you feel hotter outside.'

Sophia frowned. She looked worried, and I was shocked by her pallor and the circles under her eyes.

We went back to the morning room. Edith was just blotting a couple of envelopes. She got up briskly.

'We'll start now,' she said. 'I told Evans to bring round the Ford.'

She swept out to the hall. We followed her.

My eye was again caught by the suitcases and their blue labels. For some reason they aroused in me a vague disquietude.

'It's quite a nice day,' said Edith de Haviland, pulling on her gloves and glancing up at the sky. The Ford Ten was waiting in front of the house. 'Cold – but bracing. A real English autumn day. How beautiful trees look with their bare branches against the sky – and just a golden leaf or two still hanging . . .'

She was silent a moment or two, then she turned and kissed Sophia.

'Goodbye, dear,' she said. 'Don't worry too much. Certain things have to be faced and endured.'

Then she said, 'Come, Josephine,' and got into the car. Josephine climbed in beside her.

They both waved as the car drove off.

'I suppose she's right, and it's better to keep Josephine out of this for a while. But we've got to make that child tell what she knows, Sophia.'

'She probably doesn't know anything. She's just showing off. Josephine likes to make herself look important, you know.'

'It's more than that. Do they know what poison it was in the cocoa?'

'They think it's digitalin. Aunt Edith takes digitalin for her heart. She has a whole bottle full of little tablets up in her room. Now the bottle's empty.'

'She ought to keep things like that locked up.'

'She did. I suppose it wouldn't be difficult for someone to find out where she hid the key.'

'Someone? Who?' I looked again at the pile of luggage. I said suddenly and loudly:

'They can't go away. They mustn't be allowed to.'

Sophia looked surprised.

'Roger and Clemency? Charles, you don't think –'

'Well, what do *you* think?'

Sophia stretched out her hands in a helpless gesture.

'I don't know, Charles,' she whispered. 'I only know that I'm back – back in the nightmare –'

'I know. Those were the very words I used to myself as I drove down with Taverner.'

'Because this is just what a nightmare is. Walking about among people you know, looking in their faces – and suddenly the faces change – and it's not someone you know any longer – it's a stranger – a cruel stranger . . .'

She cried:

'Come outside, Charles – come outside. It's safer outside . . . I'm afraid to stay in this house . . .'

CHAPTER 25

We stayed in the garden a long time. By a kind of tacit consent, we did not discuss the horror that was weighing upon us. Instead Sophia talked affectionately of the dead woman, of things they had done, and games they had played as children with Nannie – and tales that the old woman used to tell them about Roger and their father and the other brothers and sisters.

'They were her real children, you see. She only came back to us to help during the war when Josephine was a baby and Eustace was a funny little boy.'

There was a certain balm for Sophia in these memories and I encouraged her to talk.

I wondered what Taverner was doing. Questioning the household, I supposed. A car drove away with the police photographer and two other men, and presently an ambulance drove up.

Sophia shivered a little. Presently the ambulance left and we knew that Nannie's body had been taken away in preparation for an autopsy.

And still we sat or walked in the garden and talked – our words becoming more and more of a cloak for our real thoughts.

Finally, with a shiver, Sophia said:

'It must be very late – it's almost dark. We've got to go in. Aunt Edith and Josephine haven't come back . . . Surely they ought to be back by now?'

A vague uneasiness woke in me. What had happened? Was Edith deliberately keeping the child away from the Crooked House?

We went in. Sophia drew all the curtains. The fire was lit and the big drawing-room looked harmonious with an unreal air of bygone luxury. Great bowls of bronze chrysanthemums stood on the tables.

Sophia rang and a maid whom I recognized as having been formerly upstairs brought in tea. She had red eyes and sniffed continuously. Also I noticed that she had a frightened way of glancing quickly over her shoulder.

Magda joined us, but Philip's tea was sent in to him in the library. Magda's role was a stiff frozen image of grief. She spoke little or not at all. She said once:

'Where are Edith and Josephine? They're out very late.'

But she said it in a preoccupied kind of way.

But I myself was becoming increasingly uneasy. I asked if Taverner were still in the house and Magda replied that she thought so. I went in search of him. I told him that I was worried about Miss de Haviland and the child.

He went immediately to the telephone and gave certain instructions.

'I'll let you know when I have news,' he said.

I thanked him and went back to the drawing-room. Sophia was there with Eustace. Magda had gone.

'He'll let us know if he hears anything,' I said to Sophia.

She said in a low voice:

'Something's happened, Charles, something *must* have happened.'

'My dear Sophia, it's not really late yet.'

'What are you bothering about?' said Eustace. 'They've probably gone to the cinema.'

He lounged out of the room. I said to Sophia: 'She may have taken Josephine to a hotel – or up to London. I think she really realized that the child was in danger – perhaps she realized it better than we did.'

Sophia replied with a sombre look that I could not quite fathom.

'She kissed me goodbye . . .'

I did not see quite what she meant by that disconnected remark, or what it was supposed to show. I asked if Magda was worried.

'Mother? No, she's all right. She's no sense of time. She's reading a new play of Vavasour Jones called *The Woman Disposes*. It's a funny play about murder – a female Bluebeard – cribbed from *Arsenic and Old Lace* if you ask me, but it's got a good woman's part, a woman who's got a mania for being a widow.'

I said no more. We sat, pretending to read.

It was half-past six when Taverner opened the door and came in. His face prepared us for what he had to say.

Sophia got up.

'Yes?' she said.

'I'm sorry. I've got bad news for you. I sent out a general alarm for the car. A motorist reported having seen a Ford car with a number something like that turning off the main road at Flackspur Heath – through the woods.'

'Not – the track to the Flackspur Quarry?'

'Yes, Miss Leonides.' He paused and went on. 'The car's been found in the quarry. Both the occupants were dead. You'll be glad to know they were killed outright.'

'Josephine!' It was Magda standing in the doorway. Her voice rose in a wail. 'Josephine . . . My baby.'

Sophia went to her and put her arms round her. I said: 'Wait a minute.'

I had remembered something! Edith de Haviland writing a couple of letters at the desk, going out into the hall with them in her hand.

But they had not been in her hand when she got into the car.

I dashed out into the hall and went to the long oak chest. I found the letters – pushed inconspicuously to the back behind a brass tea-urn.

The uppermost was addressed to Chief-Inspector Taverner.

Taverner had followed me. I handed the letter to him and he tore it open. Standing beside him I read its brief contents.

My expectation is that this will be opened after my death. I wish to enter into no details, but I accept full responsibility for the deaths of my brother-in-law, Aristide Leonides and Janet Rowe (Nannie). I hereby solemnly declare that Brenda Leonides and Laurence Brown are innocent of the murder of Aristide Leonides. Inquiry of Dr Michael Chavasse, 783 Harley Street, will confirm that my life could only have been prolonged for a few months. I prefer to take this way out and to spare two innocent people the ordeal of being charged with a murder they did not commit. I am of sound mind and fully conscious of what I write.

Edith Elfrida de Haviland.

As I finished the letter I was aware that Sophia, too, had read it – whether with Taverner's concurrence or not, I don't know.

'*Aunt Edith* . . .' murmured Sophia.

I remembered Edith de Haviland's ruthless foot grinding bind-weed into the earth. I remembered my early, almost fanciful, suspicions of her. But why –

Sophia spoke the thought in my mind before I came to it.

'But why Josephine? Why did she take Josephine with her?'

'Why did she do it at all?' I demanded. 'What was her motive?'

But even as I said that, I knew the truth. I saw the whole thing clearly. I realized that I was still holding her second letter in my hand. I looked down and saw my own name on it.

It was thicker and harder than the other one. I think I knew what was in it before I opened it. I tore the envelope along and Josephine's little black note-book fell out. I picked it up off the floor – it came open in my hand and I saw the entry on the first page . . .

Sounding from a long way away, I heard Sophia's voice, clear and self-controlled.

'We've got it all wrong,' she said. 'Edith didn't do it.'

'No,' I said.

Sophia came closer to me – she whispered:

'It was – Josephine – wasn't it? That was it, Josephine.'

Together we looked down on the first entry in the little black book, written in an unformed childish hand:

'*Today I killed grandfather.*'

CHAPTER 26

I

I was to wonder afterwards that I could have been so blind. The truth had stuck out so clearly all along. Josephine and only Josephine fitted in with all the necessary qualifications.

Her vanity, her persistent self-importance, her delight in talking, her reiteration on how clever *she* was, and how stupid the police were.

I had never considered her because she was a child. But children have committed murders, and this particular murder had been well within a child's compass. Her grandfather himself had indicated the precise method – he had practically handed her a blueprint. All she had to do was to avoid leaving fingerprints and the slightest knowledge of detection fiction would teach her that. And everything else had been a mere hotch-potch, culled at random from stock mystery stories. The note-book – the sleuthing – her pretended suspicions, her insistence that she was not going to tell till she was sure . . .

And finally the attack on herself. An almost incredible performance considering that she might easily have killed herself. But then, childlike, she had never considered such a possibility. She was the heroine. The heroine isn't killed. Yet there had been a clue there – the traces of earth on the seat of the old chair in the wash-house. Josephine was the only person who would have had to climb up on a chair to balance the block of marble on the top of the door. Obviously it had missed her more than once (the dints in the floor) and patiently she had climbed up again and replaced it, handling it with her scarf to avoid fingerprints. And then it had fallen – and she had had a near escape from death.

It had been the perfect set-up – the impression she was aiming for! She was in danger, she 'knew something', she had been attacked!

I saw how she had deliberately drawn my attention to her presence in the cistern room. And she had completed the artistic disorder of her room before going out to the wash-house.

But when she had returned from hospital, when she had found Brenda and Laurence arrested, she must have become dissatisfied. The case was over – and she – Josephine, was out of the limelight.

So she stole the digitalin from Edith's room and put it in her own cup of cocoa and left the cup untouched on the hall table.

Did she know that Nannie would drink it? Possibly. From her words that morning, she had resented Nannie's criticisms of her. Did Nannie, perhaps, wise from a lifetime of experience with children, suspect? I think that Nannie knew, had always known, that Josephine was not normal. With her precocious mental development had gone a retarded moral sense. Perhaps, too, the various factors of heredity – what Sophia had called the 'ruthlessness of the family' – had met together.

She had had an authoritarian ruthlessness of her grandmother's family, and the ruthless egoism of Magda, seeing only her own point of view. She had also presumably suffered, sensitive like Philip, from the stigma of being the unattractive – the changeling child – of the family. Finally, in her very marrow had run the essential crooked strain of old Leonides. She had been Leonides' grandchild, she had resembled him in brain and cunning – but where his love had gone outwards to family and friends, hers had turned inward to herself.

I thought that old Leonides had realized what none of the rest of the family had realized, that Josephine might be a source of danger to others and to herself. He had kept her from school life because he was afraid of what she might do. He had shielded her, and guarded her in the home, and I understood now his urgency to Sophia to look after Josephine.

Magda's sudden decision to send Josephine abroad – had that, too, been due to a fear for the child? Not, perhaps, a conscious fear, but some vague maternal instinct.

And Edith de Haviland? Had she first suspected, then feared – and finally known?

I looked down at the letter in my hand.

Dear Charles. This is in confidence for you – and for Sophia if you so decide. It is imperative that someone should know the truth. I found the enclosed in the disused dog kennel outside the back door. She kept it there. It confirms what I already suspected. The action I am about to take may be right or wrong – I do not know. But my life, in any case, is close to its end, and I do not want the child to suffer as I believe she would suffer if called to earthly account for what she has done.

There is often one of the litter who is 'not quite right'.

If I am wrong, God forgive me – but I did it out of love. God bless you both.

Edith de Haviland.

I hesitated for only a moment, then I handed the letter to Sophia. Together we again opened Josephine's little black book.

Today I killed grandfather.

We turned the pages. It was an amazing production. Interesting, I should imagine, to a psychologist. It set out, with such terrible clarity, the fury of thwarted egoism. The motive for the crime was set down, pitifully childish and inadequate.

Grandfather wouldn't let me do bally dancing so I made up my mind I would kill him. Then we should go to London and live and mother wouldn't mind me doing bally.

I give only a few entries. They are all significant.

I don't want to go to Switzerland – I won't go. If mother makes me I will kill her too – only I can't get any poison. Perhaps I could make it with youberries. They are poisonous, the book says so.

Eustace has made me very cross today. He says I am only a girl and no use and that it's silly my detecting. He wouldn't think me silly if he knew it was me did the murder.

I like Charles – but he is rather stupid. I have not decided yet who I shall make have done the crime. Perhaps Brenda and Laurence – Brenda is nasty to me – she says I am not all there but I like Laurence – he told me about Charlot Korday – she killed someone in his bath. She was not very clever about it.

The last entry was revealing.

I hate Nannie . . . I hate her . . . I hate her . . . She says I am only a little girl. She says I show off. She's making mother send me abroad . . . I'm going to kill her too – I think Aunt Edith's medicine would do it. If there is another murder, then the police will come back and it will all be exciting again.

Nannie's dead. I am glad. I haven't decided yet where I'll hide the bottle with the little pill things. Perhaps in Aunt Clemency's room –

*or else Eustace. When I am dead as an old woman I shall leave this
behind me addressed to the Chief of Police and they will see what
a really great criminal I was.*

I closed the book. Sophia's tears were flowing fast.

'Oh, Charles – oh, Charles – it's so dreadful. She's such a little
monster – and yet – and yet it's so terribly pathetic.'

I had felt the same.

I had liked Josephine . . . I still felt a fondness for her . . . You do
not like anyone less because they have tuberculosis or some other
fatal disease. Josephine was, as Sophia had said, a little monster,
but she was a pathetic little monster. She had been born with a
kink – the crooked child of the little Crooked House.

Sophia asked.

'If – she had lived – what would have happened?'

'I suppose she would have been sent to a reformatory or a
special school. Later she would have been released – or possibly
certified, I don't know.'

Sophia shuddered.

'It's better the way it is. But Aunt Edith – I don't like to think
of her taking the blame.'

'She chose to do so. I don't suppose it will be made public. I
imagine that when Brenda and Laurence come to trial, no case
will be brought against them and they will be discharged.

'And you, Sophia,' I said, this time on a different note and
taking both her hands in mine, 'will marry me. I've just heard
I'm appointed to Persia. We will go out there together, and you
will forget the little Crooked House. Your mother can put on plays
and your father can buy more books and Eustace will soon go to
a university. Don't worry about them any more. Think of me.'

Sophia looked me straight in the eyes.

'Aren't you afraid, Charles, to marry me?'

'Why should I be? In poor little Josephine all the worst of the
family came together. In you, Sophia, I fully believe that all that
is bravest and best in the Leonides family has been handed down
to you. Your grandfather thought highly of you and he seems to
have been a man who was usually right. Hold up your head, my
darling. The future is ours.'

'I will, Charles. I love you and I'll marry you and make you

happy.' She looked down at the note-book. 'Poor Josephine.'
'Poor Josephine,' I said.

II

'What's the truth of it, Charles?' said my father.
I never lie to the Old Man.
'It wasn't Edith de Haviland, sir,' I said. 'It was Josephine.'
My father nodded his head gently.
'Yes,' he said. 'I've thought so for some time. Poor child . . .'